Jayvie's Story

By Mim Eichmann

Dedication

Dedicated to my sister Cherie.

Acknowledgements

A. Bassett, Rod Brandon, Luisa Buehler, Pat Camalliere,
Odette Cortopassi, Downers Grove (Illinois) Public Library,
Robert Fliege, John Griffin, Cherie Little, Dick Little,
Neil Loewe, Doug Lofstrom, Maximum Printing,
Robert Milewski, Jon Payne, Mary Rempe, Alison Rockmann,
James Ross, Carol See, Gary Tuber, Frank Wegloski,
Lee Williams

Author's Note

The historical fiction bookshelves have been glutted for many years with novels exploring the global nightmare prior to and during World War II, especially in Occupied France. Some of these works are excellent, others quite good, others sadly mediocre romance novels masquerading as history that often stretch the negligible effectiveness of espionage and resistance movements.

When I decided to tackle this project, I was already locked into a very basic outline of Tayvie's life that had appeared in the prior novel, *Muskrat Ramble,* the timeline of which is almost an exact parallel to that within *Tayvie's Story.* In *Muskrat Ramble,* I'd written that Tayvie (aka Helen Mason Campbell) had been in a film in Memphis, TN directed by King Vidor. After the opening chapter, the first section takes us to Orange Grove (a black suburb of Memphis) and then Memphis itself. Later in *Muskrat Ramble,* I'd mentioned in a 'faux' magazine interview, that Helen had been a jazz singer in several cabarets in Paris during the Occupation in World War II, so that was a natural jumping off point for the second half of the novel.

I started searching for several lesser known, yet important, situations prior to and during the war, in order to drop my fictional protagonist's history into a timeline of true historical events. After much research, I landed on three solid leads. The first was an illegal Jewish immigrant named Herschel Grynszpan who murdered his lover, a Nazi officer, at the German Embassy in Paris in November 1938. This act was more than likely misinterpreted – perhaps deliberately -- by the Nazis and provided the catalyst for their three-day spree, known as *Kristallnacht -- the night of broken glass --* in which the synagogues, homes and businesses of Jewish citizens living in Germany and Austria were ransacked and burned.

The second event was the creation of weekly, later daily, propaganda broadcasts aimed specifically at the United States, Canada and Great Britain by a group which only existed on the air known as Charlie and His Orchestra. In these bizarre radio interludes, the lyrics to popular American jazz and show tunes were rewritten praising the magnificence of the Third Reich. Unfortunately, the

Germans really didn't have much of a sense of humor and most of the English-speaking listeners thought the music ridiculous parodies.

The third and most important lynchpin to the puzzle was the Minister of Enlightenment & Propaganda, Herr Doktor Joseph Goebbels, as well as his wife Magda and their oldest daughter Helga. Goebbels had spearheaded the massacre in the Gynszpan fiasco as well as creating the Charlie & His Orchestra programs. Among Hitler's ministers, Goebbels was intensely disliked by Hitler's inner circle. He was deemed such a duplicitous scoundrel that even the *Führer* himself frequently refrained from sharing confidential information with the man. Because of his position overseeing all the various means of propaganda: newsreels, feature length films, music, live theatre, radio broadcasts, newspapers, live public speeches and news bulletins, however, he was in many ways more powerful than Hitler. Of all Hitler's ministers, he was unquestionably the smartest, a man treacherously laying the groundwork for destruction while brainwashing countless men and women both within the Third Reich as well as throughout the world.

This all threaded together to give *Tayvie's Story* the structure I needed, and I dove in, keeping a running chronology of the European conflict timeline. I think one of the hardest things in historical fiction is to give a sense of atmosphere without going too far overboard into what's commonly referred to as 'info dumping.' That said, one man's intrigue into background information is another man's info dumping, unfortunately. So, as the writer, you go with your gut. In an example I've used frequently, when my kids were little, if four out of the five of us liked the same thing for dinner I considered the meal a resounding success.

I hope you enjoy this final book of my historical series which began with *A Sparrow Alone*, published in 2020. When I first began writing *A Sparrow Alone,* I never envisioned that its characters would beg me to create these three books … but I'm glad they did. I've learned a lot about the eras surrounding Hannah, Emma and Tayvie. I've also learned a lot about myself.

<u>Disclaimers and Clarifications</u>

- For obvious reasons, I had to make Joseph Goebbels fluent in English. Although Goebbels had studied English as a requirement to obtain his Ph.D., he was not particularly fluent in any language except German. His wife Magda, however, could carry on in-depth conversations in her native German, as well as in French and English.

- To the best of my knowledge, there were no thefts of the radium-laced drink Radithor during or after the product was pulled off the market.
- The lyrics printed in the novel for "Wayfaring Stranger" and "Keep on the Sunny Side" are in the public domain. The alternative lyrics for "You're the Top" are my own.
- Author Jonathan Kirsch, who wrote *The Short, Strange Life of Herschel Grynszpan,* never exclusively embraces the theory of Grynszpan's homosexual affair with the Nazi officer Ernst vom Rath within his book. However, he does so in a later interview available on Youtube.
- If you ever have a chance to read Hans-Otto Meissner's stunning book *Magda Goebbels,* I urge you to do so. Both Meissner and his father were part of Hitler's inner circle and served prison time after the war.

<u>The following are historic characters, works or establishments:</u>

King Vidor, *Hallelujah,* Nina Mae McKinney, Mistinguett, Sidney Bechet, William J. Bailey, Charles Johnson, Lutz Templin, Fritz Brocksieper, Charly Tabor, Josephine Baker, Lida Baarova, Cole Porter, Benny Goodman, Duke Ellington, Abraham Grynszpan, Chava Grynszpan, Herschel Grynszpan, Joseph Goebbels, Magda Goebbels, Helga Goebbels, Karl Hanke, Karl Schwedler, Charlie and His Orchestra, Adolf Hitler, Leni Riefenstahl, President Franklin Roosevelt, Winston Churchill, Tout Va Bien café, Small's Paradise, Artiste's Club, Moulin Rouge, Bal Tabarin.

Chapter 1

Helen Mason Campbell
Chicago, Illinois - December 1923

"Maman!" I shriek. *"Non! S'il te plaît!"* I run towards her, shaking my head fiercely, my tears flying everywhere. I know she will be angry I don't say the words in English, but my tongue won't fit into English right now! She is still lying on the floor … in a pile of dirty rags smashed up against the wall. I pull on her rigid arm that stretches out towards nothing. Her hand beckons like a hawk's sharp claw. Her huge blue eyes stare right at me. But she never blinks. She never moves.

She's like one of the old statues where *Maman's* friends take me in the warm place where we used to live … those old grey statues in the beautiful cemetery where the long branches of the live oaks skim along the ground like benches. The place where we eat our picnics on the faded patchwork quilt after church on special Sundays. The place they call *Vieux Carré*. I know that's not what it's called in English, but I can't remember that name right now!

But it's warm with huge red flowers everywhere. Always so warm. Always so nice. Always. Nothing like this awful cold place where *Maman* brought me a few months ago on the dark train. This awful place where almost no one understands my words. This place where the man who had been living here with us -- the man who was bringing us the food -- has now been gone for many, many days. The man I was told to call Papa. The man who made me cry one afternoon but then kissed my tears away. The man who took me to a store filled with toys all the way up to the ceiling and bought me a bright green parrot with real feathers.

But then I think he is the man who yelled at *Maman* and maybe hit her hard and knocked her down. But I don't really know this. There have been other men in our apartment too. There's been a lot of shouting by *Maman* with these other men also. They all talk in English, so I understand very little. Maybe it's been one of those other men hitting *Maman*. I don't know. I've never seen anyone hitting her at all. I've only seen her lying on the ground like she is right now. But she's always gotten up. Always.

But not this time.

I walk through our building, asking for food. *Une tranche de pain.* I finally remember the English word is bread. A slice of bread. Yes! That is what I must say if someone hears me knocking and opens their door. I hear scuffling like large mice behind many doors but only one is finally opened just a crack. The lady gives me two hard biscuits but keeps a mean face.

"How old are you?" she growls. Her breath stinks of rancid onions. My eyes burn.

I hold up four fingers.

"Go home," she spits out, her face a stained, wrinkled prune as she pushes my shoulder hard away from her door and almost shuts it on my hair. "Git now."

So now I come back to our room and open the door. Maybe by now *Maman* is better. Maybe she is on her feet walking slowly like she has done before. Maybe we can finally go and find food.

But no. She is still lying on the floor against the wall with hard eyes like marbles that never blink. Nothing has changed since the man called Papa went away. I sit down on the floor next to her and eat both biscuits. They are very stale and taste like mouse droppings.

"Leve toi! J'ai soif! J'ai faim! Up! Up, please! I thirsty … I … I … hungry!" I sob, so grateful when the English words somehow spill themselves over my tongue. Maybe this will make her happy and she will come out of this long sleep! But no, she still doesn't move. Nothing has changed. Nothing at all. I brush off a small brown bug with sticky feet that is slowly crawling over her cold leg.

I go into the bedroom. The Papa man's clothes are still here. But his suitcase is gone. Maybe he is still coming back. Maybe I should wait? *Oui? Non!* It has been too many days and I am too hungry! I see my new toy parrot on the shelf and put it in my red coat pocket. Then I carefully pull my coat down from the hook. *Maman* saw a girl with soft yellow hair leave the coat on the floor of the dark train when we came up here, so now it is mine. *Maman* says the pretty tag inside the coat has that girl's name on it, but she will cut out that tag when she finds scissors with a good sharp blade. I thought that was wrong, but *Maman* tells me to hush up. The coat was now mine. I'd said I wanted it, *non?* I remember I was so tired I fell asleep very fast in that nice warm coat on the dark train.

I walk back to where *Maman* is lying and kiss her cold cheek.

"*Maman,*" I say quietly, my wet cheek next to hers, "*je vais trouver du pain. Eh … I go … bread … us, yes? Je vais y aller! T'inquiète pas!*"

It is very cold and snowing hard out in the crowded street, but everywhere I look there are smiling black faces just like mine, lit by the bright lampposts. All the men and woman are dressed in fat brown furry coats. Most of the ladies have their hands stuffed into huge round muffs and everyone walks in small groups or hangs onto the poles of the dirty green streetcars with grimy wheels of packed snow.

After a few blocks I go into a store where I remember the Papa man has taken me once before. Huge bins filled with potatoes, onions, apples and walnuts make my stomach rumble as I walk around. A large white woman with an ugly hairnet like a big spider pulled low over the edge of her glasses is behind the counter, brushing the barnyard mess from fresh chicken eggs and then carefully placing the eggs in a wire basket. She looks up and sees my hand reaching into a bin of apples.

"Hey! You got the money fo' dat?" the woman snarls. Her blue eyes swim behind her wax glasses. "I ain' runnin' no char'ty shop fo' you half breeds runnin' wild these days! You the l'il thief stole my sass'fras sticks las' Tuesday?"

I look down at the apple and then back at her. Money! I certainly know that word even though I don't understand another word she's saying. When the Papa man brought me here, he bought other food so I could take an apple. The woman behind the counter shakes her head and then starts cleaning the eggs again. If I run out the door with the apple, she can't catch me without breaking some of those eggs, I think. What would be more important to her – one small stolen apple or several broken eggs? And what would *Maman* say if she knew? She would be very angry. *Certainement*. But I am so hungry! I grab one and race for the door.

The hairnet woman runs very fast! She is screaming words that I don't think are very nice. I hide from her view behind a small group of women in fat fur coats on the sidewalk, but when I look, she is still moving my way. A motor car is parked near an alley just a few feet away from me. No one is inside, but the door hangs slightly open. I jump in, carefully shutting the door, then scramble behind the driver's seat. The car is still warm. I curl under a thick fur coat that is on the back floor. If the hairnet woman looks in the car, I don't think she'll see me. I wait in silence, in the dark, breathing the wonderful perfume from the fur coat. There is another delicious scent as well. After a few moments I dig inside one of the pockets and pull out a twisted cinnamon and sugar roll, almost too big to hold -- and a hunk of salami! Eagerly, while waiting for the hairnet woman to give up her search, I eat until full. Then, I snuggle deeper into the fur coat and fall quickly asleep.

When I wake up the car is moving and is bouncing off a rock or maybe has hit a big hole. I only know something has jarred me awake. A man and a woman are talking. They are speaking English like you'd hear when white people talk. When I'd lived down in the warm place, there was a very pretty white lady called Madame Chenille who would visit sometimes. That is how she talked I remember. She would read me books in English, and we would pretend we were butterflies. She had a real parrot that sang lots of funny songs with me. I wonder sadly if I'll ever see Mme. Chenille or her funny parrot Monsieur Autruche again. Somehow, I don't think so.

I finally peek out from under the fur coat and am surprised to see a tall black woman sitting in the front seat. Although there is almost no light other than a bright moon, I can see the lady's hair is perfectly curled and pinned up under a large jewel-trimmed cloche. The very hat that *Maman* saw in a shop window and said she wished she could buy, but it was far too expensive.

A few minutes later we stop at a small store. I smell gasoline, so maybe that's why they've stopped. Although both people get out of the car for a few moments, I am afraid to move from my hiding spot. Other than the lights from the store, I haven't seen any light except the moon. If I get out now, I might get lost. Actually, I think I may already be lost. Nothing looks familiar.

The man starts the car up again and we continue moving. I fall asleep several more times, dreaming about *Maman* singing. She has a beautiful voice everyone says, and I would certainly agree. I hope one day I can sing like her too! She always tells me to lie down and hide behind the stage, so she won't have to pay someone to stay with me at our apartment. This way I've learned many of her songs, but I only sing them to myself since I don't know what the words mean. I've told her I'm old enough to stay home by myself, but she laughs and says not yet. I wonder if she is awake yet. If she can finally move again. Is she worried that I'm not home right now?

The car is stopping. I decide to wait until the people are gone and then get out. But suddenly, the man grabs the fur coat off me.

"Well, I'll be! Looks like we picked up a stowaway when we stopped for gasoline!" he laughs. "What's your name little girl?"

I like his hat. It looks very soft and velvety. The man and woman smile as I get out of their car. They don't seem to be angry. I look from one to the other. They both have very kind, round, dark faces shining in the moonlight.

"Can you tell us your name?" asks the woman gently, smoothing back some of my curls. "We're Dr. and Mrs. Campbell."

Thoroughly frightened, I shake my head and stare at the ground. I know that once the man checks his fur coat pockets and discovers that I've eaten the sugar roll and most of the salami they will not be kind at all!

"She's got on a beautiful wool coat," says the woman. "She must have gotten in the wrong car when we stopped for gasoline back in Milwaukee, Henry. Oh, my dear, I'm sure your people are missing you terribly right now!"

"She seems mighty shy. Check to see if maybe her name is on the coat label, Louisa," urges the man. "You know, sewn in like they do so the kids don't take the wrong coat off the peg after Sunday School. Take a look, honey."

The woman nods, then moves around behind me and gently pulls up the back collar of my coat.

"Why yes, you're absolutely right, dear! It's a beautiful hand-embroidered label, in fact. The label says: 'This coat belongs to Helen Mason.' Is that your name little one? Helen? Helen Mason?"

Slowly, I look up at her. I want to say no, my name is Tayvie — Tayvie, which is short for Octavie, although *Maman* only calls me Octavie when she's unhappy with me. But maybe this Helen Mason person will catch the blame for eating the salami and the sweet roll and no one will know anything different so then they will just let me go home without asking any more questions.

"Yes," I reply softly, the English word slippery on my tongue.

And that is how I came to be known as Helen Mason Campbell.

Chapter 2

Four years later
Orange Mound, Tennessee 1928

Something startled me awake. I felt a low metal grinding, pulsating beneath my feet as the train slowed around a sharp curve. That's when I realized I'd been having that dream once again. Some of it I remembered quite clearly, and I thought that maybe one day I might discover my original name. But just as it lay on my tongue, I would begin gliding up to the surface, the dream dissolving like a soap bubble. Sometimes I'd whisper the name Tayvie in the dark hoping that it might yield a clue. But it always swirled just out of reach in murky waters from deep within… a jigsaw puzzle of letters spilling out over the ground.

The dream usually appeared when we were riding in our car, my dad laughing over some long, outlandish tale of Mama's that would have lulled me into a light sleep. Mama was a wonderful storyteller. But we weren't in Daddy's new Model A now, with the headlamps that often shifted out of focus whenever we bounced over gravel and dirt roads thick with huge ruts. And we never would be again. The motor car had been sold to a man in the next block a few days ago, to one of Daddy's former patients, in fact. Daddy had saved enough money slightly over a year ago to buy that new motor car to replace the old tin lizzie as he called it. He'd kept it tip-top by rubbing out even the tiniest fleck of grime Mama had always commented with pride. I hoped Daddy's former patient would take good care of it.

At Daddy's funeral two weeks ago, Mama had smiled bravely through a curtain of bright tears. She'd commented quietly that we would be taking the train to her sister Lil's family down in south Memphis -- Orange Mound, specifically -- by the end of the month. She and Daddy had grown up in Orange Mound and had been high school sweethearts. They'd moved up to Milwaukee when Daddy had gotten a college teaching position up here, just a few months before I'd hidden in the back of their tin lizzie, I'd learned. Otherwise, they would never have left their beloved Tennessee. Once she had sold the car, our furniture and Daddy's medical texts, we would be on our way, Mama had replied to those gathered around us after the service.

I glanced over at Mama. She was smoothing out the edges of several old, wrinkled pictures from their wedding, carefully pressing them between the pages of her well-worn Bible. She seemed smaller now, shrunken even. Her once-beautiful, shiny black hair was streaked with thick strands of dull silver. It had been a long year for us both with Daddy's illness.

Sitting up straighter I rubbed my eyes and looked out the grimy train window. Rain pelted against the window, snaking down in little grey rivers edged in soot. Row after row of thick cornfields danced by – whispering the promise of a large harvest within a few weeks – a kaleidoscope of dark green ears with dripping wet golden tassels, Mama had whispered to me. She had such a wonderful way of making words sing, I thought. We'd soon be seeing cotton plants instead, she'd added. I didn't think I'd ever seen a cotton plant. The rain did nothing to cool the air on the train and the stiff cloth seats made my legs and back itch something fierce.

I knew there was no food left in the basket that Mama had so carefully prepared before we'd left home. I felt ashamed that she'd eaten so very little, but that I'd devoured all the meat pies, grapes, sweet tea, and cheese curds many hours ago. I was always hungry even though we were well blessed with plenty of food. One of our old neighbors, Mrs. Canfield, a lady that Mama invited over to Sunday dinner occasionally, would often poke me hard in the stomach and joke that I must have a little tapeworm whirling about in my tummy. But Daddy, frowning, had always sternly corrected her that such a thing wasn't possible. I was glad to hear that. Somehow having worms sloshing about in my middle wasn't a very pleasant thought. Those long brown worms slithering through the mud in our vegetable garden were disgusting enough.

"Try to get some sleep, Helen," said Mama quietly, smoothing my hair from my sweaty cheek. "We'll have to change trains in the middle of the night. You'll need to be wide awake in the depot for several hours to help me with our things so we're able to transfer to the next train."

"Tell me again about Orange Mound first," I begged, resting my shoulder on the scratchy seatback cushion. "And about my cousins … Charlene, Terrence and … and Beverly, right? Please?"

She had been reading passages in her Bible and probably hadn't been aware of my brief nap. I wasn't sleepy in the least right now.

"What do you want to know?" she sighed, with a wisp of a smile. "I think I've told you everything there is to tell. I haven't seen any of them now for several years. Not since you became part of our family as you well know."

"Please, Mama?" I urged.

"I'm sure you remember from my reading Aunt Lil's letters to you and Daddy, that Terrence junior was so terribly sick for such a long, long time. Diphtheria they said, but Daddy thought it might be some other kind of infection in the lining of his lung. I can't remember what he called that other infection though."

"Diphtheria?"

"Yes, an awful illness. There's a lot of dark … spit … that's called phlegm, actually … you remember your father talking about that, right?"

I nodded. Daddy had worried constantly about his patients with diphtheria. Especially the babies. So many just gave up and stopped breathing within a day or two.

"The phlegm collects in the back of the throat. Makes people cough something awful and they can hardly swallow, their throat hurts so. High fever usually as well. Little Terrence's crept almost to the end of the thermometer my sister said. They couldn't get a doctor to come out at first. And then once he did, he advised them to just let nature run its course. Said there wasn't much hope. Not a thing he could do. It was in the Lord's hands. Doctor just advised they use cold compresses, morphine, and the like to keep him as comfortable as possible. But Terrence junior was one of the lucky ones. Guess the Lord wanted him to live, 'cause somehow, he pulled through. But even so, it took him almost a year to recover. It was a miracle that Charlene didn't get sick as well. She's closer to your age … well, what we guess to be your age anyway."

I smiled and took her hand. Her palm was so rough. Like sandpaper. It had been smooth, like golden oiled silk I remembered, when I'd first become part of the family. All the chemicals she'd handled, constantly scrubbing to disinfect everything during Daddy's illness had changed that. I wondered if her hands would ever be soft again.

"Then my sister Lily was expecting again and just terrible sick," Mama continued. "She'd never been that sick while carrying Charlene or Terrence junior. Too much for her to travel up to see us and certainly not up to our coming down to visit them. Then, as you know, Daddy got sick with the cancer that next spring. And somewhere in there, Aunt Lily lost her baby and was in no shape to be on the road either. So that was the end of any kind of traveling anybody might be doing," she shrugged, patting my leg lightly.

"So, tell me about Charlene," I asked. "Beverly's the new baby, right?"

She nodded. "Yes, she's four months old now, I think."

"And Charlene? What do you remember about her?"

"She was a very pretty girl. Tiny. Small bones and quite light-skinned, kind of like you. Her hair had a little of that red in it too like yours, but darker, more of a brownish red like you'd see in a muddy creek, I guess, and very curly. Yours is more of a … well, mahogany I would call it … and so thick and straight. Kind of unusual I've always thought, sweetie."

I smiled.

"Charlene being so light skinned is surprising in a way since my sister and brother-in-law are both so dark, but these things are at the hands of the Lord as we all know. Last I saw her was just before you came in our lives, Helen, so she could have changed a great deal. Aunt Lily sent me that picture I showed you of the two children right when Daddy first got sick, remember?"

"Is that pressed into your Bible too?" I asked.

"You know me too well, my little moppet," she replied, slowly pulling out the photograph.

Terrence was very thin, tossed together like a jumble of sticks, slumped forward, his head turned partly away from the camera in the photograph. Charlene, however, was looking straight forward and smiling broadly, her teeth shimmering like little white pearls. Clouds of dark curls framed her face, which, as Mama had mentioned, appeared to be quite a bit lighter than Terrence's, at least in the picture. Huge dark eyes, again so much like my own, twinkled brightly in the sunlight. We weren't related in any way, of course. There was no way we possibly could have been. I hoped we were the same size. Maybe she'd want to share clothes. Mama had just made me some very nice longer dresses with ruffles on the sleeves and hem … Mrs. Canfield's mythical tapeworm must be creating a growth spurt Mama had commented when we discovered that all last fall's outfits were far too short.

Mama carefully tucked the picture back into her Bible.

"What about the town? Can't you tell me a little more about that? Why is it called Orange Mound?"

"Just a little more talk and then I want you to get some sleep," she scolded lightly.

"I promise."

"An orange mound is another name for an Osage or mock orange. I have to admit I don't know why the town was named for such a strange-looking fruit. Daddy always thought it was an odd choice." She took a deep breath, looking past me out the window and was silent for several moments. "Orange Mound might be the only place on this earth where we colored folk are allowed to be ourselves," she finally continued, clearing her throat, her gaze still riveted out the window.

"What does that mean?"

"No washroom signs. No drinking fountain signs. No separate waiting rooms at the trolley depot in Orange Mound. No separate restaurants or cafes. No standing high up in the balcony to watch a play or go to the picture show. You're allowed anywhere to shop or use the lending library. Excellent schools – both elementary and high schools. Excellent teachers. People are clean, homes are clean, streets are clean. Everyone is kind to everyone else. Everybody goes to church every Sunday. We always wear our best dress, starched and pressed … our nicest hat … our newest pair of mesh gloves while sitting in those well-worn, brightly polished oak pews. Always. We know that everyone has a purpose in life and that God guides us from within."

"That sounds like something you'd read in a fairy tale, Mama," I laughed softly. Go into any store to shop or any restaurant to eat or use any drinking fountain in a building? Watch a play from the main seating section? Even I knew better than that.

"Not a fairy tale," she replied, her eyes narrowing slightly. "No, it's a real place, Helen. It's a real place where a black man and a black woman can bring up their family with pride surrounded by a community of folks who feel the same. Although it's so sad that your daddy wasn't able to make this return trip with us, I know he's grinning down from above and knows this is the best road for you and me."

I hoped she was right.

Chapter 3

Orange Mound, Tennessee 1928

Lulled by the continuous rocking, I drifted into a dreamless sleep shortly after we'd changed trains, then was jolted awake as the brakes screeched to a halt several hours later. Looking out the window, I could see dozens of men rolling enormous bundles, each bundle wrapped in dark, heavy material, lashed together by thick ropes. The men pushed these bales end over end down a wide muddy path towards a large ship. That must be the Mississippi River I realized, looking out at the greyish waves, very choppy in the early morning sunlight. From where the train had stopped, a long line of horse-drawn wagons, piled incredibly high with huge bales, snaked far beyond my line of sight.

"Is that cotton, Mama?"

"Um ... hmmm," Mama answered with a sleepy nod, although I doubted that she'd slept so much as a wink during our entire trip. "Strange they're loading out onto that ship. Must have a mighty large inferior grade crop to sell. That can only be sold downriver in New Orleans as far's I know."

"What does inferior grade mean?"

"A brand-new cotton exchange building opened here in Memphis around the time your Daddy and I headed up to Granville. All the highest-grade cottons were supposed to be traded right here in Memphis. Anything below medium grade was to be sent downriver. Looks as though there are a lot of barges loaded with even more bales," she stated, pointing into the distance.

I nodded. I hadn't even noticed the long line of barges extending far beyond the ship.

"I've never seen the new exchange," she continued, shaking her head, obviously puzzled by the sight, "but I believe it's in the same spot as the old one over on Front at Union."

"Maybe there's just too much cotton to be sold in one place right now."

"Well, that might be," Mama agreed, but she seemed skeptical. "Seems odd to me though. Everyone says they always need more cotton. Looks like the rain has finally stopped for a while at least.

That's good. Once we move off this ridge, we should be at the depot in about fifteen minutes."

The train lurched as we pulled forward, curving away from the river before arriving at the depot. Hundreds of tracks threaded through one another in a tangled nest of steel in every direction. Mama took my hand as we claimed our bags and then carefully worked our way through the maze of tracks and passengers before stepping up into a large green trolley that had a sign for Orange Mound on the front window.

Orange Mound wasn't quite as grand a community as Mama remembered, but it was definitely much larger and cleaner than Granville. As the trolley clacked along, she frowned at several buildings with boarded-up windows and one small hotel with a cracked plate glass window sealed with some kind of smeary grey glue that distorted the arched words Dixie Grande Hotel into Dix Gande Hot. Next to the hotel was the restaurant where she and Daddy had celebrated all their family birthdays and special occasions, although it had apparently changed owners. A cheap metal sign swung from an uneven chain over the entrance.

"Oh dear," she murmured. "I suppose that was inevitable. The last time I saw poor Mr. Bryce he was leaning so heavy on his cane … having a hard time breathing as well, I remember. I'm sure he's a lot happier now to have joined his wife …."

Although she didn't say if the man's wife had also died, I assumed as much and squeezed her hand looking up at her. Don't leave me please, I prayed silently as she looked away from me. If you think these things, sometimes they can really happen. I'd heard that from a girl at recess one day last year while Daddy was getting so much sicker. She was talking about getting an expensive doll for her birthday, but I could only think of it in terms of losing my family – the only family I could remember.

"I didn't hear that he'd passed, however," Mama continued in a quiet voice. "I guess Lil forgot to mention it. She wrote me that the flower shop and candy store had new owners and that everything seemed to be much more expensive everywhere … or so it seemed in her letter at least. Of course, I certainly haven't the smallest reason to complain. Lil's been so busy with the baby and all, I'm surprised she's had time to scribble out anything to me at all."

Our stop was only a few streets from the Calvary Baptist Church where Aunt Lil's family attended. Mama said we'd be joining that church too. She'd told me that the church where she and Daddy were married had been torn down after a fire completely gutted the structure a few years ago. There'd been plans to rebuild, but for some reason that hadn't yet happened. The property was fenced off, topped by two lines of rusty barbed wire, standing vacant except for a sea of tall scraggly weeds and scorched bricks when we passed it.

The exterior of most of the houses looked almost identical in Aunt Lil's neighborhood. Small homes but very nicely kept up as Mama noted in approval. She said they were called shotgun houses because if someone fired a gun through the open front door the bullet would whistle straight out the back door. Each house featured a well-shaded front porch accessible by climbing five wooden steps, a trimly squared front yard that was bracketed by a sturdy tall picket fence inside of which grew a small tree, usually peach. Several rows of a garden patch were visible out back, bursting with huge late summer tomatoes, ripe blackberries and pole beans.

The inside of my aunt and uncle's house was a hodge podge of broken furniture, wooden crates, mishappen metal statues, dented lamps, and cracked urns, however. It looked as though a furniture hauling wagon had simply dumped everything off the back and no one had ever thought to organize the mess. Which was exactly what had happened when Uncle Terrence inherited the stuff from his deceased employer, an old widowed white lady with no family over in Memphis. He'd hoped to repair and sell everything, but there wasn't much market these days for such hopelessly old-fashioned junk, according to Aunt Lil.

One had to turn sideways to move between the couch and an armchair to get in the front door and carefully pry two lamps apart to walk into the tiny kitchen. I was told later that a few newer houses in another block had an indoor privy, but theirs was outside, which was a good thing since the kitchen where such an item might be placed was far too crowded with just the cooking stove and sink. Mama had already mentioned that we'd be taking all our meals out back, sitting on low wooden stools. When it was raining or cold, everybody would have to eat a bit faster of course, but it was never as cold here as up in Wisconsin, she'd assured me.

I doubted that Mama and I could live at Aunt Lil's for very long. Terrence junior slept on an old bedroll beside the kitchen stove. Mama would be joining Aunt Lil and Uncle Terrence on narrow pallets that filled the only bedroom. I would join Baby Beverly and Charlene on even smaller pallets thrown down randomly at night, wherever space permitted, between the crates and furniture jammed into the front room.

The only picture in the house was of Jesus Christ, who appeared to have sprouted a massive halo of thorns, praying as he gazed heavenward into a bright ray of moonlight in a painting that hung over the tiny fireplace in the front room. Mama mentioned that the plantation owner who had originally sold off many acres of his property to the Orange Mound land developers had insisted that this same picture adorn every house's front parlor. I already missed our house back in Granville but knew better than to say a word to Mama. Though she would never complain, I strongly suspected she missed it as well. Coming back to Orange Mound without Daddy was very hard on her no matter how enthusiastically she'd spoken about our heading home.

My biggest problem was not the crowded house, however. Right from the start it was obvious that Charlene had no use for me whatsoever. I met her only a few hours after Mama and I had arrived. She was sitting on a stump behind the house, eating a peach. She tilted her head sideways and glared at me.

"Um, hi. I'm … I'm Helen," I finally stammered. Charlene didn't bother introducing herself.

"Yeah, I figured as much. You know, school's startin' next week," she jeered, wrinkling her nose. "That the kinda dumb outfit you people wear up North?"

"Well, yes," I replied, looking down self-consciously at my dark blue cotton dress. It was horribly wrinkled and slightly stained from our two days on the train. That really couldn't be helped, but it was one of my favorites. Mama had just finished tatting the white collar a few days before Daddy had died.

"Kind of a … baby dress, doncha think?" Charlene shrugged, tossing the peach pit over her shoulder, high up into the tomato plants. She licked the juice off her fingers while still staring at me.

"Oh, I … dunno," I replied, futilely attempting to smooth down some of the larger wrinkles.

"Just what grade are you in, anyway?" she scowled, crossing her arms. Despite her unpleasant expression I thought she was even prettier than her picture that Mama had shown me.

"I should be in grade three this year. How about you?"

"I'm supposed to be in four but they're saying I might skip to upper four or even lower five 'cause I'm real smart … way ahead of the rest of the class last year."

"Wow, that's amazing!" I answered, truly impressed. I did fine with my studies, but doubted I might ever skip even part of a year.

"You know your arithmetic tables through twelve?"

"I … think I remember 'em …" I replied nervously, looking down at my wrinkled dress again. "Well, maybe. I did once anyway. When my Daddy got so ill, I missed a lot of weeks of school last year, so I might only remember them through the nines. I guess I haven't thought much about it."

"You gotta know 'em through your twelves in be in grade three at my school. An' you can't use your fingers," she snorted.

If I was behind, I would catch up. I was determined about that. If this snobby cousin was moving up to grade five, I certainly had no intention of falling backwards into grade two!

Then Charlene added: "Yeah, my mom said my uncle died. Tough for your mom, I guess."

This girl had called me a baby and was not being very nice. But why would she think that only my Mama was hurting?

"It was hard on both Mama and me," I replied quietly, but firmly.

"He wasn't even your real father!" Charlene taunted. "You don't even know who your real father is … or your real mother either, do you?"

"No, of course I don't," I stated, determined to keep from bursting into tears. "But they've always been my real parents in my eyes."

I had looked so forward to meeting this cousin and I already hated her. I started to walk away when Charlene tossed out after me:

"You sing in your church choir up North?"

"Yes, I do … or did," I replied, turning slowly to face her again. Maybe now she would be nicer. If we were both in the choir at least that would be something in common.

"You goin' to the audition after Sunday School tomorrow afternoon?"

"What audition?"

"For *Hallelujah*," she sighed. "Didn' your Mama tell you nothin'?

"What's Hallelujah? A Bible skit?"

"A talkie."

"What's that?"

"You know, a moving picture show? They're gonna make talking picture shows now … well, sometimes anyway … don't know if always."

I wondered if she was trying to prank me, maybe just telling some tall whopper of a tale to make me look stupid. A talking picture? Our family had gone to a few moving picture shows before Daddy had gotten ill. One was called *The Gold Rush* with Charlie Chaplin that was very funny. There was another one about trains where three musicians playing in the orchestra pit used their instruments to make lots of crazy sounds. Daddy and I had loved it, but Mama was not too keen and thought it quite silly. She preferred live theater concerts.

A very beautiful girl in the moving pictures named Lillian Gish had been on posters in the train depot as well as the trolley car we'd ridden in earlier. I wondered if that poster was for this talkie picture as Charlene called it. The poster had seemed every bit as exciting to me as that picture of Jesus sprouting thorns hanging over Aunt Lil's fireplace. I wouldn't ever dare admit that, however.

"No, I've never heard of a … talkie picture," I replied cautiously.

Charlene shook her head in disgust, rolling her eyes.

"Just *talkie*. Not talkie *picture*."

"Oh … sorry. Talkie."

"Do you know the hymn "Follow the Drinking Gourd?" We're supposed to sing that for the audition. We sing it in church all the time, so everybody in my choir already knows it really good."

"Sorry, I don't know it, but maybe I could learn …" I answered, my voice trailing off. I could usually learn songs pretty quickly, but I didn't want to say that in case this one was really hard. From the outside, Calvary Baptist Church had looked huge, much larger than ours back in Granville, so maybe everything they did was a lot more difficult. There was no way to know.

"Kind of like learning your elevens and twelves?" Charlene snorted. "Doubt you could memorize all the verses, though. There's a *lot* of 'em."

She sang through a couple sections of "Follow the Drinking Gourd." She had a very pretty voice.

"I like it. That's really nice. You said it has a lot more verses?"

"Yep."

"Could you maybe sing the first part through a few times? Um, please? I could learn it … maybe."

"Yeah, I could … but I won't," she smirked.

"I know 'Wayfaring Stranger,'" I replied, clearing my throat. "Maybe they would let me do that one. We sing … I mean, sang … that one back at my church in Granville. It's kind of the same idea … sort of."

"No, they only want us to do this one. That's the one Mrs. Nelson's gonna play on the piano. But you can try, I s'pose, long as you're all right gettin' laughed at," shrugged Charlene, walking towards her house. "But I don' know why you'd bother if you ain' gonna do the tune they're requiring to even be considered for the children's choir."

"What children's choir? You mean to be in your choir at the church?" Now I was confused. Maybe this talkie picture audition thing was a joke after all.

"No, of course not. Wow, you're really dumb, aren't you?"

I bristled but said nothing. *Sticks and stones may break my bones, but words will never hurt me, I recited inwardly.*

"The children's choir they're using for the talking picture," she replied over her shoulder. "Anybody can be in that stupid choir at church. Even Terrence goes to the rehearsals. He just mumbles all the time … ain' never even sung so much as one note."

Chapter 4

Orange Mound, Tennessee 1928

The audition was held in the church basement. Even though the basement was cooler, I could feel sweat trickling down between my shoulder blades. Mama had done my hair in two thick braids, fastened up tight on each side of my head with bright red plaid ribbons she had just bought, so that helped somewhat. *Don't scratch your head, she'd whispered. They might think you have lice or worse.* Charlene had taken one look at my hair, laughed hysterically, then bounded down her front steps and raced ahead, refusing to walk with me. Mama had given me good directions, though, so I found my way to the church without difficulty. Mama said she needed to stay with Aunt Lil to help with laundry. I knew she didn't think I would do well because I didn't know the hymn but thought I should at least try. *There are probably other children who won't know the hymn either*, she'd whispered gently. I knew better though. If the choir sang that hymn all the time, the other children would know it quite well. Terrence was sprawled on the front stoop whittling some kind of toy whistle out of a scrap of wood. He grunted without looking up when I said good-bye.

The basement at the church was lined with long rows of wood benches, all filled with children dressed in their Sunday best. Some children who looked far too young to audition squirmed next to their older brothers and sisters. I filled out a paper with my name and address, was given the number forty to pin on my dress and found a place at the end of a bench in the back of the room. The little girl next to me didn't smell very good. I think she might have wet her drawers. I was nervous but was glad I wasn't quite *that* nervous.

After they called each number, a tall woman with loud clacking shoes would then lead that child down a long hallway. From our seats, most of us leaned forward, trying to steal a glimpse out the door whenever it was opened. The dark hallway disappeared into a shadowy tunnel. I had hoped to hear the song a few times before my turn, but all the doors must have been firmly closed each time. Sometimes I could hear a piano thumping way in the distance but that was of no use.

Charlene's number was twenty-seven. She had been sitting in the front row with two friends who blew silent kisses as she moved out the doorway. Her friends were called next. All three girls wore dark yellow print dresses; Charlene's dress reminded me of sunflower petals. Mama always said that I shouldn't wear that color since my skin wasn't dark enough. Like me, Charlene was a lot paler than her friends and I didn't think the dress looked all that good on her. It didn't matter, though. I was certain that she would pass the audition.

The little girl with the soggy drawers was number thirty-five. She left a small yellow puddle on the bench. Good luck I whispered to her as she walked past me towards the clacking shoe woman. She shook her head, whispering "thanks", but continued staring at the floor.

I knew there must be another exit where you were taken after your audition since no one ever returned to the room. That was probably all to the good. Otherwise, those going later would have a better idea what to expect which wouldn't be fair. Kind of like not cheating on an arithmetic test. That made me think about maybe not remembering all my elevens and twelves tables and having to know them to move up to grade three. I had stumbled through my twelves for the third time when my number was called.

"Are you nervous?" the clacking shoe lady asked as we clattered down the hall. Her shoes echoed loudly off the walls.

"No, not really, ma'am." I already knew I wouldn't pass the audition so there was no point in being nervous. It was oddly calming.

"You're not?" she frowned, stopping for an instant. "Well, I must say, that's certainly unusual. You do know that Mr. Vidor himself is in the room listening to all the children auditioning today, don't you?"

"I'm sorry," I replied, looking up at her. "I don't know who Mr. Vidor is, ma'am."

"Why he's the director of this whole production!" she sputtered, obviously shocked by my ignorance. "I can't believe you didn't know that fact, child!"

We turned a corner and started down another hallway. We then passed ten doors until she stopped and knocked. Now I knew why I couldn't hear any of the other singers.

"Come in," said a muffled voice. "We're ready."

"Go on in," the woman commanded. She opened the door, then shut it firmly behind me.

There was a piano near the door. The pianist, a tiny dark woman in a bright blue dress with silver feathers in her hair, firmly pressed open her hymnal with both hands.

Three white people, a nice-looking man and two women, sat in wooden chairs at a table at the back of the small room.

"What's your name girl?" demanded one of the women, her pencil poised in the air.

"Helen, ma'am."

"And your last name, Helen? Speak up girl!" added the other woman in a loud voice.

"Helen Mason Campbell … ma'am," I replied.

"Age?"

"Eight, ma'am," I answered. I really didn't know how old I was. Daddy had thought I might be closer to five when they'd found me in their car four years ago, but Mama always disagreed and said age four.

"I'm Mr. Vidor and these are two of my assistants, Miss Dobbs and Miss Carson," said the man. "Are you also in the church choir here, Helen?" He had a pleasant face and very nice eyes. Suddenly I really wanted to be part of this talkie picture or whatever it was called. I bit my lip.

"I just moved here, sir," I said slowly, keeping my voice as loud as possible, but looking down at my feet. "I'm very sorry, sir, but I don't know the hymn that we're supposed to sing. We never sang that one at my old church, sir."

"And where did you move from?" replied Mr. Vidor, gently.

"We lived in Granville … that's … that's near Milwaukee, sir."

"Wisconsin?"

"Yes, sir."

"And how long have you been down here, Helen?" asked Miss Dobbs.

"About two days, ma'am."

"*Two days,* eh? Well, I must say, you're a brave one to try this on!" laughed Mr. Vidor.

I had no idea what he meant. Try what on? Maybe that was some phrase that only white people used. They whispered to one other, Miss Carson shaking her head. I was quite sure they were just going to tell me to leave.

"Well, how about you sing something from your old church," nodded Mr. Vidor. "Did you have a favorite? Mrs. Nelson probably has it in her book, I should imagine. I'm sure she'll be happy to play it for you."

I glanced at Mrs. Nelson. Her pudgy hands reminded me of little brown mice resting over the keys.

"It's called "Wayfaring Stranger" sir," I replied.

"That's in my book, sir," stated Mrs. Nelson, clearing her throat, "but it's in a terrible key … too many sharps for me to keep track. I would have to work this out before I could play it, Mr. Vidor. I'm sorry."

"Well, give her a starting note then," he suggested. "Can you sing it *a cappella*?"

"I'm sorry. I don't know what that means, sir."

"By itself. Without the piano."

"Oh, yes sir," I nodded. "I can do that, sir."

Mrs. Nelson exhaled loudly, then looked in the back of the book and flipped through the pages to locate the hymn.

"It would probably be best if you played the first few notes of the melody line for her, Mrs. Nelson," added Mr. Vidor. "That would be helpful, I'm sure."

"Yes sir, of course," Mrs. Nelson nodded. "That's no problem." Given her sour expression, it was rather obvious that his request *did* present a problem, however. After a couple of wrong notes and apologies to him, she played through the first line, but there was still something not quite right. There was a wrong note or an extra note or something else very strange, but despite that, I could still hear the correct song in my head.

I pictured my little choir standing like green and white penguins on the three narrow splintered steps leading up to the altar at my old church in Granville, all eight of us doing our best to sing along with the wheezing pump organ.

Always remember you're singing for God, our choir teacher Miss Beach had frequently scolded. *Sing out from the very bottom of your heart. Never scrimp on your notes, my little angels! Form every word completely before it leaves your lips and always keep that tune high up in your throat. High up! Never just dangle something thinking you're singing modern. That's simply dreadful. Dreadful, my little angels! You want Our Lord to hear every single word of praise every single time!*

"Well, girl?" scolded Miss Carson. "Do you need Mrs. Nelson to play those notes again or are you going to just stand there daydreaming, child? You're wasting everyone's time here."

I shook my head, but she played the notes anyway, again with the same mistakes.

"*I am a poor, wayfarin' stranger, while travelin' through this world of woe,*" I began singing … singing out from the very bottom of my heart as Miss Beach would have required. It was odd to hear only my voice echoing in the room. "*Yet there's no sickness toil nor danger, in that bright world to which I go.*"

Mr. Vidor gestured for me to continue.

"I'm goin' there to see my father. I'm goin' there no more to roam. I'm only goin' over Jordan. I'm only goin' over home."

"Go on," nodded Mr. Vidor, settling back into his chair.

"I know dark clouds will gather 'round me. I know my way is rough an' steep. Yet beauteous fields shall rise before me, where God redeems their vigil's keep. I'm goin' there to see my mother. She said she'd meet me when I come. I'm only goin' over Jordan. I'm only goin' over home ... I'm only goin' over Jordan ... I'm only goin' over ... home."

When I finished all three judges were staring at me. Sweat trickled freely down my neck again. After a moment the women's pencils began scratching loudly in their notebooks. Mr. Vidor tapped his pencil quietly on his lip, obviously deep in thought. The clacking shoe woman opened the door and walked inside a few steps.

"Say thank you," she scolded in a loud whisper, shaking my arm.

"Actually, just a minute," replied Mr. Vidor, gesturing for the shoe woman to wait. "I don't think I've ever heard that song, but it's very nice. Maybe you could teach it to the other children?"

"Oh, yes sir," I responded breathlessly. "I'm sure I could, sir."

Mrs. Nelson exhaled loudly, clearing her throat.

"Wonderful. Miss Dobbs, Miss Carson, mark down that I want to include this song ... uh, what was it called again ... um, Helen, correct?"

"Yes sir. It's called "Wayfaring Stranger," sir."

"Yes. "Wayfaring Stranger," right," he repeated. "I might want this as well as the children's march we're planning to use in the preacher scene where Daniel first rides into town on the donkey. As part of the children's parade. Maybe we should lengthen the children's parade in fact. Or it might even be a better song than what I was planning to use. The tenant farmers in my dad's fields where I grew up back in Texas used to sing "Follow the Drinking Gourd" ... said their grandparents used to sing that on the slave plantations. But I like this "Wayfaring Stranger" much better."

"Mr. Vidor, perhaps it might be best to see if Nina Mae knows the song and have her teach it to the other children when she gets here in a day or so," remarked Miss Dobbs. "Or maybe it's one Nina Mae could just sing by herself."

"No, no, that wouldn't work, Miss Dobbs," Mr. Vidor frowned, shaking his head. "Nina Mae will be in the crowd taunting Daniel through that entire section, remember?"

"Oh, of course!" Miss Dobbs laughed. "What on earth was I thinking? Guess I'm more tired than I realized, Mr. Vidor. But she could still teach it ... well, if she knows it, that is."

"Right, right," he nodded, frowning slightly. "Thank you again … uh … Helen, correct?"

"Yes sir."

My excitement flattened like an old balloon snagged on a twig. I'd felt certain I had passed the audition if Mr. Vidor wanted me to teach the song. Now I wasn't sure about anything. The clacking shoe lady grabbed my wrist and marched me outside, shutting the door firmly behind.

Chapter 5

One week later
Orange Mound, Tennessee, 1928

Before they'd moved up to Granville, Mama had worked as a nurse while Daddy studied for a teaching degree at the Collins Chapel Hospital in Memphis. He'd been eager to teach other doctors at a new black college outside Milwaukee and wanted to know about all the newest techniques in the medical field. Mama told me that Collins Chapel was the only hospital in Tennessee where black doctors could train properly. The hospital welcomed Mama back immediately, but even though the building was now larger and employed more nurses, they could only offer her overnight work. And, since she'd been gone for over four years, she would have to start back at the lowest salary as well.

Many patients had been desperately ill for months before seeking care. Often an entire family was admitted only to die one by one within several days. The hospital was badly overcrowded with dangerously ill patients, most of them diagnosed with tuberculosis. There were plans to add another wing, called a sanitarium according to Mama, to help those people. So far however, like her old church that had burned to the ground, nothing had happened.

Daddy's illness had left us almost destitute I heard Mama mention quietly to Aunt Lil. I didn't know exactly what that word meant, but it sounded serious, and Mama was grateful to start at the hospital two days after we'd arrived. She could now sleep in the bedroom during the daytime also, which helped immensely with the sleeping arrangements. There were still heavy bills, in some cases a year overdue from Daddy's illness. She had requested daytime hours so she could be with me at nighttime but was given no guarantee when any earlier shift hours might become available; there were many nurses who had been awaiting an earlier shift for years.

This meant I was stuck with Charlene at home, at church and at school, even though Charlene was in level four, and I was, thankfully, in level three. (No mention was ever made of my needing to know my elevens and twelves tables to be placed in level three. When all the equations were scrambled about, I still hadn't gotten my recitation quite up to scratch.)

I was also stuck with Charlene rehearsing for King Vidor's moving picture *Hallelujah*. We'd both been cast in the same two scenes. The first scene was the children's parade with a donkey, which was a terribly sad-looking beast, missing the top half of its right ear. Almost blinded by a cloud of flies, the poor thing looked as though it had been eaten by moths and kept trying to lie down rather than continue walking in the middle of our parade.

Mr. Vidor's directing assistant, Mr. Butler, explained that Brother Ezekiel, or Zeke as he was also known, would be riding on the donkey in the parade. He had accidentally killed his younger brother with a gun in a scene that would be filmed later. They said that this shooting came before the scene where Zeke was dressed like the preacher riding on the donkey. This made no sense to me. If he'd killed a man, why was he now leading a parade like Jesus on Palm Sunday with all the children praising him? Miss Dobbs and Miss Carson were standing at opposite sides of a dirt road, each wielding a huge megaphone yelling directions as we started our parade rehearsals. They told everyone that it would all be very clear when the picture was completely put together at the end.

"Moving pictures are always done in small segments … think of railroad track sections joined together finally with large spikes," stated Miss Carson, exasperated with our endless questions.

"Seems kinda dumb to me," complained one girl in a loud voice who was marching next to me in the parade. "But I reckon dese white people all messed up 'bout Jesus an' such, Him ridin' in on dat donkey. 'Course mebbe he's diff'rnt in a whitey Bible, er sumpin'."

"Quiet over there!" bellowed Miss Carson, her megaphone aimed straight at us. "We have to get this *entire* scene down perfectly today before it gets dark. The trucks with the new sound equipment arrive tomorrow night. That's Friday in case you weren't keeping track. This scene is the first one Mr. Vidor will be tackling on Saturday with the crowds lining the street and the main characters arguing with one another on the side. We must block *and* shoot both sections – the one in the field and the one at the river – that's the river baptism scene, the next day, Sunday. That's the only day the men extras are off work. It's all *very* tightly scheduled!"

Somebody asked Miss Dobbs another question that I couldn't hear.

"It's practically impossible to mix together sound and moving pictures because they spool off at completely different speeds. That was the purpose of Mr. Vidor's acquiring the new sound camera. He's very determined with this project. Can you believe he isn't even getting any money for directing? That was the only way he was able to convince Metro-Goldwyn-Meyer -- that's the name of the studio we work for back in California -- to even consider making this picture!" she'd growled into her megaphone.

"We ain' makin' much neither," mumbled a woman standing in a wide rut alongside the dirt road with several other adults. "Don' know why this fella sez he workin' fer nothin' ... gotta be *sumpin'* in it fer him. Nobody I knows does sumpin' fer nothin'! Uh uh. No suh. 'specially no white man."

The only song we were asked to sing was the first two verses of "Follow the Drinking Gourd," which I learned quickly. No mention was ever made about "Wayfaring Stranger" or about this woman named Nina Mae, who might know the song and be able to teach it. That entire conversation from the audition seemed to have been forgotten. I considered asking Charlene if she thought I should ask but knew she and her friends would just laugh in my face.

The truck with the new sound camera and equipment that Mr. Vidor had ordered never materialized. Rumors flew about that it had been stolen right out of the train yard before the transport truck had even arrived. Miss Dobbs gathered all of us the next day to say that Mr. Vidor had now rented a news reel camera in Memphis and plans were to film everything silent like was usually done. The news reel camera would be best anyway for the larger outdoor scenes where he planned to add the sounds of birds, rain, insects, and such, later. Both Miss Dobbs and Miss Carson looked very tired.

After Sunday's filming, only the main cast and a few of the men extras – we'd been dubbed 'the littles' – would be taken out to a cotton plantation over in Arkansas. There were also three young boys who had been cast as part of Brother Ezekiel's family. They bragged they'd been asked to go out to the Arkansas plantation and then on to California to add their speaking and singing voices to the picture, but Charlene claimed they were full of baloney. At any rate, the rest of us 'littles' were told we wouldn't be needed after Sunday evening.

We'd been practicing to a large kettle drum beaten by a man who was listening to an old music timing device they called a metronome. In this way we'd been kept together with the same beat in our singing and marching. They now planned to film us using this loud drum, then reset the metronome to that same speed when adding the sound at the studio out in California according to Mr. Butler. Neither he nor Mr.

Vidor was too sure this idea would work, although it was fine for animated cartoon shorts.

When I glanced up at the camera man, I thought he was even cranking the handle two times around for each drumbeat. We had to repeat the same scene with the camera man filming in front of us, next to us, behind us, on either side, as well as up on a higher platform as we marched in the parade, working hard to keep in step and singing loudly so all our mouths would look as though they were creating the same words once the sound was added. The camera might come in close on any one of us during this time we were warned -- absolutely no tomfoolery would be tolerated!

Because our clothes weren't light enough, many of us had to wear white surplices borrowed from the Calvary Baptist Church. We marched along and sang two different songs, "Follow the Drinking Gourd" and another called "Praise, Praise" for which no one really seemed to know the same words, but that Mr. Vidor insisted be filmed anyway. The poor donkey looked even more exhausted lumbering along in the middle of the parade as we sang, keeping our lines tight together and in step to the loud drumbeat. There were adults lining both sides of the parade route who weren't singing but were shouting out loud praises to Zeke perched on the donkey. It was very difficult! We were supposed to keep waving little flags as well, but these were rather flimsy, and constantly broke away from the stick. The large, slippery bows around our surplices kept untying while our arms waved these little flags. Several women cheering alongside the parade rushed forward to retie the bows.

We were thirsty and very sweaty by the time Mr. Butler announced we were finished that day. Mr. Vidor then wanted to film Brother Ezekiel, the preacher, by himself, in something he called a close-up, riding on the donkey. A few minutes later the donkey gave a loud belch and plopped down in the dust, refusing to budge any further, ignoring all bribes placed in front of his nose. Mr. Vidor decided he probably had enough of what he called footage of the donkey, so he wasn't too concerned. We'd all been singing boldly, even though our voices would never be heard, while walking on the beat keeping tight together in our lines, waving our little broken flags and trying to adjust our dusty, drooping robes for several hours. By the time we heard dinner bells ringing in the distance, reminding workers it was time to gather for the evening meal, we were ready to join that poor moth-eaten burro smack in the middle of the dirt path.

Being in a moving picture was hard work.

Chapter 6

One day later
Orange Mound, Tennessee 1928

When Charlene and I arrived the next day, we were told to join a huge crowd of men and women who were all facing a small wood stage that was partly hidden in a stand of trees. We were instructed to react to Brother Ezekiel who was standing on the stage, supposedly pleading with all the sinners in the crowd to be purified anew by an emersion baptism. He was so far away, we couldn't hear anything, but nodded eagerly. Mr. Vidor, Mr. Butler and the camera man were all on a large platform behind us, so our backs were facing the camera. We were told to sit or lie down in the field of low weeds and dirt while they filmed this part on the stage.

We'd been divided into groups and given numbers that were shouted out to stand and begin moving forward at various times, walking with our backs to the camera. It was very confusing at first but eventually made sense. Miss Dobbs had mentioned that more than a hundred more adults were coming to film the huge baptizing scene in the river at a nearby location the following day and today's work must not spill over.

The man playing Brother Ezekiel was on the stage along with a woman who was supposed to be playing the organ, although I couldn't hear any of it, and the three boys who had boasted they'd be going to Hollywood to record their speaking and singing voices. Brother Ezekiel, whose real name was Daniel I learned, was gesturing up to the sky and then out towards us. Some of the adults close to the stage were told to get up on their knees occasionally, turning to face the person next to them and shout the words *"preach it brother!"* or *"praise God"* or *"you know it!"* when cued by Mr. Butler while the camera was rolling.

Then, after this sermon, the drum began beating out a loud, steady rhythm, same as yesterday. When called, our various groups were told to slowly stand from wherever we'd been sitting. At another cue, we were then to begin moving forward towards the stage, waving our arms occasionally, while singing the old spiritual "Gimme that Ole Time Religion" which Mr. Butler assumed we all knew. We would only be rehearsing this sequence once before going to action, shouted Mr. Butler, so he urged everyone to pay strict attention. Since most of our backs were to the camera it didn't matter if everyone sang different words, different sections, or were even in the same key, continued Mr. Butler. No one would be able to tell. This was all very confusing to my ears -- rather like a flock of vultures screeching upon discovery of a fresh possum carcass.

When Mr. Butler yelled out for my group to stand and begin walking towards the stage, there were still a few people sitting on the ground beside me. Suddenly the young woman sitting slightly in front of me, who was up on her knees and had been making weird faces, sticking out her tongue and wrinkling her nose, jumped to her feet and began frantically waving her arms, shrieking, "*I wanna be saved! I wanna be saved! Please, Brother Ezekiel! I wanna be saved! Please don't leave me behind!*" louder and louder each time.

As she started pushing roughly past me, her fist smacked hard into my nose, which started bleeding. Embarrassed, I blotted it against my arm, hoping it would stop quickly. Mr. Butler shouted through his megaphone to cut the action and for everyone to back up so we could film the sequence from a different angle. I assumed this woman would be thrown out, but instead she sat down on the ground next to me again. I glanced at her, still wiping my nose, leaving a long dark streak trailing along the back of my arm. The girl was quite pretty, with huge brown eyes and nicely styled hair peeking out around a stylish leather cap.

"Nina Mae," shouted Mr. Butler through his megaphone, "did you hear me before? Nina Mae McKinney? Listen up, girl! We need you to start shoving through the crowd much faster right after you stand. Tell that little girl next to you to hold back longer before she starts moving forward. We'll do a closeup from the front in a few minutes ... that's where we'll get you in place longer."

"And Nina Mae," added Mr. Vidor, also shouting through a megaphone, standing high on the platform next to the camera, "turn slightly left when you're first waving your arms, also ... before you start pushing through the crowd. Got that? Give us a minute to move the camera and platform forward a few feet here."

"Yessir! I understand," the girl shouted as she dropped back down into the dusty weeds and turned to face me. "Did you hear what ... oh goodness! You're bleeding! Did I just wallop you in the nose, little girl? I thought I'd smacked up hard against somethin'. I am *so* sorry. Heavens to Betsy, you're even bleedin' down your chin! Here, I've got a handkerchief tucked in my belt ... what's your name? I'm Nina Mae," she continued, gently wiping off my face and arm and then handing me the cloth to continue blotting.

Mr. Butler had begun yelling additional directions through the megaphone, momentarily aimed away from us.

"Thanks," I smiled, pressing the handkerchief hard against my nose. "It's not too bad actually, but it did kinda hurt, I'll admit. I'm Helen. You're … you're the star, right?"

Nina Mae wrinkled her nose and shrugged.

"Yeah, well, up 'til a few weeks ago I was just the third girl from the right in the dancin' chorus of this vaudeville act at the Cotton Club in New York City. I had a coupla funny solo lines in this one tune. Mr. Vidor saw the show and asked if I'd wanna turn a film he was doin' down in Tennessee. I told him I'd never been in a movin' picture, but he said that didn't matter. Also, I'd never been in Tennessee, so at first, I wasn't sure. Nervous about Mistuh J. T. Crow, y'know? I mean, you see, I grew up in Georgia and South Carolina, so I know bein' this far South could be, well, downright nasty … dangerous … you know. But then I thought, well, hell, Nina Mae, why not? And I'd always thought it'd be fun to turn a film anyways but never thought they'd want 'us', you know … and one with sound? Seemed like that'd be the cat's pajamas … so, here I am," she commented.

"Do you know the hymn "Wayfaring Stranger?" Mr. Vidor thought he might want to use it, but I think he's changed his mind now."

"Um, no, I don' think so," she replied, shaking her head slightly. "And, not to criticize, him bein' a white man an' all, but Mr. Vidor changes his mind like a starling on a windy day flappin' about in Central Park … uh, that's in New York City. He's a might smart man, don' mistake me none, but sometimes he seems more like a little kid wantin' that bran' new flashy red kite or the biggest lollipop in the drugstore."

"Places! Thirty seconds 'til rolling!" bellowed Mr. Butler into his megaphone.

"Sing it to me later, Helen, ok?" she whispered, as she moved to her spot slightly in front of me. "Sounds interestin'. I'd like to learn it even if Mr. Vidor don' want it. Oh, an' keep the handkerchief just in case my next hit's a technical knockout."

"Technical knockout?"

"Boxing term. Never mind. Shhhh … here we go."

This time the filming was stopped almost immediately and followed by lengthy corrections. Then Mr. Butler, leaving a few seconds between each command, bellowed through his megaphone once again: "*Set metronome … drum … action! Camera rolling!* As had happened with the parade scene yesterday, one man hoisted the drum and metronome while several others, who were referred to as roustabouts, continuing to move the platform to many various positions around us so the same action could be shot from multiple angles. The camera man would run ahead with the camera mounted with large leather straps tethered onto three expandable wood poles that reminded me of wobbly stork legs. Nina Mae whispered to me that this weird structure was called a tripod. News photographers would be covering a hot story in New York City and then throw the tripod, camera attached, over their shoulder and race to a different location to be the first to film another story a few blocks away, she said.

"First man back with the story in the can makes the most money, of course," she commented quietly. "I been knocked clean off the sidewalk right onto the electric trolley tracks or into a hornet's nest of motor cars many times. City's *real* dangerous that way. Everybody rushin' to be first to git anywheres."

The platform and camera were then moved just off the small wooden stage to film Brother Ezekiel's sermon at close range. The rest of us were told to just continue sitting out in the weedy pasture for about a half hour or so. Then they would shoot closeups of Nina Mae and all our groups moving towards the stage as seen from the front of the crowd.

"Hey, how's the nose? Could you sing that song to me now?" asked Nina Mae. "Now's about as good as we're gonna get I reckon. You said it was called "Wayfarin' Stranger," right?"

"Yes'm," I nodded, adding, "and my nose is fine, thanks, ma'am."

"Hey, I ain' no *ma'am*, child … I jes turned sixteen!" she laughed. "Like I said before, this is my first movie. I dunno the first thing about actin' t'all, but guess that ain' much issue, I reckon. Most all Mr. Vidor's wantin' is my makin' a lot of faces for the camera an' then recordin' a coupla songs at the Cotton Club back in New York."

"That's really amazing!" I replied, truly in awe. Imagine being chosen for a leading part in a play without ever having been in a play, much less a moving picture! Other than performers in black face -- usually shown with missing teeth, old-fashioned raggedy coats and muddy boots with long hairy toes wriggling out the end -- I'd never seen a photograph of a black person on a movie poster. But a movie poster or a magazine photograph with a beautiful young dark girl like Nina Mae McKinney? I'd never even dreamed that might be a possibility. I wondered if there was any chance that Nina Mae's picture would be on a poster on that trolley to Orange Mound like Lillian Gish.

"C'mon, sing that hymn for me now. I wanna hear it. When they's finished with Daniel, you know, Brother Ezekiel, we'll be too busy. That Daniel's a nice man but he's kinda full of hisself, in my opinion. Regular on the stage, they say. Some big parts like in *Showboat*. You heard of that one?"

I shook my head.

"It ain' a bad show -- big on Broadway these days. Anyway, that fella Daniel puts on fancy airs 'cause he knows a lot of stuff the rest of us don't."

Other than a faint buzz of conversation around me, along with directions being yelled further away down by the wood stage, it was fairly quiet. I hadn't realized just how loud that drum had been all along. Although my nose felt weird, I sang through the hymn, once again hearing Miss Beach's stern guidance in my ear.

"Hey, I really like it," Nina Mae nodded. "Too bad Mr. Vidor didn' wanna use it. He tol' me he's tryin' to make everything like what our people would actually do rather than a white man's ideas. But as you can guess, there ain' no way any one of us is gonna say to him: 'hey, Mr. Vidor, sir? That ain' how such 'n such is usually done,' y'know? Man don't know much about jazz singin' or such, that's fer sure. But never mind that. You gots a whale of a voice, Helen. Guessin' people tell ya that all the time though, right?"

"Our church choir director, Miss Beach, back where I'm from in Wisconsin, used to complain I was too loud when I should've been more ... well, prayerful," I apologized.

"No, no, I mean that in a *good* way!" replied Nina Mae, looking at everyone sitting around us. "Your voice ain' half bad for a little kid. Don' you folks think so?"

Several heads nodded along with a low murmur of agreement. Everyone was tired. We were all fighting off hordes of hungry mosquitoes and flies now that the day was getting warmer. An old man, black as a shriveled prune, who was lying on the other side of Nina Mae, snorted something that sounded pretty mean though.

"Maybe one day you'll be a singer. A jazz singer like me even ... how old are you?" asked Nina Mae.

"Nine," I replied, then quickly crossing my fingers behind my back added, "well, almost anyway. I think it'd be fun to sing jazz!"

"You gots any idea what *real* jazz music even is, little girl?" the old man suddenly spat out, glaring at me as he propped himself up on his elbow.

"You mean like Mamie Smith?" I replied cautiously. I'd heard a phonograph record of Mamie Smith when a Victrola was playing in a big store just before Christmas last year. Mama didn't approve of jazz music, and I hadn't much liked the woman's voice, but that didn't mean other songs might be fine.

"Yeah, yeah. Or Ethel Waters, Bessie Smith, Ma Rainey, Ida Cox," grunted the man. "Dey's the names everybody knows 'cause dey made them records. A lot of them really good blues ladies nevuh had dat, uh, so-called means of opportunity though, y'see. Chicago style. Yeah … dat's the *real* style you want! Um, hmmm."

I nodded but Nina Mae rolled her eyes and made a face.

"So then, jest who you countin' as playin' amazin' blues or jazz music, ol' man?" she frowned, crossing her arms. "You been in New York lately? Ain' nothin' good comin' out of Chicago no more … least that's what every musician 'round me is sayin', an' they should know!"

"Dat garbage?" snorted the old man, spitting an enormous wad of green phlegm over his shoulder. "Huh, dat's all mistuh whitey's music these days like that white boy Bix Beiderbecke. Man plays cornet. Or *tries* to play cornet anyways. Pshaw! Even when them New York Negro musicians are playin' dat nonsense, it still sounds like garbage 'cause it gotta be all nice an' sanitolized for l'il miss whitey's innocent ears."

"What's that? You mean sanitized?" Nina Mae jested. "Ain' no such word as *sanitolized*, ol' man."

"You knows what I means, girl," he grunted, spitting again.

"Stop spittin' you hear me? Dat's dirty!" scolded Nina Mae. "We ain' all cravin' rollin' aroun' in your nasty brown slobber!"

Without apology the man continued speaking.

"It's like this here movin' picture … jes' a bleached-out view of who we really is. You gotta see dat, girl. Dey only want you 'cause you look like a pretty white girl, but instead, you's black. You don' see dat den you is *blind*, girl, an' you knows it! Pro'ly sing duh same way."

Nina Mae stared at the man her arms still folded. "Okay, so how did you git to be such an authority on wha's good an' wha's bad in music, mister? Huh?"

The man sat up completely and extended both hands. He was missing two fingers on one hand and his thumb on the other. I shuddered. His hands were horribly mangled.

"I was a banjo man. Most weeks I's makin' well ovuh forty dollahs. Y'know what dey's payin' me tuh roll aroun' out here today an' tomorrow? Five. Five whole dollahs for two days work. Most money I's made in the las' month. But see, here's the thing. I played wid some of the best jazz boys back in Chicago 'til I gots crippled few years back. Frost bite. I weren't even the reg'lar man, y'see, but I filled in. Don' think there's a black 'n tan in that city I didn' play at. Oh, you betcha! Louis Armstrong, Joe "King" Oliver, Jelly Roll Morton. You name 'em. All the bes' bands. Small groups – y'know, five, six, mebbe seven men at most."

"You evuh heard of Duke Ellington? He's at the Cotton Club in New York City these days. You can' tell me *his* music ain' as good as your old Chicago style! No way!" interjected Nina Mae.

"Oh Lord in heaven! Duke Ellington? Black man shrouded in a white cape, girl. Ya gotta go back to when musicians could *hear* each other an' was free to move about inside duh tune. No hot shot ice monkey writin' out dese whitey arrangements for dem big swing groups like Ellington's in New York dese days. Hot jazz meant jes dat: Hot jazz. Mmmm hmmmm."

"Well, sorry ol' man," she sighed, shaking her head. "You jes' talkin' nonsense to me. An' what's more, sounds like you never worked with much of the lady jazz singers anyway, so your opinion don' weigh much by me."

"Eh, sometimes. Nevuh much liked dat nasty Ma Rainey kinda noise, but sometimes there was one of them on a gig beltin' out some good new stuff. A few were real good."

Nina Mae frowned, muttering something I didn't hear.

"Bes' jazz singer I evuh heard was mebbe, what, five er six years ago at the Sunset Café right there on The Stroll in Bronzeville – dat's the south side in Chicago. Young gal. Name of Emma Jackson. Light-skin black girl from N'Orleans they said. Sister or cousin or sumpin' mebbe of jazz piano man Tony Jackson. Beautiful gal but hooked real bad on da shit dey said. Snow, y'know? She didn' do no recordin'; her cousin didn' neither far's I know. She died a coupla months aftuh I saw her in some kinda insane asylum I heard. Tony died 'bout dat same time."

I stared at the man. Emma Jackson. That name seemed vaguely familiar. Probably one of Daddy's patients who'd had the same name.

"Bes' place today to find black musicians playin' real jazz they sayin' is in Paris."

"Paris? You mean like in France?" scoffed Nina Mae. "You crazy?"

"Yep, dat very place. Paris, France. Dat's where I'd go, I tell ya if I had my finguhs back. I hear we gettin' better treated ovuh there too. Lots of work 'cause them whitey French musicians don' wanna play N'Orleans style jazz. They's all too damn uppity. But dem folks ovuh in Europe, 'specially Paris, love dat ole N'Orleans style jazz! So dat's leavin' it wide open for da real thing, y'know?"

"I'll believe that tale when the Lawd turns the Mississippi River into wine like in the Bible," muttered Nina Mae.

"Looks like dey's runnin' the camera back over here," the man grunted, struggling to lay down sideways once again. "Time to resurrect the real Jesus for ol' mistuh whitey, mah friend ... guess dat wine gonna hafta wait, girl!"

"Watch yourselves y'all don't go rollin' in that filthy man's slobber!" Nina Mae stated in a loud voice to everyone sitting around us, curling up her lip in disgust.

Chapter 7

Orange Mound, Tennessee 1928-1929

That following Monday after school, I had raced in the grey pouring rain to LeMoyne Gardens where we'd been working. Like a circus I'd attended with my parents so long ago, almost everything from the production had disappeared. Only a few sodden piles of wooden planks remained, marking the stage where Brother Ezekiel had delivered that sermon none of us could hear. Huge puddles sloshed within the web of ruts that had been gouged by heavy trucks, tents, and equipment.

For months afterwards I daydreamed about the movie, wondering if Mr. Vidor had finished his filming or if the missing sound camera equipment had reappeared. How long did it take to make an entire film, I wondered. Four months? Eight months? A year? Longer?

On those rare occurrences Mama brought me along on the trolley into Memphis, I studied all the announcements pasted on the walls inside the depot, on the paper borders inside the trains or on the windows of the cinema as we clanged past. My hope to glimpse a poster featuring the beautiful Nina Mae McKinney or an announcement of the new talking picture's arrival faded as weeks became months, then months a half year. There were many posters announcing movies starring Lillian Gish, Louise Brooks, Marion Davies, and Greta Garbo, but nothing about *Hallelujah*.

Curiosity got the better of me one night after supper. The mock orange trees were newly dotted with tiny buds, and spindly weeds, grasses and yellow buttercups were poking up out of the black mud in our yard. I asked Charlene if she'd heard when the film might be coming to our cinema. She'd shrugged without a reply, but Terrence snorted: "Nevuh. You's a dumb fool, girl."

"Never?" I frowned. "Why not?"

"If dat film s'pos'd to be a talkin' picture like you says, there ain' no 'lectric sound speakin' equipment in any cinema *in dis whole state*, girl! Least ways, dat's what I heard. Mebbe dem white cinemas up North gots 'em, but no way dey's showin' any kinda Negro movie up dere, you kin bet da rent on dat! Big mouth fool like Mr. King Vidor an' his money is soon parted as duh Bible sayin' goes. Says so dat right dere in Proverbs, y'know?"

I was rather surprised that Terrence knew the expression came from Proverbs, but that aside, this was the most I'd ever heard the boy say about anything. Charlene gave a halfhearted nod in agreement, then continued ignoring me as usual, working a sliver from her thumb. She now had a boyfriend, more a man, truth to tell, so she was rarely around, which suited me just fine. This man had already taken her to the cinema several times, to a local café most Saturday nights and had given her two very smart, stylish outfits on her birthday. She looked very pretty and so grown up in those clothes.

I thought it would be nice to have someone give you gifts like that, but I didn't like this creepy man at all. The whites of his eyes slithered like watery, broken egg yolks and a carpet of stubbly whiskers jutted out of his cheeks and down his neck. He blew out smoke rings from the stubby cigars that dangled from his greasy lips.

For the last several months Mama had been working much longer hours – all night into late morning six nights every week -- and the hospital had cut her pay by almost one third, so she was earning even less money. Everyone was complaining about the big pinch, Mama had sighed.

Rumors floated everywhere attempting to explain this big pinch. All my school friends shared what they'd heard after church meetings, outside drug stores, inside markets, during recess from other children and from our own families. Much of the blame was placed on excess goods such as that massive cotton crop Mama and I had seen being hauled down river when we'd first arrived. Too much of *anything* means that it's practically worthless even if it's of quality. Somehow though, there was now far too much of *everything*, from crops to automobiles to pie safes to freight cars. Those groaning shiploads of unwanted cotton were only the tip of the iceberg according to one news headline. Few businesses could afford to buy or store, much less manufacture, goods from raw materials because banks were unable to provide loans even to their best customers, the article had stated.

Nervous, people were now withdrawing every penny they'd scrupulously saved in the town's bank, opting instead to conceal their wealth at home. I'd overheard two men whispering about this after church one Sunday afternoon. Then, only a few days later, the only banks in Orange Mound suddenly shuttered their doors. Not certain how any of this could happen, I asked Mama. She explained that lending institutions had such limited cash reserves, many were being forced into bankruptcy overnight, unable to offer any advance warning.

In addition to banks closing, stores were being abandoned in downtown Orange Mound in the middle of the night. Usually the merchandise had mysteriously evaporated as well. It was said that every business owed money -- and a lot of money at that -- but because of high interest rates few were able to pay back even a fraction of their bottomless debts.

Without a word to anyone except his son, Uncle Terrence had hopped aboard an empty freight car at midnight one rainy night, heading out for a job at a coal mining camp in the Cumberland mountains. Only black men were hired as mule drivers for the Tennessee Mining Corporation he'd heard. A set of skittish mules could prove deadly for everyone on a mining team, so the mule drivers were hired to live with, feed, tend and drive the often-stubborn animals. My cousin Terrence said he planned to join his father in a month or so, but, like most of what came from the boy's mouth anymore, that seemed rather suspect.

Terrence had dropped out of school just after Christmas. He claimed to have taken a night job stacking shelves at the Piggly Wiggly store in Memphis. But Mama said she'd seen him hanging around with some rough-and-tumble trouble, as she called his new work mates, near the hospital on various occasions. Since the hospital was nowhere near the grocery Mama suspected the shelving job was a blind. Because Aunt Lil was so worried about Baby Beverly, Mama instructed me to keep quiet regarding our suspicions about Terrence. If Mama had known about Charlene's new boyfriend, she would've been concerned about him as well, but I saw no reason to mention him. The sooner that stinky man went away the better.

At Mama's suggestion, I'd started blocking from my thoughts those people who weren't very nice – like Charlene -- who were just outright mean. Charlene didn't have it within her nature to ever be nice except within the tight circle of her best friends. People like her were born hostile, and they would probably *stay* hostile, snorted my own few chums at school. Charlene had spread a vicious rumor stating that not only was I adopted, but that my real mother was a notorious, loose woman who still brazenly walked the streets in Milwaukee and that my real father was a fugitive wanted throughout the country for a score of brutal murders. Further embellishing her tale for her admirers, she'd claimed his picture was displayed prominently on the Bureau of Investigation's mural in post offices everywhere.

Her most avid admirer, however, continued to be her boyfriend, who had introduced himself to me as: "Mr. Zach B, short for The One and Only Mistuh Zackariah Brown at your service. Of course, that ain' my real name," he'd joked, winking. "Jes' one of many 'alias' monikers … I am sure you knows why."

I didn't know why but I certainly didn't *want to* know either. What I *did* know was that he and Terrence were sneaking around until very late most nights. I'd hear Terrence thumping into the house with what sounded like small bottles – too small to be bootlegged whiskey of any kind I surmised -- just as the sun's pale fingers began stretching across the horizon. I confess to having discreetly looked about but never found bottles anywhere. In Terrence's defense, however, he occasionally offered to sleep in the room with Beverly so that Mama could get adequate rest for a change, now that they were both trying to grab a few hours of sleep during the daytime. When Aunt Lil asked Terrence if he still planned to join his father working with the mules at the mine, he'd muttered he'd rather be dead than sleeping in some cave reeking of animal filth.

On those rare nights when Terrence was snoring out in the kitchen, Charlene was out enjoying the good life as she'd been whispering to her girlfriends. One of my friend's older sisters had been in on a conversation with Charlene.

"She doin' it an' doin' it an' doin' it, an' she ain' bein' careful, not in the least!" the older sister had spat out to us in disgust. "Might foolish, workin' fo' dat ugly bum. Ain' no man worth dat."

I wasn't entirely sure I understood what she meant, but I had a good idea.

Zach had told Charlene that he'd just turned eighteen, but he looked a lot older than that to me. My friend's sister confirmed that as well. "Hell, dat boy's twenty-five if he's a day!" she'd sneered. "Dunno why any girl as pretty as Charlene would believe any big promises comin' outta some nasty body louse like dat. Dunno why *any* girl would, fo' that matter!"

As each week passed, Beverly's condition worsened. Sometimes she would stop breathing, turning blue for almost a minute before a series of violent coughing spasms shook her tiny body. Gradually her sharp, ragged breathing would then return. Hot mustard plasters placed on her thin protruding ribs brought about limited results. The baby now slept with Mama during the day and Aunt Lil at night, so they were on hand immediately whenever she lapsed into these terrifying fits. For weeks now she'd refused to nurse more than a few minutes and the thinned rice gruel that Aunt Lil fed her was spit up almost immediately. Mama thought she felt unusually warm also, especially one unusual, large spot in the middle of her chest. Aunt Lil finally got her in to see a doctor who examined seriously ill children at low cost or free a couple afternoons each month.

His diagnosis seemed pretty useless though, Mama had told me quietly. Although Aunt Lil explained to the man that the red spot forming on the baby's chest was from the hot mustard plasters, the doctor disagreed. He thought the baby might well be suffering from a radiation burn and asked if we had anything containing radium in the house.

Radium was being added to everything from butter to toothpaste to cosmetics these days. He said he'd seen this identical burn on other infants in recent months. In his opinion, even a cheap alarm clock with radium dials might be enough to trigger a burn if a sick child slept close to the clock face. Admittedly, very few doctors agreed with him, but he believed that radium particles mixed in water like this expensive drink called Radithor or added to salts or food could be very harmful. Concerned by several rapidly deteriorating patients, he was among a mere handful of doctors closely scrutinizing radium exposure. He wished more would take up the concern.

We had no such clocks, toothpaste, water or salts, however.

Most of the time Beverly appeared frightened, and would thrash, screaming in pain for hours. Completely exhausted, she'd finally drop into a fitful sleep. She was still the size of a larger five- or six-month-old infant according to the doctor, even though she was almost three times that age. She couldn't sit, crawl or stand, and didn't recognize her own name even though she responded to sounds. Her cries seemed weaker with each passing day. Something was very wrong.

Before he'd left, Uncle Terrence had built an eight-inch-thick straw mattress nestled into a wide wood box with the hope of making Beverly as comfortable as possible. She looked so tiny curled up onto the stained cotton ticking, her little fists raised up close to her ears, her knees drawn up in pain high to her chest. Two weeks ago, Aunt Lil had beaten Terrence with a cast iron griddle when he'd remarked that the baby looked more like the carcass of a scrawny, burned-out chicken. He couldn't figure out why anybody would bother fussing over her. Obviously, that kid's as good as dead, he'd muttered.

Seething in rage, his mother had then locked him out of the house. Where he stayed was anybody's guess. No one claimed to have seen him. And no one seemed to care. Maybe he'd finally headed out to join his father working with the mules at that coal mine,

Mama had whispered to me, but Aunt Lil hadn't heard from Uncle Terrence either for over three months now. He'd written once and sent a little money, but since then, complete silence.

Charlene had moved her pallet out to the kitchen in her brother's absence, but I knew she rarely slept there.

Chapter 8

Orange Mound and Memphis, Tennessee
May-November 1929

Beverly died in her sleep on a hot Thursday afternoon in early May. Members of Calvary Baptist along with a few friends and neighbors had arrived at the church by early evening. In the church basement, stifling with thick humidity as though mid-summer, everyone knelt on small rag rugs, surrounding Aunt Lil and her child. At times we'd join hands, keening until exhausted. We'd then curl up on our sides, breathing hard, sometimes crying out and other times whimpering before kneeling once again. Aunt Lil wailed the loudest, shaking her fists at the heavens or wildly pinwheeling her arms and beating her chest in rage. Seated on our rugs, we echoed her rants.

Mama had worked at the hospital for twenty hours straight. Arriving last, she slipped in quietly at the back of the packed room. Charlene failed to materialize at all. If Terrence was aware of his baby sister's passing, he knew better than to show his face. Though nothing was said, no one expected the older Terrence to make an appearance.

Sweat pouring down her face and arms, Aunt Lil turned slightly to face me and began ranting: "I is in the baddest need of the holy gospel! I needs tuh *hear* my Lord's gospel! Sing me dat Lord's message, girl. He must have somethin' fo' me ... dark an' darker are dese days I is livin' ... why? Why He nevuh is listenin' tuh my honest prayers? The *honest* prayers of an *honest* woman. Why He make dis innocent babe uh mine suffer an' suffer an' suffer an' now, He yankin' her from me forever? Why? I is a good woman! Why? Why don' He be listenin'? Why He be leadin' my husband out dere tuh some Sodom an' Gomorrah abyss ... oh, Lord who 'cept You knows where?

"An' my son! God help me, but how I despise dat wicked, wicked boy an' his bad, bad, evil mouth! I know You always sayin' in the Bible tuh turn the othuh cheek, but I is outta cheeks wid dat wicked boy, Lord! An' my Charlene! Where she gone? Why ain' she here with her mama, Lord? Why she shirkin' bein' wid her mama these long, blacker den black days? Where'd she go? An' why Lord? Why?"

Aunt Lil grasped my elbow and roughly pulled me towards her. She then grabbed my face in both of her hands and began shouting: "Sing dat Lord's message to me, girl! I needs the spirit of the Lord's voice now – in my whole bein' right now! I needs tuh hear dat gospel. I needs tuh hear the Lord's message from dem angels singin' tuh me from the heavens. I needs it now, girl! If we is really created in His image, I needs to believe tha' God still cares for us, dem darkuh shadows He created down here … 'cause I jes' don' think He do care no more. Nuhssir."

As Aunt Lil's hot fingers slowly peeled away from my face, I hesitantly rose high on my knees. Against the continuing waves of weeping, I began singing "Wayfaring Stranger." I hadn't thought about the spiritual since singing it for Nina Mae McKinney out in that dusty field, alive with flies and mosquitoes, over six months ago. Murmurs rippled in a wave all around me, begging for more. A man seated much further back within the dense crowd, hidden from my view, began singing. His deep, rich voice led us into "Follow the Drinking Gourd." Some of the girls from my choir quietly added their voices as we continued with "Wade in the Water," then "Swing Low, Sweet Chariot."

Spirituals came back to me that I hadn't thought about since Daddy's wake or even earlier, from long ago at our Baptist church back home in Wisconsin. Unlike here at Calvary Baptist, we'd always done a lot of singing in my old church. Some were hymns I'd never even sung myself but had heard others perform countless times – "Balm in Gilead," "Deep Water," and "Gospel Train" -- all these and more spilled out passionately from within me.

The hidden man, his voice surrounding us like a mug of thick, warm chocolate, sang "Lord I Want to be a Christian" and then "Let My People Go". After a few moments I bravely added my voice to his. Gentle harmonies somehow tumbled off my tongue one after another without a thought. Another man whom I recognized from the choir, also joined in. On some unknown impulse I began singing a descant, a slightly different melody that rose up from somewhere within me, remembering our preacher's lilting chants and responses during prayers -- yet another dim memory from my old church. The keening background rose and fell, reminding me of icy waves crashing up onto the rocky shoreline along Lake Michigan in winter.

Abruptly, without any cue, everyone suddenly fell into an exhausted silence, as we dropped down into prayer, foreheads now touching the floor and faces buried in our palms. I caught a glimpse of the man with the voice like thick, warm chocolate.

It was the old man with the horribly mangled hands.

***

Five months later the stock market collapsed. But well before that fateful October date, we'd all been evicted from Aunt Lil's house and had moved to what was known locally as tenement alley in Memphis. This consisted of ten identical concrete buildings, each four stories high, offering a beehive of tiny, scarcely affordable apartments that stank of open sewer even in the coolest weather. Two bathrooms containing a filthy sink and toilet straddled the ends of each long hallway. Only Mama, Aunt Lil and I lived in our apartment; Mama didn't need to warn me to refrain from asking about Charlene, Terrence, Jr., or Uncle Terrence in Aunt Lil's presence. Occasionally we'd see Charlene when transferring on the trolley in Memphis. Crimson-faced, my aunt would grab my elbow and tromp fiercely in the opposite direction.

Mama worked almost non-stop at the hospital, often opting to sleep for a few hours in the nurses' dorm rather than head home. Out of necessity, Aunt Lil had taken over as my mother most days, about which I wasn't too terribly keen, but I held my tongue. If I wanted a place to sleep and have anything to eat, I'd have to help earn it, stated Aunt Lil brusquely when we were forced to move. School was a luxury, a thing of the past, she'd scoffed, having lied about my age to obtain a job at the Wonder Bread factory over on Monroe Street. My growth was stunted from a complicated birth, she'd reply when questioned about my small stature, followed by her whispering loudly in my ear: "stand up straight, girl! You ain' nevuh gonna git employed if you is always slouchin' down like an ol' rag wid no energy!"

We had to pass an x-ray exam in order to be hired for the bread company job. I passed without an issue, but a suspicious white spot glowed on Aunt Lil's x-ray, and she was denied employment. She accompanied me each day to the bakery, then stood in the daily work line hoping to obtain one of the hotel cleaning jobs. If she wasn't selected, she'd then go stand in the long bread and soup kitchen lines. Even though I worked for a bread manufacturing company, all their extra, usually stale, loaves were sent to their own thrift stores or the city's bread lines so that the manufacturer could be subsidized for their generosity by the Memphis officials. Their employees could just go stand in line after their twelve-hour workday, same as anybody else.

I was always hungry. Although the bread smelled so good as we approached the factory each day, I learned early on that snitching a raw blob of dough, no matter how tempting, only brought on severe stomach cramps. And God help you if one of the supervisors observed the act. People in the books I'd read back when I'd attended school had claimed a person would get used to that gnawing deep in your gut after a while. But that ache in my belly never quit. Sometimes it was less intense than others, but it never stopped.

Also, my back felt bruised from having to sleep tightly curled up on my side on the straw mattress that Uncle Terrence had built for Beverly. Aunt Lil couldn't part with the bedding since her baby had drawn her last breath while sleeping upon it. I was far heavier than Beverly, of course, and something resembling sharp pebbles pushed up under me. I told myself that it was like the old fable called the *Princess and the Pea*. But I felt like a filthy, hungry, stupid old crone, completely wrung out -- nothing like some exotic princess awaiting Prince Charming's arrival. On the rare occasions when Mama had the energy, she would work with me on my reading, bringing home children's books she'd secretly removed from the hospital library for a few hours.

Each time I happened to catch a glimpse of Charlene she looked so very grown up. And pretty. And clean. Even her hair sparkled. Most recently she'd had on a smart leather cap exactly like the one that Nina Mae McKinney had worn for the filming and a soft, flowing skirt that rippled like golden silk, that ended shockingly high above her knees. Despite Aunt Lil's and Mama's lowering their voices, I knew exactly what Charlene was doing – well, most of it anyway. Prohibition had been around for as long as I'd been alive; I'd never known of anything different. But even people living in dire poverty opted to get drunk on one hideous, illegal alcoholic concoction or another once they had a dollar or two in their pockets. If Charlene was getting paid by men for a few minutes of ridiculous panting, plunging, and groaning so brazenly displayed by the countless drunken men and women creeping about in stairwells or pushing up against the hallway poles in our tenement, well, so be it.

Chapter 9

Memphis, Tennessee – December 1929

As I walked out of the bakery after work one December afternoon, Aunt Lil, jobless that day, suddenly appeared out of nowhere. Without uttering a word, she grabbed my arm and shoved me along for several blocks past various restaurants and hotels she'd been hired to clean recently. Abruptly, she stopped in front of the Hotel Parisienne's wide veranda, festively decorated for the Christmas holiday with thick ropes of pine garlands woven with bright red, gold, and silver ribbons. Several men and women had gathered around two young boys who were tap dancing on the veranda. Just in front of the boys lay a small battered, open valise, boasting a handful of coins that gleamed in the late afternoon sunshine.

As they finished their dance routine they received a scattering of light applause, no additional coins, and their audience began to drift away. The boys then began singing loudly, alternately strutting and then high kicking, moving in opposing circles. One woman, laughing with her companion, then lightly tossed a penny into the valise as the audience continued slowly along its way, heads turned to watch the dancers for a few more seconds. I recognized the two boys as the ones who'd bragged that they would be going out to Hollywood for the sound filming of *Hallelujah*. Aunt Lil and I were still standing at a distance from the veranda when I began politely applauding as the boys bowed.

"Don' you be doin' that! Dey'll jes' be wantin' yo' money!" Aunt Lil growled, slapping my hands away, while vigorously shaking her head. The boys were breathless, panting loudly. They mopped the sweat from their heads with their forearms, even though there was a sharp chilly breeze.

"They were in that moving picture that Charlene and --"

"An' don' you go mentionin' dat nasty girl's name in mah presence!" Aunt Lil interrupted, hissing loudly. "She ain' no kin uh mine nor yours no more -- you hear me? You an' your sweet Mama's da only kin I gots left in this ugly, ugly world. Only ones dat mattuhs, child!"

I nodded but didn't offer an apology. Mama had attempted to reason with Aunt Lil several times that no one really knew what had happened to Uncle Terrence. Her words always fell on deaf ears, however. In Mama's view, Charlene and Terrence Jr. were trying to make a living as best they were able. Not in a way that the Lord would have approved to be sure, but it meant fewer mouths to feed every day -- a blessing at present. Although making progress paying off Daddy's medical bills, a mountain of debt remained Mama had confided in me.

"You see dat, girl?"

"Yes ma'am," I replied politely. "They're very good, Aunt Lil."

She snorted loudly and then yanked me closer to the hotel.

"Mah point bein' is this, Helen. If them boys kin do dat – an' dey's plug-ugly tuh boot -- an' makin' some good coin, you sure kin do that too," argued Aunt Lil. "Everybody loved you singin' at my po' babe's wake … seemin' like years back already … you remember?"

I frowned as she began shoving me towards the veranda. She was incredibly strong.

"Aunt Lil," I protested, resisting as best as possible, "I can't go up there into their spot -- that ain't right! Maybe they even had to pay to use it. All the songs I know are hymns anyway. I'm sure that one they just did was brand new – you know, a popular one like you'd hear on a phonograph record … in a nice shop."

"Well, phooey on dat! Dem two boys is jes restin' their skinny l'il black hides right now -- dey ain' singin' or high kickin' or doin' nothin' at all," Aunt Lil frowned, glaring at me. "You go ask 'em tuh let you sing while dey's jes' busy restin' on dem scrawny backsides doin' nothin'. Don' seem tuh me dat would hurt none. Don' you know *none* of them good songs?"

I sighed, looking at her for a few seconds before replying.

"One of Daddy's friends had a gramophone. The man brought it to our house with a few records a couple times, but Mama didn't like my listening to that kind of music. She only wanted me to hear … to sing … you know … the Lord's music."

"Hmmmph, Lord's music, mah foot," she muttered. "Fat lot uh good de Lord's music's doin' us these days! Here we is livin' in dat cesspool wid rats duh size uh donkeys swarmin' on duh countuhs an' duh huzzies swarmin' like rats in duh stairwells! Yeah, duh Lord's definitely watchin' over us, Helen … oh you betcha."

"Aunt Lil --" I started to protest, but she interrupted.

"Den you gotta learn some uh dem new-fangled songs. D'you see them coins in that suitcase? Just fer singin' a song, for heaven's sake! Hmmmph. Your poor mama is workin' so, so hard. I worryin' 'bout her constantly doin' too much. An' you, well, you gots steady work, but it don' pay spit. An' me beggin' every day for cleanin' jobs jes so's I kin wipe up othuh people's slobber -- it ain't bringin' in near enough for us. See now, here's mah idea. After you's done at dat wonduh bread fac'try – an' I's still wonderin' what's so wonnerful 'bout it -- you kin stop here an' jes' sing a few songs, make some coin, y'know? Buy us a few eggs or a sausage mebbe. C'mon, search dat smart brain uh yours, girl. Don' you know a newer song?"

"There's one called "Keep on the Sunny Side" that I heard on Daddy's friend's record that we also sang in church back in Orange Mound," I replied, hoping this would somehow appease her. "Mama didn't approve of our choir singing it – said it wasn't dignified enough -- but I always liked it. These boys probably know it. So maybe, I guess."

Before I'd finished my sentence Aunt Lil began shoving me towards the veranda. The two boys were dipping water out of a dented rusty bucket and pouring it over their heads. Although I was nervous about speaking to them, maybe I could learn something about the movie.

"Um, hi," I waved slightly, moving quickly away from Aunt Lil before she prodded me any harder.

The boys squinted into the sunlight as I walked towards them.

"I remember you from filming *Hallelujah*. Did ... did you get to finish it in Hollywood like you said?" I asked, forcing a smile.

"Yeah," answered the taller of the two, hand shielding his eyes while still squinting. "Were you there? Don't remember seein' the likes of you anywheres."

"I was next to Nina Mae McKinney when you were on that wood stage out in the field with Brother Ezekiel. Mr. Vidor was moving the camera all over the place to shoot that same scene. We had to repeat it over and over."

"Huh, yeah, ok," nodded the taller one. "Yeah, I kinda remember that. Nice meetin' ya whoever you are."

I glanced back at Aunt Lil. She was leaning forward, hands on her hips, eyes severely narrowed. I knew from experience this was not a good sign. I pressed forward.

"I was wondering," I continued, clearing my throat, "if you'd let me sing "Keep on the Sunny Side" with you ... uh, just this one time that is ... right now? I'm sure you know it, right?"

The boys shrugged.

"Maybe we do," replied the smaller boy, scratching his cheek.

"Sure," stated the taller one. "We kin take yer request. But requests cost a penny."

"It's my aunt's … birthday," I replied, surprised how fast the lie spilled off my tongue. "And, um, she asked me if I could please sing it just this one time with you. Can't I do that? I don't have a penny. It would mean a lot to her. Please?"

The boys looked at one another then motioned halfheartedly for me to join them on the veranda.

"If anybody comes by an' adds to our kitty we gits it all," said the smaller boy, arms folded. "We ain't splittin' nothin' with you over one lousy song, y'got that?"

"An' ya still owes us that penny if one shows up anyway," added the older boy.

"Okay, sounds fair."

"You know the verse?" the older boy continued. "We only knows the chorus part. An' make sure you starts in a key we can sing in, not some dumb girly key. An' you gotta sing loud … you a church singer?"

I nodded, not sure if being a church singer was considered good or bad.

"Yeah, well, this ain' church!" he snorted. "Ya gotta sing even louder. God ain't listenin' in. Got it?"

I bit my lip and took a deep breath.

"There's a dark and a troubled side of life," I began singing, glancing at them and then continuing even louder. *"There's a bright and a sunny side too … though we meet with the darkness and strife, the sunny side we also may view."*

Surprisingly, the boys joined in with perfect harmony. It sounded like we'd been rehearsing the song for days.

"Keep on the sunny side, always on the sunny side. Keep on the sunny side of life. It will help us every day; it will brighten all the way, if we keep on the sunny side of life."

Three women walking down the street stopped in front of the veranda. The boys frowned, then sharply cocked their chins for me to continue.

"Oh, the storm and its fury broke today. Crushing hopes that we cherish so dear. Clouds and storms will in time pass away, the sun again will shine bright and clear. Keep on the sunny side, always on the sunny side. Keep on the sunny side of life. It will help us every day; it will brighten all the way, if we keep on the sunny side of life."

The taller boy pulled out a harmonica from his back pocket and began playing while the smaller one tap danced. I moved to the side and stood in awe watching. The harmonica was in a slightly different key from what I'd been singing and the melody a bit different, but not by much.

"Start with that first verse again," the older boy hissed as he finished playing to enthusiastic applause, "but stay in mah key, girl, ya folluh?"

During the harmonica solo two more women had now paused to watch. I started from the beginning once again and this time also sang the third verse before the boys repeated their harmonica and tap dance sections. The older boy gestured for me to keep singing the chorus again and again. He'd tell me when to stop. By the time we'd finished the tune, several more women and one man had joined the spectators and some of them even joined in singing the chorus with us. We ended to generous applause. I was shocked to see one woman toss a nickel into the old valise! The man and a couple other women each added a penny as well. The small group applauded lightly again and then began walking away.

"Ok," snorted the older boy. "You did alright by that. We won't charge you that penny. In fact, if you come back tomorrow an' do that song and a coupla other ones wid us an' we make some good coin durin' that time, we'll split with ya one quarter of the profits."

"Shouldn't that be one third?" whispered the younger boy.

"Yeah, but she's only a girl," he retorted. "Dey don' eats as much. Ok, so my name's Milton, by the way. This here's Walter. We played brothers in that movie but we ain' really brothers in real life even though some people think we kinda look similar."

"I'm Helen," I replied, smiling. "So then, the movie's finished? Do you know when it's gonna be shown here in Memphis?"

"Yeah, it's all done. But here in Memphis?" scoffed Milton. "My guess is nevuh. Who down here wants to see a film that thinks we's all still out hoein' cotton an' cheatin' our brethren outta their hard worked dollars? Or killin' our own brother ovuh some cheap hooker or cheatin' on our woman?"

"Cheating?" I replied, feeling my face go a deep crimson. "I thought the movie was about ... well, about religion ... what with Brother Ezekiel riding in on that donkey like Jesus while us children sang in the parade ... then the emersion baptisms they were filming later. Wasn't that what Nina Mae McKinney was shouting about -- that she wanted to be saved? Be baptized?"

"Religion?" scoffed Milton. "You serious, girl? Religion don' move nobody these days! Fast money, booze, gamblin', gats, dem show gals showin' all dat nice skin – now *dat's* da only stuff I knows whats gonna get a body tuh spend his hard-earned dime at da cinema!"

Chapter 10

Memphis, Tennessee - 1930

For the next nine months, exhausted, I'd sing with Milton and Walter several days each week after having worked at the Wonder Bread factory for a twelve-hour shift that began at 4 a.m. each day. The boys would take a short break when I arrived, begrudgingly agreeing after the first month to Aunt Lil's demands to give me a one-third split of any tips thrown in their battered valise during my half hour program with them. We always ended with "Keep on the Sunny Side" for our finale. That seemed to work best for extra coins from the audience. I quickly learned more tunes, worked to sing louder, smile bigger and eventually had the courage to play up to various audience members. Since I knew Mama would not approve, Aunt Lil and I kept quiet about the situation. Every penny counted in our fragile household, and we needed the money. Plain and simple.

My work with the two boys coincided with a lot of wealthier white folks taking their late afternoon stroll for a bit of air before dinner, eager to enjoy a little impromptu music from 'those three amusing little darkies' as one lady had referred to us while laughing at Milton's antics. It gave me a view of the world I wouldn't have had otherwise, but I often felt that view ran contrary to my Baptist upbringing.

At the bread factory each morning, we were issued stiffly bleached, white cotton frocks and scarves, that were as scratchy as cardboard. We'd don these garments, which slashed painfully into my armpits, after leaving our own filthy, ragged clothing in rusted lockers. I was very envious of the hotel audience's new or perfectly mended attire as they passed, particularly the pretty yellow parasols so many young women used to deflect the late afternoon's sun from their pale, creamy faces.

Now that it was so hot every day, I stank just like our apartment in tenement alley. I'd outgrown all but two dresses which were faded, patched, badly stained, and streaked with a combination of ground-in flour and dirt. Flour dust sifted freely into the lockers at the factory. My hair, though kept as short as possible, always pinned back sharply each day, hung in sweaty clumps laced with flour by the time I arrived at the veranda. My throat seemed coated in flour dust when I'd first begin singing but would usually clear up within a few minutes. Milton and Walter didn't smell very good either … not that this made me feel much better.

I was grateful to have the chance to sing – to do something that didn't involve pounding endless mountains of dough into submission, or worse, like Aunt Lil, waiting in line for the 'opportunity' to scrub floors with a stained, rancid rag soaked in Lysol. I prayed that one day I'd own a pretty dress, a little white straw hat with long streaming satin ribbons, and a yellow or peach-colored lace parasol to twirl over my shoulder. Mama said I should be grateful and continue to praise the Lord for the things that I *did* have. She claimed that many people were in far worse shape than the three of us. All the newspaper headlines blared constantly that we were in one of the worst depressions ever experienced in the entire country. Everybody blamed everybody else. The farmers blamed the manufacturers, the manufacturers blamed the U.S. Congress, the U.S. Congress blamed the banks, and the banks blamed the farmers. And everybody blamed President Hoover.

To me, though, there sure seemed to be a lot of people out there who were clean and obviously had money. People who wore nice clothes and had enough to eat without standing in soup lines and didn't stink like rotten eggs scorching in the afternoon heat. I held my tongue from ever contradicting Mama, but I questioned the Lord's concept of fair play.

Most afternoons I would get back to tenement alley a few minutes ahead of Aunt Lil. She stood in either the employment line or the bread line for several hours every day and would join countless other women hunting for food scraps. Mama was still the main breadwinner in our household, continuing to work hideously long hours every night with little to no sleep. She very rarely complained, however. If Baptists ever began worshiping saints, Mama certainly deserved to be at the front of that line.

Late one afternoon, I entered our stifling apartment and tore off my filthy dress. Standing stark naked, I began scrubbing the material with borax on the washboard in the kitchen sink. My knuckles were raw, cracked and stung sharply. I stopped for a moment to catch my breath and suddenly became aware of rustling noises and muffled footsteps. Not from the apartment above ours, but from the bedroom. Was it possible that Mama had overslept or that Aunt Lil had returned home early? No. Mine had been the only shoes at the front door.

Had the door been unlocked but I just hadn't noticed? I shuddered. I tried to squeeze the excess water out of the dress as I listened, scarcely breathing. More rustling noises. More shuffling feet. It sounded as though something was being ripped out of Beverly's mattress. Definitely a person, however, not an animal. I quickly tugged my sopping dress over my head, then picked up a rusted knife from the drainboard. And waited.

More tearing sounds. Then I heard a young man's voice whisper "damn it." Familiar yet not familiar at the same time. I moved quietly towards the bedroom, my hand tightly gripping the knife handle. Terrence Jr. had sliced the straw mattress in half like a layer cake and was pulling out dozens of small brown bottles that had been packed tightly in wooden egg cartons. He was then repacking the bottles in shallow wood crates with paperboard liners.

"Terrence!" I cried out in disbelief, the knife clattering to the floor. "What on earth are you doing?"

"Oh, yeah, hi," he grunted, glancing at me. "Didn' hear ya come in. Jes' lookin' fo' some uh, property tha' I lef' here by mistake, dat's all."

"Where've you been all this time?"

"You mean, like anybody cares?" he scoffed, flashing a lopsided smile.

"I do anyway," I replied. Did I?

"Where? Well, I guess you could say ever'where an' nowhere," he shrugged. His voice was deep, now almost a man's voice. "Got held up fo' a bit. You know what I mean."

"No, I don't know," I countered boldly, squinting as I attempted to read the label on the bottles. What was inside them and what were they doing in Beverly's mattress in the first place?

"Held up, eh … in jail. Up in New York City. Trump up charge, y'know? Jes' like down here in Memphis, dem police ain' nothin' but nasty, rabid dogs. Dax – he's mah bus'ness partner, y'see -- an' me walk intuh a buildin' dat was already unlock an' wide open mind you, an' we starts walkin' aroun' – dat's all we wuz doin'. But dey claims we was fixin' tuh steal stuff even though we didn' have one item in our han's when them cops caught us! Put Dax in jail fo' six months an' me fo' almos' nine since I had on mah person dis jagged ol' tin can lid dey consider could be a weapon."

"I see," I mumbled, watching as he carefully extracted several more bottles from the carton buried within the straw and placed them alongside others in the crate.

"But actually, we was lucky, y'know? What I means is, a few minutes later they'd uh foun' us on da top floor of dat buildin' but, we nevuh got dat far, y'see. We figure we'd got mos' of it out befo', 'course, but dat woulda been our last haul if it *was* dere, which maybe it *wasn'* anyways, y'know? But if it *was* dere, we missed out."

Confused, I said nothing. I wondered if I could possibly repack most of the straw into the mattress halves before Aunt Lil got home. If she found out that I'd allowed Terrence to roam freely in the house she'd be furious.

"But now, see, I'm takin' the rest uh my Radithor stash tuh sell -- finally! Worth even *more* money now. Dem stupid cops up North did me an' Dax a huge favor in point of fact! People still wantin' it an' no one's got it to sell no more since they sayin' it's illegal. Some rich ofay – him bein' white trash fo' sure -- dyin' of cancer or sumpin'. Court case sayin' it gonna be da end uh sales."

He continued carefully digging out the bottles from where they'd been expertly wedged within paperboard strips among the cartons. I was surprised that I hadn't broken any of them. Each bottle had a large cork on top. Maybe that had kept them from shattering.

"What's Radithor?" I asked. It sounded familiar, but I couldn't remember why.

"You know, 'a cure for the living dead' or 'perpetual sunshine' as dey wuz callin' it in all dat advertisin' an' such ... used tuh be seein' 'em all ovuy da trolleys an' papers, 'member? Dey not bein' allowed fo' a while now, 'cause uh dat court case, like I mentioned. Radithor is said tuh give a man back his ... uh, you know ... his *oomph* so tuh speak ... proven to cure everythin' from cancer, tuh the gout, tuh burns, tuh teethin' in babies, tuh fixin' up all kinds uh female ... uh ... troubles. Why duh gov'ment makin' it illegal is duh real crime – way more a crime den us jes' stealin' it so's people can get some ... well, relief or sumpin' in mah opinion! Gov'ment plum don' wan' people gettin' da help dey needs. Dat's jes' plain wrong in mah book, y'know?"

I stepped backwards out of the puddle that was dripping from my wet dress as Terrence continued.

"So me an' Dax, he's mah bus'ness partner, like I said, we was sellin' it, on duh black market, y'know, an' gettin' us a might good price, too! Stuff sold a few years ago fo' one dollar a bottle, an' even den, dat was might expensive, lemme tell you. Some uh dem rich white folks was said tuh be consumin' a coupla bottles *ev'ry day,* kin you believe? Hoo me. But even *befo'* we was in jail we was gettin' two an' three *times* that dolluh! I 'spect it'll be even more now. People is des'pert! When it's gone it's gone, uh course, but I plans on makin' lots uh dough while I kin. Glad my product was safe pack down in duh straw, though I gotta say, findin' you people weren' so easy."

While he was speaking, he'd extracted another dozen or so small bottles from the mattress cartons.

"Can I ask just how those ... cartons ... and the bottles, got inside the mattress in the first place?"

"Well, sure," he shrugged. "Me an' my Pa built 'em in there. Built 'em in that mattress after me an' Dax stole dem cases from a warehouse where dey was first hid here in Memphis, brought down from New York. An' dem cases was originally first stole from a warehouse in New Jersey, y'see. Guess dat man who owns dat radium water company, Mistuh William J. A. Bailey, him a white man an' rich as Croesus livin' out in New Jersey, didn't do such good ... what d'ya call it ... keepin' inventory.

"Anyways, he was gettin' wind tha' maybe the gov'ment was gonna shut him down, 'cause there was already some people sayin' they's gettin' sick an' such, which is a bunch uh hogwash. So, Mr. William J. A. Bailey, he started up makin' the product an' hidin' it tuh sell. Then someone stole it from his hidin' place an' brought it tuh Memphis an' then we stole it agin and brought it over here. Mr. Bailey, he claims this water is completely safe. All natural, y'see? I mean, I even seen pictures uh dese white girls workin' in clock factories doin' up dey lips an' nails wid some kinda radium paint jes' like Radithor that glows! Last for weeks dey sayin'. No problems at all. If tha' was dangerous, dey wouldn' be allowin' for dat, now would they?"

I frowned but said nothing.

"But, anyway, mah Pa heard from a frien' dat a lot of dem cases of the Radithor were bein' hidden all the way out here in Memphis, so we jes' took uh, friendly advantage so tuh speak, y'see? An' we figured dem cork tops would be nice an' easy fer a little bit uh fluff like Bev'ly tuh sleep on, y'know? Dunno what happen' to my ol' man after we picked up dis stuff, though. He up 'n disappear a coupla days later. Ain' seen 'im since."

"Which is exactly what *you* need to do, Terrence. Your Ma'll be here any minute," I stated, attempting to hide the revulsion I felt. Uncle Terrence had been part of this idea too, I seethed within. "You don't want to be around when she shows up."

"Almos' done. Jes' a coupla short rows tuh go," Terrence chuckled. "Guess she an' ol' Bev'ly are out somewheres, huh? How old's dat kid now? Didn' know if she'd still fit in dis bed but mighty glad it's here! We made it solid dat's fo' sure."

I stared at him.

"No, Terrence," I replied slowly, taking a deep breath. "Not exactly. Beverly passed away almost a year ago. I've been the one sleeping on the mattress. Your ma didn't want to part with it since that's where your baby sister died."

"Dead, huh?" he grunted, shaking his head, showing no emotion whatsoever. "Well, dese times is pretty rottin' fo' everybody out dere I reckon, huh? I'm sure my Ma put on duh big blubber show like she always do when anybod' pass."

Furious, I somehow found the strength to hold my tongue. He continued digging deep into the mattress to extract one small remaining carton and finished filling the last wooden crate.

"Ok," he exhaled, standing up and hoisting one crate over his shoulder. "Tha' does it. I gots this batch sold in advance at a min'mum of five dollahs per bottle. Don' know wha' good people think it's gonna do 'em, since ya gotta keep on takin' it but, dat ain' my problem. I betcha me an' Dax gonna clear over uh thousand dollahs! Kin you believe you was sleepin' on a mattress wid more'n a thousand dollahs buried right under you, ya l'il runt?" he guffawed, punching my shoulder.

"You need to get out, Terrence," I stated, struggling to maintain my temper. "Aunt Lil will be here any minute. She won't approve of this --"

"You think I care what dat ol' bag thinks?" Terrence interrupted, laughing. "You kin tell her tuh go tuh hell fer all I care! An' besides, Miss Uppity, don' ferget you ain' even mah real kin to boss aroun' anyways."

"Get out. Now," I seethed.

"It'll take me a coupla trips tuh get dese crates downstairs onto da wagon I gots parked past duh alley," he grunted. "Gotta be careful. Sure don' wanna break none of 'em. Tell ya what, maybe you kin go an' uh, deflect mah ol' lady from makin' one uh dem premature 'pearances as dey say, y'know? Better fo' you 'n me both since you's duh one gots tuh live wid dat ol' boat anchor."

Refusing to look back at him, I tromped down the stairs and then continued into the narrow alley that snaked between the apartment buildings. When I returned a few minutes later with Aunt Lil, Terrence was gone. While she used bathroom at the end of the hallway, I struggled to reconnect the two halves of mattress, crazily stuffing the piles of loose straw in between. It reminded me of trying to fill a lopsided layer cake. I then tossed the original canvas cover over everything. I had no idea if I would be able to sleep on it later, but unless closely inspected, it almost looked normal.

Later that night, lying on the lumpy mattress, the top half of which kept sliding sideways onto the floor, I remembered what I'd heard about Radithor. The doctor who'd examined Beverly claimed the child was suffering from radiation burns, not a reaction to Lil's mustard plasters. He'd seen burns like that on several industrial workers who were around radioactive metals on the job. Some had handled the product, but most had not. He'd also mentioned that some wealthy people who'd been consuming the health drink Radithor, which contained a tiny amount of radium, had been recently diagnosed with fast-growing, deadly jaw cancers. He was convinced they were suffering from radiation poisoning caused by that beverage.

Beverly had been frail from the moment of birth. Was it possible that she'd been poisoned because of her own father's and brother's greed? That in fact, the mattress hadn't been created for Beverly's comfort at all? I raged within. Or then again, was it possible Uncle Terrence had intended to sell the product hoping to bring his family up to a decent level of living? Maybe somewhere in the theft of those small brown bottles he'd been discovered by others with the same idea and had been arrested ... or worse. My feelings towards him shifted slightly; his motive *might* have been noble after all. His son's motive, however? My opinion on that remained unchanged.

Maybe there'd never been any danger to Beverly at all. The doctor who had examined the ailing child had been quite adamant about the poisoning as I remembered. But no other doctor at the hospital had ever mentioned such a thing according to Mama and she'd remained quite skeptical of his opinion. I thought back on Terrence's remark that he'd seen pictures of young white girls who worked in clock factories painting their lips and fingernails in radium to go to dances and parties after work. The stuff would glow in the dark for several weeks, he'd said.

Obviously, it was completely safe, or their bosses wouldn't let them do that, right? Well, I thought, maybe they wouldn't ... or, maybe they really didn't know ...

Or maybe they really didn't care ...

Chapter 11

Memphis, Tennessee – 1930-1931

Before leaving for work the following day, I told Aunt Lil that the mattress had collapsed under my weight and was simply far too small to support me anymore. Since we had no room to store anything, she reluctantly agreed to haul it out into the hallway. A few minutes later I heard scuffling at the door as someone dragged the mattress sections elsewhere.

When I got to my spot at the factory, a new girl had replaced the woman who'd been stationed to my left all these months. That woman, a small, older lady, had been lightly coughing, but only occasionally, during the last week. The flour dust drifted freely through the air and caused most of us to lapse into brief coughing spells. Like businesses everywhere, however, the managers were quick to dismiss any worker – particularly older ones -- who might have tuberculosis. The deadly illness had continued to ravage all ages throughout the entire country according to Mama. No reliable cure was available. With so many people out of work there was no reason to keep anyone on a payroll who couldn't contribute at full measure or worse, might infect others in the workforce.

During our fifteen-minute break for lunch, the new girl introduced herself as Sylvie. She then whispered to me that she'd been told the former worker had been fired for stealing.

"Stealing what?" I'd whispered back. "What on earth is there to steal in this place other than maybe a blob of sour dough starter or a few tablespoons of flour?"

"That's all I know," Sylvie replied, looking around nervously. "I didn't ask no questions 'cause I so desperately need this job. My mama passed a year ago. She was a singer --- a good one too -- well, that is, 'til she got the tuberculosis. Then my pa, he was blinded in that blast furnace explosion 'bout six months back up near Jackson. You heard about that fire, right?"

"Of course," I shuddered. "Everyone here was talking about it. Awful."

"They said over fifty men were killed – a lot more bad injured," she added.

She'd been taking care of her dad and two younger sisters but had been fired from her factory job last month. The managers had been forced to release all the black workers at several plants and replace them with white ones, she whispered. They – the town officials in Jackson, that is to say -- said us folk belong out workin' in the fields same as how we've always done. We each measured out another few cups of flour onto our wooden mixing boards, working while cautiously continuing our conversation. Sylvie said she'd been praying every night that here in Memphis things would somehow turn out to be different.

"Ain't no one's job's safe these days, though," she'd whispered after a few more minutes. "Don't matter the color of the worker. Businesses disappearin' overnight everywhere they're sayin'. Worst part, they is still owin' most of them workers back pay. Don't matter whether them workers' skin is white, black, orange, turquoise... color don't matter one whit."

Sylvie worked at the Wonder Bread factory for less than three weeks. I never learned what happened to her. She worked hard, kept her workspace clean, and kept to herself. Most of the bread was now formed into rough-textured small loaves for distribution to the ever-lengthening bread lines throughout our area. Two huge new ovens and steel-braced kneading cauldrons had been delivered recently and were awaiting installation. These had been purchased to produce loaves at a more consistent rate using far fewer workers. Another woman stood in Sylvie's place for a few days, then she disappeared as well and had yet to be replaced. I knew better than to ask any questions.

Sylvie's deceased mother had been a cabaret singer in Paris and Sylvie loved to sing softly while she worked. I learned two wildly popular French songs: "Après de ma Blonde" and "J'ai Deux Amours" which I then performed for anyone stopping to listen at the Hotel Parisienne. Milton and Walter made goofy faces and hopped about like spastic marionettes imitating monkeys when I sang the tunes, but I refused to let their antics bother me.

I'd now been added to their duo for almost an hour most late afternoons. The hotel had also recently granted permission to two other small groups of black musicians before Milton and Walter began playing each day. The competition for attracting an audience, visibly thinned out from a few months ago, and willing to toss a few coins into the battered valise, had now grown quite fierce. The hotel had recently started demanding a percentage of each performer's earnings as well. The manager contended we were renting the space.

Money must be damned tight Milton grumbled, if grown men had to filch pennies from three kids.

On days when it was raining hard, none of us showed up. No one walking past would pause even for a moment on such a day. Because I was inside the factory well before four thirty each morning, I rarely knew if I'd be heading home to tenement alley or racing over to the hotel until I was leaving work any given day.

One Friday afternoon as I emerged from the factory, the sky appeared to be clearing after what had probably been a long grey day of rainstorms. I arrived at the hotel only to find it deserted, a heavy downpour having greeted me when I was about two blocks away. A small part of the veranda was under an awning, and, hoping the hotel's desk clerk wouldn't chase me away, I ducked under the cover hoping to wait out the worst of the rain before backtracking to our apartment.

Aunt Lil hadn't been successful in finding many cleaning jobs for quite a while. In recent months she'd stopped trying altogether. Still distraught, she'd built a small shrine to Beverly and positioned it next to our front door using a crate she'd found discarded in the alley. The crate looked very similar to the ones that Terrence had used for hiding the Radithor bottles, but I doubted it was. I'd seen pictures of Catholic votives with flickering candles wedged into mounds of discolored drippings, along with wood or brass crosses, murky stones, wide ribbons, necklaces, fresh flowers and tattered pictures of men and women with halos whom I assumed were Catholic saints. Still a staunch Baptist, why my aunt wished to mimic such imagery baffled Mama and me.

Beverly's shrine was the only thing in our apartment that was neatly tended – the only thing that Aunt Lil was willing to spend any money upon other than food. And usually, she was buying food with the money that Mama and I had earned and then eating most of it herself. If Lil had stood in the soup or bread line that day, she'd often have already eaten all three of our rations by the time we'd arrive home. I learned to disguise scraping off small bits of the bottom bread crust with my fingernails when unloading the ovens, storing the crumbs there for a few moments until I could fake clearing my throat and carefully dissolve those tasty crumbs on my tongue.

Whenever I walked in the door, Aunt Lil was praying, moaning, or shrieking in despair at her child's shrine. Sometimes she hurled herself against the walls, which were rapidly disintegrating into plaster dust in two spots. Neighbors often pounded on their apartment walls all the way down the hallway, threatening to alert police and have us evicted. Mama insisted we be patient, stating that her sister was out of her head with grief these days, reminding me of Jesus' teachings to be calm in the face of our personal storms and upheavals. In my own defense, I was around Lil a lot more than Mama and my patience had shredded like a wet newspaper many weeks ago.

Sometimes a man or woman walking by while Milton, Walter and I were performing would give us the few remaining bites of their leftover meal. We'd stop playing immediately to devour everything on the spot. I couldn't help but compare the three of us to the small pack of mongrel dogs that had appeared nightly outside our back stoop in Milwaukee when Mama had tossed out scraps after our supper. We certainly wouldn't be tossing away such meaty scraps these days.

Even once the rain had let up, I was in no great hurry to go back home to tenement alley. The dark, rumbling sky foretold yet another storm, and I opted to wait it out on the hotel porch. Mama would be at work most of the night probably, and I simply didn't have the stomach to face Aunt Lil right now. Just as a long crackling streak of lightning lit up the sky I saw the silhouette of a man, bent forward, breathing hard, slopping through the thick mud towards the hotel. He stopped, wincing in pain, then stumbled up onto the veranda in front of me.

"You da 'T's sistuh?" he panted. A tall, dark-skinned young man, he was sopping wet, dressed completely in black. Only his teeth flashed white.

"Why?" I frowned, taking a step backwards.

"The "T" ... he sen' me tuh finds you ... said mebbe you'd be here."

"The "T"?"

"Y'know, yo' ... brother," he coughed, gasping for breath. "You gotta git ... to him dere."

I stared at him.

"What brother?" I said slowly. I had no brother, of course. Was the man simply mistaken or was this some kind of trap? Had he seen me singing with Marvin and Walter on a different day and assumed those boys were my brothers? While tongues of lightning flashed viciously overhead, I doubted anyone else would be venturing outside right now. Increasingly wary, I took another step away from the man.

"No, I mean ... your cousin ... Ter'nce," he added, shaking his head and now wheezing. Several red drops splattered into the puddle in front of the man on the wet porch. A huge dark stain was spreading quickly under his arm, seeping through his shirt, then dripping off the back of his hand.

"You're bleeding."

"Nevuh you mindin' dat," he groaned. "Jes' help us. Please. Dat's all. I's Dax. Da 'T' said he'd tol' ya 'bout us. Y'know … me an' him workin'," he winced. More blood dripped onto the veranda. The man bent over further and staggered to one of the chairs, sitting down hard.

"Where's Terrence?"

"I … cain' walk dere … he down… dat freight depot … on Secon' Street … y'know it?"

I nodded slightly but made no comment. The man slumped further down in the chair and then fell forward, landing with a dull thud onto the veranda. Shaking, I backed away. The drenching rain lashed sideways into me as I stepped off the porch. Without glancing back at his crumpled body, I began running toward Second Street. I didn't want to go, but Mama's voice had immediately wedged itself firmly into my ear: *this is clearly the path Jesus is calling upon you to follow, Helen. Do not disobey His word.*

Running as best as possible through the muddy roads lit only by an infrequent arc of lightning, I finally reached the freight depot. Three low outbuildings straddled a complex network of crisscrossing tracks. Only the lightning flashes illuminated the area as I carefully stepped through dense mud towards the closest building. Peering in the building's one window I could see nothing. The door was firmly bolted. I slipped and fell onto my knees in an enormous puddle. Pushing back up out of the muck, I made my way more carefully to the next building. If it was also locked, I was determined to leave this place despite Mama's insistent voice urging me forward.

The door to the second building wasn't bolted. It scraped loudly along the swollen concrete floor as I struggled to push it open. This building seemed to be a warehouse, less than half filled with various empty wooden crates and stacked loading pallets. A long series of windows built close to the ceiling illuminated the building's interior like a photographer's flash with each lightning streak. I swallowed nervously, certain that I must be visible to anyone inside the building. A long crackle of thunder followed by more lightning brought on a heavy downpour. Water began cascading over several crates, streaming into huge puddles.

Suddenly I thought I heard my name.

"Terrence?" I called out, cautiously, yet loud enough hopefully to be heard over the waterfall.

"Go pass … dat watuh spillin'," replied the voice, hesitantly. "I's … ovuh near da … wall."

He was propped up on one elbow, lying just inside a crate. A large blood-soaked tourniquet was wrapped around his thigh. Even in the gloom between lighting flashes I could see that his left cheek was ravaged, slashed savagely into strips. One eyelid was partially torn as well.

"What happened? What's going on?" I whispered, horrified, as I knelt down beside him.

"Dax foun' ya," he groaned, swallowing hard. "Than' … God."

"What happened?" I repeated, cautiously reaching out to touch his shoulder.

"Dem men … we stole dat Rad'thor?" he panted in agony. "Dey been followin' us. All 'long … seems. We's doin' all duh work an' dey's … jes' collectin' …"

"I see," I replied, even though I didn't. The vision of those brown bottles of Radithor snugly nestled inside Beverly's mattress flashed in front of me.

"See, dey sayin' dey was cuttin' us … intuh duh deal, y'see …but dey's nothin' but … but a gang … uh goddam lyin' ice … monkeys," he rasped, pausing to catch his breath as he began coughing. "Me an' Dax … we takin' all da risk … duh sales risk … y'know? But … dem bastud whitey crooks doublecross us. Now dey's jes' … steppin' in … an' dey plans … tuh collect up … all da … da cash, y'see?" he added. "So we's plannin' --"

"What about you?" I interrupted. "I don't think Dax …"

With a trembling hand, he moved my hand off his shoulder, shaking his head.

"Dey's still aftuh … Dax' 'n my … money. We done … hid it … y'see?"

"Terrence --" I began, looking in horror at his wreaked face as he interrupted me.

"All dem … whitey bastuds see's … us jes' as … dumb coons … dat's wot dey callin' us … dey's aftuh mah fam'ly fo' dat money … doncha unnerstan'?"

I frowned. Where was he going with this?

"You gotta git … git dat cash … git it tuh Charlene," he panted. "An' den … you tells her dat she's gotta … gotta clear out … now … tonight!"

"Terrence, let me at least try to find a doctor," I begged as he slowly shook his head.

"Ain' no good … git dat money tuh … my sistuh 'n her … fancy man. Dey both help wid gettin' it."

They? He must mean that awful pimp, Zachary or whatever he calls himself. I shuddered with disgust.

"Or Mama. She's a nurse ...maybe she --" I began, hoping he'd agree to my finding her. But Terrence interrupted me again, coughing, still shaking his head.

"No! Ain' no ... time fer dat! Lissen close ... now," he continued, struggling to speak. "Y'know where dey gots da ... da dead bodies ... buildin' nex' ... tuh dat col'r'd hosp'al?"

"You mean the mortuary across the street from where my mama works?"

"Yeah ... yeah," he coughed, his words slurring. "Dat's wot's call ... yeah. Morch ... ary. So, you ... go dere. Money's in ... da Hydrol trunk. In duh 'balmin' room. Wood ... trunk where dey ..." his voice trailed off as he gasped for air.

"Hydrol," I said slowly. "I don't know what that --"

"Hydrol ... it's 'balmin' fluid. Big lettuhs ... onna top. Black. Ya cain' ... miss it."

Ragged coughing shook him, blood splattering on the floor in front of where he lay.

"Under da lid uh dat trunk ... dey's a false ... padded linin'. Buil' up in da corner ... cash's in dere .... You gots tuh git it."

I swallowed hard, staring at him.

"Dem ... bastud's ... set me an' Dax up ... no way deys gettin' dere filthy han's on dat cash, ya follah? No ... way. You git dat mon...ey an' you fin' Char ... lene ... you goddit? Ma fam'ly ... mon...ey ... mah honor!"

He moved his head slightly, vomiting a huge bloody mass just past me. I stood up slowly and looked down at him. He fell onto his back, eyes closed. Barely audible he whimpered 'go ... now 'n ... git,' blood oozing out of his mouth.

I backed away and then retraced my steps out of the building. Although it was still raining hard, only an occasional flicker of lightning now lit up the intense darkness. I hoped that the thick darkness would also make it more difficult for me to be seen as well. I wasn't so stupid as to think that these men, whoever they were, if they'd followed me here, wouldn't just torture me for information the same way they had Dax and Terrence. I truly wished that Dax hadn't found me on the veranda. I should have just gone straight home rather than wait around, I chastised myself, Aunt Lil or no Aunt Lil. Whatever all of them had been involved with had now crumbled into this deadly nightmare.

"Oh Mama," I whispered to myself, cautiously weaving down different roads from my usual path, constantly checking over my shoulder as I worked my way back towards tenement alley. "If only you and I hadn't come to this godforsaken Gomorrah, Mama," I whispered. "This is not the family or the town … not even the church you remember when you were growing up, Mama." I shook my head thinking back on that picture of Charlene and Terrence sitting on their freshly painted white fence in Orange Mound, remembering my wish that Charlene and I would become good friends, sharing secrets and trading magazines and clothes. "It's nothing like that beautiful place in those pictures you showed me when we were riding down here on the train, Mama," I continued, tears in my eyes. "Not even close. That was just a dream from a long time ago. A dream we'll never find again."

Chapter 12

Memphis, Tennessee - 1931

The door to our apartment gaped open several inches, the frame splintered all along the edge. I walked in to find complete chaos. Glass crunched under my feet in the doorway. Every scrap of the burlap flour sacks that Mama and I had stitched together for use as curtains had been savagely ripped from the windows. The kitchen and closet drawers had been dumped out, the bottoms then hacked through and thrown against the walls. Swallowing, I cautiously called out Aunt Lil's name, simultaneously stepping onto the brass cross from Beverly's shrine as I crossed into the room. The photos of the saints were shredded into small pieces. One intact paper halo eerily clung to the wall behind where the shrine had once stood, held in place by a large splatter of blood.

Our apartment had only two tiny rooms, three if you counted the narrow strip called a kitchen separately from the living room. It took me all of two minutes to pull out my only other dress from under the rubble, hastily discarding my filthy wet garments. As I buttoned the replacement, I walked through the entire place. Aunt Lil was nowhere to be found.

Once out into the hallway again, I closed the door behind me as best as possible, then saw a neighbor's door quickly click shut when the occupant spotted me. I raced down the stairs and outside into the alley. After glancing in both directions, I began briskly walking towards the hospital, head down, hands shoved into my pockets, hoping to attract as little attention as possible on the busy street. *Please, help me Lord*, I prayed over and over. *Please* don't let anything have happened to Mama! As an afterthought, guiltily, I added Aunt Lil's name to that prayer and then even later, Terrence's and Dax's.

Mama was assisting with a surgery I was told at the hospital's front desk. I'd forgotten that she was now often assigned to that task as well. Even after the procedure she would be with that patient, in addition to two other patients, for several hours yet. No visitors were allowed access to the surgical areas. These fragile folks might contract tuberculosis or diphtheria brought in from the outside, stated the receptionist behind the counter. I could wait in the lobby area, although the hospital strongly advised I wear the mask she held out to me in order to protect myself from the filth brought in off the street. Mama's shift ended at four a.m. I glanced at the clock mounted above the desk. It was almost eight o'clock. The storm had moved on fortunately, but it was already dark as I walked out of the building. Just outside the hospital entrance I spotted a gold cufflink lying in the mud. I wiped off the mud then pocketed the item thinking maybe someone had dropped it while entering the hospital. I would leave it at the reception desk when I returned.

From force of habit, even though I was quite certain this funeral parlor only dealt with the colored, I walked around to the back of the mortuary. Even when no sign was posted one could get detained or arrested for mistakenly using the front, white entrance. We'd all learned about that nasty trick early in life. Hours were 9 a.m. to 5 p.m. I knew it was easily three hours past that time but was grateful to see light weakly filtering through the back window. I rang the bell, hoping someone would be willing to admit me. After a short wait, I rang the bell again. This time a small black man, clad in a heavy dark-blue butcher's apron, shuffled into the hallway.

He shook his head, gesturing at the sign on the door that stated they were closed.

"I really need to get in," I begged. My brain whirled with foolish ideas ... what story might this man find believable?

"Sorry, miss," the man replied, shaking his head slightly, his voice muffled through the locked door. "We always close at five, Monday through Saturday. Thems the rules."

"I have the ... the missing *cufflink* for Mr. ... oh, what's his name again?" I stammered, words tumbling out of my mouth. "The minister at the Baptist church sent me here directly from the man's wife – she's so distraught because she couldn't find both fasteners at first ... oh, I'm sorry I can't remember the man's name. Please don't call the church and get me fired for not remembering his name. Wake starts early tomorrow morning, though. I really need to place it with all the other clothing so he can be dressed properly in the casket," I pleaded, then elaborated even further. "They're an heirloom according to his wife – have been in his family for two generations. She insists they're visible for her husband's viewing tomorrow!"

"You lookin' fer a white man?" grunted the employee through the glass, frowning. "Ain't got no white men in here gettin' ready to be viewed or autopsied or buried or nothin'. Never have. Can't imagine any of our corpse's needin' cufflinks for heaven's sake. Most of 'em show up ain't even got on a *shirt*! Cufflinks? Miss, I'm afraid that your minister done send you to the wrong parlor!"

"Oh no," I replied, shaking my head firmly, showing him the gleaming cufflink in the palm of my hand. "He was definite. He said this one. Across from the hospital. I'll only be a minute. He said that the man … was still lying on the table. The minister said for me to just leave the cufflink on the … the Hydrol trunk so it was ready tomorrow morning."

"Well, yeah," he shrugged, scratching his head. "We always order our bottles of embalmin' fluid in them trunks, so he's got that part right at least." Still scratching his head, he reluctantly opened the door. I stepped in quickly and mentioned again that I would only be a few minutes.

"Only one room right now has a corpse on the examinin' table, if you're sure that's what the pastor conveyed to you, miss," he replied, shaking his head. "Don' sound right by me. Anyways, you jes' follow that hallway down to the end. Room's on the left. You can't miss it."

A strange smell filled the air, burning my eyes and making it very difficult to breathe as I walked down the dimly lit hallway and into the examination room. On a white enamel table in the center of the room lay a nude corpse. A huge, dried gash across the man's throat and another long puncture that plunged deep into his stomach had been partially repaired. I quickly averted my eyes. A hole positioned at the end of the table between the man's feet drained into a regular slop bucket on the floor, although the bucket was empty. A tall white cabinet stood in one corner of the room next to a small metal table that held a butcher's scale. On the opposite wall sat a wood trunk with the large stenciled black letters Hydrol Embalming Fluid on the side facing me. On the top of the trunk, stenciled in smaller letters were the words: "*GLASS – this side up -- use care*".

I moved a half dozen murky bottles marked Bleachol and Supremol off the trunk and then carefully pried open the hinged lid. Terrence had said there was an opening in the padding under the lid. Obviously, the padding would keep breakage down to a minimum. I patted all along the lining but there were no bulges or tears anywhere in the heavy black velvet fabric. I was just about to close the lid when I noticed a slight discoloration in the fabric in the bottom left corner. I slowly moved my fingers over the material, and found that with some effort, it could be pulled back slightly from the edge. I wiggled my fingers into the space and pulled out a small, badly stained towel, folded tightly over into three sections. Each section revealed ten $50 bills. One section also contained two $20 bills. I removed the money, refolded the towel and placed it back inside the liner. Then I quietly shut the lid, replacing the original bottles of embalming fluid along the top of the trunk. Inside the tall enamel cabinet, I found a stack of small clean towels. After carefully placing the money in sections of the towel, I folded it over and pressed it firmly down into my dress pocket. I placed the cufflink on the lid, next to a Supremol bottle.

Did the Bible say anything about stealing stolen money? I didn't know. All of them, from Uncle Terrence to Charlene to Terrence and their cohorts were certainly in the wrong, that much I did know. *It is never up to us here on earth to judge others,* Mama always warned me whenever she considered my complaints to be unwarranted. *That's our Lord's duty.*

When I left the mortuary, the clerk was nowhere to be seen. The door clicked firmly shut and locked behind me. After verifying as best as possible that I wasn't being followed, I took a wide path around several back streets, then headed down through the park to return to the hospital from the back. I had forgotten that the park was bordered by a high concrete barrier that emptied out into a dark, usually deserted ravine, however. One then had to scramble up a steep hill thick with underbrush to reach the main road heading back up to the hospital. As I approached the ravine, I realized that what had looked from a distance like large rocks just off the path were two slender bodies swinging slightly, high in a live oak tree. Terrified, I pushed forward along the now treacherous stony path, as another larger body came into view at the bottom of the ravine.

Charlene and Zachary had been lynched from that first tree; Aunt Lil swung just beyond.

Chapter 13

Memphis, Tennessee - 1931

I sat in the hospital lobby attempting to steady my breathing, staring first at my shoes, then the walls, then the clock, then again at my shoes. My heart thundered in my chest. Every time the receptionist called out the next patient's name or someone new entered the waiting room, I trembled. About two dozen men, women, and children were seated on benches. Some were breathing hard, others were moaning. Several children cried softly, curled up on the floor under a bench. One man coughed up bloody phlegm into a wad of dark fabric which he then quickly folded under, hoping to disguise the result, as he glanced around nervously. Another man held a chunk of ice over his left eye. Water dribbled off his elbow into a large pink puddle on the floor.

The money weighed like an anvil buried deep in my pocket.

After about an hour, a man who'd been seated on the opposite of the room, his hat pulled low over his face, began walking slowly in my direction. I kept my head down, my eyes staring at his battered shoes as he approached, then sat next to me on the bench.

"You saw 'em ... swingin', I know," the man whispered tensely, the voice like thick warm chocolate.

I glanced sideways, saw the mangled hands carefully folded to conceal his missing thumb and fingers, then looked again at my feet.

"Help me," I whimpered, shaking, my eyes blurred by hot tears. "Please. I'm ... I'm terrified."

"You an' your mama gots tuh leave on duh firs' train tuh New York dis mornin'," he replied quietly. "She gettin' off at four, yes?"

I nodded slightly, my head still down. This man had sung God's word so powerfully at Beverly's wake. Surely I could trust him, I prayed silently.

"But where ..." I began, tears spilling unrestrained down my cheeks as my voice trailed off.

"Hush now," he replied gently, looking down at his folded hands. "Jes' lissen up. When you gits tuh New York, you takes duh subway ovuh to Harlem. Dat's a place for us coluh'd folks in Manhattan. Den you find Mr. Charlie Johnson, you got dat? He duh band leaduh of a house band at Small's Paradise -- dat's a nightclub at 134th an' 7th avenue. Right at duh subway stop in Harlem. You tell Mr. Charlie Johnson dat Johnnie 'three finguhs' Doucet sent you. Here's Mr. Johnson's card wid dat address. He'll git you in singin' wid the chorus at dat club. I guarantee. Good money. No questions. No problem. Dat's all."

I carefully buried the card in my pocket as Johnnie stood up slowly. He asked the woman behind the desk where the bathroom was located and left the room without looking back at me. I continued waiting for Mama for the next several hours. Johnnie Doucet never reappeared.

One by one the entire hospital staff had learned about the lynchings in the ravine, Mama told me under her breath when she appeared in the lobby several hours later. No one had dared venture out to cut down those thick ropes during the night, however. The police had been informed but they'd just shrugged off the incident.

"The policemen said it was probably just three dumb coons trying to swindle the wrong folks. Probably got what they deserved. My God, what a bloodthirsty town, Helen!" Mama said quietly, thoroughly exhausted, shaking her head as I hugged her.

"Mama," I whispered, still holding her close, "we need to leave this place. Now. Tonight. We're taking a train to New York City."

"Oh sweetie," she replied, an exhausted smile spreading over her face, "I promised Lil I'd --"

"No, no, listen to me, Mama," I interrupted, shaking her slightly. "We need to leave immediately. Those three people lynched out there? That's Aunt Lil, Charlene and Charlene's boyfriend."

Her eyes widened in horror.

"That's impossible! Who told you that?" she gasped.

"We need to keep our voices down, Mama. Please. I saw them myself," I whispered, firmly circling my arm around her back. "All three of them."

She stared at me, immobile in disbelief. I grabbed her arm with my other hand and pushed her towards the door, giving only the briefest account of my conversations with Terrence and Dax as we walked out of the hospital.

"Our apartment's been completely ransacked. There's nothing left. We can't return there. Ever."

We fled several blocks to the train station, boarding the train for New York mere moments before its departure.

"What about Terrence?" Mama whispered as the train jerked to a start. She held my hand between both of hers on her lap while the train rumbled loudly across the tangle of tracks. "Was there … you're sure we couldn't …"

"No, Mama," I wept quietly, new tears raw on my sticky cheeks. "Nothing. His thigh was in this … this filthy, bloody tourniquet. And there was this huge … this … *hole* in the middle of his chest. I didn't see that at first … then he started this awful retching …there was blood everywhere." I crumpled slowly and fell against Mama's shoulder.

The train gradually picked up speed, the car rattling loudly over warped trestles. A conductor came through collecting tickets after which the sparsely filled car settled into a deepening silence.

"When I left the apartment, I was terrified those men had found …" I whispered, looking up at Mama, her face a waxy distortion through my thick tears.

"Shh," Mama said, brushing my wet hair from my face as she gently kissed my forehead. "I'm here. We're here together. The Lord is with us, Helen. We have to trust in that. I do believe it's best we follow your friend Mr. Doucet's suggestion. Praise the Lord for Lil's church fellowship with the man."

We agreed we couldn't report the money to the authorities. No one would believe our story. We'd be arrested and very likely handed over to the same men who, without one whit of remorse, had brutally murdered at least three, and probably five, people within the last several hours. We'd used one of the twenty-dollar bills to purchase our tickets. I told Mama what little I knew about Terrence's deadly Radithor scheme. Sadly, we realized that Aunt Lil had simply been in the wrong place at the wrong time. Or, as Mama commented later during our sleepless sojourn, maybe she'd actually been in the right place and was now blessedly reunited with her children.

Mama always carried her Bible to work in her small leather satchel so she could pray for anyone who passed away during her shift. We carefully placed Mr. Doucet's card in the Bible and then concealed the white towel at the bottom of the satchel. Other than the clothes we wore, this satchel and its bizarre contents were now our only possessions. As I had done so many times, I read Mama's favorite underlined passages within the Bible's tattered pages and looked through the few photos she'd pressed in the back. She'd also saved the small newspaper notice the Milwaukee police had placed almost a decade ago looking for Helen Mason's parents. The fuzzy picture of a frightened little girl with huge dark eyes, holding a toy parrot, stared out of that clipping.

As our train had sped north, each mile separating us further from those grisly scenes back in Memphis, we made tentative plans. We arrived in Harlem, a neighborhood in Manhattan often referred to as the "black mecca" according to a small poster near our seats, very late the following evening. At first glance the area appeared to be somewhat cleaner than tenement alley in Memphis. We'd cashed the second twenty-dollar bill during our last train stop before arriving in Harlem, and purchased two loaves of stale bread, a small round of tasteless cheese, three plump apples and two extremely ratty, second-hand, but warm, rabbit fur coats. If we were careful there might be enough left to buy some food in New York and our subway fare, Mama hoped.

A room for several nights at a cheap hotel would have to be obtained using one of the fifty-dollar bills, Mama knew. This could easily cause a problem in Memphis, but here in Harlem, we had no idea. There was always suspicion when anyone, regardless of skin color, dressed in such tattered clothing with no luggage, produced a large bill from their coat pocket. I asked if maybe it wouldn't be better to go to a bank like Daddy had in Milwaukee so many years ago.

Mama shook her head as we descended a long set of concrete steps and boarded the subway. Once in motion the short train began shrieking through what seemed like a never-ending black sewer.

"You can't trust banks these days," Mama commented in answer to my question. "There've been countless bank crashes over the last two years if you recall. A bank clerk back in Memphis once explained to me that the Bank of the United States in New York City, an institution which certainly sounded quite impressive, but apparently wasn't, was forced to shutter its doors against an angry horde of customers who had just lost every single penny they'd invested, Helen. This happened just before Christmas in 1930, I remember."

She paused momentarily while scanning the subway walls at a stop and then glanced at the large map opposite our seats so we wouldn't miss our connection.

"The newspapers claimed those banks in New York had fallen like dominoes within a few hours. Then only a few hours later, all the banks in Memphis had collapsed as well," Mama continued, shaking her head. "I remember that day like it was yesterday! There were crazy rumors claiming that the same check was being counted twice each day – can you imagine anything so idiotic? Some banks could then claim they had twice as much money."

She glanced out the filthy window at the subway tunnel's tiles rushing by.

"You should know that's also when I stopped paying off Daddy's debts," she sighed. "Without any guarantee that my money was being applied towards that obligation, there seemed no point. And you, Lil and I certainly needed every little bit of what little I could bring in by then. I've never reneged on a debt, Helen. I'm not proud."

Our cash now lay flat beneath the lining at the bottom of Mama's brown satchel. We knew it would have to be parsed out very carefully, very slowly.

These last twenty-four hours had changed our lives forever.

Chapter 14

Harlem ~ New York City
1932-1938

Smalls Paradise was a speakeasy located in the basement of an ugly building commonly referred to as Art Deco style. A fancy, brilliantly lit display bordered the marquee *'Charles Johnson Orchestra -- No cover charge'* just outside the street level entrance. Another sign advertised a 6 a.m. breakfast dance show and boldly proclaimed the establishment served the best dinner of any nightclub or cabaret in Harlem during all late evening programs. On a lamp table at the bottom of the stairs inside the building was piled a stack of calling cards reminding patrons they were cordially invited to bring their own liquor or purchase excellent bootlegged spirits from their waiter. Like everyone, the club owners anxiously awaited the repeal of Prohibition, rumored to be ratified within a few weeks according to the cards.

Jazz music boomed around us as we cautiously wandered into the cavernous underground. An eight-piece band was set up in a far corner of the huge space. White tablecloths covered small tables that were nestled closely together on four separate tiers surrounding an enormous wooden dance floor that seemed alive with a sea of intermingled wriggling bodies … mixed black and white wriggling bodies … mixed black and white wriggling bodies dancing with one another.

My mouth dropped open in disbelief and I stepped back slightly. Mama looked shocked as well. One certainly would never witness such a crush of folks like this down in Memphis! Three men balancing oversized round trays high over their right shoulders whizzed past us on roller skates, each singing along with the band. Mama quickly pulled me out of their way although the men had already adjusted their path to avoid a collision.

"Merciful heavens, what on earth *is* this place, Helen?" Mama stammered into my ear. "Who told you to come here again?"

"His name was Johnnie Doucet, Mama. He was the man with that amazing voice who was singing at Beverly's wake, if you remember," I replied. Given the chaotic din surrounding us, I doubted she comprehended very much of my answer.

Then abruptly, the music stopped. There was some kind of announcement that we couldn't hear since loud voices from the dance floor now echoed throughout the nightclub. One of the musicians, dressed in a crisp white jacket and pants, began squeezing his way through the crowd, heading in our direction. As he passed us, I somehow found my voice.

"Excuse me," I said loudly, "do you know if Mr. Charles Johnson is here tonight?"

"Charles Johnson?" he replied briskly, scowling at our ratty attire. "Might I ask why you're inquiring?"

I cleared my throat quickly, but Mama spoke first.

"We were sent here to speak with a Mr. Charles Johnson," stated Mama firmly.

"Sent by whom?" he challenged.

"Johnnie Doucet," I replied, attempting a smile. "Mr. Doucet told me to locate a Mr. Charles Johnson at Smalls Paradise. Could you help us ... please, sir?"

"Johnnie? Huh. You folks from Chicago?"

"No, sir," I said, shaking my head.

"Well, sorry, only Johnnie Doucet I know of lives in Chicago," he shrugged, starting to brush me aside. "Look, I'm in a hurry ... once again our *prima étoile française* ain't yet got her spoiled little French fanny outta the sack. She blew up her own tour right after she landed a good gig on Broadway a few years back and it sure's hell looks like she's itchin' to repeat that experience. My regular girls'll be back tomorrow, thank God. So, if you ... uh, *ladies* ... don't mind --"

"Johnnie 'three fingers' Doucet," I stated loudly as the man pushed past us. "He *used* to work in Chicago, but then he ... moved down South. That's where we met him. He told me that Mr. Johnson would know him."

The man stopped immediately, slowly folded his arms, then turned to face me.

"I'm Charles Johnson, pianist, Smalls' bandleader," he replied, retracing one step. "An' just how d'you know Johnnie 'three fingers'?"

I glanced up to see Mama frowning, lips pursed.

"We ... we did some tunes together ... about a year or so ago."

"So, he's playin' again, huh?"

This struck me as a taunt of sorts given the skepticism in the man's voice, so I thought carefully before replying.

"No, sir. Singing. I don't think he can play banjo any more … his hands … well … you know."

"And, so he, uh … he recommended you as a singer?" questioned Mr. Johnson, obviously in disbelief, once again eyeing Mama's and my ragged appearance. "How old are you anyway? What kinda experience you got?"

"I'm almost thirteen," I stated boldly, trying to stand taller. "You know that movie *Hallelujah*? I was in it. One of the children. They gave us an audition. Mr. Vidor chose me … personally."

"Yeah, saw it back in '29 at the Lafayette Theater here in Harlem. Theater went bust right after that, of course, same as most everything around here."

"Well, that's where I met Johnnie Doucet," I replied. "Making that film."

"I didn't see Johnnie anywhere in that film, girl, an' I saw it twice."

"Well, no sir, he was just in the crowd scenes. Same as me. Then we sang later at some … uh, church functions."

"Okay," he answered, still skeptical.

"Do you remember those two boys who played Brother Ezekiel's younger brothers in the film?"

"Maybe," Mr. Johnson shrugged. He was still annoyed but listening. "What about 'em?"

"I've been workin' a" … *what had Milton always called it?* … "a 'street gig' with those two boys for almost a year. We made some real … good coin," I smiled.

Mama just stared at me. I knew I had a lot of explaining to do. Certain that Mama would never have approved, neither Aunt Lil nor I had ever mentioned anything about my performing on that hotel veranda with Walter and Milton.

The door opened at the street level admitting a frigid gush of air. Loud women's voices filled the stairwell as a large group began descending. Mr. Johnson took a few steps towards the stairs as he glanced at the group, swore under his breath, and then turned back to face us.

"I don't suppose you know any French tunes, do you?" he grumbled. "Singer I'm waiting on is supposedly the 'toast of Paris' or some such malarky."

"I know "J'ai Deux Amours" and "Après de ma Blonde" … and I could probably get through 'Mon Homme'," I added hesitantly. A lady in one of our audiences had tried to teach that one to me. I knew I didn't have it quite right, but maybe no one would be listening too closely.

"You in a good key for my brass guys?"

I knew what the term good key meant, but brass guys totally threw me.

"Of course!" I smiled bravely. Whatever he meant I was determined to figure it out.

"Any chance you sing Mistinguett's arrangements?"

I was now in way over my head.

"Er … sorry," I replied sheepishly. "I've never heard that name. Is he a composer?"

"No, that's the damned singer I'm waiting for! Her agent claims she's *the* French headliner at Moulin Rouge, Folies Bergère, and Casino de Paris in France. You book her and your problems are solved that guy told me … well, she sure as hell's created *way* more problems for me than she's solved thus far!"

"Ah," I said, nodding slightly.

"Woman's got the lousiest attendance record on the books. She'll get here eventually tonight, but only after she's poured enough cheap liquor down her gullet and sampled enough hot men to satisfy a slut in Storeyville," he snorted.

Storeyville had been the notorious red-light district in New Orleans that had been permanently shut down just prior to America's entry into the Great War in 1917, a couple years before I was born. Its scandalous reputation remained one of the nastiest debasements of any woman's character, however. Shocked, Mama started to protest, but I quickly placed my hand on her elbow, frowning slightly.

Hands on his hips, Mr. Johnson squinted at me.

"Okay, let's have you do a couple tunes to fill in," he exhaled after a few moments. "That'd help … somebody dressed in sequins and chiffon scarves floppin' around on stage. You're a little sprite, kinda like old miss fancy feathers anyway. Tell Alice up on the third floor to let you into La Miss' dressing room. You can throw on one of them hundred gowns she's got jammed in those trunks. I ain't never seen a woman travel with so many damned dresses, jewelry, and peacock feathers in all my days," he scowled. "There must be five hundred exotic birds gave up their lives for all that *frou frou* shit she parades around in! Be back to start in fifteen minutes. That's all I got left on my break. Otherwise, management'll cut into my wage this set."

He pointed in the direction of a staircase leading to the upper floor, then grabbed my elbow. "Oh, an' if you're lyin' to me about Johnnie Doucet recommendin' you, you better plan to clear outta town when you walk off that stage. I ain't fond of young light-skinned fish like you makin' a fool outta an ol' man like me -- ya follow?"

I swallowed hard. I'd only prayed that he was going to let me audition for a chorus part. Being thrown into the lion's den was not at all what I'd envisioned.

Once in the small dressing room, cramped with at least a dozen open steamer trunks bursting with a rainbow of materials, Mama bombarded me with a rash of questions. I assured her that everything I'd been performing with Milton and Walter, although truthfully not the Lord's music, was reasonably wholesome and nothing that she would have been ashamed to hear. Skepticism lined her worn face like snail tracks shimmering after a light rain.

We pulled out a green velvet dress that was crushed into the back of one trunk. It was far too large in the bodice, but Mama grabbed several hair clips off the dressing table and secured two sections under my shoulder blades as well as shortening the skirt like handkerchief points all the way around. The dress looked completely different within moments. My hair was a hideously filthy snarl from days of inattention. Mama swept up as much of it as possible and firmly pinned a small headband with sequin-studded green feathers glued on top. She dotted my face gently with the powder puff. I stared at my reflection in the mirror for a moment. A stranger stared back, oddly neither truly black nor white. Fifteen minutes was almost up.

"Do you really understand what that man wants you to sing, Helen?" she whispered, holding my shoulders so tight I couldn't wiggle out of her grasp.

"No," I answered softly, trembling. "I confess, Mama, I really don't. Please, all I ask is … just … pray for me … pray for us. We really have no other place else to go."

We hurried back downstairs, and I walked carefully up onto the stage. The hot lights pierced my eyes like blinding needles. My unwashed stench of tenement alley enveloped me anew. Mr. Johnson grumbled he wanted to start out with something in English.

"D'you know that tune Ethel Waters recorded, probably on one of those race records, called "I Found a New Baby"?"

I nodded.

"You do her same intro?"

I'd never heard the recording – in fact, I'd never actually sung the tune -- so I had no idea. I only knew the song because Walter sang it as a spoof with Milton making all kinds of stupid kissing noises mimicking a lovesick gorilla. The veranda spectators, howling at Milton's antics, had almost always thrown several pennies into the kitty whenever the two boys performed that one, so I knew the lyrics quite well.

Impatiently waiving off my reply, Mr. Johnson growled, "okay, four bars for nothin', guys," over the din of the crowded room. To me he added, "just pick it up where you can and come in. We'll vamp 'til then. Sing into the top half of that ribbon microphone, by the way. Bottom half's fussy these days … and shorten the stand."

I'd seen pictures of microphones in radio ads but had never used one. I located a protruding knot about halfway down the pole that when twisted carefully and then retightened, lowered the microphone's height.

"Ok, we take this real *up tempo* … fast swing, ya got it? Oh, what's your name?"

"Helen."

"Ellen?" he frowned.

I nodded. Close enough, I thought. He stomped off the count and the band whisked through an introduction that didn't seem to have anything related to Walter's rendition of the tune. I panicked for a moment, then on a glance from the clarinetist, dove in slightly late. Fortunately, I fell into the groove -- as Milton would have called it – quickly thereafter. The lights were so bright I could scarcely see the audience, which was all to the good.

There was a generous wave of applause as we finished.

"Get more up into the microphone … like you're kissin' it. Let's tackle "J'ai Deux Amours" next," Mr. Johnson barked at me and then signaled to the band. "Keep it tight, boys. Jabbo, you take the first ride and Bechet, you split the next one with Jimmy, ok?"

"Just straight ahead then?" asked the clarinetist.

"Yeah, yeah, that's fine, Bechet," snorted Mr. Johnson as he slammed music into several piles on top of the piano. "We'll take this in the original key, also. Miss French Poodle Tippy Toes always wants it down at least a third. No need to transpose for a change, boys."

The band slid into the tune very slowly. I caught a glimpse of men and women wrapped tightly into one another's arms out on the dance floor. The loud voices in the audience dropped to a murmur. Mr. Johnson nodded whenever he wanted me to come in with another verse after various instrumental breaks. It seemed to go smoothly without any of what Walter and Milton dismally referred to as 'train wrecks.' Once finished, as the audience began applauding, I realized a woman was standing just behind me on the stage.

"*Très bien, mon petit Rossignol* … at least better voice than Josephine," she snickered in a thick lilting French accent, her long creamy satin glove roughly patting my cheek. "You are jungle dancer, same like her also?"

Obviously, this was the French singer, quite small in stature and not especially young, but certainly a very attractive white woman. She was exquisitely dressed in an exotically low-cut, ivory brocade gown adorned with dazzling jewels that sizzled under the hot lights.

"*Je m'appelle Mistinguett*," she then added, lifting one eyebrow, "*et toi?*"

"*Je m'appelle …*" I began, the words forming effortlessly on my tongue, but then I stopped abruptly. I'd understood exactly everything she'd said, even about the nightingale – *le Rossignol* … but how?

"You go Paris one day? *Oui*? You dance?"

"No," I replied, frowning, still muddled. "I don't … dance. Not really."

"*C'est très dommage, ma petite*," she chided, patting my cheek even harder. "You learn dance like Josephine Baker, *oui*? She dirty Negro … make lots money …*avec les bananes, oui*? The banana skirt, yes? *Une danseuse qui faire le strip-tease extraordinaire!*"

She brushed past me with a snort, yanked the microphone back to its original position, while apologizing for her belated arrival to a scattering of applause from the audience. As she and Mr. Johnson began bickering over the tempo for the next tune, I gratefully backed off the stage.

Mr. Johnson engaged me later that night to sing with three other girls in his 6 a.m. breakfast show six days per week. Mama and I moved into a small apartment in a building located only a few blocks from Smalls and took in repair work from Grynszpan's Tailor Shop located just a block away. Most of our money remained untouched, firmly stitched into two pairs of socks carefully taped underneath a dresser drawer.

***

One month slipped into another; one year stretched out cautiously to the next. Gradually Mama and I stopped reacting to every deep shadow in an alley, every odd noise overnight, every sharp knock at our door. I worked at Smalls Paradise and occasionally Connie's Inn or the Cotton Club in Harlem for almost five years. For several years various musicians from Smalls had also been broadcasting twice weekly on radio station WMCA and I was occasionally included on that prestigious program.

In the summer of 1938, I accepted Sidney Bechet's contract to work with a performing ensemble he was bringing over to the Moulin Rouge in Paris for a six-month engagement. Young modern Parisians simply couldn't get enough of American jazz music according to Mr. Bechet, reiterating what I remembered Johnnie 'three fingers' Doucet having mentioned during the *Hallelujah* filming. However, many European musicians refused to play jazz, blues or swing style music. Mr. Bechet convinced me that my singing career might really take off in Paris. Now that Jim Crow had started paralyzing the U.S. northern states to the same degree as the southern ones, a lot of colored jazz musicians were heading to Europe intent on a better future.

For many of us, however, that future would come at a steep price.

Book II

Chapter 15

Paris, France ~ late summer 1938

What I hadn't been told before accepting Mr. Bechet's Paris contract, was that not only had I missed the opportunity by a mere two days to see Nina Mae McKinney, now praised in American magazines as the Black Greta Garbo, in performance, but that Mistinguett was the headlining singer at the Moulin Rouge with Bechet's swing ensemble.

Built in the late 1880s, the Moulin Rouge cabaret was located near Pigalle in Paris. The building was modeled to represent an old-fashioned Dutch windmill, although many thought the place looked more like an enormous black pepper grinder. Everyone from Hemingway to Picasso to Coco Chanel to the notoriously flamboyant couple F. Scott and Zelda Fitzgerald were said to have partied there. Female entertainers dazzled their audiences in long or short ruffled tulle skirts, flashy headdresses, and on occasion, tiny, bejeweled brassieres that left little to a man's fertile imagination.

Mistinguett had been considered the darling *chanteuse extraordinaire* of the Moulin Rouge for countless years. That said, although she certainly looked far younger than her reputed age of sixty, caustic whispers these days now demoted the performer to that of a rather well-preserved fossil of the *belle epoque*, desperate to recapture her male audience's often wandering attention. Sadly, many years back, a reviewer had compared her voice with that of a street hawker, and her dance style, once considered provocative, now paled behind that of far younger, *risqué* Paris *étoile*, Josephine Baker. Josephine, a beautiful chocolate-brown American woman, was praised for her pleasant demeanor, vibrant dancing, intelligence, and clear, lilting voice ... traits sadly marginal to nonexistent surrounding the aging Mistinguett.

By the time I'd learned of Mistinguett's involvement with the Bechet contract, Mama and I were already on board the ocean liner as the ship steamed out of New York Harbor. We began rehearsals on the *Île de France* within an hour after pulling up anchor and continued a grueling daily schedule until just prior to docking at the port in Le Havre, France eight days later. A few additional chorus members would be joining our group in Paris.

During the voyage, Mama and two other women were pressed into service refitting and repairing costumes. Some of the costumes were quite nice, others very cheap, with shockingly short skirts and embarrassingly low-cut necklines. Including the musicians, our troupe numbered fifteen on board, with three singers to be added in Paris. A few in our party admired Mistinguett, most disliked her, but we all were secretly terrified of this woman we respectfully addressed as 'La Miss'. She threatened daily to vanquish our fledgling careers with a mere flick of her diamond braceleted wrist. The woman insured her long, beautiful legs for five hundred thousand francs every year … those of us around her were of no merit whatsoever.

Arguments flared among the musicians, singers and dancers, but also with the annoyed passengers. They grumbled constantly about the endless jazz music spilling throughout the upper deck, thwarting their desire to relax with a cocktail while resting in their luxurious deck chairs, enjoying the warm, salty breezes. Many of the older Americans and Europeans on board despised jazz music; the endless bickering within our company merely reinforced that low opinion.

Late in the afternoon during our second day of the voyage, a tall, well-dressed gentleman suddenly broke into our rehearsal, grabbed the sheet music off Mr. Bechet's stand, savagely shredded all four pages and threw it overboard. I stood frozen in disbelief.

"You are all worthless heathens!" the man bellowed in perfect German-accented English, gesturing wildly. "This entire party … yes, you … and you madam, and you … *and you* … you're all headed straight to hell!"

I bit my lip, glancing at Mr. Bechet. None of us moved.

"My name is Ulrich Weber. This name will mean nothing to you, of course. But that is not of consequence. I am a proud member in standing of the Original Nazi party … do you know what that is?" he continued, his face somewhat redder. "Well, I will tell you. That is the *Alter Kämpfer*. You do not know this name?"

We remained motionless. Several curious passengers had begun to gather behind the German, and they nodded silently in agreement with one another, however.

"Well, you should. This is the founding party of Herr Adolf Hitler -- I am proud to say my beloved *Führer* for almost four years now."

Quite a few more passengers joined the original group behind Mr. Weber.

"Herr Hitler has banned this decadent so-called music in *our* country ... that is, in Germany ... a decade ago. Once our *Führer's* clean lifestyle, celebrating the purity of the mind, the body and the spirit is established throughout all of Europe -- which my good friends, is quite inevitable you should be aware, this ... this debauchery perpetuated by a horde of dirty Jewish composers feeding off talentless Negro rabble will mercifully be forever purged. This will finally remove such filth from our delicate ears so decency may prevail once and for all!"

His spittle hit an unflinching Mistinguett as the small crowd which had gathered behind the German nodded vigorously in agreement. Two women applauded briskly.

"Purged from our existence forever!" he spat out directly in front of my face. Despite this outburst, only a few tiny dots of sweat danced along his steeply chiseled brow. He shoved me out of his way and strode across the deck, his glistening black boots ringing out hollowly. The crowd followed him, many now applauding.

I expected Mistinguett or Mr. Bechet to reply with one of their razor-sharp retorts, but both stood silently as the man marched away. None of us made a sound for several moments.

"Why didn't she reply?" I whispered to Annette, a French chorus girl standing beside me.

"*Non, non. Ce n'est pas une bonne idée.* No good argue ... *avec les boches* – eh, with the Germans," she whispered back, dropping her head to disguise our conversation. "Paris now many *les Nazis.* They strong. In Berlin persons vanish. Some found *battu à mort* ... uh ... beat to death, *oui*? Some never found. This happen now in Paris too. German Embassy in Paris *est comme une forteresse.*"

"A fortress?" I frowned.

She nodded.

"*Oui.* A big Swastika flag there now. This not allow. But ... *personne font rien pour l'arretêr* ... um, no one... make stop ... bad. Very bad."

We continued with our rehearsals for the remainder of the voyage but kept far quieter.

***

Having been delayed by a series of bad storms, we docked in Le Havre very late in the evening. Our excursion to Paris began close to midnight, only allowing for fleeting glimpses of the *Arc de Triomphe* and Eiffel Tower through the dark green train windows. We were assured we'd have ample time in the coming weeks to explore those landmarks of which we'd all heard so much as well as the countless museums, cafés, and art galleries in Montmartre and along the *Champs-Élysée*. Annette had promised to take me to the *Jardin de Tuilleries*, the beautiful gardens created by Louis XIV and also to one of her favorite cafés, *Tout Va Bien*, as soon as we had a few free hours.

Other than Mr. Bechet, Mistinguett and a handful of others, most of us spent our first night in Paris sprawled out on the cabaret floor, or, if we were lucky, sleeping on one of the threadbare dressing room rugs. Our first rehearsal on dry land was scheduled for early the following morning; the show's first concert was scheduled for midnight the next night.

Our opening performance was wildly received by Mistinguett's supporters. As a result, those of us in the chorus finally had enough free hours to move to our various living quarters scattered throughout the city. Without Annette's help, however, Mama and I would never have found our destination in the 10th *Arrondissement* located not too far from our cabaret in Pigalle.

Abraham Grynszpan was the brother of Wolf Grynszpan, the owner of the tailor shop in Harlem where Mama had worked during the last several years. She had learned the trade quickly and was an excellent seamstress, highly in demand among Wolf's customers, a group comprised of all ethnicities and incomes, for both men's and women's clothing. He was not happy that we would be in Europe during his busy fall and early winter seasons, but begrudgingly reassured Mama that her job would be available upon our return in six months.

Abraham Grynszpan's tailor shop on the other hand, was located within the Marais district, a medieval Jewish quarter with impossibly difficult to navigate narrow, twisting cobblestone streets that ran at odd angles to one another rather than on any predictable grid. The area was considered the center of Jewish life in Paris. But if you weren't Jewish, it seemed particularly hostile. There existed an unusually high-pitched, endless yammering in Yiddish, a language which forever evaded my ear. The congested, bad-smelling district was completely at odds with the glamor one might experience just a short train ride away in Paris proper. A concentration of aging synagogues, schools, markets, bookstores, bakeries, and restaurants, all with signage only in Yiddish, somehow flourished within the cramped confines of the district's litter-strewn streets.

Some streets had a different name in each block, but even more confusing was the fact that many were known by completely different, unpronounceable Yiddish names which had no street sign posted at all -- not that this would have helped. When coupled with the language barrier – very few residents in the Marais district spoke any English whatsoever – Mama and I felt quite ostracized.

When Wolf had negotiated our stay within Abraham's shop, he'd conveniently failed to mention to his brother that we were Negroes. Abraham had already spent the money he'd received from us in advance, thus making it rather difficult for him to cancel the agreement upon our arrival. But it was obvious that despite Mama's reputed talent as a seamstress, he was not at all happy about us living in the tiny area he typically rented out behind his shop for extra income.

The Grynszpans two-room workspace and small frontage shop, the family's third location in less than two years, had originally doubled as living quarters for the family. Curiously, however, Abraham and his wife Chava had recently moved to an apartment around the corner completely separate from the shop. This move had occurred about three months prior to Mama's and my arrival. Every available flat surface within the *Maison Albert*, as the shop was known, located on *Rue du Faubourg Saint-Denis,* was piled high with piecework and every wall was lined by layers of tall, thick bolts of fabric standing on end.

Abraham's family, very poor Jewish refugees originally from Poland, owed Mama's former employer Wolf quite a bit of money from a long-overdue family loan. Finding themselves no longer welcomed in their native Poland, Abraham and Chava had then moved to Berlin, and, unnerved to discover that their presence as Polish Jews in Germany was even *less* desirable, had subsequently fled to Paris, a city considered at least slightly more openminded.

Wolf had coerced his brother Abraham and sister-in-law Chava to take us in for six months as a means to expedite the seriously delinquent loan repayment. The brothers' seventeen-year-old nephew, Herschel, or Hermann as he preferred to be called, also rented space behind the shop. He occupied a medium-sized closet, accessible only through a small pocket door, completely hidden behind many hefty bolts of fabric.

Communication was difficult. The Gynszpans spoke only Polish and Yiddish, along with a smattering of French. Abraham had a few serviceable words in English. Chava was prone to screaming fits whenever Mama's workmanship didn't quite please her exacting standards. Their garment construction methods were often different from the Harlem's Grynszpan shop much to Mama's dismay. We relied on charades-like gestures and crude drawings.

Mama had immediately discovered the *Église Américaine de Paris* – the American Church of Paris – a Gothic structure located in the 7th *arrondissement*, which offered twice weekly Protestant church services and fellowship gatherings in English. She insisted I attend as well, concerned that my singing at the decadent Moulin Rouge would corrupt me. The parishioners welcomed us coolly at first since few darker-skinned parishioners attended. We kept quietly to ourselves, clustered tightly, occupying the same pew each week at the very back of the magnificent sanctuary. If pressed about our employment, we simply stated that we worked at a small tailoring shop in the Jewish sector. I knew that my mentioning my singing at the Moulin Rouge would only cause a sea of scorning brows, inviting negative comparison to the *risqué* Josephine Baker.

Most importantly, the church had a radio that their head pastor had oddly installed in the church's small back storeroom. As often as possible Mama and I attended a popular BBC program broadcast from Great Britain on Monday evenings. At first amusing, we noticed that the program acquired a noticeably darker aura as the weeks progressed. By contrast, the Grynszpans radio dial in the shop was taped firmly to a static-ridden station that played a lot of giddy Polish and German folk music. Although tempted, we didn't dare try to move the dial off its designated frequency looking for the BBC station after Abraham and Chava had left for their own apartment each evening.

Within a short period of time, I became aware of the uneasiness surrounding all foreign Jews throughout the city of Paris. French Jews perhaps foolishly assumed they were fully protected simply due to their birthright. Many foreign Jews, however, now clung to one another very quietly in the deep shadows as far away as possible from the groundless taunts and maliciously swinging *matraque* or billy clubs of Nazi sympathizing gendarmes. Their presence throughout Paris had recently grown from occasional nuisance to large, unbridled threat. Those of my race already knew how to stay in the shadows.

Although the three of us occupied the same living space and he seemed a reasonably intelligent young man, Hermann thoroughly baffled me. There was the obvious language barrier, but being almost the same age, I thought he might at least say good morning or smile or even be helpful within the shop or help Mama and me on occasion.

He ran the rare occasional errand for his uncle, preferring to be out cavorting with his friends until quite late most evenings.

Aunt Chava had graciously offered to prepare dinner for us during our first night at the shop, but promptly took any leftovers with her in a rage. Mama had made the blunder of attempting to use the wrong griddle, resulting in Chava shrieking at the two of us for well over an hour. I learned from Annette that all Jews in the Marais district "kept strict Kosher", meaning they were required to prepare, serve, and consume foods in separate cooking vessels and dishes, using different utensils. We had now forever contaminated one of Aunt Chava's favorite pans it seemed. Mama and I were stunned that any woman, regardless of her religious persuasion, was perfectly willing to more than double her washing workload every night!

According to Wolf Grynszpan back in America, Hermann had convinced his Uncle Abraham as well as his immediate family that he was still attending high school. But Wolf had recently learned from a client that the impudent boy had dropped all his studies only weeks after his arrival in Paris. Hermann's father, Zindel, yet another of the Grynszpan brothers, along with his mother and older siblings, still lived in Hanover, Germany. Zindel had gone to great trouble and expense to send his ungrateful youngest son to apprentice with Abraham. The young man was expected to first complete his high school studies in the French education system and then be welcomed into Abraham's employment immediately thereafter.

Hermann had made almost no effort to learn French or anything but the rudiments of the tailoring profession, thus frustrating his father's aspirations for his son. The young man was small in stature and rather fragile in appearance. Scarcely taller than I, he was quite handsome with thick, wavy dark brown hair, deeply set, almost black eyes, and a constant brooding expression like a movie star. He struggled with stomach pains that he'd originally blamed on his Aunt Chava's greasy Kosher cooking. Mama had pantomimed that perhaps his stomach problems might be attributed to the three packs of harsh French cigarettes he consumed each week. To this the boy had snorted a curt reply in Yiddish, prompting a fierce slap from Chava. He'd mumbled 'sorry' in English and then stormed out.

As one of only two male offspring of the large tailoring family, Hermann was quite spoiled by his immediate as well as his extended family. Abraham and yet another brother, Salomon, estranged from one another for many years, competed fiercely to be of service to the frivolous young man.

Towards that end, Hermann was always very neatly attired, possessing adequate spending money (at least at the beginning of each month) provided by his various familial male benefactors who graciously scraped the linings of their own pockets to help contribute to a lifestyle of exotic restaurants, expensive cigarettes, cabarets, and various highly questionable entertainments. An avid reader, he devoured all available Yiddish newspapers each day, and when in the mood, easily drew into spirited conversations several young men of various ethnic backgrounds at his favorite cafés.

In an odd way, despite -- or maybe even because of -- his lazy, brusque demeanor, I was curiously attracted to him. He was so different from any of the musicians I'd ever worked with, most of whom, contrary to reputation, were devoted to their wives or were in long-term, steady relationships. If these men were serious about their craft, they were rarely frivolous within their private lives. Yes, there were those few who drank or gambled excessively or were addicted to various drugs. But if their music started suffering in any way, they were immediately replaced. There were many excellent black jazz musicians in Paris, all of them hungry for work.

Why I found Hermann charming was a mystery even to me. As usual, Mama noticed immediately. She'd then muttered under her breath that I'd best not get caught making cow eyes at the young man. Even though his skin was far darker than mine, that would only lead to trouble, she cautioned.

Chapter 16

Paris, France – early fall, 1938

Mama's and my finances were quite pinched. I wouldn't be receiving any money until I'd completed a full month of performances at the Moulin Rouge, and then it might easily be another week I'd been warned. Our full month in advance rent was deducted from Mama's pay by Abraham Grynszpan, this in addition to the original downpayment -- as Abraham referred to the money that we'd sent from America -- before she would receive even one sou of compensation for her workmanship.

We'd left almost all of the Radithor money in different banks back in Harlem, which we'd discreetly deposited over three or four years. During those years, we read about lawsuits against reckless companies failing to protect their young female employees from dangerous radiation exposure. Many ruthless corporations knew of these dire effects, yet brazenly claimed that the girls' painful deaths were caused by their own foolish sexual behaviors, resulting in deadly syphilis infections. Radium, at one time the darling of every product from toothpaste to baby food to virile longevity, had disappeared off the shelves overnight.

Although there were no buyers for Radithor anymore that certainly didn't mean that the men who'd murdered Aunt Lil's entire family weren't still determined to find the windfall from Terrence and Dax's sales. We planned to return to Harlem as soon as my contract with Mr. Bechet ended early in 1939. With any luck I'd be more in demand as a singer after this Paris excursion. There were far too many of us in New York vying for work and touring in America remained an expensive, risky business venture even if you were white.

Mama continued struggling with the harsh misunderstandings of Yiddish directions spoken in the Grynszpan workplace. Late at night when I'd get home, I'd sometimes find her silently praying, smothered in hot tears over some embarrassing error that would result in yet another delay of a garment to a customer. One only need glance at the hand-scrawled signage featuring a tall spool of thread speared with a long needle, posted in French -- *Le Tailleur* or *La*

Tailleuse -- as well as strange lettering I assumed to be Yiddish over almost every shop door in this section of the district, to realize there were hundreds of other tailors available who could guarantee their work, possibly for less money and in less time. Many signs had recently added the German *Schneider* or *Schneiderin* as well. The Germans milling about were a thrifty race. It was well known that a Jewish tailor was always cheapest, their handiwork dependable no matter how much they annoyingly haggled over price.

My French gradually improved since I needed to memorize a lot of French songs. Surprisingly, Mistinguett also brought in a number of jazz tunes with lyrics written in English for a few of us to sing. Most of these songs were older, however, which seemed unusual. Mixed French audiences were currently more responsive to early New Orleans jazz styles than New York's hot swing music in her opinion. I'd danced popular dances from the 1920s such as the Charleston, Black Bottom and Shimmy while performing with Milton and Walter in addition to several nostalgic sequences while at Small's back in Harlem. Newer popular dances of the '30s, such as the Lindy Hop, the Balboa, and the Argentinian tango, were all the rage in New York these days, but garnered less of a following here in Paris. La Miss always adhered to giving the public what it wanted; Mr. Bechet and his musicians were far more interested in performing the newest hot swing repertoire. This inevitably led to heated arguments during rehearsals when planning their set lists each week.

I was quite embarrassed upon learning the translation of Mistinguett's typical introduction to my newly added short solo: "*la jeune fille chanteuse que tout homme désire dans son lit ce soir*" -- "the young singer whom every man desires in his bed tonight." Then, with a deep chuckle in her throaty voice, she'd add in English that she was more than happy to step in "should a man's need arise during the evening" to uproarious laughter by the English-speaking audience members. It was rumored that her nightly sampling of men would rival that of most Parisian prostitutes working in the Pigalle district's brothels.

During our break between afternoon rehearsals and evening performances, Annette and another singer, Marie Landauer, better known as Landie, and I, would grab a coffee and a sweet roll or sandwich at one of the many outdoor cafés within a few blocks of the Moulin Rouge. Mr. Bechet jokingly referred to us as "*mes trois petites souris brunes*"– "my three little brown mice". We assumed this stemmed from our vaguely similar coloring rather than some youthful camaraderie. Both girls cautioned me against getting too friendly with Monsieur Bechet as he was always looking 'for fresh kill to drape from his belt.'

Annette's parents were dark Jewish gypsies who had emigrated from Poland to Germany during a pogrom when she was only nine years old. Landie lived not far from the Moulin Rouge with her mother, a Parisian native, and her father, a German Jew. Annette was reasonably fluent in Polish, German and French and could typically hold her own understanding English and some Yiddish unless it was spoken too rapidly. Landie was multilingual in French, German and English and understood Yiddish far better than she claimed.

One hot afternoon after being seated at Annette's favorite café, *Tout Va Bien*, I realized that Hermann Grynszpan and several of his scowling comrades occupied the table next to ours. I nodded with a brief smile, but Hermann completely ignored me and continued with what appeared to be an intense conversation with his poorly dressed, somewhat older comrades.

"Any idea what they're discussing?" I queried Annette and Landie in a low voice, my curiosity peaked despite Hermann's rude dismissal. Although we'd been fortunate enough to have been seated under the café's green and white striped awning, the late afternoon sun beat down unbearably in the dusty hot breeze. Everyone was praying for a break in this lengthy heat spell. Paris was breathtaking in the spring, so beautiful to behold even in the rain, and erotic throughout its autumn evenings. However, sometimes the city was about as desirable as an infected tooth during its relentless late summers.

"His one friend ... with the ... the smush-up hat," replied Annette, "he asking your roommate --"

"He's not my roommate," I interjected, frowning.

"Roommate, friend or whatever, you do talk about him a lot," winked Landie.

"I do not!" I insisted. "He lives in a sort of ... closet actually ... in the same apartment as Mama and me. That's all. I rarely even see him there."

"Ah, *ma chère petite ... c'est l'amour*," Annette sighed.

I shot her a dirty look.

"He was living there when we arrived," I added tersely. "I think his aunt and uncle refuse to let him live with them anymore, but I don't know why. It seems they moved out a few months before Mama and I arrived here in Paris. Anyway, we're stuck with him now. Those awful black cigarettes he smokes give Mama and me terrible headaches."

"*Merde*! I hate that stink!" agreed Annette. "I think the smush hat man name is Nathan. He asking Hermann about … not sure."

We sat silently sipping our coffees as the three young men continued talking, only occasionally lowering their voices.

"It sounds like Hermann's planning to write a letter to the President of the United States," Landie giggled.

"What? Why?" I laughed, almost forgetting to keep my voice down. "You mean President Roosevelt?"

Landie shrugged. "Well, I suppose so. He's your only president, correct?"

I nodded.

"He thinks it's demeaning that he has to live with you and your Mama in his uncle's apartment … well, *you* know why," continued Landie, rolling her eyes. "You're light so that's not an insult to him, but your *Maman* is quite dark, *oui*?"

I made no reply.

"He's writing your president looking to be granted an entry visa for the U.S. If that fails …" she paused for a moment, still listening. "If that fails, he plans to join the French Foreign Legion, or at least I think that's what he means. I'm not sure how he might manage that! Anyway, he's living illegally here in Paris. Ah, this is bad. It seems he has no documentation papers. Each day he's getting more nervous about this. If he can join the Foreign Legion, he thinks this would secure a path for French citizenship – maybe acquire an identity card to live here legally."

We all fell silent once again as our sandwiches were delivered, but I knew Annette and Landie were still listening intently. One of the first things I'd learned about working in Paris was that without an identity card, any person, especially if you were an unemployed Jewish refugee, was treading on quicksand.

"His family live still in Germany," commented Annette. "He get letter from sister … uh, last week, *peut être*?"

"*Oui*," nodded Landie in agreement.

"They – his family – told must leave Hanover and go back soon, live in Poland. But they no live in Poland many years," continued Annette.

"We'd all hoped this was only idle chatter," frowned Landie, sitting back hard in her chair.

"Did you understand it differently?" I asked, to which Landie shook her head as we each took another sip of coffee. Even though the beverage was still steaming it cooled our parched throats.

Today's rehearsal had been particularly grueling. La Miss had been in a roar of a temper from the moment she'd walked in the door.

"Annette's correct," replied Landie.

"*Merde*," sighed Annette. "*C'est partout.*"

"It's everywhere, you're absolutely right, Annette. The Germans are determined to deport every Jew living in their country to, God knows where on earth. No other countries are willing to take us in."

"I would think the United States at least," I commented, smiling slightly. "Right?"

Annette and Landie stared at me for a moment and then slowly shook their heads in unison, avoiding my gaze.

"Not … quite," replied Landie, clearing her throat. "Your President Roosevelt has no room for us either, Helen. He's made that clear in his radio broadcasts. He must stay on Germany's good side, you understand."

"Why on earth would he feel obligated to do that?" I replied rather hotly. Surely, she had misunderstood some news broadcaster!

"There's a very simple explanation, Helen," Landie continued slowly. "Germany owes many countries, especially your American government, a good deal of money yet from the Great War. Nobody wants to drop into another Depression like we all hope – we pray -- we're finally wriggling out of, yes? So, most countries are trying to -- well, I guess the English word *appease* makes the most sense -- appease the Nazis since they're now the political party controlling Germany. Most French Jews think that will be changing soon. That is, that the Nazis will go out of favor soon because their views are so fanatically extreme what with the book burnings of classic writers, and the arrests or deportation of Jewish writers, actors and composers throughout Germany. It *has* to end soon. Everyone agrees there's no way their behavior can possibly continue."

"But at same time, you understand, no person with brain want *les communistes*," interjected Annette quickly, shuddering.

"Right, right," agreed Landie. "That guy with the pipe at your friend's table -- Sam is his name, I think -- is saying the communists are our only hope. But the others are ignoring him."

I stared into my almost empty coffee cup. I was ashamed to admit that my race had often been suspicious of Jews as well. And I knew of no one who openly embraced Communism. We never think of ourselves as the guilty party harboring prejudice or as someone blind to another's persecution, I reflected.

"Nathan's now talking about a German police order that was issued last week," continued Landie, breaking into my thoughts.

"Residency permits previously issued to foreigners living in the Third Reich will be cancelled within a few weeks. That mean Hermann's family in Hanover will be forced to return to Poland."

"Well, sadly, that makes sense," I commented.

"Yes, except the Polish government now refuses to readmit any Jews into the country who haven't been living in Poland for the last five years. Hermann's parents left there for Germany right after he was born," added Landie, after listening further.

"So, where they go?" frowned Annette.

"That's exactly what Nathan, your man with the squashed hat is asking," replied Landie quietly.

"Does that mean your family is in trouble too?" I blurted out, facing Annette.

"Yes," Landie nodded, replying for Annette. "It certainly would. They're still living outside in that disgusting district outside Munich as far as you know, right, Annette?"

Eyes downcast, she nodded.

"My father is steel worker, yes? He is important for German industry so still have job, make good money. But now, the Nazis train others. What happen next, no one know. All I know is, *c'est mal*."

Chapter 17

Paris, France – fall, 1938

Several weeks later we'd just begun rehearsals on a completely revised program as demanded by the management. Like most venues, when attendance began dropping off the owners always blamed the entertainment first. It wasn't even noon yet and Mr. Bechet had already fired two musicians. An ugly mood prevailed. Mistinguett, late as usual, suddenly stomped in, grabbed my arm, and pulled me into another room. She slammed the door and thrust into my hands an official-looking envelope that had been roughly torn open.

"What this wants?" she demanded, hands on her hips. 'Why in English, eh? *Sale boches* complain my music again? None their business! We live in Paris, not Berlin!"

I skimmed over the crisply typed letter, likely written by a native German speaker considering the occasional odd sentence structure. The letter concerned rewriting lyrics of popular American swing tunes for a program to be broadcast in English to BBC listeners in Great Britain. These programs would be transmitted from Germany's radio center complex just outside Berlin. At Mistinguett's insistence, I began reading aloud:

"These lyrics carry a requirement to praise the excellent training of the pilots in our powerful German Luftwaffe, also with mention of the famous tourist attractions to be found in London, Paris and Berlin. The musical arrangements are required to be played note for note same to the original recording. Instrumental improvisations are strictly forbidden as by written decree issued by Herr Doktor Joseph Goebbels regarding acceptable swing music.

"Notification regarding this experiment has today been sent to cabaret performers with English-speaking audience at venues in Berlin, Munich, and Paris. This will make the determining of our best response. If yours is a submission we accept, you may expect adequate remuneration. Your venue is obligated to participate or face possibly severe penalties. It is ill advised to ignore this request."

"*C'est très fou!*" snorted Mistinguett, folding her arms in disgust. "What penalties Germany can do Paris? What else it say? Keep reading!"

"*The singer is to record both sides on standard shellac. Original version will be on side one. New version on side two. This must immediately be delivered to the Kurzwellensender (KWS), our transmitter facility located just outside Berlin. You may obtain this address at bottom of this correspondence. Note: it is essential this singer must have a very clear American or English accent. No other accents are acceptable.*"

"Signed by Goebbels *der Giftzwerg,*" scoffed Mistinguett, glancing over my shoulder. "Minister of Propaganda and Enlightenment. What he enlighten? This mention what they pay?"

"Yes ma'am," I nodded.

"Show me where is!"

I pointed to a sentence detailing a sizeable payment to be granted to the sponsoring cabaret.

"You our only singer with correct accent. You write lyrics. Talk to Sidney, make record. This giving me bad, bad headache. I need find tonic," she sighed, tromping out of the room.

During a brief rehearsal break later that afternoon, I spoke with Mr. Bechet about any fully notated music arrangements his band might have played on the U.S. tour they'd completed before heading to Paris.

"Wait. What? They's wantin' arrangements written full out?" he frowned. "You means, dey's wantin' the *whole thing* written down, not just usin' a lead sheet like normal? What in hell dem Kraut monkeys talkin' about? Duh whole arrangement note fer note? Ya gots yer melody line and duh chords on duh lead sheet – everythin' ya needs fo' Pete's sake! Ya cain' write out everythin' ev'ry instrument's doin' – dat's what makes it swing, girl. Dat's what makes jazz *jazz*! Ya gotta have improvisations when soloin' or it sure as hell ain' swing music. It ain't the opera! Dem Krauts are nuts!"

I smiled slightly. Nobody *ever* dared disagree with Mr. Bechet.

"Yes, sir," I replied quickly, "but that's what they're requesting. La Miss insists I'm the one who has to follow through on this … with you, sir."

Mr. Bechet muttered some French obscenity under his breath, shaking his head in disgust as he fished through his pockets for his cigarette case.

"What songs have the least amount of improvisation that are popular right now, sir? I … I was thinking maybe by … I don't know … what about something by Duke Ellington?"

Bechet snorted as he lit a cigarette, then shook his head as he blew out the match.

"Ain' gonna fly. I guarantee you they ain' wantin' no *neggermusik* as them Krauts call our early stuff. Where in hell's an ashtray when you need it? I swear tuh God, La Miss is always hidin' the damn things!" he grumbled, finally grabbing a jar lid that had been left on the windowsill.

"La Miss said something about my learning Nina Mae McKinney's song a few weeks ago … you know, "Swanee Shuffle" from *Hallelujah* because the song's popular again. Would that maybe --"

"Irving Berlin," he interrupted. "Nope. No good. He's a Jew. That film's playin' at the Palais Cinema fer a few more days. Don' know why. Y'ever seen it?"

"Actually, I was in it," I smiled. "Well, just one of the little kids, of course. But I've never seen it."

"You in that hosannah scene with that dumb runt joke of a donkey?" Mr. Bechet guffawed, taking a long pull on his cigarette.

I nodded.

"Thought you tol' me you was from Milwaukee 'fore movin' tuh New York. Didn' you say that? That filmin' was done in Memphis. "Swanee Shuffle" was filmed in New York, though, at the Cotton Club. They ask me tuh play on it but I was outta town. I remember the Cotton Club's where Nina Mae was workin' when that King Vidor fella first seen an' hired her on."

On our frenzied train escape to New York five years ago Mama and I had agreed to refrain from ever mentioning we'd lived in Memphis. I had to construct a believable story on the spot.

"Right after my … um, my adopted father passed away, Mama and I went to Memphis to visit with his mother for a few weeks. Only time I ever saw her. She died just a few months later," I lied. "Many of the children from her church were used in that film scene and they needed a few more faces in the parade, so that's why I was in it. I've never seen the film, though, because …" I drifted off mid-sentence, just barely catching myself before mentioning that it had never played anywhere in the Deep South … obviously Milwaukee was nowhere near the South. A Frenchman might not know that Milwaukee and Memphis were almost seven hundred miles apart, but

Sidney Bechet was originally from New Orleans and had toured all over the U.S. He sure as heck knew the lay of the land.

"Hmm, so you was adopted, eh?" commented Mr. Bechet, stubbing out his cigarette in the jar lid and then immediately plucking another smoke from his gold case. "Interestin'. Didn't know that. Ok. So, we still needs ourselves a composer."

"How about Benny Goodman?"

"Nope, another Jew. 'Sides, he don' write much vocal."

"Gershwin?"

"Three for three, *ma petite souris*," he chuckled. "Too bad you ain' a gambler. Most of them jazz composers nowadays ain' coons but they's Jews. An' that's worse if you kin believe it. Even if they ain' writin' swing music, you know, they's writin' marchin' band crap or ballroom puff pastry. Don' matter. The Krauts don' want 'em. Period. Nazi's been kickin' 'em outta Germany fo' 'bout four or five years now as you may know."

"Ok, who else?"

"Well, Cole Porter's got a lotta of stuff that's popular right now. He's a faggot, but married to that woman Linda whatever's her name, so most folks don' know 'bout his, uh, *liaisons amoureur* surprisingly. Least ways, doubt the Krauts know."

"I didn't know that either," I replied slowly.

"Well, at least he ain' Jewish. Episcopalian. From Peru, Indiana of all places. You ever been there?"

I shook my head.

"Yeah, same here. Anyway, I've got the original record and close enough to an original arrangement for Porter's "You're the Top." Write lyrics for that. You've sung it, right? When are they Krauts wantin' this?"

"They didn't really say," I replied, glancing through the letter even though I knew there was no specified date. "But soon."

"Yeah, Krauts'r always wantin' twenty-five copies two weeks ago. Who signed for this anyway?"

"Dr. Goebbels."

"Ah, *der Giftzwerg* himself," snorted Mr. Bechet.

"What does that word mean, please?" I asked. "La Miss called him that too."

"Means 'the poison dwarf'. Everythin' comin' out of that ugly troll's mouth's pure poison. Ok, so start workin' on them lyrics tonight. Let's aim fer Tuesday to book a session at *Le Disque Français* for recordin'. Dis ain' gonna be cheap. *Merde.* I'm sure La Miss plans to deduct it from our take this week, maybe pay us back a small percentage if it gets accepted. You better write some decent shit, y'hear, girl?"

Annette, Landie and I raced out to *Tout Va Bien* during our dinner break prior to preparations for that night's performances. Within an hour over hot coffee and teeth-rattlingly cold ice cream, we had penned an excellent start for alternate lyrics to Cole Porter's hit tune "You're the Top." We made a lot of edits and finished writing the song the following afternoon. The whole assignment, if one could call it that, struck all three of us as a hysterical farce. We laughed so hard we cried when Landie jumped out of her chair landing gracefully on one knee and theatrically delivered one set of lines without hesitation: 'You're our Charlie Lindberg and Charlie Chaplin combined -- you're the Eiffel Tower --- Man of the Hour – you're so sublime!'

I recorded both the original and new versions that Tuesday at *Le Disque Français* with six musicians from Mr. Bechet's ensemble. Microphones straddled various pipes suspended at different angles from the ceiling much like the cabaret. A thickly walled glass partition off to one side contained the recording equipment. The engineers' voices were muffled behind the partition – not that I could have understood much of what was being said in rapid-fire French even when they intermittently switched on the buzzing intercom. Just like at the Moulin Rouge, all the levels were tested, microphones repositioned and finally the recording began. The engineers had to adhere strictly to three minutes per side, recorded straight through, allowing for only a few seconds of trail off. Mr. Bechet was annoyed since newer recording equipment in America now allowed for far more flexibility. Figures the French would be too cheap to invest in new equipment he'd cursed under his breath.

As stipulated in the letter, the recordings, once pressed in shellac, were sent to the KWS facility in Berlin. None of us heard one note of anything we'd recorded. Mr. Bechet insisted that I alone list myself as the lyricist, concerned the Nazis might well look up the backgrounds of Landie and Annette, and upon discovering the girls were Jewish, penalize all of us. This bothered me immensely, but both girls readily agreed with Mr. Bechet. Mistinguett wanted my only copy of the lyrics, other than the typed version we'd enclosed with the record, but I secretly wrote out another:

> You're the top -- you're a German flyer
> You're the top -- through machine gun fire
> You're adrift above all the sunlit clouds quite grande
> You're the best around -- We so love your sound

You're in peak demand!

You're Big Ben -- You're the London Tower
You're the Thames -- Every day and hour
You're our Charlie Lindberg and Charlie Chaplin combined
You're the Eiffel Tower --- Man of the Hour
You're so sublime!

You're the top -- You're the *Champs-Élysée*
You're the top -- You're the Pyrenees (eh)
You're our grande Luftwaffe, you're J. von Goethe we're awed
You're the fastest plane – o'er all terrain
Without a flaw!

***

There was a brief piano intro along with a sixteen-bar instrumental break featuring Mr. Bechet on soprano sax after those three verses. I then repeated the last two verses, adding the lines 'you're the fastest plane -- o'er all terrain --' in a repeated three-bar tag, then finally emphasizing each of the words 'without' 'a' 'flaw' as long separate whole notes climbing up the scale as the ending, finishing out perfectly, just as the red light began flashing to indicate only four seconds were available until the trail off.

Chapter 18

Paris, France – October 1938

While I was at the recording studio, Landie and Annette had spent their afternoon break at *Tout Va Bien*. Seated at an adjacent table, Hermann and his friends had once again been arguing loudly with one another. The young men's conversation had gotten extremely dangerous, Landie whispered to me as we began dressing that evening for our performances at the Moulin Rouge. Annette was in another room rehearsing yet another set of last-minute changes for a difficult new dance sequence.

"He's … Hermann, that is," Landie remarked, carefully circling out a spot of rouge high on her cheekbone, "making a sleazy … I think that's your word for it … a sleazy deal with a Nazi officer at the German Embassy here in Paris. He's devised a dangerous plan to move his family safely out of Germany and obtain the documents illegally to live here permanently."

"Live here in Paris?"

"*Oui*," she nodded, dotting the rouge on her other cheek, then scowling, "this is much too dark. *Merde*."

"Wouldn't it be far more dangerous for the German officer? I mean, if he's caught forging documents …."

She nodded, looking into the long mirror we shared as she worked to even out the two spots of rouge she'd been massaging into her cheeks. I stared at her reflection in the mirror, my question still hanging in the air. Finally, she looked back at me, her voice barely discernable.

"His friends, especially that one who always smokes the pipe, Nathan, told him it was too risky. That it was a trap. But Hermann laughed and protested that he'd thought through the entire scheme."

I waited for her to continue, removing several clips from my hair.

"A *liaison*, same as in English, yes?" she continued, still whispering. "Hermann said he met a German, very handsome and … what is your American word … spiffy … in an expensive raincoat. They struck up a quick conversation. This was a few months ago. It turns out this was a proposition … you understand my meaning?"

I nodded, frowning.

"This man then invites Hermann to take a taxicab with him to a hotel in the Montmartre district for a sexual rendezvous. He pays Hermann with a big wad of cash. It turns out this man is a Nazi officer named Ernst vom Rath -- an *Alte Kämpfer.*"

"What's that?"

"It translates to 'Old Fighters' roughly. The first men who supported the Nazi party in the '20s are called by that name ... in fact they even proudly display the number they received when they joined the party, if you can imagine such a ... *jeu ridicule.*"

"Somehow I'm not surprised."

"Anyway, I couldn't understand if this was Hermann's, uh, *first* time with that *particular* man or his first time *ever* ... uh, you know ... the Yiddish got a little too tangled for my ear. But understand, I've no question whatever that's *exactly* what was being discussed."

"Oh, God, that boy is so reckless," I exhaled, roughly brushing through my hair, a massive nest of snarls. I'd been driven to the recording studio in an open car even though the wind had been ferocious.

"There's more. Hermann has met him several more times at this same hotel and plans to meet him again in the next few days. The money is good, he says. If things go as planned, somewhere in the next few weeks, though, he's going to demand that this Officer vom Rath illegally create the documents the Grynszpans need so they can all be brought here to Paris to live permanently. Otherwise, they face deportation to Poland in this newest pogrom. Rumor says it will begin very soon."

"But what if the officer doesn't agree?"

"Hermann says he'll expose the fact that the Kraut paid him for this 'service'. Not just once, but many times over many months. And he can prove this. The hotel even has photographs of them with arms around each other's waist or holding hands ... even one with the Nazi's head resting on Hermann's shoulder, walking down the steps into the lobby, he claims. Having sex with another man is a terrible sin in most every religion, of course. *C'est vrai.* But with a Jewish man? That is punishable by death in Germany. And for a higher-ranking Nazi official? *Le fin.* No questions asked. Also, it's common knowledge that a Jewish family would permanently disown their son for such a terrible sin as this."

"This boy ... I hesitate to call him a man ... has very bizarre ideas about ... well, ideas about everything, I think. He must see this desperate act as the only way to bring his family to safety," I replied.

"But Landie, does he really know they'll be in such a bad situation? What I've heard is that there are plans for new camps. The establishments will be much cleaner, offering far better schools and good paying work opportunities."

It had also been suggested that the Jews actually preferred to live like animals, that in fact they weren't nearly as intelligent as members of the Aryan race. A film supporting this outrageous propaganda, produced recently by Berlin's UFA studios, had been shown with limited success at a cinema near the Moulin Rouge. As one whose race had been repeatedly degraded by similarly low opinions, I'd maintained a wide berth.

"You believe that tripe?" scoffed Landie, raising her eyebrows and pursing her lips.

"I don't know. Maybe," I shrugged. In truth, since I would only be living here in Paris for another two months, I felt somewhat guilty that I wasn't more concerned about this situation. But I was exhausted just trying to placate La Miss and Mr. Bechet during our endless rehearsals and severely criticized performances day after day. And poor Mama! She'd learned a lot about European methods of tailoring since we'd lived here. Although she never complained, I knew she was more than ready to take her newly acquired skills back to America. At least the measurements and specifications would be delivered in a more civil tongue.

"Anyway, Hermann's friends say all this has been far too risky. A horrible idea that can only end badly no matter what. They say the Nazi will kill Hermann with his SS pistol before he'll let him desecrate the Third Reich's honor in so disgusting a manner."

"What did he answer to that?"

"Hermann just laughed and replied that he plans to use some of Herr vom Rath's own money to buy a gun as well, just in case there is a problem."

"Someone should try to talk with him. Maybe since you overheard the conversation --"

"*Non, non!*" Landie interrupted emphatically, her voice louder than she'd intended, after which she continued far more quietly. "I can't get involved at all. Nor can you. Anyone seen talking with him could be in danger. I don't trust these *sale boches* in the slightest."

"Trust these what? I've heard that term many times recently."

"*Sale boches.* Filthy Krauts."

"Ok. But he lives in the apartment with Mama and me," I frowned, a sobering thought settling over me. "Or he does some of the time, anyway. I don't know where he is the rest of the time. Do you think

Mama and I might be in danger from his … well, scandalous behavior?"

"I can't say for certain, Helen," Landie replied, shaking her head slightly. "You must be *very* careful around this man – around this whole situation, in fact -- from now on. He's delusional. One of his friends, that one with the stinky pipe, Nathan, called him an 'irresponsible prevaricator of the worst sort'."

"Some friend."

"*Oui.* I should imagine this is why his aunt and uncle abruptly moved out from the apartment of their own shop and now refuse to allow Hermann space under their same roof anymore. They found out. I can't believe Hermann would have been stupid enough to brag about his sordid escapades with a Nazi officer! But somehow, they know. Despite that, you may be absolutely certain that Uncle Abraham still pockets every cent that Hermann's destitute parents are scrimping to send from Hanover to pay for their stupid son's living space!" Landie spat out.

"He would do that I suppose. No surprise there," I sighed. Hermann's aunt and uncle were my poor Mama's exasperating daily trial, similar to my futile attempts to placate Mr. Bechet and Mistinguett. Maybe scrabbling for a living in Paris just bred nasty dispositions in everyone.

"No Jewish family wants to admit they have this kind of a … a 'cancer' … eating away within their esteemed male bloodlines. Hermann knows he's been thrown out for good. But since you're Negroes I'm sure he assumes you won't dare complain about the situation if *you* find out -- meaning he can stay there as long as his papa continues shelling out his rent."

A sharp knock on the dressing room door followed by the stage manager's curt ten-minute warning ended our tense conversation. As the other girls left for the stage, an obviously upset Annette rushed into the dressing room only seconds thereafter. She thrust into Landie's hands an English-printed news sheet, being sold by newsboys in front of the cabaret, which Landie read aloud.

"It seems the Nazis have just made good on their threat to deport several thousand Polish Jews from Berlin, forcing them back to Poland," she began, reading slowly. "But the Polish border guards, on order from their government … they're refusing to let the refugees enter. They've set up a huge makeshift camp outside of Poland … mostly old animal pens, this says … abandoned by some military encampment after the war ended two decades ago."

"*S'il te plaît,*" urged Annette. "Read on!"

"There's no arrangement for food or water ... some crude attempt at sanitation ... shallow shit hole dug behind some prickly bush you can bet," Landie snorted. "Overflowing with filth by the first afternoon ...."

"All *personne* be sick in days!" Annette whimpered, shaking her head.

"The refugees were dumped at this location mostly by train ... in cattle cars," Landie continued. "A lot of people are already very sick. Men and some women not moving quickly enough for the Germans were seen beaten about the head by batons or rifle butts. *Mon dieu* ..."

I quietly put my arm around Annette's shoulders. She was trembling. Landie continued speaking after taking a moment to scan further down the article.

"They're saying entire Jewish families – not just the men – have been forced from their homes with only a few minutes to pack one flimsy suitcase for all. Everyone is exhausted, hungry, confused ... *et terrifié.*"

"My family must have go too! I am sure this fact!" sobbed Annette, tears coursing down her face. She swiped her forearm under her nose. I handed her a handkerchief.

The stage manager, a small greasy man who didn't seem to speak any language very fluently, suddenly appeared in the dressing room doorway.

"*Vite! Dépêche-toi!*" he growled. "You three fixin' for gettin' La Miss bark up on you *ce soir? Ce n'est pas une bonne idée!* That woman in one hell of the temper *maintenant.* Audience keep yakkin'. Loud too. They ain't applaudin' nothin' ... not one song, not one joke. *Rien. Nichts.*"

"Lovely," muttered Landie under her breath as she and I rushed past him towards the stage. Annette said she'd try to get there by curtain. We hoped we could cover for her if she didn't.

Chapter 19

Paris, France – November 1938

"Europe always got big headache … big trouble somewhere," seethed La Miss in a loud stage whisper backstage, noting our downcast expressions as the band opened with their favorite instrumental arrangement of "Stardust". "This no excuse! You must give best work here. The hot music, *oui*? Not the dog face!"

Mr. Bechet, who typically joined the band for their second tune, had nodded silently in agreement then added, "as they say in America: 'the show must go on'."

With a melting pot of languages spoken among the musicians and cabaret staff, we traded various news accounts as they were broadcast over the airwaves. Hearing these different viewpoints was disturbing, however. Jewish radio broadcasts were the most detailed and daunting, insisting that countless Jewish men had been beaten to death in the streets of Berlin when they'd failed to vacate their homes quickly enough. It was widely rumored, traced to reliable sources, that entire Jewish families had opted to commit suicide in their homes rather than face yet another pogrom.

French radio reports were not quite as desperate in tone, but nonetheless, since Paris alone housed thousands of Jewish families, the news remained frightening. No Frenchman alive wanted to go head-to-head against the rising tide of the seemingly fearless German army. France was still exhausted from their country's massive losses, both in men as well as finance, since the Great War had ended exactly two decades ago. If you threw a large chunk of meat to a vicious mongrel, it would be sated and leave you alone was the prevailing French radio opinion. Additionally, the Polish Jews who'd been thrown out of Berlin were the Polish Jews' problem, not the French government's.

Without the slightest embarrassment whatsoever, German radio reported boldly that these new refugees had been very gently treated. Families had been given adequate time to pack their belongings, which included substantial food, medications, and other necessities, and had then been cheerfully escorted by the guards to roomy passenger trains, their luggage often hand-carried aboard by the Nazis themselves. The Germans claimed they'd also prepared several hundred Kosher meals for their new guests should any of the families keep strictly Kosher diets. Even the Nazis residing in Paris hooted in disbelief at this ludicrous embellishment.

The BBC reported the entire cabinet, prime minister, and the royal family were in anguish contemplating what Great Britain's role should be given this newest bold atrocity on the part of the Nazis. Certain broadcasters had been furious regarding England, Italy and France's foolhardy agreement at the Munich Conference just barely a month ago. They'd warned that handing over the Sudeten region, those areas specifically bordering Czechoslovakia, would merely whet this insatiably greedy Nazi appetite. And indeed, so it had -- *exactly* as the BBC had predicted! There were angry demands for the immediate resignation of the idiotic mastermind behind that ill-constructed conference, England's own prime minister: Neville Chamberlain.

The BBC had gone further to state that Hitler's treacherous work *Mein Kampf* was now included in every German soldier's kit as well as in the backpacks of all children in the Hitler Youth camps – a requirement for all Aryan youth throughout that country. Exactly as the BBC had predicted, Germany's recent march into a cheering Austria produced the final, joyous shredding of the ill-conceived Versailles Treaty that had ended the Great War – the so-called war to end all wars – exactly two decades ago. It was only a matter of time before the entire European continent might be ruthlessly trampled under Nazi boots the BBC broadcasters grimly warned.

The American radio program that Mama and I heard at the American Church of Paris gave very little information about the event, although to be fair, we weren't able to listen until several days after the pogrom. Sandwiched between two light music programs devoid of an avid listening audience, the announcer relayed quite limited detail.

***

One week later, Annette received a scrawled, badly torn letter from her mother. Annette was far too upset to read the note aloud and asked Landie to translate it for me as we sat at an inside table at *Tout Va Bien* awaiting our coffees and sandwiches. Our extended Parisian late summer had ended abruptly with cold, continuous downpours a few days before. Most of the outdoor tables had been removed and the streets were inches deep with standing water. The air stank of worms.

"As you've probably guessed by now," Landie began translating, "we are among the deported citizens from Hanover. We're now residing at a crude makeshift camp outside the Polish border. The living conditions are cramped and uncomfortable for some, but we have no such hardship. You should not believe the idle gossip that people are ill or that some have died. The Germans are providing adequate medicine, food and water every day."

Annette snorted in disgust.

"The letter ends with: 'kisses to you as always, dearest sweet Ann. We are just fine ~ Mama'," continued Landie, then handed the letter back to Annette.

"They not doing well," muttered Annette, carefully folding the letter back into the envelope. "Not at all!"

"The Krauts are obviously screening all posts before allowing them to be mailed," agreed Landie.

"You surprise this?" retorted Annette. "Nazis make all business *their* business."

"What happens next?" I asked, gently touching Annette's elbow. "Will you be able to write back?"

Annette never answered my question.

"Here how I know things no good: she never call me Ann. *Elle m'appelle* Annette *ou* Annette Adèle."

We sat silently at *Tout Va Bien*, staring at one another then into our coffee cups, murmuring thanks to a waiter who added a bit of hot water to the coffee. We'd already had our one allotted refill.

"I wonder whatever happened with Hermann's family," Landie commented after several moments, turning to face me. The entire café had been eerily hushed this week with no sign of Hermann or his friends. Someone dropped a spoon which clattered loudly for a few seconds on the worn tile floor.

"I wouldn't know," I shrugged. "He hasn't been at the shop for almost two weeks according to Mama. He usually arrives to pick up the money his father sends on the first of the month. He hasn't shown up yet though, which is odd."

"The uncle who is tailor, *oui*?" frowned Annette.

"Mama says these days when Hermann walks in the door of the shop, his aunt hands the boy any letters from his family without saying one word, then turns away. The uncle throws an envelope on the floor in front of the boy, also ignoring him."

"Your mama is always there?" asked Landie.

"She's been working extra hours recently. Some of the workers have quit and moved out to the country to be near other relatives, she thinks. I've been doing all our shopping and bringing in our food since she's been far too busy. In fact, Mama's only been to church once in several weeks. The only time I remember that was ... well... actually, now that I think about it ... never. Anyway, she's very surprised Hermann hasn't yet collected his allowance. He seems to spend everything down to *le dernier sou* as they say, each month."

"Ah," snorted Landie, adding sarcastically, "maybe your President Roosevelt answered the poor lad and has wired him *beaucoup d'argent*. He certainly hasn't been concerned with any other Jews in Europe according to last night's editions of *Paris-Soir* and *Le Temps*."

I was truly embarrassed by my country's lack of interest or involvement with this bold move by the Nazis, but honestly thought there must be some logical explanation about which we Americans living abroad were not aware. I offered no reply to Landie's accusation, motioning instead to the waiter for our bill.

An odd sense of foreboding quietly penetrated every conversation with Mama who'd become increasingly anxious to return home to America. I knew that breaking off my contract with Mr. Bechet would undoubtedly result in my being shunned by the cabaret music scene back home. Although many establishments avoided dealing with the man due to his explosive temper, Sidney Bechet maintained a powerful presence in music circles throughout America as well as Europe.

It had taken Mama a long time to warm even slightly to my singing in nightclubs. For the first three years that I'd worked at Smalls Paradise back in Harlem, she'd attended every one of my performances, sitting out in that drafty hallway, almost always knitting hats, scarves, and gloves for sale. During my breaks she insisted I sit with her and not fraternize with any of the musicians or male audience members. When I'd turned sixteen, she eased up slightly, but since we still lived in that same apartment a few blocks from the club, she appeared unannounced multiple times each week, newest knitting project as well as Bible snuggly nestled in her battered satchel. The other girls at Smalls had teased me relentlessly about being squashed like a beetle under Mama's heavy thumb. But in all honesty, I was grateful to walk out into that hallway during my breaks and find her sitting there. Newly acquired reading glasses straddling her nose, she'd cast onto her needle from a large skein of yarn while sipping a cup of tea and bringing me up to date on the evening's news.

Chapter 20

Paris, France – November 1938

The weather had been coaxed temporarily back into late summer a few days after Annette's distressing letter from her mother had arrived. Restless, and eager to enjoy a few hours of sunshine after an exceptionally blistering rehearsal that had ended quite early, I raced to the bus, then boarded *le Métro*, hoping for a long walk in the *Tuilleries* before heading back to the biblical lion's den for that evening's performances.

Mistinguett had accused the musicians of totally butchering the charts for most of her new medleys. Mr. Bechet argued the arrangements were exactly how they'd worked it out in earlier rehearsals. In true La Miss fashion, the singer denounced the professionalism of the entire ensemble, Mr. Bechet included. The musicians dumped their sheet music onto the floor and without uttering one word snapped their instruments into cases and stormed out of rehearsal. One could only hope they would be returning this evening. I was more than ready for my contract in Paris to end so Mama and I could finally get home. We were both counting the days.

Lost in thought, I'd foolishly misjudged my stop, ending up instead on the other side of the Seine. Rather than walking around four blocks to the return underground entry, I opted instead to just walk along the *Rue de Lille*, which ran parallel to and south of the sparkling river. The sea of dark umbrellas that had buffeted everyone about during the last several days' thrashing rainstorms had vanished. They'd been replaced by a leisurely strolling crowd of all ages, taking the time to examine several small delivery carts dotting the road. Many were patronizing a large sidewalk stand that carried cigars, cigarettes, a small selection of fresh fruit as well as newspapers in several languages. I breathed in the fragrant air as I continued walking past the newsstand. A few moments later I noticed several Nazi soldiers in front of a large foreboding building. Confused at first, I realized it was the German Embassy.

Suddenly a young man raced out of the building, tan raincoat flapping wildly behind him, followed closely by two more German soldiers who were yelling "*arrête! Arrête maintenant!*"

The young man whirled around to face the soldiers shrieking "*C'est un sale boche! Vous êtes tous des sales boches!*" I'd overheard many people muttering these same phrases recently: 'he's a dirty Kraut! You're all dirty Krauts!' The man had been waving a small pistol overhead, aimed at the clouds. He tossed the gun maniacally in my direction then turned to continue running. The gun ricocheted loudly off a wrought iron fence post, a red tag fluttering wildly from its handle, then skittered well under the bushes. Within seconds the two soldiers grabbed the man's arms, tackling him from behind. He landed face down with a sickening thud on the cement sidewalk. Three other guards joined the two soldiers, detaining the writhing man as he fiercely struggled on the pavement. As they clamped handcuffs across his wrists, he jerked his head sideways, facing my direction. His cheek was badly bloodied, his eyes wide with hate.

Terrified, I realized it was Hermann Grynszpan.

As the soldiers yanked Hermann to his feet, a small crowd began gathering. Several gendarmes shoved people roughly aside as they joined the Nazi guards. The officials moved Hermann away from the embassy entrance, slammed him up against the building's stone wall and began questioning him. Another official retrieved the gun from under the bushes. Within a few minutes an ambulance pulled up, its siren whooping loudly as the vehicle approached. Three French medical attendants, carrying a dark green stretcher, rushed past us into the embassy. More people had now gathered in the crowd. A din of confusion surrounded me.

The medical attendants returned quickly. A Nazi official, white-faced, moaning in agony, lay on the stretcher. Blood oozed through the sheet that had been loosely draped around his lower body. As the stretcher was being loaded into the ambulance, I could hear Hermann's continued outbursts. Someone then stuffed rags into his mouth to muffle him. The ambulance tore away from the curb, its siren whooping even louder than before, as the gendarmes began shoving their suspect towards the local precinct house located a block away. I asked if anyone could tell me what Hermann had been shouting. An older man standing near me nodded slightly.

"Yes, miss," he muttered, shaking his head sadly. "I speak English. He was saying, over and over, 'I have just shot a man in his office. I do not regret it. I did it to avenge my parents who are deported from their home'."

"Ah," I replied quietly, closing my eyes momentarily.

"What a brainless act on this boy's part!" the man moaned. "He will surely see the guillotine. His family will never see their son alive again. Today's youth are so impetuous."

***

Two days later, on Nov. 9th, the entire world had heard about a Polish Jew named Herschel Grynzspan, an unskilled, unemployed, high school dropout, given to reckless delusional fantasies, who had been illegally residing in the Jewish ghetto district of Paris. The seventeen-year-old boy had shot undersecretary Ernst vom Rath, an original Nazi party member, known as an *Alter Kämpfer*, or Old Fighter, twice in the stomach late that morning using a small handgun that the young man had purchased the night before. The twenty-nine-year-old vom Rath had clung to life for just over a day, but despite multiple surgeries, passed away in agony.

Hermann's declaration, reprinted in the newspapers was almost identical to what the man at the embassy had translated for me. But this told only a fraction of the story as Landie, Annette, Hermann's close friends and I were fully aware.

Had he approached the Nazi officer, brandishing his newly purchased loaded pistol, failing to even remove the dangling price tag, like some belligerent toddler playing soldiers with his friends? He would then have demanded that his family, very likely deported to that same wretched camp outside the Polish border as Annette's, be immediately granted visas to reside permanently in Paris as originally agreed. If not, as Landie had overheard Hermann boast to his friends, the boy would make public the fact that vom Rath had been a Jewish man's lover for the better part of a year … a crime automatically dealt with by firing squad for a Nazi official.

"Maybe vom Rath just laughed at him," commented Landie, as we compared news bulletins that morning while awaiting La Miss' arrival for rehearsal.

"Or try pull gun out his desk maybe?" added Annette, deep in thought. "Maybe Hermann no mean shoot … but then sees Nazi gun … and, well?"

"French newspapers are saying the Nazis found four bullets shot wild around the desk. They claim that two rounds loaded in the chamber were aimed point blank into vom Rath's stomach," replied Landie in disgust. "If the Kraut aimed a gun at Hermann, it seems unlikely to me that he would miss if he indeed fired. A soldier would never miss a target at such close range."

I thought for a moment.

"Maybe Hermann shot off those first four bullets as a warning to vom Rath that he was dead serious."

"Yes, you could be right," nodded Landie. "In fact, I like that. That *sale boche* maybe kept laughing and laughing and swore no one would ever believe such a far-fetched accusation about a higher-ranking Nazi officer coming from such a stupid, ignorant, illegal *kike*."

That night, for the first time since I'd been performing at the Moulin Rouge, the cabaret was suddenly closed with less than fifteen minutes' notice. All performances were canceled for that evening and the next, and possibly longer with no explanation. Landie, Annette and I quickly waved goodbye to one another, scurrying in three directions to our buses. I bought a wedge of cheese and loaf of warm bread from a sidewalk vendor before boarding a packed bus back to Mama's and my tiny apartment. As I peered out the bus window, I saw that businesses everywhere were shuttering early.

Fearful of venturing further than just down the street to obtain an English newspaper, I purchased one in Yiddish that was liberally studded with photos. Mama and I bravely tore the tape off the dial and reset the Gynszpan's shop radio to the BBC station. Between what was being broadcast and the harsh photos reprinted in the news sheets, even though we couldn't read the stories themselves, we learned that Adolf Hitler's esteemed Minister of Propaganda, Herr Doktor Joseph Goebbels, had seized upon a foolhardy Jewish boy's assassination of a Nazi officer to authorize an unprecedented massive reprisal against all Jews living in Germany.

According to Dr. Goebbels, Herr Hitler was horrified to learn of Herschel Grynszpan's willful murder of Ernst vom Rath, one of the Nazi party's most promising elite. The Jew Grynszpan, as he became immediately labeled, was known to be a member of an incestuous worldwide network of wealthy Jewish bankers, businessmen, and clergy, the vast majority leaning heavily towards communism in fact, fully intent upon the destruction of the undisputedly pure Aryan virtues upheld by the Nazi party.

As Mama and I listened to the terrifying BBC broadcasts, we learned that Dr. Goebbels had delivered an impassioned speech across the German airwaves that afternoon, unofficially urging the Hitler Youth as well as two paramilitary units, to destroy Jewish shops, rob Jewish-owned banks and torch synagogues in retaliation for the merciless killing of vom Rath. Glass from the smashed plate glass windows of department stores crunched under heavy boots as widespread looting extended throughout most of the large cities in Germany and Austria.

By the following morning this fully sanctioned rioting was being called *Kristallnacht*, meaning 'the night of broken glass' as the carnage continued unabated. To me this sounded far too whitewashed a description for the scandalous damage depicted in the photos that screamed across the front page of every early edition newspaper in the garment district. Jewish cemeteries were being desecrated. Homes were vandalized -- their expensive furnishings gleefully mutilated by the often-youthful rioters. All shockingly encouraged by neighboring German onlookers. Many of the photos were provided by German citizens in fact, proud of their neighborhood's widespread cleansing endeavors. Firemen made no attempt to extinguish the fires set in hundreds of synagogues. They were instructed instead to merely sit idly nearby, prepared to deal with any flying embers that might inadvertently land on an adjacent gentile establishment.

Mama and I listened to the BBC's continuous news stories. Occasionally, they would take a break to play a few records, but I doubt those listening had even the slightest interest in music. Each time the broadcasters returned to their microphones they spoke of new outrages. Reports stated that the police in Berlin were doing nothing to protect Jews or their property. Instead, thousands of Jewish families, supposedly arrested for their own protection, were being rounded up and then carted off to the hideously overcrowded Dachau and Buchenwald ghetto facilities located just outside the city. These families were told they would be released if they could prove they had guaranteed documentation allowing them to emigrate permanently from Germany.

"But as we've stated here on the BBC beforehand, this is a promise almost no Jew can make. Every country in Europe, including right here in Great Britain as well as France, is tightening immigration quotas. What about the United States or Cuba or Canada, you say? Afraid not, sir. Close, but no cigar. The number of countries blatantly refusing to accept additional Jewish refugees far outweigh those willing to do so. And just where *are* those few countries? Would *anybody* in modern civilized society willingly move there? I think not my good friend!

"All this outrage to justify a Nazi reprisal for a troubled Jewish teenager's impetuous act -- an act that was interpreted by Adolf Hitler and his scheming rat of an accomplice, the Minister of Propaganda, Joseph Goebbels, as a threat perpetrated by a world order of Jewry, one that's determined to exterminate all other races," the newscaster scoffed. "Utter balderdash! It's quite obvious, although we Brits dare not voice any official opinion, that this outrageous act is simply a means to further widen the Nazi's despicable agenda across the entire European continent. Had Hitler, Goebbels, Göring and Heydrich -- considered the devious masterminds behind most such acts these days -- simply been waiting for the right situation ... that is to say, the right moment, the right pawn, or perhaps even better: the right *scape goat* -- to fall into their hands? Was Herschel Grynszpan merely thrust into this spotlight as that very pawn, ladies and gentlemen? *You* my friends listening to this radio program, *you* must decide. And what's more, *you* must react accordingly and speak up!"

Ever since that German on the boat had viciously torn up Mr. Bechet's music and spat in Mistinguett's face, I'd shuddered whenever a group of Nazi brownshirts stumbled into the Moulin Rouge, ogling those of us up on the stage. Unlike the French soldiers who'd willingly leave their *matraques* or billy clubs at coat check, the Nazis sat with theirs either visibly straddling their laps or strategically nestled just outside their forks as though the clubs were part of the table service.

"You know, Helen," sighed Mama, turning down the volume, as she rubbed her forehead, "it seems very strange that there's been no mention of any demonstrations in Paris itself, don't you think? I mean, *this* is where the actual crime was committed. Well, you know that. You were right there, unfortunately."

"Yes, very unfortunately," I agreed quietly. Neither of us knew what ill might come of my having witnessed Hermann's exit from the embassy. Without question someone would have noted my standing there. "A lot of this doesn't make sense to me either. It sounds from these newest reports that this destruction is still continuing all over Germany. Wait ... wait ... that sounds like someone speaking German, Mama. Please turn it back up."

Within a few moments, the German's voice was muted as a BBC newsman broke into the man's speech. "Ladies and gentlemen, that voice you just heard was Nazi Propaganda Minister Joseph Goebbels speaking about the bulletin he issued just an hour earlier this evening declaring an immediate halt of the rampage. He praised the heroic efforts of those involved -- pshaw, what utter poppycock ... about as heroic as stepping on a foundering ant -- further stating that the resulting mess would be cleaned up by the Jews themselves! Can you believe this? And my friends, to add yet more insult to injury, Dr. Goebbels has also stated that stiff fines are being imposed on these Jews for destroying their own property. Now that takes unbelievable gall, even for the Nazis you must agree dear friends. Oh, and there's more – how could I forget? Jewish owned businesses in Germany have been told by Dr. Goebbels they can't lay claim to their own insurance policies' compensation for any of those damages."

"They're getting bolder and bolder," frowned Mama, as she turned down the radio once again as the station began playing a record. "These Nazis aim to take over the entire world, Helen."

"I fear they may very well succeed," I replied softly.

Chapter 21

Paris, France – November 1938

No workers had shown up at the Grynszpan shop for two days. No unusual taunts or overt threats had knowingly surfaced in the congested Jewish garment district where we lived, but nonetheless, residents remained inside, only scurrying to the grocery or druggists when absolutely necessary.

I left on a slightly earlier bus for the Moulin Rouge that morning, urging Mama to gather our few belongings and go immediately to the American Church rather than waiting for me to return. Since no one had arrived at the tailor shop, her abrupt departure wouldn't require an explanation.

I intended to break my contract with Mr. Bechet this morning and book our passage back to the States as soon as possible. I would probably never obtain work in the music industry again, but I no longer cared. I was ashamed that poor Mama had put up with this selfish whim of mine for all these years. We could find our way out to the hills of Pennsylvania. I'd been told that was a beautiful place to live.

We'd have to appeal to the American Church staff here in Paris to allow us to stay in their basement in the interim. It's a church – God's house – I repeated to myself firmly. I only had a little money other than what would be necessary for our return passage to New York. Surely, the church would help us … but I wasn't entirely convinced.

Unlike Mistinguett, Mr. Bechet typically arrived at the cabaret well in advance; rehearsals commenced on schedule without the singer. Only a handful of cleaning women were working inside the dark, unlit building, when I arrived, however. Mr. Bechet was nowhere to be seen. I finally located the regular custodian, a disgruntled man who spoke very fragmented English.

"*Oui?*" he asked curtly, one eyebrow raised as he wrung filthy water from his mop into a bucket.

"*Je cherche Monsieur* Bechet *ou* La Miss," I replied slowly, gesturing. "Do you know where they are?"

"*Non, mademoiselle. Je ne les vois,*" he replied, slapping the mop back onto the floor.

"*Avez-vous une feuille de papier … et un stylo?*" I asked, gesturing writing in case my request wasn't quite correct.

He fished out a crumpled receipt and pencil stub from his cleaning smock and handed them to me.

"*Merci,*" I smiled.

He nodded and continued swishing his mop from side to side down the hallway.

Mr. Bechet could only read a smattering of French and almost no English, even though he spoke both languages quite well. I addressed my letter of immediate resignation to La Miss and left it on top of the piano in the rehearsal area. None of the musicians had appeared yet. Maybe rehearsal and performances were canceled again tonight. No matter. I wasn't planning to be there anyway. I raced from the cabaret down the block to the bus stop.

My ride home was uneventful. Few shops appeared to be open for business.

As usual, a battered concrete gnome propped open the heavy door to the Grynszpan's shop. I walked in, reluctantly expecting to see several women at their sewing machines. I prayed that Mama had gotten away to the American Church before the others had arrived.

No Jewish seamstresses bent over clattering black machinery greeted me, however. Instead, three gendarmes were seated next to the silent machines. They slowly rose to their feet as I entered the shop. On the floor next to one gendarme was Mama's and my wicker suitcase, roped together with twine and tied with an unusual fancy knot I recognized as Mama's alone.

"*Vous êtes Mlle. Campbell, oui?*" asked one officer, walking towards me. He continued in rapid French about which I comprehended almost nothing.

"*Oui, monsieur,*" I replied, shaking my head slightly as I attempted a brief smile. "*Je ne parle pas très bien français.*"

The soldier muttered something to his two comrades, both of whom then snickered.

"You will sit … *ici,*" he replied, gesturing to the seat he had just vacated.

I heard soft rustling nearby, possibly from our tiny living area that lay just behind the shop itself. I silently prayed again that Mama had already left.

"You know why we here … yes?"

"No sir, I'm afraid I don't."

"You know the Jew Grynszpan, yes?"

I nodded, cringing slightly upon hearing Dr. Goebbel's derogatory name for Hermann.

"And the Jew Grynszpan, he live and work in … this same … here, yes?"

I nodded, forcing myself to stare directly at him, though very wary.

"He pay you rent?"

"No, he's not my tenant."

He raised his eyebrows, obviously awaiting additional information.

"My mother and I rent this space from Herschel's uncle, Abraham Grynszpan. Herschel also rents space from him."

"Ah, but, the Jew Grynszpan, he live here with you … *avec toi* … eh, Mlle. Campbell, *oui?*

Had this been a rather trick question of sorts? His bold implication of Hermann's living arrangement wasn't lost to me. There was a slight chance the policeman didn't understand the nuance of his question in English, but somehow, I rather doubted this. I nodded slowly. The rustling noises had gotten louder. It was coming either from Mama's and my living space or the concealed area behind the ceiling-high bolts of material beyond which lay the storage closet that served as Hermann's room. Neither Mama nor I ever needed to look for Hermann between the immense rolls of fabric as the noxious odor of his French cigarettes typically verified his presence. He was either there or he wasn't. It mattered nothing to us whatsoever. He was not our responsibility. Whatever slight interest in the man I may have harbored upon meeting him had dissolved when I'd learned of his jaded lifestyle. That said, Hermann couldn't possibly be in that room, obviously. For unless he'd been guillotined on the spot or had miraculously escaped, he was still in jail.

"He rents space from --"

"*Oui ou non*, Mlle. Campbell?" the gendarme interrupted.

"*Oui,*" I replied indignantly, my face reddening, "but he has separate living quarters. We do not live … or *sleep* … in the same room, *monsieur!*"

"I did not ask such a question," he chuckled, rattling off something in French to his compatriots which set them laughing heartily.

A fourth gendarme appeared from behind the bolts of fabric. Draped over one arm were several articles of men's clothing, a small stack of magazines filled the other. He dangled one of the magazines in front of me.

"You know what this?" the new officer inquired.

"I believe it's written in Yiddish," I replied, shaking my head. "I'm not Jewish. I can't read it."

No one spoke for several moments, one of them maddeningly flicking dirt out from under his fingernails. Then my original interrogator addressed me once again.

"You will come now with us. We have more questions," he stated, stooping to pick up the wicker suitcase. It so kind your mama pack, *oui*? She we … eh … bring in already," he stated with a shrug. I closed my eyes, grimacing. She hadn't gotten away to the American Church.

The gendarme flashed a smile with far too many large protruding teeth. Those teeth reminded me of that pack of mongrel dogs we used to feed outside our back porch in Milwaukee so long ago … before Daddy got sick … before we took the train down to Memphis … before meeting Johnnie 'three fingers' Doucet while filming Mr. Vidor's movie *Hallelujah* … before Beverly died … before singing with Milton and Walter on the hotel veranda … before seeing Terrence's and Dax's mutilated bodies as they drew their last breaths … before finding the Radithor money in the Hydrol trunk … before seeing Aunt Lil, Charlene, and her boyfriend swinging silently in the hospital's eerie black ravine … before performing at Small's Paradise in Harlem … before sailing to Paris ….

My life as I'd known it … before.

Chapter 22

Paris, France – mid-November 1938

Two of the officers shoved me into the back seat of a large black car, then sat on either side of me. The driver tore away, almost hitting an old man who was slowly pushing a rusted bicycle with a wobbly wheel over a crumbled gutter. The driver yelled at the old man. I immediately recognized the accent. Not French. German. Less than twenty minutes later we pulled up to the German Embassy on *Rue de Lille*. One of the gendarmes yanked me out of the car and dragged me over to a Nazi guard who clamped his steely fingers over my elbow. The two gendarmes then saluted the Germans and began walking briskly towards the Paris precinct as the Nazi soldier thrust me through the embassy's front entry and down the pristine hallway.

No one spoke. I was left in a darkly paneled room, dimly lit, with a small, battered desk in one corner and one heavily barred window near the other. Although of limited relief, it was definitely a room, however, not a cell. The door loudly clicked shut. I then heard the outer lock engage. A single chair was positioned almost in the center of the room. I sat down slowly and waited. I had no idea how much time passed. Occasionally I would hear the quick step of staccato heels on military boots or muffled voices outside in the hallway.

When the door finally reopened, I stood up carefully. A small man, clean shaven, his thick dark hair brushed straight back from his forehead, entered. He limped slightly, and although dressed in civilian attire rather than military uniform, wore a large red and black swastika emblazoned within a white circle on a wide black armband. He looked familiar, but I couldn't place where I might have seen him. Probably at the cabaret, but somehow that didn't seem quite right either. Carrying a folder in one arm, he walked over and sat on top of the desk.

"Please sit back down," he began, gesturing slightly as he opened the folder.

I complied.

"Helen Mason Campbell … am I correct in that assumption?" he continued, after carefully removing several papers from the folder and smoothing them out on top of the desk. He spoke flawless English with a crisp British accent.

"Yes, sir," I replied quietly.

"You are an American, yes?"

"Yes, sir."

"Information on your passport and work papers state that you are a Negress, correct?"

"Yes sir. That is correct."

"Yet you are quite light skinned compared to your mother. This is rather unusual in my opinion."

Although I desperately wanted to ask where they'd taken her, I forced myself to refrain from doing so.

"I was ... adopted, sir," I replied quietly, "at about age four."

"Adopted? How did this come about?"

"I'm told I climbed into the back of the Campbells' automobile and fell asleep. They looked for my parents for almost a year, but no one ever came forward."

"And your name? You look nothing like a Helen to me."

"It ... it was on the hand embroidered label sewn inside my coat, sir. Well, Helen Mason, that is ... I was adopted by the Campbells."

"Did anyone ever stop to think the coat might not have been originally yours?" he questioned, staring at me with a wry expression.

I made no reply. No one ever had I thought to myself.

He then glanced over at the notes spread out next to him on the desk and stood up. "You have very large brown eyes and straighter hair, long for a Negress, Miss Campbell," he continued, walking silently behind me. "It reminds me a bit of the gypsies that are scattered all about here in France, some of whom are Jewish, of course, although fortunately you are not nearly as swarthy as they."

He placed his fingers on both sides of my head and ran them slowly through my hair, his fingertips coming to a rest on the back of my neck. "And your hair is quite silky. You do not appear to use any straightening pomades or the egg white preparations of the chopped off Greek boy's cap that your American compatriot Josephine Baker uses in her greasy coiffure."

His fingers remained on my neck. I sat ramrod straight, trembling slightly. His left hand moved gently along my neck, stopping over my mouth. After lightly brushing his thumb over my lips, he then continued walking slowly back to the desk and turned to face me.

"I was required to critique your recording that was submitted to the German radio committee for your entry of "You're the Top." As you may imagine, all entries needed my approval. You have an excellent voice, Helen ... clear, expressive, richly vibrant in tone yet still quite articulate."

"Thank you ... sir," I murmured, extremely wary of the intent behind this compliment.

The man glanced once again over the papers spread out next to him, then cleared his throat.

"It has been brought to my attention that you and your mother were housing an illegal Jewish male in your apartment here in Paris for several months now. He has no visa, of which I am quite certain you were aware. I am told his living quarters were cleverly disguised behind a raft of large fabric bolts. Was it your intention to hide the Jew Gynszpan from the French authorities indefinitely?"

"No … no, sir," I stammered, thrown off by his abrupt change of subject. "My mother and I were renting the space behind Mr. Abraham Grynszpan's tailor shop while working here in Paris. Mama is employed by Mr. Grynszpan as a seamstress. We'd planned to return home to New York City in less than two months. But now we're hoping to leave much earlier, because things have been … well … not very pleasant for both of us. In fact, I … I handed in my cancellation to Mr. Bechet at the Moulin Rouge this morning."

"Hmm … odd timing, I must say," nodded the man, a cold smile snaking momentarily over his face.

"Mama and I had talked about my breaking my contract with Mr. Bechet for many weeks now … long before any of this … this current situation … happened, sir. I was very foolish to wish to stay here in Paris thinking things were going to improve for us."

"And what exactly was supposed to 'improve'?"

"Mr. Bechet thought my singing in Paris would help push my career, but that hasn't … exactly been the case, sir," I added, my voice shaking. "I assure you there was absolutely *no* other pretense for our being here. Both Mama and I are most anxious to go back home!"

He folded his arms and stared at me. His dark, penetrating eyes forced me to drop my gaze to the floor. My heart pounded fiercely in my chest.

"Yes, I am quite aware that you were brought here as a singer with Monsieur Bechet's swing music ensemble, Miss Campbell. Of course, I find that to be most unfortunate since, as you may well already know, I myself have placed stark restrictions upon what is allowable jazz music to be played in my own country."

I looked up, studying his face. There were dark hollows under his prominent cheekbones, set under a high forehead of slightly olive-tinted skin. His long, twisted mouth slithered like a worm across his face, oddly smiling and smirking simultaneously. Icy-cold fingers stretched down my spine as I recognized my interrogator: the Nazi Minister of Enlightenment and Propaganda, Dr. Joseph Goebbels. I'd seen countless photographs of the man blazoned across the headlines of newspapers in every language this past week alone.

"But I must also bring to your attention, Miss Campbell, another fact that is quite interesting to us -- to me, in particular. You were identified by several of our guards when you arrived here several hours ago. It seems that you were among the small crowd outside our embassy who witnessed the Jew Grynszpan running out the front door after having just shot *Legationssekretär* -- that is, Legation Secretary – Ernst vom Rath. Am I correct that you were indeed among the spectators of this deadly event?"

I nodded slightly, my throat dry as dust.

"Furthermore, the guards said it appeared that the murderer looked to be tossing his gun over towards your direction in fact. Fortunately, one of the guards retrieved it immediately, so no one else could intervene. Do you care to comment on these rather, let us say, suspicious coincidences? Why were you outside the Embassy?"

"Rehearsals ended in a stalemate of sorts," I stammered, my thoughts reeling.

"Stalemate? How do you mean?" he interjected.

"There was a huge disagreement between the musicians and Mr. Bechet … and Mistinguett, sir. Everyone had stormed out of rehearsal that morning."

"Ah yes, that talentless dinosaur herself, Mistinguett," he snorted, shaking his head. "As you Americans say, 'wonders never cease'. Continue."

"It was a beautiful day, so I decided to take *le Métro* to the *Jardin de Tuilleries.*"

"The gardens are on the opposite side of the river, Miss Campbell."

"Yes, sir, of course. I'm … I'm aware of that. I must have been, well … daydreaming because I missed the stop. Then when I got out a few blocks from here on *Rue de Lille*, I just … kept walking instead. You are correct that I was at the German Embassy when Hermann raced out the entry, but I swear --"

"Hermann? Do you mean *Herschel* Grynszpan?"

"I believe … he preferred Hermann to Herschel, sir."

"Interesting. Any idea why? Does his entire family call him Hermann?"

"I honestly don't know."

Dr. Goebbels pulled a pencil from his coat pocket and scribbled something on the bottom of one of the papers.

"And am I to assume since you were living in the same rooms that you retained an 'intimate relationship,' that is to say, one of agreeable sexual involvement, with the Jew Grynszpan, Miss Campbell?"

"No sir!" I replied, shocked.

"What about *Legationssekretär* vom Rath? Did you retain such a relationship with him?"

"No," I repeated firmly. "The first time I ever saw Herr vom Rath was when he was being carried out on the stretcher from the embassy after the shooting. Besides they didn't --"

"But nonetheless you knew it was Herr vom Rath, yes?" he interrupted.

"Not at that time, no. I didn't learn the victim's name until hearing radio reports many hours later."

"Besides they didn't what?"

"I'm sorry, sir?"

"You were beginning to say something that began with the words 'besides they didn't', Miss Campbell."

I exhaled slowly, looking down at my hands. If only he'd interrupted me three words earlier.

"One of my friends overheard Hermann in conversation with some of his friends at a *café* several weeks ago," I began in a low voice. "Actually, we'd both been at a table in that same *café* a few weeks prior and had overheard part of a conversation with these friends."

"So, two separate conversations, yes? And where exactly did this take place?"

"At *Tout Va Bien,* a restaurant on *Boulevard Saint-Denis.* It has reasonable prices and serves food late hours. A lot of musicians and actors go there … so it's usually quite crowded."

Dr. Goebbels scrawled several words that he then underlined on one of the papers.

"You were seated with your friend, then … your table was near theirs I presume, yes?"

"Yes," I nodded. "Just the … first time. My friend overheard the second conversation without me and told me about it later that night."

"These men were speaking English? French? Polish? Russian?

"Yiddish, sir."

"Ah. So, your friend speaks Yiddish. And what is her name, Miss Campbell? Another girl from the cabaret?"

"Marie Landauer," I whispered, swallowing.

"Landauer. So, a Jewish girl, yes?" he asked, raising one eyebrow.

I nodded slightly. Had I just stupidly placed Landie's name on some kind of deadly watch list?

"Middle name?" he asked, scribbling again on the sheet of paper.

"I don't know of one, sir."

"Just what exactly did she overhear the Jew Grynszpan and his friends saying at that time?"

"He was getting paid for … certain services … from Herr vom Rath," I replied, my eyes lowered.

"Ah, 'certain services.' Now we are getting a bit further. And just what exactly do you propose these 'certain services' to have been, Miss Campbell?"

I made no reply.

"Miss Campbell?" he repeated sternly.

"I think it may have been for … for … sexual services, sir," I whispered nervously.

"To hire a prostitute in other words?"

"Not … exactly, sir."

"Then what?"

"Just the – two men, I think. Together. Hermann said he would – expose their … relationship unless the officer obtained permanent visas for Hermann's family so they could leave Hanover and live in Paris."

Chapter 23

One minute later
Paris, France – mid-November 1938

Goebbels stared at me, a bland expression on his face, methodically tapping his finger across his upper lip. Given this unexpected reaction, he was already suspicious about vom Rath, I suddenly realized. If the Nazis could have figured out a way to eliminate the reckless vom Rath first, producing a glorious end result, they undoubtedly would've murdered him themselves! Theories regarding vom Rath's questionable reputation had been alluded to on more than one BBC broadcast. But Hermann had inadvertently solved that problem for the Nazis once and for all. And most fortuitously, the murder presented the Nazis with the perfect alibi to incite the widespread violence of *Kristallnacht* which had led to the arrest of thousands of German Jews, simultaneously bankrupting those families, while destroying their synagogues, businesses, and homes, all accomplished in fewer than three days.

"Other than Fräulein Landauer and the Jew Grynszpan's acquaintances, who else knows of these particular conversations, Miss Campbell? Was anyone else sitting at your table during either?"

"I don't believe so."

"You do not believe so, or no?" he repeated, eyes narrowing.

"No," I lied.

"There were other tables nearby, though, so others may have also overheard I presume."

"As I said, this *café* is usually very crowded. The tables are placed close together."

"But just to clarify, you are saying your friend *Fräulein* Landauer, who is fairly fluent in Yiddish, overheard Herschel Grynszpan state that he and Ernst vom Rath had an ... ongoing sexual rendezvous of some kind. She was quite certain of this exact wording, yes?"

I nodded warily, my eyes remaining focused on my hands which were tightly folded in my lap.

"One time? Occasional meetings? Multiple arranged meetings?"

"Multiple ... arranged meetings ...."

"And do you believe that Herr vom Rath was actually *paying* the Jew Grynszpan for these multiple sexual encounters, yes?"

I nodded once again, my eyes still lowered.

"You are quite certain?"

"Yes sir."

"Was it said where these encounters took place? In an alley? A brothel? A friend's apartment? The men's toilets?"

"At a hotel in the Montmartre district, I believe," I replied, cringing slightly.

"Undoubtedly one known for such nonsense as this you can be well assured," muttered Dr. Goebbels, shaking his head.

The door opened slightly revealing a guard who saluted then attempted to ask a question. Dr. Goebbels barked something in staccato German causing the man to apologize *"tut mir leid"* several times as he quickly backed out, gently closing the door. Dr. Goebbels cleared his throat and then spoke again.

"Such a relationship is punishable by firing squad for any German citizen much less a Nazi officer," stated Goebbels crisply, as though quoting from a military manual. "Without question Herr vom Rath would have been aware of this inescapable denouement. The Jews shun such men from their society's acquaintance as well if I am not mistaken. I confess I find it shocking to believe these two men would behave without any nod towards prudence. To speak so recklessly of such amorality within the earshot of others is unfathomable to me. But there it is."

Dr. Goebbels slowly rubbed his hand over his face before continuing, once again abruptly changing tactics.

"Yet apparently this knowledge was not a problem for you and your mother, Miss Campbell. You continued to live openly with this … foul individual … even though you were quite aware of his tainted moral bearing. As a stated Negress, you yourself have undoubtedly had many lovers it goes without saying, so perhaps that makes the situation tolerably normal in your view. After all, it is a well-established fact that your race is scarcely above that of the animal when it comes to crude sexual behaviors. Our own scientists have proven this time and time again. In fact, all anyone has to do is watch your film entertainer Josephine Baker jostling about in nothing but her banana skirt! I will admit that I myself have occasionally been curious for a taste of such barbaric lust … eh, what do they call it? Sweet brown sugar, I believe?" he chuckled, winking slyly.

"*Je ne suis pas une putain, monsieur!*" I retorted angrily, completely forgetting myself as I jumped to my feet. I had repeatedly been subjected to this blatant insult at the cabaret.

"I didn't say you were," he shrugged, his mouth forming that bizarre, twisted worm expression once again. "Resume your seat, Miss Campbell," he added sternly.

"Could you at least tell me where you've taken my mother?" I begged, sitting as ordered.

"You could certainly ask, Miss Campbell, but understand that I am under no obligation to reveal such information," he shrugged. "I assure you however, she is safe, clean and will have adequate meals. Well, that is, she will as long as you help me … help *us* … in moving forward."

"Help you how?" I replied in a small voice.

He stood up and began slowly pacing in front of the desk.

"I fear there are others who are aware of Herr vom Rath's … most undesirable orientation. I will first be needing for you to produce letters … *les billets-doux,* that is … professing your undying love for the Jew Grynszpan. The fact that you are a performer of low birth and would never have been considered a potential marriage partner in the eyes of his Jewish family is quite ideal you must realize. Obviously, he would never have dared mention having a relationship with a Negress to family members or even his closest friends."

This insult was obvious, but I remained composed.

"He speaks no English and I do not speak Yiddish, Polish or German, sir," I replied evenly. "I don't see how I could possibly write him."

"No matter. We will merely claim he speaks English. He will never actually receive any of these letters. They will be purposely sold on the black market for propaganda. You will state within a few letters that you are desperate to reach him because of your current situation."

"You're referring to my mother?" I asked, rather puzzled by this wording.

"No, no," he laughed, leaning up against the desk, gesturing boldly. "That you are expecting his child, of course. Instant proof of his virility … his huge prowess with women … his overt masculinity. A stallion among stallions! And this would help establish Herr vom Rath's masculinity as well, of course."

"Of course," I replied evenly, simultaneously thinking: what utter nonsense!

"My wife and I have five children. We are held up as the very model, the ultimate perfection if you will, of the German ideal family," he added sarcastically. "In fact, I am certain that at this *very* moment my dear Magda is briskly ordering the servants to get everyone down for afternoon naps while she herself is dutifully nursing Hedda, our six-month old daughter."

"Congratulations, sir," I replied, taking a deep breath, shocked at his tone of voice. "It must be wonderful to have such a large, devoted family."

"Hardly," Dr. Goebbels snorted. "This is my cross to bear as they say. I am forced to live a false life. My desire to be with the exquisite Czech actress Lida Baarova has fallen not only on my wife's deaf ears but our *Führer's* as well. I have tried to get Magda to agree to having Lida live with us − in separate quarters, of course − but that idea did not seem to be of my wife's liking."

Was he serious, I thought? What a selfish pompous ass!

"Do you know of Miss Baarova's movies?"

I shook my head.

"Ah, that is most unfortunate. She is an extraordinary actress. True perfection on the screen," sighed Dr. Goebbels. "But Herr Hitler has seen to permanently remove all of my darling Lida's films from our theaters and banish her permanently to her native Czechoslovakia. You have read about none of this I expect. I am quite sure your American-printed newspapers have no interest in reporting such stories."

That wasn't quite true. Although I'd never heard of this particular incident, Goebbels' wanton reputation as a womanizer definitely transcended Europe. Several of the highest officials in the Nazi pyramid, among them Martin Bormann, Reinhold Heydrich as well as Goebbels, were repeatedly ridiculed by the press for their scandalous behaviors that seemed the complete antithesis of the Nazi ideal of a pure race. *'Guess these gents plan on leaving dozens of less-than-desirable half breeds in their wake once the Nazi empire implodes in a few months'* broadcasters sometimes chuckled.

"At any rate, regarding this newest mewling infant, it is well past the time to be weaned in my opinion, but I am sure Magda will continue for several months yet. She aspires to be the epitome of the German *hausfrau*. Herr Hitler has blatantly anointed her as 'First Lady of the Third Reich' since he himself is unwed."

Why he spoke so openly to me about any of these matters was extremely unsettling. He began pacing in front of the desk once again.

"Fortunately, I have all of Lida's films in my private collection. I assume you enjoy watching films?"

"Yes … sir," I replied.

"Have you ever wished to be in one?"

"Not really. When I was a little girl, I was in a movie directed by King Vidor. It was very hard work, confusing, hot and dusty, and we were required to do the same thing again and again every time they moved the camera. I've never seen the film, though."

"That would be *Hallelujah* I presume?"

"Yes," I replied, startled that he would know of an American movie made a decade ago.

"You may be surprised that I have that very film in my private collection," he stated, flashing the twisty worm smile. "I will be happy to show it to you when we are at *Lanke am Bogensee*. I insisted that both my study and my cinema room be among the first rooms completed at my new summer estate so I should be able to both work and amuse myself in full. I face the dull task of moving my family out there late in the Spring from our current estate in *Schwanenwerder*."

He paused for a moment, tapping his upper lip once again.

"Let me think. What other American films do I have? Ah, yes! How about *It Happened One Night*? I have just received that one through a shrewd black-market dealer in Berlin. You are likely a fan of your Clark Gable I assume?"

I smiled slightly and nodded.

"How good is your French?"

"Not good at all, I'm afraid."

"Ah, well that is too bad," he shrugged. "Another film I have recently acquired is *Zouzou* with Josephine Baker, which is of course in French. It is not a bad film, although I do not personally care for Mlle. Baker's looks. She is always crossing her eyes and making ugly faces. I do not find these traits amusing when performed by a woman even in a comedy. You did not know her in America before you came to Paris?"

"I did not, that's correct."

"Of course, I also have Leni Riefenstahl's *Olympia*. I do not like that woman either – she is much, much too arrogant – but I confess, she did excellent film work at the Olympics in Berlin two years ago to make that film. She has included the gold medal wins of your Jesse Owens in three of his four winning endeavors, even though the *Führer* frowned upon her including such blatant American triumphs in this film. That she defied him is not in her favor I must say. If she plans to continue as a filmmaker, she will need to understand the limits of creative acceptance allowed within our Nazi regime."

I made no comment.

He sat down on the desk once again and began re-sorting the papers he'd laid out earlier. After a few moments he cleared his throat and made another abrupt subject shift.

"My wife Magda and I were recently forced to sign a four-month agreement drawn up by the *Führer* to deal with our current … eh, marital discord. This stems directly from the Baarova issue I mentioned earlier. I am not to be seen in public with any of my actresses during this, so-called respite as it were, without suffering severe reprisals with respect to my position within the Nazi party. Magda remains a favorite with Hitler, you see. In fact, she is one of his closest confidants, which I find faintly amusing. She is quite intelligent, I will give you that … but she is only a woman, of course. Why would our *Führer* care about her advice?"

I bit my lip to remain quiet. This man was one of the most arrogant, insufferable bores I'd ever encountered in my life. I felt incredibly sorry for his wife.

"Oh yes … one other important thing before I leave you for today. I should advise you to avoid arousing the anger of the *Aufseherin*. That is the Brunhilda-like woman named Gerda who has been assigned to guard you while you are my guest here in Paris. I have been told she bites!" he snickered, winking. He flashed the creepy worm smile one last time as he lightly ran his fingers along my shoulder and then walked out of the room. I shuddered as the door latched tightly behind him.

Chapter 24

an hour later
Paris, France – mid-November 1938

I was taken in a closed car with dark green tinted windows to what appeared to be a boarding house located not far from the Embassy. Within a few hours, I'd become aware that this was no ordinary boarding house, however. Given the occasional female giggles out in the hallway, I soon realized the building was a small, quiet brothel that serviced an elite clientele of Nazi officers who probably wished such visits to remain invisible to their superiors back in Berlin.

My small room consisted of a fraying grey army cot, a closet reeking of ancient moth balls decorated solely by two empty wire hangers, with more than enough shelf room for the scant contents of my wicker valise, a small dresser which yielded a few petrified beetles upon inspection, and an antique *escritoire*. Upon my arrival I'd been given a note to begin writing explicit love letters in English to Herschel Grynszpan, making use of the lavender-scented stationery found within the desk. Gerda, the tall, frighteningly muscular *Aufseherin* guarding me, grunted an occasional word in English. She seemed to have been assigned as my bodyguard as well as warden, escorting me to the bathroom down the hall whenever necessary, leaning heavily against the door. Meals were delivered and retrieved on trays twice each day.

Herr Goebbels *attaché*, or deputy, whose name was Karl Hanke, painstakingly read through and collected my letters several times each day. I was instructed by the man, whose English was almost as good as his employer's, to also write short poems, embellishing envelopes and pages with rococo curlicues of trailing vines, flowers, and hearts. Either by prose or poem I was to describe at great lengths such mythical settings as the soft pine carpeting in the forests or the wild grassy meadows filled with Queen Anne's lace and sweet clover where our breathless lovemaking had supposedly taken us on so many occasions. I was always to address the letters as 'my dearest Herschel,' and sign them 'with all my love forever, your sweetest loving D.' Why 'D'? I had no idea.

After several days penning these abstract fantasies, Herr Hanke ordered me to mention experiencing waves of nausea while frying eggs in the kitchen earlier that morning and innocently not knowing why. The Germans weren't especially creative in detailing how or what information a foolish girl would send her young lover, I thought. In two scandalous British novels that Landie had lent me recently, which I'd read without Mama's knowledge, an announcement of pregnancy by a young woman to her lover typically resulted in his scampering aboard the next train at midnight, destination unknown, leaving the poor lady to fend for herself. Maybe in German literature the men were more responsible, I mused, although I seriously doubted this.

Late one morning Herr Hanke also brought along a photographer. He snapped several pictures of me writing a letter, my head tilted forward or away from the camera lens altogether, with my hair draped in such a fashion as to deeply shadow my face. Other pictures were taken of unfinished letters and envelopes, each ornately bordered with endless chains of flowers, hearts and even a few cartoonish attempts at cupids. Several of those photos appeared in a newspaper article that Gerda brought to me two days later.

At least one news reporter had contacted Landie at the cabaret, although I was grateful the article hadn't mentioned either of our names. She agreed that yes, she had been friends at one time with an American chorus girl at the Moulin Rouge who'd claimed to be shamelessly living openly in an apartment with the Jew Grynszpan in Paris. She knew nothing about the man's intention to shoot a Nazi officer, however.

I knew my letters were intended for interception by Hermann's jailers at the Paris precinct and then gleefully sold to the French press. Following that interception, they were frivolously leaked to every newspaper in Europe while the Germans engaged in their lengthy preparations for the young man's mock trial. In this way Dr. Goebbels intended to blur whatever rumors might have bubbled up surrounding Hermann's (and by association, vom Rath's) deviant sexual relationship. A secret pregnant girlfriend? And a tawdry American showgirl at that ... certainly no surprise there since it was common knowledge that American girls were notoriously easy, even the wealthier ones who should have known better. What an incredibly desperate Christian girl to have willingly bedded a Jew! Ironically, my race had yet to be made public. I wondered when that would be taking place. In the meantime, one British cartoon stated that the story read better than a cheap drugstore novel. On reading that response, I paused. Was that statement inferring that this entire scenario was likely a complete fabrication on the part of the German press?

According to another article, the amusement value of my letters also seemed to have slightly deflected an interesting dispute within the Nazi party. Based on exclusive insider information obtained by the British press, Herr Hitler had *not* given Dr. Goebbels the order to destroy Jewish businesses, synagogues, and homes during the *Kristallnacht* pogrom blared an anonymously posted editorial column headline. *'Dearest reader* beckoned the editorial further, *I implore you to think through this: The Jews were unable to assist with, much less pay for the clean-up, or the heavy fines levied for their own property's destruction because so many of them had already been deported during the pogrom two weeks earlier to the makeshift ghetto camp outside Poland.'* Rather like first killing off the golden goose and then demanding she squat down and produce a solid golden egg mused the newspaper article further. *'Goose steppers mired in goose poop'* read another article's headline. Additionally, most of the major financial assets of Germany's wealthiest Jewish business owners had already been seized by the Nazis months ago. I wondered if Dr. Goebbels' assistant had read through those newspapers in their entirety before handing them over to me. Somehow, that seemed quite unlikely.

After a week in the musty room, I was ecstatic to receive a letter from my mother. Although the language was stilted, the note was unquestionably in her handwriting. It eerily reminded me of the note that Annette had received from her own mother. Reading slowly, I scanned for any clues to her wellbeing:

"Dearest Helen ~ I am in a ghetto camp somewhere outside Paris, I think. I work in the kitchen, so I keep quite warm and get good meals twice a day. At night I carry a hot brick with me and share a good mattress with another woman, so I am warm at night to. I prey that you are well. Please send a letter back to me soon. Sending all my love to you, Mama."

There it was, plain as day, same as Annette's mother had relayed subtle signals in her letter. Mama was an impeccable speller – far better than I. She had purposely misspelled the word "pray" as "prey" and used the incorrect form of the word 'too'. She'd also used no contractions. I had noticed this in Dr. Goebbels' conversation with me. Herr Hanke's speech was quite similar as well. Since the Germans seemed prone to lump an entire paragraph into one word, maybe the concept of shortening two small words strung loosely together with a measly apostrophe was too farfetched a concept for them. Landie howled repeatedly about the cumbersome word *Lebensabschnittspartner* which she claimed simply referred to one's 'man'.

I sank back into the chair where I'd been reading Mama's letter at the *escritoire*. I'd been so eager to devour any correspondence from her, yet right now I just felt numb. Methodically, I eased open the slightly warped small desk drawer and extracted a sheet of the lavender-scented paper. I will always associate the musky odor of lavender -- a smell I'd never found pleasing anyway -- with this room I thought bitterly.

As I tried to collect my thoughts, I pried the top off the fountain pen. Hot tears welled up. I quickly turned my head away from the desk, letting the tears splash silently on my shoulder. I knew I couldn't risk wasting even one sheet of stationery. Gerda pawed through my trash bucket at least two times every day before finally removing the contents each night. I'd had to request rags for my monthly that had begun just after I arrived, which she'd subsequently unraveled with disgustingly bizarre zeal.

This letter would be scrutinized far more closely than any I'd penned to Hermann. There was no earthly reason for me to send anything in depth within my fabricated letters to Herschel Grynszpan since he wouldn't ever be reading them in the first place. Those letters were merely intended to drift carelessly into Dr. Goebbel's voracious propaganda factory. If the Nazis truly thought Mama and I had some ulterior motive behind our trip to Paris, then they would scrupulously analyze every adverb that flowed from either of our pens − or pencil in Mama's case. I wondered if I might ever be able to convey any useful information to her. I knew better than to include any long words that their examiners would blacken and refrained from using any contractions or compound sentences:

'*Dearest Mama,*' I finally began, after staring at the blank paper for at least fifteen minutes, '*I was so very happy to receive your letter today. I am also kept warm in the home where I have been living this last week. I heard it snowed. The other guests seem very pleasant. Meals are good here to. I look forward to hearing from you again soon. Love, Helen*

For the time being, all I could say was that I was in a home (rather than a camp) and that I'd 'heard it snowed' rather than I'd 'seen the snow'. I also repeated her using the wrong form of 'to'. If she was being given any newspaper clippings that contained my blurry photos and letters to Hermann, I prayed that she believed none of this contrived nonsense.

Shortly after I'd finished my note to Mama, Gerda appeared. She had in her hand several small rag bundles and pointed at them then me saying "*oui?*" I shook my head no. She grabbed my letter off the desk and left. The door reopened several moments later and Herr Hanke stepped in.

"We are moving you now," he stated as he walked briskly over to the *escritoire*, placing the two newspapers and remainder of the lavender stationery in a small cloth satchel. "Pack your things in your valise. Bring that with you. You will find your coat outside the door."

The deputy rode with me in an enclosed car to the railroad station. He handed me over to two guards and the three of us then boarded a train I soon learned was headed for Berlin. I'd had nothing to eat since yesterday afternoon, but no food was offered, nor did I leave the small, shrouded compartment except, accompanied of course, to use the toilet. The guards left separately to enjoy their meals in the dining car, each returning enveloped within a pungent cloud of garlic.

The train rumbled into the cold, starless night. A fragment of an old dream brought me close to the surface for a moment just before I tumbled into an exhausted sleep. A woman was lying on the floor, her arm stretched out stiff like a tree branch. My face was sticky with tears as I tried to make her arm move and kept calling this woman Mama, begging her to get up. But she wasn't Mama. This woman was young and had hair the color of old abandoned corn stalks. The dream quickly faded.

Chapter 25

Bogensee, Germany – early December 1938

Almost completed on the exterior, the Goebbel's new summer home, *Lanke am Bogensee*, crouched within a sea of frozen mud, surrounded by countless stacks of wide lumber and bricks covered by mammoth tarpaulins. Outside the heavily wooded grounds themselves, the property was almost invisible, hidden within countless acres of fragrant towering pines and fir trees. Stinging needles of sleet pelted my face as the two new guards who had driven me from the small train depot propelled me around a large pallet of bricks towards a rear entrance of the house. One of the men spoke a smattering of French, but other than the occasional "*oui*" and "*non*" our communication had been largely nonexistent, my own French being equally limited.

Ladders, open crates sectioned with multiple compartments filled with hammers, screwdrivers, saws, buckets of nails, along with additional stacks of finished lumber, were crammed into the back hallway. I was guided past the construction items into an expensively decorated study complete with modern bronze sculptures depicting nude female athletes set on either side of a wall of maroon velvet curtains. Several of the curtains were partially drawn back to reveal magnificent floor-to-ceiling windows that looked out over a dismal late afternoon's deepening shadows in the pine forest.

Wide built-in bookshelves, thickly jammed with books, lined the two long sides of the rectangular room and a fireplace, logs carefully piled upon the grate but as yet unlit, straddled by asymmetrical built-in cubicles, sat opposite the bank of windows. A massive, dark oak desk, with neatly organized paperwork stood in front of the windows, comfortably nestling into the thick, dusky orange and maroon carpet.

A pair of brocade armchairs separated by a round wooden table stood in front of one wall of bookcases. Other than the desk chair, these chairs were the only seating available. I sat down to wait. Oddly, two pairs of small brass chandeliers set into the wood-paneled ceiling provided the only lighting other than a heavily shaded, highly polished, bronze floor lamp adjacent to the desk.

I stood as Dr. Goebbels opened the door a few moments later. Limping slightly, carrying a large leather-bound sheaf of paperwork, he glanced without expression in my direction as he moved towards his desk. Although he was dressed almost identically as his visit with me in Paris, he was not wearing his Nazi arm band. After placing the paperwork on the desk, he walked towards me.

Without a word of greeting, he sat in the opposite armchair motioning for me to sit as well. He pulled an envelope from his inside coat pocket, placed it on the table and then slowly slid it towards me. I noticed his fingernails were impeccably manicured, his hands far smoother than even Mistinguett's who spent a fortune each day on her manicurist. With slightly trembling hands I picked up the envelope. It bore Mama's handwriting.

"May I?" I inquired quietly.

"Of course," he nodded, settling back into his armchair.

I carefully slid my finger under the envelope flap and pulled out the letter.

My dearest Helen ~ I hope you are doing well. I have been ill these last few days – just a very small cough – but the doctor here has perscribed medicine. I am sure when it arrives, along with some good rest, this will salve the problem. I enjoyed your letter. Please write again soon and do not worry. I will be back on my feet very soon. Love, Mama

Still trembling, I slowly refolded the letter then placed it back in the envelope. I bit my bottom lip, not trusting myself to speak. Two words misspelled: prescribed and solve. Mama had been a longtime nurse, married for many years to a doctor. Words such as prescribed and solve were terms that she'd have written countless times on patients' charts. There was no way she'd have inadvertently misspelled such terms. Whoever had scrutinized her letter before allowing its posting to me had undoubtedly assumed that since she was a Negress, she was poorly educated and therefore didn't know how to spell very well. Unfortunately, I couldn't count on the same lack of observation from my end. Reading between her lines, I assumed what she really meant was that she was in fact very ill and that perhaps medicine may have been promised but as yet had failed to materialize. After a moment I found my voice.

"My mother is ill," I stated evenly, forcing myself to look up at Dr. Goebbels.

"Ah, we shall assume nothing too serious," he answered, theatrically curving the worm mouth into something that resembled a smile.

"She writes that she's to be receiving medicine for a slight cough. But as you and I both know, sir, a slight cough can so easily become much worse quite quickly. Is it possible to find out if the medicine is … helping … once it's been received and if she's getting better, sir?"

He rubbed his hand over his mouth, eyes narrowed slightly, then crossed his legs.

"That should not be difficult information to obtain," he finally replied with a shrug. Then his tone taking on something of a bitter clipped tone he added, "In fact I shall have my secretary, Karl Hanke, with whom you dealt in Paris, inquire after her. He requires to be sent out on such … ah, let us just say … such *useful* errands as this far more frequently."

"Thank you, sir. That's most kind," I smiled. It seemed an odd reply but put this to his occasional odd sentence structure. On the whole, his English was frighteningly impeccable.

"So, by now I am sure you find yourself asking: just what is next, Herr Doktor, correct?" he beamed almost childishly. "I have ordered for our dinner to arrive in the next few minutes. This cook leaves much to be desired, I confess, but she makes a decent *Kartoffelpuffer und Apfelkuchen* thank goodness. You know what those are, yes?"

"No sir."

"German potato pancakes and apple cake."

My stomach rumbled audibly at the mention of food. I couldn't remember when or what I'd last eaten. Almost as if on cue, at that moment the door opened and a large, rather unkept woman wheeled in a small cart, warm aromas immediately filtering throughout the room. Dr. Goebbels gave what appeared to be several commands in terms of how he wanted things served as the woman glowered at me. I assumed she was indignant having to serve a person whose skin was slightly darker than her own, no matter how light skinned I might appear.

She must have muttered something to that effect as well, for suddenly Dr. Goebbels sprang to his feet, hand raised as though to cuff her, shouting a curt response. Cowering, the woman turned very red, refrained from looking at me again as she quickly finished setting out our meals on the wood table. She then bowed slightly to Dr. Goebbels and hastily retreated, quietly closing the door after having pushed the cart out into the hallway. He mumbled something under his breath as he sat back down, removing the lid from a casserole dish revealing fragrant shredded beef with slivered onions next to a small mound of potato pancakes.

"I will be glad when I am able to replace that cook. She claims to know far more about me than she really does and reports such information to Magda which causes me further trouble with the *Führer*." Then, abruptly changing topics, he continued speaking. "The water here tastes of an odd bitter mineral I have yet to fully identify. It is not acceptable for the drinking. I am in the process of having a new well dug. Therefore, today I offer a choice of a French Bordeaux or a German beer. Which might you prefer?"

"The wine, please," I nodded, surprised that he would even bother offering a choice. I waited, inhaling the beef's delicious aroma, until he had finished making a cartoonish performance of opening and then pouring two glasses of wine. After a German toast to our health, he'd finally picked up his fork. I tried to match myself one forkful at a time as he leisurely chewed each mouthful, sipping his wine in between. I was so ravenous I could have tipped the edge of the plate to my lips and devoured the meal in mere minutes.

"So, I presume you have not had the opportunity to write your letters to the Jew Grynszpan while making your journey here," he stated, delicately dappling at his mouth with the corner of his napkin. As I began to speak, he held up his hand to silence me. "I realize with the train excursion that would have been quite an impossible challenge, of course, *fräulein*. Do not fret. Tomorrow you will be given more of the stationery and, how shall I say this exactly, a bit more information that we need you to include in your letters as we move forward. And tonight? Well, tonight you and I ... we are free to enjoy ourselves."

I made no comment, simply nodding my head as I continued chewing. Whatever he has in store I thought to myself dully, it couldn't be anything I hadn't observed countless times in complete disgust writhing within the stairwells and hallways when we'd lived in Memphis. Had my moral outlook so deteriorated that selling out my virginity to this degenerate Nazi in the slender hope of saving myself and my mother was now perfectly acceptable? I forced myself to take a deep breath, then smile slightly while spearing another piece of the meat. My thoughts needed to stay centered on the food. And Mama. Nothing else.

Landie had recently lent me a book translated from a hidden notebook kept by a female prisoner who'd been charged with espionage during the Great War. The book was so frighteningly graphic that I doubted it would ever be circulated in the United States. American women inevitably opted for the romantic, whitewashed versions of their own history it seemed.

I agreed to another potato pancake when offered. The cook might not live up to Dr. Goebbels' expectations, but I was delirious with appreciation for every morsel the woman had prepared despite her snub. There was a knock on the door.

"*Herein,*" Dr. Goebbels called out.

A man opened the door a few inches. After a brief conversation with Goebbels, he nodded and closed the door while quietly uttering a series of '*danke schönes, Herr Doktor.*'

"He will be returning to light the fire as needed. Thus far my personal library right here, which I am also using as my study at present, the cinema viewing room and my bed chamber are the only furnished rooms in the house. Oh yes, and thankfully, the bathroom on this floor is almost completed, at least all the plumbing is connected even if some cabinetry is not yet installed. All in all, there are quite large and sunny rooms throughout the villa. The dining room will be a good place for my children to gather for their meals to be sure."

I nodded but made no reply.

"I am awaiting delivery of tiles to fully complete the kitchen and smaller dining room. My wife and I procured these tiles when we were visiting Italy a few months ago. They are quite unusual. Magda thinks they are worth this wait, but far too much is being held up by this delay to finish the countertops, walls and floors until these items finally arrive. I am not known as a man to be kept waiting."

This revelation didn't surprise me in the least. He moved our dinner plates aside and then cut two generous pieces of the *Apfelkuchen* with a silver cake server lifting the slices onto ornate dessert plates.

"Good, yes?" he asked, after tasting his slice.

My mouth full, I nodded. After several more bites, he set down his fork, cleared his throat and sat back in his chair staring at me.

"All right, so now on to more … um … private business as you Americans would say."

I swallowed my last bite of the apple cake and carefully placed my fork back on the plate.

"I have a written order from Herr Hitler and my wife's lawyer, that I am to *abstain* – I think that is the correct English word – from appearing in public or in private with any of my usual lady friends, most of whom are actresses. Before Magda and I married we had an understanding that I should be allowed the … let us say, the *freedom* … to enjoy any relationships I wished to pursue outside of our marriage. This has not caused a problem since we got married in

1931 and I have enjoyed many such freedoms so to speak," he smiled. "However, as I mentioned to you at our other meeting, Magda did not take kindly to my long relationship with the Czech actress Lida Baarova. She claims I have been seen in public too often with the lady and my frequent trips with the beautiful actress have been met with scorn both by her and by Herr Hitler. And, as I believe I mentioned before, she was not at all accommodating with my suggestion that the actress live with us. This was most unfortunate because I did not want to give up the lady, you see. My wife had even pressed for a divorce, but all divorces in Germany these days must be granted by Herr Hitler, of course. And since Magda and I are considered the ideal model of the healthy German couple with the perfect number of adorable children, *der Führer* is not willing to grant such a request. Do you understand me thus far?"

I nodded. Some of this he'd mentioned at the German Embassy back in Paris, of course.

"Good," he replied, continuing. "So, although I am reluctant to speak of this, Magda and I have been forced by the *Führer* to live in separate households these last few months. This separation is an officially signed *order* by Herr Hitler you must understand, that won't terminate until next Spring. A six-month separation for heaven's sake! I am expected to live like your Shirley Temple!" he laughed incredulously. "Unacceptable in my eyes. Surely, the man does not expect me to forego a woman in my bed for so long. Impossible. I fully doubt he could be away from his own mistress for such a period. His intention is that I am not to be seen *in public* with any woman. In fact, can you imagine such an insult as this: during this time, I must make an appointment to visit my own darling children for a few hours during which time Magda is to be vacant from our home in *Schwanenwerde!*"

He looked at me as if expecting a response, but I had none. He reached inside his coat pocket for his cigarette case, extending the case towards me. I shook my head. Extracting one of the smokes, he lit it, inhaling deeply before continuing.

"It is good you do not smoke cigarettes. Women should not smoke. Magda smokes far too much. I have told her this is what I think brings on her nervous disposition.

"But that is not what is on the table for discussion at present. Here you are …someone who has consorted openly with a Jew … openly lived with such a man for several months, in fact. And most suspiciously, you were in attendance at the very moment that this Jew assassinated one of our German officials at our embassy in

Paris. And what is more, you are an American, complete with your mother in tow. I believe this is what is called a *decoy* in English, yes? All these elements combined create a most suspicious turn of events in the eyes of the *Führer* you must be aware."

I still kept silent, unable to look into his eyes. These were almost the same accusations he had tossed at me at the German Embassy back in Paris a little over a week ago. He acknowledged another knock at the door and the cook entered, hastily gathering up the remains of our meal on a large tray without a word before quickly exiting.

"Your letters to the Jew Grynszpan have been very well done, *fräulein*. You have a certain talent for writing words as well as your lovely singing voice," he commented, blowing out a small puff of smoke.

"Thank you … sir," I mumbled.

"But you will understand, I must continue to state that you did indeed have an affair with the Jew Grynszpan whether you are willing to admit to this fact publicly or not."

I closed my eyes for a moment but said nothing.

"Towards that end, I do have some better news, *ma chere petite.* You have done an admiral job with your love letters of helping to deflect attention from this deviant situation between the Jew Grynszpan and Herr vom Rath. For this fact alone, I have just today more favorably reviewed your own transgressions with this derelict person and have presented such a document in your favor to Herr Hitler," he stated, flashing the worm smile.

"Ah," I replied, wondering where all this was going.

"However, you must understand that you will not be leaving France until after the Jew Grynszpan's trial is fully completed. And, as promised, I will dispatch my secretary Karl Hanke to verify that your mother is receiving our best treatment available. I am a man highly valued for his word as I am certain you are most aware."

That was far from what I'd heard about Joseph Goebbels – he was about as trustworthy as a cobra – but I wasn't about to question the yardstick by which he measured his own integrity. He stood up abruptly and began walking towards the door, stopping momentarily to stub out his cigarette in the small bronze ashtray on his desk.

"I have spliced together the first two reels of *Hallelujah* and have it already on the projector in my cinema gallery. You will have the opportunity to see that part of the film you made as a little girl."

I stammered 'thank you' as I followed him through a maze of yet more piled lumber, paint buckets and assorted cloth-covered large mirrors and paintings, cautiously propped against various walls awaiting placement. Dim lighting and rich wood paneling greeted us as we entered his small film gallery. Two curved tiers, each with five sleekly upholstered, slightly curved sofas, faced a large, deeply recessed built-in screen on the opposite wall. A single overhead pole suspended high over the sofas supported a series of small stage lights, aimed in various directions.

"All seats in the house are quite good," he stated as I selected a sofa in the center of the second tier. "My few guests to date have tested them all. I designed the room myself, of course. You might be interested to know it is based on the private cinema room of your own newspaper magnate William Randolph Hearst. Did you know that Mr. Hearst is a great admirer of Herr Hitler and the magnificent achievements that our glorious Nazi party have realized within so few years?"

"I wasn't aware of that," I replied quietly. I knew the man's newspaper no longer supported President Roosevelt's policies but hadn't believed the scattered rumors circulating of late that alluded to Hearst's Nazi adoration.

"Oh, most importantly, I must point out the part of which I am most proud. The screen is recessed quite far back as you can observe, yes?"

I nodded.

"There is space at the bottom wall for my children to crouch behind so they might stage their puppet shows. They have wonderful imaginations! I have also built a small puppet theatre that can be attached behind this kneeling wall, but in front of the movie screen. Magda has taught our oldest two girls, Helga and Hilde -- they are six and four years old now -- to even sew special costumes for their hand puppets. I had wanted this little theater to be a surprise for them this Christmas, but now ... eh, of course ... that depends if their mother will even allow them to visit here without being in attendance herself. She has stated that I must take all their presents over to her house. But I still hope to change her mind on this somehow. Such an ungrateful, stubborn woman, yes?" he sighed.

Fortunately, I was kept from commenting since he'd started the projector and extinguished the lights. He sat down next to me as the film sputtered into focus. There were speakers mounted on the walls opposite the screen, but the sound boomed and was very scratchy.

"Not the best copy, I confess," he shrugged, settling his left arm around my shoulders, then pulling me closer. He was much stronger than he appeared. As the opening credits began to appear, he picked up my right hand and lightly flicked the tip of his tongue across my wrist. Involuntarily I shivered slightly.

How could this man speak so warmly about the puppet shows to be given by his children or his beautiful wife's nervousness being caused by her excessive smoking, while complaining of her neglect and unfair treatment? He'd not taken the first step to curb his unfettered philandering nor shown even the tiniest shred of remorse. I'd encountered many self-centered performers in my brief career, but not one of them, even Mistinguett, came anywhere close to Dr. Goebbels' outrageous level of self-absorption. I kept my eyes focused on the screen.

We watched in silence. At times the picture and the sound didn't quite link correctly, but only for very short intervals. The songs were matched surprisingly well with the singers' lips when the camera lens closed in. The man beating the drum to the metronome during the songs had done an excellent job obviously. Nina Mae McKinney looked darling in her leather cap and short skirt. I realized she'd been at least two years younger than I was now. I couldn't imagine carrying that kind of responsibility even today. I recognized the performance space at the Cotton Club as well as a few of the musicians in Nina's "Swanee Shuffle."

The section where we'd been lying down in the dusty field and Nina had accidentally punched me in the nose was shown with everyone's backs to the camera except for Nina's. The camera settled in for just a few seconds on Johnnie 'three fingers' Doucet sprawled out slightly in front of her on a couple of those shots. I wondered if he was even still alive. I hadn't thought about him for a long time.

Charlene was the first person I spotted in the children's parade. The camera came in close on her pixie-like face for several fixed moments. She was smiling brightly, vigorously waving her flag, obviously singing at the top of her voice even though neither her voice nor mine would ever be heard in that chorus. I was walking two rows behind Charlene, looking hot and rather disheveled, also waving my little flag. Charlene, Aunt Lil, Terrence … and Daddy.

My thoughts wandered momentarily from the film. Other than Daddy I hadn't thought about any of them recently. If you're anywhere up there where you can help Mama, I prayed silently, please let her recover from this illness … and somehow help us get back home.

The film had reached the end of the reel. A series of numbers flew by after which the newly released sprockets at the trailing end of the film began slapping maniacally around the spinning pickup reel. Moving quickly, Dr. Goebbels grabbed the reel with one hand, simultaneously switching off the machine with the other. I shivered slightly, horrified that I'd actually been enjoying the warmth of this man's body next to mine in the chilly room.

His fingers curling lightly around my wrist, he led me out of the room, then down a labyrinth of short corridors. We entered his bedroom as a newly lit fire, casting tall shadows and intense heat, roared in the fieldstone fireplace. A thick white rug lay in front of the fire, which Goebbels bragged was the single pelt of an enormous polar bear shot during a recent Arctic expedition by Russian poachers. I stood warming myself near the fire as he walked a few feet away. In the surreal flickering light, I saw him place his gun on the high chest of drawers, then pull loose his tie and unbutton his coat, carefully draping both items over the back of an adjacent chair. After turning the key in the lock, he walked back towards me.

Mata Hari would have wrestled this weasel of a man for his gun and made every attempt to kill him, I thought bluntly. I was far from being the legendary Mata Hari, however. Landie had always scoffed that the woman's exploits as a French spy during the Great War were quite doubtful anyway. *'No woman would ever take such idiotic risks and not gotten caught far earlier,'* she'd muttered. *'Soldiers just aren't that stupid.'*

Goebbels leisurely unbuttoned my dress, guiding that and my slip slowly down over my shoulders and then letting the garments fall onto the rug. My underwear followed. He took a small step back, his eyes wandering over my naked body, taking a moment to ease the small pile of my clothing off the rug. We were exactly the same height.

"Ah, just look at you, *mein kleiner Liebling*," he sighed, the worm smile twisting in the firelight while softly running his fingers over my breasts. "The circles, here, I don't know what these are called in English ... exquisite ... yet your bosom is quite small in contrast. I have never seen anything so unusual. So very lovely as I am sure you have heard from the others, yes? Perhaps this is the very treat enjoyed by your esteemed Abraham Lincoln with his woman Sally Hemmings – is that the correct president?"

"I believe that was President Jefferson," I replied quietly, eyes averted.

"Right, of course. My error. I believe most of your American presidents would have maintained far better control of your country if they exhibited even a small percentage of the discipline of German men such as myself."

Discipline? The retort almost flew out of my mouth but miraculously I repressed it.

Scarcely blinking, Goebbels stared intensely into my eyes, his smoothly manicured hands caressing my neck and shoulders. He then slipped one hand behind my head and fiercely pulled me hard against him for a deep kiss, his tongue forcing its way into my mouth. After a long moment he broke away and began removing his shirt, tossing it on top of my clothing. His chest was quite thin, his arms as well, but I knew better than to assume that this man was a weakling. He gently pulled me down onto the rug, his hands and mouth exploring, lingering, obviously enjoying himself.

"I love women, you know? All kinds, all different figures. Taller. Shorter. Blonde ones. Redheads …what is the word for a woman with brown hair?"

"Brunette."

"Yes, yes, brunette. I prefer women who haven't yet bobbed their hair, but they are getting hard to find these days, so any length hair has to suffice. Small bust. Medium bust. Large bust … always very nice. Well, on the other hand, I must qualify … *almost* all figures. Unless they are too fat. I do not like them if they are too fat. That gets in my way and is no good. Also, if they are too fat, they remind me too much of Magda when she is heavy with the bearing of yet another child. I love my children, but … I am sure you understand. So, that I must always avoid, of course. But such is not a problem here tonight. You are quite perfect. Well, in my eyes, that is! If you are indeed a Negress, you had remarkable suitable parentage I should think. Can you tell I am quite … eh, what is the word … smitten?" he murmured in my ear.

"Ah," I replied, attempting my best to sound slightly enthusiastic.

"Some men can become ready quickly and must … eh, 'complete their task' so to speak … or all is … lost immediately," he chuckled in a low voice. "I am sure you follow. But, you see, this is why my lovely young ladies, my actresses and occasionally my secretaries, are begging for my attentions, week after week, month after month, again and again … and again! I have been known to continue throughout the entire night as you may have been informed. I tell you this is no 'tall tale'," he winked.

I realized my hazy visions of the hasty sexual antics in those steamy stairwells back in tenement alley were useless in comparison to that of this egotistical creature. He avoided taking fat women in his bed because they reminded him too much of his pregnant wife! I seethed within, barely concealing my desire to slap this man's face as hard as possible. Somehow, I camouflaged my outrage. Nudging me to lie flat on my back, he leaned on one elbow next to me. He murmured how silky a young girl's skin always felt as he stroked my inner thigh. His fingers moved higher, between my legs, his mouth following.

"Yes … exactly as I had imagined …. warm honey and brown sugar combined … lovely," he sighed. His demands increased in intensity as the night progressed.

Chapter 26

Bogensee and Berlin, Germany – December 1938

A cot had been set up in a large closet in one of the bathrooms. The bathroom was finished except for some decorative tilework along two walls and was located on the other side of the house from Goebbels' bedroom. I set out the scant items from my wicker valise along the built-in shelves next to the gurgling radiator. Exhausted, bruised, discouraged, and disgusted, I'd drawn a scalding hot bath just as the sky had begun to lighten through the high bathroom window. I then crawled from the bathtub, wound myself in a large blanket, and wept soundlessly.

Scarcely an hour later the house was alive with the din of trucks grinding gears while dumping heavy loads of materials. Workmen shouted over the noise as they hammered overhead. Nervous, I quickly dressed and moved out into the hallway. Walking was painful. Raw. Karl Hanke sat reading the morning newspaper a few feet down the hall.

"Good morning," he grinned as I neared. "I trust you had an enjoyable night?"

"Very nice," I answered, fully aware of the double-edged barb behind this remark.

"I have brought along a folder with the stationery and was told to make certain you wrote another of your remarkably exquisite letters to Herschel in order to, well … earn your breakfast as it were. However, since I have been known to bend the rules on numerous occasions as I see fit, I am taking you to the kitchen first. The dining areas are a den of Polish workmen reeking of garlic and God knows what else -- not exactly a treat for one's nose at this early hour."

"Thank you."

"Of course, Herr Doktor has already been up for a couple hours. Remarkably, the man requires only three hours of sleep at night … if even that. Would that any of us possessed such uncanny energy."

I finished breakfast, grateful even though the rubbery oatmeal was badly in need of salt, butter, and honey. The cook then grunted for me to follow her to a small desk out in the hallway. A small stack of the lavender stationery sat awaiting my first scribbled nonsense to Hermann in several days. Drained of any enthusiasm or imagination, I did my best to conjure up yet another romantic fantasy, decorating the margins with the usual interlocking hearts and twining flowers. I marveled that Scheherazade was able to produce one thousand and one related fairy tales to keep from being murdered by her new husband, the sultan, a treacherous man jealous of his first wife's betrayal. It had never dawned on me until then that one thousand and one nights was just three months shy of three entire years. And during that time Scheherazade had given birth to the sultan's three children according to legend.

Later, as Herr Hanke folded the letter into the envelope, I finally felt brave enough to ask if Goebbels had mentioned verifying my mother's condition and when I might expect another letter from her.

"Yes, he did. In fact, I will be telephoning the camp just before noon to inquire about her welfare," he answered, pocketing the letter. "I will certainly let you know."

"You promise?" I pleaded, my desperation obvious, knowing my request was out of place.

He nodded with a slight shrug without comment.

"Thank you," I replied, then adding as he began walking away, "do you have any idea yet when Herschel Grynszpan's murder trial might be convening in Paris?"

"There are a few puzzle pieces that need to … um, fall into place one could say before the Jew Grynszpan's trial will make it into the courtroom," answered Hanke, grinning with a look that reminded me all too much of Goebbels' twisted worm smile. "These procedures take time as I am sure you realize."

"I'm afraid I don't quite understand."

"I am not at liberty to delve further into Dr. Goebbels' plans, I am afraid. But they will all become obvious in due course, make no mistake. In the meantime, as he promised you last night …"

I squirmed, realizing that Goebbels' and my entire evening had undoubtedly been well documented by the entire staff, thankfully small, but nonetheless all of whom were now snickering over the minister of propaganda's newest conquest.

"As he promised … what exactly if I may ask?"

"I have a car hired shortly to drive us to the Artiste's Club in the *Skagerratplatz* in Berlin," he commented, indirectly answering the question. "You have heard of this club I presume?"

I shook my head.

"Herr Goebbels opened it back in '35 in the beautiful old Rathenau-Villa. It is quite a modern cabaret with several private reception rooms, a lavish cocktail bar with bartenders trained to mix every known alcoholic beverage on the Continent, and a breathtaking winter garden which bests anything you might find along the *Tuilleries*. There is also an enormous solid wood dance floor and huge beer cellar, stocked with the finest beers here on the Continent. Oh, and most notably, the best roast beef to be found in Berlin. Both Doktor and Frau Goebbels entertain their guests there on occasion. Remarkable, yes?"

I smiled as he continued.

"What is more, you will find a sampling of the major stars -- of stage and screen -- the world press, and those citizens of the highest connection within the Nazi party in attendance on any night of the week. Well, except our *Führer* himself, of course. He is a strict vegetarian and never touches alcohol. I am quite surprised that you had not heard of our Artiste's Club over in Paris."

Something about this description did seem vaguely familiar, maybe relating to issues Mistinguett and Mr. Bechet now faced at the Moulin Rouge.

"At my request, your Sidney Bechet has sent over the sheet music for all the songs that you have been performing at the Moulin Rouge. He has also sent several of Mistinguett's songs 'in the original key' – whatever that means. He said you will know those as well. We informed Bechet, of course, that it was to his … um, profound advantage to cooperate with us. I've been assured the music will be arriving later this afternoon by special messenger. The Moulin Rouge will probably be up for sale soon. Did you know? At least one German buyer is most interested."

"When am I supposed to begin performing at this cabaret, sir?" I ignored the information about the Moulin Rouge. There had been rumors about the cabaret being on the market long before I'd even arrived in Paris.

"You're to begin tonight," he shrugged. "Oh yes, and I am certain to have acquired a new letter from your *Maman* by this time tomorrow. While you were writing your letter to the Jew Grynszpan this morning, I reminded Herr Goebbels that you were most anxious to hear if the cough was improving with the medicine our doctors had prescribed for her."

"Thank you."

And so, that evening, clad in a skimpy, faded costume that smelled exceptionally sour of mothballs and reeked of sweaty bodies, I began my career as a featured soloist, totally improvising, in a nightclub. Not in New York City. Not even in Paris. But in Berlin.

A young mixed race American woman, with almost no understanding of what was being said around me, whose backing came from one of Germany's least admired Nazi ministers, Joseph Goebbels. The ten-piece band, all white, robust Germans, of whom only the saxophonist Lutz Templin and one of their trombonists could speak any English, fortunately did an excellent job of interpreting Mr. Bechet's charts.

There was also a male singer, German by birth but exceptionally fluent in both French and English, named Karl Schwedler, whose imitation of several Maurice Chevalier's tunes was quite remarkable. The band also played a lot of instrumental music, but it wasn't quite jazz or swing or even music hall in style. I learned from Lutz Templin, who was also the bandleader, that this peculiar form was dictated by Herr Goebbels' restrictions. Specifically, no instrumentalists were allowed to play solo passages with all of the acrobatic techniques employed by American jazz musicians these days.

Bizarrely, for the first time in my life, I felt completely comfortable on the stage. My favorite tunes were warmly received by an impeccably dressed audience who applauded generously each evening. Tunes that I loved to sing, including "I Found a New Baby," "Saint Louis Blues," "Saint James Infirmary Blues," "Bye, Bye, Blackbird," and "Sweet Georgia Brown," as well as my French favorites of "Frou, Frou," "J'ai Deux Amours," and everyone's current Edith Piaf favorites "La Vie en Rose" and "Je Ne Regrette Rien," appealed to audiences night after night as the days edged towards Christmas. Bravely, I began learning a new popular waltz which had just appeared last year on German radio: "Ich tanze mit dir in den Himmel hinein." Lutz Templin claimed my American accent was charming, but I thoroughly doubted this even though he pointed out that Marlene Dietrich butchered English lyrics every time she opened her mouth.

With the exception of the German waltz, I was ordered to secretly begin recording many of these same songs each week at *Deutsche Grammophon*, most of which were then performed at the Artiste's Club later that night. I became accustomed to the musicians under this fractured microscope despite the language barrier. Their attack seemed different – neither better nor worse – compared to the musicians in either New York City or Paris. Music speaks its own language, of course, but so often the clash of egos ruins the experience for everyone. In a different milieu, I would have found the experience completely invigorating. Instead, I was cautiously optimistic that these recordings were good. I had originally assumed that Goebbels had ordered them but was informed during our first session that not only had he not ordered them, but I was also strictly forbidden to mention them to him either, according to Lutz!

But then there were my nights. I stayed in a small somewhat remote hostel not too far from the club. I was with Goebbels almost nightly, forced into a degenerate world I never wanted to experience again. He would appear just after midnight, shortly after I'd finished working, usually with a well-chilled bottle of champagne under one arm. Much like an automaton, I played my part, enthusiastically supporting the man's rabid sexual appetite while simultaneously despising myself throughout the degrading experience. We never appeared in public together, rarely acknowledging one another whenever our paths crossed, in fact. If he invited guests to the club, he lightly applauded my performance but remained in rapt conversation with the well-dressed men and women seated at his table. He had no idea how grateful I was to be snubbed.

I wrote my daily letters to Hermann Grynszpan. As allowed, I also wrote Mama twice weekly, my insides churning, my hand shaking, as I pressed pen to paper knowing she might well prefer I was dead rather than participating in this nightly debasement. From her replies, at least I knew she was still alive despite never giving me an honest answer regarding her health.

Would Annette or Landie understand? I shoved that question from my thoughts. I was just trying to … to do what exactly? My mind churned. I didn't even know anymore. Would these irrational men really release Mama and me? Would this ruse deflect their error of having used Ernst vom Rath's murder for advocating the massive devastation of lives and property known as *Kristallnacht*? So many lives were forever ruined. Centuries of irreplaceable Jewish religious artifacts, so painstakingly handed down from one generation to the next … reduced to cinders within mere minutes.

That harlot who greeted me in the mirror each morning was not one I recognized. When on stage a singer took over who wove a spell of confidence, of charm, whose broken French was deemed charming by those who understood the language. And for those who didn't, they simply laughed it off. How could I have come to accept this depraved hell in mere weeks?

And then one night someone discreetly brought a small bag of white powder into the club, looking for a buyer. An English-speaking friend of the trombonist, who had been uncomfortably attentive recently, urged me to join him and give the substance a try once we'd finished performing that night. He said I'd relax … sleep better … sing even better the next day. The invitation disgusted me. My guess was they all knew damned well I was Goebbels' current floozy. Would this powder make the pain that festered deeply in the pit of my stomach more tolerable? Lots of performers dipped into the shit as they called it for that very reason. I'd seen plenty of them in Paris and back in New York. Many times. An image of Mama's furrowed brows, pursed lips and angrily crossed arms hovered over me, even though I struggled so often now to hear her voice clearly. *'Remember, Christ never yielded to a temptation, Helen',* she whispered, her voice raspy, distant, yet still firm. *'Never.'*

But other voices circled me like piranhas. What did it matter if I spiraled down further? Obviously, this was exactly what these Nazis expected from me. Why shouldn't I just give in to it? Who was I to think I could be forgiven by Christ or anyone else? I couldn't imagine any sins worse than those I'd not only committed, but actually encouraged. After all, I'm just a temporary whore for a serially philandering Nazi official … the newest singer at one of the more popular cabarets in Berlin … a singer destined to be wrung out, discarded, and forgotten like the countless performers who had preceded her.

And, moreover, I'm an American. American girls are touted to be even easier than French ones. And French girls have been considered a loose moral lot since the Renaissance. We're rumored eager to engage in every new scandal, futilely attempting to impress a jaded crowd which has moved far beyond impressibility, let's not even discuss respectability. And mixed race? I cringed. You can still crawl out, a small part of me argued. Somehow repair your reputation. But if I got messed up with drugs, there was no chance in hell I would ever have the strength to claw my way back to the surface. I said no to the man's offer and headed immediately to the hostel.

After we'd finished performing that night, the man used about half the packet of white powder. He was found dead in the alley behind the club the following morning, having ingested what was thought to be rat poison.

Chapter 27

Berlin, Germany – December 1938

A few days later as I entered the club to prepare for that evening's performances, some of the late afternoon crowd was still lingering at several tables. This was typically the well-to-do German wives sharing a small snack and heavier cocktails with one another prior to meeting up with their husbands and others of their set for a luxurious dinner elsewhere and perhaps a night at one of the opera houses or a new play or musical. I had just set out some items on the piano, nodding hello to the bandleader, Lutz Templin, who was organizing several stacks of music into folders for tonight's program. I glanced out into the house and saw three expensively attired women, furs nudged low about their shoulders as was the current fashion, whom I recognized instantly from society photos. Even though I couldn't read German newspapers or magazines, anyone perusing such could easily match names with photos.

Walking up behind me Lutz whispered in my ear: "Lina Heydrich, Emmy Göring and Magda Goebbels."

That these women, wives of three of the most powerful ministers in the Nazi government these days, should be enjoying a late afternoon glass of wine with one another made perfect sense to me. Both Reinhard Heydrich and Hermann Göring had been spotted at Dr. Goebbels' table on recent evenings. Goebbels had mentioned later that they had enjoyed my performance.

Oddly, several high-ranking Nazis had artistic backgrounds I had learned. Heydrich was an excellent classical violinist but hadn't been permitted by his family to pursue this as a career. Instead, they forced the angry young man to join the military during the Great War. Hitler supposedly was a frustrated artist turned down by every art academy in Europe, and Goebbels himself had penned numerous plays and at least one novel in his younger days, none of which were deemed acceptable by any German publisher. His first steady paying job was in fact that as Minister of Propaganda under Hitler. I vaguely wondered if these men had been allowed to pursue the dreams of their youth if they might have been more tolerant leaders.

In contrast, Hermann Göring was the Commander-in-Chief of the *Luftwaffe*, the existence of which was in direct defiance of the Versailles Treaty that had ended the Great War. Göring was a very well-educated descendant of an immensely wealthy dynasty. Dr. Goebbels intensely disliked Göring because of the man's inherited fortune and military acumen. The Commander collected major art works from all periods of history, while displaying enough military medals pinned across his broad chest to blind one in direct sunlight. His first wife Carin had passed away after a long illness seven years ago. Second wife Emmy somehow managed to dwell in the deified bubble of her predecessor's memory. Practically everything Göring owned contained the name Carin from his exclusive hunting lodge known as Carinhall to his magnificent yachts the Carin I and Carin II.

Although all the women were exquisitely dressed, madams Göring and Heydrich paled in elegance behind Magda Goebbels, who was far more beautiful than any picture I'd ever seen of the woman. Her perfectly coiffed golden blonde hair and small, tasteful teardrop earrings dazzled in the overhead chandeliers' light. Each woman at the table had a small decorative glass of sherry along with a dessert plate featuring the crumbs of a shared cake. An ashtray with a small layer of ashes was placed at Magda's right, her delicate gold and black cigarette holder already prepared with another cigarette next to the ashtray. Her smile sparkled as she and her guests laughed with an easy unaffected composure. As I watched, Magda motioned to their waiter for the bill. Three waiters instantly appeared, simultaneously easing back the women's chairs, and offering any assistance as might be required for their exit.

I refrained from mentioning having seen Magda to Goebbels later that evening. Thankfully, his time with me was exceptionally short due to massive preparations for a hastily scheduled important meeting to be held the day after Christmas that included Hitler and his full cabinet.

Herr Hitler never emerged from his bed chambers until noon Goebbels had complained to me, nor did the man keep late hours either. What's more, he even took a late afternoon nap most days. With so much time devoted to slumber the entire world could blow up, Goebbels had grumbled despite his outrageously slavish devotion to his idol. (In contrast, Landie had mentioned that Goebbels was often referred to as Hitler's "pet monkey" in the French press.) Hitler expected to emerge from his room, be briefed by his staff regarding the last twelve hours, leisurely sip at a cup of tea and finally commence his day.

Goebbels had a weak stomach I'd learned early on and stress from this upcoming meeting had set off a serious upset. Earlier sessions had ended badly. There were too many unfettered mongrels breeding chaos among these war hungry ministers who thumped loudly on their heavily medaled chests with no regard to reason in Goebbels' opinion. He left my room in less than an hour. I was grateful for the extra hours of sleep, although alarmed that more than a week had now elapsed with no new letter from Mama.

In compliance with long-held religious ordinances in Berlin, all entertainment venues, including the Artiste's Club, would be closed for the Christmas holidays beginning December 23, a Friday, and reopen on Wednesday, December 28. Karl Hanke appeared early that Friday morning to escort me to *Bogensee*. My morning letter to Hermann, blissfully devoid of the usual floral embellishments, was handed over to another of Hanke's men before we departed, and I was told I wouldn't be expected to write any more notes until sometime after the new year. Yesterday I'd finally received a letter from Mama. The medicine had helped; her cough was improving, she stated. Despite this small reassurance, I remained skeptical.

Other than Goebbels' visit to bring his children their gifts on Christmas morning, we would be at the *Bogensee* enclave with a mere handful of the house staff in addition to the requisite two dozen private SS guards who roamed the grounds around the clock. Although loathe to admit it, I looked forward to viewing *It Happened One Night,* considered silly romantic fluff by the critics, that starred two of my favorite actors, Claudette Colbert and Clark Gable. A heavily laden truck piled with festively wrapped gifts and treats for the five Goebbels' children followed our car. Goebbels planned to leave *Bogensee* very early on Christmas morning for his wife's home at *Schwanenwerder* so that his children wouldn't be disappointed with any delay of promised treats and the much-anticipated visit with their loving father.

Once outside the city limits, the roads were extremely treacherous with thick ruts of ice, extending the hour-long trip closer to two. The winds had increased as well, thrusting blinding snow up over the long hood of the car. Hanke was furiously editing a sheaf of legal-size documents and remained quiet for the entire trip. Goebbels' arrival at *Bogensee* was anticipated an hour or so after ours, but Hanke was certain the foul weather would significantly delay his arrival. I fell asleep briefly during the drive. The fragment of the dream that persistently haunted me floated up silently, then slowly dissolved into a swirling mist.

Chapter 28

Bogensee, Germany – Christmas 1938

As we pulled into the clearing in front of the mansion, now completed except for a handful of minor details according to Hanke, lights were twinkling inside the small lead-paned, floor-to-ceiling front windows. I could see two little faces, noses pressed against the window, watching our car's arrival. The driver said something as Hanke looked up from his paperwork.

"*Ach. Scheiße.* Well, this is an interesting wrinkle as they say. It seems Magda has effectively planned a surprise for our dear doctor, which is therefore rather a surprise for us all, Helen," he sighed. "Looks like she wanted to celebrate the holiday with her husband, regardless of Hitler's stern decree that they remain separated throughout the holiday until well into next year. How exactly this separation was supposed to help their marriage in the first place is a mystery to me. Maybe she considers her husband celibate since he has refrained from galivanting with his lady friends 'on show' these recent months."

The front door opened slowly and the two children, little girls with hastily donned coats and bright yellow rain boots, came racing out towards us, stumbling through the drifted snow. The car with the presents pulled in immediately behind us.

"Well, let me see now … how are your nannying skills?" exhaled Hanke, shaking his head. "Looks as though it might well be best to introduce you as help for the children, especially with two babies in the nursery."

My mind flashed back to images of Baby Beverly, languishing in agony on top of her crib mattress, poised mere inches above dozens of tiny bottles containing cancerous Radithor.

"I … I helped care for my niece when she was a baby … the usual … changing, deep soaking, pegging diapers to the line. Sterilizing and preparing bottles, feedings, cooking … cleaning, mending rompers … lots of ironing, of course."

"Excellent! I suppose all you people had those skills beaten into you at birth in America."

Not caring to answer that question I replied, "but I don't speak any German, sir."

"Actually, that is not a problem. Frau Magda has been teaching English to the two older girls, Helga and Hildegard -- although I think they just call her Hilde. Magda herself speaks quite fluently. In fact, the woman can hold her own in a detailed conversation in French or English as well as German. Why the Nazis don't make better use of the woman and throw her faithless spouse into a deep well is rather a mystery to many."

The girls moved closer to the car which was inching forward through the snow into a parking area. They looked to be about five or six years old at best.

"Their son Helmut's three. He has recently … uh …regressed into diapers I was informed. Too much for the poor lad with these newest babies born almost a year apart, I suspect. The youngest's arrival a few months ago combined with Dr. Goebbels simultaneous disappearance. That may well have pushed the lad over the edge according to Frau Magda … quite the mess. A three-year-old boy wearing diapers, same as his two baby sisters! Can you imagine?"

I frowned, envisioning the massive loads of dirty laundry to be faced each day.

"Sir, you didn't know that Frau Goebbels and the children were going to be here though," I replied. "How do you explain knowing she would need extra help?"

Hanke shrugged, opening his car door as the two little girls waved eagerly. "Someone on her staff had to know obviously. Positively the worst gossips in the entire world, one's domestic help. I will just say they leaked the information to me a week or so back."

"*Onkel Karl! Onkel Karl!*" shouted the girls in unison, jumping up and down with excitement as he knelt in the snow, fiercely hugging them. "*Wie wundervoll!*"

"Helga, Hilde, I knew Mama would need more help," Hanke spoke slowly in English as he stood back up, "so here is an American girl to help. Say hi to Helen, please. *Sie spricht kein deutsch,* so you will practice your English -- *verstehe?*"

The girls shyly peered at me in the back seat, then waved, smiling. They were truly stunning children who looked exactly like their beautiful mother.

"*Mein Name ist Helga Goebbels und hier ist Hilde,*" stated Helga, slowly, then immediately apologized, saying, "oh … *bitte verzeih mir* … my name is Helga, and this is Hilde!"

"I'm very glad to meet you," I replied slowly, smiling. Helga, Hilde, Helmut … good heavens, did all their names begin with an "h" I wondered? If so, how on earth could their poor mother keep them all straight!

My question was answered within a couple hours: the two youngest children were Holdine, better known as Holde, and Hedwig, usually called Hedda, scarcely a year apart in age. Frau Goebbels also had a son named Harold Quandt from her first marriage, a college student who lived in Berlin with his father Günther. The five Goebbels' children all looked exactly like their mother. There didn't appear to be the faintest trace in either looks or personality of Dr. Goebbels in any of his offspring … even Helmut, who, other than the boy's frustrating refusal of late to use the toilet, seemed every bit as happy and beautiful a child as his four sisters.

By the time Dr. Goebbels had arrived that night, far later than he'd anticipated due to the almost impassable roads, all the children had long before been put to bed. Only one other nursery maid had been brought along, so ironically, my help was quite necessary. Frau Goebbels and Hanke had enjoyed a leisurely supper together in one of the intimate dining rooms while I helped the other nursery maid, Elke, whose mother was British – 'workin' class, y'know, lovie?' – feed and then prepare the five children for bed.

Helga whispered in my ear that they usually had two additional maids helping out, also that she already liked me much better than either of them. Elke was quite nice but those other two were very mean. She touched my cheek lightly and murmured *"Sehr schön. Zimtzucker."* I smiled and shook my head as she took my hand and led me to the kitchen to show me: cinnamon blended with lots of white sugar and bits of butter. She touched my cheek shyly again saying: 'a pretty color -- *Zimtzucker.*'

As we reached the hallway to the children's bedrooms, Magda appeared in time to kiss her youngest children goodnight. She then listened to Helga read for a few minutes before returning to the library where she continued in quiet conversation with Hanke until her husband's arrival several hours later. She had yet to address me directly.

Elke and I shared a modestly furnished but comfortable room warmly nestled between Holde and Hedda's bedrooms. Both babies awoke overnight for bottles but were easily coerced back to sleep after being changed and fed. While I was still rocking Holde, Goebbels strolled into her bedroom. Without a word, he gently kissed his sleeping daughter on her forehead, then, although I quietly resisted, grabbed my chin and kissed me hard on the mouth. He walked away whispering some German endearment I'd never quite understood. Shaking, I continued rocking the baby for at least another half hour, even though she was fast asleep, terrified that Goebbels might be lurking just outside in the hallway.

Was he crazy enough to think his wife wouldn't notice his absence from their connecting bedrooms … or not be aware of any noise spilling out of it? With his children roaming about at all hours as well … Helmut was a frequent sleepwalker I'd been informed! Or maybe the father's wanderings were such a frequent occurrence in their household that no one thought anything of it. No, that couldn't possibly be acceptable for this perfectly adjusted, organized and intelligent family, I reasoned sternly. This arrangement wasn't at all what I'd been dreading when I'd left Berlin, of course. Even though challenging, I was quite enraptured by the liveliness and innocence of these darling youngsters. And I now despised Goebbels all the more for his arrogant dismissal of his beautiful family while randomly sampling those of us he'd forced into sexual submission.

The following morning was a blur of breakfasts since not all the children liked the same foods, but their cook was wisely prepared. This was followed by baths, then braiding of the older girls' hair. I had never washed, much less braided, a white child's hair before, but the girls' hair was thick and quite slippery. These obligations ran into late morning bottles and first naps for the two babies, then lunch, followed by everyone's attempts to create decorations for the house. All their usual Christmas decorations were still at *Schwanenwerder*, their Berlin residence. Goebbels was working in his office the entire time. Occasionally we'd hear him shrieking on the telephone. As Landie and I had often joked to ourselves, German was such a guttural language that even the tenderest expression of love sounded more like a brutal reprimand.

Hanke and several of the patrolling SS guards had cut down a small but sturdy pine tree which we firmly braced into a corner in the enormous front receiving room. The room had been constructed specifically for the Goebbels' lavish parties yet to be given and was adjacent to the mansion's largest dining room.

The dark grey day gave way by late afternoon to another fierce snowstorm as we alternated stitching popcorn and cranberries onto long strings, folded and cut out intricate paper snowflakes, sprinkled glitter onto lightly glue-edged pinecones and added several expensive blown glass figurines which Frau Goebbels insisted she herself place high upon the tree out of everyone's reach. A brightly lit white angel topped the tree and an enormous gold, bronze, and silver *papier-mâché crèche* was positioned beneath a highly polished grand piano, all items that were heirlooms of Frau Goebbel's former mother-in-law according to Elke. The cook came into the room with a question, and Frau Goebbels followed her out to the kitchen.

One string of the Christmas lights had burned out and was discarded, but all the other bulbs blazed brilliantly in deep reds, dark blues and greens, carefully positioned quite clear of the bright paper snowflakes. A box of smashed turquoise bulbs was dumped to the side with other trash.

"Dr. Goebbels remove da duhty turq'oz ones," snorted Elke, in her odd accent. "Them's Jewish lights gettin' snuck in -- cel'brate Hanakah. Puttin' in the curse, y'see."

"I've never heard of anything like that," I giggled quietly as I helped an impatient Helmut dot glue on pinecone tips. "What would they do, wind strings of lights around their menorahs for heaven's sake?"

"Is fr'real, ducky!"

I had to remain more vigilant with my comments I scolded myself. Unlike my mindless bantering with my staunch anti-Nazi companions Landie and Annette, I was a captive in this den of national socialists. Since Elke's mother had been working class British, that might explain why she'd been swept into the ideology, although a communist leaning would have seemed more appropriate in my mind. The more I learned about Europe's muddled political tentacles the less I understood any of it.

***

It was already starting to get dark by the time Karl Hanke took the three older children out to build a much-promised snow fort after a quick snack. Elke and I cleaned up the huge mess in the front room, played with and fed the two babies, bright-eyed from their lengthy afternoon naps, and helped iron dresses to be worn by the girls later this evening and tomorrow.

After getting the children out of their snow gear and dressed for dinner, Elke and I ate together in a room just off the kitchen while the family was served by the cook and her staff in the small dining room. We could hear peals of childish laughter while Goebbels was telling some kind of outrageous story it seemed. Other than the immediate family, their only guest was Karl Hanke as far as I knew. After dessert was finished, the entire family, including the babies, moved into the receiving room once again.

"It's your turn to play this evening, darling," Goebbels smiled, as he helped Magda pull out the piano bench, glancing in my direction.

"I'm so horribly rusty," she replied, running through several sets of scales. "Well, let's hope not so rusty that I'm unable to accompany our nanny. Daddy brought her along just to sing some of our favorite Christmas songs in English tonight."

I had been sitting on the floor with Helmut on my lap. Hanke reached down for him as I stood and visibly shaking, walked over to the piano. This was the first time she had addressed my presence at all. Obviously, she knew.

"Let's start tonight with "Deck the Halls." You sing the English version and then the children and I will finish with a verse *auf Deutsch*. Herr Doktor Goebbels does not sing, although perhaps you already knew that. And for that matter, neither do I. Or at least not very well."

She played the last four bars as was custom. Never had any audition felt as terrifying as that moment singing in front of this woman who undoubtedly knew full well that I'd been her husband's lover for the last month. My tongue felt like cotton. She probably had every intention of interrogating me later, indicated by her theatrically raised eyebrows.

Somehow, I managed to get through that hymn followed by "It Came Upon a Midnight Clear," "Good King Wenceslaus," "In the Bleak Mid-Winter," "O Little Town of Bethlehem," "Away in a Manger," and a few others. Frau Goebbels never hit an incorrect note. Every chord, every rippled arpeggio, every nuance, was perfectly balanced. When Helga and Hilde knew any part of a song, they would tentatively join in, a blend of English and German. We ended with "Silent Night" sung in German, which ironically, I had learned with my Baptist church choir so many years ago.

"*Zu bette gehen, jetzt … und schließ die Tür, bitte!*" she exclaimed, clapping her hands as a distant clock began chiming the late hour. Elke had already taken the two babies to their cribs shortly after Frau Goebbels had begun playing the carols. Helga and Hilde stood immediately and took Helmut's hands. Like three little musketeers, they marched him out the door.

As I started to move to the door as well, she lightly curled her fingers over my wrist saying quietly, "I asked them to close the door. I will go to hear their prayers and kiss them goodnight in a moment. Elke can help Helmut prepare for bed, of course. I'm grateful that she was still available since my other two nannies had requested these three days off. The babies are sure to be down for the night by now."

After the door had firmly closed, she stood up, slowly pushing in the piano bench, took a few steps away and then turned to face me. I hadn't moved from my spot rooted next to the piano. The expression on her face was tired but otherwise unreadable.

"I recognized you from the Artiste's Club," she began, slightly clearing her throat.

"Ma'am, I –"

"Hear me out," she interrupted, holding up her palm.

I waited.

"When Joseph and I married it was with an … understanding … that he needed to have his … well, let's call it *freedom*, if you will … to pursue relationships with other women as he wished, so long as he didn't flaunt the relationships out in public. The man has the sexual energy of a rabid bull," she sighed. "Add that to his ludicrous attempts at charming and disarming his prey, promising these … simple-minded, talentless actresses a stunning future in those dreadful, boring movies he produces, and you have a golem, as my stepfather would have called him, driven by his nether regions. Karl Hanke is my confidant in all things Joseph as you may have guessed. My husband pens these mushy love letters to his various amours as though he were some dashing Lothario or Don Juan. And then brags of his conquests to his male friends outside of Hitler's circle like some randy teenager."

I felt my face burning. This wasn't something I'd considered. She paused to twist a cigarette into its holder, then flipped a small jet-black lighter into action, inhaling deeply.

"Joseph trusts only Karl to post these silly letters thinking he is completely safe from discovery. But Karl always shows them to me first. The man adores me and wants me to leave this ludicrous marital arrangement for his own bed, but this I must confess, will never happen."

She blew out a small cloud of smoke. I continued watching her, extremely uneasy.

"You've heard of the Baarova incident, I assume, yes?"

"Yes, ma'am," I replied.

"Of course," she shrugged. "Who hasn't? Joseph promised that scheming Czechoslovakian whore he'd divorce me and marry her. Divorce *me*! I'm practically the anointed First Lady of the Third Reich! Our own *Führer* has given me this title since he himself does not wish to commit to matrimony in order to keep pure his allegiance to our noble cause. As though our *Führer* would ever consider granting such a frivolous action as divorce to my husband!"

I nodded as she took a long drag on her cigarette.

"Instead, Adolf has challenged my husband to abide these long months of celibacy and has permanently removed 'The Baarova' from Germany. Joseph Goebbels would go utterly mad without some feckless tart wriggling in between his sheets for at least an hour or so every evening." She took another long pull on her cigarette, blowing out a puff of smoke that whistled slightly though her mouth and nose. Sensing that I was going to speak she put up her palm once again.

"As I said earlier, Karl provides my eyes and ears in dealing with the 'Emperor Joseph' as we refer to him ... as in Marie Antoinette, *verstehe*? At any rate, he wouldn't dare parade *you* around on his arm, escorting you to the theater or trotting you off on some expensive weekend excursion while squandering our country's money. Can you imagine the backlash? Only thing worse would be if he was photographed mindlessly screwing some Jewish girl while sneaking about behind a hedge. He's been known to bribe his nubile actresses with real fox stoles as well as non-existent five-year contracts."

She paused again, looking at me, then viciously stabbed out her cigarette while shaking her head.

"These damn things will be the death of me. So, Karl informed me as to how you fell into this abyss. My guess is you had nothing to do with this Herschel Grynszpan fiasco -- am I correct?"

I nodded uneasily.

"Well, speak up."

"Yes, ma'am. My mother and I were living in the back room of the tailor shop that Herschel's uncle, Abraham Grynszpan, owns in the garment district of Paris. Herschel was also renting a bedroom at the back of the shop. But Mama's and my rooms were completely separate from his."

"And?"

"And we weren't living together, ma'am. Not like that! Mama is very strict about --"

"And besides that, according to Karl's information, the boy has no interest in women anyway, correct?"

I nodded again. News travels fast in Berlin I thought uneasily.

"Basically, my husband is blackmailing you in order to save his own scrawny ass. He arrogantly authorized over the German airwaves that outrageous uprising against all the Jewish merchants and synagogues. Did you know this announcement was made *without* our *Führer's* knowledge much less approval?"

I swallowed. This was exactly the rumor I'd heard as well, but as the Propaganda Minister's wife, she knew without question that the rumor was true.

"So, getting back to your situation. You were grabbed by the SS goons and forced to write those insipid *billets doux* to Grynszpan so that my husband's blundering statement that Ernst vom Rath's murder was a hate crime -- that of a Jew viciously murdering a German officer -- was in reality a disgusting tryst between two fairies."

"There's ... there's more though," I added reluctantly. "I was also at the German Embassy when Hermann – that is, Herschel -- came running out after having shot the officer. Although no one believes this, I was only there by coincidence."

"Hmmm, well I believe it," shrugged Frau Goebbels, shaking her head. "But I must say, certainly poor timing on your part."

A light knock could be heard at the door.

"*Herein,*" called out Frau Goebbels in a gentle voice.

A sleepy-eyed Helga opened the door slowly. She looked at both of us.

"*Maman ...*"

"I will be there in a moment. Is Helmut asleep?"

Helga nodded, frowning slightly, brushing away a few wisps of dark blonde hair that were curling over her face. She shut the door quietly.

"Your children are very beautiful, Frau Goebbels, in both appearance as well as conduct," I said quietly. "I hope you'll not think me out of place by making such an observation."

She began walking towards the door, placing her hand on the knob to make one final comment before leaving.

"After gifts and breakfasts, Dr. Goebbels will be taking the older children for their Christmas sleigh ride. Well, he's not at the reins, of course," she shrugged. "Karl Hanke, Elke and several guards will accompany them. After you've put the babies down for their afternoon naps you and I will finish our discussion."

As she exited, I sank down to the ground, trembling, one hand on the piano partially bracing my descent. After a few moments I walked to Elke's and my room.

"Where'n arth yer been?" she scolded, careful to keep her voice lowered. "You'n me, we's tuh sew these dresses 'n pant'loons fo' Herr Goebbel fo' them new puppets he's boughten fo' Helga an' Hilde. I got 'em cut out from duh pattern, but there's lotsa pieces. Dere's duh apron, under petticoat, gotta gather up the shirt 'n stitch it tuh the bodice, some kinda hair needs to be cut and banded up, then stitched on … oh, an' there's even jewelry …"

"Jewelry with an apron?" I frowned. Leave it to Goebbels to order something like that, I muttered under my breath.

"Eh?"

"Nothing." I was still shaking from my encounter with Frau Magda.

"I dunno. Mebbe the jewelry's fer somethin' else. How should I be knowin' such? Me? Nevuh 'ad any puppet er doll in me whole life. Mum 'an me? Huh! We wuz pullin' taps when's I wuz jes' Helga's age. Puppets? Bloody rot!"

I remembered the beautiful cloth doll and four outfits that Mama had made for my first Christmas living with them, before they'd even adopted me. Mama had added the tiniest intricate tatting to all the necklines and hemlines, silk ribbons to clip onto the doll's long hair, a pair of cloth as well as leather boots, white and black stockings, taffeta and gingham dresses, coats, rompers, and jumpers.

What had happened to that doll, I wondered? I'd brought her to Memphis, but Charlene had called me a sissy the first time she'd seen me playing with her. I remembered stowing her in a cabinet in the church basement just before taking my seat for the *Hallelujah* film audition. I'd always intended to retrieve her after Mama and I lived in our own place but that hadn't happened until we'd fled to New York. Although Charlene certainly didn't deserve such a brutal death, I had yet to forgive her for constantly ridiculing both Mama and me.

The lamp in Elke's and my room was dim, especially for the tiny stitches needed for the puppet outfits. Within just over an hour, however, we'd basted the costumes together with plans to follow up with firmer stitches tomorrow after the girls had gone to bed. We agreed the dresses should hold together for a few hours Christmas morning.

"I started in service wid duh Goebbels fo' Christmas las' year," yawned Elke as we began cleaning up. "Dinner'll be quite ta big deal – mid-aftuhnoon, o' course, like ye'd expect – all the blimey trimmin's as dey say, although Mistress is stingy wid us as always."

Despite Elke's complaints about her employer, if I hadn't been impressed by Magda Goebbels before, her managing at the last moment to transport her entire holiday preparation from cooks to wait staff to preparations of foodstuffs to mountains of gifts and food thoroughly convinced me. Highly polished sterling silver and gilt serving pieces greeted the family at the beautifully lace-draped dining room table. This was after a morning of oranges, pears, toffee-filled bonbons, exotic nuts and rich German stollen had been consumed in front of a roaring fire while the family opened a cornucopia of gifts under their freshly decorated tree. Elke and I sat to the side with the babies, both of whom loudly protested about leaving all the excitement for their usual morning naps. Helmut squirmed uncomfortably on his father's lap and was replaced by a far more eager Hilde after a few minutes. Goebbels laughed heartily at comments made by his wife as well as the children and told several jokes which set the entire family howling that Elke tried to remember later to translate for me but couldn't.

How could this intelligent man behave with such savage lust and yet simultaneously present himself as a warm, deeply caring father and loving husband? The heartless paradox was revolting. Other than when he'd French kissed me in Hedda's bedroom, he'd only glanced in my direction a handful of times and addressed me by name only once. Not a hint of the tiniest indiscretion ever crossed his face. Yet even more baffling, his wife knew and played an even more outrageous role in actually encouraging her husband's wandering affections – or at least she had until he'd foolishly planned to leave her for the film actress Lida Baarova or have the actress join the Goebbels' household. My mind churned. What could Magda Goebbels possibly want from me?

The sleigh ride was cut short by sharp needles of sleet that had begun to fall, so my conversation with Frau Goebbels was postponed. Once changed into dry clothes, awaiting promised mugs of hot cocoa, the children raced to the theater to watch Helga and Hilde's well-rehearsed puppet show. Elke and I each held a sleepy baby who had not only foregone their morning naps altogether but had stubbornly shortened their afternoon crib time as well.

The puppet theater was mounted on a mechanical platform that was pulled out like a drawer from the wall in one piece. Like a pop-up book, it then opened out into a six-foot-wide stage with rigging for painted canvas wings and backdrops secured onto an overhead grid just like a real stage. Goebbels had built the theater himself based on one he'd seen in Brussels on a recent trip and Adolf Hitler had designed and painted the three sets of beautifully rendered backdrops and wings Elke told me. The theater was built so that the girls could stand out of sight, their hand puppets fully visible above them, elbows resting on a small lightly padded shelf. When not in use, the drawer nestled easily inside the wall, under the regular white viewing screen where Goebbels had originally shown me *Hallelujah*.

The girls' show was all in German, of course, so I had no idea what it was all about, but they had evidently written a humorous script which, not at all surprisingly, they'd practiced thoroughly at their much smaller theater at their Berlin home. As soon as the play had finished, Frau Goebbels excused herself, complaining of an intense migraine. Goebbels followed her out of the room; neither of them reappeared that evening.

Elke and I got the children bathed once again, offering any who might still be hungry crustless triangles of hard-boiled egg with grape jelly sandwiches -- quite a treat since it was winter, and the hens rarely laid in such cold weather. The babies had gone down early, scarcely finishing even half of their nighttime bottles. Helmut and Hilde barely made it through prayers before they were sound asleep as well. Helga insisted on brushing her favorite doll's hair for a few strokes as I was tucking her into bed and listened to her prayers, in German, of course, same as had been her brother's and sister's.

"What's your doll's name?" I asked.

"Deidre Marie," she replied, yawning, handing me the brush.

"That's very pretty, Helga" I smiled, as I tucked the covers up tightly under her chin. "Seems very French."

"Yes, it is French. I like French names. I am going to have lots of babies, just like Mama. My first girl I will call Deidre Marie."

Chapter 29

Berlin, Germany – December 1938

After a backbreaking morning and afternoon devoted to washing and ironing piles of laundry, I'd been curtly instructed by the cook to pack up my few things. Hanke would be driving me back to Berlin within an hour. Lutz Templin had contacted Goebbels that he would need to schedule an early morning rehearsal the next day in preparation for extensive repertoire that Goebbels insisted we include on New Year's Eve.

Elke had grumbled since daybreak that we shouldn't be made to work on Boxing Day. "Aft all, ta day aft Christmas is meant ta be celebratin'. Garn! 'Tis a grander bloody holiday than Christmas for us workin' folks," she pouted. "Scaldin' me 'ands whilst disinfectin' an' peggin' up diapers ain' my 'dea of any gift! Frau Goebbels sayin' oooh ma present 'ould be arrivin' in ta nex' day or so, but 'tween you an' me, we both knows she jes' bloody balmy forgot."

I'd wanted to say goodbye to Helga and Hilde, but the sisters had locked themselves into Helga's bedroom while rehearsing a new play for their puppet theater. A large hand-lettered sign in red paint reading: *Betreten Verboten!!* was firmly taped to the door.

Two songs I needed to learn were in German, luckily with lots of repetitive sections. Hanke helped me with pronunciations in the car as we bounced along the rugged frozen roads back towards town. I was also to write the first letters in almost a week to Hermann and Mama once we arrived. Yet again, more than a week had elapsed since Mama's last note to me. Christmas in a ghetto camp. I closed my eyes silently praying once again for some clear path to get home to America.

As we'd departed, Herr Hanke had been handed a zipped leather folder from Frau Goebbels. After helping me with the German lyrics, Hanke unzipped the folder and handed an envelope addressed to me in a woman's delicate, ornate handwriting. I opened it slowly.

"Helen ~ I am following up here. You should know that I am the one funding the series of Lutz Templin's jazz recordings being made at Deutsche Grammophon. This will be real, American style jazz, not the

repressed stuff that is allowed by my husband. He knows nothing about them, nor should you inquire of him. They cannot of course be released here in Germany because he despises American jazz music. He will not allow music of this ilk played on our radio stations nor sanction any such records sold in our stores. I am having Karl send the master copies to a small recording studio near Bordeaux. They have assured me these masters will be pressed at some time in the future and released in France. Why am I doing this, you ask? I personally am very fond of jazz music. That is, except for such painful shrieking by musicians like your dreadful Louis Armstrong.

"But my other reason is simply retaliation for my husband's irresponsible cruelty. At present you are quite powerless as well in his foolhardy schemes. And I might add, you're justifiably worried about your mother: those ghetto camps are filthy with rampant disease and rodents."

"Oh, God," I whispered. "Have you seen these … these camps? Are they that …"

"Keep reading," he replied with a small smile, placing a light hand on my shoulder. "Trust that I am working to get her released."

I stared at him for a moment then continued reading.

"Until this mock trial involving Grynszpan finally opens – and only God knows how long <u>that</u> will take -- you will be kept under my husband's thumb in Berlin. Because of your race you cannot ever be shown about with him in public without his sacrificing his professional career of course. Nor can he have his name linked in any way with yours. But you see, Dr. Goebbels thrives on this kind of misplaced enchantment and intrigue. Until he releases you and your mother, he will be free to exploit you for his sexual whimsies whenever the mood strikes – which I assure you, will strike more often than not – especially when the white kitten of the day refuses his ludicrous advances. I will stay in touch with you through Karl Hanke if I am able ~ MQG."

"I assume you read the entire letter?" I asked Hanke quietly as I placed the lightly perfumed pages in his extended hand. Without question I wouldn't be able to keep any correspondence this explosive.

He nodded.

"This seems so … so …"

"Predatory," Hanke shrugged, finishing my thought. "On both their parts. A childish game one might say."

"As much as I despise being in my own shoes, I can't imagine being in hers!" I blurted out.

"I would certainly agree with you," he replied, folding the letter back into its envelope, then rezipping it into the leather folder. "Do you know that while she was eight months along with Hedda, Herr Goebbels actually invited Lida Baarova onto their steam yacht?"

"What in heaven!"

"This is no rumor. I was right there, Helen. He brashly suggested on that trip that the three of them live together at his and Frau Magda's home in Berlin. Baarova was on the deck sunning herself in the skimpiest bathing attire I have ever witnessed outside of a burlesque house. Poor Frau Magda was so heavy with her husband's fifth child, not even allowing herself out in public anymore, that she could barely sit comfortably in a deck chair!"

No woman of means who was that far along in her pregnancy would ever allow herself to be visible in public – especially a white woman. Confinement was a term that had long fallen out of use, but the practice certainly had not.

"What happened then?"

"Frau Goebbels stood up, very pale, said she was quite tired, then went below deck to lie down on her bed. I found her weeping silently. Herr Goebbels assumed that because of her lack of interest in further discussion, his wife had agreed to this preposterous arrangement! Once again Herr Hitler had to convince the delusional man otherwise."

"Why doesn't she just leave?"

"Hitler forbids her to do so. He considers her the German ideal of womanhood, treats her children as if they were his own. She is his first lady of the Reich as it were, even though she is not his wife."

"Yes, she mentioned that when we had our ... meeting on Christmas Eve."

"There are parts of Frau Magda's relationship with *der Führer* that I do not claim to understand. I sometimes wonder if her children are not secretly fathered by Hitler rather than by her own husband. But you must understand, I have absolutely no proof of this whatsoever. No one does. I confess I do find it ironic, however, that none of the man's relationships with his extensive sampling of women has resulted in any pregnancies. At least to the best of my knowledge. And quite a few of those women have indeed borne children out of wedlock with other men."

I made no comment. Much like Narcissus in Greek mythology, Joseph Goebbels was only in love with himself.

"But I must add, Frau Goebbels has created a few amusing, awkward moments for her husband," Hanke laughed. "One time she sent a message to Goebbels' flame of the moment that he would be picking her up at midnight at a secluded park a good eight miles from town. It was late autumn and already quite chilly. The lady was to be dropped off so they could discreetly drive together to one of his favorite hotels. I need not mention Goebbels never appeared of course and the lady in question refused to have anything to do with him after that. Something about that long walk back to town rather cooled her ardor, I imagine. Remarkably, he never even suspected it was his wife's doing."

"Still, not quite enough though," I replied, shaking my head.

"On a much lighter level, I have a picture that Helga drew for you."

He handed me a small drawing, carefully designed with colored pencils. It was of her doll, dressed in a Nazi young girl's league outfit, a short-sleeved white shirt with knotted black scarf, black skirt and a little beret. Carefully printed underneath was *Jungmädelbund Deidre Marie Goebbels – Helga Susanne Goebbels, 26/12/38.*

"May I keep this, please?"

"I don't think that one is a security problem," he winked, then glancing out the car window added, "the road looks to be getting somewhat clearer finally."

Chapter 30

Berlin, Germany – 1938-39

Sensing Goebbels' disapproval, I kept Helga's drawing a secret, securely taping the picture between two sturdy pieces of cardboard, hidden inside the lining of a used suitcase that I'd purchased with my first pay from the club. I wanted no delays with Mama's and my departure whenever we'd been freed. Items such as suitcases were almost impossible to obtain and far more expensive these days.

Rehearsals for the New Year's Eve gala went smoothly. Without having to deal with the temperamental outbursts of La Miss and Sidney Bechet the hours joyously flew by. When sections needed to be rehearsed separately, we broke into small groups without grumbling and returned fully prepared within an hour eager to continue. Karl Schwedler was once again engaged to sing with Lutz's group, along with renewed contracts for drummer Fritz Brocksieper and trumpeter Charley Tabor, both of whom were extraordinary musicians.

Surreptitiously we continued recording a number of these tunes at *Deutche Grammophon*, as ordered by Magda Goebbels. Close to their original styling, with full improvisations allowed within the solos, the excitement created once those harsh restrictions had been fully peeled back was breathtaking.

A Jewish singer named Margot Friedländer, who'd worked with Lutz in Hamburg, joined us for our one rehearsal, but failed to reappear after that. Charley cautioned me not to ask questions. Margot had a wonderful voice for cabaret tunes, I thought ... so much like Landie's. If I closed my eyes, I could easily envision my fellow little brown mouse on stage at the Moulin Rouge. I wondered if Landie and Annette were still able to work in Paris; it was now impossible for Jews to find any type of employment in Germany.

Why Karl Schwedler had been hired again at the Artiste's Club thoroughly baffled me, however. Most of the time he simply talked through the lyrics with a comical, deliberately fake British accent, occasionally resorting to singing part of the chorus in a voice quite off pitch. He was well known for a regular program that was broadcast each week on German radio and was quite fluent in both

English and French as well as his native German. His program poked fun at foreign dignitaries such as President Roosevelt: *'Franklin boasts of a sweet New Deal ... let's see if this one's got more appeal'* and the British royal family: *'anyone out there want to play ... let's guess who's on the throne today?'* The program was quite popular I'd been told.

As the months drifted into summer, a daring evolution in repertoire gradually emerged. Suddenly much of the music Lutz's band was performing at the Artiste's Club – attendance to which remained by invitation only, exclusive to the Nazi elite -- was now comprised of popular tunes and hot swing music. The instrumental solos were certainly quite tame in contrast to Magda Goebbels' disparaging comment regarding Louis Armstrong's performances, but without question several musicians pushed the upper boundaries of that limit on occasion. Instead of the watered-down 'rides' as instrumental solos were known, that Goebbels had insisted upon when I'd first arrived here, far more liberty now filled the intimate space on a nightly basis. When the Promi, as Goebbels was typically called, was not in attendance, even greater liberties were taken by the club's musicians.

Very bizarrely, the works of many black and Jewish banned composers were being included as well, announced under fake titles and attributed as German compositions. Names such as Duke Ellington, George Gershwin, Benny Goodman, Sidney Bechet, Irving Berlin, among others, were thoroughly blackened out at the top of the sheet music. If no one knew who the composers were then there couldn't be any controversy apparently.

I was finally corresponding with Mama more regularly. She was now living and working at the small hospital located just inside the camp's entrance and claimed her cough was now 'the rarest tickle'. Since she had at one time been a nurse this posting was quite feasible, of course, although I worried about her constant exposure to others' serious illnesses. Karl Hanke assured me that she would have access to certain drugs for her own use, along with better food and cleaner living accommodations. In her letters she never inquired about the status of the Grynszpan trial, but she may well have been warned against asking.

A preliminary trial date had finally been set for late August or early September according to Karl Hanke. Neither the man himself nor my frivolous love letters were of any interest to newspapers these days, however. In fact, only one of my several letters detailing my having miscarried Herschel's and my child was picked up by any newspaper. The letter had been substantially edited and appeared underneath a large photo and recipe for *Kartoffelsuppe*.

The public was far more focused on the political ramifications following the Nazi's brazen move in reclaiming Czechoslovakia among other regions with almost no resistance back in mid-March. What country would the Nazis gobble up next, I wondered? And why were other governments sitting by idly, allowing such outrageous acts?

I was now being watched by at least two men in Goebbels' employ and was careful to keep all my movements completely visible each day. Typically, I took my meals at either the Artiste's Club or at a nearby *café* or, if the weather was nice, I brought a sandwich to the park near the *café*. My telescopic view of Berlin was limited to a small network of carefully maintained, stately buildings, often topped by an enormous, glistening gold eagle, from which trellised long black streamers boldly stamped with red swastikas.

The only time I felt free to breathe for a few moments was performing with Lutz's group. Our recordings for Magda Goebbels were now completed, apparently sitting somewhere in a vault until further instruction. Beyond the stage's blinding footlights there seemed to be a two-dimensional, black velvet curtain. Here I could momentarily block out reality and disappear inside the music ... by disappearing inside myself.

***

Joseph Goebbels' period of 'public celibacy' as enforced by Hitler had ended, so he was now free to roam, wooing whatever new starlet caught his eye. Magda had suffered from a possible miscarriage as well as a nervous breakdown early in the new year and had been quietly hospitalized in a rest cure home somewhere outside Berlin according to Karl Hanke, who was furious regarding Goebbels' inattentiveness to Frau Magda. The children were doing quite well despite their mother's long absence, Hanke added. Their father's absence was simply a given, as always. A new young governess was working out better than expected for Helga and Hilde he mentioned as well. She had a wonderful imagination and loved working with the girls, often helping them write scripts for new puppet shows. I smiled at the thought.

I was quite aware that Goebbels' amorous advances were coyly discouraged at first by most young actresses, meaning that little was certain from one day to the next. However, when the man was rebuffed more than a handful of times, the lady, who would most certainly have been warned in advance by the propaganda minister himself, usually found her screen career had just evaporated overnight. If she was a foreigner, her German visa was yanked as well. Goebbels' mood when arriving at my door was never predictable. For reasons unknown he thoroughly enjoyed informing me about these exploits while I sat against the headboard of my bed, scantily attired, feigning interest as I fought off sheer exhaustion ... and boredom. The man loved to hear himself talk, whether he was spewing Nazi propaganda to tens of thousands, telling jokes to an intimate gathering of friends or relating his latest tale of conquest.

"The time! The money! The promises!" he ranted one steamy late July night. Fortunately, my room was located on the opposite side of the stairs from the others in the hotel. "And then, after all that -- *all that*, mind you -- I *still* had to have her scenes removed from the film just this afternoon. Such a setback ... UFA was almost in completion of shooting the final scenes mind you."

I did my best to reflect a compassionate expression.

"Ah, but make no mistake! She cried and cried, claiming she had 'misinterpreted my motives'. She *begged* me to visit her rooms then. Even slipped me the extra key! You can be quite sure about that! She had heard the rumors regarding what pleasures I have to offer but could not believe I was making such an offer to her. Bah! But I said to her, 'well my dear, it is now simply too late'. There are too many other fish in the sea as you Americans say, to be brushed aside by some eh ... third-rate actress who thrives to remove all her clothes but only while strutting shamelessly in front of the movie camera."

"Obviously not worth your time or energy, sir," I murmured, barely stifling a yawn in time. I'd forced myself to stop feeling any guilt about my bizarre relationship with this dangerously delusional Nazi months ago.

"But I am finally going to implement an idea in which you yourself have already agreed earlier to participate," he smiled, softly stroking my leg. As always, his nails were perfectly manicured. "I have already spoken with Lutz Templin and Karl Schwedler about this exceptional proposal, in very fact."

"Sir?" I was instantly on guard. In reality I was being held prisoner by the Nazi government because of my unfortunate proximity of living in the same space as Herschel Grynszpan and witnessing Herschel's attempted escape only moments after his murder of vom Rath. But I was no fool. It could just as easily be interpreted that I was working *for* the Krauts what with my writing of those ludicrous love letters as a means for the justification of *Kristallnacht* or my entertaining Nazi officials nightly at an exclusive German cabaret or, rather obviously, my weary ongoing relationship quite literally directly under the Nazi propaganda minister himself.

Fully dressed once again, Goebbels stood up and began slowly pacing the small room.

"So, here is my idea. You remember the lyrics you wrote for 'You're the Top'?"

I nodded, pulling my robe up over my shoulders.

"Well, after much discussion, I have finally achieved some preliminary funding to pursue my brilliant newest avenue of propaganda. This will be achieved by rewriting certain lyrics to current *hits*, as you Americans call them. This is intended to introduce -- or warn in many cases -- the English-speaking countries regarding what we Germans have accomplished thus far and will undoubtedly accomplish in the near future as projected in our One Thousand Year plan."

I kept my face as immobile as possible. I could still see Landie comically dropping down on one knee in madcap imitation of Al Jolson at *Tout Va Bien* back in Paris, gesturing madly while singing *'You're our Charlie Lindberg and Charlie Chaplin combined -- you're the Eiffel Tower --- Man of the Hour – you're so sublime!'* I couldn't speak for the British, but the Americans and Canadians would certainly deem such an idea totally ridiculous. And given Goebbels' rapture in speaking about this plan he was dead serious. I'd been told that most Germans have no sense of humor; for the first time I decided this must indeed be true.

"Karl Schwedler has a remarkable command of the British accent, don't you think?"

"Yes," I replied, wrapping my robe tighter around my shoulders. I was grateful that he'd finished relaying his last romance tale for the evening.

"Indeed, even though he's a good German through and through. Did you know Herr Schwedler already has a very popular radio program?"

"Yes, although I've never heard it."

"Well, no, of course not. The day will arrive that your German will perhaps improve *ein bischen fräulein*, but ... eh, German is a most difficult language to learn. Fortunately for all you Americans, most of us here learn English. Americans rarely learn any language ... not even their own!" he guffawed, thoroughly relishing his own joke. "But our One Thousand Year Reich will have all your children fluent in our language in just a few years."

"So, what about Karl Schwedler?" I replied, returning to the earlier subject. I didn't want to think about having a child at all -- certainly not one whose native tongue was German! The fact that I wasn't pregnant yet by Goebbels meant I must be unable to bear children, which I considered a godsend.

Schwedler, although nowhere near Goebbels' level of malevolence, struck me as something of a shady character. He frequently dealt with a lot of unsavory-looking people at the Artiste's Club, suspiciously meeting up with them in the back unlit hallways during our breaks.

"Ah yes. Well, you see, Karl Schwedler is soon to begin the broadcast of an English-language program that we will beam to Great Britain once per week. The first program is scheduled in two weeks. This will include a few, eh, tasteful parodies, poking fun at Neville Chamberlain, Winston Churchill, King George VI, that dethroned disgrace King Edward, your American whore Wallis Simpson, of course, and others of their ilk, as well as that pair of silly gaggling little geese, the princesses Elizabeth and Margaret."

"I see."

"You have noticed, I am sure, that Lutz Templin has been presenting many more older jazz selections of late, *ja*?"

"I had … noticed that, yes," I replied carefully. I'd assumed Goebbels was not aware of these changes over the last several weeks since he hadn't attended any programs recently. In fact, given that Herr Hanke and Frau Goebbels had been seated together at the club almost every evening of late, I'd thought that these most recent repertoire selections were exclusively hers. Hanke was so obviously smitten with the woman she could probably have said that she loved Apache war whoops, and the man would have swooned wholeheartedly.

"Since we are at rather a standstill with the Jew Grynszpan situation at present, and your new lyrics for "You're the Top" were given high marks, you are to be presently tasked with writing lyrics for tunes as shall be funneled through Karl Schwedler."

"Meaning assigned by …?"

"By me, of course. Schwedler will make the decision who is writing what. Karl and Lutz are to locate and perform as many of these newer tunes or arrangements, with my usual restrictions … however, only for the Artiste's Club audiences, mind you. My ban on jazz music remains firmly in place for the rest of Germany naturally. But you need to acquaint yourselves with these new releases in order to … well, *modify* their content I suppose one might say."

"Of course." After a moment I cautiously asked, "does this extend to performing new works by Jewish and black composers, sir?"

"On occasion, if merited," he snorted, disgusted. "It would be impossible to leave those degenerates out. That Jewish crap is all the rage in Great Britain and America. Their fashion designers as well. Magda complains daily that I've shuttered all the better fashion houses in Germany, all of which seem to have been Jewish owned. And naturally, I must bar all imports even for my wife. I do not know why she needs to spend so much money on clothes and makeup in the first place."

"Most women like to dress stylishly, if at all possible," I commented quietly. It was extremely rare that I even mildly disagreed with him.

"Eh, I suppose. That aside, Karl has already begun writing additional lyrics or even complete verses to some of these songs. I have given him free reign to travel anywhere in Europe to gather these music arrangements. You are to begin these writing assignments as well. I intend to begin beaming radio broadcasts to American audiences within the next few months. I want the material at hand so once we begin there is no gap. The music needs to be tip top. Karl's voice is the one I have chosen to use on most of the recordings once we begin. People will identify with both his speaking and singing voice. I have thought to add your voice, that is, a female voice, to one or two songs, but that idea has not been well received by others at our radio station."

I made no comment. I would certainly prefer not to be so ... honored.

"I am calling this group Charlie and His Orchestra. There is no Charlie, of course. It will be Lutz Templin's band. And as such the ensemble known by this name will only appear on these radio broadcasts. It will not exist elsewhere. All those involved, including you, of course, will be well paid for their share of any work. And, of course, your full cooperation with this project ensures your Mama's continued ... eh, safety. On this you have my word."

Chapter 31

Berlin, Germany and Paris, France - 1939

I was forced to record my version of "You're the Top" with Lutz's group a few weeks later. Karl Schwedler was not happy with my work and said he would probably do a version using his own voice, which was perfectly fine by me. Schwedler seemed to be completely in charge of the radio scripts as well as what tunes were scheduled for each broadcast. I was instructed to write three other sets of lyrics, using songs still popular from the 1920s which had recently added new hot swing band arrangements. These songs Karl would be recording. In the meantime, oddly, I'd had no communication or visits from Goebbels himself over these last few weeks.

The first song Karl Schwedler wanted me to pen alternative lyrics was "Bye, Bye, Blackbird," a tune still popular from thirteen years ago. Without question I lacked Landie's clever way with words, spontaneous wit and vast political knowledge and gratefully opted for Lutz's suggestion that the opening verse be kept as originally written. I should attempt to rewrite sections of the chorus lyrics and then the second verse, which was about a bluebird. *'Birds flying equal planes flying,'* stated an eager Karl Schwedler, then adding *'these lyrics are specifically to demonstrate what terror will be inflicted by our Luftwaffe bombers over London.'*

For hours I sat in my room in near total darkness staring at a blank piece of paper. A ghostly full moon slid behind scudding clouds, reemerged briefly as a haunting specter, then gradually disappeared altogether. Finally, words began flowing through me, my hand seemingly forced by an unknown demon. Trembling, I regarded in horror what had just emerged from within. Why had I ever thought this farfetched propaganda was some idiotic vaudeville parody?

What in the hell was I doing?

Pack up all my cares and woes
Here I go, bombin' low
Bye Bye London
The Brits keep snarlin' fearfully
But we press ahead, no qualms have we

Bye Bye London

Now they're beggin' stop before more slaughter
Oh, what hard luck stories from their daughters
Through the night we'll light the sky
We'll be there, just look up high
London, bye bye

In disgust I'd begun scratching out the first line when someone began knocking softly on my door. My alarm clock showed it was not quite 4 a.m.

"Helen," a muffled male voice whispered urgently. "Open the door. It's urgent."

Goebbels had never materialized this late at night. I rubbed my head wearily as I walked towards the door and was grateful to find Karl Hanke standing there. He moved quickly inside my room, quietly shutting the door behind himself.

"I need to get you to Paris immediately," he stated, still whispering. "I am not able to convey to you why. This departure was not ordered by Dr. Goebbels."

"I have no papers, Herr Hanke -- everything expired months ago," I responded flatly. "How can I possibly regain entry to France?"

He shook his head.

"That issue has been attended to. Is that for Schwedler?"

I shrugged as he picked up the sheet of paper.

"Please. Make no delay. I need you to hurry, *fräulein*."

Within five minutes I had packed the battered straw valise as well as my newer case. Helga Goebbels' little drawing of her doll was still snuggly hidden within the lining. I saw Hanke frown slightly as he read what I'd just written, then fold over the paper and place it inside his coat pocket. No one was in the lobby as we walked out of the hotel. After placing my suitcases in the trunk of an awaiting official car, engine idling quietly but lights off, the driver rolled out of the parking area, lights dimmed very low, onto the roadway. We drove for at least a mile before the driver adjusted the headlamps to normal beam.

Stopping only for petrol and identification checks, we purchased food that was consumed while continuing our journey, and finally arrived in Paris near dusk. There was a field radio in the car which constantly spluttered to life, crackling with German expletives. Hanke and the driver, who was never introduced to me, then spoke to one another tersely. I had no idea what was happening.

We pulled up at the back entry of the Bal Tabarin, a cabaret considered second rate compared to the Moulin Rouge. Hanke handed me my suitcases and a folder containing necessary documents instructing me to just find the club's rehearsal room. Although I'd asked what was being said over the field radio he'd refused to comment, saying I would find out soon enough. Then, wishing me luck, he got back in the car and they sped off.

As I entered the club the hallways seemed quite dark, almost foreboding. I felt as though I'd aged nine years over these last nine months. I could hear an argument in rapid-fire French between a man and woman, neither voice sounding like Mistinguett or Sidney Bechet. I stopped just inside the open doorway, quietly setting down my suitcases.

"*Oui*?" stated the woman brusquely. "*Puis-je vous aider?*"

"My name's Helen Mason Campbell," I stated nervously. "I was working at the Moulin Rouge with Sidney Bechet several months ago. I've now been hired to work here … at least, I think that's why I'm here."

The woman looked over at one of the musicians who was viciously yanking loose strings off a large bow. A bass lay on its side next to him. There wasn't one face within the group that I recognized.

"Sent by whom?" asked the bassist, glowering at me.

I looked through the folder of documents and pulled out several pages written in French that were stamped with official-looking seals.

"I'm … not sure," I replied, handing the papers over to the woman who was holding out her hand. "My French isn't very good, so I assume one of these papers includes those … um, details."

She glanced through the documents then gave them to the bassist with a loud snort. Maybe I'd just been sent here with no job offer. What on earth was going on, I wondered for the hundredth time. The musician whispered something in the woman's ear. She nodded.

"Well, Mlle. Campbell," he began, clearing his throat, "it appears we have been ordered to add you -- temporarily at least -- to the chorus despite your having walked off without sufficient notice from your prior contract with Monsieur Sidney Bechet at Moulin Rouge. Is this true?"

Ordered by whom I wondered. Goebbels? What possible clout would he have here in Paris?

"I left a note for La Miss on the piano stating I needed to resign immediately. My mother wasn't … doing well and we needed to return to America. Maybe La Miss didn't find it --"

"Or refused to honor such a request," interrupted the bassist.

"Yes, that's very possible too, of course." I didn't dare say anything negative; all these musicians might well adore the woman.

"And you did not return to America," smirked the musician. "That is obvious."

"No. There were … problems."

For a moment no one spoke.

"You have a high speaking range. You are soprano, *oui*?"

I nodded.

"There is no interest in the high voice here in swing music. You will have to learn to push down into the diaphragm. You are of very light color. Still, women of your race should only use the low voice," he shrugged. "That has always been the style."

I held my tongue from mentioning that Ethel Waters, Billie Holiday, Josephine Baker, and my favorite singer, even though currently involved in a torrent of scandals, Nina Mae McKinney, all had clear, higher voices. True, those older matrons of the jazz realm, like Moms Mabley, Bessie Smith and Ma Rainey were still drawing interest, but their attraction had been dwindling for years even among older audiences.

"I am certain you will manage in due time," he continued. "Set your things over there near the instrument cases. You will find the sheet music somewhere under that mess of newspapers *sur la table*."

I set both of my suitcases under the table and then carefully moved several newspapers to the side. Suddenly an English newspaper's bold headlines flared up in front of me: Germany had invaded Poland earlier this morning! It was expected that Great Britain, France, and hopefully the United States, would declare war on Germany within the next twenty-four hours.

Assuming Joseph Goebbels had been part of the master plan behind this shocking invasion, I now understood why I hadn't seen anything of him in recent weeks; Karl Hanke's cryptic action might well have just saved my life

Chapter 32

Paris, France – September 1939 – 1940

One day later, on September 3, 1939, Great Britain and France declared war on Germany and Russia. The United States squatted comfortably on the sidelines to the relief of some Americans and the intense outrage of others, tentatively agreeing to send armaments to Poland.

Poland fell within a few weeks, however, and was gleefully carved up between the Third Reich and Russia as the two countries had originally conspired. Meanwhile the Brits scrambled hopelessly to reassemble their poorly organized military divisions, which had been literally lying in the weeds for two decades since the Great War … now renamed World War I.

After five weeks of fighting, not one shot of which was fired in Paris itself, France succumbed to Germany the following year on June 25th. An odd agreement ensued that bisected France into an Occupied Zone, which included Paris, and a separate Unoccupied Zone with the remnants of what had originally been the French government.

Similar to the Moulin Rouge, the Bal Tabarin was located at the heart of the notorious Pigalle district. Unlike the entertainment in Berlin – which, other than the Artiste's Club, was still under Joseph Goebbels' severe repertoire restrictions – the Pigalle district had degenerated even further in decadence within weeks after my arrival. The Nazis intended to keep the Paris entertainment district a highly erotic playground, an illicit treat for their worthy military men on leave. Men are men, the girls in the dressing room at the cabaret snorted every night as we prepared ourselves for yet another disgusting performance. But the soldiers had money to spend and the cabaret desperately needed that money.

Our repertoire was sordid, our costumes even more sordid, our encouraged behavior even *more* sordid. Shows were performed with a tiny sequined belt stretched low over our hips, disguising nothing, with a translucent chiffon scarf puffing out over our completely nude buttocks. Sometimes we had small matching sequined star patches pasted over our breasts. Other times, we were told to remain completely bared, and easily available for groping which we were expected to brazenly encourage. The later the showtime the skimpier our attire.

If photos were taken by the club's roving photographers, these would be documented and once printed, sent out to the officer, a reminder of exciting lewd moments tempting a return visit. Most of the soldiers had their own cameras, eager to grab any provocative images we might display in return for a few francs. This entertainment was available for any mid- to upper-level Nazi officer; those of slightly lesser rank could pay a somewhat higher fee for many of the same privileges. If a man wanted servicing beyond the show itself, well, that was almost always available, negotiated separately, of course.

Did I even have a choice? After what I'd experienced with Goebbels my life had lost all dignity. Did I sleep with any of these men? Maybe. Probably. The pay from the Bal Tabarin was inconsistent and decidedly stingy. We were encouraged to accept any officer's offer and drank heavily to blur these nightmares. Ration cards were issued in Paris almost immediately and items that had been in short supply already, such as butter, flour and meat, had become impossible to obtain other than through extensive, often dangerous, black-market networks. Sometimes the girls were forced to barter themselves in exchange for a loaf of bread just to feed family members. The Nazi soldiers that were stationed in and around Paris were now allocated all the available food; feeding the Parisians themselves was of little consequence. Reprisals were severe for any non-military daring to roam after midnight curfew.

Mama had now been moved to another camp and was supposedly still working as a nurse, according to Hanke who continued to appear every few weeks. He told me that Herschel Grynszpan's current whereabouts were questionable, although no one had dared yet inform the *Führer* of this discrepancy. Some claimed Herschel was still imprisoned in Paris, others said he'd been moved to one of the newly constructed concentration camps outside of Berlin. Others said the man had been guillotined at sunrise the day after he'd murdered his lover vom Rath.

Rumors yet prevailed that Hitler intended to review the Grynszpan incident when he had more time, added Hanke. The trial's commencement supposedly hung in limbo now that war had been declared. Were these rumors yet again propagated by Goebbels, I wondered? The man was an unrivaled genius at creating a whispered train of unsubstantiated information capable of wide circulation within mere days.

When I'd first arrived back in Paris, I'd received regular letters from Mama, brought either from Hanke or one of his assistants. But I'd heard nothing from her for these last two months. Was she even alive? Did I even want her to know about the despicable life I now led? I was no better than Charlene. No, I corrected myself: I was far worse. I was debasing myself for a cult … a cult of insane men with treacherously diseased minds.

Bravely, late one morning, a surprisingly shy German soldier named Dietrich let me ride on the back of his bicycle over to the ghetto camp where I'd learned that Mama had been working as a nurse. He'd told me at the cabaret that he was friends with the guards at the camp entrance and was willing to take me there. It would take at least two hours to get there but he had the day free.

It had now been almost two years since I'd seen Mama. I braced myself knowing she would not look the way I remembered. Nor did I. The girl she'd last seen had disappeared as well. A hard-looking woman, far paler, very thin, with a set jaw and suspicious eyes had long ago replaced that once innocent young girl in my mirror.

"You visit few moments only," advised Dietrich, speaking slowly. Like so many other Germans he spoke English with a British accent. "I no want put my friends bad. I had pay them *zwei* kielbasas," he added, holding up two fingers. "Each! *Das* meeting *ist streng verboten, fräulein.*"

"Of course," I smiled, so grateful for his willingness to bring me here, knowing full well what payment would be expected along the overgrown fields during our return. I'd even packed a small basket with a bottle of wine, a small round of cheese and loaf of bread, the last of any rations I'd possessed. What I'd scavenge to eat the rest of the week remained an unknown.

The emaciated woman who dragged herself to a small, fenced partition at the squalid camp scarcely resembled Mama. Neither of us said a word at first, our fingers cautiously lacing through the barbed fencing. Her fingers were surprisingly warm to mine. And dry, like ruined leather. Tears flowed down my cheeks as I gazed into her watery eyes, set within a face that resembled a dried out prune – a forgotten prune batted long ago into a filthy corner by some rodent.

"I was so worried when I … I didn't get any letters," I hiccupped through my tears.

"I've been sick again … not able to work," she nodded weakly, then coughing, quickly buried her mouth in her elbow.

Her cough reminded me of a cheap, percolating tea kettle; her voice was unnaturally slow, husky, and labored.

"There are many of us ill with pneumonia. Or maybe tuberculosis. One day I think … there'll be a cure … but now … with the war. Well, you know." She coughed again for several moments then cleared her throat, attempting a smile. "And you, my sweetheart. What's … your news?"

"I'm at the Bal Tabarin. It's a cabaret much like the Moulin Rouge … well, sort of anyway. It's not as nice a nightclub. Anyway, I've been there since the day war was declared."

"Yes, I remember … you wrote me … I think. That's been … a year now?"

I nodded.

"What's it like?"

"It's … it's quite awful in fact … an animal show … more like a freak circus. There's women's wrestling slopping about in mud and skits behind large sheets that are supposed to look like all manner of wicked goings on. There are even dancers that ride horses bare."

"You mean bare back."

"No, Mama, I mean bare … the dancers are naked."

"Oh. I see."

"It's the worst situation ever."

"Worse than working … with La Miss?" she smiled weakly, attempting some levity. She now clung sharply to the fence, as though she would topple over if she let go.

"Far worse. Could I ask them for a stool for you?"

"They won't bring one. We can't … stay long. What about your Jewish friends … Annette … and Landie?"

"I've tried to find them, but I suspect they were forced to leave Paris. No one's heard anything of them."

"Sad. But no … surprise."

"At Bal Tabarin, they're all French musicians but most sympathize with the Nazis it seems. Everyone does … indecent things … to obtain food coupons or illegal ration cards and money for the black market, Mama. You … you would not be proud of the person I have become," I stated bitterly, biting my lip, unable to look directly into her eyes.

She coughed for several seconds, unable at first to catch her breath, then stood breathing heavily for another moment before attempting to speak again.

"I can only lay blame on myself for … all … this," she began, panting deeply.

"Blame *yourself*?" I cried, incredulously. "Mama, what are you talking about? *I'm* the one that insisted we come to Paris! *I'm* the one who felt it so important that I work with Sidney Bechet to advance some worthless ... nonsense career that no one cares about! How on earth can you possibly claim that anything was your fault?"

"I took you to Orange Mound ... remember?" she replied quietly with a sad smile, speaking slowly to keep from coughing. "That's where so many of our troubles first began. But even before that ... when Papa and I adopted you, a scared, lost little girl who'd simply gotten ... into the wrong car. We should have searched harder for your parents, Helen."

I tried to speak but she waived me off, breathing hard until she was able to resume speaking.

"But I ... I wanted a child so bad. Papa and I had ... had tried ... for so many years. I foolishly ... convinced myself you were my ... my reward for such patience. But you and I both know that our Lord ... doesn't work ... like that. Now He is ... punishing me for this sin. This impertinence. It's entirely my guilt ... as I move on ... from my tiny place in this world."

"*Your guilt*? Mama, no, no!" I blurted out. "You've always been my whole life! I can't go on without you!"

She smiled again slightly, shaking her head, breathing heavily.

"You have so much yet to give, Helen. Never lose ... sight of that. One day you will find what happened to your ... real parents. I am sure." Her fingers squeezed mine tightly through the wire fencing. As I started to protest once again, she added, "I pray ... for us both."

"*Deine Zeit ist abgelaufen,*" stated one of the guards, roughly grabbing Mama's elbow – as fragile as a chicken wing. I watched them until they disappeared into the labyrinth of foreboding buildings as Dietrich whispered fiercely that it was dangerous for us to stay longer, urging me to follow him out of the area immediately.

Chapter 33
Paris, France - 1940-41

I'd received a brief letter from Mama two weeks after my visit, but for months now, nothing. A new messenger informed me that Karl Hanke no longer worked directly with Dr. Goebbels, also leaving me a notice that neither of them had been able to locate Mama. I tried posting letters to the camp but most of them were returned stamped *unzustellbar* - undeliverable. I truly doubted Mama was still among the living. Oddly though, I was unable to grieve. A tiny glimmer of hope remained. Like so many I was now living my life only in my dreams. An expression one frequently heard whispered while waiting in line for rations: *la raison d'être est morte* – the reason for living is dead.

Dietrich appeared during his next leave, but his friends were no longer posted at the ghetto camp. Although I had no heart in the idea, he insisted on taking me to the cinema to see *Die Rothschilds*. I'd heard in the cabaret dressing room that it was the usual antisemitic propaganda film released by UFA -- one I vaguely remembered Goebbels praising when he'd signed the contract well over a year ago. Nonetheless, I was grateful for the invitation.

Since the film was in German, I would only understand the occasional word. My French was certainly improving; my German lagged far behind. Dietrich had saved up enough money to buy a small bag of grape sugar candy at the theater and then dinner at an approved Nazi restaurant. I looked forward to our date. Food remained an overwhelming scarcity if you weren't in the military.

In the Montmartre district, it was now very common to see French girls on a date with a German soldier. I wasn't sure if this relaxed dating situation held true outside of Paris but gave the matter little thought. The French men, most of whom had been originally conscripted for military service with the Allies and were thus still being held under arrest in ghetto or concentration camps, were forced to harsh labor in all manner of factories, manufacturing goods exclusively for German consumption. Dietrich had told me there'd been strict food rationing in Berlin for several months before they'd even invaded Poland. Only if you were a member of the Nazi party in

Germany could you hope to feed your family at least a guaranteed ration of soup each day. Out of desperation, many had now converted to Nazism.

Before the movie began, a short film commenced that featured the Goebbels' children celebrating their father's return from a long trip according to Dietrich. Helga delivered a poem from a book she and the other children had compiled, as well as flipping through a few of the pictures she'd drawn, shyly holding them up for the camera lens. How I ached to see her other drawings and read her poems! I had no idea why this serious little eight-year-old girl, so wise beyond her years, had left such a searing impression on me. The picture she'd drawn of her doll remained safely pressed in my suitcase lining.

There were other scenes in the film where Magda was tenderly kissing each of her children – a distinct swelling of her abdomen spoke of another child on its way in the near future -- and settling them down into their beds, cribs or cots for the night. The moon sparkled brightly through the nursery windows. She looked very tired, but still incredibly beautiful. Her hair was perfectly coiffed, her make-up lightly applied.

Joseph Goebbels' visits to Paris had never directly involved me, thankfully. He rarely attended a Bal Tabarin performance, and on those occasions, he seldom even acknowledged my presence. Rumors of his recklessly brazen activities with the actresses at UFA persisted. As we cabaret performers snickered when offstage, the women he escorted to our concerts were typically more scantily dressed and far more heavily made-up than were we.

Once again, I was dumbfounded that Magda never reacted to her husband's illicit roaming. Or maybe in her own clandestine way she did. I thought back on her having privately requisitioned those jazz recordings I'd done in Berlin, secretly sending out the master disks for future publication here in Paris. Lutz Templin's band was by far the most talented jazz group I'd ever worked with. If by any chance those recordings found their way to distribution, I would be most grateful, but doubted this would transpire. On the other hand, Magda Goebbels was a very beautiful, intelligent, talented, highly secretive, resourceful, and extremely unpredictable woman who perhaps quietly enjoyed privileges behind her husband's back as well.

My cinema attendance did not go unnoticed by the Bal Tabarin's bass player, Jean Garnier. The man was sitting in the back row of the theater, supposedly absorbed in reading his newspaper. I often wondered if he weren't spying on all of us in the band, then reporting any untoward behavior to the French police. None of us trusted him.

Other than Dietrich, my only occasional visitor had been Karl Schwedler from Charlie and His Orchestra, who had assigned me two additional songs for the Charlie Enterprise as we'd been instructed to refer to the program. Schwedler had been unhappy with what I'd written as of late and assumed that this was intentional. If Mama was gone, I had no motivation to continue. I strongly suspected this was why I'd heard nothing conclusive about her. It was rather like dangling a bit of cheese outside of a mouse hole. However, this mouse was on the verge of giving up.

Having acquired the necessary coupons to purchase Jerusalem artichokes and turnips one afternoon, I was rooting through an open marketplace bin. I hoped to stretch out my purchase of a spindly chicken thigh procured earlier on the black market to make enough soup to last me for at least five days. I saw the sleazy bass player, Jean Garnier, ambling towards me as I looked up. I wondered again if he weren't spying on me.

"Monsieur," I said as he neared, lightly touching his cap.

"Do not buy the coffee -- chicory, of course," he shrugged. "But there are moldy roots ground in, I think. *C'est déplorable.*"

"Thank you for the warning," I replied, moving several tables away to begin searching through another small bin. I didn't have a coffee coupon anyway. He followed me. At the moment no one else was standing near us.

"So, I have been made aware that you are the person -- or maybe one of several persons, perhaps – writing the revision lyrics for the renowned Charlie and His Orchestra."

I glanced up at him. Nobody ever mentioned the name Charlie and His Orchestra since Goebbels had detailed his idea to me over a year ago in Berlin. The band itself didn't exist and the programs, broadcast exclusively in English, were beamed specifically for radio audiences in England and the United States according to Karl Schwedler. Was this man a spy? Sometimes, people whispered about resistance groups, but everyone knew that outside of the communists -- a loosely defined band of hoodlums who seemed perfectly willing to get themselves blown up over a few scraps of worthless outdated information -- no such groups existed.

"I'm not familiar with that group, Monsieur Garnier," I replied evenly.

"Of course, you are," he chuckled, grabbing my elbow, forcing me to look at him. "That's Lutz Templin's group over in Berlin. Schwedler visits you to obtain your new lyrics every few weeks or so. He is the one recording with Templin's band all the propaganda pieces for the

English and American radio broadcasts, as per Dr. Goebbels' orders. They say your President Roosevelt finds these programs quite amusing. Winston Churchill does as well although I must say, God help England now that they have unearthed that corpulent relic from mothballs once again."

"What do you want from me?" I asked coldly, pulling my arm from his grasp. "I'm trying to get my shopping done and return to prepare for tonight's program."

"Well, I am quite aware there is more to your story, *mademoiselle*."

"Meaning?"

"It is all quite simple. You were the one who helped Dr. Goebbels escape from the embarrassment of discovery that our dear Promi had initiated the extreme violence of *Kristallnacht* over nothing beyond a disgusting queer squabble gone amok, *oui*? Then, most sadly, it seemed that you and your mama were living in the same rooms occupied by the Jew Grynszpan. Those *billets doux* printed in *Paris Match* and elsewhere were quite the amusing little fairy tales … especially since you were never fully identified. And then that tragic loss of your unborn child! *Ahhh, c'est très drôle*! And to think that the American cartoon film *Snow White* wasn't even out yet … or was it? I confess I am not entirely sure of that particular release date."

"I repeat, what do you want from me?"

"Quite simple. Money."

"Money? You're blackmailing me? Go ahead! I haven't a sou to my name!" I laughed in disbelief. He knew a great deal of my history but nothing worth paying for in my opinion.

"No, no, not from you. Such would accomplish *rien*. Who is doing the music arrangements for Templin and Schwedler for those broadcasts? Knowing Goebbels, he must require every last note played by every instrument be fully written out, so it is not to be considered an improvisation."

"I'm not sure about …" I replied slowly. "I mean, I don't know anything about the band's arrangements."

"You played at the exclusive Artiste's Club in Berlin, *oui*?"

I nodded slightly, my eyes narrowing. This was definitely far more obscure information. How would he have known about that engagement?

"Did Lutz Templin do all his own arrangements then?"

"As I just said, Monsieur, I don't know anything."

"Or you know a great deal. I'm quite certain he does not do his own arranging. So, you need to find out and convince Schwedler to remove said person and give me that position. There is excellent money to be made there. Schwedler does not dare to double cross me."

"Might I ask why exactly?" I asked. I really disliked this weasel of a man. Outside of the money, I wondered what else Jean Garnier was hoping to gain from being a part of that group. There was certainly no hope of having such work recognized for any commendation.

"It is not obvious?" he smirked.

"No, I'm afraid it is not. Please enlighten me," I replied, scarcely masking my sarcasm.

"Herr Doktor Goebbels will be most distraught to find that there exist photos of him in … well, let us say several um, unflattering situations shot in the bedroom of his very home, the Castle Lanke … with a Negress – you, of course, in the event you harbor any confusion."

"You're bluffing. You couldn't possibly have photos of something that never occurred."

"Oh, Mlle. Campbell, trust me. Indeed, they do exist. They certainly do exist! Karl Hanke, Goebbel's highly trusted secretary at the time, was so deeply infatuated with Frau Goebbels he had a photographer hide behind the walls at Goebbels' lake house when you were Herr Goebbels' overnight guest on two occasions. As you probably recall, the house was then still under construction. There were many openings yet within the unfinished walls. Herr Hanke resorted to such spying in the hopes that Frau Magda would leave the Promi and agree to take him as her next husband, but rather sadly, Hitler refused to grant the Goebbels' such a divorce regardless of Hanke's efforts. *Eh, c'est la guerre.*"

"I still maintain that you're bluffing," I replied, cold fingers creeping down my spine.

"Very well … then there were also a few short films taken at the hotel where you stayed while you were singing at the Artiste's Club in Berlin. I love the ones in particular where you are sitting in the … altogether, as I believe you Americans say … listening to our dear propaganda minister drone on and on regarding his latest conquests among *les étoiles du cinéma*. You yourself certainly should have earned an academy award for your acting job, mademoiselle!"

I worked to keep my breathing even. Those films and photos obviously existed. On the surface it seemed far more dangerous to Goebbels than to me, but I hadn't had much time to reason this through. This weasel was not simply an annoying, talentless musician in a band of equally talentless musicians. He might well be an agent for the French police or the gestapo or even the elusive underground resistance.

"There were countless other girls too, Mlle, Campbell, that goes without saying, but the one that matters at present is you. You see, this is specifically about my desire to become part of Goebbels' unique propaganda enterprise and write out these arrangements … maybe even try my hand at some of the lyrics. It has nothing to do with you personally. Herr Goebbels would most certainly be demoted should such a long-term liaison with a Negress be forthcoming. A liaison with a Jewess would have ruined him forever, of course, but sadly we have never caught him with a Jewess, just you, *malheurheusement.*"

He paused for a moment, staring at me. I refused to flinch.

"But here is another sticky issue: you are an American. Right now, a visitor to France, albeit a reluctant one. As you may remember, I am the one who read through your work documents and entry visa when you arrived here – both of which are blatantly forged on flimsy Nazi engraving equipment as I am sure you are aware -- but I will refrain from going into that matter at the moment. If the United States joins up with England in the coming months, you will be arrested and face harsh reprisals in this country. And then, surely you realize that your position in your own country is also rather fragile … one might even say controversial if your longtime liaison with a high-ranking German minister is brought out in the open, *oui*?"

"I think you're playing with fire," I replied boldly, far more bravely than I felt. "Why don't you just hang me … like the Ku Klux Klan does in America?"

"Tut tut, such a gruesome way to die, mademoiselle, to be sure. One minute you are listening to the chattering of blackbirds high in the trees and many minutes later … you are dwelling among them. *Voila.* But here in Occupied France things are done quite differently. One is mercilessly tortured while imprisoned for weeks or even months on end awaiting one's death. Ah, now that is a *very* different story."

"As I said, I think you're playing with fire," I repeated, staring at him.

"As *you* have been all along."

I made no further comment.

"When does Schwedler return to collect the lyrics from you?"

"Next Monday. Early afternoon," I reluctantly answered after a long pause.

"You are certain of this?"

I nodded.

"What pieces have you been instructed to work on?"

"Just 'Goody, Goody.'"

"Ted Wallace and his Swing Kings?"

"That's the only recording I know of."

"Good choice, Karl, good choice," mumbled Garnier, nodding. "I will have the full arrangement ready for him. Do not fail to locate me for this meeting upon his arrival, Mlle. Campbell. And your lyrics best be tip top this time; that would be in your best interest."

He patted me on the shoulder and walked out of the market area. Distracted, my mind scattered in a hundred directions, I hunted futilely through several more bins for fresher artichokes. Many more women were now searching through the bins in the marketplace.

Suddenly I heard a commotion behind the market near the road. As I turned to look, I could see two boys, about eleven or twelve years old, feet pounding loudly in the dirt as they ran, struggling to balance a covered basket between them. Waving their pistols overhead, two German soldiers raced after the boys shouting for them to halt. I was immediately reminded of Hermann running out of the German Embassy and fully expected the boys to be thrown to the ground within a few seconds. *Drop the basket,* I whispered to myself. *There's no way you'll be able to outrun two grown men!*

One of the boys stumbled, falling to his knees as the basket's contents spilled out onto the ground. A small but plump brown rabbit was momentarily stunned as it rolled out of the basket and hit the dirt. It then hopped frantically about in a small circle and finally scampered into the weeds. One of the soldiers shot the boy who had tripped. He fell face down into the dust. The Nazi took several more steps and shot the rabbit. The animal leapt into the air from the impact, then tumbled silently to the earth.

The other soldier continued in pursuit down the road. Within a few seconds two more shots rang out in the distance. The first soldier strolled over towards the boy, kicking the motionless child to flip him over. He spit in the dead child's face and shot him again, then stooped to pick up the basket and calmly walked over to retrieve the dead rabbit. As he continued walking down the road, he shook his head muttering '*der jüdischer Schweinehund, ja?*' as he hoisted the basket over his shoulder. I knew that phrase meant Jewish bastard. Without a word, the people in the marketplace quietly resumed pawing through the various bins as though nothing unusual had happened.

Chapter 34
Paris and Normandy, France – 1941

Goebbels reminded me of a stray dog with a bone. He'd ravish every last bit of gristle off that bone before viciously flinging it aside for another animal's meal. I doubted the Promi would willingly give up on his Charlie Enterprise despite receiving flak that his intended audience thought these propaganda broadcasts so ludicrous no one took the programs seriously. I had introduced Jean Garnier to Karl Schwedler the following Monday as the musician had demanded. Schwedler was instantly suspicious of Garnier as well as my involvement with the man. He suggested Garnier accompany him on his return trip to Berlin to speak directly with Lutz Templin. He eagerly embraced Schwedler's invitation and the two men agreed to meet at the train platform early Tuesday morning.

That evening Garnier went outside for his usual cigarette during our break, leaving his bass balanced along its side on the floor as always. He failed to return afterwards. One of the trombonists set down his instrument and started playing bass after about fifteen minutes had elapsed, finishing out our final set. He then packed up Garnier's bass and left it in the rehearsal room overnight. Garnier was never seen again, at least not in Paris … nor was his bass.

The man's disappearance itself was of no concern from my point of view. His mention of the existence of those photographs and short films of me with Joseph Goebbels, however, were another matter entirely. I knew I could trust no one for guidance. Every eye that glanced over in my direction when I was out on the street, whether male or female, clad in uniform, filthy rags or fashionable attire caused me to flinch. Adding to my anxiety, Karl Schwedler never contacted me again about writing more lyrics.

Unlike my experience at the Moulin Rouge where I'd quickly become close friends with Annette and Landie, the girls in the chorus at Bal Tabarin kept completely to themselves. There would be some small banter while in the dressing room just before curtain, as well as when we'd first come off stage, but none of us ever shared the tiniest crumb of our thoughts nor the tiniest crust of our bread. During our breaks, exhausted and hungry, I would just sit in the dressing room, leaning on the long counter while staring down at my crossed arms. Helga's word for my skin color, *Zimtzucker,* cinnamon mixed with sugar and butter, would come back to me occasionally, making me smile for a few moments. One could scarcely imagine having butter or sugar or cinnamon in one's pantry these days. In just over a year, we'd all become animals. A phrase Mama had intensely disliked that was now commonplace -- survival of the fittest -- dictated one's every move.

We were now required to lead our Bal Tabarin audiences twice each night with a rousing version of "Die Fahne Hoch" which translated roughly to 'raise the flag' but was usually referred to as the *Horst Wessel Song* after its composer. After we'd finished singing, performed while perched on stools, a military-style drumroll began as we jumped down in succession on count one of each bar of music. Flipping over our stools we then donned Nazi-styled helmets and wooden rifles that had been camouflaged beneath and began goosestepping in tight formations about the stage and then down into the audience. Thunderously roaring with approval, the audience sprang immediately to its feet, madly applauding until long after the song had ended.

***

And then, on June 22, 1941, Adolf Hitler made the first of what ultimately became a series of deadly blunders which indirectly brought the entertainment industry in Paris to a screeching halt. While still pummeling Great Britain with expensive artillery mounted on his dwindling armada of Luftwaffe bombers, the *Führer* decided to attack Russia, in a maneuver the French newspapers brilliantly referred to as Operation Barbarossa. Though sustaining completely opposite views in terms of their political agendas, up until that invasion, Russia had been Germany's odd ally in the war against Poland. Germany was now fighting a war with two separate enemies on two separate fronts.

Military leaves were immediately canceled for all Nazi soldiers in Paris. Many of the troops that had relentlessly roamed the streets throughout Occupied France, were sent to one of the three Russian fronts. No one assumed that the remaining French police were any less ruthless than their Nazi counterparts had been, however. Quite the contrary. Their billy clubs often meted out deadly punishments for the smallest of infractions in full view of a large crowd of citizens as a means of dissuading any similar misdemeanors.

The German propaganda machine was in full swing throughout Paris. I envisioned Goebbels in his element, dictating one long communications dispatch after another to his fleet of young, dedicated secretaries to be distributed for radio announcements, newspaper releases, single page bulletins, live speeches, and mammoth rallies. The Promi boldly announced that the *blitzkrieg* led by the Luftwaffe over London was almost completed; a full resignation of the Allies to the glorious German empire might well be expected very shortly. Those bombers were being pulled from their missions over England's skies and now aimed to destroy the Russian army as the invincible German tanks rolled east into Ukraine, Goebbels proclaimed. New munitions factories were hastily constructed adjacent to the concentration camps that lay an hour or so outside of Paris where thousands of starving French, Polish and British military prisoners remained incarcerated while forced to work in those factories.

A former Luftwaffe pilot, permanently sidelined with burns on his eyelids that had impaired his vision, was a new audience member at the Bal Tabarin. When one of the bandsmen questioned the pilot about Goebbels' assertion that the Allies were mere days away from surrender, he had carefully replied in a low voice, "only in the *Giftzwerg*'s deranged mind, my friend. Dividing our planes between London and Russian missions is absolute suicide for Germany's cause. So many of us are missing -- presumed dead, badly injured or arrested -- with few adequately trained recruits as replacements not to mention a lack of planes. We have plenty of artillery but no way to deliver anything. But don't try to convince Hitler or Goebbels of such shortcomings. Those men are lunatics."

Possibly a coincidence, but a day or so after making this brash statement, the pilot never returned to the cabaret. I never heard from Dietrich again either but assumed he'd been sent to the Russian front. Both men joined an ever-lengthening list of people who had disappeared without a trace. One knew better than to inquire regarding their whereabouts.

As winter set in food became even more scarce. I learned to stretch out servings of soup by stirring in sawdust to help thicken the watery broth. If one added too much sawdust, however, one experienced horrible stomach cramps and vomiting. Bread often contained a light filler of sawdust I learned. This also helped camouflage the rotting stench found in the available dough starters. By mid-winter, coal and gas were in serious short supply for heating as well.

Although we had early curfews and often air raid sirens would begin wailing at night, Paris itself had not been strafed by any bombing missions. Were other areas within France and Germany being bombed by Great Britain? All allowed radio and newspaper information was completely controlled by Goebbels, meaning there was zero reliability of any news. More Parisians now privately questioned the Propaganda Minister's victorious pronouncements, but no one dared speak aloud.

My days were identical. I was now rooming with three girls from the cabaret to help with expenses but none of us were friends. I never even learned how two of the girls spelled their names. I would push back the blackout curtains from my gritty window upon rising, grateful that no bombing raid had surrounded us overnight. After fixing a weak cup of chicory coffee, I'd see what ration coupons were usable then set out to stand in various long lines with the hope some of those products might be available.

Due to shortages in rubber to repair tires and metal to replace chains, all our bicycles had fallen into disrepair. Those few who'd held onto such luxurious transportation now joined the rest of us, forced to rely on walking with ill-fitting shoes made of disintegrating cardboard. Leather was also in extremely short supply.

Fewer and fewer products were available on their designated ration coupon days. Rarely could one even hope to obtain gristly meat, butter or eggs through the increasingly expensive black market. I wondered if those living further from the city had it far worse or possibly far better. Were farmers able to hide goods from the Nazis? Or maybe the French farmers themselves were the ones withholding products in order to sell those items for more money on the black market. If the Nazi soldiers were paid off, wouldn't they just turn a blind eye to such practices? What would they care? Communication was excellent these days … unless you wanted to know the truth about anything.

Without the constant influx of Nazi soldiers celebrating their few days of freedom by squandering their money in Pigalle and elsewhere throughout Paris, most entertainment venues were forced to shutter for good or economize drastically. The number of performances we gave each week along with our salaries was severely slashed. In the first purge of personnel at Bal Tabarin, most of our musicians were sent to work at factories, farms, and public utilities throughout the greater German Reich, which in addition to France now included Austria, most of Poland and Czechoslovakia. In the second wave, I was among those sent to work at a factory.

We were not prisoners, but our accommodations, referred to as temporary barracks, although not ghettos or concentration camps, were nonetheless quite primitive. However, there were no bars on our buildings, nor were we chained, beaten or neglected. We were allowed a communal shower with warm water, a few bits of soap, and access to a washtub with a scrub board for our clothes once per week. We lined up for our rations in the morning and evening, but unlike the hardships one faced acquiring food on the outside, rarely were meals insufficient. Portions were invariably quite small, but one wasn't moving from one long queue to the next, futilely attempting to gather sufficient nourishment for the next few days.

Workers who failed to perform assigned tasks adequately, due to illness or were overheard defending radical viewpoints, were immediately arrested and removed. Without question there were spies living and working among us. Rarely did anyone speak freely. At least one large transport truck left the compound late at night several times each week, rumored to be carrying a load of newly demoted workers. I could hear the heavy gears grinding into place from my barracks which I shared with twenty other women.

I was assigned to a factory called an *Apfelfabrik*. We cooked, jarred, or bottled applesauce, apple butter, apple cider, and most importantly, a brandy distilled from the apple cider known as Calvados. The factory consisted of at least a dozen long buildings which housed immense, surprisingly modern, factory kitchens. The pungent sweet apple smell camouflaged other odors most of the time.

I'd been assigned a thickly lined, black lambswool coat with a real fur collar shortly after my arrival, which I wore all day and slept in at night. Other women in my building had also received heavy winter coats. At first, a light, expensive scent graced the fur that I couldn't identify. After a few days I realized it was the same pleasant perfume that Magda Goebbels had worn at the Lanke villa at *Bogensee … Je Reviens*, by Worth.

The coat, which had been in perfect condition before I'd begun wearing it constantly, had probably belonged to a Jewish woman with enough money to have afforded such perfume. I doubted she would have simply tossed away so stylish a wrap on some frivolous whim last summer. I shuddered wondering about the fate of its original owner.

I fully believed the whispered rumors that when Jewish workers in certain of these camps died, their corpses were dumped into huge yawning ravines and their coats handed over to those of us laboring in these heatless factories. Powdered lime was then shoveled over the bodies to help discourage any feasting by diseased rats.

There were occasionally disgusting odors that overpowered that of the apples in our complex. However, no one dared ask any questions. We'd been told we were in a camp along the Normandy coast, just a few hours north of Paris. The smell was obviously just the usual odors of any coastal fishing village.

Chapter 35

Normandy, France – December 1941-1944

During our only work break, one woman whispered to me in English that a crate of apples she'd just opened had been lined with an American newspaper. Japan had attacked the U.S. forces in the Pacific and America had now declared war against Japan she stated. Since Japan was a member of the Axis powers, this meant the U.S. was now at war with the German Reich as well, which obviously also included France. That woman, along with a few others who may have been American, disappeared without explanation that night. Was this because they were spreading unfounded rumors or because it was true? For many nights now, I'd lain awake in the bitter cold darkness, trembling in my wool coat, listening to the grinding gears of large trucks transporting droves of workers to other destinations.

A few days later, the heavy doors to the kitchen crashed open revealing a guard who called out my name. Working to keep my breathing steady I followed him outside towards the main building in the compound. Puffs of vapor framed my face as we picked our way across the icy paths. My mind raced over possible errors I'd made recently. Last week, after badly burning my wrist when a ladle filled with boiling cider slipped from my hand while repositioning the mechanical strainers, I had requested a few moments to go to the medical area for unguent. I doubted my time away from my station had been longer than fifteen minutes, possibly twenty -- there'd been several others ahead of me in the nurse's line. But once I'd returned, I'd resumed my work at regular pace immediately. The intense burning continued for days afterwards, but I'd thought it hadn't compromised my work in any fashion. I hoped this was just a reprimand and not anything worse.

We walked into the main building and then down a short corridor to an office, its door slightly ajar. The guard knocked on the door.

"*Herein*," called out a male voice.

My head down, we walked in. As the guard began to shut the door behind us the man seated behind a desk asked him to leave. I looked up to see Karl Hanke, Joseph Goebbels' former secretary, sitting there.

"Have a seat, Helen," Hanke said in English, nodding to one of the chairs in front of his desk.

"Hello, sir," I replied cautiously, taking a seat as directed. The room seemed unusually warm. A radiator gurgled slightly.

"As you are probably aware I no longer work as Dr. Goebbels secretary. I am here today as part of a temporary assignment to look over the books of this and other … similar camps," he began, slightly clearing his throat. "I am going through the current dossiers of workers at these facilities. The German Reich is now at war with the United States as I imagine you are aware."

"I had heard that rumor but didn't know if it was true, sir."

"For almost two months now, in fact. Including you, there are several Americans working here. All your workmanship has been most exemplary it would appear."

"Thank you … sir," I replied, not at all certain if this was an appropriate response.

"But obviously, any Americans working here creates a significant problem. I am authorized to immediately transfer American workers to our prison camps for obvious reasons."

Shivering, I pulled my coat tighter around me despite the warm room.

"My hand is forced to comply somewhat in this action, Helen. I am sure you understand."

"Of course, sir."

He looked down, frowning, rubbing his forehead for several moments before continuing. "Within the next few days, we will begin building out in two directions to bridge the buildings comprising this factory with several others that are almost completed in construction. This will create an important illusion of one large factory. At least from the air. These other buildings may contain certain kinds of manufacturing that I am not given license to discuss but rest assured nothing dangerous for those of you being housed here."

My first thought was manufacturing weaponry, the buildings of which could then be cleverly concealed within the apple factory complex. The Nazis had a known reputation of hiding their munitions' factories, cleverly disguising such buildings from British bombing raids.

"Because of your earlier … um … unusual relationship with Dr. Goebbels, I have taken the liberty to request that you be kept here at the *Apfelfabrik*, albeit with certain restrictions. Also, there is an additional work requirement. Dr. Goebbels has begun ordering the presentation of live soothing music several times per week to … calm new prisoners entering the camp premises as well as to benefit longer dwelling residents."

"That sounds quite ... unusual." *How could a paltry group of musicians presume to calm hundreds of new prisoners each day? People afraid to question even the smallest order, knowing that their entire extended family or village would likely face harsh reprisals, I wondered?*

"There are three men, originally musicians in Paris, working here currently to load and unload trucks among other chores. So, I am planning to assign them."

"I see."

"According to Dr. Goebbels, these small music ensembles have shown to be beneficial for morale at other encampments. They are sometimes ordered to perform while the workers wait in line for their rations, for example. I know you have performed songs in French, German, and of course, English. Many of the songs that you did at Moulin Rouge or Bal Tabarin and the Artiste's Club will not be allowed, I must warn you, however. Any music that has been decreed hot jazz or swing, especially that of the Jewish composers, is still strictly forbidden throughout the Reich. You will also perform as requested for the SS guards and for those prisoners who have -- let us say, earned the added *privilege* of entertainment -- approximately twice each month."

"So, I'm allowed to stay on here as a free worker?" I asked. He raised his eyebrow to my inadvertent emphasis on the word 'free'.

"Yes. Unless of course, you foolishly undermine your own situation. Please know I would then be powerless to intervene you must understand."

"Of course, sir."

"The musicians you will be working with are Parisians, although I was informed that the concertina player has a split French citizenship with Argentina where one of his parents was born. Two of the men are being held as prisoners because subversive literature was found in their luggage while they were attempting to board a train to Vichy last month. I am not sure of the third man's infraction."

"So, they were not guilty?"

"Well, they claimed they knew nothing of the paperwork as one might expect, although I suspect they were innocent of any complicity. The pamphlets were in Russian and of a stark communist leaning. Neither man has any known history with such groups, nor do they speak any Russian. So, the papers were most likely planted erroneously in their luggage while it was out of their sight. The intended recipient never received them. But communism is a known menace in every country so we cannot take undue risks."

"Might I request an approved song list, Herr Hanke?" I asked, changing the subject. "It isn't always easy to know whether a certain piece was written by a Jewish composer. Please forgive me, but the music all sounds so very much alike – the approved and the not approved."

With a wry smile he shook his head and whispered, "believe it or not, I fully agree with you, Helen. Yes, they all sound *very* much alike, don't they? Silly, isn't it?"

***

Days drifted into weeks ... weeks drifted into months ... and somehow, as best I could keep track, the months drifted into about two years. My work in the apple factory continued six days each week. Our entertainment ensemble as formed by Goebbels performed as requested. Whether our music soothed the other workers in any meaningful way was never mentioned. Our quartet remained the same throughout those two years even though there were many new factory workers employed during that time frame. No one spoke of their regular work.

The concertina player, André Baptiste (or Andres as he said he was known in Argentina among his mother's people), was a handsome young man with thick black hair, dark green eyes set into his somewhat weather-beaten skin, and possessed a marvelous voice. Despite the depressing conditions surrounding us, he maintained a vibrant attitude that few of us clung to anymore. When we'd first started working together, André had explained to me that his instrument was not a concertina but a bandoneon. He coaxed deeply expressive music by varying the bellows' pressures among other techniques. Within a few months I found myself mesmerized by both the man and his music but knew I must maintain an emotional distance.

André had been arrested for playing the forbidden gypsy jazz music of Django Reinhardt in a small café near the Moulin Rouge. A piece called "Minor Swing," Reinhardt's best-known jazz composition, was requested by an audience member who turned out to be a Nazi informant, undoubtedly well paid whenever he exposed a musician playing banned material.

Chapter 36

Normandy, France - 1944

The four of us were required to perform for the camp's guards twice per month as well as certain privileged audience members -- undoubtedly comprised of those fellow workers who regularly spied on the rest of us from within. From the first, these concerts included a tall glass of Calvados apple brandy, surprisingly even for those of us performing, and the opportunity to watch a recently released UFA film. The guards and that month's privileged audience were seated on long benches centered in front of the screen. After our concert, we musicians were seated on a small bench along a side wall towards the back of the room to view the film.

These newest movie plots continued to rely heavily on German propaganda, although the acting seemed a bit more sincere and the love relationships less clumsy. The actors appeared to be more human ... even for a race as heartless as the Germans, André had joked quietly. We were always next to one another whether standing to perform or sitting for the film.

On one of the movie nights, sometime in autumn, a news reel short ran first. The film featured Magda Goebbels, looking beautiful but very thin, playing piano while all six of the children – the girls expensively dressed in flowing long, white gowns, huge white satin bows in their perfectly braided hair, and Helmut in long dark trousers, tailed coat and tie – singing several German folk tunes. The children stood in a semi-circle behind Helga, who was holding a song book. Helga must be about eleven by now, maybe older, I thought. She radiated on the screen, her voice carrying easily over that of her siblings. The youngest, another girl, looked to be about age two or three. I wondered if her name also began with an "h", same as her siblings. Such beautiful, trusting little faces, all belonging to that monstrous father I sighed.

While watching the news short, André had gently slipped his hand over mine, which was resting on the bench. I'd glanced down for a second, then returned my full focus to the screen. His fingertips traced lightly, caressing my knuckles. After several minutes, nervous we might be seen, I slowly moved my hand back to my lap. He had never risked touching me before.

As the newsreel ended, while still sitting in the dark awaiting the UFA film to be threaded onto the flywheel, the drone of low flying planes suddenly began rumbling overhead, violently shaking the screen. In a flash, André grabbed my arm and pulled me under our bench. Blinding orange blasts exploded high overhead, catapulting us through the room's flimsy side partition out into the front hallway. With another series of loud explosions, we were engulfed by a rising sea of flames. André's forehead was bleeding heavily from a long, jagged cut across his scalp ending just outside his eye. Holding his head, he moaned in pain, obviously disoriented. I tried to help him stand but he was far too heavy and kept dropping out of my arms.

"Put your arm around my shoulders!" I begged. "Please! Please try, André! Hurry! I can only lift with my whole body -- my arms are useless twigs!"

He stared at me, panting, confused, blood streaming down his chin, dribbling onto his shirt and now splattering on my dress. Something from Mama's nursing days came back to me that head wounds bleed profusely, often looking far worse than reality. I prayed this was true.

My ears clogged from the bomb blasts, I couldn't hear normally, yet a chorus of men's voices shrieking in pain intensified as the flames leapt higher, surrounding us. With my support, breathing hard, André finally struggled to his feet. Limping, we made our way past the flaming walls to the door. As we moved out into the cooler night air the entry wall collapsed, throwing a shower of sparks into the column of dense smoke billowing high into the night sky.

We staggered away from the inferno, stepping over a long stretch of twisted posts and barbed wire that had been blown to the ground. In the distance I could now see the bombers returning, about a dozen planes nosed into a tight formation, so low to the ground, it looked as though they would scalp the trees. I could just make out a dense stand of firs ahead of us. Like an automaton, stumbling every few steps over the rough ground, I pushed us towards those trees.

Murmuring in spastic breaths, André glanced up at the fleet of returning planes just as we reached the small grove. "*Les Americains … gloire à Dieu … Où sommes-nous?*"

"We haven't gotten very far yet, Andre," I replied. Maybe in his mind we'd been walking for hours already.

"*Oui,*" he nodded slowly. "*Paris?*"

"No, we're somewhere up in Normandy still. That's a long way from Paris, isn't it?"

"*Ce n'est pas … terrible*. Three days walk. Maybe."

Another round of bombs began methodically pouring out of the bellies of overhead aircraft, raining down on the burning wreckage. Though slightly further away, the impact threw us both to the ground once more. I crawled over towards André then curled into a ball around his head and shoulders, covering my ears, hoping to somehow muffle these new blasts. There were no German aircraft dogfighting against the American bombers, no missiles being fired from the camp. A churning mass of billowing grey and black smoke obliterated almost everything from view.

"Incendiaries," grunted André in my ear, barely audible as he wiped a trembling hand through his hair. His sleeve was now saturated in blood. "Little bombs … four pounds … deadly."

We lay curled up, shaking, coughing in the dense smoke, as the squadron completed its deadly run. The droning engines then quickly began climbing heavenward, scarcely visible. As the shrieking of the bombs themselves died away, I could hear the roaring inferno of the entire complex crackling maniacally. We would need to start moving away from these trees within the next few seconds or risk flying sparks setting them ablaze, trapping us.

As gently as possible I helped get André to his feet once again. Like a pair of old crippled peasants, we hobbled away from the flames, now laced with occasional small explosions. Had those added buildings manufactured artillery? If so, once ignited our chances of survival would be zero. No one at the apple factory had ever known what those newer buildings were used for. I began counting our steps, breathing slightly easier with each fifty we covered.

Shuffling for the next few hours, we paused often for brief rests, making our way along a small, rutted path, surrounded by tall grasses, in the hope this path would lead to a road. Where might this road take us? I had no idea. Any sense of direction was lost to me.

A heavily veiled moon scarcely lit our way. No stars twinkled above. The sky presented a blank canvas stretching overhead. There were no night sounds -- no crickets, no hooting of owls, no slight rustling of nocturnal hunters padding along hoping for an easy meal of scurrying rodents. After the holocaust of the bombing mission, the eerie silence seemed deafening.

Miraculously, the path finally opened upon a narrow dirt road. Overcome with exhaustion, we agreed to rest until sunrise beneath some bushes. André's head wound was now thinly scabbed over, although occasionally a slow trickle of blood trailed down his cheek. We fell into a deep slumber almost immediately.

***

A loud rumbling woke me with a start. André was still fast asleep. Bright sun filtered through the leaves, warming the area. The bushes we'd chosen to hide beneath weren't nearly as concealing as I'd assumed last night. A tank had stopped just a few yards away on the adjacent road. After a moment the lid popped open, and a soldier climbed out, while another soldier pointed a machine gun at us. I don't know my uniforms unless I can see the insignia at close range, and I was clueless which tanks belonged to any given country's army. The first soldier approached, aiming a handgun at me. Even though not ordered, I stood slowly and raised my hands level with my shoulders.

"*Qui êtes-vous?*" he demanded. He spoke the words slowly, and I was fairly certain his accent was American, not French or German.

"Helen Mason Campbell," I replied carefully, then adding, "aren't you an American?"

"His name?" said the soldier, cocking his chin, as he lowered the gun very slightly.

"André Baptiste."

"A Frenchman?"

"Yes, sir."

"What are you doing here?"

"We were workers at the *Apfelfabrik* that was bombed last evening ... I believe by American aircraft. We managed to escape, but André is badly hurt. A serious head wound, sir. He needs immediate attention to avoid infection."

"I'm not aware of any such mission that was ordered last night," the soldier replied, frowning. "What's the *Apfelfabrik*? I've never heard of this military installation."

"It's not a military installation," I said, shaking my head. "It's a factory that produces applesauce, cider and apple brandies. That's all I know about it."

"You can drop your hands," he said, shoving his gun into its holster as he continued to walk towards me. The other soldier kept his machine gun trained on me, however. "You married to this guy?"

"No sir. We work together at the factory. We were also musicians there."

"So, this *apfel* place was a concentration camp?"

"A worker's prison camp, maybe. The terminology for these camps has become a little murky."

He grunted, shaking his head.

"If it *wasn't* a concentration camp, you're damned lucky, girl. You heard about them?"

"I guess … I … no."

"One of my superior officer's claims this Nazi crackpot Goebbels ordered music be performed at his death camps or 'concentration camps' as he refers to them, while the occupants are slowly starved to death. Even better, he has his prisoners march to music onto trucks, packin' 'em like sardines, or sometimes even into a large building. Then they pump the truck or sometimes even the building full of carbon monoxide they say. Takes a few minutes they claim, but the end result is a hundred percent. Like spraying mosquitoes with a lethal snout of the stuff."

I just stared at him, speechless.

"It's been whispered about for over a year now," the soldier snorted. "If I sound disgusted, believe me, I am. Wake up your friend. I'm radioing for a jeep to take you to the medics. We're camped about two miles up the way."

The soldier never did introduce himself but did call for a transport before climbing back into the tank and continuing down the road. Once I'd gotten him awake, André complained of dizziness, a terrible buzzing in his ears, nausea and a headache. Whenever he tried to speak, he rambled in a mix of English and French, making no sense whatsoever. I suspected he had a concussion. Probably a bad one. A thick wedge of dried blood, almost like the edge of a torn beret, pulsed low and ugly along his hairline. Our faces, arms and clothing were blackened with soot from the explosions.

Once at the camp, André was eased onto a stretcher and taken to the medical tent. I was given a bar of soap and towel, then accompanied by two soldiers down to a small stream to wash my face and arms. Even used sparingly, the soap stung my raw skin. The men then brought me to their commanding officer's tent.

"Have a seat," the officer gesturing to a camp stool. "I'm Captain Parker. And you are?"

"Helen Mason Campbell, sir."

"I'm told you have no papers, no visa or passport, but you're American?"

"My papers are probably incinerated now, but they were confiscated when I was sent to the *Apfelfabrik*. I believe they were kept in a file cabinet in the factory office."

"How long ago was this?"

"I don't know. I think I've been there for almost a year and a half."

He whistled, shaking his head. "Well, today's August 22, 1944. That seem about right?"

"That's impossible!" I gasped.

"Afraid that's correct, ma'am. Was this place a worker's or prison camp?"

"I've heard that those exact definitions are rather … fuzzy," I replied, shocked that more than two years of my life had simply evaporated at the apple factory.

"What about your friend? What's his name? Was he in the military?"

"André Baptiste. He's French, but not a Nazi. He wasn't ever in the military as far as I know, but I've no idea why. He worked in the cider bottling center for his regular day. We were both working as musicians when requested also. André plays concertina –"

"What's a concertina?"

"It's like a small accordion."

"I've read about those bizarre music ensembles that Goebbels concocted. Charm the beasts before they're cast mercilessly into the pit as it were. Go on."

"Anyway, he'd been tricked into playing a well-known jazz tune requested by a Nazi informant in Paris and was arrested on the spot. He thinks because it wasn't considered an extreme offense, he was sent to the work camp and not a regular prison."

"Which club?"

"Moulin Rouge, I believe."

"Hmmm, Moulin Rouge. Good place so they say, although I've never been."

"Yes, it's a wonderful cabaret … or at least it was. I worked there for several months. Could I ask where we are now, please?"

"We're just outside of Honfleur. By the time our unit had arrived here the whole Normandy province had already been liberated by the British and Canadian troops. Miraculously, Honfleur was not damaged whatsoever – strangely handed over by the Krauts with no combat. I heard that's not true for most of the other areas along the Channel though. A lot of shelling … serious destruction. Have no idea how many soldiers or civilians lost their lives. Liberating Paris is next on the horizon, although it seems Gen. Eisenhower disagrees," he shrugged. "Anyway, when were you at the Moulin Rouge?"

"I'd signed a contract to work there for six months with Sidney Bechet's band in 1938."

"I've heard of him. So, you're famous, huh? A singer, I assume?"

"Yes, I'm a singer, but not famous at all. I'd hoped to gain some popularity by singing with Mr. Bechet's band and was only supposed to be in France for six months as I said … but I was stranded here instead." I was hoping this would be the end of his questions as my voice drifted off, but I was mistaken.

"How?"

"It's something of a … complicated story, but my mother and I were living in adjacent rooms to Herschel Grynszpan at his uncle's tailor shop in the Jewish sector."

"Grynszpan … Grynszpan … you'll have to refresh my memory on that one," Capt. Parker frowned. "Sounds vaguely familiar, but …"

"He fatally shot a Nazi officer at the German Embassy in Paris in November 1938. That prompted the series of reprisals they called *Kristallnacht* throughout Germany and Austria as I'm sure you remember, sir. Herschel was being held by the Paris police for trial – they said even Hitler planned to attend this trial -- it was that important."

"What did this have to do with you?"

"Mama and I lived in the same space as him which appeared suspicious to the authorities since we're Americans. Also, by unfortunate chance, I was outside the Embassy when the shooting took place. We were detained indefinitely for questioning."

"Huh. Rumor I heard was the Krauts executed that guy around 1940 or '41. You said you'd been working at that factory for the last two years. Where were you and your mother between '39 and '42?"

"My mother was held in a prison camp," I answered slowly, my stomach beginning to churn. "I heard from her sporadically at first but nothing for a long time now. The last time I heard from her she was quite ill. I pray every day she's still with us, but …."

My voice trailed off. How on earth could I condone knowing that my mother was dying in a concentration camp while I was singing at a swanky private Nazi cabaret in Berlin? And was my name attached in any way to those dreadful lyrics I'd rewritten or that original recording I'd made for Goebbels' outlandish Charlie and his Orchestra? Propaganda programs targeted for broadcasts throughout the U.S. and England?

That didn't even begin to address the disgusting possibility that illegally obtained photographs or short films of my whoring days with one of the most notorious of Hitler's ministers might surface at any moment. And, although not nearly as damaging, reprints of the love letters I'd been forced to write to Herschel Grynszpan to help the megalomanic Goebbels' save face, were undoubtedly filed in countless newspaper archives as well. Even though unsigned, those letters could easily be traced back to my handwriting. If I were sitting on a jury, without the slightest question I would deem me guilty on all counts. I tried to remain composed.

"I sang for the Moulin Rouge for a time after Mr. Bechet and his orchestra had returned to the States. Then I worked for a similar place in Berlin," I replied, praying he wouldn't ask how on earth I'd been tapped for work by a cabaret in Nazi Germany.

"Berlin? That's sounds rather ominous, Miss Campbell. Surely, you're not going to claim you worked as a *jazz* singer in Berlin during that time!"

"Yes, actually I did," I replied, my voice thin. "Difficult as it might be to believe, there were a few, remote, very elite clubs, open by invitation only, that permitted, even encouraged such decadent American music."

"Really? Go on. Just what elite groups? I'm thoroughly fascinated."

"Some higher-ranking officers with their wives," I said quietly, clearing my throat, unsure if he was mocking me.

"I suppose you're going to tell me that Joseph and Magda Goebbels were among those frequent attendees?" he scoffed, unquestionably doubting any such experience.

"Frau Goebbels and Frau Heydrich were occasional guests as were Herr and Frau Borman. Whenever Dr. Goebbels was in the audience we played almost no jazz tunes – none by Jewish composers you may be certain."

"Jazz concerts in Nazi-purified Berlin! What was the name of this place?"

"The Artiste's Club."

"Who owned it?"

"I'm not certain," I replied. I was fairly certain that Goebbels himself owned the club, but I refrained from mentioning this.

"Where were you after that?"

The officer's stark line of questioning was making me nervous. His abrupt demeanor reminded me of Goebbels' interrogation at the German Embassy five years ago.

"Another French club, Bal Tabarin. I arrived back in Paris just as the Occupation began. All those clubs were frequented by Nazi soldiers on leave. They were encouraged to recklessly enjoy this hard-earned freedom from their duties, as I understood it. We were allowed to perform certain jazz tunes despite France being under the

Nazi flag at that point. What was allowed and not allowed was often confusing, I confess."

"Continue," Capt. Parker grunted, shaking his head.

"Then, as soon as Germany invaded Russia, all the soldiers' leaves were immediately cancelled. This was said to be the death knell for the entertainment district in Paris. The German soldiers were the only ones with any money. That's how those enterprises had survived in the first place. The Parisians themselves were poorer than church mice. And starving. We were all hungry, barely getting by with bartering soap for soup and paying exorbitant prices on the black market for a few scraps of meat."

"I think most of Europe is still hungry," he sighed. "Some of this doesn't exactly add up, miss, but I'll have to take it at face value for now. There's a mess tent just down that hill. Get yourself something to eat. I'm sure you're starving."

Chapter 37

Paris, France – 1944-45

Around midnight, the entire military outpost struck camp and began creeping south along roads outlining the banks of the Seine towards Paris. André and I rode in the back of a medical transport. His head wrapped in a wide swath of gauze, cradled in my lap, he slept most of the trip. Whenever he happened to wake, he was still nauseous, able to swallow only a few sips of water occasionally. No food. I was astounded he'd been able to walk for several hours after the apple factory bombing. Along the way we encountered several German soldiers who voluntarily surrendered and were escorted back to the base camp up the line. We were told this battalion was one of the Allies' liberation units headed to Paris as requested by a Gen. Charles De Gaulle of the Free French.

Just before dawn we entered Paris through the *Arc de Triomphe*, rumbling down the wide, seemingly deserted chestnut tree-lined *Champs Elysée* then turning down a myriad of smaller avenues. On closer scrutiny, however, I could just make out soldiers strategically positioned behind a bizarre labyrinth of barricades constructed of huge chunks of concrete, dismantled kiosks, burned out cars, crumpled bicycles, even street urinals and upended benches. A jagged line of soldiers sat motionless, their machine guns and rifles trained on targets along the rooftops and large windows of apartment buildings that lined the streets where Nazi and pro-Vichy French fighters were poised, ready to resume firing at the first smear of daylight. The gas and electricity had been out for several weeks now I was told. Additionally, the city remained in blackout overnight fearing a final destructive purge of a rumored, desperate Luftwaffe bombing run ordered by Hitler. Thus far, miraculously, the city of Paris had not been bombed.

André and the others on our transport were quickly carted on stretchers into one of the newly secured buildings that now served as a makeshift hospital. The transport had already been radioed to join a fleet of ambulances sent to pick up other injured soldiers and civilians throughout the area. The military nurses ordered the injured be taken to the back hallway where their conditions could be evaluated, wounds redressed, and medications made available. I was told to join other civilians on the third floor of the ruined building, which looked out over the street from a massive hole where a large balcony had been blown away. This had exposed a huge entertainment area, complete with a massive fireplace, dotted with dozens of shattered Tiffany lamps, scorched carpets and soot-blackened white lounging sofas.

From my panoramic view, an uncanny scene was unfolding in the street below me. Throngs of French citizens -- the women sporting their best hats, and adorned with sparkling necklaces and earrings, the men wearing their Sunday caps and coats -- lined the street behind the makeshift barricades. Many were chanting and cheering – some even applauding – as the heavy street fighting continued scarcely a few feet in front of them! Were they so inured to all these years of violence that standing adjacent to death had no relevance anymore? When a bullet struck a Nazi soldier on the roof across the street, he somersaulted slowly to a violent death on the pavement below as the crowd of Parisians almost simultaneously began cheering. En masse, the group then broke into "La Marseillaise" which echoed off the buildings along with a staccato torrent of machine gun fire aimed at another roof-dwelling Nazi guard.

Three days later, it was over. Paris and much of France had been liberated although the war intensified elsewhere. The Germans were steadily beaten eastward and then forced to retreat into their own country when the situation became intolerable. Nazi flags and street signs were vehemently ripped from Paris buildings and thrown into huge bonfires throughout many of the country's *arrondisements* as the French flag was proudly run up the flagpoles for the first time in four years.

André was finally able to swallow a bit of soft food, but his head wound was quite deep and had become infected. Shortly after the Germans vacated Paris, the Allies moved him, along with other seriously injured civilians, to various city hospitals. I visited frequently, but most of the time I don't think he recognized me. I thought back on those few serene moments together when he'd cupped his hand over mine, softly stroking my fingers, just before the American bombers had roared overhead a few weeks ago. It was a miracle that neither the Americans nor the Nazis had bombed Paris, I thought. Hitler had definitely given orders to do so but mysteriously, these commands were never carried out. Why they weren't remained a blessing given the total destruction of so many European cities.

My last few possessions had been consumed in the explosions at the apple factory. Mama's Bible with our precious family photos and the little drawing by Helga Goebbels were gone forever. Sadly, details of all those pictures were already growing faint in my memory.

Everyone needs occasional entertainment, even in the most trying of times, and I was hired back at the Moulin Rouge for a few months, having miraculously obtained a passport and temporary visa from the American Embassy. The club had recently reopened with no cover charges and very cheap drinks -- anything that might entice the public to venture inside and part with a few hard-earned coins. The cabaret had become tainted by its association as an established Nazi soldier's playground even though those carefree days had abruptly ended when Germany first attacked Russia, its former ally. However, it was certainly nothing like the old days. Food was available once again for purchase at the cabaret, but it was so prohibitively expensive that most patrons opted only for a glass of their cheapest French wine. Beer remained negatively associated with German appetites for many months.

The band was a ragtag ensemble numbering five or six rather mediocre musicians. Music charts were a hodge podge of various arrangements and not everyone's lead sheets matched for unexplainable reasons. No one among us was capable of producing exciting music arrangements and I hoped that André would be joining us in the near future since he was an excellent arranger.

Nonetheless, we put our souls into our work and the end result, if not of the highest standard, was acceptable. Because I had worked with highly respected jazz bandleaders such as Sidney Bechet and Lutz Templin in Europe, Charles Johnson back at Small's Paradise in Harlem, as well as famous musicians including Mistinguett, Charley Tabor and Fritz Brocksieper, I was considered a resource with respect to just how this music should sound after so many years of its being distorted by Goebbels' outlandish music restrictions.

André had been moved to a nearby sanitarium just before Christmas. He was still receiving therapy for double vision, as well as blinding migraines and serious balance issues. Two cinemas had reopened a few months earlier, one of which had begun showing the just-released American film *Meet Me in St. Louis,* complete with French subtitles. We opted to celebrate his transfer to the new facility by attending one evening, hoping he'd be able to enjoy the movie.

Judy Garland was magnificent, as I'd expected. But a little girl named Margaret O'Brien stole my heart the moment she appeared on the screen. She was the spitting image of Helga Goebbels, at roughly the same age as when I'd met Helga. I held André's hand tightly as I followed every move of the child whether she was the center of action or simply part of the crowd. There was an early scene where she sang with Judy Garland. My Helga has a much better voice, I said to myself, smiling. Maybe once this dreadful war is completely over, she can make films in Berlin. According to Paris newspapers, her father had flagrantly boasted recently that if the country could just hold out a little longer, that once the war had ended every German would have a Volkswagen in front of their newly constructed home, and more meat and butter than they could possibly consume over a week's time. I wondered if Goebbels' propaganda, spinning ever more outrageous promises with each passing week, was still embraced at all by his countrymen. Somehow, I doubted this.

It was said that Hitler and his ministers had built entire cities, a vibrant, connected series of bunkers snaking deep underground beneath Berlin's ruined municipal buildings. This intricate labyrinth now housed all the important members of the Nazi party, living like moles under Berlin supposedly. Even though the city was being bombed nightly by American and British aircraft, massacring entire neighborhoods in one pass, Goebbels continued to broadcast appeals to his followers. He urged them to dig in their heels in what he referred to as the Reich's Total War, alluding to a secret weapon that once unleashed would turn the tide of the war within mere hours.

I couldn't help but wonder: where was his family? Had he forgotten about them, letting them survive on their own out at his Lanke summer villa possibly? The thought made me sick to my stomach. Photos of Nazi soldiers killed on the battle fronts now showed young teenage boys, about fourteen or fifteen years of age, fighting side by side with old men -- those few soldiers who had somehow survived the first world war and were now thrust to their deaths in this one.

***

André was released from the sanitarium early in 1945, and we got married at the village clerk's office the next day. We'd only spent one long night together, André badly injured, both of us scorched and in shock, as we'd struggled through high grasses and mud hoping to reach safety ... whatever that word meant. Much of our story was identical to other wartime romances. But I knew I dearly loved this handsome, talented, and quietly intelligent man, and was so grateful that God had brought him into my life.

During his long convalescence, fearful he would cast me away in disgust, I had gradually told him about being forced to have sex with Goebbels, pen love letters to Herschel Grynszpan, and write the Charlie propaganda lyrics. I still feared that explicit films of Goebbels and me might yet surface from some German stronghold. Andre never uttered a word of condemnation, vowing to keep forever silent that which could so easily be interpreted to the outside world as my willingness to assist one of the foulest Nazis within the formerly brutal, now battered Third Reich.

André was thoroughly amused by Magda Goebbels' sponsorship of my Deutsche Grammophon jazz recordings with Lutz Templin's band. If the recording masters were still in Berlin, they'd have been reduced to rubble months ago along with all the communications buildings. But if they'd been sent to Paris for holding and final distribution as Magda had requested, there was a possibility they were intact. He envied my opportunity to have worked with Templin, Charley Tabor and Fritz Brocksieper, some of his favorite musicians, on the project.

Not that his prior life was nearly as scandalous as mine, André had fathered a son with a woman he'd then refused to marry several years ago. They'd been living together for a while and he'd felt guilty leaving when the baby was only a few months old, but knew it was the best for everyone. He'd sent money to her for a few years but had lost track of her with the onset of the war. Feeling obligated to continue contributing to his child's upbringing, he'd finally discovered that his former girlfriend was newly married and living slightly south of Paris just before he'd been arrested for performing the forbidden Django Rheinhardt music. She'd informed her husband that she'd been married to her child's father and that he'd been killed in action. She had no interest in Andre's money or any sudden reappearance in her life.

Since I hadn't become pregnant while subjected to Goebbels lurid advances for months on end, I was certain I was unable to have children. Andre was such a tender, attentive lover, there were times we just lay across the bed afterwards, fingers lightly intertwined, both of us exhausted, smiling into one another's eyes. I didn't feel that I deserved this, but I wasn't about to ever give him up.

Chapter 38
Paris, France – 1945-50

On April 30, 1945, Adolph Hitler, reduced to a raving lunatic by many accounts, and his longtime mistress, now wife of a few hours, Eva Braun, ingested cyanide capsules, followed by the *Führer's* fatally shooting his new bride and then himself within the *Führerbunker* deep beneath the ravaged city of Berlin. As they'd requested, their corpses were then hauled outside the bunker, doused with gasoline and burned almost beyond recognition as Allied aircraft fired on those men stoking the blaze. I'd just begun slicing potatoes for our supper when the first news bulletin interrupted my radio program. The propaganda minister's secret weapon – feared by many to be a new radical bomb capable of annihilating structures and populations located miles outside its epicenter -- turned out to be a pipe dream. No such weapon existed ... at least not in the hands of the German Reich.

Late in the afternoon two days later, another shocking news bulletin struck. Joseph Goebbels, his wife Magda and all six of their children had been found dead by Russian soldiers when they'd broken into the propaganda minister's bunker. The children were all dressed in white nightgowns -- the girls' hair newly washed and braided, topped with large white satin bows. They were found stretched out on three bunk beds in their bedroom in the family's bunker, adjacent to Hitler's. A doctor arrested within the bunker stated the children had been given cyanide capsules, crushed into their mouths by their mother as the children slept, after having been given a strong sleeping cocktail at bedtime. An hour after the children's deaths, Joseph and Magda Goebbels had walked out of the bunker together. Joseph shot his wife and then himself in the head. Although Goebbels' had requested their remains be burned exactly like the *Führer's*, the attending soldiers were unable to find sufficient gasoline to adequately complete the job.

Pictures appearing in the evening's newspapers were taken by the Russian soldiers who first entered the bunker. The photos showed the children in their sleep clothes, lying atop their bunk beds.

My sweet, beautiful little Helga was on the top bunk, her head turned slightly sideways, towards the camera, looking fresh as though she'd be emerging any moment from her slumber and wondering why on earth all these Russian soldiers were strolling about in her bedroom.

"You godforsaken monster! You bastard! What have you done? Why, why, why?" I seethed between clenched teeth, simultaneously punching a photograph of a smiling Goebbels, his arm raised in a '*heil Hitler*' salute while he'd addressed a huge crowd of cheering Berliners, taken two years ago according to the caption. Even though Magda's doctor claimed that she had poisoned her own children, I knew without any doubt her husband's fanaticism had driven her to complete madness during their entire marriage. He alone was responsible for this final despicable act.

In a later edition of the newspaper, there were separate pictures of each child, breathtaking headshots by a professional photographer that Goebbels had ordered as a present for Magda's birthday this past November. They didn't even have six more months to live, I whispered to myself bitterly, tears blurring my vision. I alone mourned for Helga and her brother and sisters. My grief could not be shared with neighbors, friends nor fellow musicians at the cabaret – and only in very small measure with André.

As expected, there was an immediate uproar against any extended coverage that featured Hitler, Goebbels or the many other Nazi criminals or their families who had either been executed on sight or had taken their own lives to avoid capture. *Show us their bombed-out properties, not the lavish, decadent lifestyles they led before their much-deserved, permanent descent to hell*, was the message screaming out of countless editorials.

I vividly remembered the end of Helga's and my conversation when she'd shown me her favorite doll, later the model for the picture she'd drawn for me, as I'd tucked the inquisitive six-year-old into bed that strange Christmas night:

"What's your doll's name?" I had asked.

"Deidre Marie," Helga had said.

"That's very pretty, Helga. Seems very French."

"Yes, it is French. I like French names. I am going to have lots of babies, just like Mama. My first girl I will call Deidre Marie."

If God ever sees fit to give me a child, if it's a girl I'm going to name her Deidre Marie, I swore out loud to the deep shadows flickering along the walls of my bedroom. Others will forget you, my sweet little one, but I swear, I will not. I. Will. Not.

For many years afterwards, every Christmas the movie *Meet Me in St. Louis* played for about a week at one of the Paris cinemas. I would go to see Margaret O'Brien, looking so much like my own little Helga Goebbels, exactly as I'd remembered her at that age. But I never went to see Miss O'Brien's movies as she grew older. My heart just couldn't swallow the pain.

***

André had been hired as a guitarist, concertina player and music arranger at the Moulin Rouge several weeks after he'd been released from the sanitorium. Surprisingly, he'd been able to buy reasonably good instruments at a pawn shop that had obtained them prior to the Occupation. He still tired out quite easily but was anxious to get back into playing music once again. And the cabaret's managers and other musicians were almost as ecstatic as I was to work with him. He was one of those rare talented individuals who somehow managed to get along with everybody, diplomatically smoothing out both personal and music issues.

At first, the world around us continued in a vortex of suffering, including illness, food shortages, and extremely long wait times for most products and services. Like stars slowly appearing after a heavy thunderstorm, however, businesses began reopening, meaning jobs were available once again, and with that, paychecks followed. The so-called secret weapon, that single bomb capable of massive destruction feared throughout Europe to be in the Third Reich's hands was instead developed by the Americans and dropped in August that year, first on Hiroshima and then on Nagasaki, Japan a few days later. This ended World War II. It also ended any innocence or blind trust any nation might ever again experience with other cultures.

The recording industry soon sprang back as well. André discovered that the master disks that I'd done back in Berlin with Lutz Templin's band, were all carefully stacked in a basement cabinet at a large recording studio in Paris. Someone named Maria Magdalena Ritschel, which I discovered was Magda Goebbel's birth name, had completed all the payments according to the accompanying paperwork. The studio had finally shelved the project, one of many in limbo in those days, since they'd never received any final distribution instructions from Frau Ritschel.

I was about to sign a contract to release four songs into production when one of the recording engineers mentioned that a new length record, referred to as a Long Play, was due to hit the markets by early 1948 at the latest. He suggested I release all the songs I'd done with Templin's band on this new style platter, turning at 33 1/3 revolutions per minute, assuring me that the record players everyone was buying these days would be able to play them. The players could still play at 78 rpms as had been the case with the old machines. On a whim we decided to give the idea a try. And within a year, my album *Le Jazz Chaud! Musique de Helen*, one of the first LPs to hit the market, was one of the hottest jazz records throughout Europe.

Even more miraculous, however, on September 1, 1950, on what would have been Helga Goebbels' eighteenth birthday, I gave birth to a beautiful, healthy, little girl, with glowing *Zimtzucker* skin, to use Helga's fanciful name for my own skin's hue. Crying lustily, Deidre Marie Campbell emerged into her world. Andre insisted I use my last name rather than his, quipping that if her belligerent bellowing at birth -- which he claimed was audible all the way down the long corridor of the hospital -- was any indication, our daughter was destined to be an opera singer.

Chapter 39
Paris, France ~ summer/fall 1956

André and I did quite a bit of touring throughout Europe while Deidre was a toddler, but once she'd started school I wanted to remain in Paris. My voice now tired out more quickly and I felt a burning deep in my throat after a long rehearsal or concert. Although the specialists I consulted could offer no suggestions other than the usual adequate rest, herbal teas, throat lozenges and such, one doctor asked if I'd ever been exposed to radiation, even for a short period of time. The long-term effects of the fallout from the atomic bombs dropped on Japan had appalled many scientists, shocked at a continually escalating rate of cancers even a decade later. I'd been exposed for several months, of course. The bottles of Radithor hidden inches beneath my head inside poor Beverly's crib mattress back in Orange Mound were more than likely the culprit, but I refused to mention that situation to the doctor. I often felt as though my entire life had been flimsily constructed upon fractured versions of random truths.

The doctor suggested surgery to remove any tissue that might be blocking my vocal cords. I kindly declined even though he warned me that the tissue overgrowth might actually damage my voice, even bringing my career to a screeching halt. Before André and Deidre had entered my life that would have been paralyzing news. But now? Not really.

Unlike most cabaret singers, I'd kept my repertoire alive with tunes from the 1920s, '30s and the war years. The newer music coming out of America didn't thrill me at all. The young girls were worked into a frenzy over a sexy singer named Elvis Presley and his "That's All Right" single, released on a 45, yet another new record format that had evolved since the war. Europe, as usual, seemed hot to follow the Yankees' lead. The newer jazz musicians had apparently forgotten that young people wanted to dance to their music. What they were performing wasn't even remotely danceable and hot fresh blood like Elvis Presley filled that huge void.

I did record quite a few 78s and 45s, and one additional LP. When that latest LP was hitting the record stores, I had a long-awaited interview with one of my favorite French columnists, Sarah Boulanger. She was without a doubt one of the best female journalists in the business. Even though I was exhausted after a long week of rehearsals for shows premiering in the next few months, I was eager to talk with her since we'd never had an opportunity before.

"So, fill us in, Helen, about your 'mysterious past'!" Sarah began. "I find your whole story utterly fascinating. Don't you ever wonder about your early life -- your *real* parents -- and if they're still alive over there in America?"

"Well, I was adopted around age four. I really have no memories whatsoever of my previous life. So, there's not exactly a mysterious past," I smiled. I occasionally had flashes or fragments that came over me in dreams, but I didn't want to discuss these. Not with Sarah Boulanger, not with anybody ... not even with André.

"We know you were adopted by Dr. and Mrs. Campbell. Tell us again how that all come about."

"They said I crawled into their car when we stopped for petrol in Milwaukee, Wisconsin. That's where they found me, under a fur robe on the back floor when they got home. They lived further north in a town called Granville."

"I think that sounds so ... well, so romantic!" commented Sarah, scribbling a few words in her notebook. "Like something out of a Victorian novel. Go on, please!"

I didn't agree that my story was romantic at all but chose not to comment.

"I don't remember Granville very well. My adopted father, Dr. Campbell, died after an extended illness, when I was about eight years old. *Maman* and I then moved down to Memphis, Tennessee to live with her sister's family."

"And that's quite a distance away, correct?"

"Well, yes, both in miles and in ... I guess you could say lifestyle. Tennessee is farther south in the United States. It was hard for people like us to make much of a living down there. Because of the Depression hitting just after we arrived, opportunities for colored folk weren't very prevalent, you see."

"I always forget that you consider yourself a colored woman."

"Well, I am," I shrugged, wishing I hadn't mentioned this. "At least back in America. You're one or the other, unlike here where there are a lot of darker-skinned people who are, well, just considered darker-skinned people like my husband and me."

"Tell me about working with King Vidor," said Sarah, thankfully changing the subject.

"He was shooting a film, one of the first talkies, in fact, called *Hallelujah* when Mama and I arrived," I replied. "Several children from my aunt's Baptist church auditioned to be in the film so I was just well, kind of dragged along I guess you could say. It was hard, dusty work repeating actions again and again while they repositioned the camera. I was grateful they only needed us children for a few days."

"But it was fun when you got to go see yourself, I imagine."

"Well, there were two problems. Since it was one of the very first talkies no theaters had the sound machinery necessary to show it and there were no intertitles like we always had back then in silent movies. Also, because of the subject matter – it's a cast of all colored actors – it never played in theaters in the South anyway."

"Maybe that's why you've never been interested in acting in another film. But you did finally get to view the film finally, I'm assuming. When did that come about?"

"Yes, I did," I replied slowly, looking down at my hands. "Here in Europe quite a few years later … I can't remember where, though. But, more importantly, if it weren't for the film's star Nina Mae McKinney's suggestion that Mama and I go to France if I wanted to be a jazz singer, I doubt I'd ever attempted the trip." I knew that was something of a stretch but had always presented this as a reasonable explanation when questioned.

"But you worked first for several years in New York City, correct?"

"Well, mainly Harlem, but yes. It takes some time to learn your way around, same as any profession," I smiled. "I'm sure you dealt with a lot of muck becoming a journalist."

"Oh yes, without question. We all do, especially as women. So, you were here in Paris during the war. Where were you working during that time?"

"Before the Occupation I had signed on with Sidney Bechet and Mistinguett at the Moulin Rouge but ended up staying far longer than my original six-month contract … at first it was temporarily extended and then everything was at sixes and sevens when France plunged into the war. All my identification was later burned during a bombing raid up in Honfleur."

"How did you come to be up in Honfleur? Isn't that in Normandy? I thought you were in Paris most of that time."

"Yes, you're correct. I'd been sent to an apple factory in Honfleur since the cabaret work had come to a standstill and I … obviously needed the money. When the Allies invaded up there – what they refer to as D-Day now I believe -- Honfleur was fortunate and wasn't hit directly. I was just outside the town proper, however. That's where my husband, André Baptiste, was badly injured. He wasn't my husband at the time, though. We'd met while working at the factory."

"And of course, now you and André have that darling baby girl, Deidre!"

"Well, not much of a baby anymore! She's in first grade – impossible for me to believe!"

"And is she destined to dazzle the world as a jazz singer like her famous mama?"

"Well, she definitely has other interests, Sarah. She has this *huge* voice, *huge* range. And she's incredibly serious even though she's not quite six years old! In fact, she imitates opera singers all the time when she listens to the records that André collects. I must have some moldy relative dangling from the family tree somewhere out there who loved opera!"

"So that brings me back to the United States again … don't you ever wonder about your ancestry?"

"Of course," I smiled sadly. "What adopted child doesn't? But whatever roads I might have pursued towards that end have now been closed for over three decades. And I adored my adopted parents. I was most fortunate."

***

One of André's favorite American jazz groups, on numerous records that he'd collected, was a Creole of Color musician named Kid Ory and his New Orleans style early jazz music. We'd both found it amusing that all older shellac 78s recorded by colored musicians, including Mr. Ory's, were boldly stamped *Race Record* in capital letters. Ory and his Creole Jazz Band were in the middle of their first ever European tour in October, performing at the Salle Pleyel in Paris for a week. André bought us tickets as soon as they'd gone on sale. It was a clear October night as we elbowed our way through the crowd to our seats. All performances had sold out almost immediately. Ory's French had an odd accent – not exactly American, as was mine, but just kind of unusual. He opened the program with his most well-known composition, "Muskrat Ramble." I'd always enjoyed that one on André's records.

Mr. Ory then announced that he was going to sing a Creole tune called "Eh la Bas." The Creole language was a hodge podge of French, English, African and God knows what else, he joked, so although they sounded like gibberish, the lyrics actually were French Creole, which he further explained was completely different from Cajun French. As he started singing, I realized that I knew this tune and started singing along softly with him, word for word without missing one syllable. André smiled at me, a quizzical furrow on his brow.

"How do you know that tune?" he whispered in my ear, as applause rang out through the concert hall.

"I have no idea. None whatsoever, darling. But I knew every … single … word," I whispered back.

The band performed several instrumentals and then Ory sang another piece in his Creole patois that he introduced as "C'est l'autre Can-Can." Once again, I joined in quietly singing every lyric, without giving it the slightest thought.

How on earth did I know these tunes? After the concert, André and I fought our way through the congestion down to the stage to talk with Kid Ory. He was a handsome older gentleman, not much taller than I, who seemed very nimble, almost dancing onstage with his trombone. The instrument had been cautiously placed in its open case atop the piano as he deeply inhaled on his cigarette while talking with those crowded around him.

Finally working our way to the front of the group, we introduced ourselves, mentioning my work with Sidney Bechet, who was also a New Orleans musician. I told Ory I'd known all the lyrics to those two songs but had never been to New Orleans and certainly knew nothing about Creole folk tunes! The furthest south I'd ever traveled was Memphis and no one had ever spoken or sung anything in Creole French that I could remember. He'd tilted his head sideways, just staring at me for a few moments before answering, switching to English upon hearing my accent.

"Eh, probably those songs exist in French as well," he shrugged, taking another drag on his cigarette before grinding it out in an ashtray on a side table, then almost immediately reaching into his tuxedo coat pocket for his cigarette case. After lighting his second smoke, he seemed to be studying me intently. André had wandered over to join a small group surrounding the trumpet player, a young new talent named Alvin Alcorn.

"But I knew those lyrics exactly the way you were singing them, sir," I replied, shaking my head. "I didn't know what most of the words meant, though. They didn't seem like either French *or* English!"

He laughed, nodding. "I'll agree with you on that. So, your husband said you worked with Sidney Bechet over here, yes?"

"Yes, I signed a contract back in '38 to work with Monsieur Bechet and Mistinguett at the Moulin Rouge for six months. Things got kind of skewed with the war and everything. Long boring story."

234

"Ooof, Mistinguett. Never liked that woman. Feisty ol' dame. She's gotta be somethin' like a hundred years old by now!"

"Actually, she died a few months ago," I replied quietly. "Age eighty. I heard she'd been performing up until then."

He blew out a cloud of smoke.

"So, you've been a jazz singer over here all this time, huh? Ever think you might come back to the States to work?"

"I doubt it. André, my husband, has no interest and I don't have any family over there or anything. I was adopted when I was about four years old. Both of my adopted parents, the Campbells, are now deceased."

"So, you were adopted down in Memphis?"

"No, in Milwaukee. Mama and I moved down to Memphis after my father, Dr. Campbell, died when I was eight. That was about four years later."

Ory stared at me once again, crushing out his half-smoked cigarette. A trio of women pressed forward begging for his autograph on their program booklets. After he complied, he turned back towards me.

"Milwaukee, eh? Cold up there, that's fer sure!" he commented.

"I guess that's how I ended up in the Campbell's car. It was right around Christmas apparently. I crawled onto the back floor of their car in Milwaukee to get warm then fell asleep as they continued driving further north."

"What year was this, Miss Campbell?"

I was quite surprised at Ory's interest.

"In 1923. They ran missing bulletins everywhere in Wisconsin, but my real parents never showed up. It's a mystery whatever happened to them. But the Campbells were amazing. A girl couldn't ask for anything better, Mr. Ory. Other than some pretty rough years during the Paris Occupation, I've had a better life than many girls working to become cabaret singers."

"So, getting back to your early life as a hitchhiking four-year-old," he joked, "*were* you ever in Chicago?"

I shook my head, laughing.

"You're absolutely certain?"

"I suppose there's a chance the Campbells went to Chicago when I was still little, but I don't remember any trips like that. They didn't have any relatives that lived there as far as I know. While in New York I did a few small tours, but nothing that included Chicago."

A photographer walked up to Ory and asked if he could pose for a picture for one of Paris' early edition newspapers.

"Sure, no problem. Could I ask you a favor, though?"

"Just name it," answered the photographer.

"Could you take a coupla photos of Miss Campbell and me together, please, an' give me reprints of the pictures when you've got 'em developed? I have a friend back in the States who I believe would love to have a copy. She's a huge fan of Miss Campbell's work."

I frowned. I highly doubted any of my records had ever made it across the Atlantic. Nonetheless, slightly confused, I posed for two pictures with Ory just as a thickly set, middle-aged white woman tromped over to us.

"And this would be?" demanded the woman quite rudely.

"Helen Mason Campbell, ma'am," I replied.

"Yet another hopeful chanteuse looking to attach herself as a barnacle one way or another to you, my dearest. How utterly … fascinating."

"My wife, Barbara," Ory apologized.

"Glad to meet you," I said, extending my hand for a handshake the woman ignored.

"You have just enough time to kiss the baby goodnight before she falls asleep, Edouard," Ory's wife stated as she gestured to a stagehand and clomped away.

"Your grandchild?" I smiled.

"No, our um … daughter."

A seventy-year-old man with an infant daughter, I mused. Wonders never ceased! I vaguely wondered if he had any older children.

Chapter 40

Europe and New York City, New York ~ 1960-1973

As my doctor had predicted, my voice continued to falter until I was no longer able to sing for lengthy programs. Oddly, this came as a blessing. With each passing year, traveling with Deidre so that she could study with good teachers became my passion. André supported her every step of the way as well. Occasionally he was able to take the time off to join us, but he was usually working at the Moulin Rouge. He continued to suffer with serious migraines and vision problems, complications resulting from the bomb blast, but thus far, he'd been able to continue working.

Just as Mama had done while patiently waiting through my rehearsals and performances, I'd taken up making women's vests, shawls, blankets, and hats with a fun style called broomstick crochet which looked complicated but was actually quite simple. Sales of the items netted us much needed money for food, daily transportation and the occasional treat attending the theater or cinema.

As a child, every choir Deidre joined, she enriched; almost every competition she entered she won, hands down, the money from which helped further her studies. As a youngster she learned classic art songs in English, French, Italian and German, astounding one vocal coach after another. Always hungering for even more challenging music, by age nine she'd mastered twenty-two arias in those four languages.

Her disposition remained so docile, so sweet, that her teachers, accustomed to dealing with temperamental, precocious children at this level of the music orbit, remarked that she must have descended from the angels. Audience members would come up to me in tears after concerts in which she'd been given even the tiniest of meaningless solos, overwhelmed that a child at such a tender age could bring such depth, such empathy to her music.

She received stipends that allowed her to study with teachers throughout Europe. By age twelve she'd begun appearing in small operatic roles, and by age seventeen was a much sought after soloist with small semi-professional opera houses throughout France and

Austria. After her last-minute staggering debut as an understudy tackling the hellish role of Queen of the Night in Mozart's *Magic Flute* in a small London production, job offers began pouring in from excellent opera companies all over the Continent.

But Deidre had her eye on only one prize: she wanted to join the Metropolitan Opera in New York City.

The Met wasn't willing to consider giving her an audition, however, because she was a black girl. Their reason? The company still toured frequently in the South. The riots following Martin Luther King Jr.'s assassination less than five years ago still made everyone on their board of directors nervous about having a Negro singer hired on their permanent payroll. A brief walk-on as a maid or other servant presented no problem – the same was true in the motion picture industry. But performing as a member of the actual Company? No, that was quite impossible in the eyes of the board. If she built up an international reputation with say, La Scala in Italy, she might certainly be considered to appear for a limited engagement, they pointed out. Marian Anderson had performed on their stage for two operas as far back as 1955, although it was unthinkable to offer her a full-time contract. Towards that end very little had changed.

But Deidre persisted. Darker skinned women had been pursuing contracts with the Metropolitan Opera since late in the last century she'd discovered. An opera singer named Sissieretta Jones, known as the Black Patti, whose voice was said to be identical to international opera diva Adelina Patti, had been considered for a lead role with the Met. But then, due only to her race, that invitation had been cruelly withdrawn several weeks later.

When another round of auditions became available, Deidre applied a thick, claylike foundation to her lovely *zimtzucker* complexion for a series of head shot photos and only included reviews with her application that did not allude to her race. There was only one apprentice position available and somehow, Deidre was the singer they hired since her skin could apparently be sufficiently lightened to an acceptable hue it seemed. But as an apprentice she had only one year to train with the best opera coaches in New York City to be considered for an even more grueling second year apprenticeship. Very few candidates were up to that mark and the approved coaches were prohibitively expensive. Now aged twenty-three, she was determined to make this dream a reality.

André had been suffering from constant migraines and nausea for months -- so severe he wasn't able to work any longer. X-rays of his head showed a fragment of bone, undoubtedly loosened during that bomb blast almost thirty years ago, that appeared to be pressing on a nerve. He was waiting for surgery to be scheduled and was in no shape to accompany Deidre and me to New York those frigid last few days in January 1973.

I helped Deidre move into a tiny, single furnished room in Manhattan as suggested by the Met, located within a block of a subway station. I planned to stay with her for a few days, then return to Paris, as we awaited André's surgery. Manhattan looked nothing like my memories of Harlem. On my way out the building's front door to run several errands while Deidre was at a meeting, the front desk attendant motioned to me.

"Mrs. Campbell, correct?" he asked. "A package arrived for your daughter a few hours ago. You could sign for it now or I can hold it for later."

Wondering if this was more documents about her apprenticeship that might need immediate attention, I opted to sign the register and take the parcel upstairs. The package, well-padded in thick layers of wax sheeting, looked to be a small book, however, not a sheaf of legal paperwork. It was addressed to Deidre, care of the Met, then forwarded here. A glance at the return address told me it had been sent one week ago by a Mrs. Hannah Owens Barrington at the Myron Stratton Home, Colorado Springs, Colorado.

When Deidre arrived several hours later, she tore open the package, revealing a beautifully decorated book printed in 1899 titled *The Awakening* written by Kate Chopin, an author unknown to either of us. On the title page was a handwritten inscription which read:

"To my dearest Win ~ so much of me has poured itself into this creation but I fear the bounds of propriety will soon stopper the bottle. I wanted you to have a copy before it disappears from the face of the earth.
~ fondly as always, Katie O'Flaherty Chopin."

Tucked within a few pages of the first chapter was a loose note in different handwriting stating:

Deidre ~ may your voice always soar out high above the treetops – with all our love, Win, Hannah, Edouard, Emma & Octavie.

"Well," I said slowly, looking carefully through the book to see if there were any additional clues, "since she's addressed you by name, she must have seen you perform over in Europe somewhere, don't you think?"

"I suppose," Deidre replied, frowning. "An old book by an unknown author is rather an odd gift, but who knows? I'm wondering if she didn't get me confused with someone else and intended this gift for a different girl. Do you think you could call her tomorrow, *Maman*? I know a telephone call is expensive, but I'm sure you can keep the conversation short. If it's meant for another girl, I can easily just hand it over."

After Deidre left the next morning, I collected all my change and walked to the drugstore down the street. Although expensive, I opted to go with a person-to-person phone call since it might take a while to locate Mrs. Barrington. When the call was picked up, the operator asked the receptionist if Mrs. Barrington was available.

"Well … no, um, not exactly. Would your party like to speak with Mrs. Barrington's nurse?"

"Yes, please," I replied and waited for the operator to connect me through. A few moments later the nurse came on the line.

"Hello?"

"Hello, I understand you're Mrs. Barrington's nurse – is that correct?" I asked.

"Well, yes'm, this is Betty an' I *was* her nurse."

"Hi Betty … thanks … is it possible to speak with whoever is her nurse now, please."

"Well, ma'am, Mrs. Barrington passed about a week back."

"Oh … I'm … I'm so sorry to hear that, Betty! I pray it was peaceful."

"She was a real nice ol' lady, ma'am. You a relative?"

"No, I'm afraid not. I'm calling because my daughter received a book from Mrs. Barrington yesterday. We're assuming she sent it to the wrong person. Neither of us remember ever meeting her …" I said, my voice drifting off.

There was a pause on the line.

"I helped her prepare an' post that package for a Deidre somebody, ma'am. Mrs. Barrington called directory out in New York for an address. But I'll admit, she was might worked up. I was worried then it wouldn' git tuh the person she was meanin'. She sent it off in such a big rush, y'see."

"Could you tell me anything else?" I asked. "Maybe she was confused with the name. There's probably another Deidre at the Met. We've just arrived in town -- we live in Paris -- so we don't know anyone, but I can certainly find out. Is there an address book with Mrs. Barrington's things possibly?"

"Well, ma'am, I don' think so. I got a whole trunk full of Mrs. Barrington's effects here – letters, journals, old newspaper clippings an' such. No other books. I been hopin' tuh hear from somebody er 'nother so's I could get her things settled. Myron Stratton Home won't keep unclaimed items for more'n a few weeks after the owner dies, y'see. Mrs. Barrington worked here too, a long time ago, they say. Teacher, I was tol', but none of what I found had much 'bout teachin'."

"Was she in Europe over the last few years?" I asked. There was always the chance that the woman had seen Deidre perform somewhere and thought she might enjoy this little book for some reason. Sometimes elderly people had rather odd ideas.

"Europe? Oh, no ma'am," Betty chuckled. "There's no way she's been in Europe. Not recently anyways. She's been in a wheelchair fo' as long as I been here, an' I been workin' here fo' close tuh ten years."

"I see." Disappointed, I was about ready to bid the nurse goodbye. Obviously, Mrs. Barrington had mistaken Deidre for someone else entirely. Sadly, nothing could be done.

"Like I said, there ain' no books … but there's lotsa records. She used to show me all these old 78 records she'd collected – most of 'em wouldn' even play no more, y'know, they's so bad scratched. There were a few LPs too. If you're a fan of Kid Ory jazz music or there's some French lady singer that she has one or two albums … Helen somebody-er-other. If you have any interest, I'll be happy to send 'em --"

"Helen Mason Campbell?" I interrupted with a slight gasp.

"Why, yes'm that's the name exactly! An' I wasn' thinkin' straight, but the other day, that girl's last name was Campbell. I s'pose she might've been some kinda relation."

"Yes," I replied, my voice shaking. "Deidre's my daughter, Betty. And I'm Helen …"

"My stars, ain' that somethin' ma'am! Well, given that, I'm thinkin' there just might be some othuh items here you might find interestin'."

"Could you … could you please hold on to everything for another day or two until I'm able to catch a flight to Colorado Springs?"

"Why, of course, ma'am. After all these years I'm jes' tickle' pink an acquaintance finally shows up! She was one of the nicest white ladies I evuh worked with. Even though she had a bit of an ornery side, she never once lashed out at me. An' she didn' like it when people treated her like an old lady."

"You said she was a white woman?"

"Yes'm. Don' know why she treasured all them old race records an' such, but she sure did. There was a woman here – another white woman – a week or so before Mrs. Barrington died that sure got her goat, that's fo' sure. Said she was a relative, but I dunno. In fact, that woman called the mornin' that Mrs. Barrington insisted we get that old book ready to send to your Deidre, although I sure don't know *why* she had such a bee in her bonnet about it.

"Anyways, I'm in the nurses' station up here, so jes come on over to the Mary Stratton Complex just behind the hospital when you get here, ma'am. It's a big buildin', you can' miss it."

"I'm sure I can find it. Thanks so much for all your help, Betty!"

"Glad some of these things might be appreciated somewhere, Mrs. Campbell. Well, here I am just flappin' my gums like we got all day. This call must be costin' you a fortune, too, so let me sign off. As Mrs. Barrington always used to say when she hung up the telephone: 'well, so long'."

Chapter 41

Colorado Springs, Colorado – January 1973

My scheduled pre-dawn flight into Colorado Springs was delayed by almost half a day due to snowstorms battering New England. By the time I arrived at the Myron Stratton Home it was dusk. The cab driver followed the signs once we were inside the grounds and found the Mary Stratton building within a few minutes. After paying the driver, I raced up the steps to the entrance, eager to meet Betty. She was busy with patients, however, so the receptionist gave me directions to Mrs. Barrington's room, saying the monitor on that floor would unlock the door.

But when I arrived, I was surprised to find the door ajar. A blonde woman dressed in a very short tight black skirt was in the process of removing everything from the closets and emptying a large trunk in the room.

"Where's Betty?" she shot at me, looking down her nose. "She let me in several hours ago and said she'd be back within an hour or two. Probably lollygagging about the water fountain just like all you people."

Obviously, she assumed I worked here. Since Betty had referred to Mrs. Barrington as a white woman, I already knew the nurse was most likely a Negress like me.

"I don't work here," I replied. "I'm here to look through Mrs. Barrington's items as well … but it looks as though you've already done quite a good … analysis."

She squinted her eyes, glancing momentarily at me. I was certain I was a rumpled mess after hours of waiting at LaGuardia Airport, jostling about on various subway, bus, and cab rides, not to mention the rough plane trip itself.

"Who sent you?"

"No one sent me. I'm Helen Campbell." I refrained from extending my hand. "Betty said I could look through Mrs. Barrington's old jazz records to see if my husband might want any of them."

"I'm Muriel Fiske," she stated coldly with a shrug. Obviously, my name meant nothing to her, but to be fair, hers meant nothing to me either. I could see the top half of my first LP's jacket peeking out from under a pile of towels, lying on the floor near her feet. Was it a signed cover, I wondered? If so, maybe Mrs. Barrington had attended one of my performances many years ago.

"Just how did you know Mrs. Barrington if I might ask?" asked Muriel, exhaling loudly. She had thick blonde hair that she readjusted in a large clip as she sat down heavily on the bed. "Apparently the woman decided to pass away between when I met her a couple weeks ago and my return this morning. Most ungrateful."

"I didn't know her at all," I shrugged, attempting to remain noncommittal. I'd already guessed that this was the unpleasant woman Betty had mentioned on the phone.

"So, I'll assume you know nothing about the sudden disappearance of the Kate Chopin novel?"

"Kate Chopin? Is that a book title?"

"No, the *author*," she exclaimed loudly. "I've looked through all this … worthless junk … she had stuffed into that closet and trunk. All I can figure is somebody lifted it while she was snoozing in that stupid wheelchair."

"Was it yours, ma'am? You loaned it to her?"

"No, no, nothing like that," she replied, obviously exasperated with me. "But that old rude biddy was completely oblivious to the fact that the book was worth an absolute fortune. I mean, it's worth *at least* twelve thousand dollars --- probably far more. It's the first run edition of only two hundred copies and so far ahead of its time advocating for women's rights as we know them today. Ms. Chopin, who had been a very successful author up until the book's publication, was then blacklisted – fully disgraced apparently -- for the rest of her few remaining years. It was out of print until 1968. Now it's in demand everywhere! And a first edition signed copy in mint condition … well, *none* of us can even *begin* to guess its actual worth!"

"Oh," I exclaimed, now feeling very uncomfortable. "That's quite … something."

"I had to rush back to the East Coast when the Roe vs. Wade story broke last week -- I'm an editor for *Ms* magazine, which I'm sure you've heard of. Before I left, I'd called Mrs. Barrington about the book's worth. I said I'd be here to pick it up for further evaluation as soon as I returned to Colorado Springs. She really had no interest in it whatsoever. Just said I could just stop by any time. But obviously, I'm too late. Fool woman had to up and die first and the damned book sprouted legs on me!"

"I'm so sorry to hear that," I replied, not really trusting my voice. "Is that why you were visiting her in the first place? Someone had told you about this book?"

"No, not at all," she replied, waiving me off. "I came here about something completely unrelated and just happened to notice the book on her lap while I was here. She was snoozing in her chair right out there in this huge community room where anybody could have snatched it away and she'd haven't a clue."

"Ah," I said quietly. "Did you find what you *were* looking for though?"

"No, not at all. The woman's a liar, though. She claimed she'd moved here to Colorado Springs in the 1920's because her daughter was wanted for murder by Al Capone back in Chicago!"

"That *is* odd," I replied, sitting down on the only chair in the room, slightly behind the door. My legs suddenly felt wobbly. It had been a long, confusing day.

"Now I ask you, does that sound like a statement from a woman with all her marbles intact?"

"No, I suppose not."

"Suppose not? Obviously not! That woman had more than a few screws loose most of her life if you ask me. She was downright nasty to me both times I spoke with her too."

"That's unfortunate," I replied. "You were obviously only trying to help."

Suddenly, a nurse walked into the room. I was still seated partially hidden behind the door, so she didn't see me at first.

"Sorry to keep you waitin', Mrs. Fiske. Two gals was out sick today so we been way shorthanded."

"Well, Betty, I've looked through everything in here and I don't see that book. Are you sure you didn't pack it away somewhere else already?"

"No ma'am. Everythin's still here. After the coroner an' his people was here, she was takin' directly to the morgue like we do always. As is our practice, I kept the room locked 'til next of kin can claim anythin'. We allows up tuh three weeks tuh remove items they might want. I don' know tha' Mrs. Barrington had any kin, though, ma'am."

Suddenly Betty looked over at me.

"My name's Helen Campbell," I said, standing slowly, my palms sweaty against my wrinkled skirt, heart thundering in my chest. If Betty mentioned anything about our phone conversation, Muriel Fiske would know I'd lied to her about the Kate Chopin novel.

Her expression completely unreadable, Betty looked straight at me.

"You ain' allowed in here unless you is invited," she stated coldly. "I would suggest you wait downstairs in the back hall 'til someone can be up here with you. Doubt tonight."

"I was told I could take a look through Mrs. Barrington's old records," I replied, swallowing.

"Told by who?"

"I ... I don't remember her name."

"Well, that's too bad. Someone will need to be in the room with you. You can' jes' be in here all by yourself as I'm sure you are more than well aware, girl. You git while I'm finishin' up with Mrs. Fiske here, you understan'? Maybe I can fix tuh have somebody in here with you tomorrow tuh look through them records. I ain' makin' no promises, but you kin check back then."

"Thank you, Betty," I nodded, silently praising her quick thinking as I left the room.

***

I fell asleep on a couch in the dark back hallway and was awakened a few hours later by a hand lightly shaking my shoulder. It was Betty.

"My shift's over an' since I had to work a double today, I'm not on tomorrow," she whispered. "Mrs. Fiske ain' takin' nothin' from Mrs. Barrington's room. That don' surprise me none. She lef' 'bout an hour ago. I was gettin' things back organized jes' the way Mrs. Barrington always wanted 'em. She was *real* particular about such."

"Thank you for your --"

"You don' owe me no thanks," Betty interrupted, putting up her palm. "No question in my mind tha' Mrs. Barrington wanted your daughter tuh have that book."

"Deidre was just selected for an apprenticeship with the Metropolitan Opera," I said.

"I don' know nothin' 'bout opera, but that's gotta be quite an honor!"

"It is, Betty. It really is. She's the first black singer they've ever hired, even as an apprentice, although I can't for the life of me figure out how Mrs. Barrington would have known about it. I'm assuming she sent the book, which is apparently worth a lot of money, for Deidre to sell so she'd be able to afford the best instruction possible. New York's really expensive."

"That makes good sense to me, Helen. May I call you Helen?"

"Of course," I smiled.

"I have tuh mention, Mrs. Barrington really loved your first album. That band was as good as Kid Ory's she always said."

"Thanks, Betty." How bizarre to think that the beautiful wife of a murderous Nazi, intent on recording strictly forbidden jazz music behind her serially philandering husband's back, would have catapulted my singing career just after the war.

"There's somethin' else, Helen."

"Yes?"

"Follow me up to Mrs. Barrington's room, please."

As we entered the room, I noticed Betty had set out on the bed two black and white 8x10 photographs, a long letter and Sarah Boulanger's magazine interview with me from 1956, part of which had been translated into English on a separate piece of paper.

"Even though these photos are pretty old, Helen, I definitely recognized you," Betty smiled.

I remembered Kid Ory requesting that the photographer at the Salle Pleyel take our picture and then give him copies once they'd been printed. The identifying information taped on the backs read: *'Le Kid' Edouard Ory avec la chanteuse extraordinaire Helen Mason Campbell – dans la Salle Pleyel, 17 Octobre 1956* -- followed by: *'came up after show. Singer from the States. Knew "Eh, la Bas" et "C'est l'autre Can-can" but didn't know how. Said she'd never learned any Creole patois.'*

Within the article was the photo taken by the Milwaukee Police Department, identifying me as Helen Mason, holding a toy parrot. Underneath was scribbled: *'who would have guessed that Emma's and my shy little daughter Tayvie -- your granddaughter, Hannah! -- would have hitchhiked all the way to Milwaukee at age four!'*

As I read the note, a scene flashed back into focus for the first time in decades. I was cold and hungry. I'd gone outside looking for bread. A woman – my mother? -- was lying like a statue on the cold floor of our apartment. But that was in Chicago, not Milwaukee, as everyone had always assumed. There was so much more to unravel, but all that would take time. Without question I would be taking all of Hannah Barrington's treasured possessions.

I hadn't realized I was crying until Betty put her arm around my shoulders. We both sat down on the bed as daylight began streaming into the room.

"You call Deidre," said Betty quietly. "I'll make sure all of these things are carefully packed up and shipped out to you in ... Paris, right? Might be awhile gettin' out to you, of course, but ... well, I think you've been waitin' a mighty long time already … I know Mrs. Barrington had been lookin' for you for 'bout fifty years I reckon'."

I nodded, looking up at her through my tears. We both left the room and Betty showed me where the pay phone was located down the hall.

"I'm heading back home to Paris tonight, Deidre," I said after the operator connected us. I really don't want to leave Papa on his own too much longer. You know how he is – he forgets to eat! And his surgery should finally be getting scheduled within these next few days."

"Of course," she replied.

"I'm shipping home a good-sized trunk of all manner of memorabilia, sweetheart. Sorting everything out will be next to impossible, but I plan to give it my best go. Who knows, maybe I'll start writing a book … no, let's make that two … maybe even *three* books … while *Papa* is on the mend after his surgery!" I laughed, suddenly realizing I was completely serious.

"Not much time during this trip then to explore your old haunts here in *Les États-Unis, Maman!*" Deidre commented. I could always hear her smile inside her laughter.

"Well, now that you're going to be living in the States, maybe *Papa* and I will be able to sneak in a sightseeing trip at a later date when he's feeling up to it."

"I'm so sorry to keep this short, *Maman*, but I need to leave for rehearsal in just a few minutes. Any chance you know more about that book or who the names are on the note … or why this woman Hannah Barrington sent it at all?"

"I learned that the book is an author-signed, first edition of a very small print run. It's been out of print for something like sixty years and is now worth thousands of dollars, Deidre. I believe it was sent to you by Hannah Barrington to help pay for your vocal training in New York City. She mailed it just a few hours before she died a week ago."

"So, you weren't able to speak with her," Deidre replied quietly.

"No, I'm afraid not."

"But why me? That's so frightfully generous of her but I don't understand, I'm sorry. Who is … who *was* she and how on earth did she know about me or where to send the book … or anything?"

"Are you looking at the note she placed inside the book, darling? Could you read it to me again, please?"

"It says: *Deidre – may your voice always soar out high above the treetops ~ with all our love, Win, Hannah, Edouard, Emma and Octavie.*"

"I've only pieced together a tiny part of it. I'll tell you more when we have a lot more time."

"You must be exhausted, *Maman*."

"I am, sweetheart, I am. But it's a good exhausted."

"Just one more question before we hang up: other than Hannah, whom I'm assuming was Mrs. Barrington, did you find out anything about those other names on the note?"

"Yes," I said softly, tears now flowing freely down my cheeks once again. "I think all of them … but one in particular: Octavie."

"So, who was Octavie?"

"*I* am, sweetheart. My real name's Octavie Edouard Jackson … or just … Tayvie."

About the Author

A graduate from the Jordan College of Music at Butler University in Indianapolis, IN, Mim Eichmann has found that her creative journey has taken her down many exciting, interwoven pathways. For well over two decades, she was primarily known in the Chicago area as the artistic director/choreographer for Midwest Ballet Theatre, bringing full-length professional ballet performances to thousands of dance lovers annually. A desire to become involved again in the folk music world brought about the creation of her acoustic quartet Trillium, now in its 19th year, which performs throughout the Midwest and has released four cds. Among other varied music avenues, she's recorded two award-winning original children's cds and an album of early jazz vocals.

Her debut historical fiction novel *A Sparrow Alone* was published by Living Springs Publishers in April 2020 and was a semi-finalist in the 2020 Illinois Library Association's Soon-to-be-Famous Project Competition. The highly anticipated sequel, *Muskrat Ramble*, was published by LSP in March 2021. Both books are bestsellers. Her historical thriller *Whatever Happened to Cathy Martin* was published in August 2022.

Please take a moment to visit her author website at: www.mimeichmann.com.

Bibliography and Resources

Bechet, Sidney: "**Treat it Gentle**" – *an autobiography* – Twayne Publishers, Inc., 1960

Bergmeier, Horst J.P. and Rainer E. Lotz: "**Hitler's Airwaves – the Inside Story of Nazi Radio Broadcasting and Propaganda Swing**" – Yale University Press, 1997

Brown, Daniel James: "**The Boys in the Boat**" – *Nine Americans and Their Epic Quest for Gold at the 1936 Berlin Olympics* -- Penguin Books, 2013

Chilton, John: "**Sidney Bechet – The Wizard of Jazz**" – Perseus Books Group, 1987

Kater, Michael H.: "**Different Drummers**" – *Jazz in the Culture of Nazi Germany* – Oxford University Press, 1992

Kelly, Bernard: "**Returning Home**" – *Irish ex-Servicemen after the Second World War* – Irish Academic Press, 2012

Kerr, Philip: "**Berlin Noir**" – Penguin Books, 1989

Kirsch, Jonathan: "**The Short, Strange Life of Herschel Grynszpan**" – *a boy avenger, a Nazi diplomat and a murder in Paris* – W.W. Norton & Co., 2013

Larson, Erik: "**In the Garden of Beasts**" – *Love, Terror, and an American Family in Hitler's Berlin* – Random House, 2011

Meissner, Hans-Otto: "**Magda Goebbels**: *The First Lady of the Third Reich*" (English translation by Gwendolyn Mary Keeble) The Dial Press, 1980

Moore, Kate: "**The Radium Girls:** *The Dark Story of America's Shining Women*" – Sourcebooks, 2017

Nelson, Anne: **"Red Orchestra"** -- *The Story of the Berlin Underground and the Circle of Friends Who Resisted Hitler* – Random House, 2009

Pryce-Jones, David: **"Paris in the Third Reich"** – *a History of the German Occupation, 1940-1944* – Holt, Rinehart and Winston, 1981

Rosbottom, Ronald C.: **"When Paris Went Dark"** – *The City of Light Under German Occupation, 1940-1944* – Little, Brown and Co., 2014

Speer, Albert: **"Inside the Third Reich"** – *Memoirs* -- Macmillan Publishing Co., 1970

Syberberg, Hans-Jürgen: **"Hitler: A Film From Germany"** (Originally published as **"Hitler, ein Film aus Deutschland"** – translation by Joachim Neugroschel, 1985) -- Rowohlt Taschenbuch Verlag GmbH, 1978

Vassiltchikov, Marie: **"Berlin Diaries 1940-1945"** – Random House, 1985

Vidor, King: **"A Tree is a Tree"** – *an autobiography of a great director – the Golden Age of the Movies from 2-reeler to 3-D* – Harcourt, Brace and Company, 1952

Von Oelhafen, Ingrid and Tim Tate: **"Hitler's Forgotten Children"** – *a true story of the Lebensborn Program and One Women's Search for Her Real Identity* – Penguin Random House, 2016

Wyllie, James: **"Nazi Wives"** – *The Women at the Top of Hitler's Germany* – Macmillan Co., 2019

Films/Documentaries

"Der Untergang" ("The Downfall") – directed by Oliver Hirschbiegel, 2004

"Hallelujah" – directed by King Vidor, 1930

"Zwartboek" ("Black Book") – directed by Paul Verhoeven, 2006

"How Hitler Lost the War" – written and directed by Robert Denny, 2005

"The Sorrow and the Pity" – directed by Marcel Ophuls, 1969

"Un Village Français" ("The French Village") – French television series, 2009-2017

Countless shorter film documentaries, silent and narrated film clips including but not limited to: the French Occupation, Berlin, Kristallnacht, Herschel Grynszpan, Charlie and His Orchestra, Moulin Rouge, Mistinguett, Sidney Bechet, Lutz Templin, Fritz Brocksieper, Lida Baarova, Magda Goebbels, Joseph Goebbels, Helga Goebbels, Adolf Hitler, Orange Mound, TN, Josephine Baker, Franklin D. Roosevelt, Winston Churchill, King Vidor, Nina Mae McKinney, Radithor.

on Cori's shoulders. "Hey, sweet girl. Royal and Rook just showed up."

The little girl beamed. "Rook came to see me, too?"

Cori hadn't seen my other brother since he'd been discharged from the SEALs a few weeks earlier.

Grinning down at her, Maddie gently tucked a lock of loose hair behind her ear. "He sure did. Why don't you go see them? Court will be down in a few minutes."

Cori instantly brightened. "Okay!" She whirled and raced around Maddie, her footsteps thundering down the stairs seconds later.

Maddie folded her arms and glared at me. "Are you *fucking* kidding me, Court Woods?"

Shit. First- *and* last-named.

And then, because why not make it a goddamn party, Linc popped up over her shoulder. His brown hair was mussed, and he'd clearly just woken up, but his eyes snapped open wide at the scene he'd stumbled into.

"Who the hell is this bitch?" the woman on my other side practically growled.

My eyes slid closed, but not before I saw Maddie's eyes flash and Linc mime the Catholic cross over his heart.

This wasn't gonna end well.

"You're in *my* house, *bitch*," Maddie snarled, coming into the room like she damn well owned it, because she did.

Well, she and her husband/fiancé, Ryan Cain. It was a complicated relationship. First he'd thought she was her evil twin and hated her, then they fell in love and got married. After that Maddie had been kidnapped and institutionalized by her psycho dad, who also had their marriage annulled by a shady-ass judge. But it had all worked out when Ryan shot Maddie's father and killed the bastard.

They planned on getting married again at some point, but they both seemed content to use the *wife* and *husband* labels no matter their legal relationship status.

I was happy for them, except for right now—because Ryan, although one of my best friends, was also Corinne's very overprotective big brother. The only thing he loved as much as Maddie was Cori, and the girl I'd brought into their house had just insulted them *both*.

Yeah, I was twenty kinds of fucked, and none of them in the fun way.

I glanced over my shoulder. "Look, Gloria—"

Her face pinched. *"Gretchen."*

"Totally what I said," I went on, not giving a shit. "It's been fun, but this?" I gestured to the space between us. "We're done. Time to go."

Her jaw dropped open, and I had the tiniest memory spark of her on her knees, opening her jaw just as wide as my cock sank into it.

Rubbing the back of my neck, I shivered as something a lot like shame prickled up my spine.

Maddie looked at me, and beneath the anger, I saw the disappointment. It was one thing for me to act like a fuckup on my own, but Cori had been dragged into this. Cori, who had already been dealt a shitty hand after her dad tried to kill her and then her house burned down. And that was after losing her grandfather, the one stable adult role model she'd had in her life.

She went to a special school that excelled in helping kids and young adults with autism. The past few months had been hell, but she'd slowly been turning it around. She'd been so damn excited when Ryan and Maddie planned to bring her here, to their new home, for a long weekend.

And I'd ruined it.

"You heard him, honey," Maddie practically spat. "Get out of my house."

With a huff, Gretchen got up, totally naked. Linc let out a little cough and looked away, his shoulders shaking with silent laughter.

Bending over to pick up her dress, Gretchen flashed me her ass and cunt, even giving a little exaggerated wiggle as she shimmied into the strappy green fabric. I cleared my throat and looked away, what was left of my morning wood going completely soft.

I shot Maddie another look, hoping it conveyed my apologies for all of this.

Her eyes narrowed and her jaw clenched.

Gretchen slipped on her heels and looked back at me. "Court, I—"

"I will literally drag you out by your hair," Maddie threatened. "Then I'll kick your ass for making me mess up my manicure."

Gretchen spun. "I'd like to see you try."

"Whoa," Linc snapped, all teasing evaporating as he crowded Maddie's back, his eyes shooting fire at Gretchen. "Time to get the fuck out, skankalicious. Go peddle your STIs somewhere else."

"Hold up." Maddie lifted a finger that she then pointed at Linc. "We don't slut-shame in this house, remember? We talked about this."

Linc nodded, looking properly chagrined. "You're right. I apologize to Court's consenting fuck buddy. That being said, our consent to her being in *this* house is fucking over, so time to go. Whether or not you have any sort of disease is between you and your doctor. And possibly Court, if he didn't wrap it up." He shot me a smirk. "You *did* use protection, right, man?"

I flipped him off, because of fucking course I had. The empty condom wrapper was lying in plain sight next to my bed. I *always* wrapped it up.

Gretchen gasped, a hand flying to her ample—and fake—tits. She looked at me like I was going to save her. "Court, *do* something."

"Okay." I got up, not giving a shit that I was naked, and grabbed her arm, propelling her to the doorway.

Linc pulled Maddie back to give me space to push her through the open frame. "Get out." I let her go and stalked back into the room, then grabbed my boxer-briefs and yanked them on.

She sucked in a breath, likely ready to start screeching like a pterodactyl again. I snatched her purse off the dresser and pulled out her wallet.

"Hey!"

I checked the license. "Gretchen Slutter."

Linc cracked up. "Jesus, that's really your name?" He turned to Maddie with his hands up. "This is me *not* commenting on how appropriately named Miss Slutter is. I'm sure it's a strong name, originating from the land of... Sluts? Is that a city? Country? I just need to know where all the Slutters hail from."

Maddie scoffed and looked up at the ceiling, probably praying for patience.

I ignored the fact that my best friend was an idiot. "558 Morgate Lane." I dropped the card and wallet back into her purse, then crossed the room and handed it to her. "Get the fuck out of our house, Gretchen Slutter, or I'll ruin your fucking life."

She flinched back, holding her purse to her chest like a shield.

Linc cleared his throat. "I'll show you out."

Gretchen shot me a wounded look but followed him without any further complaint, leaving me alone with Maddie.

"Don't say it," I muttered, turning away from her.

"I haven't said it, Court," she retorted. "I didn't say it when you brought the first girl here. Or the fifth. Or the twenty-seventh. You're an adult, and if you want to act like a boy who just figured out how to use his dick by fucking your way through the city, I'm not gonna stop you."

I clenched my teeth, my jaw aching as I faced her and let her lay into me.

She lifted a finger. "You want to throw your life away because you're too chickenshit to deal with actual emotions? Fine. But when your fuckups touch Cori? That's not okay, Court, and I'm not going to act like it is."

"I messed up," I murmured, scrubbing my hands over my face.

"You think?" she deadpanned.

I sighed. "I'll make it up to Cori."

"Goddamn right you will," she grumbled. "That little girl has been through *hell*. Ryan and I want this house to be her safe haven. Her *home*. When she comes here, she needs to know everything is okay and she's loved."

"I know," I said, feeling like utter shit. "I'll try... I'll do better."

"You'd fucking better," a deep voice snapped. Ryan glared at me, his large frame filling the doorway and practically vibrating with rage. He jabbed a finger at me. "You can start by explaining why my little sister is downstairs, upset that some woman yelled at her and used 'swear-jar language.'"

I winced. "Ryan—"

"I'll go check on her." Maddie moved to squeeze past him.

Ryan settled a hand on her hip, his gaze meeting hers and doing that weird-ass thing where it was like they were talking without actually speaking.

Maddie lifted a hand to his jaw, and his expression softened. "She'll be fine," she assured him, and rolled to her tiptoes, kissing him quickly.

Ryan clamped his hands on her waist and pulled her against him, devouring her mouth until she swayed a little on her feet. Only then did he let her go, watching her walk away with a private smile that vanished the second he looked at me. "What the hell were you thinking?"

"I wasn't. I was drunk and… Shit, Ry, I'm sorry."

His lips twisted into a feral snarl. "The pussy parade ends here, man. You want to bury your feelings with your dick, be my guest, but get out of my damn house. I won't have this shit touching Cori or Maddie again. My girls have been through enough."

I wasn't going to point out that Maddie had hardly needed protecting this morning. If anything, Gretchen was lucky Maddie had let her leave without needing to see a plastic surgeon.

Maddie had changed a lot in the months we'd known her. She'd gone from unsure and drowning in our bullshit to thriving and confident. But nothing brought out her protective-mama-bear side quite like Corinne.

"I got it," I agreed, my voice rough and weary. Damn, I was tired of feeling like this. I was just shy of twenty-two, and I felt like an old man.

Ryan stared at me. "Court, you saw what I went through with Mads. You had a front-row seat to all my fuckups and what it took to get her back."

Yeah, I had. But that wasn't the same—there was no evil twin in my past to blame shit on.

My spine stiffened. "Your point?"

"If I can fix what I broke with Maddie, you can fix shit with—"

"Don't." I cut him off and spun away, not wanting to hear it.

Silence lingered for another moment, so long that I thought he'd left.

"She's staying in Paris," Ryan finally admitted.

It was like being donkey-kicked in the balls as a vise squeezed my chest. All the air whooshed out of my lungs.

"After her mom's heart attack and filing for divorce from Malcolm, her grandparents convinced her to defer her final semester, since she already has the credits to graduate. Maddie hates that she won't have her best friend here for the next five months, but Bex is still planning on coming back to Pacific Cross for college."

My eyes drifted shut. It didn't matter. This was my last semester at PCU before I started law school. I'd already been accepted to Stanford. Odds were I wouldn't see her when she came back.

Which was for the best.

"I'm not going to tell you what to do," Ryan started, "but you need to accept that she's part of our lives now, and that isn't changing. This isn't like when we were kids, and you wrote her off because of what your dad did."

I snorted at the way he'd dumbed down one of the most pivotal, life-changing moments of my existence.

"She's Maddie's best friend, and Maddie's one of us now. You can't avoid her forever."

I swallowed and stared blankly ahead. "Are we done?"

He let out a snort. "Yeah. We're done. Get yourself together, because I don't care how hungover your ass is—you promised Cori you'd take her fishing. Either honor that promise, or tonight, you'll sleep with them. Got it?"

Nodding, I went into the bathroom and slammed the door closed behind me before stripping out of my boxers. I stumbled into the shower and twisted a few knobs. The water rushed out, slapping me across the face, chest, and ass from several angles. Usually I loved taking my time in the shower, but I had a feeling Ryan would drag my ass out of here if I took too long.

Bracing a hand on the shower wall, I squeezed my eyes shut as the water rushed over my head. With a groan, I popped my eyes open and looked down. A red smear snagged my attention.

What. The. Fuck?

Christ, was that *blood* on my dick?

I grabbed my cock with my free hand, sweeping a thumb across the red and wondering if I'd somehow broken the only part of me that still seemed capable of functioning. It took a second, but the red wiped off.

So, not blood. Lipstick.

I counted that as a win. Probably the only one I'd have today.

CHAPTER 2

COURT

I took the fastest shower possible before brushing my teeth. With a towel wrapped around my hips, I stepped into my bedroom. I was so preoccupied with wallowing in my bad decisions that I missed the asshole sitting on my bed.

And I was too slow to dodge the bone-crunching punch that landed on my ribs. Something shifted and popped as I wheezed out a breath. A second fist landed in my gut, doubling me over.

"Your ass is so goddamn lucky that I don't want to explain to Cori why I rearranged your face," Royal spat.

I braced a hand on the wall, trying to regain the ability to inhale. "Hey, big brother."

"Don't give me that shit," he snarled, more surly than usual, but that wasn't surprising. The man was a stone-cold killer who could terrify a death-row inmate into pissing his pants, but he turned into a marshmallow for Corinne Cain.

"Ryan and Maddie already read me the riot act," I snapped, irritation licking through my veins.

"You think I give a fuck?" Royal's voice rumbled low, practically a growl. His gaze swept down my body, his lip curling in disgust. "Jesus, what the hell is wrong with you? That bent out of shape over a girl who —correct me if I'm wrong—*you* pushed away. Again."

My hands knotted into fists, my knuckles popping. "Oh, that's rich coming from the poster boy for emotional dissociation."

He smirked, his head tilting. "Better than acting like a lovesick little bitch who's too scared to face reality."

Fury pounded in my skull, and I threw a wild right hook before I even finished letting the words settle in. Royal blocked the punch with practiced ease before landing another blow to my ribs. It hurt, but I knew he'd pulled back. My oldest brother was built like a goddamn tank and had fists the size of ham hocks. I'd seen him dent a dude's skull in a single blow.

If Royal Woods wanted me comatose or dead, there wasn't much I'd be able to do to stop him. Yeah, I knew how to fight, but I was breaking the cardinal rule: Never fight with emotion.

But it seemed like all I could do was mess up.

Royal studied me, the anger etched into his face morphing into something that looked a lot like concern. "Come on, kid. Talk to me."

I bristled at his tone. I was seven years younger than him, but sometimes he felt more like my father than Jasper Woods had ever been. My father—*our* father—was a sadistic asshole who had fallen off the grid when we took down Maddie's and Ryan's dads a few weeks earlier. I wasn't stupid enough to think Jasper was gone for good. No, he was holed up somewhere, likely plotting his next steps.

I might've hated the man, but there was no denying he was smart as hell. He'd been appointed one of the youngest generals in the history of the United States Army. He'd fought and manipulated his way to the top, even going so far as to sire his own army of sons.

Looking at Royal, I could see the similarities between us, traits dear old Dad had passed on. The straight Roman nose, the strong jaw. But I had dark eyes like my mother, while Royal's were a blueish gray that looked like *his* mother's.

Jasper couldn't even use the excuse that he'd had an affair because my mom's pregnancy with me had complications that left her infertile after giving birth. Royal, Rook and Bishop were older than me, while our other brothers, Knight and Castle, were younger. I was right in the middle. Oddly enough, Jasper had only one mistress, Holly. He'd been with her since they were teens, but she wasn't high class enough to be considered wife material, so he'd relegated her to being a decorative side piece who'd birthed him an army.

Over the course of a decade, Holly had given Jasper six sons and a stillborn daughter. Only five of my brothers were still alive. The loss of her daughter and son had broken Holly, and I knew it pissed my brothers off to no end that she remained Jasper's doormat. Holly never fought Jasper.

Even though he was responsible for killing their son.

I'd never known King, who'd been closest in age to me. He'd been born six months before me, and his death had been the catalyst that ultimately led to a naked woman shouting at my best friend's autistic sister less than thirty minutes earlier.

God, my life was fucked. I was blaming my dead brother for my world going to shit.

"Drop it," I snapped, turning away and stripping off the towel to get dressed. If Royal had an issue with having my ass in his face, he could leave.

I finished pulling on jeans and a Henley before turning back to my brother, who was watching me with his arms folded over his massive chest. After a beat, his gaze wandered around the room. "Love what you've done with the place."

I ignored the tone, because I knew he was right. Since moving in, I hadn't done a damn thing with the space. The only furniture in the room was my bed, a black dresser, a matching desk with a chair, and a black bookcase that was empty except for a single framed photograph, taken at Ryan and Maddie's wedding, of them with me, Linc, Ash, my brothers, and… her.

The photo was there only because Maddie had put it there when we first moved in. I'd tried more times than I could count to throw it in the trash, but every time I did, I put it back.

I told myself I left it there to make Maddie happy, but my subconscious was all too happy to remind me that I needed to see it when I woke up after a weekend bender and wound up cuddling the goddamn picture like it was my blankie.

All because of her.

My heart clenched, and I damn near gasped. I'd written the organ off as dead long ago, but, of course, *she* was the one who could make it beat again.

It was always her.

Following my gaze, Royal ambled to the bookcase and lifted the frame. "Talk to her."

Grimacing, I sat on my bed to pull on my socks and boots. "Are we leaving?"

Royal glanced back at me, his expression a blank mask. "Are you done being a bitch?"

I shoved to my feet. "Can we not, man? I'm tired and—"

"You think I'm not?" Royal challenged, arching his brow. "Between you and Rook, I'm ready to buy stock in Midol or Tampax."

I cocked my head. "Look at you, knowing your way around feminine hygiene products."

"With my brothers turning into pussies, someone has to," he drawled.

"What's wrong with Rook?" I asked.

Royal rolled his eyes. "Something about his dead teammate's baby mama drama or something. Pretty sure he fucked her, and now he's got his panties in a twist that he overstepped."

My eyes widened. Rook, until recently, had been a Navy SEAL. His team had been attacked and dismantled when one of their own had betrayed them, killing one of Rook's teammates and injuring others. The guy who'd died had left behind a pregnant wife, and when her life had been threatened, Rook had moved in to protect her and her newborn.

I'd never pegged Rook, basically a slightly shorter and leaner version of Royal, as one to turn into Mr. Mom, but I had copious amounts of baby pics he'd sent through our family text thread to prove otherwise. We'd all known he had a thing for the baby's mom, Emerson, but falling for the widow of a guy you'd considered a brother tended to complicate shit.

After the threat had been neutralized, Rook had moved out of Emerson's life.

Or so I'd thought.

"He told you he hooked up with her?" I stared at him.

Royal sighed, like this whole conversation was annoying even though he'd started it. "We went down to San Diego to talk to that informant and meet with Ford. I formally offered him a job with Phoenix."

"He take it?"

"He's considering it," Royal answered. "While we were there, Rook was with Emerson and the kid. A lot. Next thing I know, he's telling me we need to come back to Los Angeles."

"And from that you deduced he slept with her?" I tried to smother an amused smile.

He shot me a bland look. "Only a few reasons a man runs away from a pretty woman he's obsessed with like his dick is on fire—he fucked up, or he fucked her and *then* fucked up."

"You're a regular Dr. Phil, huh?" I glared at him.

"You saying I'm wrong?"

I scoffed. "I'm saying hearing that from a guy who's had more one-night stands than Dodger Stadium has seats is pretty fucking funny."

He moved until he was right in front of me, his boots hitting mine. "That so?"

I just smirked.

"Call Bex."

My hands came up to shove him back, a snarl pulling at my lips. He caught my wrists in his hands and hooked a leg behind my knees. My ass was on the ground before I could tell him to fuck off.

"See?" Looming over me, he arched a pointed eyebrow. "You're a fucking mess."

He held out a hand to help me up, but I slapped it away and stood on my own. "Fuck you."

"Pretty sure you've been doing enough fucking for all the Woods brothers," he muttered. "Are you trying to see if you can rot your dick off before you hit twenty-three?"

I winced, thinking of the lipstick-blood scare in the shower, and realized he wasn't too far from the mark.

"It's complicated," I finally said, my shoulders sinking.

"Then un-complicate it," he retorted, eyeing me. "Or at least figure out a way to function as a human being that's a part of this team. It'd be nice if we could depend on you to be there when shit's going down."

My spine straightened, alarm ringing through me as it dawned on me that I hadn't just checked out with my friends; I'd checked out on our damn business. "Meaning?"

He shoved his hands into his pockets and rocked back on his heels, his jaw tight. "The informant I talked to finally got back to me last night. He thinks he tracked Jasper down to a town in Kosovo."

I grimaced. "No extradition."

"Exactly, but he's still in Europe, since that's where Kent's operation is based. Word has it he'll be traveling to Brussels in a week or two for a meeting with a few of the higher ups in the European and Asian markets, but the guest list has been vague. All my contact knows is that Jasper's men are providing security on the ground."

I hissed out a breath. Rising in the ranks of the military had never been our father's endgame. No, he'd used all the contacts he'd amassed over decades in the armed forces to create the most elite group of mercenaries money could buy. Men who obeyed the person writing their check without blinking about things like laws and morals. Black Box Ops was his baby now, and he hired the best and most twisted of the armed forces to do his bidding as foot soldiers.

"Does Linc know?" I asked.

"That his father is a sick motherfucker who sells women and children to the highest bidder? Pretty sure he's aware," Royal remarked, his tone cool.

"Fucker," I snapped. Of course Linc was aware that his dad, Kent Westford, was as despicable a human being as they came. Sure he hid it well behind a billion-dollar hotel empire, but it was all a front for his human-trafficking enterprise.

It was what had bonded Ryan, Ash, Linc, and I together. Why we'd started Phoenix International, a company we all—along with Maddie, now—had an equal share in. We'd formed the company with the sole purpose of destroying our fathers, vowing that we'd never inherit our father's sins.

Months earlier, we'd had a huge win by taking out Maddie's and Ryan's dads. Gary Cabot and Beckett Cain had been handling all their dirty money, laundering it and investing it so they could funnel it right back in. Kent was the brains of the entire operation, and Jasper provided all the muscle needed to transport and deliver purchases.

Taking my father out of the equation would leave Kent vulnerable. We'd already shaken their empire by bankrupting several of their ventures, but that meant Kent had simply funneled more of his own personal finances into the hotels and seedy clubs he ran under shell corporations. If we could eliminate Jasper, then Kent would be on his own.

Layer by layer, we were making progress.

"I think you and Rook should go to Brussels. See who Dad is meeting with. If we can cut their supply lines, it'll be easier to break them," Royal said.

"You want Rook and me to go?" I stared at him, incredulous.

He inclined his head. "Okay, Bishop, too. I think you and Rook need some perspective beyond your dicks. You've forgotten what we're fighting for."

"The fuck I have," I spat. I'd seen firsthand the shit our fathers were capable of. It was the stuff that gave the boogeyman nightmares.

His hands came down heavy on my shoulders, squeezing to just the point of painful as he looked me in the eye. "You *have*. You've been spiraling since Christmas, little brother. We all thought you'd pull yourself out of it—fuck knows you always have—but this time, it's different."

I glared at him. "Your pep talks suck."

"You want pep talks, find a therapist. You want absolution for your sins, find a priest. You want to man the fuck up, then you get your ass on a plane in a week and start acting like you give a shit about people other than yourself. I'm not your keeper, Court, but I *am* the guy who will tell you it's time to grow a pair and act like a goddamn adult."

I jerked back like he'd hit me again, but the ironclad grip he had on my shoulders didn't let me go far.

"Phoenix is at a tipping point—which you know—and you're choosing *now* to live out your douchey playboy fantasies instead of acting like a grown goddamn man? I'm fucking embarrassed for you, bro. You're acting like—" He cut himself off, leaving the unspoken words looming between us.

Ice settled in my bones. "Say it," I ground out.

"It doesn't matter." Royal sighed, dropping his arms.

"Too much of a pussy to say it?" I challenged, daring him to finish the sentence.

His gray eyes cut to me, unflinching as steel. "You're acting like Jasper."

I flinched. A sucker punch to the jaw would've hurt less. Hell, a rusty icepick through my eye would've been easier to handle than being compared to that sadistic prick.

Still not done, he jabbed a finger into my chest. "*You* were the one who brought me into Phoenix. *You* convinced me and our brothers that this wasn't about some rich little boy lashing out at Daddy for not being hugged enough. You said you wanted to make a difference. Has that changed?"

I shook my head, mute and a little numb.

His head tilted. "Then get off your ass and be the man I know you can be."

"That simple, huh?" I asked roughly, my voice hoarse.

He raised his hands a little. "No, asshole, it's *not* that simple. It's a goddamn fight every motherfucking day, but it's what we do. Unless you're so far gone on the pity train that you forgot that."

I drew my shoulders back. "I haven't forgotten."

"Then get your head back in the game, Court, because it's not fair for us to carry your ass." Royal reached up to slap the back of my head.

I blocked the shot, grabbing his wrist and twisting his thumb until the muscle and tendons pulled tight.

He smiled, the unfamiliar expression catching me off guard for a beat. "Not bad, little brother." Leaning into the pressure of my hold, he popped his thumb out of its joint.

"Jesus," I swore, staring at his hand in shock. And then I was on my ass again, him having used my surprise as leverage.

Smirking down at me, he casually popped the thumb back into place without so much as a grimace. "But not good enough."

"You're a fucking psycho," I muttered, shaking my head. This time I let him help me up.

A harsh laugh rumbled from his chest. "Don't ever forget it."

CHAPTER 3

BEX

"Rebecca!"

I was halfway down the stairs when I heard my grandmother call my name, her French accent giving it a posh spin that I'd always loved. "Yes, Mémé?" I trailed my hand down the ornate oak bannister and used the scrolling loop at the bottom to swing myself around and into the parlor like I was eight, not eighteen.

Mémé looked up at me from where she sat perched on the edge of a floral wingback chair near the fireplace, her legs crossed at the ankles and a deep frown set in her face. Behind her was a large picture window that looked out on a courtyard that bloomed a riot of brilliant colors in the spring, but right now, deep into winter at the beginning of February, showcased a few random snow flurries blowing around bare branches.

"Rebecca, this blasted contraption is yet again refusing to alert me to new calls. Your Aunt Celeste has been trying to get through, but it won't make a lick of noise." With a heavy sigh, she held the top-of-the-line iPhone out to me. "You know I'm utter rubbish when it comes to these new devices."

Grinning, I took the phone and unlocked it with her passcode—her and Papa's anniversary—before checking her settings. I turned the phone over, smothering a smirk when I saw the orange peeking up at me. She'd turned off her notifications. *Again.*

I quickly righted the issue and handed the phone back. "All better."

She exhaled with a happy smile. "Thank you, chérie. Would you care to join me?" She motioned to the adjacent velvet couch, and I couldn't refuse. The soft fabric was like a hug, so familiar and precious that everything seemed a little less awful.

I'd always loved my grandparents' home in Paris. Situated on a quaint street in the 16th arrondissement, with a lush, green park at one end and gas lamps illuminating the cobblestone street at night, it was like something out of another life.

The three-story château had been in our family for over three hundred years, with some of the stone and wood inside dating back even longer. With vaulted ceilings, gold accents, and ornate lines, it made me feel as though I lived in a fairytale. My cousins and I had spent summers playing hide and seek for hours in the home's three stories and numerous rooms.

Over the years it had been updated—carpets replaced, walls painted and papered, and plumbing updated—but it had kept the same feel as the original home. It was ornate and decadent, but not over-whelmingly so.

The main parlor was Mémé's favorite, with its large fireplace and furniture that looked like it had been plucked straight out of the Regency era. At one point, the producers of some streaming company making a TV show out of a famous historical romance series had tried paying my grandparents to use the location for filming. They'd declined, not wanting to have their lives disrupted by TV crews and actors.

I'd sat in this room for hours with Mémé. She was usually reading or working on her latest crochet project. I was usually reading, too, or watching a movie on my laptop with my earbuds in. We didn't need to fill the silence with chatter; we were happy just being near each other.

"Have you spoken to your maman?" Mémé asked, arching a delicate brow. At seventy-nine years old, she was still in shape and had an elegance that commanded respect and awe. Her skin was radiant, her eyes a sparkling blue that my grandfather claimed captivated him.

"She's working late," I replied with a tight smile.

Mémé sighed, looking mildly distressed. "She works too hard. That's why she had her episode."

Episode was one way of putting it. Most people would call it a heart attack, but Mémé preferred to give things a more positive spin. It was an endearingly naive trait that everyone in the family smiled about.

But this time, Mémé was right. Mom's heart attack had been scary, and it was brought on by a genetic flaw no one had noticed. Her heart had been a ticking bomb in her chest, and years of prolonged stress had finally led to it seizing up one night a few months earlier.

When Mom had filed for divorce from my father, sold off her private practice, and decided to start over in Paris, I'd never expected to stay with her. I had a life in California. Granted, that life, up until the past six months, had kinda sucked, but still.

Okay, that was a lie.

The past six months hadn't exactly been a picnic. In addition to Mom's heart attack and my parents' divorce, I'd also learned that my father was into some seriously shady shit with some seriously messed up people. Plus I'd been drugged, almost raped, and kidnapped. Oh, and I'd almost died in a huge earthquake.

It had been an eventful few months.

I'd come to Paris with Mom for Christmas because she'd needed a break. But when we'd arrived, she'd sat me down and told me that she planned to live here permanently, and she wanted me to stay. If not for college, then at least for the immediate future.

It took a lot of soul-searching, but I'd finally realized that her reasons for needing a fresh start were why I needed one, too. At least a temporary one, and since I'd been a total nerd who devoted all her time to classes and studying—the byproducts of being a bullied adolescent at a private boarding school—I'd done enough work to be done with high school. Since I was already of age, I filled out the necessary paperwork and graduated six months early.

Staying in Paris for a few months meant I could sort some shit out before diving into college in the fall as a freshman. I'd already decided I wanted to be pre-med, following in my mom's footsteps. But where she'd focused on private practice and then built a career as a private concierge doctor to the elite, I wanted to focus on oncology. Specifically pediatric oncology.

As if sensing my thoughts, Mémé fixed me with a look. "I do wish you'd reconsider your decision, bébé."

My cheeks warmed, and I ducked my head. "I know, Mémé, but I want to help kids the way I was helped."

She made a sound in the back of her throat. "Not everyone will have the outcome you did, Rebecca. Can your heart handle that?"

She was right. I'd first been diagnosed with leukemia as an infant. But I was told I'd beaten that easily.

It was when the disease resurfaced when I was nine that it became hell. I'd gone through ten brutal months of treatments and chemo. For the longest time, I'd thought that was what had broken my parents' marriage; that my sickness and the stress of keeping me alive had destroyed their relationship.

It wasn't until recently that I'd learned it wasn't my cancer that had destroyed it at all; it was my dad and the decisions he'd made back then, including almost getting me killed.

I wished I could remember, but that time in my life was shrouded in confusion. I'd done some research, and apparently there was a thing called dissociative amnesia where the brain essentially blocked out traumatic events.

Shoving those thoughts away before I spiraled, I focused on my grandmother while twisting a lock of dark hair streaked with faded teal around one finger. I needed to redo the color. Or change it. "I want to help people."

Her face fell a bit, but she reached over and patted my hand. "Of course you do. You are like your mother in that way." Her blue eyes hardened. "And unlike your father, damn his soul."

"Mémé." I sighed, shaking my head. I wasn't going to defend my dad. Especially not since he'd made a few half-hearted attempts to reach out to me but then seemed to give up. I hadn't heard from him since he'd sent a simple *Merry Christmas* text five weeks ago.

The past six months had been crazy, and I needed a break.

My phone rang, and I pulled it from the back pocket of my jeans and grinned when I saw it was a video chat request from my bestie. I looked at my grandmother, but she was already taking her crochet project from the small basket beside her chair.

I hurried from the room and detoured through the kitchen as I answered the call. "Hey, girl!"

Maddie grinned at me, her blonde hair a mess of loose waves around her face. "Bex! Have I mentioned how much I hate that you're on the other side of the planet?"

"Only every day," I drawled with a laugh, opening one of the industrial-size refrigerators and snagging a tangerine. After I closed the door, I started jogging up the back staircase toward my bedroom.

"You left me all alone with these four," she whined, the camera jostling as she hurled herself onto the couch.

I chuckled. "Well, you're the one who asked them to move in. You and Ryan could've had your own place..."

"With all the sex in all the rooms anytime I wanted," she agreed with a wistful sigh. "Instead, I have to stick to our bedroom, unless I know for a fact the guys will be out for a while."

"Hussy," I teased, entering my bedroom. I kicked the door shut with my foot and beelined for the giant beanbag chair in the corner by my bookshelf. It easily could've fit three people, and the ultra-plush faux-mink fur was the softest thing I'd ever touched.

She ducked her head. "Guilty, but my husband is seriously talented with—"

"Lalala!" I started singing loudly, not all that interested in hearing about her sexcapades with her super-hot husband.

"Fine," she huffed, "but you know I couldn't leave them behind. They're like a matching set, and I wasn't breaking up the band."

"That was a lot of metaphors," I commented, situating the phone so she could still see me before starting to peel the tangerine. The sweet citrus scent made my mouth water.

She waved a dismissive hand, the screen again almost tumbling over. "Whatever. How's Paris? I already convinced Ryan we need to come visit you for spring break."

"Paris is…" I glanced out the large window. Beyond it I could see part of the Eiffel Tower. "Paris is what I need."

Maddie's face fell a bit. "Not gonna lie, Bex. I was totally hoping you'd say it sucked and you were coming back to California."

"Not for a few months," I said, my tone soft. I hated disappointing her. She was my best friend. Hell, she was one of my *only* friends. I hadn't been popular in school. Actually, it was the opposite. I'd been the pariah, always on the outside, until Maddie showed up and changed everything.

She sighed again. "I get it. I mean, needing the break. But I miss you."

"I miss you, too." My lips turned down in a sad sort of pout.

She sucked in a deep breath and forced a smile. "Okay, tell me all about your life."

"We just talked two days ago!" I reminded her with a laugh.

She looked offended. "And in that time, you could've been swept off your feet by a sexy Parisian man with an eight-pack and a black beret who bakes you fresh croissants daily."

"That's oddly specific." I grinned as someone spoke off camera.

Maddie's gaze flicked above the screen, her mouth dropping open and her cheeks turning red. "Ryan, I was *kidding*. I don't give a shit about sexy guys in Paris or anywhere else." She paused and winked at me. "Don't get married until you're forty, Bex. Husbands are highly overrated."

I giggled as her eyes went wide. A second later, Ryan appeared in part of the screen. He shot me a wolfish smile before lowering his lips to her ear and whispering something that made her gasp, her jaw falling open.

Smirking, Ryan drew back and traced the outline of her parted lips with his finger. "I accept, baby. But finish with your friend first." To me he added, "See ya later, Bex."

Still flustered, Maddie looked back at me, but I could see the lust glazing her eyes. "I swear, that man…"

"Still don't wanna know," I reminded her.

"Whatever. My question still stands."

Now it was my turn to shift uncomfortably. "Not really, no. I've been hanging with my grandparents and reading a lot."

She gave me a look. "Bex, if you're blowing me off for the next six months to live out your French fantasies, then I demand you at least go on a date."

"I don't date," I hedged.

"No, you didn't date *here* because of… Well, because. But you're in a whole new city. You're an amazing person," she informed me.

"Isn't *amazing person* code for homely and meek?" I snorted.

She arched a brow. "Fine. You've got a great rack and an ass you could bounce a quarter off of."

My jaw dropped.

"Want me to call Linc over for his opinion, too?"

"No," I spluttered. "Linc likes anything that has boobs and a willing hole."

"Valid," she said with a sage nod. "Now why don't—" She was cut off by an excited yell, and then grinned as a tiny human landed on her. "Hey, sweets. You have fun with the boys?"

Corinne pulled back with a brilliant smile and a nod. "Yup! Royal helped me catch the biggest fish. Rook got a smaller one, and Court didn't get any."

There was no denying the kick to my heart at hearing his name. God, would it always be this way?

Seeing the phone, Cori turned to me. "Hi, Bex!"

"Hey, Cor," I greeted, waving a bit.

Corinne turned back to Maddie. "Is that lady gone? The mean one that was in Court's bed this morning?"

Maddie shot me a stricken look before turning back to her sister-in-law. "Uh, yeah. She's gone, honey."

"Good. And who sleeps *naked*?" Corinne went on, completely unaware that she was carving into my heart with a rusty razor. She looked disgusted by the naked shenanigans, and I was right there with her. "It was so gross."

"Cori—" Maddie tried.

"I'm glad she's gone," Corinne decided. "I'm gonna go help with lunch. Bye, Bex!" She bounced away.

Maddie's eyes turned to me. "Bex—"

I cleared my throat. "Hey, you know what? I've gotta go."

"Shit," she swore. "Bex, I'm sorry."

"Why?" I forced a brittle laugh. "Court's an adult, and he can do whatever he wants, right? We both can. You know what, Mads? I think you're right. Maybe it's time I go out on a date. Try some of that awesome sex you've been telling me about."

"That's not…" She trailed off, chewing her bottom lip.

"Talk later, yeah?" I smiled again, feeling like my face was going to crack.

"Bex—"

"Bye, Maddie." I hung up and tossed the phone aside. It lit up a second later with a text from Maddie, probably apologizing *again* for something that wasn't her fault.

No, it was *his* fault. And, yeah, maybe mine, too, because I wouldn't let myself move on. I was still that little girl with a crush on the boy she could never have. The boy who'd pushed her away and then turned into the man who'd broken her heart.

"Time to grow up, Bex," I told myself, swallowing back the wave of tears that pricked the backs of my eyes.

Court Woods might have been the first boy I'd ever loved, but he wouldn't be the last. It was time to move on, the same way he had.

CHAPTER 4

BEX

If I was going to move on with my life, I needed a wingman.

Wingwoman.

Maddie, being on the other side of the globe, was a no-go, so I called in the next best thing: my cousin Camille.

My mom's older sister, Celeste, had two daughters. Jayme was the oldest, and she was currently traveling the world with my favorite band, By the Edge, as their tour director. She was awesome, edgy, and fun, but it was her younger sister, Cami, that I counted as one of my best friends.

Camille was two years older than me. After her parents' divorce when she was three, she'd split her time between Paris and England, leaving her fluent in two languages. With her pale golden hair and big hazel eyes, she had this ethereal sort of grace that I'd always envied. I lived for her stories of scandals and drama at the ballet academy where she'd trained for years.

After a falling out with my childhood best friend had left me feeling alone and sad, Cami was the one who'd started calling me Bex. She'd simply declared that I needed a change.

I had been two weeks into a summer-long moping session when Camille burst through the door and convinced me I was better off without Madelaine, the coolest girl in my school, who had been my best friend for almost three years.

I'd trusted Madelaine, and now I knew the real reasons that she'd dropped me like yesterday's trash, but at thirteen, losing her friendship had been the end of my world. And it was made worse when she went from being my best friend to being the school's worst bully, leading the charge against *me*.

Thirteen sucked enough without adding best-friend betrayals on top of it.

After that, Cami became my best friend. She'd spent the rest of the summer with me, even though she'd had a boyfriend who had ultimately broken up with her because she'd prioritized me over him. It still made my heart all sorts of fuzzy, knowing that my super-sophisticated cousin had picked me over a guy who was literally a model.

I'd gone back to California at the end of summer with a new hairstyle that Cami had found in a magazine, a new wardrobe, and a new name. That was the summer Bex was born and Rebecca was put away. Cami was the one who'd convinced my family to start calling me by the new name and had even gone so far as to send gifts and flowers to me at school under it. And because she'd wanted to make sure the world knew me as Bex, she'd had them delivered to me during classes from random names, going as far as to enlist her private school friends to help write the messages so the handwriting varied.

I finally made her stop after a teacher threatened to give me detention if my delivery schedule interrupted his class again.

Did it change the fact that I'd still been an object of ridicule and mockery? Or that Madelaine was a heinous bitch who'd devoted her life to torturing me? No. But it had allowed me to reclaim a piece of myself that had been stolen, and *that* had helped me survive the past five years.

I'd mostly kept to myself at school, but Maddie's arrival had changed that. With her, I had an actual best friend and ally. And, of course, with her came her fiancé… and his friends.

It was weird; I'd grown up with Ryan, Ash, Linc, and Court, but I hadn't really seen them since I was nine. We'd all changed. Some for the better, and some for the worse.

My mistake was in thinking we could move beyond our past. They had proven to me, yet again, that I was disposable.

I'd spent the first eighteen years of my life playing the part of the wallflower, and I was *done*. I wasn't entering college as a scared little mouse.

My bedroom door slammed open with the force of a category-five hurricane.

"Oh, darling," Cami sing-songed, striking a sultry pose in the doorway, "did you miss me?"

Unable to help myself, I giggled and jumped off my bed, where I'd been reading the newest Fiona Davenport romance. Sometimes a girl just needed a quick-and-dirty happily ever after.

Cami stalked into the room, her long legs perfectly suited for a runway in Milan. She threw my door shut with as much force as she'd opened it. "You look…"

I arched a brow and waited.

Cami lowered oversized black sunglasses down her perfectly upturned nose, her glossy pink lips bunching to one side as she looked at me. "Well, it's nothing a trip to Le Bon Marché and the salon won't fix." She tilted her head. "But I *do* like the teal streaks. Much more subtle than Jayme—she died her whole head *neon green*. She's like a walking limeade. It's insane."

I rolled my eyes but opened my arms as she surged forward to wrap me in a bear hug. She squealed, rocking us back and forth before twirling away and plopping down on the seat in front of my vanity. Without fail, she started checking out the scant amount of makeup I had on display.

"And a trip to Sephora," she added, dropping my mascara like it had Ebola.

"Are you done critiquing me yet?" I planted my hands on my hips and tried to glare at her, but a smile kept cracking my lips.

With a dramatic sigh, Cami leaned back against my vanity, crossing her skinny jean-clad legs. "Bex, honey, we both know I'm right."

I shook my head with a shrug. "Fine. You're right. Can you fix me?"

Now she frowned, sitting up straight. "You're not broken."

I dropped onto the edge of my bed. "Feels like I am."

Her head tipped to the side, a wave of cornsilk blonde hair falling over her shoulder. "Explain, please."

Suddenly on the spot, I squirmed. My gaze dropped to the floor.

"Oh, *hell* no." Cami stood up and dragged the seat closer until our knees were touching. Her eyes sparkled with ferocity. "Whose ass am I kicking?"

I scoffed. "Mine? I mean, I should know better, Cam."

Her eyes narrowed. "I'll be the judge of that. Tell me everything."

"It's complicated," I warned, not sure I had the mental bandwidth to go through the past few months of my life.

Cami shrugged a slim shoulder. "I have time. I cleared my entire night for you. I even canceled my date with Alex, so you better give me something worthy of missing out on multiple orgasms."

My eyes widened and I choked a little on my own saliva. "Camille!"

"Oh, shush." She swatted my knee. "Tell me, Rebecca Eleanor Whittier."

I cringed a little. My full name sounded so... geriatric. I shook it off and looked her dead in the eye. "It really *is* complicated."

She sobered. "Bex, I know I've been busy lately—"

I let out a little snort. "Are you kidding me? Cami, you were named the top toilet dancer."

Her jaw dropped with a shriek of mock-outrage. She pushed my shoulder. "You're *such* a twat."

I giggled. "Fine. I meant to say *danseuse étoile*." Truth be told, I knew what an honor it was for someone Cami's age to be named a premier ballerina of the Paris Opera Ballet. Camille had dedicated her life to dancing. She'd started ballet as soon as she was able to walk, and I'd seen her bare feet enough to realize she was dedicated as hell. Those toes were the things of nightmares.

At the end of the company's last season, she'd been promoted to her new position. She put in ten-hour days, six days a week. Today she'd already been up since four a.m., getting in a workout and then several choreography sessions for her upcoming season, which was slated to begin next month.

"You know I'm crazy proud of you, right?" I asked.

She grinned. "I am well aware that I'm the shining light of the Moreau granddaughters."

"Okay, first, there are only three of us," I pointed out, "and it's not like my train wreck of a life is giving you much competition."

"So? Tell me about the train wreck," Cami said with a soft smile. "I know my schedule is insane, but I love you, B. I'm always here for you."

I exhaled a long breath. "First, I need you to promise not to get judgy."

She pressed a hand to her chest, looking aghast. "I would never."

"Sure." I laughed. "Okay, let's start with the fact that I made a friend at school."

Her eyes widened with happiness for me. "Rebecca El—"

"It's Madelaine Cabot," I finished, knowing I couldn't use Maddie's real name. Did I trust Cami? Absolutely, but Maddie's real identity was a secret for a lot of reasons, and she'd trusted me with that info. I wouldn't betray her by telling Camille, or anyone, that Maddie was actually Madelaine's twin, *Madison*, who had assumed her life after Madelaine was murdered.

Camille went from elated to enraged. "Rebecca Eleanor Whittier." It came out frosty, if not outright hostile.

"That sounds a lot like your judgy tone."

Her mouth snapped shut, but she still glowered at me.

"I can't give you all the details, but Maddie isn't who you think she is." I picked my words carefully.

Cami scoffed. "Madelaine—"

"*Maddie*," I cut in firmly. "She goes by Maddie, and kinda like the way you helped me bring Bex into the world? Maddie did the same. She's not the evil psycho either of us thought she was. There was a lot going on behind the scenes, and she treated me like she did to protect me."

"Where in the abuser's handbook is that bullshit logic coming from?"

"Camille." I eyed her, not willing to budge. "I need you to trust me, okay? Maddie is... I wouldn't have survived the last few months without her."

She still didn't look convinced. "Bex, this girl once took out an advertisement for five-dollar blow jobs on the internet and gave people *your number*."

I winced because, yeah, that had sucked. Pun *not* intended. "She also saved me from being date raped at a party last fall."

Cami sucked in a sharp breath. "Oh, my God. Bex, why the hell didn't you tell me?"

"I dunno," I hedged. "I guess I was kinda embarrassed? I mean, the whole thing was stupid. I'm so not victim blaming, but I can admit I blew past the flashing warning signs. Anyway, Maddie got me out of there before something bad happened."

"One good deed doesn't undo years of torture," Cami said, shaking her head. "Look, if you want to be besties with the enemy, then... okay. But I plan to remain skeptically displeased about this arrangement until... Well, just until."

I couldn't help but smile. Cami was fiercely loyal, and I'd called her in hysterical tears more than once after Madelaine had taken her bullying too far.

"Fair enough," I muttered, running a hand through my hair. "The thing is, Maddie's engaged. To Ryan Cain."

Cami frowned. "Wait, I know that name."

"Ryan Cain is best friends with... Court Woods." I whispered the last two words, like uttering his name might invoke the man himself.

"Holy shit. *The* Court Woods?" Cami's eyes were as big as a shocked cartoon character's.

I nodded grimly. "Yeah."

Cami looked around my room. "Tell me you have some kind of alcohol in here, because I need a damn drink for this conversation."

"Cam, I'm serious."

"So am I." She stood up. "Be right back." Before I could say anything, she was out the door. When she returned less than five minutes later with a bottle of champagne, I could only shake my head.

Without missing a beat, Cami popped the cork, lifted the bottle to her lips, and drank. Five gulps later, she set the bottle at her feet and waved a hand at me. "Okay. Continue."

I eyed the bottle, spotting part of the label. "Jesus, Camille! That's a thousand-dollar bottle of champagne!"

She gave me a *duh* look. "And? It's the cheapest thing Mémé has in the wine cellar, B. You raided it enough with me over the years to know that."

"Uh-uh." I wagged a finger at her. "*You* raided. I was the idiot you conned into being your lookout."

She swiped the bottle and took another pull. "You were a shitty lookout. What kind of accomplice says, 'In the wine cellar!' when their mom calls out for them?"

"The kind who was fourteen and not ready to be grounded for the rest of her natural life," I grumbled. "If you wanted a Bonnie to your Clyde, you should have picked someone who wouldn't break under the scrutiny of maternal inquisitions."

Cami narrowed her eyes. "Don't use your big fancy words on me, Bex. And I'm freaking Bonnie. You can be Clyde."

"Fine," I muttered, shooting her a grumpy pout.

"Now stop stalling and tell me all about tall, dark, and sexy," Cami demanded.

I gave her a look.

"What? You're gonna tell me he didn't grow up gorgeous?" She snorted and took another drink. "I met him once, the summer I came to the States when I was eleven, and I'm pretty sure I was still imagining him the first time I masturbated at thirteen."

"You remember the first time you…" I hated that word, so I stumbled over saying it.

Cami arched a perfect brow. "Flicked the bean? DJ'd my downstairs?"

I groaned. "Oh, God, *stop*."

But Cami was on a roll. "Buttered my muffin? Jilled off? Pet the kitty? Diddled my—"

"Stop!" I shouted with a laugh, reaching back for a pillow and hurling it at her head. Heat radiated off my cheeks.

"—skittle," she managed from behind a wall of foam. She grinned at me as she tossed the pillow aside.

"You're such a dork," I huffed.

"Spoken like a girl who doesn't routinely do the three-knuckle shuffle," she teased.

"Where the hell did you learn all that?" I asked, exasperated.

"I went to an all-girls ballet academy my entire academic career," she deadpanned. "I can also curse in six languages. But we're not talking about my formerly pathetic life, we're talking about *yours*."

Oh, yeah. Right.

"So," she said, waving her hands, "you were telling me about how you finally got to screw the man of your dreams?"

My cheeks were now five-alarm-fire hot. "What? No. First of all, I didn't. And second of all, 'man of my dreams' is a bit of a stretch."

Cami reached over and took my hand. "B, I love you, but I also know that you've been obsessed with Court Woods since you were an infant. And I'm not giving you shit for it, because, trust me, *I get it*. Even at thirteen years old? He was so gorgeous. Tall, that chocolate brown hair, and those eyes that—"

I made a small, annoyed sound in the back of my throat.

Her eyes snapped open wide. "Did you just *growl* at me?"

I folded my arms, refusing to answer that question.

She held up her hands. "Message received. You're still just as terri-torial over him as you were when you were a kid."

"I was not," I snapped.

She shot me a look. "B, I was teasing him about losing a race to… I don't even remember his name, and you *accidentally* spilled an entire glass of lemonade on me."

I sniffed. "I tripped."

She laughed and shook her head. "Whatever you say."

Sighing, I rested my elbows on my knees. "No, he didn't grow up as gorgeous as you're thinking."

"That's disappointing."

"He's even hotter," I lamented, dropping my head into my hands as I remembered an all-grown-up Court and exactly how he looked.

Those long, gangly limbs had filled out and were thick with muscle. Every time I saw him, it looked like he was one flex away from his biceps ripping through his t-shirt. He was seriously tall, and absolutely had the dark and broody thing going for him.

But it wasn't like I was the only one who'd noticed—even Cori had met his latest bedfellow.

I rubbed my chest, a physical ache hitting me right in the feels at the idea of him with someone else.

This was exactly why I needed Camille.

"So, what's the problem?" Cami was still giggling.

"The problem is he's a goddamn liar and a freaking manwhore, and I can't spend the rest of my life hoping for something that's never going to happen." I wasn't sure if I was angry or sad. I wanted to throw the bottle of champagne against the wall and break down in tears.

Cami stopped laughing. "Oh, honey."

"I need to forget he ever existed." I took a deep breath. "And I need you to help me do it."

CHAPTER 5

BEX

The grin that split Camille's face was terrifying. One of those smiles that basically said I was screwed. Like she'd been waiting for the day I handed her the reins to my life.

Without saying a word to me, she pulled her phone out of a hidden pocket in her leggings and pressed a button before lifting it to her ear. "Hey, baby. Remember how you were asking me if I had a friend for your brother since he's back in town?"

Panic struck like a lightning bolt, and I jumped up. "No!"

She held me off with a hand and a stern look as she kept talking. "It just so happens that my cousin has decided to spend a few months in Paris, and I think Eric would love her."

"Cami! Stop it," I hissed, trying to keep my voice down.

She pushed me away and slid off the seat, dancing away like she was, well, a dancer. "I'm hanging out with Bex now, honey. I'll call you later." She hung up as I jumped and tried to snag the phone.

"Seriously? A blind date?" I demanded.

She shot me an incredulous look. "Uh, you're welcome."

I resisted the urge to grab another pillow and whack her across her gorgeous face. Instead I threw my arms in the air with a disbelieving scoff. "Cam, the last thing I want is some pity date with your boyfriend's brother. I'm not *that* desperate." *Yet.*

"Okay, slow down, B," she told me, her eyes big as she sat back down and reached for the champagne. She passed it to me.

I didn't even think before lifting it to my lips and gulping.

"First, Eric just moved back to Paris after being away at boarding school and then college, where he got his MBA or something," she started.

"Code for he looks like a bridge troll," I groused.

Cami lifted a brow and swiped through her phone until she found what she wanted, then she passed the device to me. "Does he look like a troll to you?"

I'd met Alex once, and only for a few minutes. Dark blond hair, cool gray eyes, and a build like a lacrosse player—muscular, but on the lean side. It wasn't enough to get a full impression of him, but he was definitely good looking.

But the guy next to him in the photo with light brown hair, artfully mussed, and soulful gray eyes was most definitely *not* a troll. In fact, if anything, he made Alex look like a troll. He looked like he belonged on stage with a band, crooning about heartbreak and love under a spotlight as thousands of women—and men—sang along.

Cami grinned at me as she snagged her phone. "See? The Lambert-Durand brothers do *not* have any complaints in the looks department." She pressed a dramatic hand to her chest. "The Lord truly blessed those men."

"How can a guy like *that* need help getting a date?" Maybe it was their last name that turned women off? Lambert-Durand sounded like an eighties band.

"The way Alex tells it, Eric is super smart and went to a lot of elite European boarding schools, but they were all boys only. He was always super focused on school and never had a chance to date. He's, like, a genius or something. Honestly, I think Alex is kinda jealous of his little brother, but that's just between us."

"Oh." I licked my lips, a nervous habit I'd never been able to break and also the reason I always carried lip balm in my purse.

Looking entirely too smug, she swiped the champagne bottle from me. "I haven't actually met Eric yet, but Alex said his dad is worried that Eric is too serious, so he asked Alex to help get him out of the house. You know how I told you that Alex works for his father's investment firm?"

I nodded, vaguely recalling that detail.

"Eric runs a shipping business that their late mother's family owned. Like, he's a twenty-three-year-old CEO of a million-dollar corporation," she gushed. "How insane is that?"

So, let's recap:

Broody guy who made my lady bits sit up and take notice? Check.

Early twenties and running a multi-million-dollar company? Check.

I definitely had a type.

But there was one major difference between Eric and Court: Eric *wasn't* Court. Which meant I might have a shot at my heart not getting broken yet again.

Sighing, I slumped. "Fine."

Cami brightened. "Yeah?"

"Yeah." I allowed myself a laugh, happy to see one of my favorite humans in the world beaming at me.

Setting the bottle aside, she clapped her hands. "Oh, yay! B, this is going to be epic. We're going to have so much fun. We need to shop."

I glanced across the room at my closet. "I have plenty of stuff here to wear."

Standing up with more grace and fluidity than a human should possess, Cami shot me a disbelieving look. "Okay, then, fine. I can shop and you can… watch."

"How generous of you," I drawled, even as I got to my feet.

With a squeal, she threw her arms around my neck. "Do you know how much I've missed you?"

"You realize I follow you on Instagram, right? I've spent the last year watching you live it up with your dance friends and freaking models," I pointed out even as I hugged her back.

"But none of them are *you*," she replied. "It's hard having a friendship with any of the other dancers when I'm pretty sure they'd smear oil on the stage just so I'd break a leg."

"Seriously?" I gaped at her.

She let out a humorless laugh. "Honestly, before I met Alex, I didn't have much of a social life."

She'd told me as much when we'd texted, but a text didn't capture the loneliness or longing on her face. A tight band wrapped around my chest, making it hard to breathe.

I'd spent the past few months in a whirlwind of chaos and, as a result, I'd kinda iced Cami out when it sounded like she could've really used a friend. I couldn't change the past but, moving forward, I could be the cousin and friend she'd always been to me.

"New plan," I suggested, going to my desk and picking up my purse. "How about if we go out for dinner and you tell me all about Alex?"

She gave me a suspicious look. "And shopping?"

I grinned. "And we'll totally go shopping, too. I guess I could at least use a new mascara. Pretty sure the one you picked up is from the last time I visited and you took me to Sephora." Besides, I did love shopping, too.

Cami gasped and whirled, grabbing the mascara and chucking it into the trash can. "Are you freaking kidding me, Rebecca Eleanor?"

I blanched. "I mean—"

"Have you ever seen what eye mites can do? They're grubby little things that grow in your lashes." Cami looked utterly horrified. "Six months, Bex. That's how often you change your mascara."

"I mean, I have dark lashes. I don't use it that often—"

She held up a hand. "We're not negotiating the shelf life of an opened tube of mascara. I love you too much to let little insects burrow into your eyeballs and lay eggs."

I wasn't sure that was how eye mites worked, but the idea of getting some funky eye infection from old mascara definitely gave me the creepy-crawlies.

Cami shot me a knowing look. "You're imagining bugs digging—"

"Stop!" I shouted, lunging forward to slap my hand over her

mouth, but she spun away with a laugh while at the same time opening my bedroom door.

"Let's go, Rebecca," she called, her lilting voice carrying as she hurried down the hallway.

With a reluctant sigh, I followed my cousin, my heart lighter than it had been in weeks.

This was exactly what I needed: a day out with one of my favorite humans to remind me that there was more to life than broody bad boys who ripped out your heart.

CHAPTER 6

COURT

"Damn." A sharp catcalling whistle followed the awed word.

I glanced over my shoulder to see Maddie descending the stairs in a short red dress, her hair swept up in some elaborate twist that somehow managed to look both elegant and effortless. Her heels clicked across the marble floor as she made it to the landing, but it was the way she turned bashful at his praise that made me grin.

"Thanks, Linc," she muttered, her cheeks turning a few shades pinker than the dress she wore. Her hands fluttered around her torso, patting the dress like it was wrinkled. "Is it too much? I swear, California does *not* understand winter."

Maddie had grown up in Michigan, in a town near Detroit. Usually by the first week of February, her town was buried under a foot of snow. But here in southern California, the temps hadn't dipped below seventy-two.

"Nah." Linc took a massive bite of the apple in his hand while he leaned against the railing of the staircase. "Seriously, Mads, you look hot. New dress?"

Her blush deepened as she gave a shy nod, and I was yet again reminded of all the ways she was different from her twin sister. Not that I'd ever really known Madelaine. Sure, I'd known her growing up and known that she was friends with Becca, but after I'd cut Becca out of my life, I hadn't given Madelaine a second thought until Ryan had announced they were getting married.

Ryan's father was a fucking bastard for a lot of things, but maybe the one good thing he'd done was arrange Ryan and Madelaine's engagement, because that had brought Madison into Ryan's life. Into all our lives.

Where Lainey had been callous and cruel, Maddie was sweet and friendly. She was loyal and kind, and she'd won a permanent spot in our group even before Ryan wifed her up for the first time. Besides, with her came Becca.

As much as the way we were now killed me, I would never regret the time I'd had with Becca before things went FUBAR.

Again.

Linc lifted an arm to rest on the bannister, his dark blue eyes glittering in a teasing way that was all too familiar. "Mads, if you ever change your mind, I know a great divorce attorney."

"And I know seven places to bury your body that the cops would never think to check," Ryan retorted as he came down the stairs, fastening a button at his wrist. He slapped the back of Linc's head before coming to a stop in front of Maddie. His eyes went practically feral with lust as his gaze devoured her. "Fuck, baby."

She shot him a coy smile, sliding her hands up his chest to loop around his neck. The chandelier overhead caught the several carats of colorless diamond on her finger, sending scattered rainbows across the white walls of the entrance. "Play your cards right, and you absolutely can later, Mr. Cain."

The return gaze he sent her—all heat and promises of debauchery—almost gave *me* a semi.

"Where are you two going?" Linc asked, taking another bite of apple.

"Cain Industries fundraiser," Ryan replied with a grimace. "Unfortunately the PR team said missing it would send a bad message to the board."

Maddie sighed and shook her head. "Babe, it's for the Los Angeles Food Bank."

He scowled. "I can just as easily write them a check here as I can at the event."

"But at the event you can meet more people who can write more checks," she pointed out, her tone soft. "And as someone who frequently had to rely on food banks, I know they can never have enough help."

Ryan's expression instantly changed from annoyed to pained. "Mads."

Maddie hadn't grown up like the rest of us. We'd all had our share of trauma and heartache, but we'd never had to wonder if there would be a next meal or if we'd be evicted from our mega mansions.

"I'm just saying," she continued, her chin lifted in challenge, "writing a check is good, but setting up a system to keep multiple checks coming in is better. *You* can do that, Ry. You're the freaking CEO of Cain Industries. You keep saying you're going to be different than your father, and this is where you prove it. Show the world you're more than a kid who had Daddy's company handed to him."

Ryan bristled, his icy blue eyes sparking.

Maddie's hands framed his face. "Show them who you are. Show them why you're so much more than Beckett Cain's son. Be the man I know you are."

I'd known Ryan Cain since I was an infant. We'd grown up together, and I'd seen him in every phase of his life: reckless kid who thought he was indestructible, belligerent adolescent who hated his dad and the whole world, and cold, calculating man who was the reason Phoenix International was founded.

But I had to admit, Ryan Cain ass over head in love was probably my favorite iteration of the man.

Not that I'd ever tell him that.

The way he absolutely crumbled when Maddie looked at him made my chest ache. The way he loved her was the stuff of legends. They'd overcome an evil twin, two sadistic dads, multiple kidnappings, and even a fucking natural disaster.

It was like he'd never even lived until she came along.

And fuck if I didn't know how that felt.

"Court."

I blinked and realized Maddie had left Ryan's side and come to stand in the opening of the great room where everyone usually hung out.

Clasping her hands in front of her, she gave me a worried look. "Are you okay?"

My gaze jumped past her to Ryan, who also arched a brow. Next to him, even Linc had sobered.

I gave Maddie my attention and forced a smile. "Yeah, Mads. I'm good."

The corners of her mouth tipped up. "Okay, but we're here if you want to talk."

I'd rather drink acid. "I know. I appreciate it. Have fun tonight."

"We will," Ryan answered for them both, grabbing her hand and tugging her away with a grin. He looked from me to Linc. "Don't wait up."

Maddie giggled, the sound one of pure happiness. "Bye, guys!"

Linc followed them to the door and closed it behind them. The heavy fall of his footsteps coming back was a pretty clear warning that I wouldn't be spending the evening watching reruns of *The Office* like I'd planned.

His massive body launched over the back of the couch I was chilling on, his foot damn near clipping my head. He landed with a thud, tossing me a wild grin. "What's the plan for tonight?"

"Nothing," I replied, my tone even if not a little bored.

His grin widened. "Does this mean you've finally decided to give your dick a weekend off?"

I kept my expression stony.

Not that it deterred my best friend. It took a lot to truly bother Linc. The guy was happy playing the comic relief of our quartet. Ryan was the leader, Ash was the brains, Linc was the comedy, and I was the muscle. We all had our roles.

At least, that was how most people saw us. It was the image we'd presented—cultivated—since middle school. But only the four of us knew the truth.

Ash was the neurotic one—the guy who would stay up for three days straight when he went into his manic, hyper-focused state of obsession.

Ryan was brutally efficient. The preppy, pretty boy looks hid a mind that worked, at times, like a serial killer. He used charm and charisma like swords.

I was the silent one. The one always lurking in the background, the one who was constantly trying to prove himself to the whole damn world. As a kid, finding out my dad had an entire other family had rocked me, and he'd constantly let me know that I wasn't as strong as Royal, as smart as Rook, or as committed as Bishop. And while I'd played the part of the carefree playboy, I was man enough to admit that it left me with a constant drive to show the world how useful I was.

And Linc… The ones with the biggest smiles always hid the darkest secrets. He was my best friend. I'd take a bullet for him without question, but there was a side of him that scared even me. He hid it well from us. Sometimes even from himself. But I'd seen it seep out, and we all knew that he was one push away from going full-on dark side.

For tonight, it seemed that Linc was just Linc. The guy who cared too much and was always there for me.

I punched his arm, abandoning my plans to order pizza and binge watch a TV show I'd seen a dozen times already. "I figured I should give you a shot at getting laid."

He laughed, tipping his head back. "Fuck you, dude. If you think I need your help with women, you're still drunk." His shoulder nudged mine. "Not that I haven't missed your occasional assist."

I was unable to stop the knowing grin that spread across my lips. Linc and I had always been close, so much so that it wasn't uncommon for us to share a woman for a night of debauchery. We hadn't done it in months. Not since *she'd* blown back into my life.

It was weird. Like my timeline had been divided into multiple chunks: before Becca and after Becca.

"Actually," Linc drawled, absently scratching his chest, "if you want to go find—"

"No." I shut that shit down hard. I'd avoided booze and pussy for four days, and it was a little sad how proud I was of that streak.

He sighed. "Just as well. It's hard, wanting a fast-food burger after you've been tempted by wagyu."

I frowned. "Huh? What does that even mean?"

His lips curved into a smirk. "Just that if my dick has one regret in life, it's that Bex got pissed and left before—"

I was on my feet and looming over my oldest, closest friend before I realized what I'd done. "Before *what*?"

Linc raised his hands, a knowing glint in his eyes. "Oh, did I say something wrong? You don't like the idea of me pinning sweet little Bex to my bed and—"

My fist slammed into his jaw, snapping his head to the side.

It was only the fact that I loved him like one of my brothers that had me taking a step back and not putting his ass in the local ER.

Linc stretched his jaw, carefully rubbing the already forming bruise. "Fucking *finally*."

"What the shit's that supposed to mean?" I demanded. My skin felt too tight over my muscles, stretched past the point of normal. Maybe I had some latent Hulk superpower, but I had a whole new appreciation for why Bruce Banner ripped through his clothes whenever he got pissed off.

Linc rose to his feet, the movement almost lazy. He hooked his thumbs into the front pockets of his jeans. "It means you've been living like a goddamn war widow for the last four weeks. I'm sick of your mopey ass."

I jerked back like he'd punched me. "Excuse me?"

"No, I don't think I will," he retorted, eyes flashing. "You're my best fucking friend, Court, and that's the only reason I let this shit go on as long as I have. I get it—you lost the girl of your goddamn dreams."

I reared back. "No, I—"

"Jesus, man." He shot me a disgusted look. "Stop lying to yourself.

No one has ever twisted you up the way little Rebecca Whittier has. Problem is, she isn't so little anymore. If she was any other girl and you were any other guy, I'd have made a move on her *months* ago."

Fuck me. I was going to have to kill my best friend. I'd need help burying the body, but the only guys I could ask to help were Ash and Ryan… and odds were they'd kill me for killing him.

I could try waiting until Royal and Rook came back. Or I could call Bishop, but that had its own problems. Knight was busy, too.

"Hell, I would've even shared her with you—"

I lunged for him, and he spun away too fast.

"Fuck, bro! Let me finish!" He leapt over the back of the couch, putting it between us. "I knew a menage or whatever wasn't in the cards the night you carried her ass out of the frat house."

My gut cramped at the memory of that night. Becca had been drugged and damn near raped by one of my former fraternity brothers. Maddie had saved her by alerting Ryan and the rest of us, but I'd never forget how delicate and perfect she'd felt in my arms.

And how I'd utterly failed her.

I'd pushed her away to keep her safe, and it hadn't worked.

"Is it so fucking hard for you to admit that you have feelings for her?" Linc pressed. "That you're not some emotionless cyborg? It doesn't make you weak to need her, Court. And you aren't the only one she left—I might not feel the same way you do, but I care about her, too."

I stared at him, trying to wrap my brain around what he was saying. "You really like her?"

"What's not to like? She's an amazing woman. She's smart, funny, gorgeous…"

The noise that came out of me wasn't entirely human.

Linc met my gaze. "She's also head over fucking heels in love with *you*, you fucking idiot. And I think you might feel the same way, if you let yourself."

I didn't know what to say. Trying to wrap my head around it was too much.

The door to the garage opened on the other side of the room and

Ash appeared, two pizzas and a six-pack balanced in his hands as he kicked the door shut. He took one look at us, and then his gaze zeroed in on Linc. "Started without me?"

Linc shrugged. "I saw an opening. I went for it."

Ash shot him a knowing smirk. "Pretty sure that's how you've justified hitting on every woman you've ever fucked, too." Then he looked at me. "Hungry?"

The smell of grease, cheese, and meat wafted over to me. My stomach gave an appreciative rumble. "I could eat," I admitted.

Linc slowly came back around the couch. "Truce?"

I sighed heavily. "Yeah."

Ash crossed the room and set the pizzas on the coffee table in front of the massive, U-shaped sectional sofa that dominated the room. With a huge TV that took up the majority of one wall, this was our makeshift movie theater and gaming room, and the general place we all hung out.

Linc dove for one of the boxes, flipping open the lid and grabbing a slice of pepperoni and sausage. He took a massive bite, then huffed a breath around the searing heat. "Shit. Hot."

"Fucking animal," Ash groused, shaking his head. He left and came back a minute later with three plates, which he passed out.

Linc made a face as he accepted the dish. "Remember when we could just eat pizza on our couch and no one gave us shit if we stained something?"

Ash gave him a reproachful look.

"All I'm saying is, bachelor life was a helluva lot easier before Maddie."

"So, you think life would be easier without her?" Ash challenged, looking annoyed.

Linc shook his head emphatically. "Fuck no. I love Maddie. She's like a super-hot, not-blood-related little sister. And God knows Ryan's slightly less of an asshole now that he's put a damn ring on it."

I snorted at his descriptions.

"Anyway," Ash said loudly, turning to toss me a beer, "it's good to see you coherent. I was starting to wonder if you were just going to fuck away your last semester."

I frowned, popping the top of the can. "I have independent study this semester. I already put in my internship hours with the firm when Ryan was on trial for attempted murder. All that's left now is to check in with my advisor every month before I hit Stanford in the fall."

Linc's face fell. "I can't believe you're moving to Palo Alto."

"It's three years, buddy," I reminded him. "And my law degree is something we need."

Both guys nodded, because it was true. I planned to major in international law with a double focus on criminology. Phoenix International was truly international, and our company needed a team of lawyers—that I would spearhead—who were dedicated to knowing which laws could be used in our favor and which we could bend to our will.

"I know Ryan talked to you about our expedited timetable," Ash added, taking a bite of his own pizza loaded with chicken, bacon, and roma tomatoes. The weirdo even had the pizza place put ranch on it instead of pizza sauce, which was sacrilegious to Linc but tasted pretty damn good to me.

Letting my brain shift into work mode was a welcome distraction. It was why I was secretly thankful Royal had put me on an assignment. With my light schoolwork load and the football season over, I needed something to keep me from spiraling any further than I'd gone.

Linc set his plate down and grabbed a beer. "Did you guys ever think we'd be here?"

"Here?" Ash asked, quirking a brow.

Linc waved a hand. "*Here*. I mean, for the longest time, Phoenix seemed like a pipe dream. But now it's really happening. Royal and Rook are down in San Diego on a goddamn recruitment mission."

"An interview with Rook's former CO is hardly a mission," Ash muttered. "And we all agreed—"

"I know what we all agreed," Linc said, a little too sharply. His expression softened. "I guess I just never really let myself think it would be real."

"Why?" I turned to him, wondering why he'd never voiced these concerns to me. To any of us.

Looking more serious than I'd seen him in a long time, Linc put his plate on the coffee table and leaned his forearms on his knees. "I was eight the first time my dad took me into one of his clubs."

My stomach clenched, and I exchanged a look with Ash. He looked just as concerned. Linc rarely discussed his childhood. Even as kids, he'd deflected all the shit in his life with jokes and smiles.

"I was eleven the first time I had sex," he added quietly. Ash sucked in a breath, but I knew that story. Linc's dad, Kent Westford, made my father look like Dudley Do-Right.

To the world, Kent was the man behind over a hundred upscale hotels worldwide. He was a philanthropist who donated to causes supporting orphans, widows, and the arts.

But his hotel empire was a front for a seedy world of exclusive clubs where anything went… for a price. Most of his clubs had a heavy BDSM scene where the word *consent* was missing from the dictionary. He sold people the way a baker sold donuts.

Linc had been drunk when he'd confessed to me that, when he was a kid, his dad had taken him into a club to have his first sexual experience. Two women, easily a couple decades older than him, had done some messed up shit to his pre-pubescent body under the orders of his own fucking father. All because Kent wanted to bring his son into the family business from an early age.

It had gone on for years—Kent bringing Linc with him to his clubs around the world. Sometimes he had Linc watch. Sometimes he encouraged his son to participate. As he grew up, Linc managed to put literal distance between himself and his father. Now Kent was based out of New York while Linc went to Pacific Cross in California. Linc had used damn near every excuse he could think of not to see his father, but it didn't always work, and he had to go to a club maybe once a year.

Ash leaned forward. "We're going to stop him, Linc." He met my gaze next. "All of them. Beckett and Gary were the first dominoes. We just have to put things in motion before Beckett can get to them."

When we'd started Phoenix, we'd been pawns. Chess pieces for our fathers to move around a board. Taking down Ryan's and Maddie's dads in the fall had forced our hand a bit sooner than we'd have liked, but it didn't change our endgame.

Phoenix International was the opposition to everything our fathers stood for. It protected the weak and gave the helpless a voice. Instead of falling in line the way our fathers had wanted, we were determined to break them and everything they stood for.

Somewhere in the chaos of losing Becca again, I'd forgotten that. I'd forgotten that there were people out there who needed us. Needed *me*.

That was the thing I would pour myself into. Not alcohol, not women. I'd fill the void left by Rebecca Whittier by being better. By making her proud.

Even if she'd never know I was doing it all for her.

CHAPTER 7

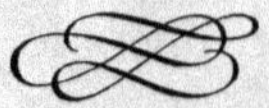

COURT

Nearly a week later, I drove to the private airport an hour from home. It was early as fuck, and thanks to Los Angeles traffic, I was running thirty minutes late. But the perk of taking a private plane was that being late wasn't really an issue.

After locking up the car, I tossed my bag over my shoulder and headed for the stairs leading into the elegant Cessna waiting on the tarmac. I jogged up the steps, already anticipating my brothers giving me shit for delaying them.

"May I take your bag for you, Mr. Woods?" The breathy flight attendant with big green eyes and red hair pulled back into a tight knot at the back of her head blinked up at me.

"I'm good," I grumbled, moving past her.

"Well, if there's anything I can do, please don't hesitate to ask," she added with a bright smile. Her gaze swept down the length of me before coming back to meet mine. "Anything at all."

Clenching my jaw, I gave her a tight nod and kept going down the aisle. The private jet technically belonged to Cain Industries, but Ryan was letting us take it to Europe. There were a couple rows of plush cream seats, two sets of four chairs around a table on either side of the aisle, and then two long couches. The back of the plane had a private bedroom and bathroom while the front of the plane had another bathroom and a galley style kitchen.

Already seated at one of the tables reading some papers, Rook barely spared me a glance.

I dropped my bag onto the seat across from him and then took the other seat facing him. "Hey."

"You're late," he muttered.

"Traffic was a bitch."

His gaze slowly lifted to mine. "I made it here without an issue."

"Not all of us had time management beaten into our skulls by the Navy," I retorted, rubbing my temples, feeling a headache building.

He set down the papers, looking way too much like Royal with his disapproving scowl. "You're right. Some of us lived the frat-boy life and didn't have to learn things like discipline and promptness."

I stared at him. "What the fuck crawled up your ass?"

Sighing, he leaned back in the seat and shook his head. "Sorry, man. It's been… It's been a rough couple of weeks."

I remembered what Royal had said, about thinking Rook had hooked up with Emerson. "Do you want to talk about it?" I asked, hesitant. I'd always kind of felt like an outsider with my brothers. Truth be told, I considered Ryan, Ash, and Linc more my brothers than those bound to me by blood.

For the majority of my childhood, I hadn't known my dad had a whole separate family living less than six miles away. It wasn't until I'd heard my parents arguing over King's death that I'd started asking questions. It had been the surprise of a fucking lifetime to find out I had six—no, make that *five*—brothers. That my dad had been with Holly since before he'd even met my mom in college.

Growing up, I'd never realized that my parents weren't in love. Sure, they'd fought, but not like Ryan's parents. My mom wasn't terrified of my dad the way Linc's mom was of his dad. And Ash's parents were so bland that I wasn't even sure how he'd been conceived. By those standards, my parents were *normal*.

The truth was my parents had married because it had been the best move for them financially and politically. My dad had never hidden

Holly from my mom, hadn't even bothered. In fact, it was the opposite. Their marriage worked because they both knew the score, and they both knew enough to ruin the other if one fucked up the balance they'd set up.

The closest they'd come was when I'd turned thirteen.

That was the year I found out about my parents' deep, dark secrets. That Dad was a sadistic narcissist. That my parents' marriage was a total farce, and as soon as they knew that I knew, all bets were off.

Not that I cared. Back then I'd been a miserable fuck who had no idea how to channel all my rage and confusion into something more productive. Not until Royal got his hands on me months after I'd spiraled out of control.

The first time I ever met my brothers and Holly, I'd taken a taxi to their house. I'd watched them play in their yard and then go inside before I found the balls to knock on the front door.

Bishop had opened the door, taken one look at me, and asked what the fuck I wanted. He'd been almost sixteen at the time, and pissed at the entire goddamn world. They knew all about Jasper's legitimate son. To them, I was the golden boy. The one who had everything while they got whatever leftovers Jasper deemed them worthy of.

Sure, they had a decent house in a middle-class suburb. One of those two-story colonial homes with four bedrooms, so they all shared their space with each other. It had a decent yard full of random sports equipment, but it wasn't the thirteen-bedroom mansion I'd grown up in. Or the seven-thousand-square-foot summer home my parents had on a lake upstate.

It was clear from the jump that Holly wasn't much of a parent. She was there for Jasper and seemed like a ghost whenever he wasn't around. After losing her daughter in childbirth and then King when he was thirteen, she'd essentially shut herself off.

The first couple years of knowing my brothers had been rough. Royal had already enlisted in the army, so I hadn't met him until later on. Rook had been eighteen and finishing his senior year. Bishop was almost three years older than me, Knight was a year younger, and Castle, the baby, was three years younger.

Watching them made something in my chest ache. They had this easy way of being together, sharing inside jokes. They were this unified wall against Dad that I wanted to be part of.

When Dad came back to their house and found me there, I expected him to be furious. Instead he took the time to point out how successful his other sons were. That Royal was on the fast-track to becoming a Green Beret. Rook was on track to graduate as valedictorian and was planning to join the U.S. Navy.

Bishop was class president.

Knight's baseball team was the top-ranked team in North America.

Castle was a veritable genius with an insane IQ. At ten years old, he was already finishing middle school.

Dad had done everything he could to make me hate my brothers. To be jealous, and I was. But I wasn't jealous of their accomplishments; I was jealous that I didn't have the family they did. That I didn't have brothers to lean on.

Rook had been the first to treat me like a brother. He'd been the oldest at home and had set the tone for the rest. After Dad and Holly disappeared upstairs, Rook asked me to come out and play football with them. He'd included me, and invited me back.

That had meant something. One by one, I'd earned their trust. Their respect. Their loyalty.

And if Rook was having a shit time now, then I would have his back, too.

Sighing, he snatched up the water bottle in front of him. He gave it a weird look. "Who drinks bottled water from a *glass bottle*?" His face screwed up in annoyance, but he took a long drink before screwing the top back on.

"Nice deflection," I intoned, wondering if I was this difficult.

Shit. I was probably worse. Even Linc, my best damn friend with whom I shared everything from cars to women, had been giving me a wide berth lately. And after the stunt with Cori? He'd flat out told me to get my shit together or he'd hold my arms as Ryan and Royal took turns kicking my ass.

With a huff, Rook fell back deeper into his seat, flicking a hand at me. "Fine, I'll tell you what happened with Emerson if *you* tell me what happened with Bex."

My teeth clicked audibly as I ground them together.

Rook arched dark brows, his expression mocking. "Not so chatty now, little brother?"

I watched him for a weighted beat. "What do you want to know?"

He looked stunned, probably because I'd shut down anything and everything that had to do with Rebecca Whittier over the past few weeks. Speaking her name was like invoking a specter I was desperately trying to put to rest.

Except the past few days of sober clarity had made me realize one important thing: that girl was embedded in the very fibers of my soul. When God had made me, he'd given me everything except a heart. *That* piece of my anatomy had been born three years and six months later in the form of my mom's best friend's daughter.

I could still remember the first time I'd met her. I'd been three and, like most humans, I didn't have a lot of solid recollections from that time in my life. But meeting her? Yeah, that shit was seared into my mind's eye for eternity.

A psychologist would probably spout some bullshit for why it was such a strong memory—maybe some chemical reaction to the lighting and smells of the room that day—but all I knew was that the first time I saw her, I spoke a word I'd never uttered before.

Mine.

My mom and Bex's mother had looked at me and cracked up, assuming the *mine* I was referring to was the tiny toy truck I'd dropped into her bassinet as I'd leaned over to get a look at her face, but it wasn't that.

She was mine, and on some primal level, my brain had recognized that.

It was the only shit that made sense, especially as we grew up. I was almost four years older than her. Sure, our moms were friends, but there was no clear reason that the draw I felt to her was so strong. Strong enough that Linc and Ryan used to tease me about it, until I'd bloodied Ryan's nose and busted Linc's lip. After that, they hadn't questioned it when I always tried to include her.

We'd grown up in the same neighborhood. It was a gated community of mansions and rolling hills, but it also had its own parks and playgrounds. We'd all had nannies, and they'd brought us to the same place to play. Some of my earliest and best memories were made with my friends and Bex.

Cutting her out of my life for almost eight years had been brutal. And having had a taste of her back in my life only to have her ripped away by my own idiocy was killing me.

I shook my head, eyeing Rook. "Take it from me, brother, don't blow it. If there's something between you and…"

He grimaced. "Emerson."

"Right," I murmured, "Emerson. Don't throw it away because you're scared or think it's what's best for her."

"I slept with her," he finally admitted.

My brow raised. "And? What? It sucked?"

He grimaced, looking down. "Best night of my fucking life, Court. It was like all the pieces of the puzzle came together."

"So, what went wrong?" I asked.

"Timing," he replied with a shrug. "She's got a daughter—"

"And you don't want kids?"

He shut that shit down fast. "Honestly? I never saw myself with kids. Wasn't something I wanted. I mean, what kind of fucking role model do I have to look up to? *Jasper*?" He looked disgusted, but the expression quickly smoothed away as he added, "But Elodie… Fuck, I love that kid, man. I can't even explain it."

"What went wrong?"

He huffed, scrubbing a hand down his face. "Everything. Em and I had this… amazing night. We'd been dancing around each other for weeks. Months. But she's the widow of one of my closest friends. Crossing that line… Fuck, man. It was a big step."

"I get that," I agreed, nodding.

"When Royal asked me to come with him to talk to Ford about joining Phoenix, I knew I'd see her, but I didn't expect to realize…"

He shook his head, lips pressed into a hard line. "I didn't expect to feel like, when I walked into her house and saw her smiling and Elodie crawling to me, I was home."

"Yeah, I'm not seeing the problem here," I told him with a low laugh.

"Em and I had an amazing night, but Elodie woke up. I mean, she's a good sleeper, but she's teething, so I got up. I wanted Em to sleep because she's been busting her ass being a single mom, you know?" He waited for me to nod. "So, I go into the nursery, and Elodie's wide awake, chattering and smiling. I swear to fuck, bro, she's such a cool kid. Super chill. I picked her up and figured I could read her a story. That turned into three, and she started getting sleepy. I went to put her down and—" He cut off abruptly, tearing his gaze away from me and looking out the window.

I wasn't sure what to say, but I knew that haunted look. I'd been wearing it myself for a while. It was the look of a man who had lost the one thing that made any bit of goddamn sense, and he had no idea how to get her back.

"Emerson decorated Elodie's nursery, and she hung up pictures for her. So, I'm putting this amazing baby girl back to sleep, and I'm planning to go wake her mom up for round… five? Six? And I see this picture of my best friend and Emerson over Elodie's crib. It's their *wedding* picture, man," he confessed, swallowing hard. "All I could do was stare at the picture of a man who was as close to me as you or Royal or… Anyway, I was like… What the fuck am I doing? Fucking his *wife*? Playing daddy to his little girl? Taking over his life like he can be replaced?"

I grimaced as he shook his head, looking utterly destroyed.

Rook met my gaze, the raw pain swirling in his navy eyes staggering. "I put Elodie in her crib and realized I was the biggest fucking asshole on the planet."

Ouch. Yeah, that was rough. "What did you do?"

"What could I do? I got dressed and left. And it clearly was the right call—Emerson texted me the next morning and said she was taking a job with her brother's band. She's going to join them as their social media manager for the rest of their world tour." He scrubbed a hand over his face.

"You know what sucks?" Rook continued. "Like just really fucking sucks? It's not just that I lost the girl of my dreams and the little girl I was head over heels for," he admitted. "It's like I lost one of my best friends. There's no more random phone calls, or videos of Elodie doing something silly or learning something new. No texts… It's like part of me was amputated."

"I know that feeling well," I muttered. It was exactly how I felt about Bex not being in my life. Yeah, I had Linc, Ryan, and Ash. I had Maddie and my brothers.

But none of them were Bex.

"Anyway," Rook said suddenly, straightening his shoulders and shoving down the rare vulnerability he'd shown. He pushed some of the papers at me. "Here's the timeline for the meeting, best as Ash could figure out."

I twisted my neck side to side, cracking the joints, before looking at the papers. It took me a second to realize what I was seeing, and when I did, I swore like a drunken sailor. Not because Ash's intel was bad— Ash was one of the best hackers on the planet, so if this was where Jasper would be, I believed it.

But he wasn't in Brussels.

"Paris," I spat in a flat tone, my head buzzing as my heart pounded. My gaze snapped up to Rook. "We're going to *Paris*?"

He gave me a confused look. "Uh, yeah. Didn't Royal tell you?"

"No," I seethed. For as much of a badass super soldier as my oldest brother was, he was also a meddling little bitch at times. "He told me we were going to Belgium."

Rook looked confused. "Why would he—oh." Then the asshole started chuckling.

"Not funny," I snapped, hurling the papers back at him as the pilot came over the speakers and declared we'd been cleared to taxi for takeoff.

"It's pretty fucking funny," Rook laughed.

Fucking Royal, sending me to Paris. Of course the dickwad had known I'd refuse to go if I knew I'd be in the same city as Bex. Probably thought it was hilarious.

"It doesn't matter," I retorted. "We're there to do a job that'll last two, maybe three, days. I won't even see her."

"Sure," Rook agreed, grinning like a fool.

"I hate you," I muttered as Bishop exited the plane's back bedroom and ambled up to us. He threw himself into the chair across the aisle from me as the plane started rolling forward.

"What'd I miss?" he asked, his dark-eyed gaze bouncing back and forth between us.

That only made Rook laugh harder.

I kicked him under the table. "Fucker."

CHAPTER 8

BEX

I had no idea who the girl in the mirror staring back at me was, but she was hot. Like, stupid hot, in a way that made me blink a million times, worried she'd vanish.

"Holy shit," I murmured, absently reaching up to touch the cropped edge of the black leather halter top that crisscrossed my chest. The built-in bra made my C-cups look a lot bigger.

Camille popped up over my shoulder, a wicked grin on her crimson lips. "Didn't I say you'd look gorgeous as fuck by the time I was done with you, B?" Without hesitation, she reached around me and adjusted the top *and* my boobs to form even more cleavage.

"Cami," I whined, twisting away.

Camille's hazel eyes sparkled as she spun away with a swish of her long blonde hair. It hung in loose waves that hinted she'd just rolled out of bed but that I knew for a fact had taken her damn near an hour to perfect.

"Time for shoes," Cami murmured, disappearing into my closet.

I shot one last look at my reflection, at the top and skinny jeans that looked painted on my body while also making it look like I actually had an ass. Well, a small ass. Between the outfit and the makeup— smoky eyeshadow with a pop of glitter on the lids and a deep berry lip color staining my mouth—I looked ready to hit up the hottest club in Paris.

Or a biker bar.

Honestly, it could've gone either way.

But the point was, I didn't look like little Rebecca Whittier, the girl who always did what people expected and rarely made waves.

No, now I looked like Bex. Category five Hurricane Bex.

"These!" Cami declared, marching out of my closet with a pair of black stiletto ankle boots with silver buckles. My aunt Celeste, Cami's mom, had bought them for me last Christmas, and I'd worn them only once.

I was usually a jeans and t-shirt kind of girl. I lived in Converse sneakers. So I was pretty damn skeptical about the pointy-toed boots with the four-inch heels that could take out someone's eye if wielded as a weapon.

"I don't know, Cam." I hesitated, wondering how comfortable those shoes would be to dance in. They looked like I'd need to spend at least a week breaking them in. "Can't I just wear—"

Camille held up a finger with a pointed gold nail, her brows lifting. "Uh-uh, B. You are *not* going to Frisson in sneakers. I forbid it. I told Alex that the girl I was bringing for his cousin was just as hot as me."

My nose wrinkled. "I think I'm regretting asking for your help."

Cami's face softened into a pout I knew well. "Bex, come *on*. You know Alex's dad is weird. He can't go out unless he brings his brother, too."

"Because *that's* not alarming," I muttered, wondering what kind of person needed pity dates set up by their dad.

Cami waved a hand, dismissing my concern. "Trust me, girl, you have nothing to worry about. I showed you pics of Eric, and he's *yummy*."

I mean, she wasn't wrong. I made a grumbly sort of noise, ceding the point.

Cami grinned, shrugging. "If it makes you feel better, you can find some other sexy Parisian boy you wanna hook up with, and I'll be the filling in an Alex and Eric sandwich."

"By all means," I said with a teasing grin. "I don't want to get in your way."

She tipped her head back and giggled. "Bex, please. I'll elbow you out of the way myself if you try to clam jam me."

A laugh burst from me. "What?"

Cami's grin stretched wider, showing the dimples in her cheeks. "You know. Clam jam. Twat swat. Damn up my beaver."

"Please stop," I begged, my sides aching from laughing.

"Have I mentioned how glad I am that you finally moved here?" She threw her arms around me in a crushing hug.

Cami pulled back and moved to the mirror to touch up her own makeup, leaving me to tug on my shoes.

Still focused on the mirror, Cami smacked her now-glossy lips together before pursing them into a smirk and meeting my eyes in the mirror. "Let's go fuck shit up, Bex."

~

When Cami had first suggested the blind date, I'd balked. Especially when she'd told me that the *date* was being facilitated by the guy's dad. I mean, what kind of guy needed Daddy's help getting a date?

I'd felt bad for Alex, thinking how embarrassing it must be to have going out with his girlfriend be dependent on his younger sibling coming along. That was why I'd said yes—for Cami. So that she and Alex could have fun, even if it meant I'd be stuck in a dark booth at the back of the club, sipping a mocktail while Cami and her stupidly gorgeous boyfriend grinded together on the dance floor.

But Eric wasn't anything like I'd expected.

In fact, when he wrapped his hand around mine and brought it to his lips, it took me a second to figure out how to form words. The fact that Alex and Cami were making out less than a foot away was barely a blip on my brain.

Gray eyes sparkled at me through a fringe of dark lashes as Eric's warm lips touched my knuckles. "Let me guess," he began, speaking with a soft accent I couldn't quite place and still holding my hand. "You thought I was some pathetic wanker who needed his big brother's help finding a date for the night?"

"Something like that," I admitted, as the car service Cami and I had taken to the club pulled away from the curb and disappeared into the bustling night traffic. My breath fogged through the chilly air.

Darkness had blanketed Paris, leaving everything under a shimmering blanket of lights from cars, buildings, and streetlamps. The bite in the air made everything seem sharper, clearer, and people waiting to get inside huddled together in groups.

The front of Frisson looked every bit the decadent nightclub, from the purple velvet ropes containing a lengthy line of people waiting to get in, to the burly bouncers dressed in black with ear pieces. The concrete under my heels trembled from the bass of the music thumping inside.

A thrill shot through me as I realized I was doing this. I was going to a freaking nightclub in Paris on a blind date with a guy who was actually really hot.

Even if his dad was pimping him out.

Eric winked at me with a boyish grin. "My father doesn't quite understand that, unlike him and my brother, I prefer to focus on quality over quantity."

My gaze jumped to Alex, and I wondered if my cousin knew that. If she did, she didn't seem to care, judging by the way his tongue was shoved down her throat and his hands gripped her ass.

"Camille seems to be special. Or, at least that's what Alex keeps telling me," Eric added, sounding sincere as he glanced back at them. Then he made a face. "Reckon they know they're in public?"

I couldn't help a soft laugh as I watched Camille's back arch. A few people in the line were starting to notice the show. "More like they couldn't care less." I cleared my throat loudly. "Uh, Cami?"

It took a second, but she finally pulled back, her hands still clutching Alex's shoulders as she looked at me with flushed cheeks and glassy eyes. She shot me a rueful smile. "I suppose we're being rude, aren't we? Alex, this is my favorite cousin, Bex."

Alex straightened and gave me his attention. He had the same gray eyes as his brother, but where Eric's were warm, Alex's were icy, almost calculating. He studied me for a beat before a smile that looked like he'd worked in politics all his life changed his expression.

One hand still on Cami's waist, Alex leaned over and extended the other to me. "It's a pleasure to meet you, Bex," he greeted, sounding genuine, but I'd grown up around enough of my dad's politician buddies to know when someone was sincere.

This guy? Not even close.

Not wanting to offend Cami, I shook Alex's hand, tamping down the sensation of spiders crawling over my skin as his gaze raked down me once more before coming up to meet my eyes. "I've heard so much about you."

"Same," I replied, forcing a bright smile.

Cami's smile only grew as she cuddled against Alex's chest. I tried not to stare, but it was kinda blowing my mind that my smart, sweet, amazing cousin didn't seem to notice anything wrong with her boyfriend.

Then again, I'd just met him, so maybe I was the one being too judgy. Maybe Alex had one of those personalities that took some time to get to know before he showed that gooey center under all the layers of asshole.

Lord knew I'd had my own experiences with *that* type of man.

No, no, no. We're not thinking about him.

"We should go in," Alex declared, letting my hand go and turning to Cami, who nodded.

"Uh, there's a line," I pointed out as Alex took Cami by the wrist and led her straight to the bouncers.

Alex shot me a look over his shoulder like I was an adorable idiot.

Eric leaned in toward me. "I don't think my brother understands the concept of lines," he whispered.

Sure enough, Alex spoke a few words I couldn't make out to the bouncer, and a second later, the man unclipped one of the velvet ropes to let us pass. Alex flicked his fingers at us to follow, and I had to fight not to roll my eyes at his big-douche energy.

"God, he's a pompous ass, isn't he?" Eric kept up the commentary as we followed them inside. "Been this way since he was born. Sadly it's a genetic trait that the men in my family are renowned for."

I shot him an amused look as we went through the front doors and stepped into a long corridor lit by sconces. "You seem to have emerged unscathed."

He shrugged. "I take after my mother, plus I had the benefit of being sent to an all-boys boarding school starting at age eight."

My brows lifted. "Isn't that kind of… young?"

"Mum died," he explained. "She had a rare genetic disorder. After she passed, my father figured the easiest way to raise me would be to let someone else do it."

"Wow," I murmured, imagining how awful it would be to have a parent die and then be shipped off to school all alone. "Did Alex not go with you?"

Ahead of us, Cami giggled at something Alex whispered. They paused at the coat check, shrugging off their jackets and passing them over. When Eric and I did the same, the attendant passed me a ticket that I tucked into my small clutch.

"You are absolutely stunning," Eric told me, sounding a little awed.

I pressed my lips together but was unable to stop the smile that started to spread. Maybe Cami's fashion sense had been dead on after all. "Thank you."

"See?" Cami called, her tone airy as she waggled her elegant fingers. "I told you my cousin was exceptionally gorgeous." She winked at me before hugging Alex's arm to her chest while he led us down another hallway with an elevator at the end.

Eric's lips pressed into a line, tension furrowing his brow for a millisecond before it smoothed away. "No. He's five years older and has always been in line to take over my father's position when the time comes. Family business, passed from one oldest son to the next."

"Sounds… archaic," I answered. I knew Alex was older than Cami, but I did the math. Eric was probably twenty-three, which put Alex somewhere much closer to the line of thirty than Cami's twenty years.

"It absolutely is," he agreed, "but it allowed me the freedom to choose my own path."

Alex pressed a button for the elevator and turned to us, his gaze hard as he looked at his brother. "Yes, your own path. And how exactly is that going, little brother?"

Eric met his brother's gaze with a level stare. "Splendidly. I mean, it doesn't come with a lifetime membership to Assholes Anonymous like yours does, but we can't all be winners, can we?"

Alex's top lip lifted in a curl as Cami chuckled.

"Oh, come on, Eric," she said, her tone light and teasing as she leaned around Alex, "he didn't turn out *that* bad. I've trained him well."

"Have you now?" Alex said, his voice quiet but with an edge that made me stiffen.

The elevator doors chimed before sliding open. No one moved.

Cami's face fell. "I was just kidding, baby."

"Quite the comedian, aren't you, pet?" Alex remarked, his jaw still tight.

Eric forced a rough laugh. "Come on, Alex. We're here to have fun. You remember what fun is, right?"

I watched the exchange with unease, waiting for something to break the tension. My gaze shot to my cousin, but she seemed intent on studying the dark wood floors under our feet.

"I'm sorry," Cami whispered.

For what? I wanted to demand. For her boyfriend being an asshole, or for him giving off serial-killer vibes?

I was seconds away from grabbing my cousin and marching us the hell out of here. When she'd told me all about her billionaire boyfriend, showing off pictures of them all over Paris, I'd never gotten creep vibes. But now that he was in front of me? Bright red alarms were flashing in my mind.

Alex leaned forward and pressed a kiss to Cami's temple. "Let's not ruin our night."

Cami nodded, the hand not tangled with his balled into a fist at her side.

Alex shot us a cocky smile. "And for the record, little brother, I know how to have p-plenty of f-fun." The acid bite of his tone made me step back, but not before I felt Eric flinch.

"Let's go," Alex added, getting into the elevator car with Camille.

After a beat, Eric went in, and I followed, albeit reluctantly. I spent the silent ride up to the third floor mentally rehearsing how I planned to grab Cami for a bathroom trip as soon as the doors opened. I needed to know what in the actual hell my cousin was thinking.

God, I wished Maddie was here. She'd know what to say.

Then again, if Maddie was here, that would've meant *Ryan* was here. And I could just imagine Ryan Cain putting Alex in his place.

But with Ryan came—

No, Bex, I mentally chastised myself before my thoughts could veer too far into dangerous territory.

Tonight wasn't about *him*, it was about *me*. Well, actually it was turning out to be more about my cousin and her horrible choice in boyfriends, but the point was, I wasn't thinking about Court Woods.

Dammit.

Just thinking his name was like having my nervous system struck by lightning.

Bad Bex. Focus on Cami.

"Are we getting off?" Eric asked me, his voice soft with amusement as I realized the doors were open. Alex and Cami had already stepped off and were watching me, waiting. Cami looked concerned, but Alex looked like someone had shoved a stick wrapped in barbed wire up his ass while he sucked off a lemon.

"Uh, sorry," I stammered, hurrying out of the car as the heavy bass of one song bled into another.

The third floor was clearly the VIP section, if the dark, decadent furniture and mood lighting were any indication. Set above the rest of the club, the VIP balcony had its own bar. Instead of the industrial style of the rest of the club, this area was high end, with cushioned sofas, lacquered tables, and a black iron railing that let the guests look out over the club.

My gaze zeroed in on the sign for the bathroom. "Hey, Cam, let's—"

"Camille," Alex cut in, turning so he was positioned between us as he cupped her cheek. "Would you dance with me?"

She smiled, her heart in her eyes as she beamed up at him. "Of course."

"We'll be back," Alex informed us, again taking my cousin by the wrist and leading her toward a staircase that I wouldn't be trying to navigate in these heels. Cami, however, was a study in grace as she floated downward.

"Guess it's just us, huh?" Eric said from my left.

I turned and gave him a one-shouldered shrug as I fought the urge to follow my cousin and ask her what the hell was going on. She was amazing and deserved a guy who'd treat her a lot better than Alex.

Huh. Maybe I could show her you could move on from a hot-yet-toxic guy and find someone with more low-key energy.

Grinning at Eric, I vowed to make the best of tonight. To give this guy every chance I could, because I deserved a nice guy, dammit.

"Do you want to find a table and talk?" I asked him, waving a hand around the crowded room. "I'd love to get to know you better."

His smile was full of warmth and hope as he took my hand. "I'd love to."

CHAPTER 9

BEX

With a soft hand on the small of my back, Eric led me toward a table in the center of the room. I appreciated that he didn't pick one of the booths shrouded in shadows along the wall. I could barely make out some of the people in them, which was probably the point. A single pendant light hung above our table, giving me enough light to appreciate how hot my date was.

Eric pulled out a chair and waited for me to sit before circling to the other side and sitting across from me. As soon as his butt hit the chair, a waitress in a tight black dress appeared with a bright smile.

"Can I bring either of you a drink?" she offered, her flirty eyes dragging over Eric with appreciation before turning to me with a slight lift of one eyebrow. Almost like she was wondering how *I* was here with *him*.

"Bex?" Eric shot me an expectant look, waiting for me to go first.

"Oh, uh." I looked for a menu, but this struck me as an *if you don't know what you want, you don't belong here* kind of place. "Can I get a virgin sangria?"

I half expected the waitress to laugh, but she didn't bat an eye before turning to Eric.

"Water for me, please. Thank you." He gave a subtle nod of his chin, dismissing her.

"Not a drinker?" I asked, kind of surprised.

"No," he replied, leaning back in his chair with a rueful smile. "I've never much enjoyed the taste. You?"

I shrugged, not wanting to admit that the last time I'd had alcohol I'd been drugged and almost raped. I wasn't looking at tonight with Eric as an actual date, but even so, that wasn't the kind of stuff I was comfortable sharing with just anyone.

But damn, looking back, that night had been the turning point that made all the difference. It had put me on a collision course with my past and present.

I'd be damned if it screwed up my future, too.

"So, are you and Alex close?" I asked, needing to change the subject. Maybe Eric could give me some insight into his big brother that would make him seem less like an entitled frat boy douche canoe.

Eric coughed and shook his head. "Hardly. Separate upbringings aside, Alex and I have never been close. He favors our father while I favor our mum… flaws and all."

I waited until the waitress set our drinks down and turned away before leaning in. "Flaws?"

His cheeks flushed an adorable shade of pink that spread to the tips of his ears as he ducked his head. He picked up the glass of water and swished the contents like it was a fine wine, watching the ice cubes clack together. "My mother suffered from a speech impediment as a child. A stutter," he clarified with a grimace. "I also had a stutter as a boy."

I remembered Alex's taunting comment in the elevator. The way Eric had flinched.

In that moment, Alex leveled up from frat boy douche canoe to ignorant twatwaffle.

"I'm sorry," I offered, not sure why I always felt the need to apologize for someone else's character flaw. Maybe that was *my* flaw. Well, one of many. Staring at the sangria, I started to wish it had alcohol in it.

"Thank you," Eric said, surprising me by reaching across the table and touching my hand.

Stunned, I blinked at him.

One corner of his mouth tilted up in a half smile. "You hear people say that they're sorry a lot in life. But you seem to genuinely mean it."

"Maybe I know what it's like to have people ridicule and mock you for things beyond your control," I hedged, not willing to deep dive into my tragic middle- and high-school years.

"That's a damned shame, love," he murmured, his fingers stroking the top of my hand in a way that wasn't unpleasant. His eyes were soft as he studied me. "I've only known you for a few minutes, and I can already tell that you're not like the others."

"Others?" I echoed.

He pressed his lips together. "Look, may I be honest?"

"Please." It would be a nice change of pace from most of the other men in my life.

"I grew up in a world of unimaginable privilege and wealth," he confided, his expression somber. "I'd imagine you did as well."

I inclined my head slightly. While my family might not have been as rich as those of some of the kids I went to school with, I'd never wanted for a thing. There'd been stacks of presents under every Christmas tree and a limit I'd never hit on my credit cards.

No, not *my* credit cards. My parents' cards, which they paid off every month without question.

Eric blew out a breath, his chiseled jaw tight. "I never asked for it, and while I can see the many things it has afforded me, it also left me with the realization that there's very little substance in my life. It's all filters and photoshop, I suppose."

"That's a good way of putting it," I agreed, and sipped my drink.

"When I talk to you, I don't get that impression."

I stilled, my head tilting as I tried to puzzle out exactly what he meant. His gray eyes seemed to glow under the dim lights, and he reached for my hand again.

"I refuse to be the type of man my father and brother are," he told me. "Constantly flitting from one pleasure to the next. One thing my mother taught me was to trust my intuition, and right now, it's telling me that you are exquisitely different from the other women in my life."

Okay, as far as lines went, that might've been the best one I'd ever heard. But it wasn't just a line; Eric was a guy who felt the way I did—utterly lost in a sea of false promises and feigned adoration.

It was why I'd come to Paris. For clarity… and healing.

My heart flipped over, and I glanced down at where he was touching my hand before flipping my palm up and lacing our fingers together.

Eric cleared his throat, the blush from before reappearing. "I expected to meet another one of Alex's friends and prepared myself to be bored to tears before making an excuse to go home early. But you… I like you, Bex."

My breath caught.

This was what I'd wanted, right? To forget… Well, to forget. To take back control of my heart. The stupid organ had made a serious mess of my life thus far. It was time for me to stop craving what I'd never have and start appreciating what I could.

"I like you, too," I finally replied, not sure I meant it the same way he did. Was I attracted to Eric? I mean, sure. Sorta. He was really good looking in a catalog-model kind of way, with a sharp jaw, piercing gray eyes, and the lean frame of a guy whose form of exercise was probably swimming or running. Maybe cross-country.

"So," he went on, a bit hesitant like he was waiting to be shot down.

I knew that feeling well.

"If I wanted to ask you out on a proper date," he continued, "you might be inclined to say yes?"

No.

The unbidden thought came with a flash of dark, pissed-off eyes that I knew way too well. It was *his* voice in my head. It was always him.

He was on the other side of the damn planet, and my gut was still keyed in to what *he* would say. Would want.

Eric's mom might've told her son to trust his gut, but I'd learned the hard way that trusting my own meant heartache and pain.

And I was over that.

I smiled back at Eric, shoving down the gnawing feeling that even considering going out with him was somehow wrong.

My heart needed to remember her loyalty was to *me*. Not the boy who'd broken her more than once.

"I would absolutely say yes to a date with you."

CHAPTER 10

BEX

"Sugar," I hissed as I stubbed my toe on the edge of my bed. That was what I got for trying to zip up my dress while kicking around piles of discarded clothes looking for my shoes.

"Are you okay?" The worried voice of my best friend came out of the speakers to the laptop I'd left open on the desk behind me.

The zipper stuck, and I swallowed a scream. I shouldn't be *this* stressed out.

"Bex?" Maddie called again, worry lacing her tone.

"Here!" I cried, managing to zip the dress and stumble back into the frame of the camera so she could see me.

Maddie's bright blue eyes blinked. "Are you wearing… plaid?"

I looked down at the black and white skirt. "It's tweed."

Her brow wrinkled. "Plaid."

"Herringbone," I corrected with a huff, sitting in my desk chair and reaching for the pearl drop earrings.

"Whatever it is… B, are you sure everything's okay?"

"Of course it is," I chirped, my voice too bright. Too forced. I paused and took a breath. "Eric's going to be here any minute, and I can't find my shoes." I glanced around my demolished bedroom with a forlorn look.

Maddie studied me in a way that broadcasted she was seeing just how frazzled I really was. "It's been, what, a week since you first met this Eric dude? You guys have gone out three times already."

"Four," I mumbled, remembering I hadn't told her about our impromptu lunch yesterday. But it was true. In the seven days since I'd met Eric, we'd gone on several dates, each one sweeter than the last.

Dinner at a trendy spot in the sixth arrondissement. A play at Théâtre Mogadore. Coffee at a quaint little patisserie. And lunch yesterday at Le Trumilou.

Every time I was with Eric, I got to know him a little better, and I liked him. I liked that he played the cello but was a fan of alt rock. I knew that he'd rescued a cat named St. Whiskers and managed to hide him at school for three years before being caught. He was terrified of puffins.

Tonight, we were having dinner and drinks with some of his old boarding-school friends. He wanted me to meet the people that were important to him, which had to mean something.

The more layers I peeled back, the more I found there was to like.

But there was something missing, and I was determined not to let date five pass without figuring it out. Which was why I was freaking out. Tonight was the night that I would know for sure.

It had to be.

I looked in the mirror and realized I looked like I was going to dinner with my grandparents and their friends.

"Fine, maybe it isn't okay." I groaned, covering my face with my hands.

Maddie sucked in a breath. "It's gonna be all right, Bex. I think. But it might help if I knew *why* you were freaking out?"

I dropped my hands. "Because tonight's *the night*."

Her eyes went comically wide. "You're going to sleep with him?"

Instant embarrassment heated my cheeks, but before I could stammer out a correction, another voice chimed in.

A voice I knew *way* too well.

"Who's sleeping with who?" Linc demanded, his tone a mix of curiosity and innuendo as he appeared over Maddie's shoulder. He grinned when he saw me, ducking so his face was level with Maddie's. "Bex! Damn, I miss you, girl. I can't believe you're staying in France." His lower lip jutted out in an exaggerated pout.

"Linc," Maddie hissed, pushing on his massive shoulder. It basically did nothing; Linc was too big and strong to be moved. "We're talking."

"Right, about sex, which happens to be my specialty," he replied, shrugging as I contemplated sliding off the chair and under my desk in mortification. His dark blue eyes, just a shade lighter than navy, pinned me through the screen. "Who're you planning on fucking, and do I know him?"

I wasn't entirely sure what kind of sound I made—a cross between a dying moose and a startled chipmunk—but I knew that this was quite possibly the most embarrassing moment of my life.

"No one," I finally managed, my hands flapping wildly as I tried to explain. "I meant tonight I'm going to kiss him."

Yeah, that actually didn't lessen my humiliation the way I'd thought it would.

Linc's dark brows shot up. "And who, pray tell, is the beneficiary of your sweet kisses?"

Maddie made a growling sound. "That's the last time I watch Bridgerton with you, Linc."

He pressed a hand to his chest, his attention on her. "Mads, you wound my very soul."

"Not as much as I'm going to *wound you* if I punch you in the nuts for not leaving us alone," Maddie snapped back, arching a brow before pointedly dropping her gaze to his crotch.

Linc twisted his lower half away, crossing his legs. "Jesus. When did you get so violent?" His eyes narrowed. "And why is the idea of you spanking my nuts so hot?"

"That's not... I didn't..." Maddie spluttered.

Linc patted her head. "It's cool, Mads. We just can't tell Ryan. He'd probably cut *off* my nuts, but it can be our secret."

"Would you get out of here? I thought you *and* your nuts were going to a party." Maddie gave him an exasperated look.

Linc grinned. "I was about to, but then I heard you talking about sex."

"No sex!" I cried, raising my hands. "No one is having sex, Linc."

His face fell. "Well that's a damn shame."

"It is?" Maddie spoke up before I could.

Linc nodded and gestured to the screen. "Hell yeah. I mean, Bex is hot. Tight little body. Awesome rack. She should be getting orgasms on the regular from places other than her own fingers. Fucking shame to hide all that pretty away." His gaze cut to me, suddenly serious. "Unless he's a douche, in which case, I'll be on the first flight to bury his ass."

Maddie groaned. "Linc, can you just not?"

"What? I'm giving her compliments," he argued. "I'd tell you the same thing, but I know—for a fact—that you get dick on the regular. And judging by the screams, it's good dick. I'm proud of Ryan."

"I am literally begging you to shut up," she pleaded, turning so red it bordered on purple.

Linc straightened as a smirk pulled at his lips. "Kinda like the way you were begging Ryan last night for—"

Maddie exploded out of her chair, this time slapping Linc's chest. "I swear to God, Linc, I'll kill you. Better yet? I'll tell Ryan and let *him* kill you. Slowly. Graphically. Starting with *your* dick."

Linc dropped a hand to cover his crotch. "I was just kidding." He backed away. "But maybe invest in a ball gag if you don't want everyone—" He spun and ran out of the picture as Maddie lunged for him.

"Asshole," she huffed, collapsing into the chair as she shook her head. Then she turned and looked at me. "Any chance I can come stay with you in Paris?"

I laughed. Yeah, my face was still flaming hot, but something about their exchange made my heart clench. I missed my friends and their crazy. "I mean, we have four guest rooms, and you have a standing invitation."

She ran a hand through her long blonde tresses. "Seriously, what was I thinking, insisting that the guys move in with us? It's like having children. And without Court here, Linc is like a puppy without a playmate."

My insides tightened. "Where is he?" The question fell from my lips before I could help myself, and I immediately tried to take it back. "Not that I care. But it's weird."

Maddie gave me a knowing look. "He's traveling for Phoenix with Rook and Bishop. I don't know the details, and honestly? I told Ryan I'm good being on a need-to-know basis with *that* stuff."

That stuff being the international company her husband and his friends had started to help people, namely those hurt by their asshole fathers. Court's half-brothers were also heavily involved, and while I didn't know all the details, I knew enough.

Enough to know that Court traveling with two of his former military brothers wasn't about sweet-talking new investors.

It was dangerous. Maybe even deadly.

Suddenly a kiss didn't seem like such a big deal.

"Bex?"

I jerked, my gaze finding Maddie.

Her face softened. "He'll be okay. It's mostly recon, from what I gathered. Minimal danger."

"That's… good." And yet, my heart didn't seem to get that memo. No. No. *No.*

This was exactly why I'd been going out with Eric all week— because I refused to spend any more time hung up on Court Woods.

"So, about tonight," I started, pushing onward.

Maddie's expression said she knew I was trying to change the subject, but because she was my best friend, she let it go. "Why is tonight the night?"

"Isn't it weird that we've been on five dates and haven't kissed?"

Her lips pressed together. "I don't think there's a timetable on that, B."

"Says the girl who got married to her husband after knowing him for a few weeks," I pointed out.

She lifted a finger. "One, we were engaged before we ever met. Two, we were being forced into it because of our psycho fathers.

Three… I mean, have you *seen* my husband? He's gorgeous. Of course I locked his ass down."

I laughed, my head falling back. "Right."

Still smiling, she shook her head. "Seriously, Bex, don't force this because… Just because."

But I knew what she wasn't saying.

Because of him.

"This is what I want, Maddie," I insisted. Maybe if I said it enough, I'd believe it.

Sighing, my bestie relented. "Okay. Whatever makes you happy, B."

I forced a smile and turned my attention back to my missing shoes.

"Have you talked to Cami?" Maddie asked.

My gut tightened into a ball of unease. "Not really." After the night at the club, I'd tried talking to her about Alex, but she'd brushed off my concerns and said he'd had a rough day. Then she'd been busy with her dance rehearsals. We'd texted, but I was hoping we'd be able to actually sit down and talk about the not-awesome vibes I'd gotten from her boyfriend.

"Sorry," Maddie murmured, looking sympathetic. "I know you and Cami are really close."

"Mads, I swear he ticks every single box for an abusive boyfriend," I told her, my heart sinking. "The way he treats her like an object, the way she defers to him? I mean, he got mad, and she acted like it was all *her* fault."

"Want me to have Ash look into him?" she offered. Ash was one of the best hackers we knew. If there was dirt on Alex, Ash would find it.

I wasn't ready to go there.

Yet.

"Let's keep Ash on the back burner," I replied. "Cami and I are supposed to hang out tomorrow. Alex has a thing with his dad." I ground my teeth, annoyed that my brilliant, talented cousin didn't see the red flags that I did.

"Good luck," Maddie said, genuinely meaning it.

My gaze swept the length of my room once more, and I spotted the tip of a shoe by the bathroom door, under a gauzy skirt. I darted over and unearthed the heels from where they'd been abandoned.

"Gotcha," I proclaimed, slipping them on my feet. Owning a pair of heels that made my legs look insanely good while also being comfortable enough to wear for hours was like finding a unicorn dipped in fairy dust.

I crossed back to my desk to finish talking to Maddie as someone knocked at my door.

"Miss Rebecca? Your friend has arrived," announced the voice of Yvette, the house manager who had been with my grandparents since before I'd been born. She was practically a second grandmother to me.

Butterflies erupted in my belly, and I pressed a hand against my stomach. "Thank you, Yvette. Please tell him I'll be down in a few minutes." Once I heard Yvette walk away, I turned to Maddie.

The butterflies morphed into a flock of crows, pecking at my insides and leaving me a ball of raw nerves. "He's here."

Maddie frowned, a deep crease forming between her eyes. "Bex, you know you don't have to do anything you don't want to, right?"

"I know that." I bristled at the implication, even if it rang a little true. "I *want* this." I quickly ripped off my outfit and grabbed a fitted navy blue dress with a boat neck and lace sleeves. I took off the pearls and grabbed a pair of diamond studs.

She sighed softly. "Then I hope it's everything you're dreaming of. But, Bex?"

I held my breath, waiting for her to finish.

"If he doesn't treat you like the princess you are, Linc won't even have enough pieces left to bury by the time I finish with him," she told me, dead-ass serious.

I couldn't help but laugh and smile. "I miss you, Mads."

"Back at ya," she replied with a grin. "Have fun, okay?"

I nodded and ended the video chat, then ran my hands down the dress, trying to smooth away my nerves like invisible wrinkles. Tonight was going to be *fun*. This was exactly what I was supposed to want.

But is it what you need?

I blinked at my reflection in the mirror over my vanity, the quiet question making my heart sink into my stomach. Until a knock at the door drew my attention away. "Come in."

The door pushed open, and Mom appeared, her dark hair pulled back into a ponytail that made her look like my big sister, not my mom. Dressed in gray scrubs, she flashed me a tired smile. "Hey, sweetie."

"I thought you were working late," I said, wincing at my accusatory tone.

She sighed and came inside. "I know, I know. I asked you to come to Paris with me so we could spend more time together, but all I seem to do is work."

"I mean, I didn't say that," I muttered, feeling guilty. My mom was a doctor. She saved lives for a living. It was kinda selfish for me to want her to go on mani-pedi dates instead of performing an emergency appendectomy on a ten-year-old.

That had been Step #3 of Betty Moreau's *New Life Plan*.

Step #1 had been filing for divorce from my father.

Step #2 was leaving all the *toxic energy* of California.

Step #3 had been to devote her surgical skills to people who actually needed them instead of getting paid stupid amounts of money to be on retainer when one of her rich clients got a nasty case of tennis elbow.

Step #4 was going back to her maiden name. Part of me wanted to ask if I could switch, too. Rebecca Whittier had seen more shit than I cared to recount.

She sat down at my vanity, facing me. "I'm sorry, Bex. I promise I'm going to make more time for us. Between the new position at the hospital and helping Mémé plan her birthday celebration, I've absolutely been neglecting you."

"Mom, I'm eighteen, not eight," I reminded her, sitting on the edge of my bed. "I don't need you to entertain me."

She arched a brow. "Clearly not. You look pretty fancy for a Thursday night."

"I have a date," I admitted, a blush heating my face.

"Would this be a date with the same boy I've seen drop you off almost every night this week?" she teased.

My jaw dropped. "You know about that?"

She laughed. "Sweetie, I'm still your mom. Of course I know when things are going on with you." She paused, smiling at me. "You look beautiful."

"Thanks, Mom."

She stood. "Then I won't hold you up. Have fun." She winked. "Be safe."

"Mom!" Humiliation burned through me.

"What?" she asked with a giggle. "I was young once." Her smile slipped the way it always did when there was even a hint of Dad in the conversation.

Mom and I both apparently had a thing for guys who had the power to break our hearts. This was all the more reason for me to keep spending time with Eric.

Eric was *exactly* what I should need. Someone safe and reliable and predictable. Someone who treated me like I was an equal, instead of making life-altering, unilateral decisions for me.

Squaring my shoulders, I lifted my chin. I deserved a guy who wanted me for me.

And, just maybe, Eric was that man.

CHAPTER 11

COURT

"Thanks, sweetheart," Douche Number Three said to the waitress, leaning over and not bothering to hide that he was checking out her butt as she walked away. The guy had been glued to his cell phone the whole time unless he was ogling the staff. "Fuck, look at that ass."

Douche Number One leaned back and gave a long, *loud* groan of appreciation. "I'd split that open like a ripe apple. She'd feel me for days."

The waitress, a tiny, curvy woman who barely looked over eighteen, hunched her shoulders and tried to make herself smaller as their words hit her ears. Her cheeks turned red, and not for the first time since we'd started watching what Rook had dubbed the Dinner of Douches.

She and another waitress, also pretty, had been assigned the table by the manager of Aubergine, a trendy, upscale French restaurant that was damn near impossible to get into without a reservation made six months prior. The clientele was elite and catered to by the staff to a disturbing degree.

Then again, the owner was Pierre Dupree, a guy on our radar for being a depraved sadist with a penchant for less-than-willing sexual partners. If it had been up to me, I'd have put a bullet in his head as soon as we'd landed in Paris. But killing a cockroach like Dupree would have lasting repercussions, and we owed it to his victims to make sure they were safe before they ended up as collateral damage.

This was the part we all hated. Playing the long game to make sure shit was handled right.

And that meant sitting on my ass, watching the security feeds from Aubergine that Ash had hacked.

I arched my back, feeling the vertebrae pop back into place. I'd been sitting on my ass for far too long, because this sure as fuck wasn't typical security. Most restaurant security systems didn't have hidden microphones seamlessly blended into the tables and booths, or military-grade cameras hovering above patrons. No, Dupree had set up the restaurant perfectly to spy on his wealthy patrons.

Ninety percent of the customers weren't up to anything nefarious. They were like the couple in the back corner who had just gotten engaged over a six-hundred-dollar bottle of champagne. Or the sleazy businessmen toasting another company they'd recently liquidated.

We were here for the other ten percent. The ones who ate wagyu beef and lobster while casually plotting murder. Or, in the case of the douchey dinner, an illegal sex-trafficking ring and the upcoming auction scheduled to take place in a week at some unknown spot in Paris for which we needed the location.

Which was why Rook and I were holed up in a hotel room with takeout containers from a local Chinese joint, eating wontons with our fingers while Bishop snored on the couch across from us.

Our hotel was a block away, but even through the screen of the laptop, I could see that the lavish, decadent restaurant was all glitz and glamor. Massive gold-and-crystal chandeliers provided warm lighting. The tables and booths, set discreetly apart to give the illusion of privacy, were made of the richest woods and leathers. Hell, there was a fucking mural of angels and demons painted on the ceiling like the Sistine Chapel. Asking for a burger was probably sacrilegious or some shit.

Waves of disgust and unease rolled off Rook. His shoulders were knotted with tension. It was like he was allergic to the upper class. He'd been like this for the past hour, watching this group of four assholes, each one smarmier than the next, hit on anything with tits that came near their table.

One leaned forward, his beady eyes magnified behind massive black glasses. "Five grand says I'll fuck her tonight."

Number Two tipped back his head and laughed, the sound like a dying donkey. "You're on. No way she says yes."

Two snorted and picked up his single malt. "Who said she has to say yes?"

That brought out a grunt from Number Three, who'd mostly been quiet. Then again, he was stoned as fuck and barely seemed to be sitting upright.

But, like a true pervert, he rallied when the threat of violence and sex loomed. "I could use a pick-me-up after this week."

Clearly I'd be following the waitress home tonight.

From the chair beside mine, Rook shot me a disgusted look. "I'm going to need to bathe in bleach."

I arched a brow. "Before or after you break some knees?"

My brother grinned, his look a little unhinged. "After, obviously."

A smirk hooked up the corners of my mouth. "I'll help you bury the bodies."

"Fuck that. Dipshits don't deserve the effort a hole in the ground would take. We'll burn 'em."

"Alive?"

He shot me an annoyed look. "Obviously. No point in killing an asshole if they don't suffer horrifically first."

A dark chuckle rumbled through my chest, and I turned my attention to the monitor to see Douche Number Four return to the table from the bathroom.

"Jesus, Henry," One sneered, looking at the red-faced, disheveled man who'd been on the receiving end of their shit all night, "can you at least try to look like you aren't a dickless sack of shit?"

The other two laughed, and Four turned beet-red. I wasn't sure of the history here, beyond knowing they'd all gone to the same bullshit prep school and university. Their families had been friends and business partners since before they were born.

"It's a family thing," Three laughed, snapping out of his drug-induced stupor and shaking his head. "Beatrice sweats like a whore in church when she's on her knees for me. It's fucking nasty."

Two made a low, hooting sound. "You've been fucking Henry's sister?"

Three looked genuinely disgusted. "Fuck no. But she's always down to suck my fat cock." He reached under the table to cup his junk. "After the week I've had, dealing with all that family shit, she's probably swallowed a gallon of my cum."

Henry looked like he wanted to say something but opted to keep his head down.

One leaned back in his chair, his toothy smile eerily like a shark's as he watched Henry. "You teach her how to do that, Henry? Teach her how to get on her knees and please a man?"

"Fuck's sake," Rook spat, looking close to hurling.

I wasn't too far behind. I looked back at Bishop, wishing like hell I'd done surveillance duty last night so I could sleep through this shit tonight. Lucky motherfucker.

"In fact," One continued, his tone dangerously soft in a way that set my teeth on edge, "maybe you should get on your knees for me now, Henry. Crawl under this table and suck me off."

Two and Three fell silent, their gazes bouncing back and forth between the two men as they seemed to realize this was a little more than giving Henry shit. Two actually put his phone down, clearly more riveted by this scene than whatever was on his screen.

One braced his forearms on the linen tablecloth, his eyes bright with a manic sort of energy as he looked across the table at a pale Henry. "I'm serious. Get on your motherfucking knees and crawl to me, bitch."

Two let out an uneasy laugh, looking around to see if anyone was around. "Fucking hell, Colby. You aren't serious, right?"

Colby didn't back down, his stare hard as he glared at Henry. "Henry knows just how fucking serious I am."

Three opened his mouth.

"Crawl," Colby growled before arching his brows. "Unless you want me—"

"No," Henry choked out quickly, shaking his head so emphatically, I wondered if it would snap off his neck. He looked close to tears. "It's… Colby, *please*."

Colby's lip curled. "The next time you open that mouth, it better be to—"

"He's here," Three cut in, looking relieved as fuck.

I shot Rook a look, because this was what we'd been waiting for. The arrival of the fifth member of their fucked-up boys' club. The leader of their group. A guy who, at twenty-three, was already making a name for himself globally. He'd recently moved back to Paris and taken over the shipping company his mother had left him when she'd died. He'd wasted no time setting up a network to transport more than just luxury cars and computers across international borders.

No, this motherfucker had figured out how to add *people* as cargo while greasing the right palms to get government and political officials to look the other way.

All four men stood as a unit, watching their friend arrive with a woman on his arm.

Of course he'd bring a girl with him. It was a power move, showing off a shiny new trophy that he'd probably offer up as a party favor for them to share after—

My breath caught.

My heart fucking stopped.

"Whoa," Rook murmured, straightening and turning to me, alarm in his expression. "Court."

But it was like he was talking to me underwater, the sounds muffled and disjointed as I stared at the screen. At the petite brunette with the big hazel eyes, smiling as she reached out her hand for Colby to drag up to his lips. He kissed her knuckles, making her cheeks blush the prettiest shade of pink.

I was vaguely aware of Rook waking up Bishop, but I was already on my feet and headed for the door, ripping it open. I bypassed the elevator and headed for the stairs, not giving a shit that we were fifteen floors up. The elevator would take too long, and I couldn't stand there and wait.

Not knowing that down the street, Bex had just walked herself into the goddamn lion's den.

CHAPTER 12

BEX

"It's so nice to meet you," I told Colby, offering him a smile as he kissed the back of my hand and winked at me.

"Eric, you asshole," Colby said, turning to his friend with a teasing glare, "where have you been hiding this delectable creature?"

God, that was the cheesiest of lines, and it was all I could do not to roll my eyes. With that smarmy grin and rich, velvety voice with a slight Irish lilt, this guy had a future in politics.

"Away from you miscreants," Eric replied, tugging me back to his side before continuing introductions. "Ignore Colby, Bex. We all do."

Colby jutted out his lower lip in an exaggerated pout that wasn't fooling me. I turned to the next guy, who gave me a long look before offering a hand.

"Brent Collingswood," he said, his pointy chin lifted in an aristocratic way that made him look more like a pompous asshole than a distinguished gentleman.

"Hello." I gave him a polite smile before turning to the next.

"Geoffry Barnes," he drawled, red-rimmed eyes a little glassy and unfocused as he shook my hand. As soon as he released me, his gaze wandered away.

I glanced at Eric, who gave me a concerned look and a helpless little smile. Like he was saying, *sorry my friends are idiots.*

Shrugging it off, I gazed at the last man. He looked like he wanted to be anywhere but here. Beads of sweat dotted his brow, and his chest heaved like he'd run a marathon.

"Henry?" Colby prompted in a tone I couldn't quite figure out. "Say hello to Eric's friend." He reached back, almost like he was going to sling an arm around Henry's shoulders, but Henry dodged him at the last second, then froze. Fear trickled into his expression.

Colby laughed, the sound forced and a little caustic. "Forgive us, Bex. Henry and I have a long history of roughhousing. He always seems to think I'm going to tackle him or some shite."

But Henry wasn't laughing.

He did, however, shuffle forward and incline his head to me. "Nice to meet you, Bex."

"You, too," I replied, not sure if I meant it or not. Unsure what to do next, I looked back at Eric and caught him frowning, too.

As soon as he realized I was watching him, his expression smoothed into something neutral. He glanced at his friends. "Give us a moment."

Without complaint, they moved back to the table and took the seats they'd had previously.

Eric pulled me to his side and pressed a kiss to my temple, murmuring, "Sorry, love. We'll make an excuse and leave if you want."

I subtly shook my head and turned my face to his. "No, it's fine. But is Geoffry okay?"

Eric smiled and bumped his nose with mine while lifting a hand to tuck my hair behind my ear. "His grandfather recently passed. They were extremely close. That's why I agreed to see them tonight. He's in town for the funeral and is clearly self-medicating."

"Oh no." I couldn't imagine losing my grandparents.

"Colby and Henry… They've got a complicated past. It's been awkward since they hooked up a few months ago," he added, his tone somber. "Their families will never allow them to be together."

I scowled. "Small-minded assholes."

Eric grinned at me. "I'm sorry I brought you, love. I knew that Geoffry needed a night with his friends, but I couldn't stand the thought of being away from you."

Warmth wrapped around my chest.

Eric's nose wrinkled. "I suppose I sound like a proper bleeding idiot, don't I?"

I tilted my head. "What? No. Why would you say that?"

He sucked in a deep breath, his cheeks turning pink. "We've scarcely known each other a week, and I can't seem to stay away from you." A hand came up to cradle my cheek. "You're becoming my favorite addiction, Bex."

My heart did a little flip, because that was exactly what I wanted to hear… right? For some reason, I couldn't shake off the feeling that this felt wrong. Maybe it was because Eric's friends seemed like a bunch of jerks, and I was putting a lot of pressure on tonight.

But Eric wasn't his friends. You couldn't help who you grew up with; I was proof positive of that.

His voice dipped. "You have no idea how much I want to kiss you right now."

My breath caught. "O-okay." Nervous butterflies erupted in my belly.

"I'm not kissing you for the first time in front of my mates, love," he said with a low chuckle. He closed the inches that had separated us. "But later tonight…"

A smile lifted the corners of my mouth as my heart beat faster. Anticipation flowed through my veins in an icy wave of nerves that left me unsteady. I needed to stop putting so much pressure on a freaking kiss.

And I definitely needed to *not* be wondering if Eric would kiss the way I'd always dreamed of being kissed: dominating and controlling, making me feel safe and precious.

I'd always been drawn to the alphahole heroes, in books and in life. But those guys weren't good in anything but fiction. Dependable. Reliable. Constant. That was what I needed.

Geez, are you finding a boyfriend or a car, Bex?

I mentally slapped myself back into the moment, shoving aside my wandering thoughts.

Eric let out a shuddering breath, probably mistaking my silence for reluctance. "Maybe we *should* go."

"No," I replied, shaking my head. "I think it's sweet that you want to be here for your friend. But I can leave if—"

"Absolutely not." He seemed insulted that I'd even suggest it. "But thank you for being so understanding, Bex."

He pressed another chaste kiss to my forehead before stepping back and lowering a hand to the small of my back to guide me to the table.

There were two empty seats, and Colby jumped up to pull out the one next to him while flashing me a winning smile.

"Thank you," I murmured, sliding into the seat and watching Eric lower himself into the chair beside me. Clearing my throat, I looked at Geoffry across the table. "I'm so sorry about your grandfather."

Geoffry paused halfway to lifting a tumbler of an amber-colored liquid to his lips. He gave me a slow, unfocused blink. "Uh, yeah. Thanks." He tossed back the drink with a grimace and signaled for another.

I looked at Eric, worried for his friend.

Eric's lips pressed into a thin line, and he reached for my hand under the table.

"So, Bex," Colby began, turning to me with a megawatt smile, "tell us about yourself."

"Uh… what do you want to know?" I hedged.

"Let's start with the basics. How old are you?"

"She completed her senior year at Pacific Cross early," Eric answered for me, pride bleeding through his tone.

Something in Colby's gaze shifted to almost predatory. He made a *tsk*ing noise and sipped his water as he leaned toward me. "Eric, I never took you for a cradle robber. How very wicked of you."

Eric shot him a look. "I'd encourage you to keep a civil tongue. Her grandparents are Laurent and Ines Moreau. If the fact that she's here as *my* personal guest doesn't remind you of your manners, then their name may."

Colby jerked back, sobering, and I flinched a little.

It wasn't that I was ashamed of my grandparents; quite the opposite. They were known across Europe for their philanthropy and patronage of the arts. The Moreau name was well established in Paris as eponymous with the leading French banking system. They were at the tippy-top of Parisian society.

But it made me cringe when people name-dropped them.

"My apologies," Colby murmured. "Eric, your brother is also dating one of the Moreau granddaughters, isn't he?" His eyes flashed. "Or did you steal this one from him?"

Eric huffed. "Of course not."

"Alex is dating my cousin, Camille," I explained with a forced smile.

Brent looked up from where he'd been typing on his phone at the other end of the table. "The ballerina, yeah?"

I nodded. "You know her?"

Brent shrugged. "My mother used to dance. She dragged me to a performance the last time I was in town and raved about her. I remember her mentioning she was Ines Moreau's granddaughter."

"My cousin is very talented," I admitted.

"She's hot. Pity Alex got to her first," Brent replied, then went back to his phone.

Okay then.

Eric stiffened and glared at Brent. "Would you put down the—"

"I thought we were meeting to discuss the auction next week," Geoffry broke in, running a hand through his messy blond hair. He let out a burp and waved a hand. "Why the fuck are we talking about—"

"Geoffry," Eric snapped, his tone sharper and colder than I'd ever imagined it could be.

I jerked and looked at him, shocked by the ruthless fury etched into his normally gentle features.

Colby laughed, the sound grating. "He's high, Eric. Ignore him."

"A little hard to do when he's behaving like a child," Eric gritted out, his muscles strung tight with tension. "Now isn't the time."

"What auction?" I asked, confused. Maybe it had something to do with the gala next month to fund a library expansion project. My grandparents had discussed it in passing, but I'd kinda tuned out. They were trying to rope me into working on more of their projects, and while I was always down to help fund a library or save the polar bears, I also wanted to keep a low profile. Dating Eric this past week was as far out of my comfort zone as I wanted to go right now.

Colby snickered. "It's a charity auction."

"What's the cause?"

Eric shot Colby a withering glare before looking at me, his expression kinder. "It's a project our families have worked on for years. We sponsor families in third-world countries that need extra funding."

"Wow," I murmured. "That's cool. My best friend and her husband do something kind of similar."

Colby started laughing. "Doubtful." At Eric's sharp look, he choked out a cough. "I just mean, our families have been working together for nearly a decade on this... project."

I frowned. "Feel free to talk about the auction or whatever else you need to. Maybe I can help?"

Eric squeezed my hand. "Thank you, love, but I think we can shelve the corporate chatter for an evening and just enjoy one another's company." He finished the sentence by shooting stern looks at his friends.

Unease rippled over me. Pushing it aside, I reached for my menu.

My fingers had just closed over the edge of the soft leather binding when something cold splashed down my back.

"Oh, no!" a horrified voice cried, and instantly Eric and Colby were on their feet.

Stunned, I turned and saw a waitress with an empty wine glass clutched in her hands. That would explain the cold liquid trailing down my spine. Smelled like... chardonnay.

"What have you done?" Eric snapped, grabbing his napkin.

"I'm so sorry, miss," the woman apologized, looking near tears. "My foot caught on the carpet and—"

"I want to speak with your manager," Eric growled.

I placed a placating hand on his chest. "No, don't." I gave her a tentative smile. "It was an accident. It happens."

This girl looked terrified, like I'd start screaming or claw her eyes out any second. The urge to try and make it better was reflexive as Eric got more and more upset.

"Really," I insisted, "it's fine."

"But she got you all... wet," Colby drawled with a snort.

"Colby," Eric ground out, his eyes flashing.

Colby held up his hands and dropped back into his chair with a smirk.

I gritted my teeth and looked at Eric, who seemed ready to pop a blood vessel. "Give me a moment to get cleaned up. At least it was white wine, right?"

His gaze cut to me. "I suppose."

"Where's the restroom?" I asked the waitress.

She pointed toward an alcove but stopped me when I started to walk around her. She wrung her hands. "I'm sorry, miss, but it's currently being cleaned. Someone was sick in it... Not food related, she's pregnant and the smells—" She rambled as she panicked.

Eric made a noise in the back of his throat. "Are you suggesting she *sit* here in the mess you made?"

"No," the waitress stammered, her eyes huge. "I'll take you to the back where our private employee restroom is, if that's all right?"

"Of course," I assured her before Eric could say something else.

We'd been... dating? Was this dating? Whatever it was, we'd been doing it for a week, and this was by far the most aggressive he'd ever seemed. Maybe he really was related to Alex. I mean, sure, he was pissed off *for* me, not *at* me, but something about how he was acting seemed off.

Then again, it had been a weird night all around.

I followed the waitress to the back of the restaurant, thankful I'd opted to wear my hair up so that it wasn't soaked with wine. Even now,

I could feel it drying and pulling my skin tight with stickiness. Hopefully I could wipe myself off with some wet paper towels and salvage the rest of my night with Eric.

The waitress moved silently, pushing through a door that led to a service hallway, and then stepped aside and pointed. "It's at the end of the hall. Last door on the right."

"Thanks so much," I told her, flashing her a quick grin to let her know I wasn't pissed off that she'd made a human error. I hurried down the hall and pushed open the door to a single bathroom.

I'd just turned to close the door when something slammed into it. I went tumbling backward, my back hitting the opposite wall and knocking the air from my lungs. I gasped in a deep breath and looked up to figure out what the hell was going on, but it took only seconds for him to get inside, lock the door, and pin me with his body.

Hard muscle pressed me into the drywall. A knee slipped between my legs as a large, calloused hand pressed over my mouth before I could scream. Dark, furious eyes framed by the thickest, blackest lashes glared at me.

"What the *fuck* are you doing, Becca?" Court Woods growled.

CHAPTER 13

BEX

With his hand still covering my mouth, all I could do was glare at Court. Glare and… stare.

Because it had been a month since I'd seen Court Woods, and a month shouldn't have made *this* big of a difference.

His dark hair was longer, falling over one eye. His sharp jaw was covered in a layer of stubble that made him look even more dangerous than usual. He was still broad—okay, the man was freaking ripped. Even through our layers of clothes, I could feel the heavy bulk of his muscles, especially where his thigh was wedged between my legs. Our height difference—I was five-five, and he had a solid eight inches on me—meant my lady business was pressed against his leg. All I'd need to do was rock my hips a little…

Bad, Bex! I mentally bitch-slapped myself because *no*. We weren't having *those* thoughts about *this* guy ever again. It was why I'd come to Paris—to put half a planet between us.

Wait.

Court was in *Paris*. Why was he here?

Some stupid piece of my heart that would always belong to him fluttered with hope.

Was he here for *me*?

Holy shit.

Was this—

"What the *fuck*, Becca?" he snarled again, his breath hot and minty against my face. "Tell me you're not this goddamn stupid."

I blinked. Okay, as far as declarations of love went, that sucked.

Now I was pissed.

I lowered my lashes, pointedly reminding him that his hand was still covering my mouth. I had the strong urge to lick his palm just to see what he'd do. Maddie had a shirt that said, *I licked it, so it's mine.*

If only it was that easy.

Eyes still narrowed, Court slowly dropped his hand but didn't back up. God, he smelled good. Like citrusy soap and faint traces of leather.

His head jerked back an inch. "Did you just *sniff* me?"

Shit. Had I?

"What the hell are you doing here?" I demanded, going on the offense because… yeah. I was pretty sure I'd leaned in and taken a whiff of him.

I'd unpack *that* slip up later, when I was home.

"I'm on a date," I added, a dark thrill shooting through me at the fury that flashed across his face.

It was quickly schooled with a callous sneer. "I'm well fucking aware, sweetheart."

"I-is that why you're here?" I stammered, shock rippling down my spine. "Are you here because…" I had no idea how to finish that thought. I slammed my mouth shut before I could do something stupid.

Well, stupider than sniffing him like I was a shifter in a romance novel.

"Because you're on a date with a lowlife scum?" He arched a brow.

I felt my cheeks flush with anger. "Eric isn't—"

"Don't tell me you're actually defending that douche nozzle." His jaw dropped open, incredulity spreading across his face.

"Court—"

His expression turned mocking. "Oh, is it love?"

"Screw you," I snapped, pushing at his wide shoulders, but the asshole didn't budge. "Get off!"

He pressed against me harder. "So you can go back out there and make an even bigger fool out of yourself? No, thanks. I'll stay here where I can babysit your ass the way you so obviously need."

"If anyone's going to watch my ass, it'll be my boyfriend," I taunted. I wasn't sure that throwing the label on Eric was a great idea, but I did love the way Court looked a little sick at my declaration. "Fun fact? He *loves* my ass."

Jesus, it was like word vomit. I couldn't stop, because I needed Court to have some kind of reaction. *Any* kind of reaction. My masochistic heart craved a flicker of awareness from him, and I'd take it any way I could get it.

And that was exactly why I'd needed to get away from Court Woods.

He was everything I wanted and nothing I could have.

"Wow," Court murmured, shaking his head like he was sorry for me. "Pathetic, even for you, Becca."

"Don't call me that!" I hissed.

Court was one of the few people who still used my childhood nickname, and it was a donkey kick to the heart every time I heard it.

"Fine. *Bex*." Disdain dripped from his tone, like my nickname personally offended him.

And just like that, I was done. Exhausted. Spent. Tired of pretending I didn't give a shit when I did. It had been a weird night, and seeing Court made me realize why.

I wasn't over him.

I was trying to force myself to feel for Eric even a flicker of the inferno I did when I was around Court, but it was as useless as a concrete parachute. My unease tonight wasn't nerves over a kiss; it was anxiety because I knew, down deep, that Eric wasn't the guy I wanted.

Sure, I could lie to my heart, but the sadistic bitch always brought me back to this singular truth: Court Woods was intrinsically woven into the fabric of my soul.

I sagged under the weight of the realization that I'd never be rid of him. Of this feeling.

Maybe it was time to just call it a life and pledge myself to a convent and whatever nuns did. Crap, did I have to be Catholic to be a nun? Or was the basic belief that there was a higher power somewhere, laughing his ass off as he played with the doll known as Rebecca Whittier?

A warm hand slid behind my neck, anchoring me to the present.

I gasped as Court touched his forehead to mine for a beat. "Focus, Becca."

It was a thing people had always given me shit for as a kid. I had this annoying habit of zoning out into a lengthy internal monologue that would've made Shakespeare concerned. My parents had called me flighty. Madelaine had called it Becca-land.

But Court... Court had never judged me. Just smiled and reeled me back in with a touch or a word.

"Why are you here?" I asked, my tone soft and resigned.

As if sensing the shift in my mood, Court finally stepped back and gave me space to breathe. "Phoenix."

My head snapped up, my spine going straight. That one word was enough explanation.

"But... *here*?" I frowned. Aubergine wasn't exactly a hotbed of criminal activity, unless you counted a shrimp cocktail that cost eighty-five euros.

He gave me a terse nod and folded his massive arms over that wide, muscular chest. "How much do you know about the guy you came here with?"

Surprise ignited in my blood, my brows shooting up. "Eric?" I laughed. "He's... He's a nice guy."

His jaw tightened. "No, he isn't. We've been—"

"We?" I cut him off. "Who else is here?"

"Rook and Bishop," he admitted. "We've been watching the group of guys you and your *boyfriend* came here to meet." He looked like he'd sucked on a lemon. "They're part of why we're in Paris. Why we've been here for a week."

My heart sank. He'd been here for a week, and no one had mentioned it? Did Maddie know?

"Maddie doesn't know where we are," Court told me, his tone soft as he read my mind.

I gave a slow nod, grateful for that. "I've only known Eric for a week, but he seems like a good person."

His features went hard. "You really think I'd be here if he was? You think we'd make that kind of mistake?"

"Maybe?" Probably not, but I wasn't ready to admit that. "We came here because Eric wanted to have dinner with his friends. One of them just lost his grandfather."

"Franklin Barnes?"

I shifted my weight on my feet. "That's Geoffry's last name, but—"

"Franklin Barnes was found dead in his flat last week." Court stared at me.

I shrugged. "Okay?"

"He was shot three times. Twice in the chest, once in the head. He was executed." His head tilted, his dark eyes gleaming. "Still think we have the wrong guys?"

I swallowed hard. "Just because one of his friends is into some dark stuff doesn't mean Eric is."

Court blew out a hard breath and tipped his head back for a second before his gaze returned to mine. "Eric isn't here to see his friends— they came here to see *him*."

"So what? That doesn't make him a bad guy. Eric's nice and sweet and…"

His brows lifted. "And?"

My cheeks heated as I lowered my gaze. "Boring."

To his credit, Court didn't give me shit for that last part. "Sweetheart, I know you're determined to see the good in people, but you're wrong."

"They were just talking about some charity auction," I started, thinking back. How could a group of guys planning an event to help people in need be evil?

Court's eyes went wide. "Wait—they mentioned the auction to you? What'd they say?"

I frowned in confusion. "Not much, really."

His hands came up to grip my shoulders. "Becca, *think*. What did they say?"

"I-I don't know. Colby brought it up, I think, but then Eric told him to shut up and he told me it was a charity their families all run together to help people from third-world countries." I stared, wide-eyed and unsure, as Court seemed to process my words.

"Fuck. But you heard the word *auction*?"

I nodded.

He growled and spun away from me, stalking the length of the small bathroom and pausing at the closed door. He didn't speak or move for a weighted moment, then his fist shot out with an explosive punch to the door.

I jerked, gasping as I looked at where the wood had splintered. "Court!" The sight of blood dripping from his knuckles as he lowered his hand with a hiss had me moving. "You idiot," I scolded, hurrying to the sink to grab a handful of paper towels.

"It's fine," he muttered even as I reached for him.

My skin crackled with electricity as I took his hand in mine. He'd split his knuckles wide open. "You probably broke your hand."

"No, I didn't." He wiggled his fingers, but I caught the barely discernible wince.

"Why did you do that?" I demanded, wrapping up his hand as best as I could.

He yanked it away and stared down at me. "Are you kidding?"

I threw my hands up. "What would I possibly have to be kidding about, Court?"

He jabbed a finger toward the door. "Do you even realize how much danger you're in here? Jesus, Bex, it's not a fucking charity auction they're discussing. It's why I'm here with Rook and Bishop. It's a major event where the items being auctioned off are *women*."

I staggered back a step.

He grimaced. "And you're apparently dating the guy who's in charge of making sure they all show up on time."

Now I was *really* lost. "Are you crazy? Eric runs a cargo importing and exporting business that belonged to his late mother."

Court gave me a look, and I froze as everything started slotting together.

Auction.

Shipping.

Business.

Oh fuck me sideways with a stick.

I turned and barely made it in time for the vomit to land in the toilet.

CHAPTER 14

COURT

God, I was an asshole. I probably could have figured out a gentler way to break the news to Becca that the guy she was dating was a monster, but I'd never been tactful. Especially not when I was pissed.

And right now? I was fucking *livid*.

But I hadn't expected the news to make her actually sick.

Every time I closed my eyes, I could see her walking into the restaurant with *him*. The way he'd rested his hand on the small of her back like he fucking owned her. Like she was his property.

She wasn't his, and she never would be.

Mine.

Oh, fuck no. I didn't have time to argue with my heart or my brain or whatever little piece of my subconscious still thought that.

With a grimace, I dropped to my knees behind her and rubbed her back in a slow circle, my heart twisting into a pretzel. "Easy," I murmured.

She rested an arm across the back of the toilet seat and lowered her forehead to it, sucking in shuddering breaths.

I reached over and flushed the toilet, then leaned toward the edge of the sink to grab a handful of paper towels. Helping her lean back, I wiped her mouth with a frown. She was too damn pale.

Eyes closed, she scooted away from the toilet and leaned her head against the wall. She drew her knees to her chest before wrapping her arms around her legs. I dropped to my ass across from her, waiting for her to speak.

"Can you just go?" she finally rasped, still not looking at me.

I frowned. "I can't leave Paris until—"

Her hazel eyes snapped open, full of humiliation and tears. "No, I mean leave the restaurant."

My spine went ramrod straight. "What about you?"

She waved a hand in the air. "I'll tell Eric I'm sick and ask him to take me home."

A low growl rumbled in my chest. "Not fucking happening, sweetheart. You honestly think I'm going to let you get into a car—*alone*—with that guy?"

"I think you're not going to *let* me do anything," she snapped back, but there was little heat in her words. She sounded exhausted, and I hated that the most. That she'd given up when the girl I knew used to fight.

The entire time I'd known Becca, she'd fought. As a kid, she'd fought for what she wanted, then for her life when she'd gotten sick. Somewhere along the way, she'd lost that, and *that* fucking killed me. I thought I'd seen a spark of it as we'd reconnected over the past few months. But then I'd gone and fucked it up all over again.

I *always* fucked it up.

I knew it, but damned if I could stop, especially where Rebecca Whittier was concerned. This girl would forever be my destruction and my salvation.

"He's dangerous," I tried, keeping my voice even and low.

She shook her head, looking more than a little distraught. I had the irrational urge to smooth her furrowed brow with a kiss. Then I wondered what she'd do if I kissed her, even on the forehead.

Probably slap me. I'd deserve it.

And it'd be worth it, a dark little voice whispered.

She rubbed her forehead. "How the hell did my life get so…"

"Complicated?" I offered with a tight smile.

She met my gaze. "Fucked up."

No, what was fucked up was my cock jerking in my jeans as her lips formed the word *fuck*.

She grimaced, rolling her eyes to the ceiling with a soft scoff. "So much for my big plan."

I cocked my head, barely catching her words. "What plan?"

She shook her head again. "Nothing."

"Becca—"

"You know what, Court? I think I've been humiliated enough for one night." She pushed herself up onto wobbly feet and glared at me when I moved to help her. "Can you tell me something?"

"Maybe," I hedged. There was a lot about my life that I couldn't—and wouldn't—tell her. Shit that she didn't need to know, and I'd protect her as much as I could from my world. She'd been hurt by it enough.

"Is it me?" The note of vulnerability made her voice crack.

"Bec—"

She held up a hand, lifting her chin. "I'm serious, Court. Is there something about *me* that just says *feel free to screw with me*?"

"Of course not," I told her, rage flaring in my system, igniting nerve endings. God, Becca was smart and kind and *perfect*. If I hadn't already planned on killing Eric before, the fact that she was in tears over his lies would've sealed his fate.

Fucker was a dead man walking.

"Then why am I constantly the idiot who trusts the wrong people?" Her hands balled into tiny fists at her sides.

"Trusting one asshole doesn't make you an idiot, sweetheart," I assured her. In fact, looking at her now, with her hair twisted into a complicated knot, her eyes glittering with fury, and the sexy as hell navy blue dress that hugged all her curves, she looked like a goddamn wet dream. Not to mention those silver heels that made her legs look impossibly long.

An image stole through my mind… her legs wrapped around my waist, those heels digging into my ass, as I fucked her into oblivion.

And just like that, my semi became a full-blown hard-on.

"It's not just one asshole," she pointed out, holding up a hand to tick off fingers as she made a list. "My dad. Madelaine. *You.*" The last one was delivered with a pointed look.

I flinched like a little bitch. Only this girl could make me do that.

Put a gun to my head? I didn't even break a sweat.

But having Becca pissed at me? I was ready to shit my pants. The power she held over me was downright dangerous. The fact that she was my weakness had been exploited enough by my father, and I wouldn't let it happen again. If that meant I had to push her away to keep her safe, then I would.

When Ryan and Maddie had gotten together, it had brought Becca back into my orbit. I'd done a damn good job of erasing her from my mind, but one moment was all it took for her to become the center of my universe yet again.

And, *yet again,* she'd walked unknowingly into my world and paid the price.

It wouldn't happen a third time.

Sighing, I shoved my hands into my pockets. "None of that was your fault. You can't blame yourself."

She arched a brow. "I have a clinical diagnosis of anxiety that says my brain can, and will, blame me for anything."

I frowned. "You were diagnosed with anxiety? When?"

"Suddenly concerned about my welfare, Court?" The mocking edge to her voice made me want to punch something else.

Or toss her over my lap as I spanked her ass.

I narrowed my eyes. "I'm always—"

A knock on the door cut me off, and I spun to face it, pulling the Glock from where I'd tucked it into the back of my jeans. Becca inhaled but didn't say anything. She stayed quiet and let me handle things.

Fuck if I didn't wish it could always be that way.

"It's me." Rook's voice was muffled, and I unlocked the door and yanked it open.

He stood on the other side with the waitress I'd paid to spill a drink on Becca. Neither of them looked happy.

Rook hooked a thumb at the waitress. "Eric's asking what's taking so long."

"I tried to stall," the waitress added, looking guilty.

I felt Becca come up behind me but blocked her when she tried to move around me.

A faint smile lifted Rook's lips as he spotted her over my shoulder. "Hey, Bex. Long time no see."

"Hey, Rook." A small hand curled over my bicep. "Court, let me by."

I whirled so fast that she lost her balance. Without hesitation, my hands grabbed her around the waist to steady her. "No."

She tipped her head back to look at me but didn't fight my hold. Instead, she placed her hands against my chest. "He's going to get suspicious if I don't go back out there."

"I don't care," I gritted out.

Sighing, Becca turned to the waitress. "Please tell him I'll just be a moment."

With a nod, the waitress scurried away.

I drew in a deep breath, readying for a fight.

Her fingers dug into the cotton of my black t-shirt. "Let me go back. I'll finish dinner, and he'll drop me off at home. I'll tell him I think we're better off as friends." She shrugged with a sad smile. "That'll be the end of it."

I snorted in disbelief. "You really think he's going to let you go?"

"Yes," she replied, guileless and innocent as ever. She truly didn't understand the walking temptation she was. "Even if—" She cut off abruptly, her face going pale. "Oh, no."

"What?" Panic spiked in my blood, and I dragged her closer, eviscerating the scant space between us.

"Cami, my cousin," she croaked out, her eyes huge, "she's dating Alex, Eric's brother. Is *he* involved in this? Is Cami in danger?"

I looked back at Rook. We knew who Alex was. He'd never been flagged in our system, but it wasn't a stretch to think that Eric's brother could be involved as well.

Rook grimaced. "It's not like these guys have a fucking membership roster. We haven't gotten any intel that he is. Just Eric."

Becca let out a scoff. "Please. Of the two of them? *Alex* is the asshole. Wait—maybe it's really Alex, and he's framing Eric?"

"Then why is Eric here, talking about an auction, with these guys?" I reminded her gently.

She visibly deflated. "Oh, right."

"Which is why going back out there is a horrible idea," I added.

"Actually…" Rook mused, rubbing his jaw.

I glared at him, wishing like hell I'd gotten mutant laser beams I could shoot out of my eyes at him. Was he fucking serious?

He pressed his lips together. "I don't like putting innocent people in danger either, little brother, but we can't afford for these guys to get spooked for *any* reason. They've already pushed the auction date back because of Barnes's murder. They push it again, they may cut their losses."

Fuck. That meant they'd get rid of the women currently being held somewhere in Paris like livestock waiting for the auction block. They wouldn't keep them alive indefinitely. No, they'd kill them and focus on the next auction.

"I'll be okay." Becca's soft voice didn't waver.

I stared down at her, searching those gorgeous green and gold eyes for any sign of fear or panic. Any hint that this was too much. If it was, I'd walk away with her right now.

That was why what I felt for her was too dangerous. Why I'd never be the hero. Because if push came to shove, I'd let the world burn to protect her.

"I have a tracker," Rook spoke up. He held up a small device and handed it to her. "Keep this on you so we know where you are." He looked at me. "You can follow her home. Make sure she's safe."

I groaned and looked at the ceiling.

"I'll be okay," Bex assured me, giving me a small smile. "I mean, you'll have my back, right?"

"Always," I vowed.

"Then it'll be fine. Trust me."

Her I trusted.

It was the rest of the world I didn't.

CHAPTER 15

BEX

I couldn't stop staring at Eric, but judging by the grins he kept flashing me and the hand resting on my thigh under the table, he didn't know it was because I knew his dirty secret.

I went through dinner on autopilot. Thank God for all the mindless dinner parties and galas I'd attended growing up. I was practically a professional at smiling and nodding at the appropriate places. But the whole time, my mind was whirling with the newfound information.

Looking at each of the men I was sitting with, I kept wondering at what point they had decided people were commodities that could be traded and sold. Then again, my own father had gotten tangled up in this world, too.

When given the option, I declined dessert, even though I'd eaten barely a quarter of my dinner. Everything tasted like cardboard and dropped like lead into my belly. Not wanting to be sick again, I stuck with sipping water and refused to drink the wine paired with my meal.

Relief sank into my bones when Eric tossed his napkin onto his plate. He smiled at his friends. "Gents, it's been a pleasure, but if you don't mind, I'd like to spend some time alone with my lovely date."

I forced a sweet smile onto my lips before neatly folding my own napkin and setting it on the table.

"Alone time, eh?" Colby teased while leaning into me. "You know, Bex, if you ever want a real man—"

"Enough, Colby." The bark in Eric's tone was jarring and not at all on par with the mild-mannered, almost timid guy I'd been dating for a week. And now, instead of plotting how to end this evening with a goodnight kiss, I was trying to figure out how to end things entirely.

So far, I'd surmised that Colby was a Grade-A asshole, Brent was a sniveling little bitch who hadn't gotten over some high school bullshit, Geoffrey was a barely functioning addict/alcoholic, and Henry…

Well, Henry honestly kinda stumped me.

On the surface, he had the same sort of bloodlines and connections as the others, but the way they talked down to him didn't sit right. Henry seemed to be the butt of the joke more often than not, and sometimes the teasing turned downright vicious before Eric called his friends off.

Then there was Eric, whom I was still having trouble wrapping my head around as the bad guy. It didn't add up; he was kind, attentive, and even over-tipped the waitresses who'd dealt with us all night. He'd stopped Colby when Colby had intentionally dropped his fork so one of the waitresses would have to bend over and pick it up for him.

What kind of criminal mastermind who supported sex trafficking bothered to help a waitress?

But in my gut, I trusted Court.

Even if I wanted to strangle him, I knew he wouldn't lie to me. Not about something this important. And I knew that if Phoenix thought there was a problem here, there was a freaking problem. The guys were too good at what they did to make baseless accusations.

Which meant that the guy escorting me from Paris's premiere dining experience was a sociopath.

Not exactly comforting.

I jerked as hands landed on my waist and pulled me in. A moment later Eric feathered a soft kiss over my jaw.

"Thank you for tonight, love," he murmured, his voice like warm honey. His eyes found mine, and he smiled. "You were spectacular."

This was the part where I should be pulling away. No, *running* away. But instead, all I heard were Rook's words.

They may cut their losses.

I wasn't an idiot. I knew that people who trafficked other people didn't "cut their losses" by making it a line item on their tax returns.

Court had said he'd been in Paris for a week now as he and his brothers tried to figure out where the auction would be held.

And I was currently on a date with someone who *knew* the details of said auction.

The wheels slowly cranked in my head, formulating an idea that was potentially a disaster… but worth a shot.

Sliding my hands up the front of Eric's shirt, I wound my arms around his neck and tipped my head back with an apologetic smile. "I wouldn't call this evening a total loss. Even if I *am* questioning your choice in friends."

His grin gave him a boyish look. "They're my oldest mates, you know how it is."

"I absolutely do," I agreed with a laugh. "We don't get to choose who we grow up with."

"Spoken as though from experience," he replied, his hands tightening for a moment on my waist.

I shrugged. "I'm Malcolm Whittier's only child. You'd be surprised by the things—and people—that I know."

He hesitated just for a heartbeat. "Oh?"

I patted his chest, hoping that I was infusing the right amount of mystery into my words. Enough to make him curious. "Of course." A coy smirk lifted my lips. "Every year we used to vacation with—" I cut myself off with a giggle. "It doesn't matter."

His arms slid around my waist, pulling me closer. "Actually, I'd love to know about how you grew up. I'll admit, I *have* heard of your father. Then again, most of the world runs on computer chips manufactured by Whittier Corp."

I resisted the urge to shudder. "I'm well aware. I swear, growing up my dad and his friends would have dick-measuring contests based on whose business did the best that year. If I had to listen to Kent Westford brag about another hotel opening, or what nuclear conflict General Woods stopped in Iran, I would go crazy."

"Sounds positively tedious," Eric mused as the valet pulled up with his car. "Shall we?"

I nodded and stepped out of his embrace, smothering the urge to shake off my nerves as I moved toward the car. Eric opened the door for me and waited until I was situated inside to close it and move around to the driver's side. I watched as he tipped the valet and exchanged an easy smile with the man before sliding behind the wheel. He flashed me a grin and then pulled into traffic.

Holding my purse on my lap, I watched the facades of buildings and shops blur past while trying to come up with something to say to bring up the auction again. Something to make him give away some detail that might help Court.

"General *Jasper* Woods?" Eric's question came so suddenly that I thought I'd imagined it.

But when I turned my head, he was glancing at me, his brow furrowed.

I smiled. "One and the same. I'm surprised you know him. Or do you make it a habit to keep up with the American military rankings?"

The corner of his mouth twitched. "Not quite, but we are… acquainted."

"So you'll be meeting with him while he's in town?" I kept my gaze as neutral as possible.

Eric's eyes narrowed a fraction, his fingers unfurling and closing around the steering wheel.

Fuck it. Gamble big, win big, right? That was a saying?

I made an *ah-ha* sound. "I mean, it makes sense. The *auction*."

His gaze whipped to me so fast the car swerved. I gasped and threw out a hand to the dash for support. Several cars honked behind us, tires squealing as the evening traffic tried to avoid collisions. Finally, Eric got it together enough to pull over, idling near an upscale lingerie boutique.

"You know about the auction?" His voice was low, controlled.

I barely held back the urge to swallow as I met his gaze, stunned by the blazing intensity. Slowly, I arched a brow. "Did you miss the part where I said my father is Malcolm Whittier? The same Malcolm Whittier who created the cybersecurity systems currently used by men like General Woods?"

God, this was such a gamble. My heart was pounding in my chest like a war drum, and if Eric decided he wanted to hold hands now, he'd find my palms dripping with sweat.

He still looked skeptical.

I shrugged one shoulder and studied my nails. Hopefully he was buying my *I-don't-give-a-damn* bravado. "The only reason I even know about the auction is because Daddy is missing Mémé's eightieth birthday celebration." I rolled my eyes with a dramatic flair as the lie slid off my tongue like ice. "Business."

"But the auction is two days after her party," Eric pointed out. "Wouldn't he have time?"

Holy shitballs.

He'd told me the goddamned date and it was in less than a freaking week!

Stay calm, Bex.

"Uh, he usually would, but he's finishing up some other deals and the timing is just off." I winked at Eric. "Honestly I think it's because he can't stand to be around my mother. And seriously, I'm so sick of them fighting. It's easy to see why she filed for divorce, but it's about eight years too late. It's a shame, because my grandparents still think of him as their son."

Total lie. I'd hear Papa ranting about how Dad had never been good enough for his baby girl. If Dad showed up at the party—which he definitely had *not* been invited to—Papa would probably punch him.

Eric shook his head, a slow grin creeping across his lips that made his eyes sparkle. "Bex, you never cease to surprise me. Just when I already think you're incredible, you reveal a whole new layer of utter perfection." He reached out and grasped the back of my neck. "You're everything I've been looking for and never thought I'd find."

My breath caught in my lungs as he leaned in and I realized, in horror, that he was about to kiss me. The very thing I'd gone into this date wanting was now a revolting idea.

His eyes darkened as his tongue darted out to lick his bottom lip, and I knew I'd have to make a choice—let him kiss me, or fake a heart attack.

And I really sucked at acting sick.

The one time I'd tried to fake the flu to avoid going to school—courtesy of Madelaine making middle school a living hell—I'd blasted my forehead with a hair dryer for a few minutes before going to find my mother. My mom, with all her medical powers of deduction, called me out for faking when she put her hand against my head and almost got second-degree burns.

Not my finest moment.

But when I'd broken down—literally—and told her why I couldn't go to school, she'd let me stay home, and we'd spent the day together, shopping and bonding. It was one of my favorite memories.

The sharp honk of a car horn behind us had Eric jerking back with a scowl. He glared in the rearview mirror at the car flashing its lights, waiting for us to move from where he'd double-parked.

"Keep your knickers on," he groused, waving a hand to acknowledge the other driver as he pulled back into traffic. He shot me an apologetic smile. "Sorry, love. What can I say? You've utterly bewitched me."

Three hours ago, I would've loved to hear him say those words. But now, knowing what I did, the heart sank like a lump of charcoal in my gut. My skin crawled where he'd touched me, and I forced down the urge to shiver.

He kept talking as he drove, mostly mundane topics, but every time he shared something about himself, I wondered when he'd gone from poor little rich boy to monster. What did it take for a person to make the decision to become evil? Or maybe he'd been born that way, and if so, what effed-up genetics were part of his cocktail?

I responded with as many answers as possible, but it was like a switch had been flipped. Like my acknowledging his dark, depraved secret meant the veil of formality had been ripped away.

He wasn't some guy who'd been cast out by his father and brother. He was a shark, silently moving through turbulent waters and using the chaos to disguise his moves. The look of disdain in his eyes when he talked about his father and the cutting way he referred to Alex as inferior made one thing painfully obvious: Eric Lambert-Durand was a stone-cold sociopath.

The more he relaxed, the more I started to wonder what I'd ever seen in him.

Well, mostly I'd seen that he wasn't someone else. That was the only prerequisite I seemed to require nowadays.

I did know that, by the time he pulled the car into the circular drive of my grandparents' house, I was ready to lose my shit. My nerves were shot, and I was over the small talk. I needed space to think through my options.

Putting the car in park, Eric turned and grabbed my hand. "Bex, I'd love to see you again."

I forced a smile onto my lips, wondering if he felt the tremble in my fingers. "Me, too." I could keep up the lie for a few more minutes. I lived with my mom and grandparents; it wasn't like I could invite him in to spend the night.

Oh, God.

A fresh wave of nausea welled up in my stomach. Had he been with any of the women he'd trafficked? Forced them?

A phantom memory of hands unbuttoning my shirt punched the air from my lungs. It had been months since I'd had a flashback to the night I'd been assaulted. Well, almost assaulted.

I'd been saved just in time by Maddie and the guys. The drugs I'd been given had messed with my memory, but every now and then, a glimpse would surface like the words in a Magic 8 Ball before sinking back into my subconscious.

Like the scent of fresh soap and leather as Court had carried me home and tucked me safely into bed.

I'm sorry, Becca.

Sometimes I thought those were the only words he knew how to say.

"Bex?" Eric squeezed my fingers again, his expression concerned. "Are you all right?"

I placed my free hand over my stomach. "Honestly? I'm feeling kinda off."

"You barely touched your dinner," he mused, his brow furrowing.

"Probably something I ate at lunch," I replied, reaching for the door handle. "I'm sure I'll be better tomorrow."

"Wonderful. The weather is supposed to be clear—I was thinking of taking my family's helicopter to Brussels tomorrow. I have business there, and thought it would be wonderful for you to join me. There's a fabulous restaurant where we could eat before returning. Or… we could stay at my family's flat for an evening or two."

I stared at him for a beat, not sure how to reply.

Concern trickled into his expression. "Bex?"

"Uh, sure," I stammered, unable to form an excuse for why this was never going to happen. Right now I just needed to get out of this car. "What time?"

He grinned. "I'll pick you up at ten, does that work?"

"Absolutely," I assured him, gently pulling away and opening the car door.

"Bex?" he called as I was about to close the door.

I froze and peered inside.

His dark eyes were fathomless pits. "I can't tell you how happy I am to have you in my life. You're extraordinary."

A weak smile tugged at my mouth. "Eric, I can honestly say I've never met anyone quite like you, too."

"Get some rest, love. I'll see you tomorrow."

"Yeah. See you tomorrow," I echoed as I stepped back and closed the door. I turned and headed for the front door and used my key to unlock it. Once inside, I quickly set all the locks and leaned against the heavy wooden barrier, catching my breath.

Inside my purse, my phone buzzed with an incoming message. I already knew it would be from Court, but I wasn't ready to deal with him.

The house was dark and quiet, with only a few dim lamps lit downstairs and along the curving staircase. I needed a shower and my snuggliest jammies before crawling into my bed. Tomorrow I'd text Eric and tell him I'd gotten worse and had to cancel.

I was mentally rehearsing my excuse as I walked into my bedroom. I kicked the door shut and reached for the light switch. Warm light flooded my space, illuminating the man waiting on my bed.

My heart jumped into my throat, and I fell back against the door with a gasp. "How the hell did you get in here?"

Court stood up with a slow smirk. "Your grandparents' idea of a security system is a joke, sweetheart." His dark eyes swept the length of me. "You okay?"

I opened my mouth to say yes, but the word stuck in my throat. All of the stress and emotion of the night—hell, of the past *year*—crashed over me at once.

A pit of darkness opened in my mind, and then I was freefalling into it without any idea where it would end. The world spun as I slid down the door, tears flooding my eyes as I started to shake hard enough for my teeth to chatter. I caught the flash of fear in Court's eyes a second before I squeezed my eyelids shut.

Before my ass could hit the floor, I was caught and lifted up, cradled against a warm chest, and held by strong arms.

CHAPTER 16

BEX

I buried my face in the fabric of his jacket. The supple leather absorbed my tears as I sniffled and breathed in the scent of the coat mingled with fresh soap.

Tomorrow I would mentally bitch-slap myself for falling apart all over Court Woods, but tonight I was going to leach comfort from him like a sponge, the way I had when I was little. Once upon a time, he'd been my protector, the one who made the bad things better.

I still remembered the day Doug Pearce had pushed me down when I'd tried to take the last swing on the playground. My ass had barely hit the ground when four shadows fell over me. Court, Ash, Ryan, and Linc stood behind me, having seen what was about to go down from the other side of the playground, where they'd been playing a game of pickup soccer with other fourth graders.

Court had helped me up and checked me for injuries while the others threatened Doug until he pissed his pants in front of all of Cloverleaf Private Elementary Academy. I knew for a fact Ryan, Ash, and Linc hadn't touched Doug, but he'd had a black eye the next time I'd seen him at school, and the knuckles on Court's right hand had been split.

No one gets to hurt you, Becca.

But then everything had changed, and the guy I'd thought would always have my back had abandoned me. He had been the one who hurt me.

Rubber bands wrapped around my chest, squeezing until I was sure my lungs would pop. My breaths came in choppy pants as tears clogged my throat and I turned my face into Court's neck.

His arms tightened around me, a silent promise that he would keep out the world for tonight. "Becca," he murmured as my sobs devolved into hiccups, "sweetheart, I need you to look at me. Come on, let me see those gorgeous eyes."

I lifted my head and blinked up at him.

He moved a hand to my cheek, his thumb stroking away the last tear that tumbled free. "There's my girl," he whispered, his dark eyes like twin blocks of burning coal. "Baby, did something happen?"

A hysterical laugh bubbled out of me. "You mean other than my life?"

His jaw tightened. "I mean with that asswipe. I never should've let you go with him. Did he—"

"He didn't hurt me," I assured Court, smoothing a finger across his jaw until it relaxed.

He exhaled long and hard. "Thank Christ for that." His lips pressed against my hair, and I snuggled closer to his chest without thinking. My ear pressed against hard muscle, and I focused on the steady thumping of his heart.

"Sorry," I whispered, sniffling again.

He snorted. "For what?"

"Breaking down like an idiot?" I couldn't keep the self-deprecation from my tone.

"Baby, I'm here anytime you need me," he murmured, running his hand down my back.

"I just… I guess it all caught up with me," I went on, resisting the urge to remind him of all the ways he'd abandoned me over the years. For tonight, I'd let myself believe the lies.

Just one night.

With a shaky laugh, I covered my face with my hands. "I'm a freaking disaster."

Gentle fingers wrapped around my wrists and tugged. "No, you're not. You're…." Court blew out another breath, his dark eyes pained. "You're fucking amazing. I promise we'll get this punk out of your life. How'd he take the breakup?"

I sat slowly on the edge of my bed, knowing I must look guilty.

Court's eyes narrowed. "Becca."

"Hear me out, okay?"

His expression went cold, flat. "Tell me."

Maybe if I started with the good news? "I know when the auction's happening," I blurted out.

He stiffened, the air around him going still. "And how would you happen to know that info?" His voice remained deadly calm, almost terrifyingly so.

I bit my lower lip. "I might've played up that my dad didn't exactly keep that world a secret."

Something dark and unreadable flashed in his eyes. "Becca."

"And maybe I also name-dropped your dad, and Linc's… *and* the fact that we all used to vacation together," I finished, pushing the words out so fast that they ran together.

Court took a breath, then another. He paced a few feet away before turning back. "What. The *fuck*. Were you thinking?"

My heart slammed in my chest. "I was thinking I could help! Eric—"

"Is a motherfucking psycho, Becca!" Court snarled. "And you just basically gave him a free pass to show you his crazy."

I ducked my head, my shoulders hiking up. "Yeah, he actually seemed pretty excited that we were on the same team."

"Of fucking course he was," he spat, sparks practically flying from his eyes as he pinned me with a ruthless stare. "Do you have any idea what you've done?"

"Helped your ass out?" I snapped, suddenly cranky. Jesus, it wasn't like I'd married Eric. I'd fudged a few truths to get info from a seriously bad guy to help Court and Rook.

"More like put yourself directly in his crosshairs," he hissed. "Jesus, how could you have been so stupid?"

I jumped up. "I'm *not* stupid."

He shook his head, jaw tight. "No, Becca, you're not, which is why I can't for the life of me figure out why you further insinuated yourself into a situation you wanted out of."

I snapped my mouth shut. Okay, I *had* done that, but I'd done it to help *him*.

"What? No answer?" he mocked with a snort. "For someone who doesn't want shit to do with me or Phoenix, you sure as hell are good at finding ways to keep yourself in my orbit."

I jerked back like I'd been slapped, his words cutting through me like a thousand knives. "Are you kidding me? I left my home and an entire freaking continent to get away from you! Until tonight, I had no idea that Eric was mixed up in your shit."

His jaw clenched, a muscle ticking.

"You want me done, Court? I'm *done*. Get out and forget I ever existed. That's what you're good at, right?" I arched a brow at him, wanting—no, *needing*—to make his heart ache the way mine did.

Instead, he took a step toward me, his long legs eating up the distance between us in a single move. His toes bumped mine as he towered over me. "Oh, sweetheart, you have *no* idea."

Something in his dark gaze made me shiver, my insides lighting up with anticipation. I balled my hands into fists at my sides so I wouldn't do something *really* stupid. Like kiss him. Right now, I was a trembling ball of emotion.

There had always been a connection between Court and me. It was as undeniable as the ocean being blue and grass being green. No matter what I did or how far I went, that wouldn't change.

But I still never could've imagined what he'd say next.

"Pack a bag."

I blinked, not sure I'd heard him right. "What?"

"Pack a bag," he repeated, his tone firmer. "Unless you want me to start packing for you."

"Where exactly am I going?" I asked, too confused to keep on being pissed.

"With me," he replied, like the answer was obvious.

An astonished laugh burst from me. "Excuse me? No. No *way*."

"Let's recap what's going on," he started. "You met a guy who is a known human trafficker." He ticked up a finger. "You started dating said asshole." Another finger, and another. "Then you decided to not only let him know that you like him, but you cosigned on his lifestyle."

"I didn't—"

He pressed the final finger to my lips. "You *did*, which, to a guy like that? Is like finding a unicorn wrapped in bacon. Plus, you doubled down by letting him think you're in with the big players—my and Linc's dads."

"I… I'll still break things off with him. I can text him tonight and say I'm sick. I'll be sick for a few days and then say I've had a chance to rethink—"

He scoffed and shook his head. "Sweetheart, Ash did a little more digging into Eric. Did you know his last girlfriend filed a restraining order and pressed charges for assault?"

My heart sank like a rock. "What?"

"The case was officially put on hold when she went missing a month later. The girl before that? Also gone without a fucking trace." He paused, his lips pressed together. "You starting to see how bad you messed up yet?"

A sense of dread settled low in my belly as I remembered the almost manic look in Eric's eyes. He'd been so excited… Oh, God, what had I done?

And his last two girlfriends were *missing*?

Court's hands settled on my shoulders, wrenching my attention to him before I could fully spiral into panic. "Pack a bag, Becca." His words were softer, kinder now. "I can't keep you safe while you're here."

"Where am I going?" I mumbled, numbness setting in. "Back to California?"

"No, you're staying in Paris," he replied, "but you'll stay with me."

"You?" The word came out like a squeak, and I knew I must've looked like a googly-eyed cartoon character with the way I was gaping at him.

He tensed like he was readying for a fight. "Yes, me. I can't protect you if you aren't near me, and I'll be damned if I let you get hurt again."

Again.

That word echoed between us like the clanging of a gong. We hadn't spoken about that summer, but maybe now we would. Maybe it would give me the closure I finally needed on that part of my life so I could move on for real.

Well, after my life wasn't in danger anymore.

Also, again.

My life was like a soap opera. Just when things couldn't get any crazier, the long-lost evil twin surfaced. Then again, my best friend was currently living the life of her long-lost evil twin, so I guessed I could kinda check that box off?

"Becca?" Court's hands tightened on my shoulders.

Crap, I'd totally spaced out. "What about my family? Will Eric—"

He shook his head. "I doubt he'll come after them. Your grandparents are too high profile in this city, and your mom is, too, in her own right. You'll tell him that you had to go finalize some things at PC. Ash will create a paper trail in case anyone looks into it," Court finished, shoving his phone into his back pocket. His dark brows lifted. "Bags aren't gonna pack themselves, baby girl."

I scowled. "Don't call me that."

An amused smile drifted across his full lips. "You really want me to stop calling you that?"

"Yes," I retorted, though I wasn't entirely sure. He'd started calling me baby girl when I was, well, a baby. He'd known me *that* long. Then it had been Becca. Now it was still Becca, but he liked to sprinkle in the occasional *sweetheart* or *baby* to really fuck with my ovaries.

Court Woods was gorgeous. I knew that. With dark hair that always looked perfectly mussed, a body that would make a Greek god envious, full pouty lips, and a killer jawline, he looked like he'd just stepped out of a fantasy. Like G.I. Joe and Adonis had a baby.

Having him say anything in that rumbly voice of his was cause for an IPE. Instant Panty Explosion. But the reverence and adoration he usually reserved for when he called me Becca... Yeah, *that* messed with my head. Every wall I'd meticulously built to protect myself went crumbling into dust the second he spoke my name.

And now I'd be staying with him? As in sharing a bathroom and sleeping under the same roof?

"What am I going to tell my mom? My grandparents?" I asked, shaking my head. "No, Court, I can't just leave."

"Tell them that you're going back to the States for a week or two because there was a mix-up with your credits," he replied with a shrug. "If we need, Ash can—"

"Yeah, yeah," I grumbled. "Ash can work his magic and *un*-graduate me." I glared at him.

He gave me a little smirk. "If you're tossing around words like *un-graduate*, you might actually need to head back to PC."

"So, why don't I do that then? I can go back to California and hang out with Maddie until this blows over," I argued.

"Which, again, puts you on another continent. I can't protect you from that far away," he reasoned.

"Why do *you* have to protect me?" I challenged, crossing my arms. In this dress, the small movement pushed my boobs up and out.

And Court one hundred percent noticed.

His focus dipped to my cleavage and lingered for a moment before he lifted his gaze. The stark hunger in it almost had me stepping back.

Or leaning in.

God, he messed with my head like no one else could.

"Truth?" He tilted his head, studying me.

I nodded, my mouth dry as cotton as I stared up at him.

Slowly, like he was afraid I'd spook and bolt, his hands reached for me and settled on my hips. "I'm not going to pretend you and I don't have shit to wade through, Becca. There's a lot of stuff you don't know—"

"Because you never told me," I cut in, frustrated and still hurt by all the lies and deception that littered our past.

He gave a single nod. "I know, baby. But I think it's time we fixed that."

"Meaning?" I whispered, and snagged my bottom lip between my teeth.

His gaze snapped to my mouth, and his grip on me tightened as he tugged me closer. Close enough that I felt the hard length of his cock against my belly. I sucked in a gasp, every muscle freezing as my mind went into a freefall.

"Meaning I'm done running from this. Us," he clarified. "I've spent the last few weeks miserable as hell because I thought I was doing the right thing by pushing you away. Fuck, make that the last few *years*. All I ever wanted was for you to be safe, Becca. And tonight, I think I finally figured it out."

"Figured what out?"

My entire universe hinged on his next words. Something shifted in my soul. A feeling that whatever came next would alter me forever.

Court lowered his forehead to mine, inhaling the air I exhaled like he was devouring me. "That the safest place I can keep you is with me."

CHAPTER 17

COURT

Sometimes, I really needed to fucking think before I acted.

I absolutely knew that Becca would be safe with me, but I hadn't thought it out beyond shooting down the few very valid points she'd made. And now that she was in my car and I was taking her back to the hotel, I was starting to have doubts.

"You're quiet," she remarked from the other side of the car.

"I'm thinking." Not a lie.

Her big hazel eyes were wide. "About?"

"My next step," I replied.

It was quiet, but I heard her huff. If that wasn't enough, she turned her body away from me.

"What?" I finally demanded when the silence felt like a guillotine hanging over my head.

"Nothing," she snapped, her voice frigid. "Just let me know when *you* figure out what *you're* going to do."

I frowned, turning down the road that led to the hotel where we were staying. "You're pissed." That was nothing new, but this time, I wasn't entirely sure why.

"Gee, ya think?" She rolled her eyes so hard I was pretty sure I heard it.

Sighing, I drummed my fingers on the steering wheel. "What did I do now?"

She twisted to face me. "You're aware that I'm here, right?"

Why did this feel like a trick question? I flicked my gaze at her, unsure. "Yes?"

"Does it ever even cross your mind to talk to me?" She stared at me for a beat, disbelief and hurt in her eyes.

"Becca—"

"I'm serious, Court," she interrupted, holding up a hand. "You routinely make unilateral decisions for me because you think you know what's best, but did you ever think to just stop and ask me what I want?"

Okay, well when she put it like that, it sounded bad. What sucked was I knew she was right. I did tend to make decisions that directly affected her, but only because I knew she'd make the wrong choice.

Oh, fuck. That sounded bad even in my head, so I knew it would be even worse if I said it aloud.

But how did I explain to her that watching her walk around was like watching my heart beat outside my body? That nothing else mattered if she wasn't happy and safe?

Then again, she didn't look happy now. And while being with me was safe, she wasn't out of danger yet.

"Okay," I said, my voice soft. "The plan right now is to get you to the hotel I've been staying at with Rook and Bishop. Once we're there, you can tell us everything you know about the auction, and we'll all talk about our next steps. Does that work for you?"

Her lips formed a tremulous smile. "Yeah, Court. That works for me." She hesitated and then added, "Thank you."

I drew to a stop at a red light and turned to give her my full attention, watching the way shadow and light played off the angles of her face. God, she was so beautiful that it hurt to look at her.

I'd done a lot in my life—played Division 1 college football and created an empire with my friends and brothers. I was on the verge of graduating from an elite college with a degree in pre-law. I'd already been accepted into Stanford Law for the fall semester. I could actually say that I'd helped save people's lives.

And yet, none of it mattered unless Becca was looking at me the way she was now—a small smile, her eyes soft and pleased.

I'd give it all up for her, and that scared the shit out of me.

Linc and Ash had frequently given Ryan hell when he'd fallen for Maddie. They'd pushed him and teased him, encouraged him to work for her. I'd never really joined in, mostly because I'd understood how he felt. I knew what it was like to desperately want to be good enough for the girl next to you but know you'd never measure up to what she truly deserved.

No, I'd never deserve Rebecca Whittier. In fact, I was done even trying to earn the right to be at her side.

The one good lesson I'd learned from my father was that if you really wanted something, you had to take it. Damn the fallout. Fuck the consequences.

I wanted Becca.

Now.

Tomorrow.

Forever.

And starting tonight, that's the way it would be.

Even if that meant doing grown-up shit, like talking about secrets I wished could stay buried. Truths I knew would break her heart.

Then again, maybe if I did it just right, I'd break her heart open in the perfect place that would let me finally slip in and claim it as mine.

I bypassed the valet stand at the front of the hotel and opted for street parking. Once I killed the ignition, I turned to her. "Wait for me to open your door."

Her lips quirked up at the ends. "Is this your attempt at chivalry?"

Resting an arm along the back of her seat, I leaned in close enough to hear her breath hitch. "No, sweetheart. It's me needing to make sure there isn't someone I need to shoot first."

She gulped down a breath and gave me a shaky nod. "Okay. I'll stay here."

Huh. Was it really that easy?

I slipped out of the car and walked to her side, my gaze moving around the mostly empty city block. I'd intentionally parked on a street that was off main roads and away from touristy hubs and popular restaurants like the one she'd been at tonight.

While I didn't think anyone knew we were in town, I wouldn't risk her life on it.

"All good," I finally told her, holding out a hand. When she didn't hesitate to wrap her fingers around mine, I was barely able to hide my smile. I reached into the back and pulled out her stuff, stacking the duffel on the suitcase to wheel with one hand while I reclaimed hers with my other.

"I'm sorry." She spoke so quietly that I almost missed it.

I turned, one eyebrow lifting. "What?"

She looked up at me, the streetlamps catching the golden flecks in her eyes. "I said, I'm sorry."

"What could you have to be sorry about?"

She gave a tiny shrug. "Complicating your life?"

I stopped us by one of the side entrances that opened into a court-yard with seating and smoking areas for hotel guests. "Don't ever apol-ogize for being in my life," I told her, dead fucking serious. "I'll take you any way I can get you."

Her eyes widened for a second. "Court—"

Leaning into her, I pressed a kiss to her forehead. "Becca, we've got a lot to talk about. There's a lot of stuff I should have told you that I didn't."

"Stuff about my dad?" Fear trickled into her eyes, and she nibbled her bottom lip.

Fuck if I didn't want to kiss the worry away. But she wasn't ready for that, and I hadn't earned the right.

Yet.

I stiffened on instinct as the door was pulled open. A second later, Bishop popped into view.

He grinned. "Bex!" He swept her into a massive hug, lifting her off her feet.

And I wanted to punch him in the dick.

Asshole.

"Mind if I get this shit inside?" I groused, as she wrapped her arms around his shoulders and giggled.

Bishop walked backwards, still carrying Becca, and gave me space to get inside.

Finally over it, I snapped, "Put her down. We need to get upstairs, not draw attention."

Bishop slowly lowered her to her feet. "God, he's a moody fucker. You look good, Bex."

She blushed, ducking her head so innocently it was all I could do not to pull her into my arms and take her straight back to the car. Drive her as far away as we could get. Find a place where no one could ever find us.

"He's had a rough night," Becca agreed, shocking the shit out of me when she came back to my side.

Bishop's brows lifted as he shot me a curious look. Without missing a beat, he grabbed the suitcase from me. "Rook filled me in a little."

"There's more," I said, my tone grim. This wasn't a social visit; Becca was here because she was in danger. "Let's get up to the room."

Nodding, Bishop led the way. He used his keycard to activate the elevator and access our floor.

Ash had scouted locations and picked this property. While we weren't sure of the exact location of the auction, we knew a lot of deals between these fuckers went down at Aubergine. There were too many meetings there with too many players we'd identified as part of the network of flesh peddlers. Staying close to the restaurant seemed like the best idea.

The hotel itself was smaller and decidedly less ostentatious than a lot of other Parisian hotels. But that also worked in our favor. The boutique hotel was lax on things like cybersecurity, which let Ash slide in and do his thing, essentially erasing any traces of us in the city by using aliases and glitching security feeds to keep our faces hidden when we left our room.

It wasn't a foolproof plan, but it was good enough to handle recon.

I knew the day was coming that I wouldn't be able to hide behind anonymity, or bank on some of the sleazeballs seeing me as just an extension of my father. One day I wouldn't be the guy doing the groundwork. I'd be the guy with the law degree untangling red tape and knowing just how far I could bend certain laws.

We all had our roles to play in setting up Phoenix.

"How've you been, Bex?" Bishop asked, leaning against the elevator wall and giving her a lazy once-over before turning to smirk at me.

Fucker knew exactly what he was doing. Instead of taking the bait, I exhaled and leaned against the opposite wall before averting my gaze toward the ceiling.

"Oh, you know," Becca chirped, a false note of happiness souring her tone. "Parents getting divorced, moving to the other side of the planet. Oh! But I did meet this guy. Seemed pretty cool for a sex trafficker."

Bishop chuckled. "Yeah, some of them are real charmers."

She let out a heavy sigh. "Too bad. I really saw us going places."

"Oh?"

Becca nodded, keeping up the game. "Yeah, you know. Marriage. Babies. Maybe a cat?"

"You're allergic," I reminded her, my tone sharper than I'd intended, remembering the time she was five and tried to befriend a stray kitten. Her eyes had swelled shut, and hives had sprouted all over her arms and hands.

"A dog then," she corrected, sighing dramatically. "Buzzkill."

"He really is," Bishop chimed in. "I begged Royal to send Knight with us, but *nooo*. He had to send Mr. Ray of Fucking Sunshine."

Becca giggled, the sound doing funny things to my chest while making me pissed that I wasn't the one making her laugh. Why was it always so goddamn complicated?

Bishop leaned in closer to Becca, cupping his hand around his mouth to stage-whisper at her. "Personally? I think Royal knew—"

"Let's go," I snapped as the elevator door opened onto our floor with a chime. I motioned for Becca to exit first, and when Bishop followed, I elbowed him in the ribs.

"Oof," he hissed, glaring at me.

Becca turned, eyes wide. "Everything okay?"

"Perfect, sweetheart," I assured her with a smile, stepping up and placing a hand at the small of her back to guide her down the hall to our room. I let out a relieved breath when she didn't move away from my touch.

"Touchy bastard," Bishop groused behind us.

"Pretty sure *my* mom is the one he married," I pointed out with a smug smirk over my shoulder.

Bishop flipped me off while Becca slapped my stomach with the back of her hand and told me, "Be nice." She gently shook out her fingers and mumbled something under her breath. I wasn't entirely sure what she'd said, but it sounded a lot like, "Are your abs made of bricks?"

I fought back a grin and pulled up short at the last door in the hallway across from the emergency stairs. Never hurt to have a quick exit if needed. I reached back and grabbed the keycard from Bishop to unlock the door.

After rapping my knuckles against the door in a quick pattern, I pushed the door open.

"What was that?" Becca gave me a strange look.

"What was what?"

"The weird knocking thing," she replied, gesturing to my hand.

"To let me know who was on the other side of the door," Rook said, appearing out of one of the bedrooms.

The hotel room was a decent size for Europe. Not the palatial size of most US suites or even some of the more modern European and Asian ones, but it had two bedrooms and two bathrooms. The bedroom I had was the master, with its own en suite and king-size bed. The other room had two full beds and a bathroom that was also attached to the main living space. There was a tiny kitchenette and a desk that we'd turned into our command hub.

I'd offered to give Rook or Bishop the solo room, but they'd joked they were used to sharing space with other guys and I was the entitled prince who needed his own space.

It was bullshit, but I'd taken the solo room nonetheless.

"Whoa," Becca murmured, her gaze sweeping the space and lingering on the four computers and six burner phones all plugged in on a couple of power strips.

"Drink?" Rook offered, walking to the small fridge and grabbing a beer.

"Yeah," I replied, needing something to take the edge off.

"Definitely," Becca chimed in.

I gave her a look.

"What?" She planted her hands on her hips and glared at me. "I think, out of everyone in this room, I'm the one who has the most solid reason to get shitfaced."

Bishop laid a hand over his heart. "You don't have to convince me, babe."

I resisted the urge to deck my brother, instead focusing on watching Rook pass a beer to each of us. I didn't open mine until after Becca cracked hers and lifted it to her mouth. She tried to hide it, but there was no missing the way her nose scrunched up and her mouth twisted.

Smirking to myself, I opened mine and chugged half of it. I set it on the edge of the coffee table and carried her bags toward my room. "You can stay in here." I wheeled her suitcase into the dark room and flipped on a light for her.

She crowded against my side to get a look, her gaze snagging on the solitary bed. Her swallow was audible. "Uh, cool. But I can always get a room of my own—"

"No." All three of us shut that idea down.

Rook walked around and sat down on one of two matching armchairs. He sprawled out and scrubbed a hand over his face with a yawn. "It's safer for you here."

"You can share my bed," Bishop offered.

I finished drinking my beer and hurled the empty can at him. He dodged it easily with a laugh.

"It's safer for you to be nearby," I told her, ignoring the way she gaped at me in shock. Gritting my teeth, I flashed her a tight smile. "I can sleep on the couch."

She nibbled on her lower lip. "Are you sure?"

I nodded. "Yeah, of course." I met her eyes, wishing I could just say *fuck it* and tell her we were sharing the bed. But she was already skittish, and I wasn't a complete asshole.

But having her in my space was one step closer to admitting exactly what I knew—we were inevitable.

"Court mentioned that Eric told you about the auction?" Rook spoke up.

Becca looked past me. "Yeah. I don't have a ton of details, but maybe it'll help?"

"Better than what we have now, which is jack shit," Bishop replied, frowning.

"The auction is happening a week from tomorrow," she said. "Two days after my grandmother's birthday celebration." She blanched, her face going pale as she turned and looked at me. "I can't miss Mémé's birthday party, Court."

I looked at Rook over her head. He shook his head, but I knew what her grandmother meant to her. "We'll figure it out, Becca."

"Let me put it another way," she tried, her eyes hardening, "I'm *not* missing her birthday."

"Is Eric invited?" Bishop asked.

She frowned. "Well, yeah. I asked him if he wanted to come before I knew he was a psycho. His brother will be there with Cami, too."

Bishop switched his attention to me. "How are you selling her absence?"

I leaned against the wall. "She has to return to California to tie up some loose ends with graduation."

Bishop nodded. "That could work."

"What could?" Rook looked at Bishop, somehow seeming the most in charge despite being the only one sitting down.

"You two have a past," Bishop pointed out. "Let's say Bex goes back to your fancy-ass school, sees you. You two... reconnect. You agree to come out here as her date. With your history, you could sell that you two are together."

"Except Eric thinks she's hung up on *him*," I pointed out.

"Okay… then you followed her here, but make it clear you finally want to be with her," Bishop reasoned.

I tipped my head to the side. "And that accomplishes what exactly?"

He held up a finger. "One, it puts you in play. We don't have to hide you being here."

"Actually, if we could create enough chatter about there being a divide between you and the guys, our dad might reach out, if he knew you were in Paris," Rook agreed.

My brows shot up. "Now we're bringing our dad into this?"

Bishop held up another finger. "Two, *not* having to hide your presence gives us a lot more flexibility. You can hide in plain sight *next* to Bex."

"So, you want to sell that Court decided to give up his friends, his school, and his entire life for *me*?" Becca let out a belly laugh. "No one would ever believe that."

Rook and Bishop stared at me, the challenge blatant in their gazes. I shifted my weight from foot to foot and turned toward her, dropping some of the shields I'd always kept up where she was concerned. I'd convinced myself they were necessary to function, but now I was starting to see that by trying to protect us both, I'd only been hurting us.

"Court, tell them this is ridiculous," she insisted, her eyes searching mine. "You're not… we're not… This is stupid. It'll never work."

I lifted my hand and cradled her cheek, grinning softly as her breathing hitched.

"Oh, I don't know, Becca." I swept my thumb across her soft skin, feeling her tremble slightly. "I bet we could sell it."

Her lashes fluttered for a second as her eyes closed. "Court…"

I turned us so my back was to my brothers and they couldn't see her. Couldn't see *us*. "We really need to talk, Becca."

Her eyes opened, and the uncertainty in them was like a dagger to the gut. "We do. But…"

"But not now," I finished for her.

She nodded mutely and stepped back, breaking my hold and peering around my arm to see Rook. "Can we finish planning how to save the world in the morning? I've had a really long day."

None of us pointed out that it was after two in the morning.

"Yeah," Rook said, pushing to his feet. "Get some sleep, Bex."

Her gaze lifted to me once again, her lips parting like she was about to say something, but then she stopped. That perfect mouth closed, and she retreated into the bedroom, grabbing the door and slowly closing it.

I moved back so she wouldn't hit me with it before turning to face my brothers.

Bishop was grinning like an idiot. "Feel free to thank me, little brother."

"Fuck off," I snapped, glaring at him. "You put her on the spot, and—"

"—and got your ass in the game?" He snorted and shook his head. "Jesus, Court, I'm helping you out."

"I don't need your help," I muttered, rubbing the back of my neck with a groan.

Rook looked back and forth between us before sighing. "This isn't a blind date, Bishop. Leave him alone."

Bishop's face fell.

Rook glared at me. "And you, get your shit together. She's a sweet girl, Court."

"Meaning?" My muscles tightened, coiling as I readied myself to knock his ass out. I was barely hanging on to my sanity.

"Meaning figure out what you are to each other, and either let her go, or…"

"Or?" I challenged.

He met my gaze. "Or man the fuck up and lock her down."

CHAPTER 18

BEX

Snuggling deeper into the soft sheets, I inhaled the rich, comforting scent that surrounded me. For a moment, time was suspended and I was content. Safe. Happy.

And then my scent memory kicked into gear, and I shot up in bed, damn near falling off the edge as my heart threatened to gallop out of my chest. I looked around the room wildly, probably looking like a caged animal. But not a sexy animal like a tiger or a jaguar. I no doubt looked more like a deranged cockatoo with my hair sticking up all over the place.

I wasn't a delicate, light sleeper like the princess of some fairy tale. I was known to thrash and starfish in the middle of the bed. And I sometimes woke up the next morning wearing less clothes than I'd gone to bed in, with no memory of how I'd taken them off.

Glancing down, I sucked in a sharp breath because, yeah. I was totally naked.

My clothes were strewn around the room—my tank top tossed over the chair by the window, my flannel bottoms at the foot of the bed. And my panties were…

Oh, hell. Where *had* they gone?

A knock on the closed door almost gave me a heart attack.

"Becca? Hey, can I come in and grab some clothes really quick?" Court called, his deep timbre muffled by the door.

"No!" I shouted.

"Everything okay?" His tone took on a concerned edge. And then, because of freaking course, the doorknob jiggled ever so slightly, like he'd put his hand on it, preparing to breach the perimeter.

Which wasn't the only perimeter I kinda wished he'd breach.

I slapped my forehead. Literally slapped it with an audible crack, like that would set my hindbrain back on a much safer path.

"Ow," I yelped, rubbing the sore spot on my brow. I needed to remember that slapping sense into myself was a freaking metaphor.

"Are you okay?" The worry in Court's voice ratcheted up another notch, and the elegant doorknob tipped down. "I'm coming in."

"No, no! You can't come in!" I flailed in a desperate lunge, trying to grab my pants from the bottom of the bed, but the damn sheets twisted around my waist and legs.

"What's going on?" he demanded, but didn't push the door open.

"I… I… uh…" I grabbed for the pants again, praising all the baby cherubs when my fingers touched flannel. I gave a quick jerk, but they were freaking stuck. "For real?" I huffed, pulling again with all my strength. It took a second, but they came free with a *whoosh*. The cuff of one leg—which was soft and fuzzy and comfortable—suddenly became a weapon as it slapped my open eye.

"Fuck, shit, damn!" I swore, dropping the pants and covering my eyes as tears instantly started welling. I was blind. I'd have to go to the doctor and explain that I'd lost my vision because of a freak flying flannel incident.

"What the fuck?"

I froze, realizing Court's voice sounded way too clear to be on the other side of the door. Lowering my hands, I looked up at him from a single, watery eye.

Court stood a foot away from the bed, looking like he had no clue what to do next. His hands opened and closed at his sides while his gaze slid from my teary face to my very naked chest. He swallowed hard and slowly dragged his gaze back up to my face. The lust in his eyes was momentarily eclipsed by concern. "What the hell happened?"

"My pants attacked me," I said, sounding utterly pathetic. "I think I'm blind."

"You can't see me?"

I blinked my open eye. "Partially blind," I amended.

He stepped forward and halted. "Can I... I need to check your eye."

"Sure," I muttered, dropping my hands to the sheets pooled around my waist. I quickly yanked them up, situating them so my boobs were covered.

Court sat gingerly on the edge of the bed and twisted to face me. "Let me see."

I took a shaky breath and tried to blink my injured eye open. The air hitting it burned, and I hissed out a breath.

"Easy," he murmured, reaching for my face and holding it between his large hands. He leaned in, his gaze clinical as he searched my gaze. "Can you see me?"

"Yeah," I mumbled. My left eye was throbbing, but I could see, so maybe I'd be spared that trip to the doctor.

The corner of his mouth tipped up, and I pressed my lips together to hold in any morning breath. While I looked like a recently reanimated zombie when I woke up, Court definitely *didn't*.

The extra stubble shadowing his jaw gave him a killer bad-boy vibe. This close, I could see the gold flecks in his walnut-colored eyes. There was a small scar under his right brow that I didn't remember. He smelled like warmth and cedar, and I wanted to snuggle into him like my favorite blanket.

"I think you'll live," he deduced with a soft smile, but he didn't let me go. His calloused thumb gently wiped a tear from my cheek.

"Okay," I whispered, not wanting to break whatever spell had woven itself around us. This moment was perfection, and I wanted to bottle it up and save it forever.

"Becca?"

I leaned into his touch without thinking. "Yeah?"

His brows pulled together. "Why are you naked?"

And just like a pretty, iridescent bubble popping on a summer breeze, the peace around me shattered, and I realized that the only thing keeping Court from seeing my naked body was a white Egyptian cotton sheet.

I jerked back. "Uh…"

He grinned and got off the bed like a gentleman, even if his hungry gaze dipped down to the sheet wrapped around me. "Not that I'm complaining. If you feel like getting naked in my bed—"

I cleared my throat. "Where are your brothers?" My voice was pitched to a decibel just shy of the screech of an eagle.

His tongue darted out to wet his lips. "Rook has a meeting with a source from his SEAL days. Bishop is grabbing breakfast."

"Oh. Okay." At least I wouldn't be flashing all the Woods brothers my kibbles and bits.

Cutting me a break, Court turned away. "Hey, is it cool if I take a shower? Unless you want to go first."

Crap. I'd kicked him out of his room *and* his bathroom. "Yeah, sure. I need to call my mom and let her know what's going on."

He arched a brow.

"I know," I huffed. "When I said 'let her know what's going on,' I meant I'll lie to her face using the crazy-ass story you came up with."

He grimaced. "I know you hate lying, Becca, but it's for the best."

My spine stiffened. "Of course it is. That's how you always justify it, right, Court? You decide what's best, and the rest of us are expected to go along with it."

He bowed his head. "Becca, I don't want to fight."

"Right," I muttered. "Because it's not worth fighting over, is it?" I wasn't sure exactly what I was saying, but by *it*, I meant *me*.

Yeah, I'd left California—more like fled—to put space between us, but there was some dark, hidden part of my heart that had been hoping he'd come after me. That he'd fight for me.

That hadn't happened.

Even now, he was here only because he had to be.

"You know what?" I said suddenly, "maybe a trip back to California is a good idea."

"What?" His eyes narrowed.

"Yeah," I continued, forcing the words through my teeth, "I can stay with Maddie and Ryan. Linc and Ash are there, so I'll be safe."

"I already said you're not going to California, Becca," Court replied, his tone firm.

The only thing keeping me from getting up was the fact that I was literally naked under the covers. "I need to be safe, right? I can be safe there. I bet Linc would bring me back for my grandmother's birthday. He could even be my date, to spare you."

"*Spare* me?" he snarled. "No one, least of all Lincoln mother-fucking Westford, is coming near you."

"He's your best friend," I snapped.

"Exactly," he shot back, "which means I know *all* the ways he'd love to fuck you."

My mouth dropped open. "Linc and I are friends," I spluttered. "*Just* friends."

His disbelieving expression had me flipping through my memories of all the times Linc and I had goofed off. Yeah, he was an incorrigible flirt, but it was harmless.

Right?

Court shook his head and blew out a hard breath. He tipped his head back, looking at the ceiling for a long moment. "Becca... Can we not do this right now? Please?"

Dammit. All it took was a *please* and those big brown eyes to have me considering that maybe *now* wasn't the time for this fight.

Then again, maybe Court felt like it would never be the right time. He could just keep pushing off all these uncomfortable conversations indefinitely, because I didn't matter enough—

"No." He moved back to the bed and sat, grabbing one of my hands.

Surprised, I looked down at where he'd laced our fingers together. Had his hand always been that big? Or was mine just stupidly small?

"This isn't me trying to get you to drop it," he added, his tone kinder and gentler. "This is me asking for a ten-minute pause so I can take a shower, you can get some coffee, and then we can sit down and talk." He squeezed my fingers. "Really talk. There's a lot that I think we need to say to each other."

And suddenly, talking was the *last* thing I wanted to do. Nope. I actually preferred my ostrich way of handling things. Head in the sand had worked for me for eighteen years, right?

"Becca," he murmured, using his other hand to lift my chin. "I mean it. No more running away for either of us. I can't keep doing this."

My eyes widened. "Oh, *you* can't do this anymore? Well, since *you* can't, I guess that fixes everything."

He had the decency to look ashamed. "I know it'll take more than words to earn back your trust, but I'll do it. I swear I will."

"Why?" I blurted out. "Why *now*? Court, I'll stay here, okay? It's stupid to fly back to California for three days and then fly back. Carbon footprint and all that, you know? The environment—"

His index finger feathered over my bottom lip, rendering me speechless. His mouth curved into a wicked, devastating smile. "You're rambling, baby."

"You shouldn't call me that," was all I could think to say.

His head tilted. "I think I like calling you that."

It was like I could hear my synapses attempting to fire, to form a response, but I couldn't. As always, being around Court was like being restored to factory reset. Instead of remembering all the ways he'd hurt me and let me down, I was ready to trust him with my heart.

"Do you need the bathroom before I take a shower?" he offered, leaning back but still holding my hand and touching my face.

I blinked once. Twice. Then nodded.

"All right." Letting me go, he stood up.

I started to get out of the bed and froze when I remembered that I was *still* naked. "Uh."

Court did that guy thing where he grabbed his shirt by the back of his neck and yanked it off in one smooth tug. If his nearness caused my neurons to misfire, him shirtless was going to liquefy my brain.

Tan skin stretched taut over hard muscles that looked like they'd been created using the same mold as a Greek god. Each ab was perfectly outlined, and it took all my willpower not to let my gaze follow the trail of dark hair that disappeared into the waistband of his sweatpants.

But it was the gold, orange, and red phoenix tattooed on his ribs that snagged my attention. The mythical bird wrapped in flames, that rippled across his skin as he breathed, looked ready to set the world ablaze.

"Becca?" He sounded utterly amused.

My gaze snapped up to see he was holding his shirt out to me. I stared at it dumbly for a second before grabbing it. I tried not to focus on the fact that it was still warm and smelled like him as I pulled it over my head.

"Fuck," he murmured, heat flaring in his irises. "You look good in my clothes."

I adjusted the collar, which had slipped off one shoulder, but then it slipped off the other. I was basically swimming in his shirt, but I was woman enough to admit I liked it.

Fine.

Loved it.

I rose from the bed, feeling my cheeks heat as the cool air brushed my bare legs. The shirt landed a few inches above my knees, but I still felt exposed and raw in front of him. Especially when he flashed those hungry eyes at me.

Ducking my head, I hurried into the bathroom and closed the door. I leaned against it for a moment as I took a deep breath and looked at my reflection in the large mirror over the double vanity.

"Breathe, Bex," I ordered myself. I slowly counted to five in my head and then pushed off the door and hurried into the separate toilet area of the bathroom. I'd unpacked some of my toiletries last night, so I washed my hands and brushed my teeth when I finished emptying my bladder. Locating a hair tie, I twisted my unruly hair into a knot on top of my head and braced myself to leave the space.

Court was standing near the foot of the bed, a pile of clothes in one hand. He smiled at me as I walked by, careful to keep enough distance so we wouldn't touch.

But then he caught my wrist. "Can you do me a favor?"

"Uh, sure," I managed.

He handed me his cell phone. "Ash is supposed to text me, and it's important. Can you knock on the bathroom door and let me know what he says?"

My brows shot up. "Isn't that, like, need-to-know type stuff?"

His lips twitched. "It's not that kinda stuff. It's the not-so-official summons for you to return to Pacific Cross. In fact, forward it to yourself so you have it, just in case you need to show it to anyone."

"Like Eric?"

Storm clouds gathered behind his eyes. "If that fucker contacts you, I need you to tell me immediately, okay?"

I nodded. "I will. What's the code to unlock it?"

He gave me a strange look before finally saying, "Zero-eight-twenty-two."

I paused, the number registering in my brain. "My birthday?"

His face relaxed into a softness that I rarely got to see. "Yeah." He started to move around me.

"Court?"

He stopped instantly, giving me his full attention. "Yeah, baby?"

I caught my bottom lip between my teeth, suddenly embarrassed and unsure. "You..." I took a deep breath. "You really want to talk later?"

He moved in front of me, his hands framing my face and holding me like I was the most precious thing in the world. "Yeah, Becca. I've let you go twice now, and I hated myself every time. I can't do it a third time. I won't survive it, baby."

I swallowed hard, working not to cry.

"I know I've let you down before, but I won't. I'll do whatever it takes to prove that I need you in my life."

I shrugged. "Sure, Court. Whatever you say."

His eyes slid shut, and he leaned forward to press a kiss to my forehead. "Give me ten minutes." Then he was gone, disappearing into the bathroom.

Letting out a wobbly exhale, I hurried up and grabbed a change of clothes before wandering out into the main living area to the kitch-enette. A fresh pot of coffee was waiting for me along with my favorite hazelnut creamer. Smiling, I made myself a cup and took it to the couch.

I'd just settled in when Court's phone pinged with an incoming message. Setting the coffee aside, I typed in my birthday and saw he had a new text. "Damn, Ash." I did the mental math—if it was eight in the morning here, it was two a.m. in California.

I hit the text icon, and the message opened into an image.

It took me a second to realize that what I was seeing was a perky set of very naked breasts attached to a blonde with big green eyes. Her lips were stained crimson and slightly open, her eyes hooded.

UNKNOWN: I miss you, baby.

Before I could *nope* my way out of the text thread, a second one came through. This time it was a waxed va-jay-jay with a silver piercing spread wide open by long, pointed green nails.

UNKNOWN: My pussy needs you.

Horrified, I exited the text thread, but stopped cold as I realized there were other texts in his phone. Ash's name was in there, but it was buried under several others.

Nicki. Sarah. BethAnn.

Knowing I shouldn't but unable to help myself, I clicked on the first one.

Nicki was a tiny redhead who seemed to have an affinity for black lingerie.

Sarah had pierced nipples.

And BethAnn? She just wanted to let Court know that she and her cousin were "DTF again" whenever he was free.

Nausea roiled in my gut. I stared at the phone until the screen went dark, mentally willing away what I had seen.

But there was no denying it. And if the texts weren't enough, I could hear Cori asking Maddie about the woman she'd seen naked in Court's bed.

I didn't know how long I sat there, my coffee growing cold as my insides went numb.

I was such an idiot.

Court flashed me a smile and said a few sweet things, and I crumbled. Every. Single. Time.

I won't survive it, baby.

Tears of humiliation burned my eyes.

"Did Ash text, baby?" Court's voice was like a bolt of lightning zipping down my spine. He came up behind me, his hands settling possessively on my shoulders as he bent to kiss the top of my head.

How many other women had he kissed like that? Called *baby*?

"No," I finally managed, my throat tight as I shook off his hold and stood. I pasted a cold smile on my face and handed him the phone. "But you got a few other messages."

Frowning, he took the phone and unlocked it. His thumb moved over the screen, and I saw the second he realized I knew. His face went pale under his tan skin. "Becca."

"Save it," I snapped, storming around the couch.

"Fuck. Becca, wait. You don't understand."

I whirled around. "You know what, Court? I might not be the smartest person in the world, but even I know what sexting looks like."

His eyes were wild. "They sent *me* those pictures."

"Oh," I laughed coolly, "so it's *their* fault? You're just a helpless victim? Because you certainly gave enough of a shit about them to save their contact info."

His jaw clenched. "Let me explain."

"No," I snapped. "I'm done letting you explain. I'm done letting you tell me how I'm so important to you, but all you do is lie to me. And I'm… I'm done being the idiot who keeps letting you do it."

Spinning away, I raced into the bedroom and slammed the door before locking him out of the room and my heart, once and for all.

CHAPTER 19

BEX

Every time Court knocked on the door, threatened to break it down, or called my name, I caved a little more. My brain started rationalizing all the ways that maybe I had misread the signals that multiple women sending him nude images gave off.

I considered calling Maddie and waking her up to talk, but that seemed like a shitty way to wake up my bestie. It was after eight, so Cami was in the studio rehearsing by now. I didn't want to bother her.

After taking the time to come up with lame-ass excuses that my mom and grandparents would let slide to excuse my absence for the next few days, I headed into the bathroom, where I put another locked door between myself and Court before climbing into the shower.

There wasn't much that a hot shower couldn't fix, or at least make a little better.

Thirty minutes later, I felt a little more human as I towel-dried my hair and pulled on fresh clothes. I balled up Court's shirt and hurled it under the sink. I left the bathroom feeling slightly better than when I'd gone in, but relief hit me hard and fast when I heard voices other than Court's on the other side of the door.

Banking on Rook and Bishop giving me a buffer from the asshole, plus missing my morning coffee fix, I opened the door and stalked through like a woman on a caffeine-fueled mission.

The three brothers stood in the center of the room, and they all turned to look at me as I emerged.

I flashed Rook and Bishop a big smile, pointedly ignoring Court. "Morning, guys."

"Becca," Court started.

I lifted the still mostly full coffee pot and turned to him with a saccharine-sweet smile. "Unless you feel like being treated for second degree burns, I suggest you back all the way up." I lifted my hand with the pot, unafraid to use the liquid gold as a weapon if needed.

Court somehow managed to look hurt, frustrated, and pissed off. "Can we just talk?"

"Nah," I returned, pouring myself a fresh mug. "I'm good. If you need someone to talk to, try Nicki or BethAnn. Personally I thought BethAnn had the nicer smile, but Nicki's definitely hotter."

"Oh shit," Bishop muttered, his dark eyes wide.

Rook shot Court a death glare. "What the fuck did you do?"

Snarling, Court turned to them. "I didn't do shit. I got a text—"

"I'm sorry," I interrupted, arching a brow, "but I'm pretty sure I counted higher than one."

He ground his teeth together. "It's not what—"

"Question," I posed, ignoring him again and walking around to stand in front of his brothers. "If multiple women are sending you naked selfies, would you think that was an accident? A coincidence? That the naked selfie fairy shot the wrong asshole in the ass?"

Bishop snorted a laugh. "Tell me you're not that fucking stupid, man."

"Jesus fuck," Court swore. "Can you stop acting like a child for a goddamn minute and let me explain?"

"Oh, *hell* no," I snapped. "You don't get to act like I'm some delusional girlfriend acting like a paranoid idiot. I know what I saw, Court. Maybe stop covering your ass for five seconds and own up to the truth."

"That's a valid request," Bishop chimed in, coming to stand behind me.

"I can't do this. I have a call with Royal in fifteen," Rook muttered. He stabbed a finger at Court. "Fix this." And then he stalked away to the other bedroom. He slammed the door hard enough that the decorative table on the wall between the bedrooms trembled.

"Those girls meant *nothing*," Court insisted.

"And yet, you keep their pictures," I pointed out.

Bishop wandered to the couch and perched on the edge, watching us like we were his new favorite reality show.

Court threw his arms up. "Because they sent me those pictures last night. I didn't have a chance to delete and block them like the others."

"Oh, bad call, bro," Bishop muttered with a wince.

"Don't worry," I assured him, my tone acidic. "I'm well aware that Court had an extremely active social life lately. Cori told me *all* about meeting one of his sleepover buddies."

"Goddamn it," Court growled. "I haven't been with anyone since her! And I sure as shit haven't talked to anyone since I started talking to you."

I set my coffee down just so I could give him a slow clap as I eyeballed the clock. "Congratulations, Court. You haven't talked to another woman in sixteen hours."

His phone gave a chirp from the dining table, then started to vibrate with an incoming call.

"You should probably get that," I suggested. "Don't want to keep your harem waiting."

"Becca," he snarled, a tendon in his neck throbbing.

"How does it work?" I asked, tilting my head as I feigned curiosity. "Do they pick days? Or do you have someone assign them, like shifts?"

He spun and grabbed his phone before hurling it into the wall. It shattered into a hundred pieces.

My heart pounded, but I forced my outward appearance to stay calm, unruffled, as I grabbed my coffee and took a sip. "I thought you were waiting on Ash to send you something."

"I can't win with you," he hissed, shaking his head.

"Wait, have you actually been trying?" I asked, not willing to give him another single centimeter.

Court pinched the bridge of his nose. "What do you want me to say, Becca? I never claimed to be a damn monk."

"Did I ask you to be?" I shot back.

"Seems like that's what you want," he returned, just as pissed as I was now.

Good. It was easier to hate him when he was mad at me.

Bishop cleared his throat. "Maybe you guys should take a step back. Neutral corners and that shit."

"No. Court wanted to talk, so let's talk," I retorted.

"Not about this," he gritted out, crossing his arms. "You know what? Let's just do what Bishop said. We'll take a minute and cool off."

I pointed to my chest. "I don't need to cool off. What could I possibly need to cool off for? I didn't do anything wrong."

"Except jump to the wrong conclusions," he said flatly. He scrubbed a hand over his face.

"Why does it matter?" I pressed. It was kinda like when you had a bruise and you kept pushing on the spot to see if it still hurt.

It totally did, but I couldn't seem to stop fighting with him.

Before he could answer, I plowed on. "It's not like *I* matter, right? I'm just that kid who used to follow you around before you realized she was too annoying to keep around."

"That's not even close to the truth, and you know it."

"No, Court, I *don't* know it because *you* could never be bothered to tell me the truth about what happened that summer," I hissed. "The only time you came close was after *I* found a video where Madelaine claimed she knew some big secret you'd been keeping from me, which… not surprising, considering you also kept to yourself the fact that my dad was involved in all sorts of shady shit."

"I made mistakes, Becca," he said. "I fully admit that, and I want us to move forward with everything out in the open."

"Maybe I don't want to," I replied with a nonchalant shrug. "Maybe I want…" Shit, what did I want?

"What?" he challenged, waving his hand in a *go ahead* motion.

"Make it good, Bex," Bishop whispered.

Court glared at him. "Shut the fuck up."

"You know what?" I started, the dumbest of all dumb ideas forming in my head. "You're right, Court."

He gave me a wary look. "I am?"

"You have a past, and that's fine."

"Everyone does, Becca. Even you." He gave me a hard look.

I frowned. "What?" Uh, unless kissing counted, I was underwhelmingly without a past.

He scoffed. "What was it you said when we were in Montana? I wasn't your first, second *or* third?"

I quickly searched through my memories of the time we'd spent in Montana, hiding out from Maddie's and Ryan's insane fathers and creating a plan to take them down. And yes, that was when Court and I had had our most intense falling out—after I found out he'd lied about why he'd abandoned me years earlier.

Not just Court, but everyone had been lying to me. I'd been hurt, angry, and embarrassed that everyone seemed to know more about my own life than I did. That people kept making decisions for me, especially ones that I thought had my back.

Court and I had said a lot to each other that night. But I'd never forget the moment he said *You've always belonged to me.* The truth was, he was right. My heart had always belonged to the boy next door. My hero, my friend, my everything.

But then he'd doubled down by reminding me, *I was your first kiss, remember? I was meant to be your first everything.*

He'd been right, but I'd been hurt and pissed, and I'd lashed out the only way I'd known how. *I'll give you that you were my first kiss, but you weren't my first. Or my second. Not my third either.*

The pain in his eyes had been worth the tiny momentary triumph that had surged through my veins. But my claim had been a lie.

Well, unless you counted me, myself, and I, then sure. I'd had three sexual partners.

But I wasn't about to tell Court he was right. That even when I'd tried dating or getting close to other guys, no one held up to the ideal of the perfect guy that my childhood self had invented.

No one except him.

It was stupid. I mean, I'd been a kid. What did I know about love and forever? But something in my bones knew that every guy I'd ever held hands with, kissed, or touched who wasn't Court Woods felt wrong.

At this rate, I was going to need an exorcism to extract him from my DNA.

Unfortunately, that meant I needed to either come clean… or keep up the lie.

It was a no-brainer.

"What? Only guys deserve orgasms?" I folded my arms and shifted my weight, popping one hip out in defiance. "Did you expect me to enter a convent? Die an old, virgin spinster? Oh, or maybe I should be waiting for my one true love to sweep me away."

Court's eyes flashed. "Don't."

"Don't what?" I needled. "I may not have been with hundreds of people, but I guess some of us prefer quality over quantity."

"Oh, I'll give you quality," he growled, moving closer to me.

"No, you won't. Not now, not ever. I'm not interested in you, Court." I sucked in a breath, praying he wouldn't see through the outright lie.

He smirked. "You're lying."

"Don't believe me?" I challenged. I spun and looked at Bishop. "How would you feel about going out with me?"

Bishop's eyes went wide. "Uh, what?"

"A date. You. Me." Oh, God, I hadn't thought this through. If he said no…

Well, the convent was still an option.

Court snorted. "Becca, come on. My brother isn't going—"

"Okay."

I don't know who was more shocked at Bishop's decision—me or Court. But I recovered fastest, flashing Bishop a big smile that felt too tight across my face. "Awesome. Tonight?"

"No fucking way," Court spat. "Even if you two were serious, you can't just go running around Paris, Becca."

"Just so happens we're conveniently staying in a hotel with excellent room service," Bishop replied, grinning.

Court glared at him with enough ice to freeze fire. "You're going on a fucking date with her in our hotel room? What, are Rook and I the chaperones?"

Bishop scoffed, pulling out his phone. "Bro, give me a little credit. I may not be racking up the notches on my bedpost as fast as you, but I *do* know how to date a woman. And… done." He winked at me. "I just booked us our own room here. We can be alone all night."

Wait.

What?

All night?

Court turned and studied me, no doubt waiting to see if I'd crack and retreat.

Instead I lifted my chin, defiance rolling through my veins. "Awesome. I can't wait."

CHAPTER 20

COURT

In the years I'd known I had brothers, I'd gone through an entire spectrum of emotions. Shock, longing, annoyance, anger, happiness. Even love.

Apparently blistering hot rage was a whole new thing.

After Becca practically danced back to her room, I rounded on my brother, absolutely intent on breaking every one of his appendages, starting with his dick.

"Are you out of your goddamn mind?" I hissed, my hands clenching at my sides. I could already imagine the satisfying way the cartilage in his nose would shatter under my fist. "This isn't happening."

Bishop barely spared me a glance as he looked up from his phone. "Yeah, it is."

"No, it fucking *isn't*."

He stood up, not that it mattered. We were almost the exact same size, making him eye level. "Yes. It is." He paused. "Unless you give me one good reason why it shouldn't."

I let out a frustrated growl. "How about because we're in the middle of a goddamn op?"

A brow lifted. "And we're also in a holding pattern until we know more. We're not even leaving the damn hotel. Hell, I requested a room on the same *floor*."

"She's—" I cut myself off.

"She's *what*?" he pressed, edging closer until his boots touched mine. "Yours? She's a person, not a toy, Court. You don't get to call dibs."

I snorted in disbelief. "So, what? You're into her now?"

He met my gaze and held it. "She's beautiful, smart, and fun. What guy *wouldn't* want to date her? Until there's a ring on her finger, or you grow the fuck up, then I don't see how it's any of your concern."

Fury pounded in my veins, so blinding that my vision went unfocused. "Are you serious right now? You know we have a history."

"And?" He cocked his head.

"This isn't some damn game," I hissed, poking his chest with my finger. Fucker had pecs made of goddamn iron. "Becca is a sweet girl."

He threw his arms in the air. "Jesus, she's not a *girl*, Court. When are you going to wake up and realize that *Bex* is all grown up? She doesn't need you protecting her from schoolyard bullies anymore. She's a grown-ass woman. Maybe your problem is that you can't see that."

No, my problem was that was *all* I saw.

The round, perky curve of her tits. The full ass. The flat stomach. The wicked glint in her eyes when she smiled. Even down to those slim fingers that I'd imagined wrapped around my cock way too many times.

All the muscles in my back tightened. "I see her just fine."

Bishop gave me a hard look. "Then do something about it, Court."

"Maybe I'm trying, but my brother is cockblocking me," I snapped.

He snorted a laugh. "Bro, the only thing cockblocking you is your own cock."

"What's that supposed to mean?"

"It means, you're a dumbass and she's right—you really did expect her to sit around with a chastity belt on, waiting for you to finish getting your dick sucked and fucked by half the female population of

California." He gave me a disgusted look. "It's the twenty-first century, dude. Women can have casual sex, too."

"Did I ever say they couldn't?" What the fuck was going on?

"You implied Bex couldn't," he responded.

"That's different," I insisted, but the argument sounded shitty, even to my own ears.

Bishop clapped his hands down on my shoulders. "Court, you can't have it both ways. Either you want her, or you don't. If you do, go tell her right now, and I'll cancel the room. But if you can't? Then get out of her way."

"You mean *your* way?" I knocked his hands away.

He grinned. "That, too. I'm not going to apologize for appreciating what you're intent on throwing away."

"You're my brother," I finally snapped. "Aren't you supposed to have *my* back?"

"Who the fuck says I don't?" He moved around me. "So? What'll it be? Are you going to talk to her?"

I ground my teeth together, my jaw aching as my gaze cut to her closed bedroom door. My eyes dropped, but not before I caught Bishop's smirk.

"Exactly what I thought." He made a *tsk*ing sound under his breath as he walked by me, and that was all it took for me to spin and shove him.

Bishop stumbled forward a few steps, surprised but regaining his balance quickly. He turned and glared at me. "Don't."

I shifted my weight to my back leg, bracing myself for him to fight back. My blood craved the violence, needed it to soothe some savage part of me that was going apeshit at the idea of Bishop and Becca alone in a hotel room together.

"Stay the fuck away from her," I ordered.

The door across from us opened and Rook leaned a shoulder against the frame, watching us with annoyance. "You two fuck up this room, and it's coming out of your paychecks."

I glared at him. "He—"

Rook held up a hand. "I don't give a fuck. We have more than enough shit to deal with without you two whipping out your dicks to see whose is the biggest."

"Mine is," Bishop chimed in.

I snorted, not even bothering to reply to that.

"Bishop's right," Rook added.

Bishop blinked in surprise, then smirked. "See? Told you mine was bigger."

"Not *that* you idiot," Rook muttered, shaking his head. He looked at me, holding my gaze. "Either you're in or out with her. If you're out, then it shouldn't matter what your brother or any other guy does with her."

"And if I'm not?" I glared at them both.

"Then say so, and I'll never look at her again," Bishop told me, his voice conveying absolute honesty.

"What happened to the good, old-fashioned bro code?" I mumbled, not wanting to deal with these annoying feelings and what they meant.

"It absolutely applies, but only if you're willing to admit that you have feelings beyond friendship for her." Rook made it sound so simple.

I'd been ready to do just that. I'd thought she and I were on the exact same page when I'd gone to take a shower, then I'd come out and everything had gone to shit. Now she was going on a date with my damn *brother*?

Bishop and Rook watched me, neither willing to give an inch. As if making me face up to the feelings I had for Becca would lead to some kind of miraculous revelation. Like this was one of those bullshit primetime teen soap operas where the main character suddenly realizes he's in love with the girl next door.

I didn't need a special moment to know I'd been head over heels in love with Rebecca Whittier since the day I'd understood what love was.

And I'd been running from it ever since.

But if this was what she wanted… Fine. I'd been an idiot for thinking we could actually, what? Be happy together? Just *be* together?

I pulled my shoulders back and let out a heavy breath. "You know what? Do whatever you want, brother. As far as I'm concerned, she's fair fucking game. I've always felt a little protective of her because she was like a little sister, but she isn't. She isn't anything to me."

The sharp inhale at my back made me die a little inside, but turning to see Becca standing behind me broke what was left of my cold, dead heart.

Her hazel eyes swam with tears, the slender column of her neck working as she tried to swallow around the emotions.

I forced a cold smile. "Have fun tonight, sweetheart, but make sure he wraps it up. I know how concerned you are about numbers and all that shit, and Bishop's count might be higher than mine."

She stumbled back a step, looking at me like I was a stranger.

Good. As soon as this was done, I wouldn't see her again. And it would be easier for her to move on if she hated me.

I looked over my shoulder at Rook, who looked pissed. "I have an errand to run for Ash. I'll be back tonight unless you need me here sooner."

He wordlessly shook his head.

"Perfect." I grabbed my wallet from the side table near the door, brushing past Bishop.

"You're making a mistake," he warned me, too quiet for Becca to hear.

I paused. "No, I'm not. This is what's best for everyone."

"Idiot," he muttered at my back as I yanked open the door and slammed it shut behind me.

On that we could agree: I was absolutely an idiot.

Becca could never be mine. I'd been a damn fool for thinking we could ever move beyond our past.

CHAPTER 21

BEX

Court's words haunted me the rest of the day. They played on an endless loop, slowly driving me insane.

She isn't anything to me.

Part of me wanted to call Maddie, talk to my best friend about how much Court had hurt me—yes, *again*—but there was a quieter, darker part of me that couldn't do it. That couldn't bear to hear the pity in her voice, the apology on her lips.

It was humiliating.

You'd have thought that, by now, I'd be used to Court Woods humiliating me, but it seemed there was never actually a rock bottom. Each time I thought I'd hit it, it turned out there were another twenty levels or so of my pride left that he could shred.

What did it say about me that I kept giving him chances to hurt me? That I kept showing up at his feet like some deranged puppy that could be kicked a million times but was still looking for a little bit of affection? A glimpse of love…

Disgusted with myself, I opted for distraction. I pulled out my Kindle and flopped down on the plush mattress, tugged the sheets and comforter up to my chin, and dove back into a fictional world where the alphaholes ended up head over heels in love with the main character.

Yes, multiple alphaholes, because sometimes a girl needs her own harem.

I finished one book and started the next without a pause. My stomach gave a slight rumble, and when I checked the clock, it looked like it was almost time for my *date*.

As if I'd conjured him with my thoughts, Bishop knocked at the door. "Bex?"

Clearing my throat, I sat up and ran a hand through my rumpled hair. "Yeah. You can come in."

The door cracked open, and he stuck his dark head in a minute later. He flashed me a tight smile. "You okay, gorgeous?"

I gave a half-hearted snort because I was pretty sure I looked the antithesis of gorgeous. Unlike Bishop, who somehow looked like a combination of a dashing rake from a Regency romance and an MC biker. The mix of devilish gentleman with more than a hint of danger was enough to send most hearts—male and female alike—into palpitations.

Honestly, the Woods brothers were unfairly hot. They had insanely muscular builds, and none of them was under six-two. And because they all were former elite members of the armed services, they were ripped as hell. Dark hair ran in the family, thanks to their dad, but Court was the only one with dark eyes. The others had shades ranging from almost turquoise blue to gunmetal silver.

Bishop's were a gentle deep blue the color of the ocean. His cheekbones were a bit sharper than Rook's or Court's, giving him an almost pretty-boy look. Especially when he flashed a charming grin.

"I'm okay," I finally answered.

He came into the room and closed the door before leaning against it. He crossed his legs at the ankles. "We don't have to go out tonight. I know you were just trying to get at Court."

I bit my lower lip, embarrassed at how easily he'd read the situation. "I mean, kinda. But I *do* like you."

"But not the way you like Court," he finished with a kind smile.

My shoulders slumped. "I'm sorry."

"Shit, girl." He chuckled, pushing off the door and coming to sit on the other side of the bed. "Don't apologize. Heart wants what the heart wants. I'm just sorry my brother's too goddamn stubborn to see what's right in front of him."

I dipped my head, but my inner masochist had me asking, "And what's that?"

He leaned over and touched my chin with his index finger. "You're an amazing woman, Bex. And he's a fucking moron."

A tremulous smile twitched across my lips. "Pretty sure the only moron is me. I'm the one who keeps setting myself up to be let down again and again."

He exhaled a heavy breath. "Can I be honest with you?"

"Please."

"None of us had a great upbringing, but I think Court had it the worst." He pressed his lips into a tight line for a beat. "The General is a fucking asshole. He's exacting and demanding and outright sadistic. I mean, look at the shit he put all of us through. His test *killed* my brother. And damn near killed *you.*"

I rocked back. "You know about that?"

He gave a grim nod. "Yeah. I mean, Court doesn't talk about it much, but I know the gist."

"That's more than he's told me," I muttered.

He cocked his head. "You two have never talked about it?"

I met his gaze. "Until a few weeks ago, I had no idea it even happened."

His brows shot up. "You forgot getting kidnapped for a week?"

My spine stiffened as irritation swirled in my blood. "Yeah, but in my defense, I was also really sick."

He inclined his head, ceding my point. "I only heard about it after the fact, and I definitely don't know the details, but I know it was bad."

"I'm sure it was." There was no masking the bitterness in my tone.

"Did you know Court was sent to military school for a few months after?"

My head snapped up, my jaw dropping open. "What?"

Bishop grimaced. "You aren't the only one who paid a price, Bex. I'm not trying to excuse him or the shit he's done to push you away, but what happened to you fucked him up in a lot of ways."

I frowned, my forehead wrinkling. "But *military school*?" It was one thing for General Woods to want his son to be *in* the military, but military school basically spelled out juvenile delinquent in our world. I was stunned that he'd take the hit to his family's social status.

Lauren Woods, Court's mom, came from old money. Like the kind that started before the United States was even an idea. They were proper and believed strongly that indiscretions were handled privately.

"He sorta… shut down after what happened to you. I think you were still in the hospital for a good chunk of it. The General was at our house one night, and I heard him yelling on the phone. Before he left, he told my mom that Court had gotten into another incident. He was livid and kept mentioning he was sending Court away to get him straightened out." Bishop sighed heavily.

"I had no idea," I whispered, my hand drifting up to cover my mouth. That year was still a blur. The doctors claimed it was because I'd been so sick and so close to dying that my brain had barricaded the memories away.

All I really remembered was needing Court, and him never showing up except once to tell me I needed to leave him alone. I'd been young and ill, and I'd just lain in that hospital bed as my heart shattered.

Now, looking at it through adult eyes, I realized that the boy who'd come to visit me wasn't the boy I'd known.

His eyes had been hard and flinty, somehow icy and fiery at the same time. He hadn't smiled—in fact, his lips had been pressed into a line so harsh that the skin around them was white. And his cheeks had been hollow, while his normally carelessly windswept dark hair had been buzzed short.

Like he was enlisting in a thirteen-year-old's version of boot camp.

"The General came to see us a couple of times a month, and it was hell," Bishop confided, his voice low. "He was mean—he'd hit us when we were too loud or asked questions. He wanted little toy soldiers, silent and obedient as they waited for his next command. We hated when he came over, but we didn't see him every goddamn day. Not like Court did."

My heart sank like a boulder.

Growing up, Court had always had bruises, but I'd seen the way he played with his friends. They'd treated me like I was made of glass, but they'd tackled each other off the deck for fun.

"He *hurt* Court?" My voice wobbled.

"He hurt all of us," Bishop amended, "but I think he hurt Court the most, yes."

I wasn't sure what to do with this information. It was easier to be mad at Court when I didn't have to think about the hell he'd been through as a kid.

And I'd never known any of it. Court had kept that part of his life hidden from me.

He was always keeping secrets. Wasn't he tired of it? Of all the hiding? I knew I was exhausted from always being kept in the dark.

I drew in a long breath. "It doesn't excuse him for spending the entire fall lying to me. If anything it just proves that he has a pattern of dishonesty, especially when it comes to me."

"You're right," he agreed without flinching, "but us Woods brothers aren't exactly stellar at sharing our emotions or feelings. I mean, I trust my brothers with my life, but there's a lot of shit I keep from them."

I arched a brow. "Really?"

He nodded. "Yeah."

"Like what?" I asked, genuinely curious. Then I quickly backpedaled. "Forget I asked."

"No, it's cool," he replied with a soft smile. He blew out a breath and looked up at the ceiling. "I haven't told my brothers that I'm bisexual."

My eyes rounded. "Why not?" As much as Court and his brothers were alpha men to the extreme, I couldn't see any of them being bigoted and rejecting Bishop.

He chewed on his bottom lip. "Honestly, I realized it when I was in high school, but the idea of the General finding out was enough to make me keep it to myself. And as evolved as the United States Marine Corps claims to be, guys who come out as gay or bi are often treated differently. I guess I just got used to hiding who I am, and now it's been so long that I don't want it to make things weird."

"Thank you for telling me." I reached for his hand, humbled that he'd entrusted me with his truth.

He squeezed my fingers, but there was no spark. No chemistry. "Don't give up on him, Bex. I know it's asking a lot, but he's been through shit none of us even know about, because he keeps it bottled up."

I leveled a gaze at him. "I get that, but I can't let myself keep hoping for something that will never happen."

His lips quirked. "Did you see how pissed he was when he left?"

I nodded.

"Trust me," he finished with a grin. "I think today was the kick in the ass Court needed to realize he's out of chances with you."

Hope flickered in my chest, a single tiny flame that threatened to turn into a bonfire if left unchecked. "I don't know."

"Please, Bex," he whispered, those soulful eyes searching mine. "Don't write him off yet."

I exhaled, suddenly bone weary even though I hadn't done anything all day except read and chill out. "Fine."

He gave my fingers one last squeeze, then got off the bed. "Hungry?"

"Starving," I admitted.

"Rook is ordering some pizzas. They'll be here any minute, and maybe you can talk to Court when he comes back."

Nodding, I climbed off the bed and stretched. I followed him into the living area and ate dinner with them. We watched a movie, and by the time I went to bed, Court still wasn't back.

I could tell Rook and Bishop were nervous about it, until Rook got a text that seemed to relax and piss him off at the same time. When the brothers exchanged a look they thought I'd missed, I knew the truth.

Court wasn't coming back for me. Whatever bridge we'd started building this morning had been burned to the ground. This time I wasn't sure which one of us had struck the match.

That little bubble of hope inside me popped, and I crept back into my bed.

I wanted to be angry, to rage at the world. But I just lay in silence as tears dripped down my cheeks until sleep was the only thing left that would claim me.

CHAPTER 22

BEX

I was cold.

No, I was freezing.

Shivering, I pulled my knees to my chest and wrapped my arms around my legs. Tucked into a corner of the small room, I heard only the roar of the wind through the trees. It slammed against the sides of the house, battering it like a hurricane.

Squeezing my eyes shut, I dropped my head to my knees and swallowed a sob. My throat ached from all the screaming and crying I'd already done, and the heat of my forehead seared through the jeans and burned my knees.

My head felt heavy, muddled. My bones ached. I just wanted to sleep.

Something crashed outside, and I jerked. My head snapped up to see a tree bent nearly in half outside the lone window in the small space.

I'd pulled the comforter off the single bed in the room and wrapped it around my thin shoulders as best as I could, but I was still so cold.

My eyes stung with the need to cry, but I was out of tears. My throat burned, and I reached for the bottle of water. My fingertips brushed it, knocking it over.

"No, no!" I cried, clumsily grappling for it before it could fall over.

It was like watching a disaster in slow motion.

The clear plastic teetered on the rim, wobbling for a moment before tilting away from me. What was left of my water splashed onto the dusty floorboards as the bottle rolled away.

I scrambled forward. The fabric of my jeans tore as they snagged on a rough piece of wood. A splinter pierced my skin, and I recoiled with a cry. The bottle tumbled under the bed and out of sight, leaving a thin trail of droplets in its wake.

That was my last bottle of water. The other empty containers mocked me from a few feet away, where I'd arranged them in a neat row of three. The empty box of crackers was next to it. I'd licked all the crumbs from the bottom hours ago. How long had I been here? When would it end?

A sob ripped from my throat as I started to cry again, my insides tumbling around with fear, hunger, and exhaustion. I wanted my mommy. I wanted my friends. I wanted—

The glass of the window exploded into the room, shards skittering across the floor as a tree branch smashed into it.

I screamed again, rolling to my side as the wind howled louder. A deafening roar consumed me, threatening to rip the walls of the cabin apart as the storm raged on.

With nothing left to do, I tried screaming for help one more time. Only one name came to my lips, because he'd never let me down. He'd always saved me. He was my hero.

Something else slammed into the tiny space, and then the floor was shaking as something thumped across it. Something grabbed my shoulders, wrapping around my tiny arms and lifting me.

"No!" I screamed and wriggled, curling tighter into a ball. "Let me go!"

"Becca."

I knew that voice, but my brain was beyond comfort. Beyond comprehension. I slapped out. "No!"

"Becca."

My chest heaved with heavy, gut-wrenching sobs as I tried to curl into a ball. "Please, no!"

"Becca!" Strong hands grabbed my shoulders, shaking me into awareness. My eyes snapped open as I gasped.

"Hey, hey," Court whispered, his face inches from mine. He hovered over me, his dark eyes wide with concern. "You were having a nightmare. Wake up, baby."

"I…" I swallowed roughly, sniffling back tears. I blinked a few times, the tears blurring my vision. I managed to focus and saw Rook and Bishop crowded in the open doorway of the bedroom, each holding a gun. Light from behind them spilled into the space, casting shadows that made me anxious.

"I'm sorry," I gasped, humiliation burning through me as I turned back to Court. My chest heaved as I cried. "I'm so sorry. I—" My voice cracked.

Court made a soft, strangled sound and lifted me into his arms. I wrapped my arms around his neck and my legs around his waist like a toddler, burying my face in his neck as I tried to slow my heart rate. He turned us, sitting on the bed and leaning against the headboard with me curled around him like a spider monkey.

"Can we do anything?" Bishop asked, his voice uncharacteristically solemn.

Court's hand calmly rubbed up and down my back in soothing strokes. "No, I've got her, guys. Go back to bed."

"We're here if you need us," Rook murmured, and then the door closed, enveloping us in darkness again.

My breath caught, and Court shifted.

"Don't leave!" The words tumbled out of my trembling lips before I could snatch them back. Panic held my lungs in a vise as I clutched at him, my nails digging into his bare shoulders.

Both his arms wrapped around me, steel bands that would keep out the world. "I'm not going anywhere, baby. I was going to turn a light on for you. Can I do that?"

I nodded against his neck, embarrassment rolling through me as more tears fell from my eyes and landed on him.

"Okay," he murmured, slowly peeling one hand off me. The bedside light flickered on a moment later. His hand came right back to my hip, anchoring me in the present.

The thundering roar of my pulse pounding in my head started to slow. My sobs turned to soft hiccups. Eventually I relaxed the death grip I had on Court, embarrassment surging in like a tidal wave on the heels of my panic. I tried to pull away, but he seemed content to keep me right where I was.

I sank into his hold, once again soaking up his comfort.

A shudder rippled down his massive frame, and this time he pulled back just enough to duck his head and meet my eyes. "Want to tell me about it?"

I dropped my gaze, humiliation burning my cheeks. "Just a nightmare."

But it wasn't *just* a nightmare. It was a recurring night terror I'd had since I was ten. It felt so real that I'd gone to therapy over it. I hadn't had this dream in months.

"Becca, you were screaming like someone was after you," he remarked softly, his thumb brushing the bare skin of my hip where my pajamas had twisted. "Jesus, you scared the shit out of me."

I still couldn't meet his gaze. "Sorry."

His hand lifted, gently pushing my chin up so I had to look at him. "Talk to me, sweetheart."

"You left," I blurted out, my heart aching like a bruise.

He winced and ducked his head. "I know. I just couldn't be here and watch you with my brother. Not when…"

After a heavy silence, I pressed, "Not when what?"

"Does it matter?" His tone was bitter. His gaze collided with mine, and the agony in his eyes was like a thunderclap going off in my head.

"Nothing happened," I finally whispered. "Bishop and I are friends."

His brow furrowed. "Then why—"

"I was trying to piss you off," I muttered.

He let out a humorless chuckle. "Mission accomplished, baby. I can't remember the last time I was that furious."

"Why didn't you come back?" I asked.

"I did, but after you were asleep." He shut his eyes and shook his head. "I had Rook text me when you went to bed. I couldn't stand seeing you. Or *not* seeing you, if you and my brother put that hotel room to use."

I sighed. We really were a fucked-up pair.

"I came in about an hour ago and was lying on the couch when I heard you screaming." His gaze pinned me to the spot. "Wanna tell me what that was about?"

I shrugged, trying to play it off. "It was a nightmare, Court. I had a bad dream. I—"

"Tell me about it," he cut me off, but his tone was so gentle. So kind.

I studied him for a moment. The way his dark hair was mussed like he'd been stabbing his fingers into it over and over. The five o'clock shadow of stubble that made him look older, sexier. His eyes were fathomless, endless pools of darkness, ready to devour me. Those plush lips that I knew for a fact could be soft and teasing or hard and dominating.

Suddenly I was acutely aware of the fact that my core was centimeters from his cock. He was wearing only a tight pair of black boxer briefs, and my yellow ducky jammies consisted of a thin pair of shorts and a camisole. Awareness cracked through me like a lightning bolt, my nipples pebbling.

To his credit, Court didn't say anything. Didn't move—hell, he barely *breathed* as he waited for my reply.

Sighing, I dropped my chin to my chest. "It's always the same. I'm in a tiny little cabin in the middle of a storm. I can hear the wind outside, and it's so loud. Like the freight-train roar they talk about before a tornado. I'm alone and scared. A tree breaks through the window and glass sprays everywhere."

I shivered, the details slamming back into my skull. "I'm cold, and I'm hungry and thirsty and…"

"And?" He prompted when I didn't keep going.

I lifted my gaze. "And I think I'm going to die. But I keep yelling for help, because I know that someone is coming. Someone will save me if they can just hear me. Find me."

He swallowed hard, his Adam's apple bobbing as his hands tightened on my waist. "Becca, you were screaming—"

"I know," I muttered, shaking my head.

"You were screaming my name," he finished. His brows pulled together. He looked conflicted, in pain. Uncertain in a way I'd never seen before. "Becca, fuck. I swear, I got to you as fast as I could."

I wrinkled my nose. "Court, you were asleep in the other room."

"No," he whispered, shaking his head. "I mean when you were a kid, and my dad kidnapped you. When you almost died so he could prove a fucking point."

My muscles locked up and, as if he knew I was getting ready to bolt, Court's arms wrapped around me again. "Don't."

I drew in a shallow breath, feeling like a deer that had been spotted by a hunting party. "Court—"

"Becca," he countered, "please, let me tell you what really happened that night. That week. Hell, what happened to *us*."

I studied him for a long moment, not sure I was ready to hear the whole truth. I knew fragments. But I had been sick back then. Really sick. And I'd nearly died.

Memories were a funny thing. Some were crystal clear, like watching a movie in 4K high definition. And others were like trying to grab sand in a windstorm. No matter how hard I tried, the grains kept slipping through my fingers.

My memories of Court were the clearest, though. Always had been. It was like my brain had decided he was worth the effort of capturing as much detail as possible. Like the way he'd smiled after he'd lost his two front teeth. He must have been seven, which would have made me three. But I remembered the color of his shirt—green-and-white striped with a smear of chocolate from the ice cream cone he was trying to eat before it could melt under the broiling August sun. The dirt caked under his fingernails from a day spent playing in the backyard with me. The fact that his left shoe was untied, like it often was.

And that was just one of a thousand memories of him.

But things got confusing right after my ninth birthday. That was when I was diagnosed with cancer for the second time in my life. More specifically, acute lymphocytic leukemia.

I'd first been diagnosed with non-Hodgkin's lymphoma when I was an infant. I'd been told how I'd easily beaten it after six months of treatment. How my scans for the next five years always came back perfect. Enough so that doctors told my parents I no longer needed them. That if it hadn't come back in five years, then odds were it wouldn't.

Only cancer hadn't been done with me, and this time when it came back, it hit me worse than before and had spread by the time it had been caught. I'd needed a bone marrow or a stem cell transplant, but neither of my parents were a perfect match. Everyone we knew was tested, but I had a weird blood type, which made finding a donor hard.

I went through chemo and miraculously didn't lose my hair. I lost a lot of weight. I couldn't keep anything down. More than once I'd had a feeding tube inserted to get calories into me.

The cancer ate away at my body for months, and I lived in this weird limbo state. My parents started fighting more. My mom cried all the time.

Oddly enough, Court and I got really close. His family still lived next door to mine back then. Our schools were connected under the same prep-academy umbrella, so we even rode to and from school together.

When I passed out on the playground, Court heard and left his history class to come find me just as the ambulance was loading me in. He jumped inside and refused to leave me until we got to the hospital and the doctors told him that he had to stay back so they could run tests on me.

Nights were the hardest, but Court would stay up late texting with me when I couldn't sleep. When I told him I was having bad dreams—a byproduct of chemo and stress—he began sneaking into my room each night. He started out sleeping on the floor, but then moved into my bed when he realized he could sometimes chase away the nightmares just by being close.

One night, when I couldn't sleep, we turned on my favorite movie, *Little Women*. When we got to the scene where Teddy promised to kiss Amy before she died, I sniffled and lamented that I'd probably never get my own first kiss.

That night, I had.

Court's kiss had been gentle and tentative, full of the awkwardness that came from him being just barely thirteen and me being nine. It was innocent and sweet, and that was the moment I knew I loved Court Woods.

Less than a month later, he'd disappeared from my life and broken my heart.

No, not broken my heart. Because what we'd had wasn't just puppy love or a crush. He was the other half of me, and he'd crushed my very soul.

I didn't remember much about the next month. It was a blur of twisted memories that never made sense. Mom had always told me it was because I'd been at my sickest and had nearly died. The doctors had told my parents to brace for the worst when, in the eleventh hour, they found a donor match that saved my life.

But that month had forever changed my life, and I'd never quite known why. I had an idea, thanks to a cryptic message left for me by a dead girl, but Madelaine hadn't had all the answers.

No, if I wanted answers, the only person who could give them to me was the man whose lap I was currently cuddled on.

I'd been too angry, too hurt, to hear him out before. Or maybe too scared. My life had been rocked by a lot of revelations over the past few months, but it was better than the alternative. I was so sick of being protected and lied to.

"I need you to tell me the truth," I told him, barely managing to get the words out around the lump in my throat.

His eyes drifted shut like he was in pain, before he gave a terse nod. "I'll tell you anything. Everything. Whatever you want."

"No more lies?" I whispered, half begging.

His gaze locked on mine. "Never again, Becca."

"Okay. Tell me."

COURT

Eight years earlier

The slam of the front door made the walls of the entire house shake. It was like a gunshot going off, followed by a roar I was all-too-familiar with.

"Court! Get your ass down here!" Dad bellowed. I could picture him standing in the middle of the marble foyer, bracketed on either side by the dual curving staircases as the massive bronze-and-crystal chandelier above him swayed, not immune to his wrath.

I looked up from my science homework and glanced out the bedroom window, wondering if it made more sense to bail and take my chances with the twenty-foot drop. I could probably hide at Becca's. I'd seen her dad's car leave hours ago with her in it, probably on their way to another appointment.

My stomach clenched, remembering how pale she'd been when I'd left her this morning. The bluish bruising under her eyes was getting worse. She'd lost so much weight. Every time I saw her it was like she was shrinking. She was so tiny—*too tiny*—and always looked so down. I hated it. I missed the girl who always made me laugh.

Nine-year-olds shouldn't worry they were going to die. It wasn't fair.

Her bedroom window faced mine, and despite the distance between our large houses, we still talked on the phone at night, sitting in front of our windows so it was like we were together.

Anger built in my chest as I heard Dad yell for me again. I hated him so much. Hated the way he yelled at Mom and me. The fact that he was a giant liar and had a whole other family on the other side of town.

I had five brothers. Five. It had been six, but one of them died a few months ago. Mom and Dad had been fighting about it when I'd come home from soccer practice. They hadn't known I was there, but I'd heard it all. Mom had been screaming, yelling that I wasn't going to end up like King; that Dad couldn't hurt me if he still wanted access to Grandpa and Nana's money.

It had taken a lot of listening to figure out that it meant Dad had been part of something that killed a brother I'd never known existed until after he died. Something he wanted *me* to do, too, but Mom wouldn't let him. Dad had slammed the door so hard the walls shook when he left, and he didn't come back for almost two weeks.

He'd gone and stayed with his other family. I knew because Ash helped me find them, and I'd gone over there. I'd watched Dad leave, kissing a woman who wasn't my mom like he was one of those guys who went to work and was saying goodbye to his family.

I watched from the shade of the bushes across the street as the woman left next, driving away in a shiny red SUV. I waited until the boys—my *brothers*—trickled out into the yard to play football together. I waited until they'd gone back in before I'd finally sucked up the courage to go over and knock on the door.

"Court! Where the fuck are you?"

I pushed back from my desk and took my time crossing my large bedroom and opening the door. I knew he hated it when people didn't jump to obey his every command—a byproduct of being a general in the United States Army for several decades—which made this little rebellion one I particularly enjoyed.

It was a few minutes after he'd shouted that I appeared at the top of the steps, arching an eyebrow. "What?"

Dad—or the general, as my brothers called him—glared up at me, his cheeks mottled red. He was in his early fifties but still in great shape. I knew he hit the gym every day, determined to stay in top physical condition.

"Get down here," he growled, stabbing a finger toward the floor.

I arched my brows. "I'm doing homework."

"I swear to fuck, Court, if you don't get down here—"

"What?" I challenged, squaring my shoulders. I'd hit a growth spurt last year and shot up to eye level with him. I was still mostly arms and legs, but I'd been using our state-of-the-art gym myself. Not that it seemed to do much yet.

Besides, Mom would have his balls in a vise if he laid another hand on me. She'd gone out of town with Mrs. Whittier for a spa weekend yesterday, but we both knew all it would take was a call from me, and she'd be on the phone with a divorce attorney before I could say *parental abuse*.

And dear old Dad would be fucked. Or, rather, his shiny new company would be. The U.S. Army didn't pay much, which was why he needed Mom. He needed her money and the billions her parents had left her when they'd died.

After the argument, Mom sat me down and explained a few things about herself and Dad. The big thing I'd learned was that Mom didn't give a shit that he had six kids with another woman. Their marriage had been arranged between their families when they were in college, or so she'd told me. She didn't love him, and didn't care if he didn't love her, but she did love me, and that was where she drew the line.

She told me how my brother, King, had died because my dad made him do some wilderness survival test in the middle of nowhere. All of my older brothers—Royal, Rook, and Bishop—had done it when they turned thirteen. But earlier this year, King had fallen in a ravine when it was raining and hit his head on a rock. King had only been six months older than me, and Dad planned on me doing the same test they had.

Turned out all those times he took me camping and showed me how to build a fire and track deer weren't just to spend time with me. It was to make me into the man he wanted.

But I hated him. I'd never be that man. I'd *never* be like him.

My parents had a complicated past, but I didn't give a shit. I was counting the days until I was eighteen and could live my own damn life. In the meantime? I decided Mom was right—I didn't care what Dad did as long as he left me alone.

"It's time," the General hissed, breathing hard like a pissed-off dragon.

An icy chill swept across my skin, because I knew what time he meant. I'd turned thirteen last week. Dad had casually mentioned a "camping trip" at dinner last week, and Mom had thrown a glass at his head. She'd said absolutely not, and I'd figured that was the end of it. "No. Mom said I'm not doing it."

He glared at me. "It's time to be a man, Court. There's a car waiting outside."

My hands shook. "No." I lifted my chin, defiance and bravado twisting my guts. "I don't want to."

He sneered up at me. "Of course. Too fucking scared. What a little bitch I managed to sire."

"Well, thank God you have six other sons," I drawled, then snapped my fingers. "Oh, wait. You're down to five now, right?" I shot him an openly mocking look.

He bristled, his chest puffing up. "Your brother was too weak to handle the one test I gave him." The cruel twist of his lips showed just how little he cared that he'd been directly responsible for his own son's death.

I clenched my jaw. "Fuck you. I'm not going."

"Yes, you are," he gritted out, his steely blue eyes flashing.

"No, I'm not," I retorted, shoving my hands into the pockets of my jeans. "I can always call Mom."

Threatening to call my mom was pretty pathetic, but I knew it would work. I'd heard them arguing about the test for the majority of the week. Mom had put her foot down and said absolutely not. My father might've commanded thousands of men in his decorated career, but he didn't control my mother. Not even a little bit, and especially not after King had died last year.

Dad had grown up in a military family that was obsessed with strength. Apparently *the test* had started with my grandfather. Some fucked up survivalist trial to make sure his sons were man enough to be worthy of the Woods name.

My dad carried out the same fucked-up tradition.

Until my mom stepped in after King's death. Her father had been an attorney, like her, and had crafted an iron-clad prenup for my parents. Mom threatened to expose Dad's cheating and enact the prenup, which would've left him with absolutely nothing.

He countered that she'd been just as unfaithful, to which Mom reminded him she had plenty of money, for her and I to live on, in accounts in the Caymans, plus I would come into parts of my massive trust fund when I hit certain age milestones—sixteen, eighteen, and twenty-one. It was enough money that my great-grandkids were set for life.

But of course Dad would wait for Mom to be gone to make me go. I should've known something was up when Dad suggested Mom and Mrs. Whittier should go on a weekend trip because Mrs. Whittier needed a break. I'd even told her that I'd make sure to check on Becca while she was gone.

"I can't," I told him, my stubbornness and fear mixing together into something that felt a lot like denial. This wasn't happening, and maybe if I ignored him, he would forget.

"Court."

Something in his tone made me stop. It was almost like he was… happy?

Frowning, I looked back and, yeah, he was fucking smiling.

An uneasy feeling twisted in my gut. It was the smile he wore when he was about to beat me at chess. The smile he wore when he had someone backed into a corner and knew he was about to win.

"Come down here, son," he beckoned, waving a hand.

"Dad—"

"I promise you'll want to see this," he vowed, still grinning. He reached into his pocket and pulled out his phone.

I took a step forward and stopped, narrowing my eyes. "I'm not playing your games."

"Aren't you?" He lifted a quizzical brow. "I tell you what—I bet that you'll be on your way to the airstrip in the next ten minutes."

I frowned. "I'm not going, Dad. Mom said, remember? You can't make me."

"And you, son, are entirely too predictable," he mused, rubbing his jaw thoughtfully. His eyes glittered as they looked up at me. "What's rule number one, Court?"

My dad had a lot of rules that he'd drilled into my head, but I knew instantly which one he was talking about.

The more you have to love, the more you have to lose.

His smile widened. "Nine minutes."

"Who?" I breathed the question, fear spiking in me. Was it one of my brothers? Mom? Linc, Ryan or Ash?

"Come and see," he entreated, holding the phone out to me.

I wanted to be strong, to tell him to fuck off, but I wasn't the monster he was. I cared about people. Loved people. And if he hurt one of them because of me?

I thundered down the steps and swiped the phone, expecting to see my mom or one of my best friends tied up.

My heart stopped beating at the tiny form in the middle of a cabin. Tears streaked her cheeks, her big hazel eyes wide as they looked around the small room in desperation and terror.

"Becca?" I croaked.

"Well, since your mother and Mrs. Whittier decided to take a break, I told Mr. Whittier that you and I would take Becca camping to our cabin this weekend so she can have a little vacation, too."

All I could do was gape at him and then stare back at Becca. *My* Becca. She was so scared and all alone.

Dad's hand came down heavy on my shoulder, drawing me closer. "There's one small complication," he said, almost sadly.

I looked up at him, my vision blurring from rage. I'd never hated him more than I did in this moment.

Dad reached into his pocket and pulled out an orange bottle of pills. He gave a soft sigh. "It seems we forgot her meds."

Horror curdled in my stomach as my vision tunneled. *No, no.* Becca *needed* those meds. It was the only thing giving her a fighting shot against the cancer that was ravaging her tiny body.

Dad handed me the pills. "Be a good boy and get these to her, would you?" When I didn't move, he took my hands and wrapped my fingers around the bottle. He turned to walk away.

I lurched forward a step. "Dad." My voice cracked.

"It'll take you thirty minutes to get to the airstrip." He checked his watch. "Flight's two hours. Another hour to be dropped off at the starting line. Then you just have to get to the cabin where she's waiting for you. And her medicine."

I had no words. I knew the exact cabin he was talking about. It was a ninety-minute flight to a private airfield, but the cabin hadn't been used in recent years except when my brothers had gone through their trials. That was the point: they were left at the base of the mountain with nothing and had a week to make it to the cabin, where they'd find food and water and a satellite phone to call for an airlift out.

There were no trails. No roads. Just dense forest, a few mountain stream runoffs, and some sheer cliffs. If you made a wrong turn, you had to backtrack and find the right way. The fastest anyone had found the cabin was Royal; it had taken him three days and two hours. That beat our father's previous record of four days and eight hours.

"Oh, wait. You said you had homework, didn't you? Too bad. I actually just found a bone marrow match for Rebecca. I'm having them flown in from Guatemala in five days. They can do the procedure next week… if she's back by then." Dad winked at me.

I wanted to scream. To punch the shit out of him. But none of that would help Becca. I was frozen in place, my mind whirling as I gaped at him.

"Since you're my son," he went on, "I arranged for the driver to come back and give you a ride to the airport. If you want to go." He looked at the Rolex on his wrist. "But I also told him to give you until five to get in the car."

My gaze swung to the grandfather clock in the entryway. It read 4:58.

I watched as the long hand slid over the 59 notch. I glanced desperately up the stairs, wondering if I had time to pack. To grab my phone and send a text to Mom or—

"Don't even think about it," Dad snapped. "One phone call to your mother or anyone else, and Becca will never make it back. And it will be all *your* fault."

Shoving the pills in my pocket, I bolted for the door. It took me less than ten seconds to get in the car.

The motherfucker had been right. I'd been heading to the airstrip in less than ten minutes.

CHAPTER 24

BEX

Present Day

I thought I'd seen Court Woods experience every possible emotion —happiness, sadness, fury, playfulness—but I'd never seen him look so ashamed. It made me ache to hug him, to make it all better.

He cleared his throat. "It took me a little over four hours to get to the drop-off spot. And then another four days, twelve hours, and sixteen minutes to find the cabin. The storm that hit came out of nowhere, and I kept getting turned around. I thought I'd never find you… then I heard you screaming."

A shudder rolled down his frame, his dark eyes full of anguish. "At first I thought it was the wind. When I realized it was you… Becca, I'll never forget that sound. You aren't the only one who has nightmares— I have them, too. And in them, I hear that scream. Then it goes quiet, and when I find you, you're…" He shook his head with a sniff.

"I'm right here," I reminded him, my voice soft.

"Yeah, but I still close my eyes and see the girl I found. Becca, you were so sick. It took them almost another six hours to get to us because of the storm, and the whole time, all I could do was beg you not to die.”

My eyes widened.

Court’s jaw was tight. “Baby, you were burning up. Then you had a seizure. They didn’t know if you’d survive the medevac flight back to Los Angeles. It took them almost a week to get you stable enough for the transplant.” His eyes drifted shut. “And it was all my fault.”

“What? No, it wasn’t. Court, that was your dad, not you.” I frowned at him, but he wouldn’t meet my gaze, so I tugged on his hair until he looked up.

He shook his head. “He told me that caring about people left you vulnerable, but I never believed it. I mean… Fuck, we were kids.”

“Exactly,” I agreed. “We were *kids*. I can’t believe my dad was part of this.”

He grimaced. “I didn’t know about that until later when I heard our moms fighting. Well, it was more like your mom laying into my mom and threatening to go to the cops.”

“Why didn’t she?” I wondered.

Court looked like he wanted to sidestep the question, but then he sucked in a deep breath. “Fear. My dad threatened your parents. Plus he had the donor lined up for you when you were strong enough… They did what they had to do.”

“It broke their marriage,” I whispered. “And when I came home from the hospital, we moved. I missed being the girl next door.”

His eyes shut, as if pained by my confession. “Every time I looked out my window and saw your house, it made me sick. Sick and angry. I was so furious for so long.”

“Bishop mentioned military school?”

His lips twisted into a sardonic smirk. “Yeah. That was a fun few months. Hell, I was so twisted up, even Mom agreed to send me away.”

“What changed?”

“Royal,” he admitted. “He came to talk to me. Told me I could keep acting like a punk, or I could put in the work and do better. *Be* better. So, that's what I did. I focused on being better, bigger, stronger. Making sure my dad couldn't ever hurt me or anyone I loved ever again."

"Court," I murmured, my heart aching for him. For *us*. For what we could've had.

"Becca…" He sighed, his hands tightening on my hips like he was ready to push me away.

Not happening.

Not tonight.

Not ever again.

I looped my arms around his neck, linking my fingers behind his head. "I don't blame you for what your father did, Court."

"Don't you get it? As long as I care about you, you'll always be a target," he insisted. "Pretending not to care was the only way to keep you safe."

"You realize we haven't been friends, or whatever you want to call it, in a long time, and that didn't stop bad shit from happening to me," I pointed out. "Madelaine made my life hell for *years*. I was bullied, treated like crap, and pushed around for pretty much my entire teenage life."

His eyes flashed.

"I was drugged and almost raped. I was freaking kidnapped by Maddie's dad." I let out a sharp laugh. "And let's not forget that I decided to date a guy who thinks it's normal to buy and sell human beings like dolls. You didn't play a part in *any* of that."

"I should have," he hissed, his fingers digging into my hips. "I should've protected you—"

"So, which is it?" I demanded. "You're never supposed to let me out of your sight? Or you're supposed to stay as far away from me as possible?"

He opened his mouth to answer, but then snapped it shut. A frown creased his brow.

"Exactly," I murmured, loosening my fingers to delve them into his thick hair. The strands were shorter at the nape of his neck, and I pressed the pads of my fingers against his skin to massage away the tension.

He let out a shuddering breath before leaning forward to rest his forehead against mine. "I'm sorry."

"For what this time?" A soft smile pulled at my lips.

"For not being honest with you years ago," he admitted. "Pushing you away was a mistake. I thought it was for the best, and maybe in some ways, it still is."

I tensed, bracing for another round of being pushed away. "No," I told him. "Stop trying to do what's best for me and just give me a chance. Court, I don't blame you for what happened to me back then. I never did, and I never will."

He watched me, his expression wary.

"But I *do* blame you for how you've handled things lately," I admitted. "For the way you just act like I'm a doll you can put on a shelf and expect to stay still. I'm not a little girl anymore. I haven't been for a long time. I'm stronger, and I know what I want. It's what I've always wanted."

His gaze held mine, the fire in them catching me off guard. "Don't say it if you don't mean it, Becca."

I blinked, my breath catching at the intensity pouring off him. "I don't understand."

One hand left my hip and wrapped around my chin, his long fingers easily holding my jaw in place. "I'm not a kid anymore, sweetheart. The things I want, the things I *need*, might be more than you can give."

My heart slammed against my ribs, my body prickling with awareness. "I'm not a little girl anymore either. I can handle it."

A pale version of a smile ghosted across his full lips. "Think you can handle me?"

I straightened my spine. "You're still expecting me to be the sick, broken girl from when we were little, but I'm all grown up now. And I'm *not* afraid of you."

He smirked, his hand sliding down my neck to wrap around my throat. He applied the lightest pressure to my pulse point, letting me feel the power of his hold. Making me aware of the fact that he could cut off my air with a flex of his fingers.

A dark thrill shot through my blood like lightning. I stayed impossibly still even as my pulse pounded in my chest, throbbing all the way down to my core. I had the urge to rock against him, knowing he was hard beneath me.

"Do you know the real reason I wanted to get you away from Eric?" His voice was soft, almost teasing. But the edge to it had my breath catching.

"Because he's the bad guy?" I guessed.

"Because I saw the way he looked at you," he corrected. "Like he owned you. Like you were *his*."

I licked my lips, my throat suddenly bone-dry.

"See, baby, I know the look of a man who wants to see you naked, spread out under him as you shatter." His thumb pushed down a little harder on my windpipe.

I swallowed, the sound audible. "Oh, really?" It was all I could think to say; my brain was being short-circuited by his touch.

One corner of his mouth hooked up in a feral, wolfish smirk. "Fuck yeah, Becca." He leaned in, his lips brushing my ear as he added, "I look at that man in the mirror every goddamn day."

I gasped, the sound sharp and desperate as he thrust his hips up, grinding his hard length against my core.

"Court." His name left me as a needy whimper. My fingers curled into his hair and pulled hard. I tried to roll my hips against him, aching and pulsing with a kind of need I'd felt only in my dreams.

The hand on my waist stopped me from moving. From rubbing myself against his erection like a cat in heat.

"You need to be sure this is what you want. That *I* am what you really want," he said, his teeth catching my ear lobe and biting it. A streak of pain melted into warm pleasure as the nip turned into a soft suck.

Who the hell knew earlobes were a freaking turn-on?

He pulled back, meeting my gaze. "See, I'm not sure you *can* handle me, princess," he murmured, his voice a guttural rasp that I felt between my legs. His dark gaze flicked over my body, his tongue darting out to lick his bottom lip. "You talk a big game, but if you think I'm anything like the two-pump chumps you've let between your legs, then you're out of your beautiful fucking mind." His lips brushed my ear once more. "I'll fucking wreck you, Becca. I'll ruin you for any other man, and I'll never let you go."

Oh, God. My blood heated, simmering in my veins as my head spun. He straightened, still keeping a possessive hand around my neck as he stared down at me, his expression full of fury and fire.

I sucked in a deep breath, squaring my shoulders. "I've *always* been able to handle you, Court Woods."

His hand reached for me again, tracing my jaw. "Think so? Care to prove that point, princess?"

I lifted my chin, wordlessly accepting the challenge. Daring him to do his worst.

He smiled, the look almost feral. He gave a low chuckle. "Be sure, baby girl, because if you're mine, every motherfucking inch of you belongs to *me*. That tight ass, these perfect tits, and that sweet cunt will be *mine*. Hell, your fucking period is gonna need permission to come if it wants to touch *my* pussy."

My insides clenched with need, wanting what he was describing.

Was his speech supposed to send me running? Because all I wanted to do was make him prove it.

He cocked a brow. "So before you go thinking you can handle me and saying shit you're clueless about, keep those pretty lips shut unless you're ready to wrap them around my cock."

My eyes went wide as I stared up at him, barely breathing.

His expression was knowing, but there was a look of uncertainty in his gaze. Like he was waiting for me to realize this was too much and go running. To let him off the hook from exploring this chemistry between us.

Heat unfurled low in my belly.

Game. Fucking. On.

I stared him dead in the eye and blinked once.

Twice.

My past, present, and future teetered on the edge of a knife.

It had always been this way for us.

All or nothing.

My gaze jerked to where his cock was threatening to punch through his boxer-briefs before flicking back up to him. I slowly lifted a single brow.

And opened my mouth wide.

CHAPTER 25

BEX

Court studied me, his dark eyes alight with an intense lust that I felt like a caress. The hand wrapped around my throat slid up my neck, his thumb pushing into my open mouth. "Suck," he ordered. "Show me what this mouth would do to my cock."

My lips automatically sealed around the digit, my cheeks hollowing as I sucked his thumb deep, imagining it was something a lot bigger. I squirmed a little as arousal flooded my pussy. Under me, his cock was long and thick, hard and ready.

He made a soft, humming sound before pulling his thumb out partially and then thrusting it back inside the wet heat of my mouth.

My tongue curled around his skin, my lashes fluttering shut as I put all those years of reading romance novels to use, calling upon all the erotic imagery that the authors made seem so natural.

Romance authors deserved way more credit than they got.

I gently scraped my teeth against the pad of his thumb, smiling around him when a judder rippled through his frame.

"Fuck, Becca," he rasped, pulling his thumb out. His dark brown eyes blazed. "Say it. I need to hear you say it."

It was like standing on the edge of a cliff, staring out into the void.

I had no idea what lay beyond, but I had to trust something would be there to catch me when I fell.

That Court would catch me.

"I'm yours, Court," I told him. "I've always been yours."

He surged forward, his lips claiming mine in a bruising kiss that felt like a dam finally breaking free. The resulting torrent swept me away, and all I could do was cling to him as he kissed me.

I parted my lips with a gasp, and he took full advantage. His tongue tangled with mine, stroking it into submission, and I let him take control. A low groan vibrated from his chest as he pulled me closer, angling my head exactly where he wanted me.

Needing more, I tried to grind myself against his lap, but he let go of my face to clamp his hands down on my hips, halting my movements. His kiss slowed from the initial frenzy, turning lazy and gentle.

With a frustrated whimper, I pulled away. "Court. Please."

His eyes snapped open. "You'll get what I give you, baby. Unless you've changed your mind and can't handle it?"

I gave an annoyed huff and shook my head.

His lips curved into a grin. "Do you have any idea how adorable you are when you're pouting?"

"Do you have any idea how much I really need you to—" I started to blurt out, but cut myself off.

His eyes lit up. "Oh, no. Finish that thought, Becca."

Heat crept across my cheeks. "I just need *you*."

His brow lifted. "I'm right here."

If I'd have been standing, I would've stomped my foot. "I need you to touch me."

"I *am* touching you," he pointed out. But then, just because he could, he leaned in and kissed the tip of my nose. "You mean like that?"

"Court," I whined, my skin feeling pulled too taut.

Still grinning, he lowered his lips to my shoulder. "Like this?"

I let out another aggrieved sigh, wondering if it was possible to combust from embarrassment or need.

A hand glided up my ribcage before his fingers lightly pinched one of my nipples. "That?"

I sucked in a sharp breath, feeling the echoes of his touch like there was a direct line between my nipple and my clit. "More." His hand squeezed around my breast, holding it through the fabric of my cami. He kneaded the sensitive flesh in his palm, but it wasn't enough. "*Please.*"

"Since you begged so nicely," he murmured, his fingers tugging the neckline of my top beneath my breasts, baring them to his view. "God, I can't wait to fuck these tits."

I'd barely had time to let *that* visual settle in when his head lowered and he caught one tight bud into his mouth, sucking hard. I arched into him, letting out a strained cry as his teeth nipped at the aching tip of my breast.

"Oh, fuck, yes," I managed to get out, my head spinning as he turned his attention to the other nipple. I clutched his head to my chest, wondering if my nipples would bruise from the sucking and the biting.

Some baser instinct hoped he would leave marks. I wanted to see them in the mirror tomorrow for proof this wasn't another dream my brain was tricking me with.

Court picked me up and flipped me onto my back, his hips pressing my thighs open so he could settle between them. I wrapped my legs around him, trying to tug him down.

His teeth bit a little too hard into my nipple, and I yelped.

He glared down at me, reproach in his eyes. "Unless you're saying 'stop,' I'm in control, sweetheart. Got it?"

I nodded and willed my body to relax, even though it felt like I was being decimated by an inferno that made my blood boil. My insides felt raw and scorched, aching for more.

His lips curved into a smile, and he lifted up, planting his hands on either side of my head to brace his weight. "That's my girl. Let me take care of you the way I always wanted to." He lowered his head, kissing me again as the hand that was on my hip slipped around to splay across my belly. A finger teased the elastic waistband of my shorts, the smooth glide making my tummy flutter.

"So soft," he murmured, his tone reverent as he looked down at where he was touching me.

I followed his gaze, not surprised to see fading teeth imprints on my pale chest. My nipples were an angry shade of red, the color of raspberries in the snow. I watched his index finger lift the band of my shorts, and then his hand dipped inside the fabric and into the lace of my panties.

The first brush of his fingers against my slit had me trembling.

"Fuck," he groaned, sounding pained. "So fucking wet for me." He cupped my pussy, grinding the heel of his hand against me as he gave me another deep kiss.

He licked into my mouth, tasting me again with a throaty moan. Just when I was positive I was going to scream, he slid a thick finger inside me. He broke our kiss with a pant. "Jesus, you're tight."

I let out a strangled cry as he worked his finger in and out of my body with shallow thrusts. My heart slammed against my ribcage at the foreign sensation. I was suddenly, glaringly aware of how tiny my own fingers were in comparison to his.

And this was just a *finger*.

I'd felt the size and length of his cock when I'd been on his lap. I knew that biology said it would work, but my brain was having serious doubts.

His thumb slipped in lazy circles around my clit, making my hips buck up. His finger sank even deeper, and when he curled it inside of me, my eyes fluttered shut.

"Mmm," he hummed in approval and added another finger, stretching me wider.

With a groan, I embraced the unfamiliar burn, rolling my hips to match the slow, steady rhythm he'd started. My toes curled as he pressed harder against my clit, stroking the nub firmly.

"Oh, God," I managed to gasp out, feeling like my lungs were going to shatter. Or collapse. My release spiraled higher and faster than it ever had. My thighs started to shake as everything south of my belly button coiled.

And then it stopped so abruptly that the world tilted around me.

I let out a plaintive, "No." The desperate whine in my tone shocked me, but Court just chuckled. The warm sound vibrated between us. His mocha-colored eyes were alight with amusement.

My eyes went wide as he lifted two glistening fingers to his mouth and sucked them in deep. His eyes flared. "Sweet as a peach," he rasped, coming down to kiss me again.

Tasting myself in Court's kiss was strange and kinda hot. I wrapped my arms around him, greedily clinging to his touch however he offered it.

"I want to hear you scream," he whispered against my lips.

My body flushed as I remembered we weren't exactly alone. "Your brothers—"

"Will leave us the fuck alone if they know what's good for them," he replied. "But if you're still thinking about my *brothers*, I'm doing something wrong here."

Before I could figure out how to answer that, he lifted himself away from me and got off the bed.

Pushing myself up to my elbows, I missed his weight pressing me into the mattress. "Court—"

With a smirk, he grabbed my ankles and yanked me to the end of the bed. I let out a wholly undignified squeak as my ass stopped halfway off the edge. His hands were immediately at my waist, stripping off my shorts and underwear.

His gaze darkened as he drank in the sight of me. My top was still pushed down under my boobs, and my lower half was completely naked. Feeling exposed and vulnerable, I tried to close my legs.

With a growl, Court wedged his body between them, keeping them splayed. "No," he snapped.

"But…" I started.

He arched a brow and slapped a hand over my pussy. My entire frame jolted at the contact, my core clenching at the sharp sensation.

I gaped at him. "Did you just spank my lady bits?"

His eyes narrowed. "No. I just spanked *my* pussy. I warned you, Becca—now you're mine. Every single delicious inch of you."

Oh, hell. It was like he'd dumped a package of pop rocks into my veins. A full-body shiver swept through me, and I took a big breath before releasing it and sinking onto my back.

The curl of his lips made my heart feel too big for my chest.

"Now, where were we?" he mused softly, thumbing his bottom lip as he eyed me.

When he dropped to his knees, my breath caught. His massive shoulders pushed my thighs wider, spreading me open. He leaned in, licking up my slit with the flat of his tongue in one long swipe.

"Fuck, yes," he muttered, his hands wrapping around my thighs and pulling my pussy onto his mouth. He sucked my clit into his mouth, repositioning his hands so one was splayed flat across my belly, pinning me down. When he pushed two fingers back into me, the pressure of his hand pushing my pelvis down as his fingers pumped into me was almost my undoing.

Electricity shot through my limbs, making my toes curl and my hands clench. His teeth gently nipped at my clit before he sucked it into his mouth once more, flicking his tongue over it.

I exploded with a sharp cry, my back arching off the bed. My hands fisted around the covers as I convulsed, the walls of my pussy spasming around his fingers so hard that I worried they'd break.

Court's pace never slowed, and I somehow tumbled headfirst into a second orgasm. I forgot how to breathe as he kept sucking and licking my clit, curling his fingers to hit that mythical spot I thought only actually existed in romance novels.

I was still twitching, my brain shooting off pathetic attempts to get my muscles back online, when he stood up. I didn't even bother attempting to push myself up. My head lolled to the side as I panted, watching him shove his sweats down.

"You're so perfect when you come for me," he praised, his eyes glowing with pleasure and hunger as he reached inside his boxer briefs and wrapped a fist around his length. The corded muscles of his forearm flexed as he squeezed his cock, and all I could do was lick my lips.

"Ready for more, baby girl?" He pushed his boxer briefs down, his cock jutting out toward me like an arrow aimed right for my pussy.

A tendril of panic wrapped around my heart as I watched his fist close over his cock again, giving it several rough strokes that left him groaning.

Could I do this? Was I actually going to have sex with Court Woods right now?

Hell, yes, my hindbrain answered for me. He touched me with his free hand, his fingers slipping through my folds as he collected my arousal and spread it all over his cock with a grunt.

"Shit." He froze over me, grimacing. "I need to grab a condom."

"Uh… I'm on the pill," I confessed. Not that I'd started it because I needed it; I'd just always had irregular periods.

His dark eyes studied me. "Have you ever had sex without a condom?"

I shook my head. Not technically a lie, because I hadn't had sex at all, so the condom was kinda irrelevant. Unease trickled in as I remembered all of his previous conquests. "Have… you?" I cringed inwardly as I waited for his response.

His mouth tightened, and I got the feeling that he was embarrassed about the other women. "I've always used protection," he admitted. "And I was tested before I came to Paris–we all get full workups before we go into the field."

I exhaled hard in relief. "Do you… I mean, we don't *have* to use a condom?" Why was I posing it like a question? Ugh, talk about unsexy.

An animalistic glint entered his eyes. "So, in a way, I'd be your first and you'd be mine," he murmured, moving closer and dragging his cock through the wetness between my legs. "I'll definitely be your last."

The feel of his bare shaft rubbing against my core was perfection. This was everything I'd always wanted. This wasn't just something physical—though the physical was pretty freaking great—but it was knowing Court and I were on the same page. That this insane attraction I'd battled wasn't just one sided. That we could finally be together.

"Yes," I breathed, accepting his declaration as truth.

I pushed back a tiny spark of alarm as he stood between my legs, his cock poised at my entrance. The soft, blunt head of him pressed into me and my breath caught.

I could do this. I *wanted* to do this.

Court leaned down, one hand holding my hip as the other cradled my face like I was the most precious thing in the world. "This is how it always should've been, Becca," he whispered, pressing a soft kiss to my lips. "You always should've been mine." His hips flexed and he surged inside of me, burying himself balls deep in one thrust.

The scream that tore from my lips wasn't sexy. It wasn't erotic. It was pure pain, because holy forking shitballs, I was pretty sure his cock had just split me in half.

Of all the ways I'd ever imagined dying, death by cock strangely hadn't made the list.

Court froze above me, his body coiled tight with tension. He slowly dipped his head, eyes wide as he stared at me. "Becca?"

A tear tumbled down my cheek, the agony between my legs pulsing in waves. "Okay, I might've lied about how many guys I've been with." My frame trembled, and it was all I could do not to shove him away.

"Fucking hell," he swore, looking horrified. "How many guys have you been with?"

"Counting you?" My eyes slid shut, mortification heating my face. "One."

CHAPTER 26

COURT

Holy *shit*. What had I done?

My cock gave a jerk, reminding me that I was still balls deep in the tightest pussy I'd ever had.

Because she was a fucking *virgin*. And I'd just rutted into her body like a goddamn psychopath.

"Becca," I rasped, shaking my head like that could somehow make what she'd said less true. But I could see the pain making her jaw tight, the tears shimmering in her eyes. Her nails were gouging into my shoulders enough that I'd be shocked if I wasn't bleeding.

Oh, fuck me.

Was *she* bleeding?

I started to pull out, only to stop when she winced. "Ouch—please don't move. That makes it worse."

I dropped my forehead to her chest for a beat, taking a breath and trying not to move a muscle. "Baby girl, why the hell didn't you *say* something?"

"I—"

She was cut off by a frantic pounding at the door.

"What the fuck? We heard a scream," Rook called.

"Bex, are you okay?" Bishop demanded.

"Oh, God," she whispered, more tears falling as she twisted her neck to look upside down at the door across the room. Panic filled her eyes. "We're fine!"

"We heard you scream," Bishop pointed out again. "Bex, if you're hurt—"

"Jesus Christ," I muttered, wondering if this could get much worse.

The doorknob twisted then, and I realized that, yeah. It could get worse.

"Don't fucking come in here!" I roared, making Becca jump under me. Her pussy rippled around my dick, and I ground my teeth together to keep still as she whimpered in pain.

There was a beat of silence, and I could picture my brothers on the other side of the door, debating whether or not to come in.

Becca shot me a scared look, but I had a feeling it was less about me defiling her perfect body and more the idea that my brothers might come spilling through the damn door any second like a pair of amateur detectives.

She opened her mouth and stunned the shit outta me when a throaty moan left her lips. "Oh, fuck, Court. Yeah. Right *there*."

My eyes went wider—if that was even freaking possible—as I stared down at her. Was she…

"Uh… shit," Bishop said quickly.

"Sorry," Rook added. "We'll just… yeah."

I listened to the sound of them retreating and their bedroom door slamming shut. I had no doubt they were each reaching for a pair of noise-canceling earbuds.

Letting out a long breath, I glanced down at the woman in my arms. My fucking dream girl.

That I'd treated like a blowup doll.

"I'm so sorry," I whispered, unable to stop myself from kissing her cheek. I tasted the salt of her tears and felt like an even bigger asshole. "Why didn't you say something?"

"To be fair, I thought it would be okay," she offered lamely.

I gave a frustrated huff. I wanted to kiss and strangle her at the same time. "Sweetheart."

"Fine," she huffed. "I was afraid you'd stop, and I didn't want you to. I wanted this."

I arched a brow. "You wanted your first time to hurt as much as humanly possible?"

"Okay, maybe not *that*," she amended, "but I wanted to be with you, and for the first time in over a decade, it felt like we were *us* again."

Sighing, I gave a slight shake of my head. "But you said you were…" I couldn't finish the sentence without snarling. The idea of her with the three guys she'd claimed had been enough to send me into a dimension of pissed off that seemed solely reserved for anything Becca-related.

Her lashes dropped. "I lied."

"Why the hell—"

"Because I didn't want to seem like some little kid," she snapped. "I mean, you're *you*… Freaking sex god of Pacific Cross."

I shot her a disbelieving look. "Seriously?"

"Do you know how many times I heard about the girls you'd slept with around school? Almost every girl on campus worships at the altar of your dick. Well, yours and Linc's. There were even bets to see who could sleep with you two together."

"I really don't want to talk about my best friend while I'm in the middle of fucking you. In fact, new rule—we don't talk about anyone else when my cock is inside you." Grimacing, I looked down between our bodies to where my cock was still inside her. When she clenched around me, I let out an inhuman sound. "Don't do that."

"I don't even know what I did," she protested.

I closed my eyes, counting to five. "Okay, let me get off you and—"

"What? Hell, no!" Her eyes went wide.

My heart gave a painful squeeze. "I promise I'll be as gentle as possible. I won't hurt you anymore."

"I don't give a crap about that," she replied. "I want this. I want *you*, Court. I've always wanted you. I can handle this."

"Sex isn't something you should have to *handle*," I told her. "It should be something you want."

"Something I've dreamed of? Imagined in detail?" She licked her lips, her eyes going slightly hooded. "Something I've gotten off to from just the thought of it?"

I swallowed hard. "Yes."

Her eyes met mine, fierce and confident. "I've dreamed of you being inside me since I was old enough to know what sex was, Court Woods."

My hips gave a small, involuntary thrust that made her gasp. "Fuck. Becca, I'm sorry—"

"No," she cut me off, her fingers digging into my shoulders again. "Can you… can you do that again?"

Watching her carefully for any signs of discomfort, I gently withdrew an inch or so and then rocked back into her. The resulting moan she gave was throaty and made my dick even harder.

"We can stop," I reminded her, even as my instincts were screaming at me to pound her into the mattress. There was some deep, primal part of me that was fucking thrilled I was her first. That I'd claimed what no one else could. No one else ever would.

Becca was finally mine. It was the way it was always supposed to be.

"Please don't stop," she murmured, lifting her hips. Her eyes went a little unfocused. "Oh, wow. That felt… nice."

My lips curved. "I think we can do better than *nice*."

She blinked, her gaze locking on mine. The amount of trust shining in her eyes was staggering. It made me feel invincible and unworthy all at once.

I leaned into her, capturing her lips with mine once again. They were soft and supple, this kiss dizzying in its power as she opened for me. Whether she realized it or not, her thighs parted more, allowing me more space to move. I pushed into her, bottoming out and swearing I saw stars.

She was perfect. *This* was perfect.

I reached between us, my fingers finding her sweet little clit, swollen and begging for my attention. I gently rubbed the side of it, and she tore her lips from mine with a ragged cry.

"Oh, God," she whispered, her eyes screwing tight as her face contorted in pleasure.

But I wanted more. Needed to see the look in her eyes as I made her come again. Watching her shatter was my newest addiction. One I would feed as many times a day as she'd let me.

Going slow was a whole new form of torture. Every time I dragged my cock out of her cunt, her walls clamped down on me, tightening enough to make the edges of my vision blur. All I could do was grit my teeth and roll my hips into her, keeping my pace as gentle as possible.

"Court," she finally whispered, her delicate hand coming up to touch my jaw.

I managed to grunt a response.

"I'm not going to break." Her hazel eyes were glazed, her plump lips open as she sucked in a deep breath that made her perfect tits brush my chest. "I've waited eighteen years to be yours."

"I don't want to hurt you," I murmured.

Her lips curled into a smile that made my pulse pound. "And I want you to fuck me like I'm yours." She paused, eyeing me. "I am yours, right?" She wrapped her legs around my waist, arching into my touch.

My control snapped like a dry rubber band. I pulled out of her before thrusting back in, my fingers pinching her hot little clit. She jerked in my arms, writhing with the moan of a woman loving being fucked.

I lifted up a little, changing the angle, hitting her deeper. I smirked as her lashes fluttered, her throat exposed as she tossed her head back. The strands of dark brown and teal blue fanned out across the white sheets made her look angelic.

"You're mine," I reminded her with a growl, picking up my pace and setting a relentless rhythm as I let my inner caveman take over. "You've always been mine, sweetheart, and you always will be. Yesterday, today, and every single goddamn tomorrow for the rest of your life."

She bobbed her head. "I'm yours. Harder, Court. *Please*." She gave a pathetic little whimper that sent a shot of adrenaline down my spine and into my cock.

"Whatever you want, baby," I vowed, pistoning my hips in and out of her. Changing my balance, I grabbed her leg and pulled it up, then sank in deeper yet. Her wet heat gripped me like a vise, fighting to keep me locked inside her.

She swore under her breath in frantic little pants, the wild look in her eyes letting me know she was close.

"Come on, baby. Come for me," I demanded before kissing her again. I rubbed firm, tight circles over the swollen nub of her clit and felt the moment she exploded around me. I swallowed her cries in my kiss, pumping into her until I felt my own orgasm gather at the base of my spine and spurt out of my cock, painting her inner walls with my release.

When the last of my cum dripped from my cock, I dropped onto her, letting part of my weight hold her down as we both gasped for air. I nuzzled the side of her face and kissed the fluttering pulse point of her throat.

Her hands stroked down my back to my ass and squeezed. My hips gave a half-hearted jerk, and I felt a shudder ripple through her pussy. I kissed her shoulder next, then trailed kisses up the column of her neck until I found her mouth again.

"I'm never letting you go," I whispered against her lips, hoping she knew how dead-ass serious I was.

She gave me a soft look. "Good. That's all I ever wanted."

In a minute I'd need to get up. Clean up the mess we'd made and tuck her into bed. But right now, I wasn't moving. Even as my cock started to soften in her, I refused to pull out. Refused to move an inch.

In this moment, I had everything I wanted. Everything I *needed*.

I'd finally tasted the girl next door. The girl I'd been obsessed with for as long as I could remember. Now she was mine.

And I didn't fucking share.

CHAPTER 27

BEX

Shafts of light streaming around the edges of the drawn curtains woke me. I opened my eyes slowly, blinking the room into focus as my brain came back online.

I was surrounded by hard, hot muscles.

I remembered Court grabbing a washcloth from the bathroom and gently, almost reverently, cleaning between my legs before tossing it aside and climbing back into bed with me. But what had happened next had shocked the hell out of me.

Court Woods was a cuddler.

He'd tugged me into his arms, my head winding up pillowed against the divot between his chest and shoulder. After he'd stroked my hair for less than a minute, I'd been out like a light.

And waking up now? I'd turned onto my side while I was sleeping, and he was spooning me from behind. He'd managed to stretch one arm under my pillow while the other arm was wrapped around me, his hand cupping my breast like he was protecting it from the world. He'd wedged a leg between mine, the heavy press of his morning erection nudging my ass.

I wondered if I could angle my hips a little so he'd slide back into me. My thighs and everything between them ached like I'd run a marathon, but I wanted more. I loved the feel of him inside me, owning my body.

The hand around my breast flexed, his fingers lazily rolling my pebbled nipple. "Morning." His voice was rough and sleepy.

The sense of rightness was like an anchor for my soul. I snuggled my back against his chest, a smile already tugging at my mouth. "Morning."

He let out a gruff sort of sigh and pressed an absentminded kiss to my shoulder. "How're you feeling?"

"Good," I replied.

"How good?" His voice had a teasing thread that I'd missed for a long time.

I pushed my hips into his cock. "Could be better."

"Right fucking answer, baby girl," he practically growled, the hand on my breast giving a harder, more possessive squeeze. He plucked at my nipple and then slid the hand down my stomach until his fingers brushed my slit. I almost protested when they bypassed where I wanted them and kept going until he grabbed my leg. He picked it up and dragged it back over his thigh, spreading me open. Only then did his fingers find my center.

"Fuck," he groaned, and sucked at the skin where my neck sloped to my shoulder. "Already so wet for me."

I lost the ability to formulate a response as he slid two fingers into me with ease. In the quiet of the morning, all I heard were our breaths —his soft and steady, mine raw and ragged—and the sound of his fingers sinking into my soaking pussy.

"More," I whispered, not above begging as I tried to roll onto my back.

Court didn't budge, the length of his frame pressing against me and keeping me on my side as his fingers stroked in and out of me with unhurried thrusts. Occasionally he'd brush them over my clit, but never enough to get me off.

"Court," I whined, desperate for more.

He made a soft humming sound, still pressing idle kisses across my jaw.

I reached down and grabbed his arm to try and make him move faster, harder. Something. I couldn't even get my fingers to touch when I wrapped them around his wrist. And then he just stopped.

"Becca," he warned.

Huffing, I couldn't help myself. "Can't you just—"

Suddenly he rolled us, him on top and me gaping up at him, wondering how this had happened. Damn him and his secret ninja sex moves.

Straddling my waist, he quickly grabbed my hands, transferring them into one of his and pinning them above my head. My back arched, boobs pushed up on display for him. Dipping his head, he took full advantage, sucking one into his mouth.

I tried to buck him off, but he was too heavy. My feet just slid against the soft sheets, unable to find purchase. When I kept squirming, he used his teeth, biting my nipple until I squeaked and stilled.

Satisfied, he sat back and met my gaze. "Do you mind? I'm trying to enjoy my morning."

"So am I," I snarled, shaking my hair out of my eyes.

Making a soft *tsk*ing sound, he shook his head. "Come on, honey, I know for a goddamn fact how smart you are. I already told you—your body is *mine* now. I get to play with it however I want, whenever I want."

I blinked. "Uh, I don't remember *that* part of the agreement."

"It was in the fine print," he assured me, but his tone was amusingly dismissive.

"So I... what? Just lay back and take it?" I glared at him.

"Sometimes," he replied with a shrug. "Right now, I want to enjoy driving my girl crazy, until she's begging for release."

Okay, no denying that a big part of me warmed when he said *my girl*.

"Tell you what," he added, a wicked gleam in his dark eyes, "I'll make you a deal. You tell me exactly what you want, and I'll give it to you."

My pulse thundered as I contemplated his offer. I knew what I wanted, but did I have the lady balls to voice it? I could feel my face going red just thinking the words.

Judging by the growing grin on his face, he was loving my shyness.

I sucked in a deep breath. Fine. He wanted me to tell him exactly what I wanted, then game freaking on.

"I want you to turn me over and fuck me from behind while you finger my ass," I told him, proud of myself when my voice didn't wobble. I'd read a scene where a girl had a guy doing that, and she'd loved it. I'd never even attempted ass play, but whenever I read about anal, I knew it was something I wanted to try.

Of course the book girl was also being throat-fucked by another guy, but unless Court was down for inviting Rook or Bishop in to help complete *that* fantasy, I didn't see it happening.

His jaw dropped open a bit. "You… What?"

Now *he* was the speechless one. Oh, I liked that. No wonder he liked making me blush so much.

"Was I not specific enough?" I asked innocently, batting my eyelashes.

His gaze sharpened as he let my wrists go. "Turn over."

He didn't give me much room to work with, but I managed to roll onto my stomach. He backed up enough to help pull my knees up so my ass was in the air and on display.

The groan he let out made me feel like a sex goddess as he kissed one cheek and then the other. "I love this ass. Like a fucking ripe peach to match the way you taste. My fucking peaches," he murmured. "One of these days, I'm going to fuck you here."

"Yes," I whispered, loving that plan. It seemed so primal, so base, to be taken that way, and I craved it with Court. I wanted him to take me every way he could. I *trusted* him to take care of me.

I heard the sharp crack of his hand hitting my ass half a second before it burned. I moaned into my pillow as he repeated the action, careful not to hit the same spot. He peppered a series of slaps across my ass, then dipped his fingers back inside of me.

"Like that?" he rasped, moving into position behind me. His

fingers were replaced by the blunt tip of his crown, pressing against my entrance.

"Yes," I sighed, feeling like I could melt into the mattress. I gasped as he pushed inside of me, this angle making him sink deeper. The sense of fullness nearly overwhelmed me.

I was about to beg him to move when I felt his fingers probe at my tight ring of muscle. He spit against the rosette of my ass, and the contact of the hot liquid made me jerk. It was dirty and amazing. Using my own arousal and his saliva as a lubricant, he slowly worked a finger into my ass. A whole different set of nerve endings lit up.

"Fuck me, your ass is so goddamn tight," he muttered, rolling his hips into me as his finger thrust in and out of my back hole, slowly stretching me open. "Let me in, Becca."

I gasped, squeezing my eyes shut against the onslaught of sensations. It was almost too much. My toes curled, the arches of my feet cramping. "Oh, God, yes. Like that."

He added a second finger to my ass, and I wasn't sure I could handle a third. It felt so good. So freaking right.

"Court, please." I didn't even know what I was asking for.

"I've got you, baby girl," he said, his free hand going to my hip and holding me as he increased his tempo. His hips pistoned against me, his balls slapping my pussy with each thrust, hitting my g-spot and making my core spasm

Breathing became a struggle as my entire being devolved into pleasure. It wasn't quite enough, though. I wiggled a hand between myself and the mattress until I was able to rub my clit.

Court gave a groan. "Fuck, yes, baby. Touch yourself. Come for me, sweetheart." He managed to add a third finger, his cock hitting me just right as I frantically rubbed the bundle of nerves between my legs.

The orgasm barreled into me like a freight train, decimating me. My legs gave out, and only Court's strong hold on my hip kept me from collapsing. My hips jerked erratically as I came hard enough to see little sparkles of light dance across my vision.

"Shit, yes," Court hissed, his grip on my hip turning bruising as his cock surged inside me with his release. When he finished, he let me fall onto the bed, awkwardly splaying out with my head to one side. I puffed out a breath to dislodge strands of hair from my eyes.

"Holy shit, baby," he panted, dropping onto his back beside me, his chest heaving. He turned and looked at me, awe in his eyes. "Where the fuck did that come from?"

I lowered my gaze, suddenly bashful once more. "Uh, just something I read in a book."

"Remind me to buy you a gift card to the bookstore," he told me. "Fuck it. I'll just give you my credit card. Get whatever you want."

"You didn't think it was… weird?" I'd always hidden the covers I bought on my e-reader by keeping the books organized by list, and the majority of the books on my shelves had discreet covers.

"Fuck no," he retorted, turning to look at me. He reached over and tucked some hair over my shoulder as he rolled to his side and kissed me. "If you'd asked me to dress up in a chicken costume and spank you with a drumstick from KFC, *that* might've been weird."

I cackled at the image.

"But I still would've done it," he finished. "Fuck, Becca, I'd do anything for you. I…"

My heart skipped a beat. "You what?"

He looked away before muttering something that sounded a lot like, "Fuck it." He focused his intense gaze on me, his hand cupping the back of my head. "I love you, Becca."

I gasped audibly. "You what?"

He shook his head, his lips set in a stubborn line. "Don't tell me it's too soon or I'll change my mind—I've been in love with you for months, Becca. Maybe my whole goddamn life. I spent too much time being a little bitch and trying to stay away from you because I thought it was what was best for you."

"And now?" I watched him closely.

"I'm done fighting this. Us. Call it destiny or fate or dumb fucking luck, but you were always meant to be with me," he replied, his fingers tangling in my hair.

"Court…" I didn't know what to say to that. What to do. My gut told me to throw myself into his arms and declare I loved him, too, because I did.

But admitting that would give him even more power over me, and my brain wasn't ready to make the leap my heart was. I'd been hurt by this man too many times to blindly jump and expect him to catch me.

"Don't say it," he murmured, like he sensed my hesitation. "I haven't earned it yet."

He leaned in and kissed me. "But I will."

CHAPTER 28

BEX

I leaned my head against the edge of the claw-foot bathtub, hot water soaking away the aches from the night before. Okay, and from the morning too. Grinning to myself, I sank deeper into the water, letting my chin brush the surface as the bathroom door opened.

Court eyed me in the tub, where I was submerged under several thick inches of bubbles. When he'd offered to run me a bath, I hadn't known it would have bubbles. Or that Court had no idea what a proper water-to-bubbles ratio was. Still, he'd left me in bed and turned on the water before coming to get me and depositing me in the bath with strict instructions to relax.

A girl could get used to this.

Except for the scowl on his gorgeous face, everything was awesome.

"What's wrong?" I asked, sitting up. The bubbles clung to my skin, blocking my breasts from view.

"Nothing," he muttered, placing a stack of folded clothes on the counter. He turned back to me, forcing a smile that didn't smooth away the frown lines on his brow.

"Court," I warned, lifting an arm to lean on the side of the tub. "Please don't lie to me."

He sighed. "Your phone keeps ringing."

I frowned. "You want me to put it on silent?"

"It's Eric," he spat, like the man's name alone was poison in his mouth.

"Oh." I sat up straighter. In my little blissed-out bubble of the last twelve hours, I'd forgotten that I was kinda, sorta in hiding from a guy who was kinda, sorta my boyfriend. Well, in *his* mind. "I guess… I mean, should I talk to him?"

"Fuck no," he retorted. "I never want you speaking to that prick again. And, if things go my way, he and the rest of his sick-fuck friends will be dead in a week."

I winced, because I knew he wasn't kidding. For some guys—hell, most guys—a death threat would just be annoying male posturing. For Court? It wasn't an idle threat.

Huh. I'd never really considered the fact that the guy I'd fallen for had killed people.

I let that thought tumble over and over in my head.

Oddly enough, I couldn't bring myself to care. Maybe because I knew he only killed people who deserved it. I didn't think that would hold up as an excuse with the police, but as long as he wasn't caught…

Yeah, I could live with that.

Court leaned against the counter, crossing his legs at the ankles. He still hadn't put on a shirt, which was totally fine in my book. I wasn't sure I'd ever get tired of looking at that tan skin stretched over hard muscles. I had the urge to lick every divot I saw, mapping his skin with my mouth to learn all its secrets.

He had put on a pair of pants; however, they were gray sweatpants —AKA God's gift to womankind—and they barely stayed up on his narrow hips. When he leaned back on the counter, the material clung to the curve of his long cock. It was a thing I wanted to see again and again.

"My eyes are up here, gorgeous," he teased.

I didn't lift my gaze, watching in fascination as his dick went from soft to half-hard before my eyes. "I'm well aware of where your eyes are."

Chuckling, he pushed off the counter and sauntered to me with some major big-dick energy. He paused beside me, and I had to tilt my head all the way back to see him until he sank onto the edge of the bathtub. Without invitation, he dipped his hand under the bubbles and cupped my right breast, giving it a firm squeeze.

I moaned, my lashes fluttering as I felt the correlating pulse of need in my clit.

"I need to ask you a question," he said, slowly pulling away.

It took a second to focus my attention back on him. I already missed his touch. But something in his tone leached the arousal from my system. "Okay."

His expression was carefully schooled into blankness. "How would you feel if we left Paris tonight?"

"What?" I frowned, not sure I'd heard him correctly.

Sighing, he slid off the edge of the tub and sat on the floor so we were at eye level. "I talked to Rook and Bishop," he started, his tone low and serious, "and they agreed they could handle things until Royal could get here. He could take my place, and we could leave. Get you out of here before the auction."

"You're really that worried?" I watched him closely.

Concern wrinkled his brow before he got it in check. "I really think I don't want you anywhere near this shit when it goes down. We can leave, go back home to California—"

"I can't go back right now," I interrupted him, but made sure to keep my tone gentle. I lifted a hand, sloshing water and bubbles as I reached for his fingers. "Why are you saying this now? What's changed since yesterday?"

He shot me an incredulous look. "Everything has changed, Becca."

"Because we had sex?" I couldn't help but glance down at my body.

His cheeks flushed just a smidge. "That was more than sex, baby. You're mine."

"Right," I said slowly, still not getting it.

He rolled his eyes. "I'm not about to let you put yourself in danger."

"Whoa." I pulled my hand back and leaned away from him. "I'm sorry—did you say you aren't going to *let me*?"

He shook his head, almost like he was annoyed. "You know what I mean."

"No, I don't think I do," I replied. "Court, last night was amazing, and I love where this could be going, but I'm not going to stay home and just wait in bed for you every day."

"I didn't ask you to. I'm not sending you away—I'm going with you," he pointed out. "We'll be together."

"And you're cool with leaving your brothers here?" I spluttered.

His jaw tightened. "It's not ideal, but you're more important."

"Court, my mom is here. My grandparents are here. Hell, my cousin is dating Eric's brother," I said, my panic rising as it sank in just how fully entrenched in this world I was. Even if I wanted to run, I couldn't leave my family at risk while Eric was loose.

He frowned. "We can—"

"Take them with us?" My laugh was slightly hysterical.

"Well, no." He grimaced, his frustration becoming clear. "Becca, *you* are my priority."

"And I lov—" I cut myself off. "I *appreciate* that, but we can't run away from our problems, Court."

"Fine. Then you leave, and I'll stay. I'll handle Eric and the auction and my dad," he reasoned, like that was an answer. "You can stay with Ryan and Maddie for the time being."

"No. *Hell* no," I retorted. "I'm not leaving my family or you."

"Becca—"

"I said no," I snapped, standing up and grabbing the towel waiting for me. I used my foot to lift the stopper, and the water started to drain.

Court watched me rise and offered me a hand to step out of the massive tub. I held on to him only long enough to not slip and fall and break my neck. I tried pulling away, but he didn't let go.

Standing up, he drew me against his chest. "I don't want to fight, sweetheart. I just want you safe."

I melted a little, looking at our reflection in the mirror. "I know you do, but I can't leave. And if I can help, I want to. Please don't make me choose between you and helping them."

He sighed, the sound reluctant. "I won't. But I don't like it."

I turned and looped my arms around his neck. "I know this is all new, but we'll figure it out. I promise I won't take any unnecessary risks, okay? And I'll stay back and let you and the guys do your thing. I just need to be here in case my family needs me."

Nodding, he gave me a soft kiss. "Fine. I'll try not to be an overbearing ass."

"Look at that," I mused with a laugh. "He *can* be taught."

Court rolled his eyes and swatted my ass. "Get dressed. I have food waiting for you in the living room."

"Sir, yes, sir!" I chirped with a mock salute.

His gaze heated. "Smart ass."

"You can spank the insubordination out of me later," I teased with a wink.

His look went from amused to hungry in half a second. "I fucking plan to." The slight growl in his words made my belly swoop. He kissed me hard, his tongue sliding into my mouth and dominating mine until I was breathless and achy for more.

"Court—"

A banging on the bedroom door had us both turning.

"You two need to get out here," Rook called, his voice all business.

I exchanged looks with Court and quickly finished drying off before tugging on my bra and a shirt. I searched for my panties under the leggings he'd brought. "Where's my underwear?"

"Gone," he replied with a shrug. "You don't need them."

"What? Yes, I do," I insisted, but I was already rolling the leggings up. Luckily I'd pulled my hair into a messy bun for my bath, so other than a few damp pieces clinging to my neck, it was dry.

"You really don't," he replied, following me out of the bathroom and through the bedroom. I yanked open the door to see Rook waiting with a worried look.

"What?" Court asked for both of us, his hands landing on my hips.

I leaned against his chest without thinking, absorbing his heat and strength into myself.

A sad smile played at the corners of Rook's mouth before he looked at Court. "I'm happy for you guys."

"But not everyone will be," Bishop called from his seat on the couch. He turned, holding up my phone. It was ringing, Eric's name showing as the caller. "Fifth time he's called. I think he's having sepa-ration anxiety."

I frowned. I'd texted him yesterday with the story that we'd worked out—me being back in California to straighten out my gradua-tion status—and I'd pretty much ignored my phone after that. Why would Eric be blowing up my phone?

"Maybe something's wrong with Cami?" I wondered, glancing back at Court.

"Your mom or grandparents would've called," he pointed out, shaking his head.

"Okay, maybe something's wrong with Alex, and Eric can't get ahold of Cami?" I tried. My brow furrowed as I tried to work out the urgency.

"Dude, it's almost two in the morning in California," Bishop wondered aloud. "Why is he calling now?"

"He's *been* calling, like, every hour. Now he's upped it to every minute." Rook's lips twisted to the side.

"You said he only called five times." I gaped at Bishop.

He shrugged. "He's only called five times *this* hour."

That made zero sense unless someone was dead. "But—"

Court snarled a little. "He's fucking obsessed with you, princess."

"I've barely known him a week," I argued, utterly mystified.

"Not sure that matters to guys like him," Rook murmured, rubbing the back of his neck.

I bit my lower lip. "I should answer it."

"The fuck you should," Court spat.

"I kinda agree with Bex," Bishop offered.

Court turned his annoyance to his brother. "You would."

"What the hell does *that* mean?" Bishop demanded, his normal easygoing nature dissipating.

"Enough," Rook snapped, shutting them both down. He looked at me, his expression softening. "I think you should talk to him. The last thing we need is him spooking and calling off the auction. This is the closest we've been in months."

Court made a sound behind me, but Rook shook his head. "It's just a phone call, bro. She's not going to his house. Bex can handle a phone call."

"I can," I confirmed, turning to look at Court.

He stared down at me, clearly unhappy, but he eventually nodded just as my phone stopped ringing. After a beat, it started again. I pulled away from Court and took the phone from Bishop, then swiped my thumb across the screen to answer.

"Hey!" I forced a bright, cheery tone. "What's—"

"Where the fuck have you been?" Eric's voice was a dangerous snarl that took me aback.

I'd *never* heard him sound so furious. Something in my expression must've given away my shock because Court was right in front of me a second later, his face concerned while his eyes flashed fire.

"Uh, I've been busy," I said slowly. "Is everything okay?"

Eric made a huffing sound. "I was worried when I didn't hear from you."

"I was with my friends," I hedged, backing up to sit on the arm of the sofa. Court followed me, mirroring each step and standing between my legs. He casually linked our fingers, and the show of support helped steady my nerves.

"When will you be back in Paris?" he demanded.

"I'll be back for my grandmother's birthday," I replied, keeping my tone even and calm.

Eric sucked in a sharp breath. "No, that won't do. I need to see you before then. Where are you in California? I'll get on my company plane within the hour. I can be there in twelve hours."

My jaw dropped. "You… you want to come to California?" I shot Court a wild look.

His brows shot up and he shook his head vehemently.

"Eric, that's really sweet—" I struggled to find the right words.

"I miss you." He made it sound so simple, and if he was anyone other than a human trafficking psycho, it might've been sweet. "I'll be there by… tomorrow morning your time. We can grab breakfast."

"No!" I shouted. "You can't."

"Why not?" His voice had taken on an icy tone that sent shivers up and down my spine.

I pushed out a broken laugh. "Well, because I'm coming home in a few hours." I couldn't look at Court as I said it, but I could feel the frustrated rage coming off him in waves.

"You are?" Eric didn't sound convinced.

"It was supposed to be a surprise," I improvised, sounding disappointed. "It didn't take long to wrap things up here. I just needed to sign a few forms in person and meet with the dean. I already have a flight booked for first thing in the morning. I'll be back in Paris by the evening."

"What time? I'll get you from the airport." He made it sound like a foregone conclusion instead of an offer.

"Oh, no," I insisted. "Our driver will pick me up."

"No, I insis—"

"How about we plan on a late dinner?" I suggested, railroading through his protest. "Say eight o'clock? Think you can grab us a table at Aubergine again?" At least the restaurant was close to the hotel, which meant the guys would be nearby.

Court squeezed my fingers to the point of pain, but I refused to look at him. I knew he wouldn't be on board, and I'd deal with the fallout of his wrath after I hung up.

"Of course," Eric replied, sounding more in control. "I'll pick you up at eight."

"Great," I said, trying to tug away from Court, but he wasn't letting go.

"Oh, and Bex?" Eric began, his tone softer.

"Hmm?"

He paused. "Don't ignore my calls again, love." There was a frosty note of warning in his tone that made my blood run cold. "I'll see you tomorrow."

"See you tomorrow," I mumbled, still a little in shock as I hung up the phone. I lifted my eyes, dragging them up Court's body until I met his very pissed-off gaze.

"What. The. *Fuck*?" he demanded.

CHAPTER 29

BEX

Court was pissed, and I couldn't blame him. I'd unilaterally made a decision that affected us all, but if anyone should understand that, it should be him. How many choices had he made for the both of us?

I winced inwardly because, shit, I didn't want our relationship to be some kind of tit-for-tat game where we were constantly getting back at each other. We had to be better than that.

"I'm sorry," I told him, meaning it.

His nostrils flared, still pissed, but willing to hear me out. I noticed Rook backing away and joining Bishop on the sofa.

"I should have talked to all of you before making that decision with Eric," I added. I reached for Court, not sure if he would take a step back. But he stayed still, letting my hands slide up the hard planes of his chest and loop around behind his neck. His hands went to my hips and pulled my body flush to his.

"I don't want you anywhere near him," Court hissed. "He's fucking unhinged, Becca."

"I know," I agreed with a nod. "But what else was I supposed to do? He was going to fly out to California. It would've blown everything up."

His lashes fluttered shut, his jaw tight. "I get that but… fuck." He looked over my shoulder at his brothers. "What are our options?"

"I know you hate it, but she made the right call," Bishop said, uncharacteristically serious. Concern creased his forehead, but the set of his mouth was all business. "The only other option was getting Bex's ass on a plane within the next hour, which is doable, but then it puts her a continent and an ocean away from us."

"I could go with her," Court argued. I stayed quiet, letting them work this out between themselves, because Court needed that.

Rook grimaced. "I mean, you could. But our best chance at getting Eric is here in Paris at the auction. I heard from my guy this morning. He's part of an international task force that's been working this same organization from another angle. He thinks he can get his team to play nice with us."

"Play nice?" I echoed.

Bishop tossed me a grin. "Phoenix isn't exactly a by-the-book legal enterprise, Bex. We bend, and sometimes outright break, laws to get what we need to do done. Ultimately we've operated under the idea that what we do is more important than bureaucratic bullshit, and even though there are plans in place to make it legal in some ways, we'll never stop doing what we need to in order to protect the people who need it."

"That being said, it doesn't mean we can't work with international organizations," Rook pointed out. "They have funding and resources that we don't always have access to, and most governments get what we're doing. They can't outright condone us, but they also aren't looking to stop us either."

"Huh." I looked up at Court. "That's why you're becoming a lawyer."

He nodded. "Specializing in international law will help us on a global level. When we decided to set up Phoenix, it wasn't on a whim. We did our research, and we all have roles to play. It's just a crazy time right now, because the main people we need to eliminate first are related to us."

"Beckett and Gary falling were the first dominoes," Rook said.

"The General will be the next, and after him, we can go for the one we want the most—Westford. He's the head of the snake."

Linc's dad. I'd met him only a handful of times growing up, but he'd always seemed so *normal*. He was the dad who actually wore jeans and a t-shirt. He'd played baseball with the guys when they were little. When all of our families had gone on vacations together, he'd snuck me cookies.

Finding out Kent Westford was at the epicenter of this whole nightmare had been almost as shocking as learning my dad also played a part.

"And that's it?" I asked.

Court let out a humorless laugh. "Hardly. Someone will take his place, the same way someone will take over Black Box Ops when our dad is gone. There's always going to be another asshole looking to take over the fucking world. It'll never end, baby. But that doesn't mean we don't fight it with everything we've got."

The note of fire in his voice stirred something in my chest. They were so passionate about what they were doing. So driven. It made me want to do the same thing, to be better. I wanted to help.

And maybe I could. I could be the link to Eric that set everything in motion.

Court looked at his older brother. "He's coming today?"

Rook nodded. "He'll be here—" A knock at the door cut him off. Grinning, Rook pushed off the couch and went to answer it, checking through the peephole to make sure who it was before yanking it open. "Hey, man."

The guy on the other side of the door was huge, like every other guy in the room, with a full beard, tanned skin, and a full sleeve of black and gray tattoos on his left arm. He looked utterly relaxed in khaki cargo pants and a tight black shirt that showed off an impressive amount of muscle. But it was the furry companion at his feet that made me smile.

"Trick," Rook greeted, extending an arm. They did that patented guy half-hug, half-back slap thing, then Rook turned to the gorgeous dog sitting patiently at his friend's side. He crouched down. "Hey, Wanda."

Wanda looked up at Trick with soulful brown eyes, waiting for Trick to give her a nod before getting up and butting her head against Rook's chest. Her thick brown-and-black tail wagged furiously.

Bishop stood up, extending a hand. "Good to see you again, man."

"You too." Trick glanced at us, smiling. "Hey, Court."

Court nodded. "Trick. Glad you're here."

Trick's gaze landed on me and lit up. "I don't think we've met."

"I'm Bex," I said, leaning over to extend my hand as far as I could while Court looped a possessive arm around my waist and pulled me back to his side.

"My girlfriend," Court added, eyeing where Trick and I had clasped hands to shake like normal humans.

I gaped up at him. We were throwing around labels now?

Trick didn't seem phased. "Dude, congrats." He looked at me. "Good luck, sweetie. If he fucks up, let me know. I'll kick his ass for ya."

Court scoffed. "Yeah right. Last time I checked, I kicked *your* ass."

"I'd also downed half a bottle of tequila," Trick retorted. "Sober me would end you. Tell him, Rook."

Rook stood up. He eyed his friend and then his brother before shrugging. "Honestly, you're pretty well matched. Trick's faster, but Court plays dirty."

Trick looked a little bummed by that. He looked down at the dog nudging his hand as she sat patiently. "*You* know I'd kick his sorry ass, don't you, girl?" He scratched behind her ears.

"So this is the infamous Wanda?" Bishop started to reach over to pet her.

Wanda spun faster than my eyes could track. Her ears flattened to her head, her lips pulling back in a snarl as she let out a growl.

Bishop froze, eyes wide. "Uh…"

Trick settled a hand on her head. "Down, girl."

Instantly the dog relaxed, her tongue lolling out. She gave a small thump of her tail as she looked at Bishop almost like she was apologizing.

"I'm good," Bishop muttered, stepping backward and sitting back down.

Trick chuckled, the sound low and warm. "She's a working dog, bro. You can't just approach her like a damn Labrador the first time you meet her." He looked at Court and grinned. "*She* could kick your ass."

"I'm inclined to agree," Court replied with a smile.

"She's beautiful," I remarked. "She's a German shepherd?"

"Belgian Malinois," Trick corrected, rubbing her black muzzle. She leaned against his side.

"She's yours?" I asked.

"Technically she belongs to the Navy," he answered with a rueful smile. "But yeah, she's mine."

"Trick found Wanda when we were on a mission in Europe," Rook jumped in. "She was this half-starved little thing that he had a soft spot for. He spent three weeks sneaking her rations and shit."

"Yeah, that was the best decision I ever made," Trick said. "She saved all our asses."

"She did?" I glanced at the dog, who looked utterly content beside Trick.

"Wanda." Trick spoke her name, and she stood with a slow swish of her tail. He pointed at me. "Greet."

The dog turned from him and wound her way through the furniture until she was in front of me. She sniffed my hand, then nudged it with her cold, wet nose.

I smiled and looked at Trick. "Can I…"

He gave me a nod, and I pet the top of her head. Her fur was soft as velvet, and when I rubbed her ear, she gave a loud groan and pressed her head into my hand. I couldn't help but smile.

"We were finishing up our mission and getting ready to roll out," Trick told me. "I was saying goodbye to her, and she fucking attacked me."

I froze mid-ear rub. "She did what now?"

"Bit the shit out of my arm." Trick grinned and laughed. "Rook and Ford were pulling her off me when all of a sudden, she lets go and hauls ass to our teammate, Cooper. Coop's trying to load our gear into the Humvee so we can leave, but Wanda knocks his ass down next.

"It wasn't until Cooper was lying in the dirt that he saw the explosive device someone had strapped under the truck," Rook finished. "She fucking knew it would kill us the second we started the damn engine."

"I brought her back with me, and we all pushed to have her trained as an official bomb dog in an ATF-sponsored program they were doing alongside the Navy," Trick went on. "She tested off the fucking charts, but unless I was around, she didn't seem to give a shit about working."

"Trainers finally agreed to let Trick become her handler. She's been with him ever since. That was three years ago. Wanda's family," Rook said.

I rubbed the top of her head, loving how she leaned against my legs. "Why'd you name her Wanda?"

Trick grinned, looking boyish. "Because the Avengers are the shit, and Scarlet Witch is a fucking badass. Duh."

I laughed, shaking my head as I kept petting her.

"Guess we should talk this shit out," Rook finally started.

Trick nodded and snapped his fingers. "Wanda, place."

The dog got up and trotted to the door, then lay down against it, her head resting on her paws. She huffed out a big breath and closed her eyes, but I had a feeling one wrong move, and she'd be ready to rip my throat out.

"I only have an hour," Trick said. "So we need to get this going. I'll debrief my team."

"They're good with us joining the party?" Bishop looked skeptical.

"They're accepting that you'll crash the party," he amended, sitting in the chair across from the sofa. Resting his forearms on his knees, he leaned forward. "We're all on the same side, but you know the drill— shit goes sideways, and they'll deny ever agreeing to a partnership. You'll be on your own."

"We won't fail," Rook told him, all business as he sat on the couch. He grabbed a file from the coffee table and passed it to Trick.

Trick opened it and flipped through the papers. "How sure are you on the auction date? Our source still hasn't confirmed it."

Rook's gaze flicked to me. "We're sure. Bex actually knows someone attending."

Trick looked up, surprised. "You do?"

I nodded. "I was sorta dating a guy who's organizing it." I cringed.

He blinked at me. "I have questions."

Court squeezed my hip. "Let's sit down," he murmured to me. He guided me into the other armchair across from Bishop and Rook, then stayed standing at one side, like my own personal bodyguard.

"Bex got tangled up with Eric Lambert-Durand," Rook explained.

"As in Lambert-Singh?" Trick's gaze latched on to me. This close I could see that his eyes were a gorgeous shade of dark blue that lightened to a pale gray around the pupil.

"Uh, yes?" I wasn't sure who Singh was.

"Lambert-Singh is the name of Eric's shipping company," Bishop told me. "Lambert was his mother's maiden name. She inherited the company from her father, Colton Lambert. His partner was Mikhail Singh, but Singh sold off his shares to Lambert when he was diagnosed with Alzheimer's while Eric was an infant."

I nodded, trying to keep track. I was going to need a flow chart. Or one of those murder mystery boards with the red string connecting people and places together.

"How the hell did you meet him?" Trick asked.

"Blind date," I replied with a sigh. "His brother, Alex, is my cousin's boyfriend. Cami, my cousin, set us up."

"Well that's some shit luck," he muttered with a shake of his head.

"You have no idea," Court added, his tone dark.

Bishop grimaced. "Yeah, Eric's recently turned into a full-blown Bex stalker."

"And why exactly did he volunteer the auction info?" Trick looked at me.

I shifted in my seat, my stomach doing little flips from anxiety. "I, uh, might've let him think I know more than I actually do."

"She mentioned knowing Dad," Rook clarified. "She also name-dropped Westford and let it slip that her dad also loops her in on this shit."

Trick studied me for a beat, then snapped his fingers. "You're Malcolm Whittier's kid. Rebecca."

I nodded, my heart sinking. "You know my dad?"

Trick started to give me a look like *duh* but then seemed to catch sight of Court behind me and schooled his expression into something unreadable before nodding. "Yeah." He glanced at Rook, almost like he was silently asking a question.

Rook gave the smallest shake of his head, and the lines around Trick's mouth tightened for a beat. I wanted to ask what I was missing, but Trick swallowed his reaction and started asking me more questions. "You're still in contact with Eric?"

I nodded, unable to brush aside the uneasy feeling. As if sensing my distress, Court sat on the plush arm of the chair, his hand coming around to cup the back of my neck. I leaned into his touch, soaking it up.

"Eric has made it abundantly clear that he's interested in Bex," Rook added, concern in his eyes. "Unfortunately, Bex is tied to this shit until we can neutralize it."

"Knowing *when* the auction is going to be helps a fuckton," Trick said. "Any idea of a location?"

I shook my head. "No. But I'm seeing Eric again tomorrow."

Court's hand tightened on my neck.

Trick looked at Court in surprise. "You're cool with that?"

"Not even a little," Court bit off. He relaxed his hold. "But Becca can make her own choices, and I'm going to support her."

"I can try to press Eric for more details," I offered, wanting to be useful.

Court swore under his breath. "Becca—"

"Only if it comes up naturally," Trick cut him off. "We have a couple ideas of the location, but nothing solid. Worst-case scenario, we'll split our resources."

"That sounds dangerous," I said softly.

"It's not ideal," he replied, inclining his head. "But we'll do what we have to. Is it just the three of you?"

Rook straightened. "Knight's out of commission for a bit, but Royal can be here if we need extra manpower."

"Ryan, Linc, and Ash said the same thing," Court added.

I turned to him. "They're coming to Paris?"

His gaze dropped to me, softening. "If we need them. Yeah."

"Honestly, it might help to have them close." Trick rubbed the back of his neck. "We're being careful, but our team isn't big."

"How many?" Rook demanded.

"Six," Trick admitted. "Seven if you count Wanda. We can call in Paris police to assist after the fact, but not leading up."

"Leaks?" Bishop's stare was hard.

Trick nodded. "Up to and in the Ministry of the Interior. In fact, there are a few upper officials that would be huge if we can get to them at the auction."

"That's why you kept it small," Rook mused, rubbing his jaw.

Trick's expression went arctic. "You and I both know your team is only as good as the men you can trust."

Rook's entire body went rigid, his eyes flashing in a way that made me want to hide under a chair. "Yeah. We both learned that fucking lesson, brother."

"Then you know why we kept it at six men. Made sure we were all vetted and tested," Trick added.

Wanda lifted her head, looking at Trick.

That broke the tension holding Trick's body tight. His shoulders relaxed as he looked fondly at the dog. "Say the word V-E-T and she gets nervous. Not a fan of needles. It's okay, girl." He glanced at the rest of us. "I should get going. We have a team meeting tonight."

He stood, as did the rest of us. Wanda yawned and pushed herself into a sitting position.

"Thanks for stopping by," Rook said, shaking Trick's hand again.

"Anytime, man." Trick nodded at Court and Bishop before giving me a kind smile. "I guess I'll see you around, Bex. Stay safe, okay?"

"Will do," I replied with a smile that felt forced. Standing in the middle of these four guys—three of them trained by the military to do things I'd never be able to comprehend and one who owned my damn heart—I was struck by how out of place I was in their world.

As we watched Trick leave with Wanda, I wondered how I could ever fit into this world. How I could make a difference the way they were.

CHAPTER 30

COURT

After the night I'd spent with Becca, it was hard returning my attention back to the reason I was in Paris, but there was shit that needed to be done. After a lengthy phone call with the guys and my brothers to bring everyone up to speed, we split up.

Rook and Bishop each had their own leads to follow, and while I could've been doing the same thing, I decided instead to focus on my girl.

Fuck. The grin that thinking of her gave me was undeniable.

Pushing back from the laptop in front of me, I turned to see Becca still curled up in a corner of the sofa, her Kindle on her lap. Her brows were pulled low and she was chewing on her thumbnail. At some point she'd dragged the fluffy blanket off the back of the couch and wrapped it around herself. She'd snagged one of my old football hoodies earlier, and the overall look was fucking adorable.

She gave a tiny little gasp, her hazel eyes going wide. Her dark hair was still in a messy bun, the streaks of teal shooting through it not as vibrant as they'd been a few months earlier.

"Good book?" I asked.

She didn't look up, utterly entranced by whatever she was reading.

"Becca," I tried again.

After a beat she gave a half-hearted hum of acknowledgement.

I stood up. "Are you about done?"

"Mmm," was the only response.

I scratched my stomach, watching her with amusement. "Do you need anything?"

"Okay," she agreed, still not looking up.

That wasn't an answer to my question, so I tried something else. "I think I'm going to go jerk off in the shower."

"Sure."

"Then I might hit up a sex club and let someone peg me," I added.

She flicked her fingers in my direction. "Whatever you want."

Chuckling, I shook my head and ambled over to stand in front of her. "Becca?"

"Yeah?"

I reached down and gently tugged on a corner of the device.

Her head snapped up, eyes flashing with warning. "Don't touch the Kindle. Don't *ever* touch the Kindle."

I froze, my thumb and middle finger still holding the corner. "Uh."

Her eyes narrowed, her tiny nose twitching. "There are two things in a girl's life you don't touch without permission—her body and her book."

My brows lifted. "Noted. But what if I'm trying to get my girlfriend's attention when she's reading?"

She gave me a smirk. "Then you need to match or beat the energy of her book."

"What're you reading?"

The barest hint of a blush creeping across her soft cheeks gave me all the info I needed. I gave another yank, pulling the Kindle away.

"Court!" She tried to scramble off the couch but got tangled in the blanket. She fell back with an outraged squeak.

I looked down at the screen, only able to catch a glimpse before she lunged and grabbed the reader back. But I definitely saw the words *dripping, pussy,* and *cocks.*

Hold up.

"Baby, did that book say *cocks*? As in two?" I shot her an incredulous look as she cradled the Kindle to her chest like a kitten.

"Yes, cocks," she retorted, lifting her chin even as crimson spread to her ears. "But there are *three* cocks, if you must know."

"Okay, yeah," I said. "Now I *must* know."

She sighed. "It's reverse harem omegaverse."

I blinked. "I know what those words mean separately, but I'm not sure about throwing them all together."

She turned off the screen and set her Kindle aside before glaring at me, hands on her hips. "Reverse harem."

"Okay," I said slowly.

"One girl. Multiple guys."

"And you're into that?" I'm not sure if this conversation was turning me on or concerning me.

"In fantasy? Sure. In real life, it sounds like a freaking nightmare," she replied, making a face. "I mean, we've been together for less than twenty-four hours, and I already know that you're more than enough for me to handle. I'd go nuts if I had to juggle the needs, wants, and moods of three guys."

"Right. And what's the other thing? Omegas and verse? Is that, like, poetry?"

Her gaze darted away. "Uh, no. One word, actually. Omegaverse. It's a type of... fantasy."

"Unless you have a secret hobbit fetish I missed," I started, a grin spreading across my face as she kept her gaze averted, "I'm guessing it's not the kind of fantasy Tolkien wrote."

She cleared her throat loudly. "Was there something you needed? Or did you just want to give me shit for my choice in books?"

I stepped into her space, following her as she walked backward until her ass hit the closed door of our bedroom. Then I caged her with my arms and leaned in to bury my face against her neck. A delicious shiver rippled through her.

"Rook and Bishop are gone for a few hours," I murmured, lightly kissing under her jaw.

Her breath caught. "Uh huh." Her small hands came up to clutch the hem of my shirt.

I drew back to look her in the eye. "So I thought I'd let you pick."

Her gaze dropped to my lips. "Pick what?" she asked in a breathy tone that made my cock harden.

"Where I fuck you," I answered, kissing one cheek. "*How* I fuck you." I kissed the other cheek, then I pressed my mouth to hers. Her lips parted instantly, a surge of triumph hitting my veins like a bolt of electricity.

I kept my weight off her, my hands pressed to the door on either side of her head, as I devoured her mouth. My tongue stroked hers into submission before I turned the kiss softer, sweeter. I dragged the kiss out, sensing her impatience grow.

With an annoyed little huff, she wrapped her arms around my neck and tried to pull my body against hers. When I didn't budge, she arched her back, brushing those full tits against my chest.

"Court..." She whimpered my name as I kissed her jaw and as much of her neck as the damn oversized hoodie gave me access to.

"Yeah?" I mumbled against her throat.

"Can— I want—" She kept cutting herself off, and I wasn't sure if she was too shy to admit what she wanted, or if she was just as affected by my body as I was hers.

"Tell me." I tried to cajole the answer from her, needing to hear her pretty mouth say dirty things.

"Me on top," she blurted out, cheeks now stained bright red. "But first— First, I want—"

I cupped her face with my hand, keeping her eyes focused on mine. "Whatever you want, baby."

She sucked in a breath, and I could see her rallying the courage to tell me. "I want to taste you first. I mean, can I?"

I thumbed her bottom lip, my dick ready to punch through my sweats. "Princess, you never need permission to suck my cock. Let's just make that a rule, deal?"

Eyes bright, she smiled and nodded. "I think I like that deal, as long as turnabout's fair play."

I snorted a laugh, and my hand left her face to slip between us and cup her pussy. "Fuck, yes. I can't wait to wake you up with my tongue between your legs."

She rocked her hips, pressing her hot center against my fingers. I teased her through the thin fabric of her leggings until her breath came in choppy, needy pants. Unable to hide my grin, I finally took her hand and walked backward to the couch. When my calves hit the fabric, I sank down, leaving her standing between my open knees.

Uncertainty flitted across her face, but it was quickly squashed by hunger as her gaze drifted from my face, down my chest, and landed at my groin. When her pink tongue darted out to lick her lips, I groaned and reached into my sweats to fist my cock before I came in my pants like a damn kid.

"Have you done this before?" I rasped, needing to know how much she could take of what I was desperate to give. The idea of fisting my hand in her hair and fucking her throat was too strong to deny, but I wouldn't make the same mistake I had last night. I would go at her speed.

For now.

I planned on fucking this woman for the rest of our lives. Of making her mine in every primal way a man could mark his girl.

Becca gave me a shy look and shook her head slightly. She still looked uncertain, but determined. Like sucking my dick was her own personal Everest to conquer.

My chest swelled with the knowledge that I was getting another of her firsts. Clearing my throat, I forced my hands to my sides, then I said the words I'd been dying to say for fucking years. "On your knees, Becca."

She fell to her knees before me like it was where she was always meant to be. Those pretty hazel eyes lifted to my groin, and she reached for the waistband of my sweats before pausing, her gaze flicking up to my eyes as she silently seemed to ask for permission to touch me.

I gave her a nod and wondered—not for the first time—if she was more submissive than she let on. Sure, she had an independent streak a mile wide, and while a lot of her hesitation in the bedroom could be due to inexperience, there was something in my gut telling me it was more.

I'd been to plenty of sex clubs in my life. I wasn't a stranger to BDSM, but I'd never been invested in that lifestyle, mostly going when Linc had dragged me along with him. That was more his scene, but I had to admit, there was a part of me that wanted to dominate Becca. That needed to own her orgasms and cries, that wanted to show her a whole world of pleasure that she'd never known.

Watching as she tugged my pants down, I helped her only by lifting my hips. She wordlessly stripped off the sweats. I grinned as she swallowed hard, now eye level with my erect cock.

Looking up at me again with big eyes, she placed her hands on my thighs for balance before leaning in and licking a stripe up the underside of my cock.

"Fuck," I hissed, my hips giving an involuntary thrust.

The corner of her mouth hooked up in an impish grin before she repeated the action. The tip of her tongue caught the bead of precum leaking from my slit. She gave a soft little hum, like she enjoyed the flavor.

Little minx.

I touched her jaw. "You can do more." It was a request, a plea, and an order all rolled into one statement, but it did exactly what I needed.

She sucked my tip into her mouth, the wet heat almost as good as being buried inside her cunt.

I couldn't stop myself from putting a hand on her head and gently guiding her down to take me deeper. I kept my hold loose so she could back off for air when she needed, but each time she bobbed her head up and down, she took more of me. When my cock nudged the back of her throat, the edges of my vision turned hazy.

And then she swallowed around my length, shocking the shit out of me.

I sucked in a sharp breath, the air hissing between my clenched teeth. "Shit, yes. Just like that, baby."

She kept going, sucking and licking. When she cupped my balls and pressed a finger curiously against my taint, I grabbed her hair and yanked her off my cock.

She blinked at me, her gaze a little unfocused as her nails dug into my thighs, the bite of pain exactly what I needed to get my release under control.

"You're way too fucking good at that," I told her, my chest heaving.

Looking entirely too pleased with herself, she bit her lower lip. I tugged her on top of my body and kissed her. The breathy little moan she gave made me feel like the king of the fucking universe.

My hands were frantic as I pulled her clothes off. She yanked at my shirt until I took it off too, leaving us both naked.

My brothers would shit kittens if they knew what we were about to do on this couch. The place where they sat and had coffee and discussed upcoming plans.

I grinned as Becca straddled me, her legs on either side of my hips. My cock slipped easily between her soaked folds, coating my length in her arousal.

The urge to taste her again was too much to resist. Hooking my hands under her thighs, I lifted her slight weight easily until her knees were perched on my shoulders, her pussy right at my mouth.

With a squeak of alarm, Becca pressed her hands on the wall above us for balance. "Court—" Her argument was swallowed in a moan as I used my thumbs to spread her wide and suckled her clit into my mouth.

I ate her out like a man starved, each one of her cries making me impossibly harder. She rocked her hips, riding my face with abandon as I fucked her with my tongue and repositioned my hand so my fingers could torture her swollen clit.

She shattered, her thighs shaking on either side of me. It was easy to hold her up, but if she'd smothered me with her cunt, I would've died a happy man.

My dick, however, was another story.

She was still twitching from her climax as I dragged her back down the length of my body and positioned my cock at her entrance. With one thrust, I was balls deep inside her.

"Oh, God," she gasped. Her hands found my shoulders, her nails cutting into my skin as she held on, rippling around my cock.

"Ride me, baby," I ordered, my hands on her hips.

She started slowly, lifting her hips and sinking back down. It took a few seconds for her to find her rhythm, but then her eyes hooded as she rode me, grinding herself against me each time.

"Look," I told her, jerking my chin down at where my cock disappeared into her body.

Her eyes snapped open, and she looked, smiling a little as she watched the way she took me.

"That's it," I encouraged. "Fuck me, Becca. Use me to get yourself off."

Her head tipped back as her movements became more frantic. Instead of bouncing on my dick, she rolled her hips, grinding her needy clit against my groin to get herself off. I kept my hands light on her hips, letting her do all the work.

"That's my girl," I said, my voice rough. "Just like that."

A startled cry fell from her lips, and she convulsed around me, her inner walls milking my cock hard enough that my vision blurred from the effort to hold back my own release. She jerked and bucked on my cock, her movements now wholly uncoordinated.

She collapsed, her head dropping to my shoulder, and that was my cue.

My hands tightened on her skin as I fucked into her from below, unleashing everything I'd wanted to since I'd felt her tongue on my cock. I chased my own release like a man possessed, barely aware of her cunt fluttering around me yet again as I railed her.

Lightning shot down my spine, my balls drawing up as I pressed myself into her once more. My cock jerked, my release painting her insides. I was vaguely aware of her gasping through another orgasm above me.

"Holy shit," she breathed, sounding like she'd run a marathon.

My heart thudded in my chest, my pulse pounding as I turned my head and found her lips. I coaxed them open with a slow kiss, savoring the taste of her on my tongue as she melted against me.

I smoothed a hand up and down her spine, feeling her muscles going slack as we caught our breath.

"Court?" she whispered, breaking the stillness.

"Yeah?"

She lifted her head. "We're going to get through this, right?"

The uncertainty in her voice cracked something in my chest. "Yeah, baby. We're going to get through this. I promise."

I'd never meant anything more in my entire life. No matter what happened tomorrow or next week or in the next decade, Becca was mine. Mine to protect, mine to adore, mine to love.

And I'd do whatever it took to keep her.

CHAPTER 31

BEX

My hands trembled as the car turned down my grandparents' street. I'd sent them and my mother a quick text that I'd be home tonight, and I'd rehearsed the cover story in my head and out loud with Court several times.

Thinking of Court had me pressing my fingers to my lips. I could swear they still tingled from when he'd kissed me before I'd left him at the airport.

Just in case Eric was extra-suspicious, Rook had come up with the plan to deliver me quietly to the airport an hour before my "flight" was scheduled to arrive. Obviously I wasn't on said flight, but Ash had worked his magic and made it look like I was. I'd ordered a private car from the service my grandparents always used to take me home.

My stomach had started knotting the second I'd left Court's side and disappeared into the travelers in the airport, wheeling a suitcase filled with the stuff I'd taken to the hotel only a few nights before. Well, all of my stuff plus Court's hoodie, which I'd stolen.

So much had changed in such a short amount of time, and sitting alone in the car gave me nothing to do but remember and think.

Remember all the ways Court had fucked me through the night and morning.

Remember the desperate way he'd kissed me, his eyes promising that if I said the word, he'd take me and run.

Remember the way his eyes seemed to glow when he told me he loved me.

And think about what the hell I'd gotten myself into.

I'd texted Eric when I'd gotten into the car, but he'd been oddly silent. I wasn't sure if that was a good thing or a bad thing.

I was exhausted; I'd barely slept the night before, thanks to Court. Okay, thanks to me, too. Now that I knew what it was like to be with him, I couldn't imagine going back. I'd spent two nights in his arms, and I'd need at least two *lifetimes* with him before I'd get enough.

It was taking everything in me not to call Court now. I needed to hear his voice, but the burner phone that Bishop had given me to contact them was stowed safely in the lining of my suitcase. I thought it was overkill, but the guys all seemed to think it was necessary.

As the car turned up the half-circle drive, I peered at my grandparents' estate with trepidation. I loved their house. It had always felt like home to me, but at that moment, all I wanted was Court and our room at the hotel.

The driver put the car in park, and I waited for him to come around and open my door. I slid off the bench seat and stood up as he moved to the trunk and pulled out my bags.

"Thank you," I murmured.

"Anything else, miss?" the driver, an older gentleman with kind eyes and white hair, asked.

I shook my head. "No, thank you."

"Goodnight, miss."

"Goodnight." I started up the stairs, pulling out my keys as I went. Exhaustion settled into my bones. I didn't have long to get myself together before Eric would be picking me up for dinner. Hopefully I'd have enough time to call Court and check in.

Huh. I was a girl with a boyfriend to check in with.

For some reason, that put a soft grin on my face as I pushed open the front door.

I heard voices, and my smile grew as I heard my grandfather's deep baritone laugh. I wheeled my suitcase into the foyer coat closet to grab later. Right now, I wanted to see the two people who always made me feel cherished and loved.

"Mémé? Papa?" I called, heading for the parlor room that they tended to use when entertaining guests. I rounded the corner… and froze in the stained-glass archway to the room.

Eric was sitting on the settee across from Mémé while Papa was at the wet bar, pouring himself a bourbon.

"Can I get you one, Eric?" he offered, holding up a crystal decanter.

"No, thank you, sir," Eric refused, the epitome of politeness. He turned and spotted me, his eyes lighting up as he stood. "Welcome home, Bex."

Mémé turned to me, her eyes bright. "Darling, why didn't you tell us that you were dating such a fine young man?"

"Indeed," Papa added with a smile that reminded me of Mom. "Did you get everything sorted back at your school?"

I managed a nod, my throat dry. Panic made my stomach clench and my palms sweat.

Mémé made a soft sound of annoyance. "Absolutely absurd that you had to traipse halfway around the world in this day and age. I've half a mind to call your headmaster and remind him of just who provided the grant for the new science lab last year."

"Not a bad idea, my love," Papa told her with a serious nod.

"No," I blurted out. "It was my mistake. I, uh, was so preoccupied with leaving school and Mom's heart attack that I missed the form. It was my fault."

Mémé frowned but sat back in her seat. "Very well. Eric tells us that the two of you have big plans."

"It's just dinner," I mumbled.

Eric flashed me a winning grin. "I might have another surprise up my sleeve, love."

My heart palpitated as Mémé all but giggled. Papa came to stand beside her chair and rested a hand on her shoulder. The look that flashed between them was the kind of thing I'd always wanted for myself.

"Ah, to be young and in love," Mémé said in a wistful tone.

Panic washed through me like fire. "We've barely known each other a week."

Papa chuckled. "Oh, *ma fille*. You know your grandmother." He looked down, utter adoration on his face. "She just wants you to be as happy as we've been."

Mémé beamed at him before looking at me. "You two go on. Don't let us keep you."

"It was truly a pleasure to meet you both," Eric told them, turning to shake Papa's hand and kiss the back of Mémé's.

"No, darling, the pleasure was all ours," Mémé replied, beaming at him. "I'm so glad you stopped in to introduce yourself. Our granddaughters are entirely too secretive about their romances."

Papa gave a nod of agreement. "But we'll see you at Ines's birthday celebration in a few nights."

"Yes, sir. I'm delighted to be invited to such a momentous event, even if I'm not convinced the age is true." Eric winked at Mémé, and I felt sick.

Mémé waved a dismissive hand, unable to hide her delight. "Oh, shush. You do wonders for an old woman's heart." She looked at me and winked. "This one's a keeper, Rebecca. Charm, looks, *and* brains? Don't let him go."

"It's me who won't be letting your granddaughter go," Eric whispered conspiratorially. "Now that I've found her, I'd be a fool to lose her. But I'm sure I don't have to tell you just how spectacular she is."

"No, you don't." Papa gave me a warm smile that did little to thaw my insides. His expression turned into one of concern. "Are you all right, sweet girl? You look a little pale."

Probably because I felt like I was going to have a stroke. I wanted Eric as far away from my family as possible.

"Darling?" Eric crossed the room to me, his hands coming up to frame my face. It was all I could do not to flinch and jerk away. "Are you all right?" The question seemed genuine enough—maybe I was imagining the hard glint in his eyes.

"Just tired," I finally answered, giving him a weak smile as I pressed a hand to my stomach. "And famished. I didn't eat on the plane. I was afraid to spoil our dinner."

Looking satisfied, Eric leaned in and kissed my forehead. "Then we should get you some food. Can't have you wasting away on me now, can I?"

I gave a small shake of my head, my smile fading as Eric studied me, his gaze scrutinizing before he seemed to shake himself out of whatever thoughts he was having. He took my hand and pulled me from the room.

"I've already reserved a table at Aubergine as you requested," he told me, ushering me through the house and toward the front door. "We have so much to discuss."

"We do?" I was unable to keep the surprise from my voice.

Eric spun, looming over me as he squeezed my fingers. "We do, my love. Missing you these last few days brought some things into perspective for me."

"I was only gone a couple of days," I pointed out, barely able to resist the urge to back away.

His gray eyes were bright, almost manic, as he looked at me. He let out a heavy breath. "Let's discuss this while we eat. I can't have my girl withering away."

I wasn't *his* girl.

I was Court's girl. Always had been.

Always would be.

Even if, for the rest of the night, I had to pretend I'd fallen for a monster.

Eric pressed a possessive hand to my back and guided me out into the night.

CHAPTER 32

BEX

Aubergine was just as packed as the first night we'd gone there, but unlike that time, we were shown to a private booth in the very back corner of the restaurant. The lighting was dimmer back here, and when Eric indicated for me to slide into the booth, my stomach gave an uncomfortable flip.

Taking a deep breath, I slid across the bench and waited for him to join me. He boxed me in against the wall.

He took the menus from the hostess but didn't bother handing me one. Once the hostess turned and left, he shifted to look at me, once again grabbing my fingers. "I've missed you."

"I was gone barely three days," I pointed out.

His brow furrowed. "Bex, I think you misunderstand my intentions here, so let me be perfectly plain. I see a future with you."

"Oh. Uh, okay." I wasn't sure what to say, because I knew I had no future with him. I was playing a game of cat and mouse, and I wasn't sure if I was the cat or the mouse.

Right now, I felt like the mouse.

His thumb stroked the back of my hand. "I know this must seem sudden, but I'm not a man who entertains casual relationships, and this is the first time in my life that I've found a woman who is just like me. Who won't judge me. A woman who can help me."

My throat and mouth went dry.

"I never expected to find someone like you," he went on. "Someone who can understand my business while helping me build connections. Do you see it? The power we could have?"

Shit. I might've oversold my connections to General Woods and Kent Westford. "I think you're overestimating my reach. I grew up knowing these people, but that doesn't mean we're friends."

"You and I both know friendship is a fairy tale sold to people who can't afford to face the realities of life. Everything is a transaction, and the currency is information. Connections." He gave me a wolfish smile that made my insides shiver.

"Eric, I'm not entirely sure what you're getting at," I admitted.

"Bex, I need to know if you feel the way that I do. That we could truly be something." His expression was so earnest that I almost forgot what a psychopath he was.

I rolled my bottom lip between my teeth, considering how to respond. Unless I wanted to blow everything for the guys, I couldn't shut him down outright. No, I had to play the damn game.

Besides, there was also the very uncomfortable reminder that his previous girlfriends hadn't fared so well.

"Of course I want that," I agreed.

A smile lit his face. "I was hoping you'd say that. I'd like you to attend the auction with me. Not just as my date, but as my partner."

"P-partner?" I echoed.

He nodded. "Yes. With the people who will be in attendance, I think you and I presenting a united front will be just the push I need to get Westford to see me as someone to rely on."

"Rely on." It seemed all I was capable of was parroting his words back, but my brain was struggling to connect the dots.

"My company does well, but I want to expand. I've struggled to get an audience with Westford, and your connection to him is exactly the angle I've been looking for," Eric explained, like the answer was so obvious. "Considering all the ports I have access to, it will be extremely lucrative for him and me to combine our reach."

I couldn't find words.

Grinning, he leaned in and kissed the tip of my nose. "You and I will be unstoppable, don't you agree?"

I nodded slowly. "Absolutely." I could do this. I could fake being supportive for a few more days. "Have they finally decided on a location for the auction then?"

His shoulders straightened. "They have, and I'm happy to say they've taken my suggestions into account."

"That's great!" I gave a weak laugh. "Where will it be?"

He gave me an odd look. "Only members receive that information an hour prior to the event's start."

"Right. Of course," I mumbled.

"Don't worry, my love, you will be at my side when it happens. That's why it's so imperative I have you nearby," he finished as the waiter approached.

"Good evening. My name is Jacques, and I'll be serving you this evening," he greeted with an ultra-white smile. With artfully arranged blond hair and sparkling brown eyes, he looked like a frat somewhere was missing a brother. "Would you like to hear the chef's specials of the evening?"

I opened my mouth to reply, but Eric shut me down. "No. We'll both have the beef Wellington. Bring a bottle of Cristal and a bottle of flat water. That will be all." He flashed the waiter a hard look until he turned and left.

"Um," I started, uncertain, "I can order for myself."

"It's more efficient this way," Eric dismissed. "Besides, I enjoy taking care of you, and I plan to do so for the rest of our lives."

Tiny alarm bells went off in the back of my head.

"Eric, I can take care of myself," I said, trying to be careful with my tone and words. It felt like I was walking on eggshells laid over a minefield.

"But you won't have to," he replied with an indifferent shrug. "It's convenient that you've already finished school. Such a clever girl."

"I'm going back to California to go to college," I told him.

"There's no need. If you truly insist on continuing your education, I have connections at the Sorbonne, but with the amount of travel we'll be doing—"

"What?" I couldn't hold in the note of incredulity.

He shot me a confused look. "Darling, one of the many requirements of my job is that I travel and routinely inspect ports, warehouses, and more sensitive locations for various shipments. I prefer a hands-on approach to business, and since you'll be at my side, attending a regular university will be impossible."

I leaned as far away from him as I could. "Eric—"

He gave a rueful chuckle and rubbed the back of his neck. "I'm mucking this up, aren't I, darling? Maybe I should've started off with a more specific question." When he reached into his pocket, I wasn't sure what to expect.

It sure as hell wasn't a ring box.

"Eric." I choked on his name as he pried the lid up, revealing a sparkling princess-cut diamond that had to be at least five carats, surrounded by a ring of sapphires.

"I know this is sudden for most people, but I've learned that if there's something I want, then I have to take it." He looked me in the eyes. "Rebecca Whittier, will you marry me?"

No.

I wanted to say it. Hell, I wanted to *scream* it. To close the lid and hurl the box away from the table.

"It's too soon," was all I could manage to squeak out.

He laughed, the sound warm and inviting. "I know we've known each other for less than two weeks, but I've already shared more details of my life with you than anyone else. You *understand*, Bex. We fit."

Love wasn't puzzle pieces fitting neatly into perfect shapes. It was messy and chaotic, passionate and consuming.

"I won't lose you," he finished, his tone taking on a harder edge that caught my attention.

My gaze snapped up to meet his, and I swallowed hard at what I saw. He looked possessed. Like a child who'd just been given a toy he'd always wanted and would fight to keep.

I was the toy. I was a thing for him to own. To be his.

The irony wasn't lost on me that, forty-eight hours earlier, I'd let myself become someone else's possession. I'd told Court I was his—that every piece of me belonged to him.

The difference was, I knew Court would treat me like someone to be cherished and protected. Eric? Yeah, he looked like he'd put me in a glass case on a shelf and occasionally bring me out to play with when the mood struck.

I wanted to say no. I *needed* to say no… but then I thought of the auction. Of the girls and women who were likely suffering, people I could help if I just played along for a few more days. That's all we needed—a few more days, then it would be over.

"Bex." His hand tightened around mine, squeezing my fingers together until the joints popped.

I couldn't hide my wince. "You're hurting my hand."

"We're made for each other," he went on, ignoring the fact that he was grinding my bones together. "Surely you see that."

I looked up, took a deep breath… and spotted a red light blinking in a corner of the ceiling.

There were security cameras in here. Cameras that the guys had hacked. There was a good chance that Court was watching us right now. The hand Eric was strangling was under the table between us, but I knew Court would see any sign of distress and come running. He'd blow up the entire operation for me.

Then it would all be for nothing, and I couldn't be the reason innocent people were hurt.

"You caught me off guard," I whispered, keeping my tone light and soft. "I wasn't expecting a proposal tonight."

Eric frowned. "I know it *is* a bit sudden."

A bit? I wanted to laugh in his face. The guy was freaking delusional. And dangerous.

"You're right," I said. "We haven't known each other long, but I can already tell how special you are. This is like a fairy tale. I never expected to find my own Prince Charming."

He grinned, relaxing the crushing grip on my hand. "And I never expected to find my princess, but here we are. And I want us to spend the rest of our lives together."

"Me, too," I demurred after a beat, lowering my lashes and hoping he'd see the expression as bashful and not I'm-going-to-throw-up-if-I-look-at-you-much-longer. I drew in a breath, centering myself, before I lifted my eyes. "Of course I'll marry you."

"Oh, my love," he breathed, letting me go so he could take the ring from the box and slide it onto my finger. He leaned in and pressed his mouth to mine before I had a chance to come up with an excuse.

Oh, shit. Oh, shit.

Please don't let Court be watching right this second. He'd lose his shit. He'd storm in here and probably kill Eric.

"I'm going to make you so happy," Eric vowed, pressing another kiss to the corner of my mouth.

I forced a smile onto my face as he drew back, and the waiter appeared with our drinks. As soon as my champagne was poured, I grabbed the glass.

"A toast," Eric declared, lifting his flute. "To our future. May we get everything that we deserve."

My smile turned more genuine as I agreed whole-heartedly with his toast and clinked our glasses.

I absolutely hoped Eric got everything he deserved.

Caught by the police, a lengthy prison sentence, and a life stuck in a box sounded exactly like what my temporary *fiancé* so richly deserved, and I was more than happy to help him get it.

CHAPTER 33

BEX

"This isn't the way to my house," I said as Eric turned another corner. I'd managed to make it through dinner without any missteps.

"I know." He held my hand over the console and raised my fingers to his lips. "I planned a celebration for us tonight. I reserved a special room for us at Westford Towers."

I swung my head to gape at him. Westford Towers was one of the most exclusive, expensive hotel chains the Westford family owned. Judging by the heat in his gaze and the way his lips lingered on my skin, it didn't take a genius to guess the type of celebration he had planned.

"Eric, I can't," I said, shaking my head.

"Why not?" His tone took on that cool edge that gave me the impression he wasn't happy.

"I…" Shit, how did I get out of this? "I'm tired, and it's been such a long day."

He let out an incredulous snort. "How often do you get engaged, Bex? We need to celebrate. I promise you won't be too tired for what I have planned."

I tried pulling my hand away, but he wouldn't let go. "Eric."

"Bex," he snapped, stopping at a red light and scowling at me. "I think I've been pretty fucking understanding."

I jerked back like he'd hit me, stunned by the rage in his eyes.

"You just up and left," he snarled, the transition from calm to furious giving me whiplash. "You didn't tell me where you were. I had no idea if you were hurt or sick. I almost missed my meeting in Brussels!"

"I'm sorry," I murmured, trying to get him to calm down. "I didn't think it mattered—"

He slammed a hand on the steering wheel. "You didn't think *I* mattered?" He practically roared the question.

"I didn't say that—"

He grabbed my wrist, hard. "You won't do that again, Rebecca. I won't stand for it."

Fear licked up my chest as I watched him unravel in front of me. "Eric, please."

He sneered, stomping on the gas when the light turned green. The car surged forward, the back tires chirping in protest as they struggled to find purchase on the asphalt.

My heart pounded in my chest. "You're scaring me."

"You scared *me*, so I suppose we're even," he hissed. "You're my fiancée. You'll be *my wife*. I won't have you running around like some common whore."

Whoa. *What?* Where the hell had that come from?

"Eric, stop," I ordered, trying to sound like I wasn't on the verge of a panic attack as he weaved in and out of traffic like a madman.

"I think it's time we got a few things straight, darling," he growled. "You will *not* disappear again, or you won't like the consequences."

I wasn't sure if I was supposed to respond or not, but when he squeezed my wrist harder, I gasped out, "I won't. I promise."

He gave a curt nod and slammed on the breaks as another light turned red. The car skidded to a stop. "I gave you a stunning diamond —do you know how much it's worth? And you don't want to show your appreciation?"

Was he actually insinuating that I owed him sex as a thanks for a ring I never asked for? No wonder women ran from him.

Unfortunately, running away wasn't an option for me as he hit the gas the second the light turned green. I pressed myself against my seatback, praying we wouldn't crash.

"You don't understand," I tried again. "It's not that I don't want to—"

He let out a scoff. "Don't fucking lie to me."

"I've never done this!" I shouted, screwing my eyes shut as he narrowly missed a woman stepping into a crosswalk. "I've never… I'm a virgin."

Miraculously, his foot came off the gas.

"What?" he asked, sounding curious.

I pried one eye open and saw him staring at me. "I've never… I've never had sex."

He pulled the car over to the shoulder. "You've *never*…"

I shook my head, letting the fear knotting in my chest seep out in the form of tears. My eyes welled up. "I never had time for a boyfriend in school," I whispered, letting the truth mingle with the lie. "And my grandmother always said how special it was to wait."

"You're pure," he breathed, his eyes round with wonder. Like I'd announced I was an angel or a unicorn. "Of course you are."

"I don't want to lose my virginity in a cold hotel room, on a mattress that's been shared by so many other people," I added, dropping my gaze. "I want it to be special. Magical."

Not a lie. It was what I'd wanted. And my first time had definitely been special and memorable. Maybe not as magical as romance novels made it sound, but I wouldn't change it for anything because of *who* I'd been with, not where we'd been.

"Of course," Eric agreed, touching my chin and lifting my face. "My sweet, beautiful girl. Of *course* you're innocent. Like you knew waiting for me was exactly what we'd both need."

I nodded and expelled a breath. "Eric, I want our first time to be perfect. It's the start of the rest of our lives. And while there's a part of me that wants to wait until we're married—" insert gagging noises *here* "—I have a feeling I won't be able to wait." I let out a breathy chuckle.

Eric's eyes practically glowed with animalistic pleasure. "I understand completely, my love."

"What about after the auction?" I suggested with a bright smile. "We'll have so many reasons to celebrate that night... Could we go back to *your* place? Not a hotel?"

He leaned in, pressing a kiss to my lips. "Absolutely, dove."

I swallowed down a wave of bile at the feel of his dry lips on mine. "You're not angry with me? I know I was wrong, running away from you, but I was just so... overwhelmed. I was scared of how deeply I felt for you." I batted my lashes, playing up the innocent virgin act.

And because Eric was a narcissistic chauvinist, he ate it up.

He wrapped a hand around the back of my neck and pulled our foreheads together as we shared the same air.

Don't throw up, I mentally ordered myself. My skin felt like a thousand ants were crawling over it wherever he touched me.

"I understand completely," he said, his tone now reverent, with no trace of the irrational rage from moments earlier. "I love you."

He *loved* me? He barely *knew* me. And seconds ago, I was pretty sure he'd wanted to kill me. Eric was dangerously unstable. It was like playing tag with a rabid wolf.

I cleared my throat. "I know you do. I feel the same way."

My heart wouldn't let me say *I love you* back to him. The words got caught in my throat.

"I'll take you home," he murmured.

I nodded. "Thank you. Mémé's party is in two days. I have to find a dress. I was going to ask Cami to go shopping with me tomorrow."

"I'll speak with Alex. Perhaps we can all go out to lunch? I'd love to see the dress you select."

"Sure," I replied, even though I hated the idea. But lunch with his brother and my cousin would give us a buffer.

He gave me another kiss that I barely returned before he withdrew and focused his attention on driving back to my house.

On the way home, I sat back and listened to him talk. He told me a bunch of details about himself and growing up that didn't seem relevant to the auction, but I mentally filed them away just in case. Whenever he asked about me, I gently turned the conversation back to his favorite topic—himself.

How had I missed how self-absorbed he was?

By the time he pulled into my grandparents' driveway, I was exhausted and just wanted to sleep. I hadn't had a chance to call Court before we'd left, so who knew what he was thinking by now? Probably the worst.

Eric parked the car and slid an arm around me, angling me toward him. "I'm so happy that you're mine."

Everything inside me rebelled at his statement. I *wasn't* his. Never would be.

But I grinned. "I am. I'll let you know where Cami and I decide to go shopping so you and Alex can meet us nearby."

"Perfect." He leaned in to kiss me, and I let it happen even as I felt nothing. How had I once been excited to have this guy's lips on mine?

It made me want Court all the more. I missed the way he kissed me—like he couldn't get enough. I felt safe with him. It just felt right.

Eric pinched my chin. "You're distracted," he accused.

"I'm sorry," I replied instantly. "I'm so tired, and it's been a lot of excitement for one day."

He studied me carefully before letting me go with a thin smile. "Of course. You should go inside and rest. I'll see you tomorrow."

"Tomorrow," I echoed as I got out of the car. I smothered the urge to run to the front door, instead taking my time and pausing to blow a kiss at Eric before going in.

Once inside, I slumped against the door. The ticking of the clock in the hall was nearly drowned out by the sound of the blood rushing through my ears.

I'd done it. I'd survived.

I looked down and sighed.

I'd also gotten engaged.

The diamond sparkled in the overhead lights as the clock chimed, striking eleven o'clock. My grandparents were long asleep. If Mom was home, she probably was, too, which meant I was alone.

I hated it.

I opened the hall closet and noticed my suitcase was gone. One of the staff likely took it upstairs. I shrugged out of my coat and hung it up before locking up and heading for the large staircase.

Trudging up, I reviewed everything that had happened tonight.

Mémé's birthday celebration was in two nights. The auction was slated to happen two nights after that.

So, in five nights' time, I'd be back in Court's arms.

Five more sleeps, my brain whispered, reminding me of when I was little and that was how I'd measured time. Exhaustion pulled at my bones. I needed a shower and to talk to Court before going to bed. And I needed to text Cami to find out if she was free to shop for dresses.

My bedroom was at the end of the hall, and I pushed it open with a yawn. After closing the door behind me, I kicked off my heels with a groan and hit the light switch, bathing the room in a soft yellow glow that illuminated the person on my bed.

I gasped as Court stood up, my eyes drinking him in even as I wondered if I was dreaming.

"Are you okay?" His voice was low, tight with concern.

"You're really here?" I whispered, still stunned.

He crossed the room. "Becca, are you all right? Did he do anything?"

My hands landed on his chest, feeling the hard muscles under his Henley. The leather scent of his jacket mingled with the warmth of his cologne. "Why are you here?"

He gave me an *are you serious* look before his hands gripped my shoulders. "Did you think I wouldn't be?"

"Yes?"

A corner of his mouth curved. "Baby, you honestly think I could go back to not sleeping next to you after the last two nights?" He shook his head. "Fuck, no. It's you and me. If that means I have to sneak into your house every goddamn night until this is over, I will."

Tears pricked my eyes. "I really love that answer."

"Good." He chuckled.

"Have you been waiting the whole time?"

"No, I got here about ten minutes ago. I followed you to the restaurant, and then I had to run an errand for Trick." He frowned. "Rook and Bishop kept an eye on you from the security feeds, and Bishop followed you home."

I'd known they wouldn't leave me unprotected, but hearing him confirm it made my heart give a happy *thump*.

And the fact that Rook and Bishop were the ones watching my proposal explained why Court hadn't busted into Aubergine and killed Eric on the spot.

He leaned forward. "Now can you please answer my question before I lose my shit? Are you okay?"

"I'm perfect now," I breathed, meaning it. This was what my heart needed. To see Court. To be with Court.

"He didn't do anything?" he pressed.

I shook my head, still a little dazed that he was actually freaking here.

He sighed, visibly relaxing as his hands slid down my arms to take my hands. And then he froze. "Becca?"

Oh, yeah. Shit.

I followed his gaze down to where his thumb hovered over the engagement ring.

"What the *fuck*?" His horrified gaze jerked back to my face.

I winced. "Okay, so maybe *something* happened tonight."

CHAPTER 34

BEX

"Explain," Court demanded, his voice a dangerous growl that really shouldn't turn me on as much as it did. His dark eyes glittered with fury.

"Eric asked me to marry him," I replied with a shrug, trying to downplay it. "I said yes."

"What the—"

I pressed a hand over his mouth. "Court, I didn't really say yes. I only agreed so he wouldn't think anything was wrong. I couldn't exactly say, 'the only reason I'm here is because I'm spying on you for my friends.'"

His jaw clenched, and I worried he might break some teeth. He looked up at the ceiling, and I wondered if he was silently counting to ten. Finally he turned his gaze back to me. "Take that thing off."

My brows lifted, but I tugged the ring off my finger and set it on top of the dresser near the door.

Court exhaled slowly. "I fucking hate this."

"I know," I murmured, stepping into him and wrapping my arms around his waist. My head fit perfectly beneath his chin, and I could feel his heart beating against my cheek.

His arms came around me as he nuzzled the top of my head. "But you're okay?"

I nodded. "I'm okay." Then I wrinkled my nose. "I could definitely use a shower, though. Hanging out with Eric makes me feel gross."

Probably best not to mention I wanted to scrub away his touch and possibly create some sort of bleach-based lip balm.

"Okay. Let's get you in the shower then," Court agreed and kissed the top of my head. "Then you can tell me what's going on before we get some sleep."

"I can't believe you're really staying," I admitted. We'd gone from zero to a million in the blink of an eye. Sometimes it was still hard to believe.

He gave me an odd look before casting his gaze across the room to where a black duffel sat beside my desk. Hope fluttered in my chest as he took my face in his hands. "I'm not going anywhere, baby. If I can't be with you during the day, I'm damn sure going to be with you all night long."

Heat unfurled low in my belly at his words, and I wordlessly pulled away to walk toward my attached bathroom. As I went, I started stripping off my clothes, starting with my shirt.

I heard his sharp intake of breath as I dropped the top on the floor and reached behind myself to undo my bra. I shimmied out of my skirt and kicked it aside before looking back over my bare shoulder at him.

"Coming?" I asked, my voice sultry and low.

"Fuck yes," he breathed, snapping out of his daze and stalking after me, shedding his jacket as he went.

My bare feet hit the cool tiles, and Court was immediately behind me, kicking the door shut and crowding me against the edge of the counter. I looked at our reflection in the mirror and smiled as he slipped his arms around my waist.

One hand reached up to play with my bare breast and rolled a nipple through dexterous fingers as his other hand slipped into my panties. He groaned when he touched my center, toying with my clit as his mouth kissed a path from my shoulder to my jaw.

I leaned against him, widening my stance to give him room to work.

He worked a finger into my core with shallow thrusts, warming my body up. "Fuck, you're so tight," he murmured. He changed the angle of his hand and added a second finger, hitting me deeper.

My knees started to tremble, and I reached out for the counter to steady myself.

He pinched my nipple, the tiny bite of pain making me gasp.

His chest rumbled as he chuckled. "I love that sound." His fingers dipped in and out of me languidly, the pressure building between my legs but not reaching what I needed to come.

"Court," I whined, trying to rock my hips and give myself the friction I so desperately wanted.

He nipped my earlobe. "Relax, baby girl. Let me take care of you."

I turned my head, needing to feel his lips on mine. As soon as our mouths touched, I parted my lips to let his tongue sweep in. I moaned into his mouth as his thumb rubbed tight circles around my clit.

My legs trembled, my knees giving out as my climax crested, washing over me like a wave in the ocean. My hands braced against the counter, holding up my weight as I bit my lip to keep from crying out.

The last thing I needed was my mom or grandparents coming to check on me.

Court worked me through my orgasm, gently stroking between my legs and occasionally brushing his thumb over my sensitive clit. Each time he did, a shudder rippled down my spine.

He gave me a single kiss between my shoulder blades and then turned me in his arms. He shoved my underwear down to my ankles and helped me sit on the counter. I flinched as the cold stone met my bare ass.

"You're too dressed," I told him with a pout. His dark-wash jeans and black shirt were molded to him like a second skin. He even still wore a pair of black boots. "But I am feeling the whole tall, dark, and sexy vibe you've got going on," I added, licking my lips.

He flashed me a wink before turning to the shower and starting the water for me.

The house was old, but the plumbing was new, and it wasn't long before the bathroom filled with steam. After testing the water with his hand, Court turned back to me. His gaze heated as it raked down my naked body, and I couldn't help but give him a sassy little smirk and push my boobs out a bit.

"Shower," he ordered, and I wasn't gonna lie—the bite to his tone sent a delicious shiver down my spine.

I slipped off the edge of the counter and intentionally brushed against him as I stepped into the shower. The heat wrapped around my body like a hug as the spray beat down on my head. I went to pull the glass door shut, but Court caught it. He stepped inside, somehow having managed to strip off his clothes in record time.

I blinked water out of my eyes as he filled the space, pressing my back into the tiles as he kissed me hard. His thick cock pushed against my stomach as he devoured me. His hands were everywhere—holding my face, then playing with my breasts before sliding down to grab my ass.

Court groaned. "Fuck, I love your ass, Becca." His fingers delved between my cheeks and prodded at my back entrance. "I can't wait to fuck you here." Using the water sluicing down my body, he eased a finger through the tight ring of muscle.

I grabbed his arms as my eyes fluttered shut, the sensations over-whelmingly forbidden and decadent at the same time. My head dropped back against the tiles as he stretched me open with a second finger.

His lips found the curve where my neck met my shoulder, his teeth nipping before he sucked on the spot. After a beat, he tore his mouth away with a snarl. "Fuck."

"What?" I gasped, my eyes snapping open.

His lips pressed into a tight, annoyed line. "I can't mark you."

Yeah, explaining hickeys to Eric might get a little complicated.

"Then mark me where he can't see." I reached between us, wrapping my hand around his length and giving it a firm stroke. "Where he'll never touch me." I kissed the underside of his jaw, smiling to myself when a shudder rippled through his massive frame. "I'm yours, Court. Remind me what that feels like."

He quirked an eyebrow. "Forgot already?"

I shot him what I hoped was a coy smirk.

His eyes flashed with a dangerous heat a moment before he grabbed my legs and lifted me like I weighed nothing more than a feather. He butterflied my legs open, his cock notching at my entrance as he pinned me to the wall with his weight.

"Yes," I hissed, desperately needing him between my legs and buried inside me.

"Mine," he snapped, his hips driving forward and impaling me on his cock.

I dropped my head to his shoulder and bit him to avoid screaming in pleasure and waking up the house.

He grunted as he pulled out and thrust back in. "That's my girl. Mark me, Becca. Show the fucking world who I belong to." His groin collided with mine, somehow grinding against my clit with each pump.

Lightning coiled low in my belly, the shower hammering us with water from above. My chest ached as my release built, the pressure inside me close to detonating as he pounded into me, his long cock hitting at just the right angle, just the perfect spot, to have starbursts dancing across my vision.

"Oh, God," I whimpered, my pussy contracting around him. "I can't... I need to—"

"Come for me," he demanded, snapping his hips.

It was like a chain reaction. With his dick hitting inside me and his groin rubbing against my clit, I detonated like a damn bomb. I bit into his shoulder again as my orgasm ripped through me, decimating every coherent thought and even my ability to breathe.

Court rode me through my climax, never letting up until I was breathless and boneless. He pulled out of me, still hard.

"On your knees, baby," he ordered.

My knees had pretty much turned to jelly, so it was an easy command to obey. I sank down in front of him as he turned us, blocking the stream of the shower with his back as he loomed over me. His hand touched my jaw. "Open."

Like it was on a hinge that he had total control of, my mouth opened, and I watched as he gripped his cock and gave it several rough tugs. He worked himself from root to tip, the corded muscles of his forearm, abs, and chest flexing as his head tipped back in pleasure. As he breathed, the phoenix on his ribs rippled like a living thing.

The first spurt of cum on my cheek made me flinch. I closed my eyes, letting him paint my face and chest with his release. Unable to stop myself, I darted my tongue out to taste him on my lips, savoring the salty essence of Court.

Blunt fingers smeared his cum over my skin before it was scooped up and pushed into my mouth. I opened my eyes, meeting his gaze as I sucked his fingers clean. He repeated the process on my chest, gathering his release and feeding it to me. His hot gaze watched me, a mix of awed and ravenous.

When he was satisfied, he pulled me up, supporting most of my weight as he kissed me slowly. I melted against him, sated and happy.

All the stress seemed to wash away, and neither of us spoke while Court maneuvered me in the shower and washed and conditioned my hair before squirting strawberry-scented body wash onto my loofah and cleaning my body. I leaned against his chest, feeling him hardening at my back, but he seemed to ignore it as he focused on cleaning me.

After he was done, he shut off the water and wrapped me in a fluffy towel before securing one haphazardly around his waist and blocking my second favorite part of his anatomy from view.

He snorted a laugh. "Which part gets first place?"

I blinked and realized I'd spoken that last thought aloud. Hopefully he'd chalk up my pink cheeks to the heat in the bathroom. "Uh, your smiles."

"My smile?" His lips pulled up into a confused sort of grin that reminded me of the boy next door.

I shook my head. "Your *smiles*, plural."

"I have more than one smile?"

"You have five smiles," I replied. "One when you're really happy.

One when something makes you laugh. One when you see something cute, and one when you think no one's looking."

He stared at me and then swallowed. "That's only four."

"My favorite is the one I don't see that much," I admitted.

His head tilted, a soft smile forming on his lips as he studied me. It made his eyes sparkle in a way that caught my breath.

"That one," I whispered, touching his lips. "That's my favorite smile. It's the one you get when you look at me. I've missed it."

Understanding lit his eyes, and he pulled me against him, wrapping me up in a hug that I never, ever wanted to end.

CHAPTER 35

BEX

The early morning sun slanted through my curtains. I blinked into consciousness, feeling utterly relaxed and content as I snuggled deeper under my sheets.

"Hey," I murmured, spotting Court's naked back across from me. He'd pulled on a loose pair of black gym shorts and seemed to be busy looking at the books on my shelves.

Oh, shit.

"Uh…" I pushed myself up on one arm, wrapping the sheets around my chest.

Court turned, and I wanted to fall through the bed when I spotted the book he was casually perusing.

"Court—"

He turned and gave me a look that would've disintegrated my underwear, if I'd had any on. The morning light framed him, casting a golden glow around his body. My mouth went dry as I looked over every inch of exposed, tanned skin.

"Becca, Becca," he murmured, closing the book and giving me a knowing look. "I gotta say, princess, I'm shocked you'd bring these books into your grandparents' home."

Screw it. I loved my books, and I'd own that shit.

"That's not even the kinkiest one," I told him.

His dark eyes lit up. "Really?" He dragged the word out with a grin.

I nodded.

He put the book back on the shelf before coming over and sitting beside me. He pushed my hair back and leaned in to kiss my shoulder. "So you have a thing for… what the hell was I even reading?"

I lifted my chin. "Merri Bright. She's freaking phenomenal. She writes omegaverse, but you were looking at her angel series."

His brows shot up. "Those were angels? Jesus, no wonder the earth is so screwed. All the angels are too busy having massive orgies to bother helping us mere mortals."

"Not how it works," I retorted lightly with a little scowl. "But what's wrong with an orgy?"

He gave me a look. "Baby, I'm gonna guess you've never actually seen an orgy."

"And you have?" I winced at the way his eyes glittered. "Never mind. Don't answer that. I heard the rumors."

"Which?" He looked genuinely curious and innocent until I noticed the glint in his eyes.

"Ugh." I grabbed a pillow from his side of the bed—because apparently we had *sides*—and hit him in the face. "You know exactly which rumors. And I'm not judging at all. I bet it was… nice," I finished lamely, my face heating.

"Nice?" Court echoed.

I let out a huffy breath. "Fine. I bet it was fucking amazing for whatever girl you and Linc had sandwiched between you."

He gave a noncommittal sound.

"All I'm saying is that I'll have to live out my menage and reverse harem fantasies through books, unless you're cool with sharing," I finished, unable to resist teasing him.

"Becca, I really need you to hear this," he said, his voice gravelly and serious. "There's no fucking way I'll spend my life sharing you. I'm too goddamn possessive, and we both know it. You're it for me."

"And you're it for me," I insisted, reaching for his hand. "It's a *fantasy*, Court. One that I am totally fine playing out in my dreams. I don't need anyone but you."

He leaned in, his forehead touching mine as our breaths mingled. He gave me a grin. "What other fantasies does your deviant mind have?"

I hesitated, feeling weird and vulnerable. "Are you making fun of me? I mean, I know I'm not experienced like you—"

He instantly sobered. "No. Becca, I'm not making fun of you. I'd never…" He exhaled hard. "Baby, I fucking love that I was your first, and I sure as shit plan on being your last." His hand came up to trace the slope of my shoulder, his fingertips grazing down my arm. "I just want to make sure you're getting what you need, and I don't want to push you."

"I don't *know* what I need," I admitted, still a little embarrassed. "But that doesn't mean I don't want to try things."

He gave a soft hum. "Such as?"

I bit my lip, pretty sure I was going to burst into flames and be incinerated on the spot.

Court tilted his head. "Okay, so we've already covered your threesome curiosity. Or foursome. Fivesome?"

I laughed a little. "It's off the table. But for the record, I'm not sure of any woman who isn't fictional being able to handle more than two dicks at a time, so my fantasy has always been limited to three people, including me."

His eyes glittered with mirth. "So you wouldn't object to toys?"

My breath caught.

"You know, in case I wanted to get a dildo to fill up your tight, little pussy while I'm fucking your throat?" His fingers ghosted across my neck.

I swallowed hard and shook my head. "Y-you want to do that?"

His gaze heated. "Sweetheart, the things I want to do to you are illegal in a lot of places." He pulled me toward him. The blankets and sheets tangled between us as I awkwardly straddled him. A hand grabbed my bare butt. "I can't wait to fuck this ass. As soon as we have the time, I'm going to start with a plug you'll wear all goddamn day. We'll work up to my cock fitting inside you."

Rubber bands seemed to wrap around my chest, constricting my air. "Seriously?"

The corner of his mouth pulled up. "Hell yes."

"What else?" I breathed, my gaze flicking to his lips.

He leaned in, kissing my jaw. "I think we've already established I have a thing for your ass, and I can't wait to see it red and hot from me spanking it."

I nodded with an appreciative moan, my hands coming up to loop around his shoulders. "Definitely interested in that."

He smiled against my skin. "So spanking is good. How do you feel about being tied up?"

"Is this the part where you tell me you have a St. Andrew's cross in your basement?" *Please say yes.*

He chuckled, the warm sound rolling between us. "No basement, but I do know of a few clubs with a private room I could reserve."

"Private room?" I squeaked.

He drew back. "Or public, if that's your thing."

The idea of people watching as Court tied me up and did unspeakable things sounded so sinfully perfect.

"Huh," he mused, giving a small nod. "My girl has a little bit of an exhibitionist in her."

"Is that... wrong?" I asked, once again hit by a wave of uncertainty.

He shook his head. "There is no right and wrong, Becca. Our relationship and how we interact in bed and out is ultimately up to us. If you want me to fuck you missionary style in the dark for the rest of our lives, I will. If you want me to strap you to a cross in the middle of a club so people can watch as I torture your sweet little body, then I'm game for that, too."

I squirmed on his lap, feeling exposed and sexy. "Yes, please."

"To which?" He arched a brow.

"The second one," I whispered, almost afraid to admit how much I wanted that. It felt like I was supposed to be embarrassed for wanting something so primal, so vulgar. Societal norms dictated that sex stay behind closed doors.

His hand came around to the back of my head, fisting my hair and tugging my neck back. I gasped around the bite of pain that licked up my scalp.

"Too much?" he asked, his voice like liquid chocolate.

"No," I gasped, the pain burning a path down my neck and spine before pooling between my thighs.

Court pulled my head back more, my chest arching. He swooped in and took a pebbled nipple between his lips, sucking it hard before biting it.

"Oh, fuck," I whimpered. I tried to grab his head, to make him turn his attention to my other needy peak, but he tugged my hair tighter. Tears blurred my vision for a second.

"No touching," he murmured. "Hands behind your back."

I was quick to obey, folding my arms behind my back and holding on to my wrists.

"Such a good girl," he rasped.

I blushed and fought a grin as heat unfurled in my chest. Who knew I got off on praise?

He kissed and licked a path between my breasts before nibbling on the other nipple. My breath caught as I clenched my teeth to keep from crying out.

"So fucking responsive," he said with an appreciative groan. "I can't wait until we're somewhere that you don't have to be quiet."

I panted, my head bobbing as I agreed. It was so hard to swallow the cries that desperately wanted to come out.

"Can you be quiet, baby?" He looked up at me, waited for me to nod. "Lie back and put your hands up. Hold on to the headboard."

I toppled backward off his lap, my arms shooting up and my fingers wrapping around the elaborate wooden spindles of my headboard. Clenching my teeth, I watched as Court peeled the sheets away from my body and tossed them aside.

He pushed my thighs open and stared hungrily between my legs until I started to squirm. Suddenly shy of him eye-fucking my pussy, I tried to close my legs.

"Don't move," he snapped, pushing my legs even wider as he lay between them. His broad shoulders wedged my thighs open, parting the lips of my sex.

"Court." I was going to combust if he didn't do something soon.

He leaned in, his nose right above my clit as he inhaled deeply. "God, this smell is everything." His finger traced my slit. "You're fucking soaked for me, baby. I wish you could see yourself the way I do, your pretty pink pussy all shiny."

The whimper I let out was almost inhuman. He kept dragging a finger around my pussy but refused to touch me where I needed him to. I opened my mouth to tell him to hurry the hell up before I died of whatever the female version of blue balls—*blue ovaries?*—was.

"Uh-uh," he told me. "You need to be quiet, remember?"

I pressed my lips together until they hurt, burying the need to demand he do something or beg him to fuck me into the mattress.

"You said spanking was okay, right?" He asked the question almost absently, a finger tracing a pattern on the inside of my left thigh as his face nuzzled my right.

Was I supposed to answer that? Roll over so he could slap my ass?

I was still trying to figure it out when his hand slapped my pussy.

A strangled sound vibrated in my throat as I worked to swallow it down while my hips jerked.

"Hmm," he mused, and that was all the warning I got before his hand came down again, this time on my clit.

The air whooshed from my lungs as my pussy clenched and my thighs trembled. My head spun as I tried to make sense of what I was feeling.

Pain? Not really.

Heat? Oh, yeah.

Court hummed as he rubbed his fingers against my clit, making my body jolt as the heat turned into a throb.

I squeezed my eyes shut, surrendering my body to his control, but I almost lost my vow of silence when his tongue pushed into me. My entire body trembled as his fingers worked my clit while his tongue rimmed my entrance and dipped back inside.

"So fucking delicious," he murmured before going back again.

The feel of his tongue and his fingers, my legs splayed impossibly wide as I gasped for air… it was too much. He gave my clit a firm pinch, rolling the sensitive nub between his thumb and finger, and I shattered.

Eyes closed, I hurtled through the abyss of my mind, my breaths coming in ruined, ragged pants through my nose as my back arched off the bed. Swallowing my pleasure was like trying to contain lightning in a bottle as my lungs screamed for oxygen.

I was still twitching, barely catching my breath, when Court straightened to kneel between my legs. I scarcely had time to realize what was happening when he thrust in, his wide cock tunneling inside me. The instant sensation of fullness stole my breath once more.

Court leaned over me, one hand braced on the bed as the other wrapped around my wrists, pinning me under him as he ruthlessly used my body.

It was freaking incredible.

I lost myself to the feel of him moving in me, his cock hitting every spot just right. He grabbed my thigh, pulling my knee closer to my chest. I gasped as he went even deeper.

A tsunami of pleasure was building in my center and rippling out through my limbs. My skin felt hot, too tight. Like I was going to burst apart at any second.

La petite mort.

Death by orgasm.

Every muscle in my body pulled taut, hovering at the edge of shattering. I clenched around his cock, and he swore softly under his breath. I opened my mouth, unable to stop the cry that welled deep in my soul.

Court's mouth sealed over mine, kissing me and swallowing the noises I made as I flew apart. He jerked inside me, and his warm release coated my walls.

When he was finished, he collapsed on me, letting his weight press me into the bed. I lowered my arms, wrapping them around him as his head rested on my chest. Our sweaty bodies stuck together.

I'd just opened my mouth to say something when my phone chimed next to my bed. I wanted to ignore it, but when it started ringing a moment later, I knew who it was. And if the way his body tightened was any indication, Court knew it, too.

"I have to answer him," I whispered, regret lacing my tone.

"I know." He sounded pissed and resigned. He pushed himself up and looked at me, watching as I grabbed my phone and answered Eric's call.

"Hey," I greeted, forcing as much enthusiasm into my tone as I could. I reached for Court, threading my fingers through his soft hair. He leaned into my touch, kissing the inside of my wrist.

"Good morning, my love," Eric returned, a smile in his voice. "I tried texting you, but you didn't answer."

Because you gave me less than a minute, you damn psycho.

"I was in the shower," I replied.

He gave an appreciative hum. "I can only imagine how gorgeous you look naked and wet."

I gritted my teeth. "Was there something you needed?"

"Only to let you know that I've spoken with Alex and Camille," he informed me. "I'll pick you up in thirty minutes. They'll meet us later so we can shop for your dress and then have lunch. I have an errand to run this morning, and I want you to come with me so we can spend more time together."

"Oh," was all I could manage. I'd been planning to call my cousin myself this morning to ask her about dress shopping, but apparently Eric was now the secretary of my social life.

"Bex? Is everything all right?" Suspicion gave his voice a hard edge.

"Yeah," I quickly assured him. "I'm just... not a morning person." I winced a bit at the lame lie.

"We'll stop for coffee," he cooed with a chuckle. "Anything for my girl."

Court, clearly hearing what he'd said, narrowed his eyes with a small hiss.

"Sounds good. I'll see you soon." Even as I spoke, all I could do was watch the guy who had my heart. I didn't really hear Eric's reply, and I quickly ended the call.

"You're not his anything," Court spat, looking furious.

"No, I'm not," I agreed, running my fingers through his dark hair.

His hand found the inside of my thigh and went higher until his fingers brushed my slit. I blushed, feeling his release trickling out of me, mixed with my own arousal. My eyes widened as he used his fingers to push our combined juices back into my pussy.

"Mine," he growled.

"Yours," I assured him, my heart full even as I resigned myself that I had to convince another man I was his for the next few days.

CHAPTER 36

BEX

"Bex!" Cami's face lit up when she saw me walking into the boutique alongside Eric.

I went to hug her, but Eric's hand tightened on mine, keeping me at his side.

Since he'd picked me up, we'd run a few errands for him. Well, he'd run errands. I'd gotten the simple pleasure of sitting in his car and waiting for him to return.

Slowing my pace, I matched his stride while walking to my cousin. I spotted Alex sitting in a chair near the dressing rooms, playing on his phone.

When I was close, Cami pulled me in for a hug, and Eric reluctantly let me go.

"Hi, Eric," Cami chirped, flashing him a warm smile.

He gave her a polite nod. "Pleasure to see you again, Camille."

Cami turned her attention to me. "Girl, I've already started pulling dresses for you. There's this stunning black Monique Visset gown with a low-cut back—"

"Are we attending a funeral?" Eric cut in with a sardonic chuckle. "Bex, you look amazing in yellow. Why not try that?"

Somehow it didn't seem like a suggestion, but I pushed a smile onto my lips and nodded with as much enthusiasm as I could fake. "Great idea, honey."

Eric practically preened at the term of endearment before pulling his own phone from his pocket and going to join his brother. Alex barely looked up as Eric sat, but I did notice him scoot away slightly.

"Yellow." Cami made a face. "Seriously?"

I touched her arm. "It's fine."

"You'll look like a freaking canary," she whined, rolling her eyes. "Besides—whoa. Hold the hell up!" She snatched my left hand, holding up the ring and staring at me with big eyes. "Holy shit, Bex! You got engaged?"

Now Eric and Alex were both watching us, Eric looking smug and Alex looking… uncertain.

"Yup," I told her. "Eric proposed last night when I got back to Paris."

Cami looked utterly stunned. "But you've barely known him for two weeks."

"What can I say? When you know, you know," I replied, shooting Eric a warm smile.

Cami's brow furrowed. "Okay, I know you wanted to get over Court, but getting engaged? That's a huge step." She shook her head and lowered her voice. "Talk to me, girl. What's really going on?"

I grabbed her hand and squeezed a bit harder than necessary. "I need you to just support me right now, okay? Can you do that?"

She studied me carefully, and I worried that she'd press the issue. But Cami was nothing if not on my side. "Okay, babe. Then I guess I call dibs on maid of honor?"

My shoulders dropped in relief. "Deal. Just don't tell Jayme I gave you first dibs."

Linking her arm with mine, Cami towed me toward the dressing rooms, where a woman waited for us dressed in a teal cocktail dress with a chunky belt and large earrings. Her brown hair was pulled back in a severe bun, but she had a wide smile.

"Bex, this is Janice," Cami introduced. "Janice has helped style me for more after-parties and benefits than I can count."

Janice's gaze scanned me from head to toe as she tapped a pale pink nail on her chin. "Nice proportions. 32 C?"

I blinked in surprise as she guessed my bra size. "Uh, yeah."

She slowly circled me. "Hmm, might need a bit of a lift for your rear end, but you've got lovely legs."

"Thanks?" I shot Cami a look, and she shrugged in return and flashed me a thumbs up. Clearing my throat, I looked at Janice. "I'm interested in something yellow."

Her lip curled. "Yellow?"

"It's my favorite color," Eric spoke up, giving Janice a hard stare. "Besides, she looks ravishing in any color, unless you're implying this store doesn't have the proper attire for my fiancée?"

Alex's head shot up. "Fiancée?"

Eric ignored him, instead looking at me. "Don't you agree, my love?"

"Of course," I replied quickly.

Janice huffed softly. "I have a few options. I'll bring them to your room." She whirled away with a flourish.

Cami gave me a slightly uneasy look, but I studiously ignored her. Instead I went into one of the dressing rooms and started to strip off my clothes. After folding them, I looked at myself clad only in lilac lace panties and a matching bra.

I fingered the lacy edge of one cup, remembering the way Court's eyes had flashed with appreciation as he'd pushed my hands away to do the clasp behind my back for me. The way he'd dragged his nose up the back of my leg as he tugged my underwear up.

Something caught my eye, and I turned in the full-length mirror to see a small purple bruise on my hip. It looked innocent enough, like I'd bumped into something. But I knew exactly where I'd gotten that bruise. Even now I could feel the possessive way Court had gripped my hips as he'd thrust into me last night.

My clit gave a needy throb, and I wished more than anything that he was here with me right now.

I jumped as the curtain was drawn back and Janice stepped inside, her lips pressed together over the mountain of yellow and gold fabric draped over her arm. She began hanging the dresses, muttering about yellow being a spring and summer color and this being a winter event.

But when she turned to me, she gave me a weak smile. "Let's see if we can find you a proper dress, shall we?"

I nodded, even as I knew my opinion wouldn't matter. And sure enough, Eric shot down almost every dress I tried on.

The first one showed too much cleavage.

The second made me look like a nun, all covered up.

The third was too marigold.

The fourth had feathers, and apparently he was allergic.

I could sense Janice getting ready to explode when I tried on the fifth dress, a pale champagne that sparkled and fell to the floor. I'd definitely need heels to keep from tripping over the hem, but it was stunning.

I exited the dressing room once again, and Eric looked up from his phone.

"Oh, my God! Bex!" Cami cried, standing to one side in a crimson dress with a slit up to her hip and an intricately laced corset. The straps fell off her shoulders, leaving her decolletage bare. She looked like a movie star.

"This is stunning," Cami gushed, coming to stand in front of me. She turned to Eric. "Doesn't she look amazing?"

"Beautiful," he agreed, getting up and walking to me. "Do you like the dress?"

I had to admit it was freaking gorgeous, and probably something I would've picked for myself. "I love it."

"It looks made for you," the woman who had been assisting Cami mentioned. When the door opened, the chime signaling a new customer had come in, she headed for the entrance.

Eric leaned in and kissed the tip of my nose. "Perfect. You and Cami can check out, and we'll go to lunch."

Cami shook her head. "I have one more dress to try on."

"Why?" Eric looked confused as he waved a hand at her. "Red is clearly your color, don't you agree, Bex?"

"Uh, yeah. The dress is totally you, Cam," I assured her, noting that

Alex was watching the exchange but didn't speak up. In fact, judging by the tight set of his jaw and his dark eyes, he seemed pretty pissed about something.

"Forgive me for saying," Eric added, "but might I recommend a heel that will accentuate your legs? With the color and the high slit, it will highlight all the work you've done as a dancer."

Cami and I exchanged baffled looks. When had Eric turned into the fashion expert?

Finally, Cami let out a soft laugh. "I mean, you're right."

Janice nodded. "I have just the pair in mind for the dress."

"Alex?" Cami looked at him, clearly reading her boyfriend's mood.

Alex's expression was still pinched. "I'm certain I'll love whatever you select."

"You mean you'll love peeling it off me later." Cami grinned and looked at me, but the look Eric exchanged with his brother made goose bumps erupt across my arms.

Alex pushed angrily to his feet. "Excuse me. I need to make a phone call." He spun on his heels and stalked through the boutique to the front door, then shoved the glass open and stepped outside.

Cami's face fell. "I should check on him," she murmured, hurrying back into the dressing room with Janice at her heels to help her out of the gown.

I turned to Eric, trying to play it off as amusing, even though something in my gut was warning me there was a problem. "Should I be concerned with how much attention you're giving to Cami's dress?"

Eric flashed me an indulgent smile as his hands came up to frame my face. "My love, are you jealous?"

"No," I replied, genuinely meaning it. To be jealous, I'd have to care about Eric, and that wasn't happening.

He chuckled. "My sweet love *is* jealous." He swooped in for a quick kiss that turned my insides to ash. "There's absolutely no need to be. I just thought her dress was appropriate for the... occasion."

"For my grandmother's birthday celebration?" My brows rose.

He gave a noncommittal hum as Cami came out of the dressing room. She flashed me a tight smile before chasing after Alex.

Janice exited after her and passed the red dress to an associate before looking at me. "Will you need shoes to match?"

"Yes," Eric answered for me. "A low heel. Nothing too high. Can't have my future wife looking like a whore." He flashed me a wink, but my stomach soured.

So, *I* couldn't wear heels, but Camille could?

That didn't make sense.

"Eric…" I started, but I wasn't sure where to go from there.

He held my gaze, his eyes sparkling with a glint that made me shudder. "It's going to be a spectacular night, my love. The start of the rest of our lives together."

CHAPTER 37

BEX

Eric dropped me off at home later that afternoon, citing a business meeting he couldn't get out of. I didn't fight him; I'd take any and all chances to get away from him.

Lunch had been strange. Alex barely paid attention to anyone, including Cami, which only worried my cousin more. Eric had kept the conversation going, asking my cousin about her upcoming dance performances and talking about our wedding.

I did manage to get everyone to agree to keep our engagement under wraps until after Mémé's event, telling them all that I didn't want to detract from my grandmother's party. Plus, I told Eric that we deserved our own moment to announce our news, and he seemed to love that idea.

As I trudged up the front stairs, pausing to blow Eric a kiss, I realized how utterly drained I was. I hated lying, and I'd spent the day lying to one of my favorite people in the world.

I pushed open the door and saw the house manager, Yvette, in the front hall. Yvette had been part of my life for years. She was only a few years younger than my grandparents and had worked for them almost as long as they'd been married. Yvette wasn't just an employee; she was family.

Which was why she had no problem speaking her mind when she saw me.

"Rebecca, cher, you look exhausted," she chastised, her brow furrowing as she came over and pressed a hand to my forehead. "Are you coming down with something?"

"No," I assured her. "Just didn't sleep all that well."

"Ah, well, perhaps it would be best to tell your late-night suitor to take an evening off?" She gave me a pointed stare.

Of course she'd noticed Court, because as good as my guy was at breaking and entering, Yvette knew this house like the back of her hand. Nothing escaped her attention.

"Please don't say anything," I whispered.

Her expression turned annoyed. "You know I won't lie for you. If you're old enough to entertain a nighttime visitor, then you're old enough to be honest with your grandparents and your mother. Besides, your grandmother hasn't stopped raving about your gentleman caller, so I doubt she'd be upset."

"It's not him," I confessed. "Eric isn't the one who… It's complicated, Yvette."

She sucked in a sharp breath. "Rebecca, what are you doing, cher?"

"I know what it looks like," I admitted, adjusting the gown in my arms, "but it's not that."

"And how do you plan to explain *that*?" Yvette's gaze dropped to the ring on my finger.

"It's—"

"—complicated," she finished for me with a frown. "The little Rebecca I knew would never lie or cheat. What has gotten into you?"

"Eric is… He's not the guy for me" I confessed. "But I need him to think he is."

Her blue eyes widened. "Cher—"

I grabbed her hand and squeezed. "I promise I'll tell you everything. I'll tell Mom and Mémé and Papa too, but for right now, I can't. Please, Yvette. I'm not asking you to lie for me. I'm just asking that you not bring up the guy in my room. Or the ring."

Yvette sighed. "All right, cher." She cupped my cheek with her hand. "I've known you since you were a babe, and I suppose I can trust your judgment."

Relief sank into my bones, and my knees almost gave out. "Thank you, Yvette."

She didn't look happy, but she nodded. "Is that your dress for tomorrow evening?"

"Yes."

She held out her arms. "I'll see that it's ready for you tomorrow."

"Thank you," I murmured, passing her the dress.

She gave me a final stiff nod, and I whirled and ran up the stairs before she could take it back. I didn't breathe again until I was in my bedroom.

I looked around my room, my heart sinking when I didn't see Court or his bag. Tugging off the ring, I tossed it onto my dresser and spotted a folded piece of paper.

B-

Had to take care of some things. Be back later.

-C

The simple message wasn't exactly what I needed, but it would suffice until Court was back tonight.

Still feeling edgy, I pulled out my cell phone and dialed Maddie's number. She answered the video chat on the second ring.

"Hey, babe!" she greeted, her smile bright. Judging from the background, she was at home and in her bedroom, propped up against the headboard. "By the way, welcome to the club."

I frowned. "The club?"

"Yeah. The *I'm fake engaged* club," she replied. "Although, I'm kinda annoyed you didn't tell me the not-big news yourself. You can make it up to me by letting me *not* be your maid of honor."

"Ha ha," I deadpanned. "And Cami already took that spot."

"Eh. Just as well. But enjoy your new almost-wifed-up status."

"You're hysterical," I drawled.

"Hey, all I'm saying is, it worked out pretty well for me." She waggled her eyebrows.

"Ew, no." I shuddered at the idea of really being engaged to Eric.

"Even if I didn't find him morally reprehensible, I'm not on the market."

Her blue eyes widened. "Uh, what now?"

I didn't bother hiding my grin. "Court and I are together."

She let out a shriek. "Bex!"

Off camera, something slammed like a door being thrown open.

Maddie ducked her head, shooting someone I couldn't see a small smile. "Sorry, Ry."

"Jesus," he swore. "Don't scream like that, baby. You scared the shit outta me."

"Did you know Bex and Court are now a thing?" she demanded, glaring at her husband.

"Seriously? About time he nutted the fuck up and got the girl," Ryan remarked. "And for the record, no, the dipshit didn't mention it, but it does explain why he was more pissed off than usual during our debriefing."

Maddie's expression shifted, her eyes taking on a decidedly puppy-dog, begging quality.

Ryan sighed heavily. "Don't make that face."

"But, Ryan," she whined.

"You're not coming to Paris with us," he snapped. "It's too dangerous."

"Wait, they're definitely coming to Paris?" I asked.

Maddie nodded at me. "Yeah. Ry's packing now. So are Linc and Ash. I want to come, but *someone* thinks it's too dangerous."

"Because it is," Ryan gritted out.

"Fine." Maddie let out a sad breath and turned her attention back to me. "I guess I'll just sit in this house all by myself. Go to school by myself. And if something goes wrong, I can call—oh, wait. There's no one I *can* call, because you'll all be on the other side of the planet!"

"Goddammit," Ryan hissed.

Maddie winked at me, keeping her voice soft and wobbly. "So, if I fall down the stairs or get into a car wreck or accidentally eat a freaking peanut—"

"Fuck. Fine. Pack a bag, but you're staying in the goddamn hotel, Maddie," Ryan snapped.

"Of course," she agreed instantly, but somehow, I doubted my best friend could or would be contained to a hotel room.

My heart lifted. "You're coming to Paris?"

She nodded with a grin and seemed to wait for Ryan to move before whispering, "Seriously, bringing up the peanut incident is my golden ticket."

"Mads, you almost *died*," I reminded her. Maddie had a severe peanut allergy, and at her eighteenth birthday party, she'd eaten a peanut-contaminated cupcake.

One bite was all it had taken to have her throat close up. I still remembered the way she'd passed out. Linc stabbing her leg with the EpiPen. All of us hauling ass to get her to the hospital.

"Eh." She shrugged like it was no big deal, and maybe to her, it wasn't. After all, the girl had switched lives with her dead twin, been locked in an institution by her psycho dad, and then almost burned to death in a house fire set by her father-in-law.

I bit my bottom lip. "Court didn't mention the guys were all coming. He said maybe, but—"

"They literally decided an hour ago," Maddie told me. "Apparently Rook's friend got some intel about several big-name douche nozzles showing up in Paris, and he asked the guys to come over."

I nodded, relieved that Court wasn't keeping stuff from me.

"So, you and Court?" Maddie smiled. "When did this happen?"

"Four days ago," I admitted.

Her jaw dropped open. "Rebecca Whittier! You finally decided to get the guy of your dreams, and it's taken you four freaking days to call me? As your bestie, I'm not sure if I should be pissed that it took you so long to tell me or jump up and down because you two finally got together."

"Definitely the latter," I said with a small laugh.

"I want all the details," she demanded, sitting up straighter.

I gave her the rundown of everything that had happened. From the disastrous dinner with Eric and his friends to Court interrupting the date. I told her about moving in with Court, and the stupid fight we'd had when I'd seen the text messages.

"He's *such* an idiot," she seethed, shaking her head.

"He is," I agreed. "But he's *my* idiot now, I guess."

"Yet another club we can both be in," she giggled. "The *I'm with an alphahole who thinks he knows best* club."

I inhaled sharply and nodded. "Definitely."

"So things are good with you guys?" she asked.

A dreamy smile touched my lips. "Yeah. We're really good. We talked out everything. I'm not saying there's a magic wand to fix a decade of bad shit between us, but...."

"Just a magic dick?" she offered with a wry grin.

"No," I replied, shaking my head. "You know that's my least favorite thing in a book—when a girl is magically fixed by a guy's dick. Like, really?"

"Okay, fair," she conceded. "A magic dick can't fix real-world problems. But... sometimes it makes them easier to handle."

I tried to fight a smile and lost. "Valid."

"Ryan gave me a synopsis of what's been going on with you in Paris," she said, "but seriously, Bex, are you okay with all of this?"

"I have to be," I answered. "If I can help stop Eric, help stop some of these guys, then I want to. I *need* to."

"I get it, trust me," Maddie responded, her tone soft. "Even now, I've been talking to Ryan about college. I always thought I wanted to be an architect, but the more I learn, the more I want to help Phoenix. Maybe I'll go into social work."

"You can still help Phoenix, and others, with an architecture degree," I pointed out. "You can help design buildings and homes for people that need them."

She tilted her head. "Yeah, maybe."

My bedroom door opened, and I looked up as Court slipped inside. My heart gave a little kickstart. He looked all sorts of sexy in ripped jeans, a white t-shirt, and his leather jacket.

But then I saw the look in his dark eyes, and I froze. That look told me I wasn't going to like what came next.

"Mads, I've gotta go," I said. "Court just got back."

"Yeah, I should pack before Ryan changes his mind," she said. "But I'll see you soon, B."

"See you soon," I echoed and hung up. I slid off my bed and waited for Court to come to me.

He sat on the edge of my bed and tugged me between his spread legs, burying his face against my chest. My hands instantly delved into his soft hair, the strands still cold from the freezing temperatures outside.

"What's wrong?" I finally asked, bracing myself for the worst.

"I need to talk to you," he said, his tone somber as he looked up at me, those whiskey-colored eyes uncertain.

"Okay."

"Becca, we've been keeping an eye out for guys coming into town. Men and women that we know are affiliated with the clubs and parties that Westford organizes," he started.

I nodded, following along. "Right. Maddie mentioned Trick saying as much. That's why she and the guys are coming to Paris."

He looked surprised. "Maddie's coming, too?" He gave a slightly bemused smile. "Never mind. I can see her being very convincing."

"Yeah," I agreed. "Now tell me the news I'm not gonna like."

His gaze met mine, and his hands tightened on the backs of my thighs. "One of the men we saw come into town last night—a man who met with some other people of interest today—it's your dad, sweetheart."

My eyes drifted shut as the news leveled a part of my heart.

"I'm sorry," Court added, standing up and pulling me fully against his chest.

My head fit perfectly under his chin, and I burrowed against him as the news rolled over me like a tidal wave.

"I guess he didn't tell you he was in town?"

I pulled back. "You think I wouldn't have told you? You know I've been ducking his calls. And it's not like he'd leave a voicemail and say *Hey honey, I'm in town to commit a bunch of felonies—let me know if you're free for brunch?*"

He cupped my face, his long fingers cradling me. "I'm not accusing you. I just didn't think the guy was enough of a douche to come to Paris and not at least try to see you."

I let out a bitter laugh and twisted away from him. "Yeah, well, clearly I mean a lot to him."

"I'm sorry, baby girl," he murmured.

I wrapped my arms around myself and turned back with a shrug. "You'd think I'd be used to people I love not giving a shit about me, but it still hurts every damn time." Tears burned my eyes and spilled over before I could blink them back.

Court grimaced. "He's an asshole, Becca. That's not on you."

"He's my dad," I croaked.

"And?" His eyes blazed as he closed the distance between us and grabbed my shoulders. "Baby, we're *not* our fathers. You're not, Ryan's not, Linc's not… I'm sure as shit not, and neither are my brothers. Just because we got thrown into the shitty end of the genetics pool doesn't mean it defines us."

I looked up at him, my heart still broken even as his words hit home.

He pressed a hand flat against my chest. "You have a good heart, Becca. You always have. That won't change because your dad is a fuckup. Nothing can change the woman you are. The…" He sucked in a deep breath. "The woman that I love."

It was like storm clouds drifting apart for a ray of sunlight after a hurricane. His words hit my soul, sinking in with a warmth that helped something click into place. A piece that I'd been missing since I was a little girl.

Twice now he'd admitted to loving me. "I feel like I keep waiting for you to take it back," I confessed, speaking my biggest fear into existence.

"Becca, I've loved you since I first laid eyes on you," he told me, his tone fierce. "I loved you before I even knew what it meant to love someone. Don't you get it? I've been a fucking disaster since I tried giving you up, because how can a person live without their heart?"

"Court." I was at a loss, emotions overwhelming me to the point of crippling me.

"It's okay," he assured me with a tight smile. "I still haven't earned it."

I pressed a hand over his lips. "Love isn't something you earn. It just *is*, Court. And I love you, too. I always have, and I always will."

He released a shuddering breath, his shoulders falling like I'd removed a massive weight from them as he dropped his forehead to mine. "I won't let you down again, Becca. I swear."

"I know," I answered, and I did.

I knew it in my heart, in my soul, in every fiber of my being.

Were we perfect? Absolutely not.

But we were perfect for each other.

CHAPTER 38

BEX

"Happy birthday, Mémé." I leaned in, kissing the soft, pale skin of her face as I wrapped her in a hug.

"Thank you, bébé," she returned, her smile radiant as she looked around the ballroom. I followed her gaze, taking the time to see what she was seeing.

The ballroom of the Montpelier Paris was draped in swaths of gauzy white fabric with twinkling lights, giving it a celestial look. The large central dance floor was surrounded by round tables with crisp white linens and candlelit centerpieces, and an eight-piece orchestra was playing on a dais, their music flowing easily through the packed space.

I hadn't been to this hotel in years, but it was owned by one of Mémé's oldest friends. Considered a luxury boutique hotel, it was set in the heart of the 6th arrondissement and was always booked solid a year in advance. Cami had once mentioned it was her dream to get married in this very ballroom.

Mémé's party was the It event of the winter season. I'd spotted several ambassadors, heads of state, and a few royal family members from neighboring European countries in the crowd. As part of the family, I was let in before all the other guests, but I knew for a fact that there was an endless parade of limos waiting to drop off guests at the formal red carpet.

"Mrs. Moreau." Mémé's personal assistant, Gianna, appeared behind her with a warm smile for me. Gianna had been handling Mémé's affairs for over two decades now. With her hair in an angled silver bob and her critical blue-eyed gaze that missed no detail, she was a woman who knew how to get things done. "It's time for pictures with the board."

In lieu of traditional birthday presents, my grandmother had opted to tie her birthday gala to her favorite charity, a local Parisian organization that helped at-risk youth find alternatives to the city's growing crime statistics.

Mémé gave a nod. "Of course. Excuse us, will you, bébé? Perhaps you can find your young gentleman." She waggled her eyebrows at me, and I gritted my teeth around a smile.

I'd pushed off Eric arriving early with me as part of the family by telling him Mémé needed my help getting ready, but he'd already texted me five times to let me know his position in the limo queue.

Taking a minute to just breathe and enjoy the moment, I watched Mémé and Gianna wander off to join Papa.

"Look who I found," Cami squealed from behind me.

Turning, I saw my cousin flanked by Alex and Eric.

There went my peaceful minute.

Eric's smile was brittle as he pulled me into his arms. "You look spectacular," he announced, then lowered his voice to add, "Though, I am a bit annoyed at the wait time to see you, my love." His hands squeezed my hips as if in warning. "And I thought we discussed a *low* heel."

I gritted my teeth. "I know," I simpered for his sake, "but I kept tripping over the dress in the low heel. I needed something more."

He looked pissed but gave me a tight nod.

I squared my shoulders and prepared to win my Oscar nomination. "I'm so sorry for the delay getting you inside," I whined, letting my expression crumple. "It's all my fault. I got so caught up trying to help Mémé…"

Seemingly pleased that I was upset, he kissed my forehead. "All is forgiven, pet."

Pet.

Why did that particular term of endearment rankle so damn much?

Looking past him, I caught Cami giving Alex a bright smile… that he resolutely ignored. He snagged a glass of champagne from the tray of a nearby waiter and downed it like a shot.

I shot Cami a quizzical look, but she shrugged it off, her blue eyes sad. "Cam—"

Eric grabbed my hand. "I see the chief justice. We should say hello." His gray eyes glinted with enthusiasm as he pointed out a tall, slender man, who had to be pushing eighty, leaning heavily on a cane.

I let Eric lead me toward the chief justice, who gave Eric a knowing smile and dismissed the two men in suits he'd been talking to.

"Eric, my boy, look at you," he said with a grin, his gaze moving past Eric and raking down my body in a way that sent goose bumps skittering across my flesh. "And who is this lovely creature?"

"Rebecca Whittier," Eric responded, his hand resting against my hip like I was a prize poodle he was showing off. "She's Mrs. Moreau's granddaughter."

"Ah. The one from the States."

"Bex, this is Chief Justice DuChamps. He's a… close friend," Eric finished with a conspiratorial smirk.

Chief Justice DuChamps returned the look. "Quite right." His shrewd gaze landed on me once more. "Whittier."

Eric's grin increased. "Yes, she's Malcolm's daughter."

The chief justice chuckled. "I had lunch with your father earlier today."

"Did you?" I tried to keep the surprise from making my voice squeak. "I've been so busy with my grandmother's event that I haven't had time to see him yet."

Eric squeezed my hip. "I think you'll see him sooner than you think."

DuChamps straightened. "It's confirmed then?"

Eric nodded. "Seems like an ideal time, doesn't it? Half the police are either here or controlling traffic in the vicinity. Having so many heads of state in one place was just what we needed. Many are sending buyers on their behalf."

As they spoke to each other like I'd ceased to exist, warning bells went off in the back of my mind.

DuChamps clapped Eric on the shoulder. "I won't be one of them. I prefer to inspect my merchandise myself to make sure it's exactly as ordered." He lifted a bushy dark brow.

Eric straightened. "I can assure you that it is, and I've already arranged transport back to your island in the Pacific for it."

DuChamps looked at me. "This one's going places, young lady. You picked a fine horse to *ride*." The insinuation felt oily and wrong as he grinned and wandered away.

My brain whirled as I tried to fit the pieces together. "Eric—"

He turned to me, his gray eyes sparkling. "I should've told you, pet, but things just came together today. There was a complication I didn't want the chief justice to know about, but you handled yourself brilliantly." His lips crashed down on mine, his kiss bruising.

"C-complication?" I stammered as he pulled back.

His face twisted into a scowl. "Apparently there's been a task force assembled to stop our event. Something the bloody Americans cooked up. Stupid wankers don't even know that one of their own team is one of *us*." He let out a caustic laugh.

Trick. Someone on his team was working with the bad guys, even though he said they'd been hand-selected to avoid corruption.

Holy shit, how deep did this go?

Like dominoes falling, the pieces clicked together.

"You're having the auction tonight," I whispered.

His face twisted as he grabbed my elbow and pushed me back several steps until we were tucked into a small alcove. "Shut up. Discretion is key in this business. Never, *ever* say words that can be construed as anything other than a business deal."

I shuddered, recalling the easy way he and the chief justice had discussed *merchandise*. Nothing they'd spoken of was illegal. They hadn't said they were trading humans, just that a shipment had been arranged. Legally they could've been talking about a couch that Eric's company was having delivered.

After a beat, Eric's expression softened. "Brilliant, isn't it? With as many foreign dignitaries˙and diplomats as your grandparents have invited, the Paris police have thrown most of their resources into protecting people here. No one will ever know what's taking place less than a mile away."

My heart slammed against my ribs, threatening to gallop free. I wondered if Eric could see the shock and horror that must be written on my face.

I needed to call Court. To tell him and the others what was going on. They needed to warn Trick that his team was compromised. My phone was tucked into a small clutch, and all I wanted to do was yank it out and call Court.

Eric whirled me in a fast circle, grinning like an absolute maniac. "Bex, this is going to change everything for us. After tonight, they'll see how valuable I am. We'll rule the European sector and be invincible." He pressed his body against mine, a prominent ridge poking into my belly.

In an instant, my blood seemed to turn to ice, but I had to fake excitement. Couldn't let him know that I wasn't Team Take Over the World.

Instead, I looped my arms around his neck and smiled up at him. "Sounds like you've got it all figured out, honey."

He nodded, swaying us as he dipped his head to whisper the rest of his diabolical plan in my ear. "Offering to host the event at my warehouse by the pier was precisely what I needed. It allows me to showcase just how fully integrated an experience I can provide the buyers, from location to delivery."

I toyed with the ends of his hair while swallowing a wave of bile. "That sounds incredible. I can't believe you pulled it together so quickly."

He glowed at the compliment. "I hope you don't mind cutting the evening short. I'm sure you'll be able to make an excuse with your grandmother—"

"You want me to leave?" I jerked in his hold.

His eyes narrowed. "Of course I do. We're partners, Bex. You and I… With my abilities and your connections, we'll be unstoppable. I need you at my side tonight."

I swallowed hard. "Okay, Eric. Of course. Let me go tell my grandmother I need to leave. I'm sure I'll come up with a reasonable excuse. Do we need to leave now?"

"We'll all leave in a few minutes," he replied.

"All?" I echoed.

He smiled. "One of the buyers requested something… specific. Delivering on it will help prove my point."

Before I could ask what the hell *that* meant, he lifted my hand to his lips and kissed it. Then his gaze darkened, and he nearly crushed my fingers. "Where is your ring?"

I hissed a breath, instinctively trying to pull away. "Ow! Let go— you're hurting me."

"Where the *fuck* is your ring, Rebecca?" he snarled.

"I left it at home because we both agreed to wait until after this event to announce the engagement," I retorted.

A muscle in his jaw ticked. "I suppose I did agree to that, didn't I?"

I watched him the way I would a dog with rabies, wary and ready for him to attack. "Let me go," I repeated, my voice low.

His nostrils flared slightly as he tossed my hand away before digging his phone from his pocket. Whatever he saw brought a terrifying smile to his face, and I was rapidly realizing how completely unhinged he was.

"Meet me in the underground parking level in ten minutes, pet," he murmured, tucking the phone away. "We'll leave then."

I nodded and had taken one step away when he grabbed me yet again, this time grinding the small bones in my wrist until I was sure they were dust.

"Don't make me come and find you, pet," he warned before leaning in to kiss me hard before releasing me with a small shove.

I stumbled away from him and hurried from the alcove. I had no idea where my grandparents were, and honestly, I didn't care. Right now, I needed to make a phone call.

I was almost to the bathroom door when it opened and my mom stepped out. She beamed when she saw me, until she took me in.

Concern lined her face. "Sweetie, what's wrong?" She took me by the shoulders, looking into my eyes. Our irises were the same shade of hazel, but deep lines had appeared around hers during the past few months.

"I just… really need the bathroom," I lied, knowing it sounded lame.

"Becca, honey." She frowned at me. "If something's wrong—"

"It isn't," I insisted. "Just got done dancing, and I'm a little flustered."

"Does this mean I finally get to meet the infamous Eric?" she asked with a soft laugh. "I'd love for you to introduce us."

"I will," I told her. "I just need to fix my makeup and use the bathroom."

"All right," she replied with a sigh, letting me pass.

I ducked into the ornate bathroom, thankful it was a private one. Granted, it was the size of a small apartment, with a separate toilet and bidet, a massive mirror framed in gold, and a chaise lounge in addition to the pedestal sink.

My hands trembled as I locked the door and pulled out my phone, almost dropping it. It took three tries to hit Court's contact. He answered before the second ring, probably wondering why I was calling him from *my* phone and not the emergency one. This stupid little clutch had room for only one phone, and I, shockingly, hadn't expected to cut out of the party and go to the auction.

If Eric was watching my phone or checked it… Shit, I'd deal with that later.

"What's wrong?" His warm voice almost sent me to my knees. The concern in his tone ramped up my own anxiety, and I yearned to be curled up in my bed wrapped in his arms.

"It's tonight. The auction is happening tonight," I gasped, gulping down air.

"What the fuck?" he swore, then covered the mouthpiece to shout something I couldn't make out. "Baby, where are you?"

"At the Montpelier, but I have to leave for the auction with Eric in a few minutes." I dropped onto the chaise lounge.

"The fuck you are," he growled. "Are you alone?"

"I locked myself in the bathroom," I admitted.

"Good. I'm coming for you. Stay put." I could hear him moving now, his breaths coming in sharp pants as he hurried.

"Court, I *can't*," I whispered. "He'll come for me. If I don't go, it'll mess everything up."

"Becca, listen to me," he snarled, "do *not* fucking leave the bathroom. If he comes after you, make a fucking scene, baby. Scream, fight, slap him. Whatever you do—do *not* go with him. We have no idea where the auction is—"

"It's at a warehouse he owns near the pier. He's planning on using his ships to transport people," I shot back, tears clogging my throat as I realized how completely out of my depth I was. "Court, he said someone on Trick's team is working with him."

"Motherfucker," Court ground out. "Becca—"

"Do you know where the warehouse is?"

"What?"

I shut my eyes. "Do you know where the warehouse is?"

He was silent for a beat before admitting, "Yeah. It's one of the places we had flagged, actually. The location makes sense, but, baby, we're easily twenty minutes away. Maybe more with traffic, and if Trick's team is compromised… We can reach out to Paris PD."

"Considering Eric's people have Chief Justice DuChamps in their back pocket, I wouldn't be surprised if the police are compromised, too." Hopelessness settled around my heart like a lead blanket.

"Fuck."

"I know," I murmured. "If I don't go, if I stay here, what happens?"

Court was silent.

"What happens, Court?" I demanded.

"They'll cut their losses," he rasped. "They'll kill everyone. And

Eric will come after you. Westford, my dad… Fuck, Becca, they'll all come for you. But I can protect you, baby girl."

"And my family?" A tear tumbled down my cheek.

"Becca." His tone was anguished.

"They'll kill my family, won't they? To get to me?"

His silence was all the answer I needed.

"I'm going to play this thing out," I started, my voice sounding a hell of a lot stronger than I felt. "I'm going with Eric, and you're going to come riding in with the cavalry. This is one of the only times I'm down with you saving me like a damsel in distress."

"No," he bit out. "Fucking *no*. I'm not risking you."

"Court, do you trust me?"

His hesitation wasn't because he didn't trust me; it was because he *did* trust me. Just like I knew he'd always have my back. It just sucked that this was the stress test I was about to put us through.

"You know I do," he finally said, frustration lacing his words. I could picture him stabbing his fingers through his dark hair.

"Then you're going to trust that I can handle myself. You're gonna tell me you love me and trust me to do this, because you believe in me."

"Becca."

I barely swallowed a sob. "Tell me you love me, Court."

"You're my entire fucking reason for existing, Becca Whittier," he vowed. "I trust you. I love you."

I choked on my tears. "I love you. I'll see you soon."

"Becca—"

I hung up before he could talk me out of it.

Every single cell in my body wanted to hide in this bathroom and wait to be rescued. I wanted to bury my head in the sand and forget this nightmare. But if Eric suspected I was betraying him, he'd lose it. He'd kill all those people they had lined up to sell, he'd come for my family… He had to be stopped.

I stood up and looked at my phone. Before I could overthink it, I made the judgment call to delete my call logs and texts with Court.

Maybe I was being paranoid, or I'd seen too many spy movies, but I had to see this through to the end.

After washing my hands and using a damp paper towel to blot away the eyeliner smudges under my eyes, I straightened my spine. Staring at my reflection I whispered, "You can do this."

God, I hoped I could do this.

I turned and unlocked the bathroom door, sending up prayers for a miracle to whoever might be listening.

CHAPTER 39

COURT

I picked up my coffee mug from the end table beside me and hurled it at the wall. It shattered in a spray of ceramic shards and lukewarm coffee. "Fuck!"

Rook looked up, his expression tense as he talked to Trick on the phone, relaying the latest shitshow. Bishop shot me a grim look from where he was reloading a magazine clip.

A familiar hand clapped down on my shoulder, and I turned to see my best friend behind me.

"We'll get her out, bro," Linc vowed, his tone solemn. His blue eyes, usually full of mischief and laughter, were cold and lethal. He'd arrived with my oldest brother and the rest of my friends only twenty-two minutes earlier. They were jet-lagged and exhausted.

And ready to kick some ass.

Behind him, Ryan and Royal were loading the last of our weapons. Ash was sitting at the computer, monitoring the roads and finding us the best route to the pier. And on the far side of the room, Maddie hovered in an open doorway, her face pale.

"I want to come," she insisted.

Ryan whirled. "Mads, no. We talked about this."

"But Bex is in trouble," she pressed. "She might need me."

Ryan pinched the bridge of his nose, likely praying for strength to deal with his wife. "Madison, I will literally tie you to the bed to keep your ass here."

"Ry—"

"Maddie," Ash cut in, his tone gentle, "you'd be a liability. They'd have to split their focus between keeping you and Bex safe."

I barely suppressed a snort, because he was wrong. My focus was entirely on my girl, and as much as I loved Maddie, if it came down to her or Becca… There was no choice to be made.

That being said, Becca would be heartbroken if something happened to her best friend.

"I don't care who's coming or not, but I'm going," I announced, heading for the door.

"Court—" Royal began.

"I swear to Christ I will lay you out if you even think about stopping me," I threatened, wondering if this was how the Hulk felt before he turned into a green beast that could level cities. Furious energy roiled in my veins, adrenaline and fear a toxic cocktail that threatened to undo me.

Royal, calm and collected as ever, just shot me a *who the fuck are you kidding* look. He held up a hand, keys dangling from it. "I was going to offer to drive."

I exhaled a hard breath, my brain spinning with how much shit could go wrong in the next thirty minutes. Panic clawed up my throat, and I wondered if it was possible for a twenty-two-year-old to drop dead of a heart attack.

"We're all going," Ryan said, then looked at Maddie. "Except you."

Her jaw set in a mulish line as she huffed, pissed that she was being sidelined.

"I'm staying, too," Ash reminded her, his gaze never leaving the monitor.

"But you're at least doing something," she muttered, running a hand through her blonde hair. She turned to me, aqua eyes flashing. "Get my bestie back, Court."

I nodded. "I will." I'd never meant anything more in my life.

Except when I'd told Becca that I loved her, but that wasn't a promise. It wasn't even a vow. The word hadn't been invented yet to explain the soul-deep covenant that bound us together. She was mine, and I was hers. That was now the sum of my entire world.

I'd just been the idiot who'd been too scared to risk his heart before. Too blinded by my own ideas of how to keep her safe and coddled.

But she wasn't a fragile little girl anymore. She was a vibrant, incredible woman who hadn't let the world beat her down. Who, even at this very minute, was putting herself at risk to help others. If that was who Becca was, I would embrace it. I'd stand in the shadows, forever the guardian who fought the monsters so she could thrive in the light.

"Got 'em," Ash called, leaning in and tapping a few buttons to enhance a screen.

I pushed my way through the room and leaned over his shoulder to see a nondescript black limo gliding through the Parisian streets toward the city outskirts.

"That's the car Lambert-Durand arrived in," Ash added, his green eyes narrowed as he concentrated. "It left the parking garage five minutes ago and is registered to Lambert-Singh Shipping."

"She's in there?" I demanded, my chest giving a painful squeeze.

Ash grimaced. "I mean, I can't see inside the car, but I'd be willing to bet on it." He spun in his seat and looked at a separate laptop with a bunch of gibberish on the screen that I didn't understand. "I tapped into her phone. The trace puts her inside the car or running alongside it."

Or shoved into a trunk. Or…

Air hissed through my teeth as I bowed my head, fighting to stay in control and not surrender to the overwhelming panic building in my chest.

"Just got off the phone with Trick," Rook announced, his shoulders bunched with tension. "They have an idea who the mole is now, but they have to contain and isolate him before they can meet us at the warehouse."

I pressed my lips into a tight line, irritation licking up my spine. "We need to go now."

"Agreed," Rook replied with a tight nod.

"Be careful," Maddie whispered, fear in her eyes.

Ryan crossed the room and kissed her, holding her face in the palm of one hand. "We'll be back soon *with* Bex. Stay with Ash, okay?"

She nodded, a tremulous smile on her lips. "Go get our girl."

No.

I was going to get *my* girl.

CHAPTER 40

BEX

"We're here," Eric announced, smiling at me in the dark interior of the limo.

The engine cut off, the driver getting out and coming around to open Eric's door. He got out into a dimly lit parking lot before reaching back and extending a hand to me. As much as I wanted not to touch him, I grabbed his hand and let him pull me out of the car.

Cold air whipped across my cheeks and stung my eyes. I caught the faint scent of water and trash that marked the Seine and blinked through icy tears to look at the brick building looming ahead.

A quick glance around showed we were in an industrial area that, as Eric had promised, ended at the riverfront with a private pier. Different size boats were docked alongside what looked like a massive cargo ship. Metal crates in various colors were stacked four-high on the deck.

The warehouse was a three-story rectangle with thin slivers of windows that seemed blacked out. A few low-wattage lights cast an eerie yellow glow, illuminating the dark, reflective lines of several parked cars. Ahead, a large metal door was pulled open to allow entry to a couple dressed like they'd been at the party. The woman's red dress shimmered in the lights as she disappeared inside and the door closed.

In the distance, I could make out faint outlines of other buildings, but there was no sign of life. This was an area of Paris I'd never been to. It had a slightly haunted feel, like you could tell no one ever came out here.

"Eric!" a voice called, and I turned to see Colby heading toward us, his hands shoved in the pockets of his peacoat.

"Colby," Eric greeted, his tone warm even as his grip on my arm tightened.

Colby rubbed his hands together in front of his face. "Ready for the festivities?" His gaze raked down me, an appreciate leer in his smile.

"Of course," Eric replied with a breezy chuckle. "I assume the others are inside?"

"Brent is," Colby answered. "Geoffry was passed out with a bottle of tequila when I left his estate this afternoon. I doubt the fool will wake up."

"And Henry?"

My skin prickled as Colby's gaze turned vicious with a side of homicidal.

"Detained for the evening." Colby's voice was more chilling than the bitter wind coming off the water. "I'll see to him later. If you'll excuse me, I must join my father. He's looking for a new toy to add to his collection."

"Of course," Eric said with an indulgent smile, and we watched as Colby sauntered away toward a group of men several yards away.

My insides twisted with fear and worry. "Eric—"

"Shall we, my love?" Eric held out the crook of his arm for me, and I went to take it. My clutch brushed his arm, and he glared at it. "Leave that in the car."

A nervous laugh escaped me. "What? Why?"

"No phones inside," he replied, his tone curt. He jerked his chin back toward the interior of the car.

I hesitated, and he ripped it from my hand and hurled it back into the car, then slammed the door. He crowded me against the side of the car, caging me in with a snarl.

Instinctively I looked at the driver, but he was staring straight ahead, studiously ignoring me. Great, he clearly wasn't going to help me out. "Eric—"

He pounded a fist on top of the car, right next to my head. "You will *not* disobey me. When we walk into that warehouse, you are my pet. My prize. You will behave the way a woman is supposed to behave. You will be quiet and do exactly as I tell you. You represent *me*, dove. Don't forget that."

Holy shitballs. Did he really think that was how women were supposed to behave? Like we were dogs that could be made to heel?

Eff that noise. This bitch would totally bite back.

Just maybe not at *this* moment.

Seething, I pushed my rage down deep and reminded myself I needed to hold on. Court was coming for me, and I wouldn't want to be Eric when he got here.

"I'm sorry," I whispered, lowering my lashes and trying to look as penitent as a Catholic schoolgirl who'd been busted smoking by the nuns.

He rolled his shoulders. "That's better. Truly, I think you like provoking me, pet." He stroked my head, toying with the curled ends of my hair.

I shook my head. "No."

His smile was predatory. "Now, let's try this again." He held out an elbow and gave me an indulgent smile when I slipped my arm into his.

My heels clicked against the asphalt as I let him lead me to the warehouse, my gaze roving over the structure and drinking in every detail. Aside from the windows, there was an emergency fire escape with rusted bars leading from the roof. Other than the single door at the front, there was a small door near the back right corner. Probably another emergency exit.

When we reached the door, it opened again, revealing two men in suits with guns. When they saw Eric, they gave him a nod and let us inside.

Inside wasn't much better than outside. It was better lit, but the concrete floors and cinder block walls were cold and stark. There were walls partitioning the space, but they didn't reach all the way to the exposed, industrial ceiling. A metal catwalk lined the outer walls with guards positioned in several locations, and I spotted more men with guns walking around the main floor. The entryway split to the right and left ten feet ahead.

No one seemed to be in the entrance area now, but I could hear loud conversations coming from the other sides of the partitions.

Eric pointed left. "Look in here." He pulled me forward, and when we rounded the left corner, I was stunned by what I saw.

A large stage, complete with a podium and spotlights, took up the far wall. In front of it were rows of seats. To the right, a bar had been set up. A few people were sitting, and several men were gathered at the bar. To the left a staircase led up to a more private area with mirrored walls as its front, and I suspected it was one-way glass.

"That's my office, where we monitor everything," Eric told me, following my gaze. He pointed to the front of the seating area, where a section had been cordoned off with honest-to-crap red velvet ropes and gold stanchions. "Our VIP section."

Next he showed me a series of tables and laptops at the back. "We also stream the event for those who can't attend in person." Half a dozen men wordlessly manned them, never glancing up at us.

"Wow." It was all I could manage to squeak out without asking him exactly how many times he'd been dropped as an infant. Seriously, how did a person get this fucked in the head?

I mentally counted the rows of seats. It was at least ten deep and seven across. Were they really expecting seventy people to attend?

My grip on Eric tightened as the room seemed to tilt. I gasped for air, feeling like the world was collapsing around me.

"Come with me." Eric didn't give me a choice, pulling me with him like an errant child. We crossed back through the foyer, where more people were entering, and paused at the opening of the next space. The entryway was covered by a black velvet curtain that partitioned off this room from the other.

A ball of ice formed in my gut as I caught my breath. I could hear muted conversations, and somehow, I just knew that I wouldn't like whatever was on the other side.

With a flourish, Eric grabbed the edge of the curtain and pulled it aside for me, revealing the large space all at once.

"Holy shit," I whispered before I could stop myself.

Eric chuckled. "Impressive, isn't it?"

Honestly, yes. It *was* impressive.

Impressive that people could be this freaking cruel to other people.

Women and children were assembled in lines, chains wrapped around their wrists and ankles, all attached to each other and locked into eye bolts welded into the concrete floor. There were maybe a couple dozen, all shapes and sizes and races. Some as young as maybe ten and others old enough to be my grandmother. But the vast majority were near my age. More than a few had vacant, glassy eyes and looked like they'd been drugged. They shivered on the unforgiving floor, barefoot and dressed to show off maximum skin, most clad in skimpy bikinis, but several were just flat-out naked.

And all around them? Men and women, dressed to walk a red carpet, wandering down the line, surveying them. A few even had notebooks and were writing as they walked by.

Armed guards were stationed throughout the room, watching everything with blank expressions, but four of them stood in a row near the back wall in front of another black curtain.

Words caught in my throat, but I managed to get them out. "What's back there?" I pointed at the curtain that partitioned off a separate area.

Eric turned and gave me his full attention, taking my hands. "That's where we've put our special-request orders."

Static buzzed in my brain. Special requests? Like, for food?

"Pet, you understand that some of the buyers have... particular tastes. It's a business."

I was a statue, incapable of processing thoughts or sounds or oxygen in my lungs.

"Bex?" Eric's expression hardened as a man came up behind him puffing on a cigar. He blew a cloud of noxious fumes into the face of a scrawny teenager nearby.

"Eric," he greeted, his warm tone rich and throaty. Dressed in a well-fitted charcoal gray suit, he looked like he'd just stepped out of a board meeting. His slicked-back hair glinted in the lights.

Eric shot me one last look, the meaning pretty damn obvious —*behave*.

"Ambassador Nielsen," Eric returned, shaking his hand. "Have you been here long?"

"Long enough to know that you delivered exactly what I asked for," he replied, tapping the ash from the end of the cigar onto the floor. His beady brown eyes gave me a quick once-over before I was dismissed. "She's spectacular."

Eric smiled, all teeth and smug satisfaction. "It took a bit of extra effort to secure her. Thank you for your patience. Will you be leaving now?"

"No," the ambassador replied, waving off the idea. "I plan to stay. Who knows? I might find a gift for my brother. Bastard's marrying an absolute bitch of a woman. A political match, you know. He'll need someone else when his frigid ice queen can't be bothered to spread her legs."

"Let me know if I can assist you in any way," Eric said.

"You know I will." He wandered off, pausing to watch as a man pulled back a teenager's gums to check her teeth like she was a fucking horse.

No, no, no. This was too much.

I wasn't prepared for *this*. There was no way to fake my way through being okay with any single part of this. Maybe there was a fire alarm I could pull?

"It had to be this way," Eric was saying, still pulling me past the row of prisoners. He hesitated at the black curtain, looking uncertain. "You trust me, right?"

My gaze snapped to his. "I... Of course."

"You're absolute perfection, love," he breathed, pulling back the black curtain and revealing...

I frowned. Were those... dog cages?

Five of them, all wired metal and boxy shapes, but—*oh, sweet holy mother of baby Yoda*—there were women inside them. Three were asleep. The fourth was sobbing, curled into a ball. But the fifth... The fifth looked at me with big hazel eyes, a bruise forming around one of them. Her blonde hair was a wreck, and her red dress had been torn. Scratches crisscrossed her arms, and a chain with a padlock had been wrapped around her slender throat.

She whimpered, the sound ripping me apart as her thin fingers wrapped around the bars of her cage. "B-Bex."

I gaped, stunned.

Horrified.

"Cami?"

CHAPTER 41

BEX

Without thinking it through, I lunged forward and fell to my knees in front of Cami. My hands touched hers for a brief second before grabbing frantically for the padlock. I yanked on it uselessly and turned to Eric. "Open the door."

He was frowning, looking genuinely confused. "Bex, I told you, this is business."

"No," I snapped, "*this* is my *cousin*. Get her out of here."

"She's already been paid for. I can't." He spoke slowly, like I was a little kid he had to explain this to.

I shot to my feet, hands balled at my sides. "This isn't a game, Eric. Let her out."

"No, pet, this *isn't* a game," he replied, folding his arms and glaring at me. "It's business. She belongs to Ambassador Nielsen. He put in a request for a thin, blonde woman. Either a gymnast or a dancer. Camille fits his preferences almost perfectly. Ideally, she'd still be intact, but her notoriety adds a certain flair to the acquisition."

Behind me, Cami let out a soft sob. She threaded her arms through the bars and grabbed the hem of my dress. "Bex, help."

"Eric, no. She's not a freaking piece of art—she's practically my sister," I snapped.

His dark brows lowered. "Bex, you're making a scene."

"You haven't *seen* a scene yet," I spat.

He moved so fast that I didn't have time to react. His hand wrapped around my throat, squeezing, as he bent me backward over Cami's cage. My hips slammed painfully into the bars, my spine arching as I cried out.

"I thought you understood how this business operates," he hissed in my ear.

My gaze flicked around the room wildly. The only people paying attention were the guards covering the cages, and none of them were going to help me. Unless I could take down Eric and a bunch of armed guards—not to mention guys like Senator Nielsen—all by myself, I was screwed. At least until Court showed up.

Eric gave me a hard shake, my teeth clicking together. "You will *not* embarrass me. Get yourself together, or I'll throw you in the cage beside her like another common bitch."

I let my body go limp, all the fight draining from me.

"Bex!" Cami cried below me, sounding hysterical. She tried slapping at Eric's pants, but it was hopelessly ineffective.

"I'm sorry," I rasped, keeping my eyes on Eric.

He stared down at me, his expression a mask of icy rage. "You disappoint me, Bex."

"I know. I… It won't happen again." I swallowed around a cry. "You caught me by surprise—she was supposed to be the maid of honor at our *wedding*."

He squeezed my throat, cutting off my air just because he could. When I started to panic and was on the verge of thrashing, he let me go.

Lightheaded, I crashed down on all fours, gasping.

A fist tangled in my hair, wrenching my head back. "I mean it, Bex. Tonight is too important for you to fuck up. Can you behave?"

"Yes," I gasped, tears stinging my eyes. "I'll behave. I promise."

Still using my hair, he pulled me to my feet. His gray eyes were like a tempest on the sea, churning and violent. "We have things to do now, my love. But first, I think I'm owed an apology."

It took everything in me not to knee him in the balls, and I made a mental note to start self-defense training the second I was free of this psycho.

Instead, I licked my lips. "I'm so sorry, Eric. Forgive me."

Still looking annoyed, he loosened his hold on my hair. His index finger notched my chin up. "Of course I forgive you. I love you."

His love wasn't a gift; it was a threat.

He kissed my lips softly, almost reverently. "I suppose I also owe you an apology. Perhaps I was wrong to not alert you that Camille was going to be part of tonight's offerings."

"Bex," Cami begged at my back.

I stiffened my spine. "Can we please leave this area?" I wouldn't be able to fake it if I turned around and saw Cami stuffed in the damn dog cage again, makeup wrecked and dress torn.

"Of course," Eric assured me, wrapping an arm around my waist and leading me from the space as Cami started to scream.

Eric stopped and turned to the guard. "Shut her up."

I bit the insides of my cheeks until I tasted blood, watching in horror as the guard withdrew a syringe from the inner pocket of his suit jacket. He headed behind the black curtain, and a moment later, Cami's cries stopped.

My heart stopped beating. "Did he kill her?"

Eric laughed. "Heavens, no. She's worth too much. He simply gave her a sedative that will keep her calm for the rest of the evening. We're not savages, darling." He tweaked my nose. "Now, let's fix your hair." He smoothed my hair back from my face, stroking the loose waves back into submission.

"Thank you," I murmured like an obedient girl when he stopped and shot me a pointed look.

"You're welcome," he cooed, and then he pulled me through the crowd yet again, pausing to speak to a few people.

I stayed mute at his side, doing my part by politely smiling and nodding while inside I was shattering. I didn't see a clock anywhere, and I had no way of knowing where Court was or when he'd be here.

All I could do was hold on to the bone-deep, gut-level certainty that he would be here. He was coming *for me*.

It was amazing how much a week could change a person's life.

This time a week ago, I was vowing to cut Court Woods out of my life forever. Now, he was the only person I wanted. The person I needed. The one who made me feel invincible and precious, valued and strong.

Where are you, Court?

Eric led me through the crowded room and back toward the stage until we were near the VIP section. It was then that I noticed the room had another door near the stage, probably opening to the other side of the lot where we'd parked.

A few men were seated in the section, all holding drinks and laughing. All but one turned as Eric and I approached, but when we came to a stop in front of them, I realized the man who hadn't bothered glancing at us was none other than General Jasper Woods.

Court's father.

The guy who'd used me like a chess piece, almost killing me in the process.

My breathing quickened as my pulse accelerated. I hadn't anticipated coming face-to-face with Court's dad. It had been years since I'd seen him. Maybe I'd get lucky and he wouldn't remember me. Or, maybe he wouldn't care at all about me being here, since he and my dad were still working together.

"General," Eric greeted, his tone hinting at polite reverence as he inclined his head. "My name is—"

"Eric Lambert-Durand," General Woods drawled, looking wholly unimpressed. "I hear you were quite instrumental in arranging all of... this."

"Indeed," Eric replied, not seeming put off by the other man's tone.

The general scuffed his toe on the dirty cement floor. "Interesting accommodations."

One of the men to his left snickered. "I've seen cleaner chicken coops." He had a thick Southern accent and a red handlebar mustache that twitched as he spoke.

Eric's cheeks flushed. "What it lacks in decorative charm, it makes up for in convenience and security."

"We'll see," the general replied, sipping his drink and effectively dismissing Eric.

And then his gaze landed on me.

It took me aback, for a second, how much Court looked like his dad. They had the same bone structure and jaw and hair color, but the eyes was where they were different, and not just because the general had green eyes and Court had brown. The general's lacked any sign of compassion, where Court was all heart.

I knew how they sparkled when he was amused. Went flat when he was pissed. And softened when he looked at me.

"Well, well," General Woods murmured, slowly standing up. He was a few inches shorter than Court, but he was heavily muscled and took care of himself. "I can't believe it. Little Rebecca Whittier."

"Hello, General Woods," I replied, my spine stiff. So much for him not remembering me.

The corner of his mouth tipped up. "What in the world are you doing here?"

Before I could speak, Eric cut me off. "She's my fiancée."

The general's brows shot up to his hairline. "Fiancée?"

Mustache man leaned around to peer at me. "Whittier, huh? Related to Malcolm?"

"His daughter," the general replied with an amused smirk.

"Ah," Mustache said with a nod.

"The last time I saw you, you were… quite ill." He shook his head, looking sad. "Had my son worried to death."

"I don't really remember much from when I was sick," I told him and shrugged with what I hoped was an innocent smile. "And Court and I haven't been friends in a long time."

Not a lie.

Sometimes I wondered if we'd ever been friends, or if we'd just always belonged to each other. What we had was deeper than friendship.

"Of course," General Woods murmured, his expression unreadable as he kept his gaze on me like a laser. "And how did you and Eric meet?"

"My cousin is… *was* dating his brother," I admitted, unable to keep some of the bitterness from seeping into my tone.

His shrewd gaze turned to Eric. "And you had no idea who she was?"

"I knew she was related to Malcolm Whittier, but I had no idea how deep her connections ran to the organization prior." Eric beamed at me. "Talk about a fortuitous coincidence."

The general gave a slow nod as he rubbed his jaw. Then he looked at me, hate and scorn in his eyes. "Well, at least you're consistent. You find young men with a modicum of potential and ruin them. Just how golden is that cunt of yours?"

I instinctively stepped back, sucking in a sharp breath.

"Excuse me, General, but that is my fiancée you're speaking to," Eric spluttered. "A woman you've known since she was a girl."

"What the fuck would you even know about that?" he demanded, rounding on Eric.

Eric's gaze jerked to me for a beat. "She told me that your families were friends. That—"

General Woods's caustic laugh cut him off. "Fucking hell. You're just as stupid as my son. He thought he loved her, too, you know. But he was wrong, and she *ruined* him. Destroyed his potential." He glared at me, his expression full of venom.

"Ruined?" Eric sounded confused.

Jasper pushed a finger into my face. "He was never the same after he saved you. Went off the rails, an absolute disappointment to the Woods name. All because his mind was so twisted up over *you.*"

"It must kill you, huh?" I asked, finally done with the whole farce of the evening. "That your precious son is absolutely *nothing* like the person you are. Court is good and kind and loyal."

"*Is*, huh?" He arched a brow at me. "I wasn't aware you and my son were once again on speaking terms."

I gasped, realizing I'd slipped up.

"Where *is* my son? He seems to have forgotten how to answer a damn call these days," he snarled. "Perhaps history will repeat itself. Think if I take *you*, he'll come running to save you once more?"

My gaze darted around as I looked for a way out, my fight-or-flight instinct landing firmly in the *flight* category.

Mustache laughed and sipped his drink, watching like this was the best show he'd seen in years. Even Eric seemed absolutely stunned at the way Jasper Woods and I were going at it.

"Let me ask you a question, Eric," General Woods snarled. "How much is she worth to you?"

Eric looked stunned. "Excuse me?"

"Her worth," the general repeated, enunciating each word like Eric was a dimwitted kid. "Is she worth your place in this organization?"

Eric's jaw dropped. "General, sir, I'm not entirely sure—"

"Let's say we're starting the auction early," General Woods cut him off. "And the first purchase is this little bitch. So? How much will she cost me? Or, I suppose I should ask, how much is she going to cost *you*?" He jerked his head, and two guards peeled away from the wall to come over and flank Eric.

Eric's gray eyes went wide as he looked at me. "I thought you said that you were friends with—"

General Woods's laugh boomed through the space. "Jesus, you're a pussy-whipped sack of shit, aren't you? Do I need to repeat my question yet again? Or perhaps remind you just who is providing all this security? One snap of my fingers, and you're just another bloodstain on the ground."

Eric studied me for a beat and then shook his head.

My eyes slid shut, and I braced for what I sensed was coming next. I'd been betting the odds, pretending I was important to men like the general, to get on Eric's good side.

Well, it had worked.

Eric had bought every lie I'd told. Enough so that he'd brought me straight into the lion's den.

And now I was going to be devoured.

"Take her," Eric said, his tone cool.

The general snapped his fingers, and the two men behind Eric grabbed me, one on each arm.

"Good choice," the general told him. "Mind if we use your office?"

Before Eric could reply, General Woods turned on his heel and stalked toward the rear staircase. When I didn't move, the guards dragged me. My heels slipped over the concrete, catching on the hem of my dress until I heard it tear.

"Wait—stop!" I tried to fight back, but the two men's grips tightened even more.

The general turned, his arm flying as he backhanded me.

Stars exploded across my vision as my head snapped to the side. My face throbbed, tears instantly gathering. Holy *shit*, that hurt.

"Do you have any idea what you've cost me?" Woods hissed. "My son turned into a little bitch because of you. But not anymore. As long as I have you? He'll do exactly what I want." His thumb and index finger crudely grasped my chin. "Maybe I'll even let him have a little fun with you when he behaves."

"General—"

The second slap shouldn't have come as a surprise, but shock still struck me like lightning.

"Shut up," he seethed. "If I want you to open your mouth, I'll have my cock ready to shove in it."

Dazed, I let myself be pulled up the stairs to the office. My feet tripped on several rungs, but I never went down, thanks to the two assholes keeping me moving.

General Woods pushed open the door at the top. "Oh, honey. I'm home," he called out loudly, the mocking edge to his tone sharper than a sword.

I was pushed into the space by the idiots, my ankle twisting as one heel slipped. This time, when I fell, no one bothered to catch me.

I landed in a graceless heap on cracked linoleum flooring, then braced myself on my hands and took a breath.

It couldn't be much longer now. Court would be here any minute.

"What the hell are you doing?" a horrified but familiar voice asked.

I shook my dark hair back… and looked right up into the face of my father.

CHAPTER 42

BEX

My father wasn't tall. He was average height and average build. He wore wire-rimmed glasses that he was constantly pushing up the bridge of his nose with one finger. His dark hair was thinning on top, and I knew he was self-conscious about it.

At least, he had been when I'd last seen him, several months ago.

"Becca?" Dad gaped at me from where he sat in front of a row of monitors and a keyboard. He twirled around in his chair and started to stand, but General Woods shoved him back down, hard enough that the chair would've toppled if the back hadn't been against the desk.

"Jasper, what in the hell do you think you're doing?" Dad glared at the man he'd once considered his best friend.

"Just making sure you hold up your end of the deal, Malcolm," the general replied indifferently. He crossed the room to stand beside me, petting the top of my head like I was a labradoodle. "I had no idea your daughter grew up to be so stunning."

Dad's face was ashen. "Jas, no."

Fingers teased the ends of my hair. "She'd be popular at The Palace."

I'd never seen my dad get angry so fast. "Don't you fucking dare even *think* it. I've done everything—"

"You think I don't know about those side deals you've been cutting in Washington?" The general left me to stalk back to Dad, looming over him. "You think we don't have men inside every single facet of that city? Even the fucking president knows who's really in charge."

Dad's chest heaved, but he didn't speak.

"You always were a fool, Malcolm," Woods went on, sounding disgusted. "You may be a genius around a computer chip, but with everything else in the world? You're useless. It just so happens that Kent and I still need you, and, to make sure you do as you're told, I'll teach you the same lesson I taught my son."

Turning, Woods nodded to his goons. They were on me in a second, picking me up until the tips of my shoes barely touched the floor. The one on the right twisted my arm behind my back.

I cried out, sure my bone was going to pop out of my shoulder.

"Stop!" Dad exclaimed, getting up. "I'll do what you want. I'm sorry, Jasper. I just… Fuck." He stabbed his fingers through his hair. "I promise. I'll do what you and Kent want, okay? Just don't hurt my daughter."

Another snap of the general's fingers, and my arm was released.

"I'm so sorry, sweetie," Dad said to me, his eyes pleading for me to understand.

"Don't do what he wants," I hissed. "I don't care what they do to me—this is *wrong*."

General Woods got in my face, blocking my view of my dad. "Think you'll be saying that when I have you strapped to an altar in The Palace? While I'm picking the biggest, fattest cocks to split your pussy wide open? Letting men and women impale that asshole on whatever they want? Did you know that with the right amount of pressure, an asshole can fit a baseball bat inside?"

I tried to pull back, but there was nowhere to go.

Woods sucked on his teeth, making a soft *tutting* noise. "Can't say it looked too pleasant. There was a shitload of blood involved, but it was entertaining. I wonder if your pussy could—"

"Jasper, *stop*!" Dad roared.

General Woods whirled like a viper and punched Dad in the face, sending him crashing back into the desk.

I gasped and tried to move forward to help my father, but one of Jasper's goons pressed a heavy hand on my shoulder, keeping me still.

The general didn't let up, raining punches down on my father's head until Dad slumped to the ground, blinking groggily. Crimson was smeared across the general's knuckles, and it dripped onto the floor.

"You," he seethed, glaring at Dad, "don't *ever* tell me what to do. Don't forget who owns your ass, Malcolm." A smirk twitched across his lips. "And now I own your daughter's ass, too. Behave, or I'll sell it to every sick fuck I can think of."

My stomach pitched, nausea rolling through my gut.

Dad gave a weak nod and bowed his head in surrender.

I wasn't sure what to think. Seeing my dad literally brought to his knees was awful, but knowing I was being used as a pawn—*again*—was pretty twisted, too.

The general brushed the wrinkles from his shirt and straightened. "Now, Malcolm, you and your daughter are going to stay in here. I have shit to deal with." He looked at one of the guards. "Watch the door. If either of them tries to leave, break their legs."

The goon responded with an excited smile. "Will do, boss."

Nodding, Woods jerked his head at the other guy, and they both stalked out of the room. After a beat, the one they'd left as our babysitter edged out and closed the door behind him.

I stumbled forward, dropping to my knees beside my dad. "Are you okay?"

A sob wrenched from his chest as he buried his head in his hands. "I messed up, Becca."

He really had, but he was still my dad, so I wrapped an arm around his shoulders and tried to comfort him. "It'll be okay." *Please don't let that be a lie*.

"Why are you here?" Dad asked, his voice hitching as he stared at me with a wild look.

I grimaced. "It's a long story, but, I think the better question is, why are you helping these people?"

Dad's head lowered once more. "I'm so ashamed of myself. You have to believe that I never wanted *any* of this."

"And yet, you're here," I replied, not ready to let him off the hook. I looked at the computers. "You're part of this."

"Not by choice," he quickly replied. "I tried to get away from them, truly I did. I even met a congressman who was going to help me. But then Jasper and Kent found out. They were already on edge after Gary's death and Beckett's disappearance, but when they heard I was planning to betray them, they threatened you and your mother after they killed the congressman and his entire family."

Not surprising.

I pushed myself up, looking around the small space.

Aside from the desk and the rolling chair, there was a beaten-up wooden coffee table and two vinyl armchairs. A skewed framed certificate proclaiming the factory had once passed inspection was covered in a layer of grime and filth.

"We need to get out of here," I murmured, going to the window that overlooked the auction floor.

The auction seemed close to starting. People had begun taking their seats, filling the space with noise. To the right I could see the small landing area outside of the office where our guard was. He was picking at his nails, oblivious to me peering at him through the one-way glass. When he turned, using the mirror side to inspect his teeth, I turned away with a grimace.

"What time is it?" I asked.

Dad got up slowly, wincing and touching his already purpling cheek. "Almost eleven."

"Come on, Court," I whispered, knowing he had to be close by now.

"Court?" Dad blinked at me. "Court *Woods*?"

I nodded.

"I wasn't aware you two were friends again."

I shot him a baleful look. "Well, Dad, you'd have to actually be part of my life to know who my friends are." I didn't bother keeping the acidic bite from my words.

"Becca—"

I held up a hand. "Don't. Are you really trying to stop Jasper and Kent?"

He nodded.

I looked past him to the screens, realizing they were surveillance feeds. "What are you doing up here?"

"Monitoring the local channels to make sure we have a heads up if law enforcement gets wind of this event," he replied.

"Auction, Dad," I snapped, pointing a finger at the window. "They're selling people down there. So, why not just call the cops now?"

He looked uncomfortable. "Because, Becca, I would be held responsible, too."

I threw my arms in the air. "News flash, Dad, you *are* responsible, too."

He looked at the floor. "I'm not a man equipped to handle prison, Rebecca."

I gaped at him, wondering how he'd ever been my hero. He had the spine of a jellyfish; no wonder the general was so easily able to control him. "Well, make a decision fast, Dad."

He gave me a quizzical look.

"Court's on his way here," I explained. "He's coming for me, and he's bringing friends. The kind with badges and guns and the power to lock you away for a lifetime."

He paled.

"Cami's downstairs in a cage," I added. "She's been sold off to some sick freak who plans on doing God-knows-what to her. General Woods is about to do the same to me. So, you need to ask yourself— can you handle going to prison if it means saving me? Saving Cami? Or are you going to tell your friend *Jasper* that he's about to be in a world of shit?"

Dad looked horrified. "I can't... Becca, you don't understand the—"

"I understand plenty." I cut him off, bitter and hurt. "I understand more than you could ever know, but now you need to make a choice, because Court *is* coming for me."

Clearly conflicted, Dad looked everywhere but at me.

It was like being stabbed in the heart with a rusty knife. "What am *I* worth to *you*, Dad?"

Finally he looked at me, hopelessness in his gaze. "I'm sorry I'm such a disappointment, Becca. I'm so sorry for the pain I've caused you. Your mother. All I ever wanted to do was help people."

"You can do that now," I insisted, tears blurring my vision as I laid my heart on the line. This was my *dad*. The guy who'd taught me how to ride a bike. The one who'd read me bedtime stories. I had to believe there was something in him that would do the right thing.

Shoulders slumping, Dad turned to the desk and peered at the screens. He enhanced one, showing an image of several men sneaking along a shadowed brick wall, balaclavas covering their faces and weapons drawn.

"They're here," he said in a wooden voice.

"Dad, *please*," I begged.

He reached forward, turned off the screens, and shut down the computer just as someone welcomed the outside room to the auction over a microphone.

Clearing his throat, Dad met my eyes. "I choose you, sweetheart. I'm sorry if I ever made you doubt that."

Relief hit me as I heard the first loud *bang* ring out. Someone screamed... and all hell broke loose.

CHAPTER 43

BEX

I raced across the room and pressed my palms flat against the window. All the assholes in their finery were starting to freak out.

Smoke billowed in from the emergency exit, and several men with guns ran from different areas, converging around General Woods, who looked pissed as he barked orders.

My gaze jerked to the door. This might be my one chance to get to Cami, but I'd need help getting past the guard.

"Dad." I turned, my heart plummeting when I saw Dad's laptop open and him typing furiously, his fingers flying over the keys. "What are you doing?"

He hit one last key and flashed me a grim smile. "The right thing. I just sent out an alert to local and international law enforcement. They'll be here in minutes. Then I sent out a tip to local news syndicates. The bigger the impact, the less likely they'll be able to hide."

I knew my dad was good with computers, but that was some Ash-level hacker shit. "You did that?"

He hung his head. "The disbelief in your tone tells me all I need to know. I'm so sorry I've disappointed you, sweet girl. I'm sorry I let you be hurt by this world. Hurt by my actions."

Emotion clogged my throat, and I had to try several times to swallow it down. "Thank you." Gunshots peppered the air in rapid bursts. We both dropped to our knees on instinct. "I need to get to Cami before someone else does."

"You can't go out there," Dad insisted, crawling to me.

"I have to," I replied, pushing up into a crouch.

"Rebecca!" he hissed as I crept toward the window again.

The guard was gone, likely having abandoned his post to join the others in fighting. A few people were hiding under the seats, but for the most part, the main room had cleared. I could hear pandemonium in the foyer and wondered how bad the room where the girls were was.

Another round of shots cracked through the night, followed by a *boom* that sent shudders through the building.

"Holy shit," I whispered, wondering if the plan was to bring down the whole warehouse.

"That sounded like it came from the docks," Dad muttered. He gave me a worried look. "We need to get out of here."

"That's what I've been saying," I snapped, exasperated.

His jaw tightened. "We'll go down the stairs and out the side door."

"What? No. Cami's in the other room, behind a black curtain," I replied, shaking my head. "She's already been s-sold." I choked on the words.

"Camille isn't my concern—you are." Dad stared at me.

Why was he being so stubborn about this? He'd picked a helluva time for his paternal instincts to kick in.

Unless…

Aw, hell.

I lifted my chin. "Is that it? Or are you hoping Court will let you make a run for it if he finds us together?"

The guilty look was the last twist of the knife I could take. He was still thinking of himself.

"Think of all the good I can do to help people, Becca," he pleaded as he grabbed my hands. "Locked up, I'm no good—"

I yanked away. "Screw you, Dad. Do whatever you want. I'm

going to save as many people as I can." I spun away and pulled open the door, then thundered down the stairs before Dad could stop me.

Not that he tried.

He didn't even call my name, though I knew he followed me down because I heard his thundering footsteps. When I looked back, I saw him split off from me at the landing and run for the door on the opposite side of the room. He ripped open the door and ran into the night.

Fucking coward.

My heart splintered, another piece breaking off and falling into the abyss, but I'd unpack those emotions later when I had time. Not while people were shooting guns a few yards from me.

Over the chaos of people scrambling and guns firing, I heard the low, familiar whine of sirens in the distance. Another blast went off, this one seeming to come from the direction of where the cars were parked.

A woman hiding under a seat to my left shrieked, her shrill cry bouncing off the walls until the man beside her slapped a hand over her bright red lips. He dragged her backward until they were out from under the seats. Then he grabbed her hand, and they ran for the side door, disappearing into the night after my father.

Tiptoeing toward the foyer, I peeked my head around a partition and gasped when I came face-to-face with Alex. The foyer was empty except for him and two bodies dressed in the dark tactical gear of General Woods's men. The front door gaped open ominously.

"Alex—"

He covered my mouth with his hand and propelled us backward into the room I'd just come from. My heels tangled in the hem of my dress, and we toppled to the ground, Alex landing heavily on top of me.

I struggled, fighting to get his weight off me.

"Stop fighting, dammit," he snarled, grinding the side of my face against the dirty gray floor. "I'll fucking leave you here."

I stilled, even as my heart thrashed inside my ribcage, my eyes wide as I tried to look at him.

"Don't scream," he warned, slowly peeling his hand from my lips.

"Get off me," I demanded as soon as I had the ability.

He scoffed, narrowing his eyes. "Looking for your boyfriend?"

"Fuck Eric," I snarled.

His left eye twitched. "You might not be as stupid as I thought."

"Where is he?" I demanded, realizing how quiet things had gotten. I tried pushing him off again. "I need to get Cami."

His eyes hardened. "Cami's gone."

Panic unlike anything I'd ever known exploded in my chest. Suddenly not being able to breathe had absolutely zero to do with the guy on top of me. "*No.*"

Alex got up and reluctantly offered me a hand. "We need to get out of here while they're fighting out back. They blew up the dock and half the cars in the lot, but I know for a fact my little brother keeps a spare car half a mile from here. The key's in the wheel well."

"Why would you help me?" I got up by myself, ignoring his hand.

He looked down. "Because I couldn't help Cami, but she'd want me to help you."

I watched him, studied the self-loathing and regret in his eyes. "You brought her here."

"I didn't have a choice." His words were bitter. "Eric—"

"Save it," I snapped, over men and their excuses. And they claimed *women* were the weaker sex?

I was calling bull-fucking-shit.

Alex glared at me, his hands balling into fists at his sides.

"I'm going after my cousin," I told him, leaving zero room for arguing.

He sucked in a breath and shook his head. "Fine. Let's go."

My brows flew up. "You're coming?"

"Believe it or not, I care about Cami," he muttered, turning to go back into the room where the women had been chained.

"I don't believe it," I retorted. "You let your brother sell her off to some sleazy perv."

He winced, jaw tight, and then followed me through the foyer.

I took a deep breath before darting across the open space and pushing aside the partition to see into the room that had been set up like a preview for the buyers. Less than thirty minutes earlier, this room had been full of people. Women and kids, chained to the floors and walls.

Now it was empty.

The sirens were closer, likely out front by now, but none of that mattered if they were gone.

"Where are they?" I whispered.

Alex snorted before tapping my shoulder and pointing toward the curtained-off area where Cami had been. "The door behind that curtain leads to a hallway. There's a staircase at the end they'll use to access a series of tunnels connecting all the buildings on this pier. When this place was operational, they used them to move different goods and shipments. That's how they'll get everyone out. None of the tunnels are on the public schematics—they'll just pop up in one of the other buildings." Alex shrugged.

"You know a lot about this place," I remarked.

He winced. "We played here as kids before... Well, before."

"Okay, let's go." I took a deep breath and readied myself to rip back the curtain. My hand brushed the black fabric a second before an arm wound around my chest, hauling me back against a wall of unmovable muscle.

A gun cocked, the barrel flashing silver as it was aimed over my shoulder at Alex's head.

Oh, shit. We'd waited too long.

CHAPTER 44

COURT

I couldn't wait any longer.

"I'm going in," I said in a clipped tone, the earpieces that Ash had outfitted us with communicating my plan to the rest of the team. We were split up, but Ash was keeping us straight. I glanced up, spying the blinking red dot of the drone recording everything. It was how Ash was protecting us all.

"I'm coming with you." Linc's voice sounded in my ear, but I knew my best friend's frame even in the inky darkness.

From several yards away, I spotted the wide shoulders of either Rook or Royal. At this range and time of night, it was impossible to tell who.

"Be careful." Okay, it was Rook.

"Who called the fucking cops?" Ryan snarled as red and white lights lit up the other end of the mostly gravel road leading to the warehouse.

I had to give it to Eric, the setup was smart. The property backed up to the water and was situated dead center in a dilapidated industrial park that hadn't had a tenant in a decade. The only people who came here were vagrants and criminals.

We'd lit the place up like the goddamned Christmas tree in Rocke-feller Center.

To my right, cars were burning, thanks to a handful of Molotov cocktails Bishop had made. The guy had a serious hard-on for explosions, and he'd taken a lot of joy in setting up some carefully selected cars to go *boom* and essentially block the auction attendees from using cars to get away.

Sure, a few had managed to pile into cars, but the rest were on foot and easy for Trick and his team—the ones he knew for a goddamn fact he could trust—to corral.

When Rook had made the call to tell Trick he had a viper in his nest, he'd apparently already known who. They'd isolated the man—whatever that meant—before hauling ass to meet us here.

Taking out the dock had been Royal's idea. We all knew what those barges meant, and if they made it to international waters, they'd be gone, along with anything and any*one* on board.

Without the firepower to take down all the boats, the dock had been the best idea.

We hit the warehouse, Royal and Rook engaging and drawing out some of the guards from the front where the rest of us picked them off. The attendees made our jobs easier by dressing up in flashy clothes that couldn't be confused with the dark tactical gear the guys from Black Box Ops wore.

But things were quiet out here—aside from the literal fire burning and the approaching stream of cop cars—and that meant it was time to head inside.

I hadn't seen Bex, though I'd looked for her in every face of every person who exited. Some had fled through the side exits, straight into the crosshairs of members of Trick's team. They'd been rounded up, but no one had seen Bex.

No one had seen the women being sold off either, which meant they were all inside together, along with the majority of my father's men.

Something twitched in my gut—a feeling that something wasn't right.

"Where the fuck is everyone?" Bishop hissed.

Yeah, that.

Even if some had gotten away, we were missing too many people.

Like my father and fucking Eric.

"Sweep inside," Royal ordered. "Trick's team can handle the police and red tape. Our priority is the women and Bex."

No, Bex was *the* priority, at least for me.

I glanced at Linc, and he gave me an affirmative nod, reading my mind. Ryan joined us as we met my brothers at the entrance.

The foyer was empty, save for two bodies. I didn't give a shit about them, worried only about finding my girl. At the end of the entryway, there was a split. The double doors to the left were wide open, but a black curtain hung in front of the opening to the right.

"Rook, Court, Linc, go right," Royal commanded. "We'll go left."

It took all my willpower to fall in line behind Rook and let him take the lead. He had all the experience in this area and had swept through more buildings as a SEAL than I'd ever know. He moved like a panther, all stealth, as he crept forward, nudging the curtain aside with the muzzle of his gun before stepping into the space.

"You know a lot about this place," a familiar voice hissed, drawing my eyes to two people on the opposite side of the room, standing by a dark curtain.

My feet were moving, my long legs eating up the distance between us. I missed whatever the guy said as my heart pounded, blood roaring in my ears.

She took a step toward the curtain, and I reached out and grabbed her, pulling her into my arms.

Right where Becca Whittier belonged.

CHAPTER 45

BEX

Time stopped as the warm body at my back held me prisoner. I inhaled deeply, and my knees almost buckled in relief as I recognized the soft scents of leather and citrus.

I knew that smell.

I knew these arms.

"Court." I choked on his name. My knees wobbled as I leaned against him.

"Hey, princess," he greeted, his voice a low rumble that reverberated through my body. His hand tightened on the gun aimed at Alex. "Get on the fucking ground, asshole."

Alex shot me a look. "Uh, Bex? Can you—"

Court spun me away, into the arms of someone else, before stalking forward and pressing the gun to Alex's temple. "Get. The fuck. Down."

"Hey, Bex," Linc murmured, angling himself in front of me. I spotted a third guy but couldn't tell who it was. Just that he was prime panty-melting material—tall, dark, and muscled.

"Wait, Court, it's okay. I think," I added as an afterthought.

Alex lowered himself to the floor, and Court glanced back at me. His dark eyes were empty voids behind the black mask over his face.

"He's helping me," I continued.

Linc scoffed. "Like fuck he is. That's Eric's brother."

"I know," I replied. "He was helping me find the women. Eric sold Cami."

"Fuck," a voice that sounded a lot like Rook grumbled.

"Where are they?" Court demanded.

Alex let out a weak cough, sending a puff of dust and debris tumbling across the floor. "I already told Bex—they're in the tunnels by now."

"Tunnels?" Linc asked.

"Apparently there are tunnels that connect the buildings underground," I informed them. "It's how they're moving everyone."

"There aren't any tunnels on the schematics." Yeah, that was definitely Rook.

Alex let out a humorless laugh. "No shit, genius. They're secret for a fucking reason. Hey!" he cried out as Court ground the gun against his head. "I'm trying to *help*!"

I snorted and shook my head before looking at Court. "We need to go. If they get away—"

I'd lose Cami.

I couldn't lose her.

Rook sighed. "Royal, we need you in here. We have a lead on the women."

I gave him an odd look. "Uh."

Court tapped his ear. "Ear piece."

That made more sense. "Your dad is with them," I added.

"And the general," Rook added to Royal with a snarl. An automatic rifle hung from a strap wrapped around his torso like a G.I. Joe accessory, but I knew that weapon was the farthest thing from a toy.

Moments later, three more guys dressed head to toe in black burst into the room.

"Where?" Royal demanded, his voice just this side of human. I'd read enough paranormal romance to question whether or not Royal was a bear shifter; the guy was that big and growly.

I pointed at the curtained area. "Door back there."

"Court—"

"You're *not* sidelining me," Court hissed, his gun still aimed at Alex as he pressed a boot into Alex's back to hold him still.

I couldn't *see* his face, but I got the distinct impression that Royal was pissed. Maybe because that was his default setting, but still, he didn't like anyone questioning his orders.

"What building will they come out of?" Rook asked, crouching by Alex's head.

"You think Eric's stupid enough to tell me that shit? I have no idea, man," Alex whined. "There are five different buildings, so five different options." He hesitated. "But there's one that leads to the other side of the pier. I doubt you guys hit it. There's a small boathouse they could use."

"Goddammit," Royal swore.

"How long would it take them to get there?" Rook asked.

"It's almost a mile away," Alex offered.

I turned to Royal, assuming by default that the guys flanking him were Bishop and Ryan. "They have almost two dozen women and children with them, including my cousin. I'm going too."

"The fuck you are," Royal snapped.

Court stiffened. "Don't speak to her like that."

"This isn't a fucking democracy," Royal retorted. "And we're losing time standing around here. Civilians stay the fuck out."

"He's right, Becca," Court said. "You need to go somewhere safe."

"Fuck that noise," I challenged. "I'm going."

"Fuck me sideways," Royal hissed. "Trick, can you hear me? Yeah. I need backup, if things can be managed out there by the cops." He paused, listening for a minute before angling his body toward Court. "You want your girl safe?"

Court nodded.

"Then you get her the fuck out of here," Royal told him. "Goes for you two as well."

Linc sighed. "Guess that means it's time."

"You sure that's smart?" Ryan asked. "You might need the support."

Heavy footsteps clomped from inside the entryway. A moment

later, Trick, Wanda, and seven more guys who looked like a terrorist's worst nightmare stormed into the room, armed to the freaking teeth with weapons. They looked ready for war.

"National Police and Europol are here," Trick said, Wanda sitting at his side. Her head tilted up to watch him. "My CO is working with them, setting up a containment zone. I heard what you said about the boathouse—we're sending people that way to pin them between us."

"Then let's go," Linc growled, bouncing on the balls of his feet.

"Phoenix protocol," Royal snapped, sucking the wind from Linc's sails. "We're going. Court, get that fuckwad in the hands of the cops." He motioned with his gun to Alex. "Get your girl safe, and then all of you get the fuck out of the public eye before the press shows."

"Ask for Lieutenant Striker," Trick advised, ripping back the first curtain. He tore down a second, revealing a simple wooden door that led to the tunnels Alex had described.

"What's Phoenix protocol?" I asked, confused, as Court yanked Alex to his feet.

"It means Royal's in charge," Linc replied with a weary sigh. "And we're getting benched."

Bishop cackled as he ran by, following Trick and Royal into the curtained area. "Catch you on the flip side, Bex."

"Bishop," I called, grabbing his arm. "They have Cami." I didn't need to voice what I was begging for.

"I'll get her," he swore, giving me a nod.

I stayed, watching them disappear behind the wooden door into a void where I couldn't follow.

"Take him," Court snarled, shoving Alex in Ryan's direction.

Ryan caught him with ease and pushed Alex ahead, then followed him with the barrel of a gun pressed between his shoulder blades.

"Fuck," Alex complained. "I'm not fighting you. We're on the same team."

"No, we aren't," I shot back, still furious that he'd given Cami to Eric.

Linc touched my back briefly as he followed Ryan, leaving me alone with Court.

Court pulled his mask up, revealing his stupidly symmetrical, gorgeous face. His chocolate brown eyes were molten as he holstered his gun and yanked me to his chest. His lips descended, and he kissed me hard as his tongue swept into my mouth and he devoured me whole.

I wrapped my fingers around the straps of his bulletproof vest as my legs started to tremble.

He pulled away from me. "You're shaking, baby."

"C-cold," I managed to get out between chattering teeth. My skin pebbled like I was in a freezer. Even my bones rattled.

"Shit," Court murmured, hugging me to him. "Becca, you're in shock."

"N-n-no I'm n-not," I forced out, even as a strange buzzing sound filled the space between my ears.

"Yeah, you are," he countered, swinging me into his arms with ease.

I hated the hard Kevlar that kept me from burrowing against him, but I settled for tucking my face against his neck and inhaling his scent.

"Can you pull my mask down, princess?" He kissed the top of my head.

It took a few tries to remember how my arm worked, but I managed to clumsily tug the mask back over his face, hating that it hid him from view. It was the best damn view in the world.

"In the world, huh?" he teased me with a soft laugh as he started to walk.

Crap. I'd said that out loud? I needed to get it together before I admitted those pants made his ass look utterly biteable.

"You can nibble on my ass all you want later." His chest shook with laughter.

I huffed a sigh.

"Keep your head down when we go outside, okay? I don't want anyone to see you," he warned.

I didn't know why. I honestly didn't care. I did as he requested, letting my hair fall around my face as we stepped into the chilly night air. There were so many sounds—sirens, yelling, arguing—but at least no gunshots.

"Hey!" someone shouted, and Court paused.

"Does she need medical treatment?" a raspy female voice demanded in a heavy French accent, and I peeked through my hair to see a woman dressed in a three-piece business suit, her strawberry-blonde hair pulled back into a ponytail. A gold badge was clipped to the front of her jacket.

"No. I'm looking for Lieutenant Striker," Court told her in a detached voice, angling his body to show her his shoulder. I peeked around, spotting a small phoenix patch sewn into the material.

The woman studied me for a beat, noting the way I was holding on to Court like he was my lifeline, before nodding. She pointed some-where behind us. "She's back there."

Court spun on his heel and stalked in that direction.

I tried to clench my teeth together, but they wouldn't stop chatter-ing. I couldn't stop shaking.

"Almost there, Becca," Court whispered. "Hang on, princess."

I managed a small nod, the burning urge to cry building behind my eyes. I squeezed them shut but was immediately flooded by the memory of the viewing room. Of the women and kids. Of the cages and Cami begging me to help her.

A sob ripped free of my throat before I could stop it.

"I know," he murmured, his arms tightening around me.

Night had long since fallen, but the sky was bright with colored lights streaking through the darkness. Fire glowed in several places, and I spotted a few burning cars. Farther away, it looked like the fire had spread from the pier to engulf one of the vessels.

Fancy-dressed people were clumped in groups on the dirty parking lot and patchy grass, some with their hands zip-tied behind their backs.

"Lieutenant Striker?" Court asked, bringing us to a stop.

"You are?" a brusk, no-nonsense voice demanded.

"Court Woods," he replied. "Trick said we should ask for you."

"Ah," she mused. "Part of Phoenix?"

I felt him nod.

"Is she one of the rescued women? We're setting up triage over there. Social workers are on their way to help with housing and treatment."

"This is… She's not one of them," Court finally answered.

There was silence, and I got the sense that the lieutenant wasn't a fan of vague answers.

I looked up, taking a gamble that this was safe ground, since Court had spoken his name and Trick had vouched for the lieutenant.

"My name is Rebecca Whittier," I supplied. "I came here with Eric Lambert-Durand."

Lieutenant Striker was a tall, leggy brunette with sharp eyes that appeared almost violet. The smattering of freckles across the bridge of her nose might've been cute, if I didn't think she'd punch me in the teeth for saying so. She commanded the very air around us, even if she was a few inches shorter than Court.

Her brows lifted as I spoke. "You're the inside girl."

Court stiffened.

"Relax," Lieutenant Striker assured him, then sighed and cracked a tiny smile for me. "Are you all right, Rebecca? Do you need medical attention?"

"No, ma'am," I answered. Even though she had a decade on me at best, I felt compelled to be as polite as possible. "And it's Bex."

"Bex," she confirmed with a nod. "We need to debrief you—"

"I'm getting her the fuck out of here," Court snarled.

The lieutenant huffed out an annoyed breath, her eyes flashing. "If you would let me finish," she said, her tone sharp as a razor before softening as she spoke to me. "That can wait until tomorrow, when this circus has cleared out. Trick, Royal, and I already came to an agreement. You're free to go with your friend."

"Friends," I corrected.

Her strangely purple eyes flicked to Court, a perfectly sculpted brow raising.

"Thank you, ma'am," he said in reply.

She planted her hands on her trim hips. "Thank you for your

assistance tonight." She jerked her head behind her. "I believe you know where to catch your ride?"

He nodded.

"Take care of yourself, Bex," she said to me. "We'll speak soon." Her gaze moved behind me. "Motherfucking, cock-sucking roaches." She swore enough to make a sailor blush. "When I find out who called the press, I'm making earrings out of their balls."

I swallowed the answer, not sure where my dad was.

The lieutenant stormed away, looking like she was going to raise hell.

"Let's get out of here," Court told me, already moving away from the scene.

"Wait," I protested. "She said friend—what's going on?"

Court sighed and shifted me, his gaze meeting mine. "Ryan's meeting us at the car. Linc's not coming."

"Why?" I demanded.

He cursed softly under his breath. "Because we have a plan to catch his father, but we need to make it look like Linc isn't one of us."

"But… That…" I was at a loss for words.

"Baby, I promise to explain it all in detail, okay? But right now, we've gotta go."

I shook my head. "I can't leave until I know Cami's okay."

"I promise that we'll find out what happened to Cami, but I need to get *you* out of here, princess."

I pushed at his shoulders. "Put me down, Court."

He hesitated, and for a second, I thought he might actually do it. But then his grip grew harder, tighter, and we were moving through the darkness again.

I began to struggle, fighting to get out of his hold.

"Enough, Becca," he snapped, stopping short and glaring at me. "Be pissed at me if you want, but we aren't going back."

"You don't get to make that call!" I bucked, trying to break free.

"It's not *my* call!" he shouted. "We have a plan, and we have to stick to it. They'll get Cami, but we need to get the fuck out of here before we get caught up in this shitstorm and it blows the plan to fuck."

Tears spilled over my eyes. "I hate you right now."

He flinched like I'd slapped him. "If you need to hate me, fine. Fucking hate me. But you aren't going back, Becca."

There were too many emotions hitting me too fast. Everything I'd suppressed all night—fear, pain, heartbreak, terror—all manifested itself in a total meltdown. I sobbed in his arms as he kept walking.

Darkness swallowed us up as we walked, and I let myself drown in it until I felt Court go rigid beneath me and stop.

"Princess, I need you to be quiet," he murmured, yanking his mask up and off. His dark eyes scanned the area, searching for an unseen threat.

Something in his tone instantly shut down my crying. I swallowed a hiccup and lifted my head.

"Can you stand?" Court demanded, his tone low and urgent.

"Yeah," I replied, my gaze darting around, but all I saw was darkness. "What's going on?"

"Pretty sure we're being followed," he said through gritted teeth as he lowered me to my feet.

I tottered in my heels, my ankles threatening to buckle, but I locked my limbs and stayed upright as fear churned in my chest.

Court maneuvered me behind him. "Becca, listen to me. The car is about two hundred yards ahead. Keys are in the front driver well. I want you to run for it when I tell you."

Was he insane? Even if I wasn't in the heels from hell and wobbling around like a newborn deer, the ask was too great.

Leave Cami? I'd done it.

Leave Linc? Fine. I'd done that too.

But I drew the line at leaving him.

I opened my mouth to argue... and heard a soft *click*. The sound broke the stillness of the night, and time seemed to crawl to a stop.

"You always were blinded by this girl," Jasper Woods said with a chuckle as he pointed the barrel of a gun at Court's head.

CHAPTER 46

BEX

Court's gaze slid to mine. I saw the concern in his eyes as he realized we were in trouble. "She has nothing to do with this."

"You know," Jasper mused, "this is quite the coincidence. First, I run into Rebecca here, and now I see you? If I didn't know any better, I'd think you joined my other disappointments in rebelling against me."

Court didn't reply. He didn't move a muscle.

"General..." I'd try begging. "Please—"

"Shut up," he snapped, his dark gaze flicking to me. "This is all your fault, you little bitch. Should've killed you when I had the chance back when you were an annoying little brat fucking up my son's future."

"Fuck you," Court hissed through clenched teeth, the heavy rise and fall of his chest showing he was close to losing his shit.

General Woods sighed and looked at me. "See? Even now, I have a gun to his head, and he's more concerned about me insulting *you*. Be a good girl and come stand the fuck in front of me."

I moved on wooden legs, watching as he used his free hand to grab the gun tucked into the back of Court's pants. He hurled it away from us.

Court grimaced. "Just let her go. You don't need her. You have me."

"Weak," General Woods muttered. "So fucking weak. Such a damn disappointment."

"Then let's settle this once and for all, *Dad*," Court offered. "You and me—unless you need a weapon to beat me."

The general gave a dark laugh. "Court, this isn't going to be a fair fight. This is going to be *you* doing exactly what *I* say for the first time in your fucking life."

"How did you find us?" I asked, not sure what I could do except keep the general talking. I looked around, praying that Ryan or someone else on our side would materialize.

General Woods looked at me like I was insane. "You honestly think I didn't have an escape plan? I didn't get where I am in life by taking chances, little girl. Though I must admit, I wasn't expecting to run into the two of you out here. Talk about *fortuitous coincidence*."

Court let out a slow breath. "I'll go with you. Let Becca—"

"No!" General Woods cut him off. "We're all going together."

"Just take me," I offered, hoping to de-escalate this situation. "I won't fight back."

"Becca, *no*." Court had never sounded so pissed off.

"That's an interesting proposition," the general mused, looking like he was considering my offer. "You'd definitely be easier to handle than my son. And more... *fun*."

I stepped back as his gaze raked over me. Fear pulsed in my veins, but I'd go with him if it meant saving Court.

"I accept your offer, Rebecca," General Woods finally decided, his hand tightening around the gun. "I'll even let you say goodbye to my son before I end his pathetic life."

"No!" I screamed, my desperate cry ripping through the night. I moved toward them, not sure what I was going to do, but I'd do *something*.

Everything happened in slow motion. Jasper started to turn the gun on me, and the very second Court seemed to sense the gun wasn't on him, he spun and grabbed his father's wrist. The gun fired, the muzzle flash illuminating the dark as a bullet zipped by me.

Court knocked his father to the ground, and the gun went flying as they traded blows.

Shock held me in a stranglehold. Then I realized the gun was lying a few feet away. I'd never held a gun before, but I wanted to grab it now. To aim it at Jasper Woods and fire until all the bullets were gone. To protect Court.

I lunged forward, already envisioning his father's end even as Court caught a foot to the stomach and staggered back.

Pain ripped through my scalp as something jerked me backward. Instead of falling forward and grabbing the gun, I was tumbling down.

"I've got you, love," Eric whispered against my ear.

My eyes watered as I fought him. "Let me *go!*"

Court, hearing my scream, looked up and gave the general the opening he needed. General Woods kicked out and swept Court's legs from under him, knocking him to the ground. The general climbed on top of his son and began raining punches down on Court's head.

"No!" I twisted and fought, feeling strands of my hair rip free of Eric's hold.

"Dammit, Bex," Eric hissed, letting go of my hair to wrap his arms around me in a frighteningly strong reverse bear hug. He dragged me back a few steps. "You're safe now. I've got you."

I couldn't break free. All I could do was watch in horror as General Woods lifted Court's head to bash his skull into the asphalt and gravel.

I'd heard of women doing incredible things when they were in untenable situations, like a mom lifting a car off her kids. Where the hell was that strength now?

Eric's hot breath hit the back of my neck, and I snapped my head back, catching him in the nose and mouth. He howled in pain, releasing me.

I hit the ground on my hands and knees, then scrambled forward to grab the gun. The second I felt the cold metal in my hands, I swung and aimed it at General Woods. "Stop!"

Woods looked at me, freezing in place, and then his lips curled into a snarl. "You don't have it in you."

Court slammed a fist into his father's temple, knocking Woods off him. He rolled to his feet and came to me. When he held out a hand for the gun, I wordlessly passed it to him as Eric screamed about his broken nose.

"No, she doesn't," Court agreed, "but I do."

Woods pushed himself to his knees. "What now, son?"

I leaned against Court's legs, adrenaline thrumming in my blood. To my right, Eric was still holding his hands over his face, blood dripping between his fingers.

"Now I live the rest of my life with my girl," Court told his father.

"And I spend the rest of mine in a prison cell?" Woods smirked.

"Sounds good to me," Court agreed. "I like the idea of you in a cage, being someone's bitch."

The general growled. "Fucking shoot me, you pussy."

No, my mind said. I didn't want Court to kill his own father; I didn't want him living with that. Did Jasper Woods deserve a bullet to the skull? Absolutely. But killing him wouldn't undo the past.

"And let you get off easy? Fuck that," Court replied. "I want you to spend the rest of your pathetic life knowing your sons are out there, undoing everything you've ever done. We'll dismantle Black Box Ops. We'll petition the government to strip you of all your titles and awards. The world will forget the name *Jasper Woods*. You'll be nothing. You *are* nothing."

The sound of footsteps pounding across the deserted parking lot hit my ears, and I could only pray it was the good guys and not the general's men.

Eric turned and started to run.

A snarl ripped through the night, followed by a blur of fur and fury as Wanda launched into the air and landed on top of Eric. She tackled him to the ground with a ferocious growl, grabbing his forearm. He screamed as her teeth sank into his skin.

"Game over," Court said to General Woods.

Royal, Trick, Rook, and Ryan ran toward us. Trick kept going until he got to Wanda's side and spoke a foreign word that had her releasing Eric and backing away to sit beside Trick.

Royal got to us first. "Good job, little brother."

General Woods glared at his oldest son. "Fucking ungrateful pricks. I tried to give you all the fucking *world*."

"We don't want your world," Rook informed him, a hand on his gun.

Ryan knelt by my side. "You okay, Bex?"

I nodded, still pressed to Court's leg. "Where the hell did you come from?"

Ryan gave me a lopsided grin. "I handed Alex off to the cops and heard the shots when I was heading over to meet you and Court."

I looked over at where Trick had handcuffed Eric. "Is it over?"

"Yeah, princess," Court told me, passing the gun to Ryan as Rook handcuffed their father while Royal kept a gun trained on him.

I looked around. "Where's Bishop?"

Court bent and picked me up once more, holding me against him. A tremor ran through his body as he kissed the side of my head.

"With Cami," Rook told me, yanking Jasper to his feet. "We found her in the tunnels, but when we figured out the general and Eric weren't with them, we started searching for them. Wanda must've heard you guys, because she took off running this way."

As if summoned, Wanda trotted over to us and nudged my thigh with her wet nose. I reached down and ruffled her fur.

"Everything secure?" Court asked.

"Yup," Royal answered. "We'll get these two to Striker and meet you guys back at the hotel, okay?"

"Bex, please," Eric was begging. "Tell them who I am. I love you—"

With a growl, Court handed me to Ryan like I was a bag of groceries. Ryan and I watched Court stalk the five feet over to where Eric was and deck him. One punch, and Eric was on the ground.

"Dammit," Trick sighed. "Now I've gotta carry the bastard."

"Drag him back," Court snapped. "Let his head hit every fucking rock in the damn parking lot." He took me back from Ryan and cuddled me to his chest. My head found that perfect spot between his shoulder and pec to rest on.

I needed a freaking shower and a bed. "Is Cami okay? The others?"

"There's a team of social workers and therapists already gathering to help everyone we found," Royal assured me. "Some of them have a few injuries…" He trailed off, his gaze locking with Court.

"What?" Anxiety sliced through my exhaustion. "What happened?"

Royal gave me an unreadable look. "When we found Cami, she wasn't with the others. They'd left her behind."

"Why?" My mouth went dry.

"In the chaos of evacuating, she must've fallen. Looked like she broke her ankle. Bishop was taking her to the medical team—"

"I need to see her," I told Court.

Court grimaced and looked at his brother. "Is she still here?"

"No way of knowing," Royal replied. "Might be best if you head to the hospital later. That's where they'll take her."

"But—"

"He's right, princess," Court said softly, meeting my gaze. "We need to get out of here before it becomes a three-ring circus."

"Pretty sure we're way past that point," Trick commented, hefting Eric over his shoulder in a fireman's carry. "But you should go unless you want to be dragged into an international incident."

My brows shot up.

"Pretty sure a few of the men we collared are foreign ambassadors. This is shaping up to be a political nightmare," Rook added.

"Just wait," General Woods seethed, not done yet with spewing hate. "You'll all pay. Especially you, bitch."

Royal swung around and punched his father in the mouth, knocking him down again. "Shut the fuck up."

With his arms cuffed at the wrists behind his back, Woods had no way to break his fall. He hit the ground like a bag of bricks, his head bouncing off the cement. He slumped, eyes rolling back as he lost consciousness.

"Guess we're carrying two," Rook muttered, bending down and

picking up Jasper. "Let's go." He and Trick started back toward the lights glowing in the distance.

"Get out of here," Royal told us again, but this time his tone was gentler, his focus on me. "It's going to be a long night for all of us."

"We'll see you soon," Court told Royal, nodding at his brother.

One of my shoes fell off, and Ryan wordlessly picked it up and carried it for me as we started walking in the other direction.

I barely noticed when we arrived at the car, and it was like I wasn't connected to my body when Court sat us in the backseat, keeping me on his lap as Ryan drove us away.

"It's okay, princess," Court said, his lips against my hair. "Just rest. We're all okay."

Exhausted, I closed my eyes.

CHAPTER 47

BEX

The steady hum of the car engine went silent. Panic speared through my chest, and I jolted awake. "Cami," I gasped.

"Easy, baby," Court murmured against my head, his hand stroking my back.

I twisted away, putting a few much-needed inches between us. My eyes felt heavy and swollen as they filled with tears all over again. "Court—"

"They found her, remember? She's at the hospital," he told me, not moving as Ryan exited the car.

"I need to see her."

Court's expression tightened. "We will, but first we need to get you cleaned up."

I sucked in a sharp breath, my eyes going wide as every worst-case scenario pummeled my brain.

"She'll be fine," he added, his voice reassuring and somber.

But would she? Would any of us? Right now it just seemed so overwhelming.

Ryan knocked lightly on our window before pulling open the door. "Maybe we can talk about this inside?" His blue eyes flashed as he looked around the street for threats.

Aside from a couple walking away from us to the intersection at the end of the block and a taxi rolling by, the side street next to the hotel was empty. But I understood his unease.

Court helped me slide off his lap and onto the pavement, wobbling on one heel.

Ryan reached out and steadied me. "You okay?"

I peered up at him. "No."

He gave me a grim nod, letting me go as Court got out of the car. Once he'd closed the door, Court tugged me to the curb and turned around. "Jump on."

It had been years since I'd hopped on him for a piggyback ride. When I was little, my legs had been so much shorter than all of theirs that it had become our go-to mode of transportation when we were all together.

He was a lot taller now than we were as kids, and I was still a lot shorter. I had to jump, but I threaded my arms around his neck and wrapped my legs around his hips, losing my second shoe in the process.

"I've gotcha, Cinderella," Ryan muttered, grabbing my other shoe so he now carried the pair.

We approached the side door of the hotel, and I was surprised when Maddie opened it.

"What the fuck are you doing down here?" Ryan growled, glaring at her.

Maddie didn't even flinch. She tossed back her long swath of pale blonde hair and returned his look. "Letting your ass inside. Ash is watching the monitors."

Ryan looked pissed as he rubbed his forehead.

"Hey, Mads," I said.

She brightened and moved to hug me, but Ryan cut her off.

"Reunion inside where we're safer," he told her, but his tone was gentle.

Maddie gave me a small smile and nodded at Ryan before turning and leading the way to the service elevator.

Taking the keycard from her, Ryan swiped it over the panel and ushered her, then us, inside before joining us. Maddie hit the button for our floor, and Ryan pulled her into his arms as we started to ascend.

"You okay, Bex?" she asked me, her head against Ryan's chest.

"Not really," I admitted, my chin resting on Court's shoulder as the elevator chimed and the door slid open. We headed down the hall toward the hotel room we'd stayed in before.

Using another keycard, Maddie opened the door and held it as we all went inside.

I tapped Court's shoulder, feeling like a toddler who was done being carried around. He let me slide down his body, and then Maddie was all over me.

"Don't ever scare me like that again," she demanded, squeezing me hard.

"Sorry," I whispered, clinging to her.

"Where are we at?" Ryan demanded. He tore off his Kevlar vest and tossed it aside. Court did the same, the sharp sound of the ripping velcro almost too loud.

Ash spun in his chair, looking exhausted. He tugged off a headset and set it aside to gesture at the TV. A local Parisian news station was muted, but the camera was showing the scene at the warehouse from behind a police barricade.

It cut to shots of men and women in cuffs being escorted into police wagons, victims wrapped in blankets with their faces blurred, and back to an aerial shot of the dock, still smoldering.

"Jesus," I whispered, stepping around Maddie and going to stand in front of the TV.

"It's gonna be a long night," Ash mused, scrubbing his hands over his face. His bright green eyes were alert but weary. "They saved twenty-six people." He looked at me. "Including your cousin."

Maddie gripped my hand.

"Eric?" I demanded, needing to know what happened to the asshole.

"In custody," Ash confirmed. "Apparently unconscious, but in police custody nonetheless."

"General Woods?" His name tasted bitter in my mouth.

Ash smirked. "Also confirmed as in custody, but *not* unconscious."

"Should've hit the bastard harder," Ryan said.

"Or shot him," Court added with a glower.

I shook my head, my gaze on Ash. "What happens next?"

"Well, we're looking at a bureaucratic nightmare," Ash admitted. "Everyone's trying to figure out what the fuck happened tonight while simultaneously trying to take credit. The news is crediting Paris PD at the moment, but someone's going to have to make a statement."

Ryan sat down on the edge of an armchair. "And our guys are ready for that?" Maddie crossed the floor and climbed onto his lap, snuggling against him. Ryan held her like she was a living, breathing teddy bear he could use for security.

Ash hesitated. "Actually? We might've dodged a pretty big fucking bullet."

Court moved behind me, looping an arm around my waist and anchoring me to his chest. "How so?"

Ash leaned back, the chair creaking as he stretched. "Because someone tipped off every international and domestic agency in Europe *and* called the damn press. The top law enforcement agencies in this corner of the world are fighting over who gets the credit. They're already calling this the largest human trafficking bust this century. With this much press, they *can't* sweep this shit under the rug, even if they try."

"How does that help us?" Ryan demanded, all business even as his fingers lazily drew circles on Maddie's hip.

"This many people, they're going to take the U.S. task force at their word. Lieutenant Striker is planning to keep *our* involvement to a minimum in the public eye. She likes the idea of having—and I quote —'an elite task force in my back pocket.'"

Court scoffed. "We're not dogs that she can bring to heel."

Ash arched a brow. "No, but she *is* in a position to help keep us secret and let us work in the shadows. The longer we can keep Phoenix International quiet, the better it'll be for all of us. Eventually someone will draw the connection between us and what we do. When that happens…" He sucked in a sharp breath through his teeth.

Court's arm tightened around me. "It'll put us and the people we love in danger."

Ash nodded. "Exactly."

Ryan exhaled and rested his forehead on Maddie's shoulder. "Okay. Maybe it's not a bad thing that someone tipped off the press."

I cleared my throat. "It was my dad."

All eyes turned to me.

"You saw your dad?" Court asked softly.

I nodded. "Yeah."

Ryan's eyes narrowed. "Maybe start at the beginning?"

"It can wait," Court told him. "She needs to rest."

"It's okay," I assured him, even as a weary shudder rippled through my bones.

"Bex, you look exhausted," Maddie pointed out, biting her lower lip as worry filled her azure eyes.

"What if we table this for an hour or so?" Ash suggested. "Royal, Rook, and Bishop will be back by then, and you won't have to repeat the story."

"I could really use a shower," I murmured, tipping my head back to look at Court.

He didn't look happy but gave a single nod. "Fine. Shower, *food*, and then we'll chat."

"Hospital," I reminded him.

"Okay," he gritted out. "But then your ass is in bed for the foreseeable future."

"Yes, sir," I quipped, loving the way his eyes heated.

His hand covered the curve of my hip, his thumb stroking my ass. "Let's go."

"Wait. What about Linc?" I needed to know that he was okay, too.

Ash grimaced. "Linc is fine."

"But—"

Court turned me in his arms. "We'll tell you the whole plan when we're all together." He looked over my shoulder at Ryan. "Can you guys order some food?"

"I'm not hungry," I mumbled, my stomach the last thing I wanted to think about.

"On it," Ryan responded, ignoring me.

"Do you need help, Bex?" Maddie offered, her voice sweet and kind.

Court shot her a baleful look. "I've got her covered."

Maddie barely hid a smile as she leaned back into Ryan. "Just making sure."

Court took my hand and led me into what I'd always consider *our* room. He nudged the door shut and leaned against it, his dark gaze boring into me. "I need the truth, Becca."

I paused, watching him.

"Are you… Did you get hurt?" His jaw clenched as he tried to tactfully ask the question haunting him.

I sighed and moved to stand with him, my arms going around his waist as I tipped my head back to look at him. "Other than a few bruises and scrapes, I'm fine. I promise. Your dad has a helluva right hook—"

"He *hit* you?" Court's voice was low, lethal. It charged the room with an anticipatory sort of electricity that made the fine hairs on my arms stand up. Murder flashed in his eyes, making them cold, dark pools of fury. He pushed back my hair, hissing at whatever he saw. "Fuck. I didn't notice it before. That son of a bitch. I'll kill him."

"Court," I started, meeting his gaze and holding it, "I'm *fine*. Bruises heal. I'm here with you now. We're okay."

That was all that mattered. Not revenge or fear or rage. Right now, I just needed the guy I loved to remind me that we were together and nothing would change that.

His gaze searched my face, his entire body pulled taut. "Becca—"

"Right now I need a shower," I said slowly. "And I need you to help me out of this dress. Can you do that?"

He swallowed reflexively and nodded. "Yeah. I can do that."

I turned my back to him so he could access the zipper. His hand found the piece of metal and tugged it down. The dress loosened around me, and I didn't stop it from slipping off my shoulders and pooling around my feet.

Court's warm breath ghosted across my neck as he brushed my dark hair over one shoulder. His blunt fingers traced the edge of the white corset I'd worn underneath before he started to open each clasp.

I was painfully aware of the way my breaths quickened the more skin he exposed until he reached the end where the corset matched the white panties that hugged my ass.

"Becca," he rasped, dipping his fingers into the elastic of my underwear and dragging them around to my front.

My eyes fluttered closed as he brushed my slit, a soft gasp leaving my lips as need pulsed between my thighs. I fell back against him, my corset landing on the floor with my discarded gown.

His lips pressed against the curve of my neck, lightly sucking on the flesh there. He peppered kisses up to the curve of my jaw, and I turned my head toward him.

His mouth covered mine as he worked a finger between my folds. I gasped into him as his tongue swept in to take control and his finger fucked me with slow pumps.

I widened my stance, the heady thrum of arousal soaking into my bones and making my blood pound.

When he added a second finger, my knees started to shake. As if sensing I was close to breaking, he banded a strong arm around my chest, locking me against him as he used his fingers to drive me crazy.

He swallowed every sound I made, feeding off my pleasure like it would give him all the energy he'd ever need. His thumb rubbed tight circles over my needy little clit as he crooked his fingers inside me, rubbing that magic spot that sent a cascade of sparkles bursting behind my eyes.

I shattered in his arms. My sex convulsed around his fingers, greedily trying to suck him in deeper. He caught me as my legs turned to jelly, unable to bear my weight another second.

I'd barely come down from my high as he carried me to the bed. He spun me in his arms, his lips crashing against mine with dominating force. All I could do was cling to the front of his dark shirt, my back arching into him.

Then I was falling. My back hit the mattress, and I looked up at Court, dazed. My stomach clenched at the feral glint in his eyes as he gazed down at me and licked his lips.

He reached behind his neck, fisted his shirt, and yanked it over his head. He tossed it aside and toed off his boots, then reached for his belt buckle.

I scooted higher up on the bed, my mouth going dry as I watched him strip. Every piece of clothing exposed more tanned skin. The phoenix tattoo inked on his ribs seemed alive as it moved when he did.

Each flex of his muscles reminded me how strong he was. And, in some stupid little way that made my heart go flippity-flop, reminded me how safe he made me feel.

"You're staring," he teased, pushing his dark pants down.

I couldn't hide my grin. "What can I say? It's my favorite view."

He palmed the hard length of his cock through his boxer-briefs, the corded muscles of his forearm flexing as he gave it a hard squeeze. Like he was seconds from losing control if he didn't figure out how to rein it in.

I let my legs fall open, positive my panties had a massive damp spot.

Court groaned. "Fuck, what you do to me, baby."

I coasted a hand down my body, my fingers slipping into my under-wear. "I could say the same thing."

Like a rubber band being pulled too tight, his restraint snapped. One second he was at the foot of the bed, and the next his body was covering mine. His hips settled between my thighs like we'd been created for one another. Two pieces that fit together to make something whole.

My arms went around his shoulders. "I love you." I needed to say it. Needed him to know I meant it. That in all of this craziness, he had become my constant.

His palm cradled my jaw like I was the most precious thing in the world. "I love you, Becca."

We managed to work my panties and his underwear down, kicking them off in a tangle of limbs that made me smile. But all humor vanished when he pushed himself inside me with one smooth thrust.

My eyes screwed shut as pleasure whipped through me with the force of a hurricane. Every nerve ending flared to life. I wrapped my legs around his waist, letting out a happy sigh when he slid in a little deeper.

"Oh, fuck," Court groaned. He reached down, hooking an arm under one knee, drawing my leg up higher, spreading me wider. "I can't be gentle, Becca. I need you too damn much."

My fingers tangled in his hair. "I'm yours, Court. Take what you need."

His hips withdrew, and then he plowed back in. The utter fullness nearly stole my breath. All I could do was hang on and enjoy the literal ride as he fucked me… as he *loved* me.

Tears gathered in my eyes as he moved in me.

His hand came up, his thumb catching a tear that tumbled down my cheek. He slowed down. "Am I hurting you?"

"No," I managed to choke out, shaking my head emphatically. "I just… You and me…"

Understanding lit his eyes, his expression somehow fierce and tender at the same time as he gazed at me. "I know, baby girl. I feel it, too."

His gaze held mine as he resumed thrusting, his hips pistoning in and out of me as my thighs started to shake. My back bowed off the mattress.

"Eyes on me," he murmured, bumping my nose with his.

With a gasp, my gaze snapped back to his. "I love you."

His eyes hooded, a small smile hooking up the corner of his mouth. "Not as much as I love you."

I raked my nails down his back to grab his ass, feeling the muscles tighten as he flexed into me. "Court."

"Let go, princess," he whispered. "Come for me."

My body seized, my pussy greedily clamping around his cock as I came with a strangled cry. My vision went unfocused as waves of pleasure rocked through me. His cock jerked inside me, and then he was coming with me. My center milked his cock, clenching and convulsing around his length as he rode me through my climax with jerky thrusts.

"I love you," he whispered again before capturing my lips with his once more.

I sank into his kiss, reveling in the way he held me and the knowledge that I was loved by the man I'd never thought I'd have. That we were together, and nothing would ever change that.

CHAPTER 48

BEX

When we emerged from the bedroom nearly an hour later, I was swimming in a pair of Court's sweats and one of his old Pacific Cross football hoodies. Court had tied the waistband strings as tight as he could, but one strong breeze or me tripping on the dragging hem, and they'd be around my ankles. Luckily the hoodie was practically a dress on me.

I snuggled into it, comforted by the soft fabric and the scent of the guy I loved. It was like being hugged by him, but with fewer muscles.

He was officially never getting this piece of clothing back. I was invoking the girlfriend's right of eminent domain, adding the hoodie to the list of his things that now belonged to me.

Like his cock.

Just thinking that had me smiling as I wrapped my arms around myself.

As we came back in, Maddie looked up. At some point, Ryan had gotten up, and she'd taken over his seat while he was on the phone, pacing in front of the window that overlooked a desolate side street with a healthy dose of the roof next door.

Ash was still at the computer, this time with Royal and Rook hovering over his shoulders. Bishop was sprawled on the couch. It looked like he was asleep, but I had a feeling if he heard one small move, he'd be up and ready to go.

"Do you want me to get you some clothes?" Maddie offered, swinging her long legs where they were draped over the arm of the chair.

My best friend had a good five inches on me, but her clothes would definitely fit better than the ones I had on.

And yet…

"I'm good," I said with a smile, tucking my head into the loose neck of the hoodie to take another hit of Court's smell.

Court smirked at her before kissing the top of my head. "Food," he ordered, gently pushing me toward a stack of boxes piled on the table in the kitchenette.

I scowled at him. "You need food, too."

He grinned. "I ate earlier."

I gulped down air, and my cheeks heated as I remembered the way he'd sunk to his knees in the shower and eaten me out.

My gaze instinctively shot to his dick, wondering if I could get away with the same excuse if I dragged him back into our room.

His brows lifted, and he shot me a look that said his cock wasn't an approved food group. He was wrong, but I wasn't going to argue that point in front of our friends and his family.

I pawed through the boxes of pizza and other stuff before snagging a garlic knot. I ripped off a chunk, then popped it into my mouth and chewed the doughy garlic and butter concoction.

Bishop swung his legs off the side of the couch, putting himself in an even more awkward sprawl by giving me a place to sit. He cracked an eye open. "How ya doing, Bex?"

I shrugged and ate another bite as all eyes turned to me. "Thank you for taking care of Cami."

He gave me a sad smile. "Of course. I wish I could've done more."

"Was she okay? I mean other than her ankle?"

He looked away. "She's gone through a lot tonight, Bex. She'll need time and for people to just love her and let her heal."

Tears gathered in my eyes. "Fucking Eric and Alex. They got Alex, too, right?"

"I handed him off to Striker myself," Ryan assured me.

Good. I knew Alex had kinda been trying to help me, but he was the reason Cami had been there. He was the reason her ankle had been broken.

Royal pushed away from Ash. "Okay, let's—"

"Wait." I held up a hand. "I need to know what's going on with Linc first."

Royal looked annoyed, but Court stopped him from complaining by asking, "Do we have confirmation?"

Ash sighed and nodded. "He's currently being taken to La Santé. They'll arraign him, and his name will be leaked as one of the people arrested."

"Linc's going to prison?" I gasped, my mind blanking at the name of Paris's maximum security prison. "But he's one of the good guys. How…" I turned and glared at Rook. "Did Trick betray us? Lieutenant Striker?"

Rook shook his head. "No one betrayed us, Bex."

"It was Linc's idea," Ryan added, but frustration bled through his tone.

I looked at Court, needing answers.

He sat on the edge of the coffee table in front of me and took my hands. "Remember how we were worried that going after Gary and Beckett would accelerate our timeline for Phoenix going public?"

I nodded. "But that doesn't matter, right? Ash said—"

"I know," he interrupted gently. "But we went in tonight thinking we were still working under a tight deadline. We can't keep Beckett in the dark forever, and if he's able to get word to Linc's dad that we're setting them up, then we'll lose our chance of getting to Kent."

"Right," I agreed, remembering that flimsy plan that had seemed like it was being held together by prayers and clearance-bin duct tape. "Kent Westford is the head of the snake."

"He's the head of *this* snake," Rook corrected with a weary exhale.

Court shot him a dirty look.

"What?" Rook didn't back down. "This doesn't end with Kent Westford. Once we end this group, there's another waiting to step into the power vacuum it'll create."

"Fuck," Ryan muttered, rubbing his temples, "can we just take the win for tonight? We all know we're in it for the long haul. It's why we started a company instead of a fucking club."

"Lieutenant Striker made things better, though. We don't have to rush things," I said, cutting through the tension.

Court glanced back at me with a soft look. "We, huh?"

My eyes narrowed. "You're not cutting me out of this, Court Woods. I'm part of the team now."

"Baby, you were always part of the team. I was just too fucking stubborn to admit it," he confessed, squeezing my fingers.

Royal scoffed. "Can we get back on track? This isn't couples counseling."

Maddie tipped her head back and looked at him upside down, pointing an accusatory finger. "Hey, you. Chill out. We're all stressed, but you don't have to be a butthead."

Royal glared at her while Bishop cracked up.

"Butthead was really the best insult you could think of?" Rook asked, sounding amused.

Maddie shrugged. "I got used to censoring myself because of Cori. She's freaking relentless with that swear jar."

Court drew in a deep breath. "Linc had the idea to get caught. Grab Kent's attention, and get him to pull Linc back in. Let him think he can control Linc, so we have a guy on the inside."

A pit opened in my stomach. "No. Court, what if Kent doesn't go for it? What if Linc's stuck in prison?"

"He won't be," he promised me. "Worst-case scenario, Striker will help us acquit him and say he got lost in the mess of the night."

"Wait, what's to stop Court's dad from telling everyone what he saw tonight?" Maddie demanded, eyes wide with worry. "He saw all of you. He knows—"

"He's known about *us* all along," Royal interrupted. "Well, not Court and Ryan, but that doesn't matter. Jasper won't be in some random-ass prison with everyone else. He's going to be held in a top-secret facility run by Interpol."

Rook shot Maddie a reassuring look. "And on the very slim chance the general is able to make contact with the outside world, that might work in our favor."

"Why?" she asked.

"Because he never saw Linc," I murmured, realizing that because Royal had sent us away, Linc had already been in "custody" when General Woods got to us.

Rook nodded. "Exactly. It gives Kent more incentive to help Linc. At this point it looks like Linc's on his own. Like we all abandoned him."

Ryan leaned on the back of Maddie's chair. "Kent's been looking for a reason to make himself invaluable to Linc. He has all the power and the money in the world, but Kent can't bring his only son to heel. Bailing him out of a shitty situation is just the opening a guy like Kent has been praying for."

"Then what?" I asked.

Court pressed his lips into a tight line. "We have to wait for Linc. We'll monitor things from a distance, but he says he has this under control, and we have to trust him."

"That's a horrible plan," I blurted out.

Maddie snapped her fingers. "I said the same thing."

"Anything can happen to him in prison," I added, worrying my lower lip. "Look at what happened to Ryan." Last year, Ryan had been wrongfully incarcerated, and in the week it had taken the lawyers to get him out, he'd been stabbed and had nearly died.

Ryan winced. "Unlike Maddie's father, Kent's not going to pay someone to try and kill Linc."

Maddie looked stricken, the same sick look on her face that always showed up when we talked about her dad. Gary had been an absolute monster, and he'd done a lot of damage to the people in this room.

"Now that we're all caught up on Linc," Royal said, his gray eyes piercing as they flashed at me, "can we get back to what you saw tonight? What the fuck happened in the warehouse?"

The events of the evening played out like a horror movie in my mind. I told them everything that had happened once I'd gone inside with Eric. When I got to the part about the general and how he "took" me from Eric, Court changed our sitting positions.

Plucking me off the couch, he sat down and arranged me on his lap, holding on to me like I might vaporize and blow away any second. Royal, Rook, and Bishop looked furious, but for me, everything with the general had taken a back seat to the shit that had gone down with my own dad.

Disappointment weighed heavily in my gut as I remembered him choosing himself over me. Over a few dozen innocent people, and who knew how many others during the past decade.

"So he's the one who called the press? It was a good call," Ryan mused, looking thoughtful. "It gave everyone attending the auction nowhere to hide. We were so busy trying to keep everything an organized secret, but maybe we should've gone for maximum chaos instead."

"I think I want that on a t-shirt," Maddie quipped, flashing me a wink.

Royal let out an undignified snort. "Chaos is never a good thing."

"I don't know, big guy," Maddie teased. "You could probably stand a little chaos in your life."

Rook chuckled. "I'd pay to see that."

Bishop nudged me. "See? Your dad did help. Kinda."

"Yeah," I drawled, my stomach sour. "My dad's a freaking genius." Actually, he was. It was why men like General Woods wanted him in their pocket. His technology had helped them do a lot of illegal shit over the years.

"He didn't get away," Ash told me with a sympathetic smile.

My eyes widened. "Wait—what?"

"Trick's team had the side exits covered," Bishop confirmed. "Your dad was caught early on. He's being transported to La Santé, too."

"The general is the only one getting the VIP experience," Royal said with a humorless chuckle. "He's going in a black hole somewhere in Siberia."

"Siberia?" I echoed.

Royal's lips twitched. "Hell yes. They'll put his ass on ice. Literally."

"Knight said we'll celebrate that win when we all go back home," Bishop chimed in. He looked at Royal. "*When* are we going home, big brother?"

Royal frowned. "We still have shit to sort here, but a couple days, tops."

"That gives us time to explore the city," Maddie told Ryan with a hopeful expression.

He smoothed her hair back with an indulgent smile. "Whatever you want, baby."

Ash turned to Royal to discuss more stuff on the computer while Rook wandered toward the bedroom he'd been using. Bishop turned to Maddie and Ryan and started suggesting places they should visit in Paris.

"You're quiet," Court remarked.

I turned on his lap, giving him my full attention. "A lot to think about."

"Your dad?" he asked, his expression cautious.

"No. Well, kinda. I guess I'm not sure what comes next," I confessed.

His head tilted. "In terms of..."

"Us? Me?" I let out a brittle laugh. "I didn't really think past what we'd do this week. Stopping Eric and your dad. But now... Court, I moved my whole life to Paris. My mom put our house on the market, and I'm willing to bet that my dad's stuff is going to be seized by some government."

He gave a slow nod. "True."

"And, shit, I need to talk to my mom. My grandparents. I need to see Cami." It was all so much, the weight of responsibility crushing me under the enormity of it all.

"Princess, you're spiraling," he murmured. "You don't need all the answers tonight. We'll figure it out."

A hysterical laugh bubbled from my chest. "Court, I don't even have my *phone*. It's in Eric's limo."

"We'll get you a new one," he replied. "You can use mine right now if you need to."

A stupid thought struck me. "I don't even know my mom's new phone number! I just programmed it into my phone—"

Court pulled his phone from his pocket, unlocked the screen, and hit a few buttons. When he turned the device to me, my mom's contact info was in it.

"You have her number?" My brows pulled together in confusion.

"Of course. I covered all my bases in case I needed to get to you or —*oof*." The air slammed out of him when I dove at his chest, hugging him as hard as I could. His chest shook as he laughed.

"Can I call her now?" I asked, peering up at him.

"Of course," he answered, like my question was ridiculous. He pushed his phone into my hand, and I hit the green button to initiate the call.

Mom answered after three rings. "Hello?" She sounded exhausted and uncertain.

"Mom?"

"Rebecca Whittier," she gasped into the phone. "Where the hell have you been? We've been worried sick!"

"I know, Mom," I whispered, emotions knotting up my throat. "It's a long story, and I promise I'll explain it all. Where are you?"

"The hospital," she replied. "Cami was in an accident and, well, her ankle was broken in two places. She's in surgery now."

"Surgery?" My heart sank. That didn't sound like it was a simple break.

"Yes. Honey, where are you?"

I glanced at Court. "Not far. I can be at the hospital in about thirty minutes. Are Mémé and Papa there, too?"

"Of course," she answered, sounding baffled.

"We'll be there soon," I told her.

"You're with Eric?" she pressed.

I met Court's eyes, finding my anchor in the hurricane. "I'm with my boyfriend."

His gaze warmed with approval.

"I'll see you soon." I hung up and handed the phone back to Court.

"Ready to go to the hospital?" He cocked a brow.

"Definitely. I need to see my family before I can sleep. They need to know everything that happened."

His lips turned up. "Already taking me home to meet the family, huh?"

Bishop laughed. "I hope you can win them over, Court."

"Doesn't matter," I said with a tiny shrug. "They can either accept him or not. It doesn't change the fact that we're together."

"Damn right, baby," he growled before kissing me hard.

CHAPTER 49

COURT

Becca and I left the hospital hours later, arriving back at the hotel as the sun was rising over Paris. I could make out the curve of the Eiffel Tower's peak in the distance.

"I feel like I've been put through a blender at high speed," Becca moaned, taking my hand and letting me pull her to her exhausted feet. I pushed her car door shut, and she leaned against it while eyeing the hotel.

"That was a lot," I admitted. I hadn't done much except stand by her side as she told her family everything that had happened during the past few weeks.

She'd glossed over parts of it for her grandparents' and mother's sakes, but she'd revealed enough that they were rocked. Dr. Whittier had also been made aware that her soon-to-be ex-husband was staring down the barrel of a lengthy prison sentence.

"At least Mémé and Papa insisted on a prenup when Mom married Dad," Becca murmured.

I nodded. "And their divorce is almost finalized. She won't have to worry about assets being frozen while shit gets worked out."

Becca nodded, her hazel eyes exhausted. "Is it wrong that I never want to see my dad again?"

"I mean, I feel the same way," I admitted with a smirk.

She lightly punched my chest. I caught her hand and dragged it to my lips, then kissed her knuckles.

She was quiet for a long moment, the sounds of the city filling the morning air. It was cold, but in a refreshing sort of way. Like starting over with a clean slate.

"I can carry you inside again," I offered. She'd borrowed clothes from Maddie for the visit to the hospital but was still wearing my hoodie. I liked seeing her in my clothes.

She grinned at me. "I think I can handle walking inside. I just…"

"What?" I tipped my head to the side, moving closer to rest my hands on her hips.

"I don't know what to do," she admitted.

"About?" Everything in me went cold, wondering if she was going to pull away. If, now that the craziness of the past few weeks was over, she was rethinking us.

She hooked her fingers around my belt loops. "I came here with my mom to help her get a fresh start. I'll feel bad if I leave and go back to California, but I don't want to be away from you."

Relief hit me in a dizzying wave. She wasn't trying to end things; she was trying to find a way for us to be together.

Not realizing I'd been bracing for my worst fear only to have it vanish just as fast, she kept talking. "I miss being with you guys. I miss Maddie, but I also think I need to stay here for a while. Cami's going to need a friend."

Camille's ankle had been broken in two places and required a plate and two screws to put it back together. That would be followed by a lengthy recovery and physical therapy. She wouldn't be dancing for months, and that was *if* her ankle healed right.

"I mean, I'm sure we can make the long-distance thing work, but is it wrong that I just don't want to?" Her nose scrunched up adorably as she peered up at me. "We're finally in a good place, and I *really* hate the idea of not seeing you every day."

My lips twitched as I tried to hide a smile.

"Oh, God. I'm being *that* girl, aren't I? The needy, stage-five clinger who can't get out of bed without texting her boyfriend." She looked horrified.

I chuckled. "I don't think you have to worry about that, because I have zero plans of you waking up in any bed that doesn't have me in it, too."

She softened in my arms, the trust in her gaze staggering. Like I had the answers for her problems. Or, at least, for *this* problem.

"I only have my internship this semester," I reminded her, "and technically I've met all the requirements for that already. I can check in remotely and fly back if I need to for a few days."

Her eyes sparkled. "You'd stay in Paris?"

"Princess, I'd stay in a goddamn *shoebox* with you," I told her, leaning in to kiss the top of her head.

"What about Phoenix? And Linc?"

I sighed. "Phoenix can run just fine without me, especially if we have people like Lieutenant Striker in our corner. Royal and Rook handle most of the day-to-day shit, and they're bringing on one of Rook's SEAL buddies, too."

"Trick?" she asked.

I shook my head. "His contract isn't up with the Navy yet. It's Rook's old CO."

"CO?"

"Commanding officer," I explained. "Royal met with him a month ago and offered him a job. I haven't met him yet, but his wife's a nurse and they have a kid. Rook's trying to convince him to move closer to Pacific City, but we'll see."

"You'd really be okay living in Paris until I go back to the States for college?" She sounded so unsure. What was it going to take to prove that I was all-in? That she was it for me?

"I'd really be okay living in an igloo at the North Pole with you," I assured her.

She giggled. "Okay. So you'll... what? Find an apartment?"

"*We* will find an apartment," I corrected. "Somewhere close to your grandparents and mom."

"And when I go to college?" she pressed.

"We'll figure that out, too," I answered, confident in the answer because there was no alternative. Just because I'd been accepted into Stanford didn't mean I *had* to go.

"I don't have to go to PCU," she added, her voice brightening with hope. "I can apply at schools near you, too."

"Or," I countered, "I can find a law school near PCU. We have options, baby."

"I guess we have a few months to figure it all out," she murmured. She stared up at me, wonder in her eyes. "I can't believe it."

"What?"

Her body pressed against mine. "That we're here. Together. That we all survived *and* I got the guy."

"Princess, you've always had the guy," I told her. "I can't believe I got my girl."

She pursed her lips. "Keep that in mind the next time I drive you crazy."

My hands palmed her round ass and squeezed. "You can drive me crazy any day of the week, Becca." I leaned in, nuzzling the side of her neck. My lips feathered a soft kiss over the skin under her jaw, and I felt her shudder in my arms. "Just as long as I can drive *you* crazy."

She let out a breathy giggle. "Deal. Now how about you take me inside and show me just how crazy you can make me?"

I pulled back, arching a brow. "Is that a challenge?"

"If you're up for it," she replied with a coy smirk.

Pressing my already hard cock against her stomach, I growled, "With you? I'm always *up* for it."

She tipped her head back and let out a full laugh that did funny things to my heart.

This was it. This was the moment I'd been waiting for; the moment when my entire damn life just made sense. And it was all because of this woman.

She was mine, and I was hers.

For-fucking-ever.

ACKNOWLEDGMENTS

If you've been following any part of my journey the last year, you know what a struggle it's been. I'm talking *uphill in the rain, pushing a boulder with a broken leg* hard. I flat out wouldn't have survived it without my tribe of people.

Mom and Dad, you've been there for every single high and low. Thank you for being my constant support. For picking me up from the airport, literally holding my hands as I tried to figure out my next steps, and encouraging me to ride the waves. Micah, Lauren, and Sherry for rallying behind me. Nora and Aria for always making me smile.

My besties in the world: Krista, Lori, and Chris. Thank you Bella, Tracy, Nicole, and Katie.

My incredible editor, Tashya Wilson and my proofreader, Ricarda Berger. You two are the absolute best.

The biggest of thanks to my Inner Sanctum group! Y'all have sustained me in ways you'll never know. Your support means the freaking world.

ABOUT THE AUTHOR

USA Today bestselling author Hannah McBride has been many things in her life: a restaurant manager, a clinical research coordinator, a dreamer, a makeup brand ambassador, an event coordinator, a blogger, and more. But at heart, she's always been a writer, and in 2020 she decided to make it official. Good luck stopping her now.

ALSO BY HANNAH MCBRIDE

Blackwater Pack Series:

SANCTUM

BROKEN

PREY

LEGACY

SCARS

REQUIEM (coming 2024)

Mad World Series:

MAD WORLD

MAD AS HELL

MAD LOVE

INTO THE WOODS

By the Edge Series:

EDGE OF FOCUS (coming 2024)

Anthologies:

A Bridal Party To Remember

Hell Hath No Fury

Devour